Books by
Carole Cummings

Sonata Form

Blue on Black

The Aisling Trilogy:
Guardian
Dream
Beloved Son

The Wolf's-own Series:
Wolf Ascendant
Raven Inconjunct

Don't Fear the (Not Really Grim) Reaper

The Queen's Librarian

RAVEN INCONJUNCT

WOLF'S-OWN — PART TWO

CAROLE CUMMINGS

COPYRIGHT INFORMATION

"Maybe no one finds it, or even misses it, but fairness is like love. What is given has nothing to do with what we seek."
— *Author, Haruki Murakami*

RAVEN INCONJUNCT

WOLF'S-OWN — PART TWO

- Book 3 -

Kōan

1

Malick had always been enamored with aesthetics.

Even in the time he thought of as Before—back when he was mortal; back before he'd seen the terrifying delicacy and elegance of life, of the Balance of the gods, of the universe, of a single beat of a mortal heart—he'd admired beautiful things, beautiful people. He collected them, studied them, until he found something yet more beautiful and redirected his attention. Umeia told him quite often his attention span was that of a two-year-old child; she would change her opinion eventually and tell him it was actually that of a gnat.

His mother was the first to have held his attention. Not for aesthetic reasons, though yes, she'd been quite beautiful. Then again, didn't every son think so of his mother? Still, the lines of her face and the drape of her hair had not been the things Malick had heeded.

The carefree nature with which she'd approached life; the hard practicality with which she'd lived it; the gentle but stern hand with which she'd led her children—those were the things Malick had seen beneath the near-perfect set of her cheekbones and the supple tilt of her mouth. But the ferocity with which she'd tried to defend herself and her children, when their father decided he wanted his family back and that a knife and a cudgel was a good way to get them—that was what had solidified her place in Malick's heart forever. Turned a poor, mortal woman into something tragic and iconic, an ideal to which none could even attempt to aspire.

Malick thought perhaps he'd caught Wolf's eye that same night, when his thirteen-year-old self—still all knees and elbows, but under the delusion that shock and grief and rage really could turn him into a giant—had driven off their father with his own cudgel. Malick was only sorry he hadn't killed him. Sorrier he'd taken the time to grieve his mother and let his father slip away like a ghost into the darkness. That single regret kept his attention for years.

Umeia had been rather secondary in Malick's attention 'til then.

She was beautiful in a different way, almost up there on their mother's pedestal in Malick's heart, but not quite. More their father's daughter, really, with his looks and his disposition, and that streak of temper that turned to violence in their father, but in Umeia veered into protective instinct. She'd get violent, surely, if anyone threatened her own, and Malick was certainly her own. But she'd also come into their mother's pragmatism somewhere along the way, and she was wily, Umeia, so she hardly ever had to opt for violence. Brains, brass, and boobs, Malick would tell her, always laughing and with a snarky grin, and he'd generally get a healthy swat for it, but he'd also get real smiles and cackles, and sometimes even a hug.

She'd been sixteen when their father killed their mother and Malick had almost killed their father. She'd had four genuine offers of marriage by then, even without a dowry or a swath of fallow dirt to bring to a binding bed, and then another three afterward. She'd refused them all, taken Malick out of Kente and to Thecia on money she'd made selling everything they owned, taught him cards and charm and petty fraud by the time they'd got there, and set him loose on the unsuspecting.

Malick had known he was aesthetically pleasing; now he knew what to do with it.

He'd loved all his marks. Every one of them. Strange, though, how their beauty didn't seem to hold up to constant scrutiny. Blemishes of the soul were a lot harder to see than those of the flesh, but they almost always revealed themselves eventually. And then the beauty would fade for Malick, and the love would go with it, and he'd move on to a new love, a new purse to plunder, a new body to debauch, because none of them ever complained about the debauching. Malick had always made it a point to be very good at everything he did, and sex was just something else he did.

He didn't have to trick or steal their purses from them. They handed him fortunes without him ever having to ask.

Beautiful women had left their husbands for him. Beautiful men had threatened to lock him up and keep him for themselves. Only one ever actually tried it. Umeia helped to dump the body in a swamp when Malick was through with him.

"Someone like that doesn't deserve the fire," she'd told Malick, satisfied. In that moment, she'd been one of the most beautiful women he'd ever seen.

He didn't know if Wolf had been watching him all along, but he thought probably. It had been Desi, though, that made Wolf decide that perhaps Malick might have his uses. Malick knew this because he'd had the audacity to ask.

Beautiful, of course; they all were, in their own ways. Desi had been special. Malick supposed that might just be because Desi had been taken away before Malick had found her flaws, and so she would therefore remain always beautiful in Malick's memories. Still, though, Desi had been something else.

Sold to a Thecian lord when she'd been six, coddled, really, perhaps even a bit spoiled, and taken to the old man's bed when she'd been twelve. She'd been seventeen when Malick had first seen her, her purse heavy and her dark eyes handing him an easy in.

She'd learned her art just as thoroughly as Malick had, and that bit of fractured steel inside her, covered over with layer after layer of silk, had bitten him deeply. She had fire in her, did Desi. Smothered to near suffocation beneath the oppression of captivity disguised as wealth and favor, but it was there, and she'd kept it kindling for over a decade. Here was one whose beauty was her strength, and whose strength was her beauty, he remembered thinking. Here was one who could laugh and bite and moan and snarl, and yet he thought she might—*maybe*—accept a cudgel to her beautiful face for her children, should she ever be blessed with them. Or cursed. Her lord was rather an old, ugly little man.

Malick had Desi twice, and then he didn't see her again until her mutilated body had been displayed on the gates of her lord's manor. *FAITHLESS*, the placard had stated.

Malick hadn't wept. He hadn't lost control. He hadn't done anything but stare, mark each score and welt on what had been flawless ebony skin, mark each bruise and slash on her bloodied, disfigured face. Knowing, *knowing*, that Desi would go unavenged and unmourned, because she was chattel, and a man could do as he pleased with what he owned.

Malick wouldn't understand it for many years, but he thought now that was the moment he became Kamen, even before Wolf had turned him. Back then, he'd only understood that justice didn't come for everyone; sometimes you had to go and get it.

So he'd watched.

He'd waited.

And then he'd hunted.

It wasn't easy. It took patience. It took charm. It took finding the right people and asking the right questions. It took amiably bedding those he didn't even want to touch and wringing secrets from their mouths as he wrung orgasm from their bodies. It took finding that sliver of cruelty, a legacy of his father, and letting it blossom, take root, flourish.

Malick didn't only take care of Desi's lord in her honor—he took care of every man in the lord's employ who'd marked her, who'd taken her broken body and used it as she'd spent her last breath on a cry of agony. Malick made them scream just as loudly and desperately as he was sure Desi had done in the end.

Malick was thorough. Malick was methodical. Malick hunted them down, one by one, and showed them what "merciless" really meant.

And when the last two had divined the too-obvious pattern and fled, Malick had stalked them across two cities and the reach of a sterile wasteland between, and taken care of them too. Thoroughly and methodically.

Wolf had taken him then, made him Kamen, and Malick-now-Kamen had dragged Umeia with him.

A whole new sort of beauty opened up to the *Temshiel* Kamen, Wolf's-own. The beauty of vastness and things unseen by mortal eyes, and knowledge impossible to attain within the narrow stretch of a mortal life.

Hunting was easier now. It took him almost two decades to learn how to use the spirits properly, how to be just cruel enough to be sure you were getting the answers you needed, but not so cruel as to hasten their slow slide into true insanity. Malick did Wolf's bloody work while he learned, and when he'd learned enough, he'd hunted down his father—an itch in the back of his mind for *years*—and made his mother's murderer look him in the eye, know his son, as Malick strangled him. A knife would have been quicker, a simple surge of power easier; Malick had wanted to feel the pulse slow and sputter beneath his hand, wanted to watch up close as the life sparked out of eyes that were too like his own.

Malick generally got what he wanted.

Wolf's law wouldn't allow Malick to bury the corpse and so bind his father to the earth. Malick sulked a bit as he watched the pyre, but he obeyed. He was Kamen Wolf's-own, and he respected his god.

And then, out of the blue and all unlooked-for, there had been Skel.

Malick hadn't been impressed by Skel's perfect face. Malick hadn't been impressed by Skel's raven-black hair, or his cobalt eyes, or the lines of his body, or the way he moved it.

Malick had been impressed by the carefree nature with which Skel approached life; the hard practicality with which he lived it. Skel was fierce and beautiful and whimsical and foolish. When he'd tested Malick in a seedy tavern—Malick somewhat drunk and grieving his mother all over again, grieving all those he'd already outlived, still smelling of the smoke and incense from his father's pyre, and wondering if acquiescing to being the bloody hand at the end of Wolf's long arm on mortal lands had been such a brilliant idea after all—Malick had been struck not by the pleasing angles of Skel's face, or the open invitation in his too-blue eyes. Malick had been struck by the tiny hints of fracture behind the reckless audacity. By the singular pinpoint of satori that Skel was just as broken inside as anyone else; perilous enough to be interesting, and yet still strangely safe.

Skel was *Temshiel.* Skel couldn't die.

He'd been beautiful in his way, in more than the aesthetic sense, though he was, of course, extraordinarily aesthetically gifted. His sense of justice was perhaps a bit rigid, to Malick's mind, but it lit his soul with such a bright fiery blaze sometimes that Malick couldn't look away. Blinded. Skel was beauty and distraction and laughter and forgetfulness. Skel was friend and sometime-lover; touchstone and confidant; role model and bad example.

Malick had thought Skel wouldn't take a cudgel to the face for anyone. He'd been wrong.

There'd been Asai and foolish choices and betrayal and bewildered grief, and then there'd been no more Skel.

Malick finally felt the true weight of what he was. What he'd chosen. What his god had made him, and what he'd allowed himself to become. Malick looked Kamen in the eye, and… flinched.

He retreated.

Umeia didn't need to. Umeia was much better than Malick at being what they were. Still, Umeia had come with him. Malick would regret that eventually, but at the time, he'd been grateful.

Always enamored with beauty, and now it hovered just out of Malick's reach. No matter how many drinks he poured down his throat, no matter how many beds he fell into. He searched for it in the wrong places—pink lips, light-stubbled chins, firm breasts, muscled backs, pleasing faces, sweet-scented skin—he *knew* he was looking in the wrong places, but he couldn't bear to look within. If he found it, he might lose it. He loved with little splinters of himself he didn't mind risking, and nursed with liquor and more liquor the shriveled part of his spirit that hunkered inside him and hardened into a snarling little knot.

He observed the world around him with ever-growing contempt, nurturing his useless craving for vengeance, while he watched and waited.

And then, out of the blue and all unlooked-for, there had been Fen.

Malick had thought, right up until Fen had shot him that first hate-filled glare, that he'd been waiting for a chance at retribution. He'd been wrong.

He'd thought at first he was enamored with Fen's aesthetic beauty. Angular and sharp-boned, every slant and slope in exactly the right place. Eyes like storm clouds over a roiling sea, flecked through with the light of the suns forcing their way from the other side in scattershot amber. And oh bloody hell, the fucking *hair*.

He'd thought it was Fen's face: perfectly proportioned, perfectly angled, perfectly exquisite. He'd thought it was Fen's body: deliberately sculpted and honed, and all the more beautiful for the intrigue of the scarred map of self-inflicted sanity. He'd thought it was Fen's hair: an outward symbol of inward bondage, and the bit of rebellion in the choppy fringe that hid his eyes, but never well enough. He'd thought it was the way Fen moved and glared and spoke and sneered. He'd thought it was the way Fen snarled and spat and fought and came *this close* to actually winning.

And it was. It was all those things. Except all those things Malick could have walked away from. Yet somehow, he couldn't walk away from Fen. Malick told himself it was because he just didn't want to.

Fen was not whimsical. There was no laughter with Fen. Fen's approach to life was not carefree. Fen's approach to life was wholly self-destructive, and yet Fen wouldn't permit that destruction until he'd saved everyone he loved. The *way* Fen loved was, in and of itself, a prelude to suicide. Fen was not safe.

Fen was a black hole, all unknown and unwilling, sucking those around him into hopeless orbit. Malick had passed the event horizon almost the moment he'd plunged into amber-shot gray banded by indigo.

Not merely fractured inside, but shattered, and yet Fen wouldn't just accept a cudgel to his beautiful face for those he loved; Fen would wield one. Fen would learn the heft of it, how to swing it with the most precision, which point of the body to target, and he'd do it better, faster, and with a strange elegance that wasn't elegant at all, but still dangerously seductive. He'd take your cudgel to the face, then snatch it away from you and very efficiently set about killing you with it. And then he'd make you thank him for letting you take the image of his terrible radiance to hell with you.

There was a feral beauty in that sort of brutality, one that took that pedestal Malick had set in his heart, decades and lifetimes ago, and rocked it. One that made it all too imperative for him to irrevocably accept Kamen into his skin.

Kamen was necessary to save Fen and Jacin and Jacin-rei. *Malick* was necessary to care enough to keep the trinity from splintering into irretrievable pieces. *Kamen Malick* was necessary to show Fen that living in the same skin with all the parts of himself, without losing any of them, was possible.

It had, apparently, never really been about aesthetics for Malick.

There were probably some things Umeia would tell him, things about broken dolls and wanting to fix them, or damsels and wanting to rescue them; Shig would speculate that Fen's unwilling and oh so carefully hidden vulnerability appealed to Malick's predatory instincts. Malick knew some of those things might be a little bit true, but they weren't all of it.

It was the beauty in the shards of a riven soul; it was the beauty in watching that soul pick up each jagged piece, examine it, judge its worth, then discard it with learned indifference, or fit it back into the mosaic of Self, use it. The very *tragic* beauty in watching Fen do all of that not for himself but for everyone else.

A cudgel to the face was nothing, when compared to forcing life and sanity you really didn't want on yourself because someone else needed you to.

Malick would've liked to say he'd known he was in trouble from the start. He'd dismissed it when Samin warned him, scoffed when Umeia did. Umeia thought she knew him, but she only knew Malick; she'd never understood Kamen. Malick had told Umeia she was being absurd, she didn't know what she was talking about, and in many ways she hadn't. Still, in that one thing, she'd seen when he had refused to, and it had almost cost him everything.

He'd denied he was in deep when he'd watched the trinity that was Fen shatter then rebuild itself on a lonely road in the middle of the night; he'd denied it when he'd watched Fen put a knife through the eye of the man he'd loved nearly all his life then pry his heart from his chest and stomp it; he'd denied it when he'd spoken the words and told himself he'd only said them because Fen needed to hear them. He'd even denied it when he'd found himself not just willing but eager to break the laws of his gods to save Fen.

When Fen stepped in front of Kamen's sword, Malick couldn't deny it anymore. When Malick understood what had been hidden beneath "Untouchable" as life bled from the wound Kamen had inflicted, Kamen stepped in again and forced life where it was not wanted.

He remembered wondering if Wolf had known all along, if it had all been planned exactly as it had played out, and he supposed it was likely. If Husao had seen all the esoteric and mercurial reasons why Fen would become life and breath for Malick, it was almost blasphemous to imagine

Wolf hadn't. Just as blasphemous for Malick to raise his fists to the sky and curse Wolf for it, though he sometimes did it anyway.

Kamen never did. Kamen understood. Malick grudgingly admitted that he did too.

Asai had failed mostly because he'd underestimated Fen, but partly because he'd only glimpsed Malick through Skel. Asai had known Kamen; he'd never known Malick.

Kamen was Wolf's, but Malick was Fen's, and he would no longer deny it. For Fen, Malick could be just as fierce and merciless as Kamen ever was.

It wasn't going to be easy, showing Fen what he was now, watching as Fen came to understand the necessity of living. The onus now strapped to his back of doing so for others yet again. It was hard and cruel and just fucking tragic, and Malick bled with it.

Cruelty had never come easily to Malick; Kamen, however, had been born of it, had suckled at the teats of ruthlessness and brutal malice.

And he was, after all, neither Kamen nor Malick, in truth. He was one or the other and neither and both. He was Kamen Malick. He was Wolf's-own.

So, then. Wolf's will be done.

There was a vicious sort of beauty in that.

Change-month, Year 1322, Cycle of the Wolf

"It's a panther." Samin nodded, fairly confident, though he'd never seen a real one. The fact that this one seemed a docile, playful thing, and not the sly, vicious beast he remembered reading about once upon a time, gave him some doubt. But the black, glossy coat and the teeth were rather indicative, so he stuck with his assessment.

Morin was wide-eyed, fascinated. *"Panther."* He peered up at Samin, asking.

Samin merely shrugged then watched as Morin crossed the street and approached the woman who held the big cat's leash. The apparent mascot of The Lucky Panther Theater in front of which it lounged, the panther's ears pricked up as Morin neared, its yellow eyes attentive but only mildly so, its concentration more on the thorough stroking the woman was giving its lazily switching tail. Several men waited in the queue for a serving of vinegary rice rolled in spicy tuna from the little booth next door; they eyed the panther with interest, but appeared to be more intent on lunch than entertainment. The street was too noisy to hear what Morin said to the woman as he pulled up in front of her, but her laugh was honest and pleased when she nodded assent. She winked over at Samin as Morin dared a touch to the panther's head. The great, rumbling purr of the thing—*that* Samin could hear.

He gave Shig a nudge. "Aren't you going to pet it?"

Shig squinted over her shoulder with a twist of her eyebrows then followed the tilt of Samin's chin across the street. She looked the panther over critically for a moment then dismissed it.

"Naw. Too tame."

Samin snorted. If it was tearing through the streets and ravaging innocent passersby, *then* Shig would probably try petting it.

With a shrug, Shig went back to teasing a rat-sized monkey. The monkey chittered from its perch atop its owner's fruit stall while Shig waved the last piece of her fried sticky dough on the end of a stick in front of its nose.

She only looked up when Morin ambled back across the street, flushed and grinning.

"Aw, that big thing with all those teeth and you still have all your fingers?" Shig finally let the monkey have the pastry, chuckling when it snatched the stick from her, too, then waved it at her with an indignant squawk. "How are you gonna get yourself any lovely battle scars to attract the girls if you won't tease vicious animals properly?"

"Shows what you know." Morin's smirk was sly. "I tease my brothers all the time."

Samin ruffled Morin's hair then gave him an affectionate cuff. He was glad they'd come along. Besides getting accosted every five seconds by some hawker or stall owner trying to shove their wares down his throat, Samin was having fun.

"C'mon, then." He chivvied Morin and Shig ahead of him along the market's crowded thoroughfare. "I think the smoke shop is down that way."

The day was getting on, and Joori would probably be fretting by now. Not that Joori fretting was anything unusual, but they'd been out and about long enough for Samin's feet to start hurting anyway, and he didn't like to cause any of the boys distress if he didn't have to. Balancing Morin's wish to go everywhere and see everything *right now* with Joori's inability to leave Fen on his own while also keeping both Fen and Morin in his sight at all times was somewhat taxing, but Samin did what he could. Anyway, Samin agreed that Fen shouldn't be left unsupervised just yet, and with Malick out for the morning on some mysterious errand, Samin had approved of Joori staying behind. At least this time. Samin rather thought—

"Seyh! *Seyh!*"

Samin didn't growl as the young man with the funny little spectacles caught his sleeve. He must've scowled, though, because he was let go immediately, and the strange young man backed up a pace with a quick assessing glance at Morin and Shig.

"Ah." The young man dipped his head. "I apologize, but…" He trailed off and shot Shig a speaking look.

Shig smiled, all friendly welcome. "It's your business, after all."

Samin had no idea what that meant, but he followed Shig's gaze to the little stall from where the young man had leapt. *Necessities* was written on a small placard and nailed to one of the posts holding up the stall's roof.

The man was on the small side, slim and wiry, and dressed in loose tunic and trousers that looked like he'd put them together with a disparate array of eye-wateringly bright handkerchiefs. Dark, sleek hair was gathered neatly into a long, loose tail at his nape. His smile was small but sincere enough beneath those strange violet spectacles, and he offered a deferential manner to Samin that Samin was still trying to figure out when Morin stepped in.

"Ooh," said Morin. "Lookit the fish."

The booth was rather plain, compared to the others they'd seen down around the main square where the temples sat. As they got closer to the Ports District and the inn where Malick had put them, the atmosphere grew just a touch seedier, but still not seedy.

Bamboo shelves stood prominent in this man's shabby booth, one lined with little bowls containing a single fish each. Ruby-colored and cobalt, velvety black and silklike jade—their fins were long and flowing, as though decked in the formal robes of the Adan. Samin privately decided they were pretty enough, but they looked rather bored and sickly, and he hoped he wasn't going to have to talk Morin out of one.

Shig was rather bolder than Morin: she stepped around him and right up to the young man, who watched her, patiently expectant, with a serene smile on his rather pretty face. Shig turned her grin on him and dipped her colorful head in a respectful bow. She offered her hand, but not as though she meant to shake with the young man.

"Seyh." She turned her hand palm up in front of her and merely waited.

The young man's mouth split in a dazzling grin, and his small hand settled atop Shig's.

"Ah." He tipped a knowing nod. "A child of Wolf, with the kiss of your god upon your brow. You've the mark of the spectral domain all around you like invisible skin." He closed his eyes, a light frown beetling his thin brown eyebrows, before he peered at Shig with keen interest. "You've lost your cursed gift, girl. Have you come to seek it again?"

Samin's eyebrows shot up, and he leaned in to make sure he didn't miss anything. Did that mean what he thought it meant?

Shig lifted her chin. "I'm here to learn from my god if he wishes me to have it."

That was certainly news to Samin.

Shig was still grinning, but her tone was strangely somber. "I didn't lose it, seyh—it was taken from me when the Ancestors went home."

"*Ah!*" The man's eyebrows shot up, making the spectacles slide down the bridge of his nose. "Not Jin, though." He enveloped Shig's hand in both of his. "Half-Blood, then." He turned an interested look on Morin. "I've not seen a full-Blood before." Morin took a small step back, wary, but the young man didn't look offended. "Fear not, young Jin. You are not in Ada, where I hear even now your kind struggle for that which they know not how to grasp."

Morin frowned; he looked like he was trying to decide if he should be insulted or not. "What does that mean?"

It meant that just because the Adan had no more cause to fear and imprison the Jin, it didn't necessarily mean the troubles of the Jin were over. The gossip Samin had heard coming from across the sea had not been entirely good news, and with every additional report, he was just as happy to be well rid of it all. He'd seen no reason to trouble the boys with it, and definitely not Fen.

"You will know when it is time, I've no doubt." The young man slid a knowing smirk at Samin then patted Shig's hand before releasing it. "Fate is not yet done with any of you, I think."

Morin huffed, derisive. "Well, I'm done with Fate." Scowling, he snatched up a walking stick propped against the support post beside him. He gripped it tight, as though ready to whack someone with it.

"That, young seyh," the young man chided, "is not what you need." He took the stick from Morin, a protective hand set to the wolf's head that topped the stick. He gave it a squint-eyed onceover, as though looking for damage, before he slipped it under a table weighted down with what Samin could only think of as junk. "Someone else will be by for it eventually, no doubt." It was said softly, more to himself, as the young man pushed up the spectacles and peered at Samin as though waiting for him to say something.

Except Samin had nothing to say. He gave Morin a little nudge.

"Come on, have your look so we can go. D'you want a fish or not?"

"Eh." Morin's attention was once again diverted to the bamboo shelves and their bowls. "I just thought they were interesting. They looked better from farther away, anyway."

Samin nodded. "Is that all they do? Just float about and stare?"

"You thought they might juggle?" The man's smile was not unkind as he loosed a thready little giggle into his sleeve. "Here now, girl, back away before you bring it all down on my head." He shooed Shig away from where she'd been dipping her fingers into one of the bowls. "Think you they serve no purpose, eh?" The young man seemed to be talking to himself again as he pulled down two apparently random bowls and brought them carefully over to set them on the table before Morin. "Sometimes the purpose of a thing is merely to share its beauty with the world." An impish grin spread across his face as he scooped his hand into one of the bowls, dumping a satiny garnet fish into the bowl of one that looked like liquid turquoise. "And sometimes, the beauty merely hides its purpose."

The reactions were immediate: droplets splashed up and out as the fish went for each other with a viciousness that surprised Samin. From floating placidly in their separate bowls like lumps of pretty jewels, to blood in the water in a second and a half. Morin only stared steadily, thoughtful, as though analyzing tactics.

The young man turned his attention back to Shig. Bold, he tugged at a stray green curl that had come loose from the striated tail at her nape.

"Such a beacon to the spirits you must have been, girl. Bravery or arrogance?" He dropped a quick, knowing wink. "Or brave arrogance?"

Shig's smile turned coy; if Samin didn't know better, he'd think she was flirting.

"Necessity." Shig shot a sly glance at the placard that apparently was meant to describe the young man's business. "The spirits can be difficult, but also useful, if one can master them."

"Mastery!" The man's eyes went wide. "It is no wonder, then, that Wolf looks so fondly upon your own spirit." He dipped his head, an echo of the respectful bow Shig had given him a moment ago.

"Um… I think…" Morin's face was screwed up in mild revulsion. He peered at the young man, then gestured him over. "I think the blue one won."

Ech. Samin's lip curled at the bloody bowl, and the blue fish once again floating placidly in the middle of it, the mangled fins of the other fanning down over its back from where it hovered, dead, just beneath the skin of the water.

Morin only stared, a deep furrow in his brow. He didn't shift his glance as the young man wordlessly dipped his hand into the bowl, caught the victor and dumped it unceremoniously into the empty bowl and set it back on the shelf.

It took a moment, but Morin eventually shook himself. "What are those made from?" He cut a meaningful glance at a row of amulets. He didn't seem to want to dare to actually touch them.

"From the earth, the sweat of my brow, and the blessing of my gift," the man answered.

Morin narrowed a skeptical look upward. "No Blood?"

The young man nearly choked. "Never!" He swept his hand out, imperious. "The Adans' ways are not ours, young full-Blood. Look away from your past oppression, or you may lose forever the ability to see beyond it."

Samin's mouth thinned down. It was quite possible that the advice was good, but this man had no idea what a Jin's life was like in Ada. It wasn't his right to chastise Morin for bearing scars and keeping his—in Samin's opinion—healthy suspicions because of them.

"The oppression is not so long past," Samin put in, warning. "The boy's got a right." Before the young man could sputter a reply, Samin jerked his chin at the table. "Do these come with the spells to use them, or is that extra?"

Because that was how these hawkers worked: the product was usually cheap, but the key to using it dear.

"Not spells." The man gathered his dignity around him like a cloak. "Prayers." He stepped behind the table, dismissed Samin, and shifted his attention to Morin. "You will find many things the same here, but also many things different. We do not command our magic with spells; we ask of it. We ask the gods to bless us in its use. Only *Temshiel* and maijin have the right of control. We merely pray for the blessing of favor." He picked up an amulet made of ruby that sparked like blood when he held it up to the light. "Merely focus. An orison from my hand to yours. You will find no one of the Craft who will promise an answer to all of your prayers—only that the gods will hear them."

An abrupt upswell of music blatted from across the busy street where a small stage was nestled between a cut-rate fish market that smelled cut-rate, and a candle shop that was apparently trying to overpower the nasty fish smell with nasty perfumed wax. Morin immediately lost interest in the vendor and turned his eyes across the street, wonder and pleasure blossoming over his expression at the puppet show just beginning.

Samin only sighed as Morin bolted away, the young man and his booth and his fish forgotten completely. Shig smiled before running to catch up with Morin and take a place in the watching crowd beside him as the puppets began their larking.

With a polite nod to the booth's vendor, Samin ambled leisurely up to the outskirts of the audience, watching not the show but Morin and Shig. Faces shining, they were instantly rapt, thoroughly enjoying themselves, and elbowing each other like siblings as they laughed at the japery on stage. Samin smiled over them like a proud father, and he didn't even let that thought embarrass him. A man could do worse than this brood.

A tug at his sleeve pulled his gaze down to see the young man from the booth giving him that serene, knowing smile over his spectacles. He pushed a fishbowl into Samin's hands.

"For the boy."

Samin scowled down at the fish flopping around in the bowl. What the hell?

"The lad needs no luck or protection." The man shrugged. "Wolf has already marked him. No small thing, that." He set his hands around Samin's and forced a firmer grip on the bowl, paused as laughter at the puppets' antics swelled and drowned out whatever he was going to say, then continued, "The obvious is almost always a mask." He paused again as music started up, then patted Samin's hands and released them. "If there is equilibrium to be found, it will be the Kurimo that finds it."

He was making absolutely no sense, and yet so serious, so sure, like a bloody fish in a fishbowl could explain the secrets of the universe.

"Uh." Samin tried to push the bowl back. "I don't think—"

"A gift, seyh, a gift!" The man wheezed his weird little chuckle, hands held up and back. "To refuse on the cusp of the New Year…"

Was dishonor and insult and bad luck besides, right, terrific. Samin made himself tip his head in a shallow bow, and kept back the growl.

"As you wish, seyh. Blessings on you for your generosity, and luck in the New Year."

The man merely bobbed his head and chuckled some more as he retreated back to his booth, pushing the spectacles up the bridge of his nose again.

Samin did *not* throw him down on the ground and start kicking his head in.

※

"It's our birthday soon." Joori tried to put buoyancy into his tone, but the statement still came out hesitant, too forced. He took a step away from the door, trying to gauge Jacin's mood. You just never knew with Jacin anymore. "Malick says they have fireworks at midnight on the Turn here. And there's a bloody-great festival. He said we'd all go."

Jacin just kept staring out the window, slumped on the bed he shared with Malick, slats of shadow from the crisscross pattern of the muntins on the windowpane bisecting the too-sharp planes of his face. There wasn't even anything to see—the weathered boards of the pier on which the inn sat, the water, the suns in the sky—but Jacin watched some kind of inner landscape anyway, so it didn't seem to matter.

He'd been getting better. He *had*.

Joori tried not to sigh, tried to just accept it and pretend at patience. Sometimes Jacin was just like this.

It had been almost three months now since that horrible day and night. A whole new world had been opened to them, and then at least some of it presented in more tangible ways—a new land, new people, new lives. The grief and shock weren't quite as fresh. The scars were beginning to cover over all the past hurts for Joori. Still there but not so sharp, not so sensitive to the accidental touch anymore.

Jacin's hurts didn't seem to be scarring over, or even scabbing. Jacin still seemed... raw.

He wore a braid now. Only a small one, plaited neatly back from his left temple. Joori kept wanting to ask him why, but he was afraid of the answer he might get, so he didn't. He never offered to braid it for him, either.

"They keep the traditions of the shrines here. Did you know that?" Joori didn't wait for an answer, because he knew he wouldn't get one. "Tougei's right across the bay, where it's said the *Temshiel* got the marble to build them. There's a temple in the city's center for each god, and then a whole great shrine for the ashes of—"

He stopped. He probably didn't need to be going on about the dead right now.

"Malick asked Morin yesterday if he'd want to go see Tougei. He said there are ferries just for people to go across and explore, but no one's allowed to actually live there but the priests. Sacred, and all."

Joori might not have even been there, for all the reaction he got. Jacin just kept staring, that blank-empty thing that made the hairs at Joori's nape prickle and his stomach curl. Joori looked down at his hand, at the scar across his palm that matched the one across Jacin's.

"Please." Joori crouched down by Jacin's hip and set a hand to his knee. "Come back, Jacin. I want my brother back."

Not a word, not a twitch, but Jacin's eyes slid shut, a suspicious glimmer catching the light at his lashes. It was abruptly difficult for Joori to swallow.

It had seemed like Jacin turned some kind of corner on the voyage here, come to a somewhat tranquil equilibrium, or at least calm acceptance.

He'd still had his bleak days, but the lighter ones had outnumbered them, and Joori had hoped. And then they'd reached Mitsu, Tambalon's teeming capital, and the nightmares had hit and Jacin's "ghosts" had come back, his mind rebelling against contentment with vicious force, punishing him for things over which he'd never believe he didn't merit punishment.

Now the days Joori was coming to think of as Jacin's Good Days were like heartbreaking teases, reminders of possibility that seemed to drift further and further from realistic hopes for the future with every spate of Jacin's Dark Days that stretched too long between them.

Joori dragged in a breath, followed Jacin's blank gaze out the window, and moved his hand to Jacin's shoulder. Jacin didn't flinch away, but that might just be because he didn't even know Joori was there, so Joori didn't let it bolster the agony of hope.

"It'll be all right, Jacin."

Joori said that a lot. He couldn't think of anything better to say.

⛩

This, Dakimo thought with a tight set to his mouth, was going to be interesting. Entertaining, perhaps. Irritating, most probably. But definitely interesting.

He cleared his throat politely, waiting until Emika lifted her frown from the scrolls and missives littering her table. Hand at his breastbone, Dakimo tilted a respectful bow.

"Madam Governor. Kamen awaits you in the receiving room."

"Kamen?" Emika lifted her eyebrows. "The summons was for Kamen and his…" She paused, glanced down at something on the table and then back up to Dakimo. "He's come alone?"

Not only come alone, but nearly spitting and snarling about it too. He hadn't been happy that Dakimo chose not to disclose how he'd managed to find them. Even less happy when Dakimo had dryly inquired if perhaps Kamen shouldn't be a bit more circumspect about throwing his power around inside the Statehouse itself. Of course, it had been rather strained and lost some of its acerbity, what with Dakimo pinned to the peak of the vaulted ceiling as he'd been. But still.

As if Dakimo didn't have his own tricks and contacts. As if he didn't have too many years on Kamen that he'd be so put off by a little Null magic. And Kamen had let him down eventually.

Dakimo put out a hand. "He has come alone, Madam."

"And should I take this to mean he is everything I've been led to believe he'd be?"

Insubordinate? Arrogant? Disrespectful, rebellious and uncooperative? If Dakimo's past experiences with Kamen were any indication—

"I'm afraid so, Madam."

Emika scowled. "Brilliant."

She shut her eyes, running a hand through silver-shot mahogany before pausing to rub at her temples.

Dakimo traced the scrolling patterns of the henna wards on the backs of her fine-boned hands, noting their depth and detail, checking his work. Just a touch faded, but these were precarious times. He'd have to be sure to clear her schedule for a few hours to renew the spells before the week was out.

He tried not to get attached to mortals. But he liked this one very much. Perhaps even loved her a little. As Wolf's emissary here in Tambalon's capital, Dakimo had worked with Emika since her installation as governor, and more closely, once Wolf entered his Cycle.

Beautiful, in the way of mortals, with a brilliant mind and a sincere desire to do well by her people and her office. She would make a fine *Temshiel*, should Wolf ever decide he had a use for her. Perhaps Dakimo would test those waters before it became too late, before that silver in Emika's artfully arranged dark hair turned to brittle white, and the fine lines at her mouth melted into folds and furrows. She certainly had the sort of heart Wolf sought.

"Fine." Emika sat up straight. "*Fine*, damn it. What's one more arrogant immortal in a city full of them?" She peered up with a wry twist of her lips at Dakimo's delicate cough and subsequent smirk. "Present company excepted, of course."

"Of course."

They shared a small grin before Emika slumped back on her cushions. "He'll be able to help."

Spoken evenly, a statement, but Dakimo had known Emika for quite a long while, and had no trouble recognizing the underlying plea. He sighed.

"Madam, he is our best hope."

It would've been better, though, if Kamen had brought the Incendiary, as he'd been ordered to do. Dangerous though they were, the Incendiary's arrival in Mitsu two weeks ago had sent futures-possible into a murky state of flux that Dakimo had seen only once before, and it would be wise to gauge intentions and opportunities before moving ahead with any of the myriad proposals and risks now before them. What he'd heard of the Incendiary's state of mind did not fill him with confidence, and he'd have preferred to see the man for himself.

Incendiary were dangerous enough, but this particular Incendiary…

Dakimo could only trust in his god, he supposed. He'd been entrusted with the knowledge of what this Incendiary was—*who* this Incendiary was—and whether or not Kamen was informed was up to Dakimo's discretion. Today was to have been a test of the Incendiary, more than of Kamen, but the way things were working out… well. So far, Dakimo wasn't finding himself tempted to relay the information. Powerful though he was, Kamen was not known for his even temperament and careful consideration.

"Kamen is the only Null in existence." Dakimo shrugged. "And he is in his own Cycle. If he cannot root out the *banpair* and put an end to them…"

Emika waited for Dakimo to finish, but when he didn't, she pursed her lips in an unhappy line.

"Right." She stood. "Let us meet this Null, then."

⛩

"I was *busy*." It snapped out of Malick, angry and insolent. It was annoying enough to be summoned—by a bloody mortal *governor*—but to be summoned *now* was just… infuriating. And considering Fen's state since they'd arrived here, possibly unwise. "In case you hadn't heard, things got a little messy in Ada, and I was a bit occupied with trying to follow my own orders. I *don't* appreciate the implication that I'm responsible for *you* letting *your* problems get out of control."

Dakimo merely lifted an eyebrow. The condescension in it made Malick's teeth set tight.

The governor, Emika, held up a hand, placating. "Tambalon's problems are the problems of all *Temshiel* and maijin, and of the gods. As Dakimo said, we've been asking for Wolf's blessing since his Cycle began. You are, perhaps, late in bringing it, but Tambalon is grateful for your presence now."

Malick almost snorted. He was pretty sure he'd just been very diplomatically spanked. He wished he knew how to diplomatically pummel.

"Kamen." Emika sighed. "We need help. Dakimo has been keeping a very close watch on the potential outcomes to what's happening, and every day the possibilities grow more worrying. Their numbers are growing, and so is the roster of the missing. And now the dead. What's worse, no *Temshiel* or maijin has thus far been able to find either the *banpair* themselves, or the spirits of the missing." Her mouth twisted in mild revulsion. "*Or* those of the dead."

Malick narrowed his eyes and stood a little straighter from his deliberately impudent slouch against the wall. "Are you telling me these *banpair* are somehow managing to steal the souls of the victims too?" He hadn't heard that one before.

"We can't tell." Dakimo shrugged off Malick's glare. "No one can speak to the spirits as well as Goyo of Snake. He's worked doggedly with the Patrol for months, and yet he must have a direction to look to locate just one of the countless souls that walk the world. We have yet to find that direction."

"And how long has that been going on?"

Malick had only been told there were *banpair* operating in some kind of coven and managing to hide themselves from even the eyes of the gods—he hadn't been told they were stealing souls as well. And considering what Yakuli had been able to do, kidnapping countless Jin and using their own magic against them to imprison their spirits, this was a lot more alarming than Malick had thought. It was a damned good thing he *hadn't* brought Fen.

"Possibly since the beginning." Dakimo opened a hand. "We have had dozens of disappearances over the past several—"

"Four hundred and three." Emika's hazel glance moved from Dakimo to Malick. "That we know of. We can't be sure exactly when they began, nor can we know which were victims of these *banpair*, and which met other fates. Nor do we know if that count is optimistic. Mitsu is a large city, and our ports are swarming at even the thinnest of times. People come and go."

"Of those discovered dead, we believe more than half of them were victims of these creatures." Dakimo paused and fixed his dark blue gaze on Malick. "The method has become quite obvious. We believe they keep their victims alive for as long as possible, to prolong the torture and enhance the... taste." He looked like he wanted to hit something.

Malick studied them both carefully. "And you looked—"

"I assure you, every *Temshiel* and maijin with a talent for employing the spirits has looked within their realm. Goyo, as I said, is the best there is, but even he's been stymied. Those who have been lost remain so."

And not even the gods could find them.

This was... really bad. And not at all what Malick had been expecting.

"Tell him all of it, Dakimo." The tone was almost gentle, but the look in Emika's eyes was limned in steel.

Dakimo met it for a moment, but not with challenge; more like resignation. "I had no intention of doing otherwise." He turned to Malick. "Of all the *banpair* now roaming the world, only twelve are unaccounted for. The oldest. Maijin turned to the Six before the One was thrown down."

Meaning the last remaining maijin from when the world was still called Daichi, and before the moons had come.

Malick frowned. There should be some kind of conjecture to go along with the way his stomach had just plunged, but there was nothing there, just the knowledge that this was a lot bigger than he'd been led to believe. Than anyone but a very small circle of those involved had been led to believe.

"And what do you suppose this all means?" he asked slowly.

Dakimo's teeth clenched. "We don't *know*."

"You don't suppose…" Malick hated to even think it, but this was old magic they were talking about. "I imagine you've thought to speak to Rihansei?"

"Well, of *course*." It was too obvious that Dakimo was holding on to his temper with both hands. "He's been as helpful as he possibly can be, and as cooperative as always. More so. He says he knows even less than we do, and I believe him."

Yes, but the magic of the gods didn't work on Rihansei, so there was no way to *know*. Rihansei had only ever given away exactly as much as he had to and no more. He held the Gate between the old world and the new, and so enjoyed a sort of cooperative status with the gods' servants here in Mitsu; but he was a practitioner of the old magic, powerful in his own right, and as manipulative as any *Temshiel*. Malick trusted him as far as it went, but Malick trusted very little he couldn't get his hands on and squeeze for truth. And Rihansei and his monks had made it a mission to coax initiates away from the temples since… well, since forever, as far as Malick knew.

"All right." Malick sucked a tooth, thinking. "I'll have a look myself and see if I can find anything that doesn't feel right."

Dakimo's mouth flattened. "If Goyo hasn't been able—"

"*Not* the spirits." Malick rolled his eyes. "I'll leave that to Goyo and those who can be bothered to do it properly. I was talking about actually going out and looking—you know, with my eyes. Like people do. Hunting."

"Alone?"

Dakimo asked the question with so little query in the tone Malick almost missed the too-casual slide to it. He managed to keep his expression bland.

"No, I think I'll bring a companion along. Samin is a good man to have about. And it's always wise to have backup."

And Samin could do with a little mayhem.

Emika shook her head, impatient. "The Incendiary?"

Malick hoped the reflexive closing down and tightening of his shields wasn't visible on his face.

"Incendiary?" Threat and warning, all in one.

Dakimo sighed. "Kamen, please. Did you really think word wouldn't spread?"

No, he hadn't, not really. He'd just hoped he'd have a bit more time. Fen *needed* a bit more time.

"Maybe not. But I *had* thought a *Temshiel* of Wolf would understand and perhaps try to *keep* it from spreading." Malick shot a meaningful glance at Emika and then back to Dakimo. "Exactly where are your loyalties in this, Wolf's-own?"

"My loyalties lie with Wolf and my duty to Tambalon, as charged by Wolf himself." Dakimo was very obviously offended, indignant. "You've no right to question—"

"I've every right, when it comes to the wellbeing of my own, and the Incendiary is—"

"He is not *your*—" Dakimo stopped then sucked in a long, steady breath. "He is your charge, yes. But you've brought him to Mitsu, and while you're here, you must obey Tambalon law." He gestured to Emika. "The governor *is* Tambalon law."

Yeah, which was why Malick had chosen not to let anyone know he was here. The one place in the world where *Temshiel* and maijin both had to obey mortal law also, somewhat unhappily, happened to be the one place Fen needed to be to become what Fate had made him. Anyone who'd been paying attention, anyone who hadn't slept through the past six months, had to know Kamen would have no choice but to bring the Incendiary here eventually. Malick had just hoped that doing it immediately, before anyone might expect it, and doing it veiled, would keep his presence beneath notice until after Fen was... better.

"Kamen." Emika's tone was gentle. "His presence has already changed fates in ways not even Dakimo can see. Surely he would be useful in—"

"*No.*" Just that one word, low and quiet, but Malick managed to make it drip with malice. Damn it, he'd *known* they were up to something.

"Wolf made him for a reason," Dakimo said. "You can't just—"

"*Fate* made him. And you know as well as I do where that led with the last Incendiary. I'm *not* watching it happen again."

Emika cut a glance over to Dakimo. She was very good, a years-long diplomat, so her expression gave very little away, but Malick was pretty sure she was taken off guard by that last.

Not Dakimo, though. He shook his head, ever so slightly, then turned to Malick.

"Many of our kind know of the Incendiary. You can't pretend you didn't know talk would spread quickly. And you can't pretend you're not aware of the dangers. Perhaps only we few know where he is now, but… Kamen, you cannot do this alone."

Malick snorted. He couldn't help it.

All right. Fine. Malick didn't have to be on his own with this one; he could draw some allies, should he need them. And he might. If nothing else, he could wheedle one or two of Wolf's into helping him mow down the *banpair*, once he found them, so he could get back to concentrating on Fen and his latest turn into depression and apathy. Because an apathetic Fen was not a Fen who was going to care much if every minion of the gods started sniffing around to see which way he'd jump, some of them likely determined to make the decision for him, one way or another. The one advantage Malick had here in Mitsu was that no one could get through his veil and find him, which meant they couldn't find Fen by looking for Malick.

Which reminded him—

"How did you even know I was here, anyway?"

Dakimo rolled his eyes. "You mistake strength for talent and power, Kamen. So many of the young ones do."

Yeah, yeah. That's what all the old immortals harped. Some of them spent more time in the temples learning that "talent" than they did actually out in the world, doing what they were supposed to be doing. No wonder they lost touch with mortals.

"The point…" Emika trailed off, peering curiously between Malick and Dakimo. She shook it away. "The point is that there is an Incendiary in Mitsu, and Mitsu is in need of assistance. As I understand it, the Incendiary draws Fate's players to himself, and his influence—"

"I said *no*." This was a point on which Malick had no intention of giving even an inch. "The man's still getting over having lost half his family, not to mention what Asai did to him, and then having to deal with Yakuli. I'm not risking—"

"Was he not a fairly accomplished assassin?"

"You have rather a talent for understatement, Madam Governor. You have *no* idea what the man can do with a knife. But right now? He can't even walk without a limp. And you want me to get him to put himself out there as some kind of bait for *banpair* who've been managing to slip through the magic of the gods and their servants for *years*? No. This man saved the Jin. He needs rest, he *deserves* rest, and I'm not going to allow you to—"

"He is so very fragile?" Dakimo's tone was bland, deliberately goading.

Malick almost choked on the anger that surged in his chest. He held it back.

Yes and no, he didn't say. *Wouldn't* say. Not in front of these people. Fen still had that diamond-hard core somewhere in there, its facets just beginning to pick up a glimmer of a shine on the voyage here, but once they'd hit Tambalon and Fen's "ghosts" reawakened...

No. This wasn't going to happen, Malick wouldn't allow it. Not until either Fen showed Malick he was ready, or until Wolf grabbed Malick by the scruff of the neck and made him tell Fen what he was and why people like Dakimo and Emika were going to be wanting to use him as their personal tool.

"No one touches him." Malick kept his voice deadly soft. "And no one talks to him. I'll take care of your bloody *banpair* for you, and you'll leave me and mine alone. Anyone tries to come for him, they'll have to get through me." He stared evenly at first Dakimo, then Emika.

"I... see." To her credit, Emika didn't flinch or look even the slightest bit cowed. "And you will see to it that the Incendiary's presence does no harm to Mitsu or its citizens. I want no repeat of what happened in Ada."

"Don't enslave his people or try to take what's his, and you won't have to worry about it." Malick shot them each one last glare. "Stay away from us. No interference. You don't want to piss me off."

He didn't wait for a response, and he didn't wait for a formal dismissal. He slammed through the door of the governor's receiving room and out into the wide hallway, glaring at the polished marble beneath his boots as he stalked. *Temshiel* and maijin everywhere, he could feel them, and he checked his veil again to make sure they couldn't feel him.

Thing was, he admitted as he strode out of the Statehouse and down the steps to the crowded street, none of this was a surprise—just an annoying inconvenience, when he had other, more important things on his mind. He'd known someone was going to twig to his presence here eventually—and, as a result, to Fen's—he just hadn't counted on being so admittedly unprepared when it happened. And now that there was a pack of rabid *banpair* gumming up the works, Malick's time was going to be more in demand than he wanted it to be.

Then again, his timing had always been shit. He really shouldn't be surprised.

He hadn't been paying attention as he stalked and stomped about the teeming streets of the capital, face set like thunder and eyes narrowed to slits so that anyone who got in his way quickly amended their misstep. He'd thought he was merely wandering aimlessly, walking off some steam before heading back to the inn, so he was a little surprised and mightily put out to realize his feet had led him all unknowing to the short iron gate that marked the entrance to the grounds of Wolf's temple.

Maybe it was just as well. He'd been thinking only yesterday that maybe he should track down Imara, that she could maybe do… something for Fen. She was a healer, after all, and she was old. *Old* old. And claimed quite frequently that she'd seen it all. Imara might be able to give Malick a direction to point himself. Not that Malick needed *help* when it came to Fen. Not from anyone, including bloody Joori, the annoying little prick. It was just that—

Oh hell. Malick was such an idiot. Imara. Of course. *That* was how Dakimo had found them. There wasn't a *Temshiel* in the world who spent more time in Mitsu than Imara did—she probably knew every shop owner and dock worker in the entire city. She wouldn't have needed to look for Malick with magic; all she had to do was pay some fisherman to watch for arriving Jin, because Malick could veil Joori and Morin from prying eyes, but he couldn't veil Fen. And Imara would know that.

Fuming all over again, Malick glared up at the fountains and the priestess in her painted wolf's mask who tended them, and then past all of it through the shade of the hackberry trees to the open arches that led into the temple itself. The priestess's head lifted, turned toward him; for a moment, Malick thought she somehow knew him, sensed him, until he realized her gaze was pointed just over his shoulder. He sighed, quite purposely loud and longsuffering, and set his hand to the gate before he turned with a scowl.

"Imara." Damn it, he hated it when she sneaked up like that.

Imara dipped her dark head. "Finally come to pay your respects to your god?" She was smirking.

Malick *did not* roll his eyes. As if he didn't pay his respects with everything he did.

"Oh, I know you *think* you know why you've come." Imara gestured Malick through the gate. "So it'll be that much more fun for me when you find out why you're actually here. And you thought you had a lot of work to do *now*."

"You like to live dangerously, don't you?" Malick strode up the path, valiantly not giving in to the impulse to shove Imara into the fountain's pool as they reached its near edge. "If you've forgotten the sting of having your ass handed to you, I'll be happy to refresh your memory for you."

"Ah, Kamen." Imara linked her arm through Malick's and tugged him along. "I've missed you. I don't have enough arrogant asses in my life."

She was nearly bubbling, like the twentyish young girl she appeared to be, instead of the centuries-old *Temshiel* who'd given Malick the fight of his life the one time they'd tested each other. Whatever she had in mind this time, it wasn't going to be pleasant, Malick could tell just by the gleam in her topaz gaze.

Malick rolled his eyes. "And I don't have enough annoying immortals who think they know better than me just because they're older, *or* who think they're my mother. Just cut the bullshit, Imara, and tell me what you want."

"What *I* want?"

"Yeah, and don't pretend you didn't tell Dakimo how to find me, because that innocent trick doesn't work on me anymore. And thank you, by the way, for turning on me when I was coming to you for—"

"You should've reported to Dakimo yourself. He is Wolf's voice here in Tambalon, and while we run in Wolf's Cycle, Emika is Wolf's law."

"Unless Wolf himself has ordered otherwise."

Imara's eyebrow went up. "And has he?"

Fail the Fool and fail the Cycle.

From Fen's mouth, but it had been Wolf's voice. And regardless of what Malick had thought it meant at the time, he knew too well what it meant now.

"Yes."

"Because you're just *that* special."

"Pretty sure that's already been well established."

"Oh, for the love of—"

"Look, I know how disappointed you are that I haven't yet managed to fuck myself over completely and trip myself into the suns, but I'm not—"

"You haven't told the Incendiary what he is yet." Imara's voice had turned cool, just like that, but her expression was… hard to read. "Have you."

"And neither will you, so don't even think it."

"It's your job, Kamen. By all means, you should do it." It had the ring of threat more than concession.

Imara stopped just on the far edge of the fountain's pool. With a look, she dismissed the priestess, waiting until she was on her way up the temple's steps and out of earshot before turning back on Malick, stern.

"I want to meet this Incendiary."

"No."

"The choice is not—"

"*No.*"

Malick had just been thinking Imara might be able to help; now, he locked everything he had down tight, daring her to try to wriggle through the veil that cloaked thought and feeling, leaving only the set of his jaw and the hardness of his gaze by which to measure his reaction. Because it would not be a good idea to let Imara touch the bit of fear her request—demand—had stirred down deep in his belly.

He pulled his arm out of Imara's grip. "The Incendiary is mine, until either he decides different or Wolf does. You don't know him, *I do*, and you're just going to have to trust that I know what I'm doing. *I* will tell him, when *I* decide he can take it."

"Take it."

…Shit.

"It's a lot for a man to accept, is all. He's still grieving. Let him finish that before springing this on him."

Imara stepped away and set her stare on the ripple of the pond. "So, he is unwell?"

"He is…" Malick paused, tried to do that thing Fen did, where he looked like he was ripping out his heart to give you an answer, when really he was giving you a very blatant nonanswer that you didn't recognize as nothing at all until after he'd coerced you into fucking him unconscious. And then it was too late. "Fen is unique. He has his own ways of dealing with things. I just want to let him. He needs time."

"For what, Kamen? To grieve his own? To undo what the Ancestors did to him?" Imara paused, but she still didn't look at Malick. "To forget his first love?"

Don't kill her, don't kill her, don't kill her.

Easier said than done. Malick's hands ached to wrap around someone's throat, and since Asai wasn't an option, Imara would do. He restrained himself.

"All of it."

Imara just kept staring at the water, watching the mottles of the bright-colored sakou slither and flash as they flittered just below the surface.

"What are you hiding, Kamen Wolf's-own?"

Malick didn't flinch or move, didn't even shift his glance. He kept his gaze fixed on Imara's profile and breathed evenly. He couldn't afford to give anything away, not to Imara. She was old, she was smart, and she was ruthless when she needed to be. If she thought Fen was "fragile," as Dakimo had wondered, she might very well try to take him from Malick. And it wasn't only Malick's own wants and desires that recoiled at the thought. Fen needed Malick, whether Fen knew it or not. Asai's persistent "ghost" was only a part of it.

"Just keep your nose out of it, Imara." Malick let the warning in his tone ring clear. "He's mine until one of us is dead, or until he chooses otherwise. Don't test me on this."

"Ah, but testing you is so very… educational." Imara stepped back from the pond, snagged Malick's arm again and started steering them for the temple. "You can't put it off any longer, Kamen. It's your job. You may have until the week's turning, and then the matter will be taken from your hands. He will begin at the temples. If you'd like to maintain your hold on him, I suggest you ensure his cooperation."

"He's not ready."

"*Make* him ready."

"I can't *make* him ready, damn it, there's more to—"

"Then make him *think* he's ready. Tell him what you must, give him what you must, but get him to the temples, and make sure he ends up in Wolf's."

"I'm not pushing him to—"

"Push, wheedle, fuck him into compliance, since you think you're so bloody good at it, just do—"

"—make a choice like that, not now, not Fen, I can't—"

"*Can't.* You're *Temshiel,* Kamen—a *Temshiel* of Wolf in Wolf's own Cycle. Are you telling me you're not as good at getting someone to do what you want as Asai was?"

Cheap fucking shot.

Malick stopped at the temple's bottom step, anger flooding his chest. He hated being pushed, and Imara knew all his sore spots. He was surprised she hadn't thrown Skel at him too. But Malick would be damned if he was going be pushed into pushing Fen—not by Dakimo, not by Emika, and certainly not by Imara.

Damn it, she *owed* Malick. He deserved better than this. *Fen* deserved better than this.

"He's borderline suicidal, Imara. If I push him too hard before he's ready, he might—"

"Then you'll just have to make sure he doesn't."

So bloody ruthless Malick could have strangled her.

"Imara…" He tried entreaty this time. "I know what I'm doing. Just leave him alone for a while. I'm taking care of this. He'll be what's expected of him, but he needs—"

"If you knew everything you think you know, you'd indeed be a creature to be feared by even the gods themselves." Imara tugged on Malick's arm. "Come along, Kamen. You know you have to. Wolf's not through with him. Wolf's not through with any of you."

Bloody fucking *hell*. She had to be talking about Morin, what Wolf had planned for him. Which was likely going to be harder for Fen to take than the whole Incendiary thing, and for which Fen would probably end up outright killing Malick, unless everything happened in exactly the order Malick intended. Incendiary first; Morin… sometime after that. A long time after that, probably. It all depended on Fen.

Imara was watching him carefully, though Malick was sure nothing was showing on his face. Still, she smirked and leaned into him, pressing up against him, intimate, like a lover.

"If you make me, I'll just go directly to his brother and start there. I doubt 'your' Incendiary will thank you for it, but it might be fun to watch."

That was it. Malick was done with this conversation. If he stayed here any longer, he really was going to kill her on the temple steps.

"Fuck off, Imara." With a growl, Malick shoved Imara away and stalked off in the other direction. "If I need your damned interference, I'll jostle your web. Until then, just stay the hell away from anyone named Fen. Don't make me kill you."

2

The absolute nothing of the suns, Jacin thought, really couldn't be worse than existing in the penury of life without meaning. *Couldn't be.* Not that he'd be finding out anytime soon. They all still watched him—making sure he didn't drown himself in the washbasin, probably, or go at his wrists with a rice paddle. They hadn't left him alone the whole voyage here, and he supposed he was only alone now because they thought Malick was watching him. He didn't think he was ever getting his knives back.

He could tell them they needn't bother. He was just a little too cowardly for that. Even if he moved himself to say as much, they wouldn't believe him anyway.

Dying in battle, for a purpose, that was one thing, but… well. He'd been told living was his sacrifice, and the gods had already fucked him over. He didn't want to chance being reborn into a life even worse than the one he had. He had just enough courage to try to start again, but not enough to do it as someone else.

Now, if he could just get someone to show him *how* to start again…

You need your beishin to see to you, Jacin-rei. You always have done.

Perhaps, but Jacin didn't say so. If he answered, Beishin would only get more insistent, so Jacin tried to ignore him. He took a drink instead.

The liquor left a pleasant tingle in the back of his throat, warm and rough, but it didn't dull like he would have wished, which rather pissed him off. Not enough to stop drinking it to spite himself, but still.

The ember at the tip of his smoke flared and sparked as he took a heavy drag. He held the breath in his lungs, puffed short bursts one-two-three, watching carefully.

Circles, but not perfect. He tried every time, though. Just in case.

Distended rings flittered and drifted in the chill whorls through the cracks in the panes, skimming toward the ceiling. He let them expand and ripple outward into almost nothing before gusting the rest of the smoke out his mouth, obliterating the imperfection.

Shig could blow smoke rings, pink lips puckered in a supple O-shape and a crack of her jaw. Jacin tried, but he just got vaguely circular clouds and blobs, and then he got annoyed, so he didn't try anymore. At least not in front of Shig.

They were moving on—all of them—starting again, and all Jacin could do was watch them and wonder why he couldn't seem to. He'd thought he was. He *remembered* thinking… *maybe.*

But then.

It had been almost three months. And yet all it took was one careless moment of allowing remembrance, and body-memory kicked in and set him tense, adrenaline swamped him and shortened his breath, pounded through his heart, and then he was there, watching himself do it all over again.

Betrayal and failure and fear and more betrayal and grasping at treacherous hope and death all around him—

Your fault, little Ghost.

His teeth clamped tight and he shut his eyes, forcing encroaching memory away. He held his breath, waited for his heart to stop pounding in his throat.

Physical pain was one thing. He could live with that, seek it, even, those bright little sparks of controlled sensation that focused his mind and told him he was real, *they* were the ghosts. *This*, though, this… pain of the mind, of the heart, of the soul… he had no idea what to do with it. And no one seemed to want to tell him. Not even Malick.

He pushed the last of the smoke through his nostrils as he took another sip of the liquor, flicked the ash onto the saucer that had been under the teabowl, and shoved his shoulders more firmly into the mattress. The teabowl had held tea when the inn's maid brought it. Jacin was sick of tea. There'd been a mostly full bottle of something dark and strong-smelling sitting on the washstand, so he'd dumped the tea in the basin and replaced it with… whatever this stuff was. He accepted the faint buzz as a good sign.

Your emotions make you weak and foolish, little Ghost, Asai told him. And the Temshiel *knows it. Why do you suppose he's so afraid to tell you what you are? What you've always been? Great things await you, my gentle mercenary, but you have not the greatness in you to reach them. Your* Temshiel *knows it. I can help you rise above what you are. I can help you truly become Fate's hand.*

Jacin just sneered and took another drink, said, "Fuck you, Beishin," to the ceiling and set the smoke at an angle between his lips.

You were so much more to me than that.

Beishin's voice sounded sad, but Jacin remembered that tone very clearly, and he knew the eyes that went with it were watchful and calculating, looking for weakness, even if he couldn't see them.

I would have given you everything. Your sister did not have to die, Jacin-rei. That was not my doing, but yours. You have refused to be what you are, you refuse it still, you refuse perfection. Can you not see the failure you have allowed yourself to become?

He shouldn't have answered, shouldn't have acknowledged. He'd opened the floodgate and now he had to deal with the deluge.

"No, I see." Jacin shoved the smoke out through his teeth and shut his eyes. "I didn't kill you quick enough."

Beishin laughed, a warm, kind thing that *still*, even after everything, curled a sick knot in Jacin's gut and spiked his chest with regret. He clenched his teeth so hard he bit off the end of the smoke. With a curse, he took it from his mouth and spat the loose paper and leaf into the saucer. He stubbed the smoke out, hauled himself up, and lit another.

Perhaps, little Ghost, you should ask your Temshiel *what you are.* A soft chuckle, mockery slinking at its edges. *See if he will tell you. Then you can know what you really are to the gods. What you are to treacherous Wolf. What you are to his own.*

Beishin *tsked.* Jacin could almost see the disappointment in dark eyes, the slow, sorrowful shake of the head.

He doesn't love you. Why do you go on lying to yourself, Jacin-rei? Why do you go on letting them *lie to you?*

Jacin tightened his jaw and shut his eyes again. "Because I can't care enough not to."

And he didn't *want* to know, damn it. Why couldn't Beishin see that, if he thought he saw so much? And why couldn't he just shut the fuck up about it?

You can't care enough about anything. It's why all your trying amounts to nothing more than a lake of blood on the dirty cobbles of an alley behind a whorehouse.

Which was true, except it wasn't really, and it made sense, except it didn't. But Jacin was more or less used to that.

You need your beishin to show you what you want, little Ghost. Only I can love the unlovable. Your Temshiel *pretends at it, all the while hiding from you what you are, keeping perfection from your grasp, because it suits his god, because he wishes to keep for himself what—*

"Why d'you listen to them, Jacin?"

Jacin didn't jump. He was used to Caidi showing up abruptly. He even guiltily hoped for it sometimes. Caidi always chased Beishin away when she came.

"They're not real, you know."

Jacin watched the stratum of smoke shift across the ceiling. "Neither are you."

"How d'you know I'm not?"

Her voice was quiet, kind. Jacin kept waiting for it to turn accusing, but it hadn't yet.

Caidi sat primly on the windowsill, just looking at him, sunlight sparking through the panes and glinting off her hair. She was as lovely and loved as she'd ever been.

Sometimes Jacin liked to sit and watch her for hours. Sometimes he didn't want to look at all.

"Because if you were real…" The smoke's ash was getting long; he flicked it into the saucer, thought about trying a few more smoke rings, but decided there was no point. "If you were real, you'd know how you died. And you wouldn't be here."

"I know how I died."

Jacin's eyes burned as he lifted his bowl in an ironic toast and emptied it. He waited until the prickly sting at the back of his throat ebbed into pleasant warmth and the fire in his gullet tamped to a steady tingle.

"You'd know why."

"I know that too."

"Yeah?"

Jacin couldn't think of anything to say, so he didn't say anything. He could tell her everything—how it all evolved, how he'd failed her so spectacularly, how his need and his sick, impotent maybe-love-maybe-hate had made him too slow and uncertain. How she'd died because he hadn't been able to make himself believe how thoroughly he'd been betrayed until he'd watched her silent descent from the sky. But then she might go away, or start agreeing with Beishin, and Jacin didn't think he could take that.

He set the empty bowl on the mattress beside him and stared at his fingers, running his thumb over the tips. They were losing their calluses, going soft. It was… terrifying. In a bizarre way. He didn't understand it, so he stopped looking. He set his hand to his torso instead, settled his fingers over the scar from Malick's sword, and gave it a light swipe through his shirt. An almost complete absence of sensation. Scars he knew. Scars were old friends. Stripes of desensitized remembrance that blanked out feeling.

It had taken weeks for this one to heal properly. Malick had been frustrated, cursing more than once through his teeth about magical healing and Tatsu's perceived failure to use it with the precision and motivation necessary. Jacin hadn't said anything. Malick wouldn't have wanted to hear it. Malick would've looked at him the same way Joori did, and Jacin could barely stand it from Joori. So Jacin had just kept his mouth shut and eventually stopped picking and poking at the scabs, seeking that bright pinpoint of pain whenever he needed to know if he was real or not. Anyway, Malick always seemed to show up seconds after the blood started to ooze, like he could smell it or something, so it never did Jacin much good.

Sometimes, he thought about asking Malick for his knives back— partly to see if Malick would hand them over; partly because Jacin *needed* those little doses of *here* and *real* sometimes—but Jacin wouldn't be able to hide the cuts now; they all watched too closely, and he didn't want to see the way they'd all look at him if they knew. And he wasn't really sure if he'd stop once he'd started that first satisfying slice, so it was best he didn't have them. Anyway, he'd found other ways to confirm his reality, and Malick was nicely obliging.

Jacin thought maybe Malick knew, probably even understood. He wanted to take some twisted kind of comfort from that. He didn't let himself. Every time he reached for something real, it was taken from him, destroyed. He'd learned not to reach. He might not be perfect, but he wasn't stupid.

He started a little when the ember of his smoke seared into his fingers. A low curse rumbled from his mouth as he jammed the butt into the saucer and swiped at the ashes he'd let fall to the bedding while he hadn't been paying attention.

Caidi smirked. "You put another hole in that, and Malick will kick your ass."

Jacin wheezed a snort, said, "No, he won't," and settled back in to stare at the ceiling.

Malick wouldn't kick his ass. Malick wouldn't do anything to him except for those things Jacin asked him to. Malick wouldn't even touch unless Jacin touched first, even when he *knew* Malick wanted to, because Jacin could see it, and Malick didn't bother to hide it. Still, Malick waited for permission, even when Jacin *needed* it all taken from his hands, *needed* someone to tell him, show him, lead him, make him.

Jacin scrubbed at his face. "*Fuuuuuuck.*" He was exhausted, and all this *thinking* wasn't helping. Also, his bowl was empty. He thought about going over to the washstand for the liquor, but he had a bit of a haze going now, and he didn't want to ruin it. "I don't know what he *wants* with me." It came out hoarse and through his teeth. "What am I to him?"

He'd been wondering that for a while now. He didn't think it was for the obvious reasons, or Malick would've found a way to lose Joori and Morin along the way. Malick was *Temshiel*—he didn't need a mortal with whom to pass his time, and certainly not one as unpleasant to be around as Jacin knew he was. And yet, here they were, living on Malick's koin, this little inn holding more luxury than Jacin knew his brothers had ever seen, and there was the promise of an actual house, a home, in the next day or so.

Jacin kept waiting for the other shoe to drop, and he thought waiting for the betrayal was perhaps more painful than the betrayal he knew *had* to come.

"He's told you what you are to him." Caidi sounded a little annoyed, but Jacin didn't look at her to confirm it. "Why can't you believe that he loves you?"

"Because he can't." Jacin should've gotten that bottle after all. "Because he doesn't. Because I made him… it was part of the trade." And Malick was still holding up his end, for some reason, and Jacin didn't think he wanted to know why. "He doesn't know what it is, he's said as much, and I don't…" Jacin trailed off.

Even if Caidi was a figment of his imagination, he didn't really want to say that part out loud. Even if he knew it was true, he didn't want to give it power by speaking it and *making* it true.

"You don't deserve it?"

Jacin only shut his eyes. Figured. He couldn't even trust his own delusions to not betray him.

"Everyone deserves it, Jacin. Even Asai deserved love once. Except he used it when he got it, because that was what he was."

A snort he couldn't help gusted from Jacin's mouth. He lit himself another smoke.

"And Malick won't, I suppose. If I were to offer it."

He eyed the bottle again before he flopped back down to the mattress and took a long drag. Fuck it. Liquor only drove the lethargy deeper, and the temporary muffling of his thoughts never made the headache worth it. Anyway, Caidi wouldn't go away just because Jacin was muzzy.

She'd been waiting for him, here in this too-luxurious room at this too-luxurious inn, when they'd arrived in Mitsu almost two weeks ago, and so far, she only seemed to go away when Malick was around. Otherwise she just hovered about, nattering at Jacin, making him think about things he didn't want to think about, tricking words and confessions from him he didn't even know were down there somewhere. The only good thing about Caidi not-really-haunting him was that she somehow managed to silence Beishin once she started in on Jacin, so Jacin just kept not asking her to go away.

"Do you know why I love you?" Caidi's tone was soft, the words spoken kindly.

It still sent a bit of a frisson up Jacin's backbone. He didn't answer. Couldn't.

He'd never been able to figure it out. She'd only been a little thing when Asai had taken Jacin away—no, when Asai had bought him, bought him from his father, and that *still* stung like fire, but it was the truth, and dressing it up in less appalling words was worse than useless; it was gutless. Still, Caidi had been far too young to have formed any attachment to Jacin back then. Jacin had been surprised she'd even remembered him when they'd been reunited. Doubly surprised when she'd latched on to him the way she'd done.

Jacin had loved a half-remembered image of a towheaded toddler, but Caidi had been a reality for which he hadn't been prepared, and so he'd been helpless to shut her out. He wanted to regret it but he couldn't. Wanted to shut her out now, because knowing she wasn't real was killing him, but he couldn't do that, either.

"Because," Caidi told him evenly, "you love so big, even when you don't want to. Because you can't help it. And because you need it back, but you don't know how to take it." There was a pause, but when Jacin didn't fill it, Caidi went on, "You stepped in front of a sword for him. You saved his soul. But don't forget why he was risking it in the first place."

Jacin shut his eyes.

That was actually the one thing he'd never been able to explain away, where Malick was concerned. He almost wished he could, so he could finally settle everything into neat lines with predictable end points, know what to expect. But that one too-big-to-ignore fact loomed over the conclusion and made one plus one equal four hundred and seventy-two.

Malick had been forbidden to even touch Yakuli. And yet he'd meant to kill him. For Jacin. It was... inexplicable.

Hope crouched at its edges. Jacin stubbornly shied away. Hope had never done anything but fuck him over in the end, and that was the worst kind of hurt.

Caidi *tutted*. Jacin could hear the heels of her shoes knocking against the wall beneath the windowsill, and he thought it was a little strange that his mind would conjure something like that. Then again, he'd learned not to too deeply analyze the things his mind came up with. He never liked what he found.

"You think Malick doesn't know how to love, Jacin. But his problem is that he loves too much, just like you. It's why Wolf chose him. And everything he threw around so carelessly for over a century is now narrowed down on you. *Your* problem is that now you have to figure out what to do with it."

Sometimes Jacin thought maybe this really was Caidi, maybe she really was a ghost who just knew too much, because there wasn't a single word in what she'd just said that could possibly have come from Jacin's own mind. It threw him, clogged up whatever he might have been thinking of saying into the back of his throat where it tangled with the smoke and the remnants of the liquor and *burned.* His eyes teared.

"I don't know what I'm supposed to be here. I don't know… *how* to be." His hands fisted. "And he won't *tell* me."

"That's because you're supposed to decide that for yourself."

Jacin rolled his eyes. "That's what *Malick* says." It was very nearly a sneer. Because Jacin really, honestly hated Malick for it sometimes.

"*Well.*" Caidi sighed, all put-upon. "I guess since there seems to be a consensus, maybe you should start trying to figure out how to do that, instead of wallowing in why you think you can't."

Right. *There* was his guilty conscience talking. Maybe she was half ghost and half Jacin-being-self-pitying.

"He wants something from me." It sounded so weak, so shaky, that Jacin was almost ashamed, but *fuck,* it seemed to be Caidi's purpose to drive him to this kind of lost despair-through-hope at every opportunity; shame seemed rather beside the point. "Maybe he does… love me…"

He doesn't love you. Why do you go on lying to yourself, Jacin-rei? Why do you go on letting them *lie to you?*

Not Beishin, but an echo of him, and yet somehow it didn't hurt any less.

Jacin swallowed and squeezed his eyes tight. "But it won't matter in the end, because he brought us here for a reason. I just don't know what it is yet."

Malick might be all kindness and gentle acceptance now, but he was a predator right down to bone. There *had* to be something else coming.

"He wants something from me."

"And you'll give it when he asks," Caidi told him gently. "Because that's what people do for each other. You don't know your own heart, Jacin, and you have no idea that it's not really yours anymore."

Jacin's eyes snapped open, and he narrowed them over at Caidi. "What the hell's that supposed—?"

She was gone.

He didn't know why it surprised him when she did that, but it did. It kept him guessing—*was she real? was she a ghost? was she his own sick mind making sure he didn't forget what a failure he was?*—and he hated the doubt more than he thought he hated the dreams that Caidi's recent presence had seemed to stir. Joori thought it was some kind of new, cyclical depression, but it was really just exhaustion, because Jacin would much rather not sleep than watch Caidi splatter on the cobbles over and over again, with Beishin's accusations still ringing in his ears and Beishin's blood warm and sticky on his hands. Nothing seemed quite so effective at dredging up things Jacin didn't want to see-remember-think-about-know as Caidi telling him none of it was his fault, that he could be an actual person, that he deserved—

He cut that one off and flicked the ash from his smoke into the saucer. Believing he deserved it would make him want it, which would make him see it where it wasn't. He didn't know what it looked like when it was real, and he was too cowardly to risk what was left of him on something that wasn't.

Of course you know what it looks like, Caidi had told him just yesterday. *Your brothers love you. Why can't you believe others could too?*

Because they don't, Jacin had snapped back, and she'd shaken her head at him in frustrated disappointment, but he'd known at least *that* for truth.

Joori loved someone who didn't exist anymore, maybe never had; Morin tolerated his "freaky" brother, because what choice did he have when his "freaky" brother's pseudolover was the one feeding, housing and clothing him? Jacin sometimes wondered if the too-intense obsession-fixation-halfway-hysteria he had with keeping them close and safe and alive was actual love or just some new twist on his own circuitous delusions.

Maybe if Jacin had had the opportunity to see Joori and Yori together, he'd have some idea what that sort of love was supposed to look like. Because Joori really had loved her, which was something else Jacin couldn't think about. Because if he'd been just a little quicker in that alley, Yori would still be alive too.

"You put another hole in that quilt," Malick said from the door, low and carefully neutral, "and I *will* kick your ass. The inn's already going to charge me for mending it the first time."

Jacin only flicked more ash into the saucer and took another drag. He didn't jump because he wasn't surprised. When Caidi disappeared like that, Malick generally made an appearance not long after. Which was one more tick in the not-his-imagination column, because how the hell would he know to make his own personal phantasm disappear before he even knew Malick was going to show up?

Then again, Malick also managed to banish Asai, too, like he used to silence the Ancestors, so maybe it was just the way it was with him. Jacin wouldn't pretend to understand *Temshiel* magic, even if it wasn't supposed to work on him. He had a scar that should have been a fatal wound just below his ribs that said otherwise.

Sometimes he still hated Malick for it.

"Who were you talking to?"

Malick was still at the door. Jacin couldn't see him unless he shifted from his sprawl on the mattress, which he didn't, so he didn't know what look Malick was giving him. He rather suspected it was one of those compassion-with-a-shovelful-of-wariness ones, though, so it was just as well.

"Fen." Soft but stern. "Who were you talking to?"

Jacin thought about answering… decided he didn't want to. He dragged himself up off the bed, shambled slowly over to the washbasin and refilled the teabowl. He sucked on the smoke until the ember was bright and long, almost to his fingertips, then dropped it into the stale water and diluted tea in the basin.

Malick watched him take a gulp of the liquor. "How many have you had?" He waved through the trail of smoke as he followed Jacin toward the bed.

Jacin shrugged, dropped diagonal across the mattress, and shut his eyes. He could feel Malick staring down at him, trying to figure out how to "handle" him, no doubt. Malick usually figured it out before Jacin did, so Jacin just waited.

"I thought you were doing all right today." The mattress dipped as Malick sat down. "You seemed fine when I left. What happened?"

Jacin's jaw stiffened, and he clamped his eyes tighter, lifting his bowl to take a drink—

"Fen." Malick stopped him, hand warm though firm. "Who were you talking to?"

He wouldn't be ignored—that was the thing about Malick. Talking at Jacin, all the time, or touching him, or just doing that staring-and-smirking-knowingly thing he did. Malick *never let up*. Anyone else Jacin probably would've killed by now, but from Malick it was almost a bizarre comfort all by itself, and Jacin didn't know why.

Eyes abruptly burning, Jacin tugged at his hand—not too hard, so as not to spill the liquor, but just hard enough to let Malick know he was serious.

Malick let go, so Jacin told him, "Caidi," by way of conciliation.

There was a pause. Jacin slitted his eyes and peered at Malick sideways. Malick's eyebrows had jumped up to his hairline. Mild surprise, but not shock. Jacin thought the surprise was actually due to having got an answer, rather than the answer itself. He wondered what Malick would look like if Jacin had admitted to Beishin as well. He almost snorted. He took a drink instead.

"Did…?" Malick shifted on the mattress. "Did she talk back?"

In other words: *Exactly how crazy are you right now?*

Jacin did snort this time. "Yeah, she talked back." He turned his gaze back up to the ceiling.

"And, um…" Malick pushed the ashy saucer out of the way and folded down on his side, facing Jacin. He propped himself up on his elbow. "What did you talk about?"

There was no easy way to answer that, and anyway, Jacin didn't want to. So he didn't.

Malick waited for several silent moments before he sighed, unhappy. "Fen, these…" He scrubbed a hand through his hair. "Caidi isn't there. You know that, don't you?"

Jacin wasn't sure, he kept going back and forth on that one, so he still didn't have an answer. Except he knew how these conversations went, he knew what came next—*it's only your own guilty conscience, you can't listen to what your "ghosts" tell you, blah blah blah*—and he didn't want to hear it. He didn't want Malick to voice a denial of the things Caidi said, even if Jacin was doing it himself the whole while, but it would be different coming from Malick, and Jacin didn't want to have to hear it in Malick's own voice.

Cowardly, just as cowardly as pushing away the knowledge that one father had sold him to another and neither of them had seen him as anything but a means to an end, but this threat of knowledge was *right here*, and Jacin… he just *couldn't*.

Fuck, he was pathetic. He really did want to believe. Wanted to pretend he was flying, even if he knew he was falling.

A creeping pressure-fist closed around his heart, and it was abruptly hard to breathe.

"She looked like my mother."

It just… came out, ill-conceived and entirely against Jacin's will.

"Oh?" was all Malick said, expectant. He stretched out on the mattress, peered at Jacin with those tawny, too-knowing eyes, and waited for more.

Except Jacin didn't have more. He didn't even know why he'd blurted it in the first place, except maybe because Malick usually didn't insist that Jacin talk actual sense, only that he respond, that he recognize reality. Maybe something in Jacin thought the shock of an answer—any answer—might forestall Malick from making declarations Jacin didn't want to hear. But that was it, all Jacin had. He didn't have the excuse of the Ancestors anymore, but he hadn't forgotten the lesson about keeping as much of the crazy as he could locked behind his teeth.

"Fen. Was, um…?" Clear hesitation, which was surprising from Malick, before he sucked in a rough breath, as though bracing. "You've been… seeing Asai too. Haven't you?"

Cautious. Gentle. Because Malick had said more than once there were no ghosts hovering around Jacin. He'd checked.

Jacin thought about answering this one, because he hadn't been seeing Asai, only hearing him. It didn't seem like a distinction that would make much difference.

With a snort that was flat, defeated, Jacin tossed back the rest of his liquor and dropped the bowl to the bed.

"I don't want to talk about it."

He didn't look Malick in the eye as he said it, or as he turned on his side to face him. Instead, Jacin snaked out his hand and ran the tip of his finger over the lines of Malick's open collar, keeping his eyes on his hand. Invitation, but Malick wouldn't take it as such. He never did. It always had to be Jacin's idea, Jacin's *choice*. Jacin thought Malick was making some kind of point—

Make a fucking decision, Fen.

—and Jacin sort of got it, but sometimes it just made him want to scream and beg, *please just take it all away, I don't know what to do with it.*

Jacin had perhaps had little choice when he'd woken to reality one day and found himself in the middle of the ocean and bound for Tambalon, but he'd nonetheless made that choice—retroactively, granted, but he'd thought pretty clearly—when Malick had invited him to share his bed as well as his house and Jacin accepted. Wordlessly accepted, but still. He was here, wasn't he?

Slow and careful, Malick took Jacin's hand, stilled it, and settled it flat over his breastbone. Jacin could feel Malick's heart beating against his palm, and he thought, *I was supposed to cut that out*, and instead he'd cut out Beishin's. It still set a light quiver to him that wasn't wholly unpleasant. It still made him wonder what would have happened if things had spun out the way Beishin had wanted them to. Would Caidi still be alive? Would Beishin have loved "his Ghost" if Jacin had fulfilled the destiny that had been invented for him?

"I don't want to talk about it." A whisper this time, hoarse, as Jacin tugged at his hand.

Malick didn't let go. In fact, his grip tightened. "Are you trying to get around me, Fen?"

It was light, with very little rebuke inside it. Because yes, Malick understood, Malick *knew*.

Still, it set Jacin's teeth on edge. "Trying to get around you would imply you've some sort of right to expect answers from me that I don't want to give." He gave up trying to get his hand loose. Instead, he just shoved in right up close, comforted by how the lines of his body met and melded with Malick's. He pushed his face into Malick's chest, breathed in pine and sage, and shut his eyes tight. "I just don't want to talk about it."

Malick let go of Jacin's hand, finally, slid his arms around Jacin and hauled him in tight. Jacin's breath caught, a clogged up little sob that came from nowhere, because it felt so fucking *good* he didn't know what to do with himself.

"Fen."

Just that, just that one word whispered into Jacin's crown, and it wasn't even really his name, but it was the one Jacin had given once upon a time, Malick wouldn't use another until Jacin gave him that, too, and it burned at the backs of Jacin's eyes, because he didn't know why he hadn't.

"Oh, *hell*."

Jacin had got so abruptly lost he almost didn't realize Malick was pushing him onto his back, turning him so he could see Jacin's face. Jacin didn't know if he fought it because he didn't *want* Malick to see, or if it was just because he didn't want Malick to let go. It didn't matter; the "fight"—such as it was—was useless, because Jacin hadn't been expecting it, and Malick was too much of an opportunist not to take an advantage when it was handed to him. Jacin's hands were pressed to the mattress on either side of his head, and his hips were pinned by Malick's thigh before Jacin could muster the wits to look for leverage.

Caught, trapped, which was stupid, because wasn't this where he wanted to be anyway? Except he didn't want to have Malick *looking* at him like that, so Jacin turned his head and shut his eyes.

"This." Malick's voice was soft as he let go of one hand and traced the hollow of Jacin's eye with a gentle fingertip. "This is where you hide yourself when it all gets too much. I only wanted to find you."

Jacin frowned. He knew it was exactly what Malick wanted, but he couldn't help doing it anyway: he opened his eyes and peered into

Malick's. He didn't ask, *What the fuck are you talking about?* but he suspected it came out in the glare.

Malick smiled, because glares amused him, which irritated the shit out of Jacin, but this smile wasn't smirky or predatory or even knowing—it was soft and as gentle as Malick's fingers sliding into the hair at Jacin's temple. The fingers of his other hand laced through Jacin's where his hand was still pinned to the bed.

"I admit that I had to learn to look." The low tone slicked and sloped over Jacin's nerves while Malick's fingers set a light, heady fizz to Jacin's scalp. "You live so deep inside yourself that sometimes I think you get lost in there. And I think some of the time, you want someone to come and find you. So, you need to tell me, Fen…" Malick paused to set a tender kiss to Jacin's mouth, all fleshy, yielding lips, and the tiniest swipe of the tip of his tongue. "Would you like to stay in there with your ghosts for a while?" He slid his mouth lightly just below the line of Jacin's jaw. "Or would you like to be reminded that you're not one?"

Jacin could've answered this one. He knew exactly which he wanted. Somehow it all clotted in the back of his throat, and his mouth couldn't form the right shapes to make the right words. *Please*, it wanted to spew, and, *Take it away from me, just this once*, and, *I don't know how to do this. I've been faking it and not very well, clinging to a shattered life, and I don't know how to let go. Pleasepleaseplease show me how to be something other than desperate and directionless and useless. It's so fucking lonely in here.*

"Malick," was all he said, weak and small, because it was all he *could* say, but he opened his eyes when he said it, because he thought it important that Malick know Jacin was *here.*

Tea-colored eyes looked back, stripped Jacin with a peculiar depth he couldn't read but could somehow *feel.* It was almost like something breaking, something hard going soft, but it wasn't pity—*not* pity—so it didn't make Jacin gag.

Malick's face twisted, and he shut his eyes. "Oh, hell, Fen." Tender, he slid his fingertips through the tears Jacin hadn't known were leaking down his temples and into his hair. "It doesn't have to be like this."

Then show me how it can be, but nothing would come out Jacin's mouth except "Malick." Reckless entreaty. Desperation voiced in the arch of his body and the tears that wouldn't stop coming. "*Malick.*"

"Shh. Just let me." Gentling, comforting, controlling—*controlling*—as Malick stretched his body over Jacin's, trapped him, stilled him, and took it all away with breath and touch and the mute command implicit in one long, driving kiss.

Pleading and imperative like it had been that first night when Jacin had both blooded and bled and finally bent his neck to this same need that had crouched in his corners then and clawed at his walls now. By no means slow, and by no means solicitous. Malick's hands were fierce on him—*grippingtakingholding*—and his kiss was pristine power, deliberate dominance, threading like lead into Jacin's bones that sank him like an anchor into *here* and *now*.

Malick didn't ask Jacin to move, neither with words nor without, he simply did it himself, forcing reaction, demanding response. Jacin rocked his body with Malick's because he had no choice, and when Malick pulled his mouth away for a shaky breath, Jacin spent his own on begging—"Please. Malick, *please*"—until Malick shut him up again.

No shame in this—this naked supplication, this absolute *necessity*—not right now, because Malick wouldn't let Jacin have the time or the wits to look for any. Jacin was existing only inside this single moment, living for the next touch, dying for the next kiss, and Malick just kept it all coming, he wouldn't let up, wouldn't give Jacin time to think or even breathe, so Jacin just stopped trying.

He was stripped of his shirt roughly, but with a strange reverence he couldn't credit. Each scar was touched and stroked as it was revealed, a hard press of fingertips that dug down deep for sensation and didn't relent until Jacin was forced to feel it. He couldn't protest, Malick was drowning him in kisses, and every time Jacin gathered enough fury to shove through the outrage of dead flesh brought back to life, Malick drove it away with a press of his thigh to Jacin's groin. Jacin was being played, manipulated, and there was an appalling erotic relief in knowing it was out of his hands, not his choice.

He had just enough wits to try to help when Malick went for Jacin's trousers, but Jacin's "help" was more like disconcerted flailing, and more begging every time Malick let him breathe. So, Malick took both of Jacin's hands and pinned them above his head, kissed him into silence again and did it himself.

The position, the near-violence, the urgency and the helplessness—it took whatever sense Jacin might have held in reserve and throttled it down to raw, simple *need*. He was wild with it, trying to drag his hands away just for the reassurance of knowing that he couldn't, moaning like he was dying, and kissing Malick back with a desperation born of every single rejection he'd suffered since he'd known what rejection was— rejection of his kiss, of his touch, of his love, of his *self*—because Malick had never rejected him, had never looked at him like he was nothing.

"Please, please, please, *fuck*, Malick, do it, just—" Jacin had to snap in a choppy breath as a hard knot of sensation opened up inside him and set fire to his spine. "Just… uhn, do it, please, I… *Malick*."

Malick did. It hurt at first, but Malick had meant it to, because he knew Jacin needed it to, needed the focus, needed the reality.

Jacin somehow didn't have his hands again, so he couldn't claw and drag as Malick shoved into him. All he could do was arch and try to tilt his hips, *get more*, until Malick stopped him from doing that too with a firm hand to his torso and a look that was so intense Jacin thought he might smolder to an oozing puddle of slag beneath it. Malick's palm was right over the scar beneath Jacin's breastbone, flaring a heat that didn't belong there just beneath Jacin's skin. Malick's gaze was so concentrated it felt like he'd opened up the wound and Jacin was bleeding out all over the place.

It was too much, except it *wasn't*. It wasn't *enough*. Jacin's eyes filled and spilled over again, because he didn't know what all the things churning and stoppered up in his chest meant, but he thought Malick did, and he knew Malick was waiting for him to ask, but he couldn't, he just *couldn't*.

"Please," was all Jacin said; it seemed it was all he *could* say anymore. He knew there should be humiliation tangled in it somewhere, but this was all on Malick now, that was the whole point, so Jacin pinned it down just as firmly as Malick pinned Jacin's wrists to the bed.

"Tell me," Malick bid him, rough and demanding. And then he waited.

A bright flare of panic ripped through Jacin's gut, because he didn't know what Malick wanted him to say, had no idea what Malick wanted to hear, and Malick wasn't going to tell him, he wanted Jacin to *know*.

And Jacin didn't.

He could bluff, maybe—snarl and curse and snap his teeth. Except bluffing didn't work on Malick. Almost nothing worked on Malick but for those answers he saw as necessary truths, the ones that ripped a hole in the spirit in the giving. And stopping now before Jacin got what he needed out of this… unfathomable. He was too close to that terrifying edge he couldn't see or define, but he knew it was there. He could fall or he could fly, but one way or another, he *would* go over.

Jacin had no choice. He took all the unnamed, unknowable things that were driving in his chest—all the chaos, all the terrifying emotion that was too unfathomable and just *too much*. He let it all leak out his eyes with the tears that wouldn't stop, bound them to two words—"I *need*"— and shoved them from his mouth on a breath that was meant to be forceful but trickled out on a wretched little sob instead.

Malick shut his eyes. "*Damn* it, Fen."

That was it, that was all he said, rough with impossible emotion and shoved out through his teeth, before he laid his body fully to Jacin's, pinned him, stilled him, and took his breath again in a deep, hard, soul-scouring kiss. His grip on Jacin's wrists relaxed, but he didn't let go; he slid his fingers through Jacin's instead, and pressed his hands down into the bedding.

"Show me, Fen." Malick breathed it into Jacin's shoulder, humid heat that swept down Jacin's chest and bloomed beneath his sternum. "Show me what he wouldn't take from you. Give me what you hide inside yourself because he told you it's not worth having."

Jacin stiffened, bared his teeth on a snarl. "Shut *up!*"

All at once *furious*, Jacin bit at Malick's lip, sucked him into a kiss that was rough and spiteful, and refused to give in to the impotence of position. He pulled back with a glare, tears still leaking, burning like fire behind his eyes. "You never let up. You just can't ever *shut* the fuck *up.*"

"Oh, I can." Malick dipped in and sucked the lobe of Jacin's ear into his mouth, puffed hot breaths through his nose into the shell, and set a light nibble to Jacin's throat just below. He lifted his head and looked right into Jacin's eyes, like he was seeing through to bone. "But then you'd never show me, and I wouldn't know." He smiled, too deliberate for it not to be at least a little bit cruel. "And you want me to know. Don't you? Because you know bloody well that *I* want it, and to me it's worth it all."

He didn't wait for Jacin to answer, which was good, because Jacin wouldn't know how. He moved, a long, slow thrust of his hips, pushing in, pushing down, pushing, pushing, pushing, because that was what Malick did. Pushing until he got what he wanted out of Jacin, and Jacin somehow ended up both grateful and resentful at the same time.

It was all right, though. It was good. It was a relief. *Finally* there was something to surrender to, something to force away the creeping shame of surrendering at all, the rabid need for the profound reprieve of having no control. And if Jacin couldn't have physical pain to sharpen his mind, he could have *this* to blank it, could dissolve beneath Malick's steady force that pressed into Jacin's heart and mind as he pressed Jacin's body into the bed. Jacin was just a mess of nerve endings and reactions, held together by the grip on his hands, the pressure of blood and bone surrounding him, shoring up the fissures and keeping them from winnowing into fractures.

It started out slow, so slow Jacin thought he'd scream if Malick would let him, but that was the point—Malick wouldn't let him—so he just rode along into oblivion, let Malick push and prod his body into sensation that didn't terrify him and reaction that wouldn't end in rebuff.

Time stretched out into long, sticky threads, each touch, each movement, each kiss spinning into its own web, binding mind to body to soul to heart. Jacin had just enough time to take hold of that thought, close a mental fist over it, before it wasn't slow anymore.

He didn't know where his mind went while Malick fucked him into a clutter of raw need and animal want, but it was somewhere pleasant and free of constraint, a perfect contradiction to the constriction of his physical self. His body was slave to Malick's tempo; his breath was captive to Malick's kisses. His pleasure climbed with the hard strokes of Malick inside him, and ebbed with every rhythmic retreat.

Helpless. Powerless. Vulnerable.

No loved ones to save, no souls to salvage, and even if there were, he was trapped and just as defenseless.

It shouldn't have spiked the pleasure to new levels of intensity, but it did. And Jacin didn't even care that Malick knew it.

Jacin let go. Jacin *flew*, riding on the current of the rhythm into which Malick forced his body, spreading the wings of his self on the cooling wind Malick slipped through his mind. Uncertainty was forgotten, grief was an unknowable thing, and madness was something that looped his body into its feral desires, and shaped it into craving that wasn't shameful or base or twisted, but met and heightened and mirrored by another.

"Yeah." Malick's breath striated all over Jacin, runneling over throat, shoulder, chest and sliding deep down into his gut. "Like that, baby, there you go, c'mon, love." Soft, soothing counterpoint in Jacin's ear to the near obscene things Malick was doing to Jacin's body, the filthy reactions he was coaxing out from a core that opened like an aperture and spilled Jacin into the free fall of the universe.

The tears hadn't stopped, not once, and fuck, Jacin was going to drown himself in them, but they'd changed, they didn't hurt and sting. They leaked steadily as Malick held him down, held him together, drove his body toward bliss and his mind toward somewhere cool, calm and dark, where there were no ghosts waiting to ambush him with the accusations of his own guilt. He was free there, while his body was pinned to the bed, his back scraping against the sheets and his chest slick-sweated and fusing with Malick's. Like the physical imprisonment enabled the mental liberation.

It was forever inside, and full of colors he could taste. The bliss was so intense—sparked that much brighter with every hard shove of Malick inside him, every breath that was driven from his lungs with the force of Malick's thrusts—that he thought he might die of it. He almost laughed at the irony that it seemed this was the only time he really didn't mind living.

"There it is, Fen." Malick stared right down into Jacin's eyes, gaze a soft counterpoint to the ruthlessness of his rhythm. "That's it, yes."

Jacin didn't know what Malick was seeing, and he thought he should be a little scared that maybe he was giving too much away, but Malick wasn't rejecting it, whatever it was, he wasn't turning away, so Jacin just let him keep looking. It spiked the intensity somehow, roped sensation all through Jacin's body like jags of lightning.

"Perfect," Malick breathed, sonorous and so replete with brutal authenticity. "Perfect, just like this, you have no fucking idea, Fen."

And save him, it *hurt*. Jacin wanted to sob out loud, and he had no idea if it was from the words—*that word*—or the way it caught on his building climax and twisted it sharper. Maybe both, all, he couldn't suss it, all snarled together, that was it, just bloody *it*, Jacin couldn't take another single second.

He almost didn't need Malick to touch him to slip him into orgasm, but he was grateful for it anyway. He shouted as he went over, something guttural and grinding, his body seizing in pleasure, and his mind completely white, completely blank. Bliss sparked and sputtered all through him, heaved him around inside it, then threw him down, gasping. He could only try to breathe through it as he rode on the tail of Malick's orgasm, the hard jerking of Malick's hips and the muffled curses into Jacin's shoulder just another chunk of sensation that sent fizzy little ripples up and down Jacin's backbone.

They were both wheezing, shaky and weak, residual shudders breaking through Malick's body as he panted into Jacin's hair. He finally released Jacin's hands and slid his arms around Jacin's ribcage, squeezed.

"*Fuck*, Fen." Another shiver jolted through him, leaking into Jacin through osmosis.

The joints in Jacin's arms were a little stiff, but he made himself move them and wrap them around Malick's neck. If he didn't, Malick might move away, and it was too soon, Jacin didn't want to let go yet.

"Just... *fuck*."

Jacin rumbled something slurry and incoherent but agreeable nonetheless, and shut his eyes, breathed deeply the scent of pine and sage and sex. He thought it was probably strange and perhaps even unhealthy that he could only seem to reach this sort of contentment in the aftermath of practically begging for domination, then giving submission over without even a token fight, but... well. He wasn't perfect, he'd never been perfect, and he'd never be perfect. If he was right about nothing else, Beishin had pegged that one, at least. Anyway, Jacin was batshit, right? This was probably normal for him.

"Fen, this…" Malick let the whisper drift off as he pulled out, turned it into a hissed little "*Shit*" with which Jacin agreed, but Malick didn't pull away, like he knew Jacin wasn't ready for him to yet, so Jacin didn't say anything. "Everything's about choice, right? Yours, mine… other people's. This doesn't have to be as wrong as you think it is."

Jacin frowned. Malick had assured him hundreds of times he couldn't read Jacin like he could read just about anyone else if he tried, and Jacin mostly believed him. Because if Malick could see what was inside Jacin's head most of the time, Jacin thought he wouldn't right now be lying beneath Malick, trying to catch his breath after being fucked halfway stupid. But then there were times like this.

"What does that mean?" It didn't come out angry, because Jacin wasn't willing to let go of the contentment yet, but it was perhaps a touch wary.

Malick sighed, propped himself up on his elbows, and peered down at Jacin, too sober for what they'd just done together. He stroked a finger over the small plait at Jacin's temple.

"Your choices are yours." He said it calmly, like he was expecting Jacin to freak out any second. "Not mine. Not… his. You can't keep letting *his* opinions influence what you think of yourself. It'll matter one day. It matters now, really."

Ah. Right.

Now Jacin was ready to let go. He clenched his teeth and wrenched his gaze away, turning his head to the side.

"I told you I don't want to talk—"

"Fen, just listen to me for a moment, all right?"

"*No!*" Jacin shoved at Malick's shoulders, trying to shimmy out from beneath him, but Malick still had the advantage. "Why d'you have to bring *him* in here?" Jacin snarled, helpless to escape, helpless to keep the tears from burning their way back out again, just… helpless in general. "In *here!*"

In here, where Jacin handed Malick everything Asai refused, and Malick pretended to want it and accept it. In this room where Asai taunted him, in this bed where Malick fucked him and where Jacin forgot to pretend Malick's eyes were dark and mocking.

Jacin couldn't make himself fight before, and now he couldn't stop. He growled as Malick pressed him down into the bed, snapped his teeth when Malick took hold of his jaw and forced Jacin to face him. Jacin didn't want to, *wouldn't*, so he shut his eyes like a five-year-old.

"Fen, look at me."

"*No*. I don't want to hear it and I don't want to see you when you say it. Just get the fuck *off* me, I don't want—"

"I'm trying to tell you that he's *wrong*, Fen. I'm trying to tell you that whatever he says to you in that twisty little head of yours, whatever he tells you to make you think you're not worth the effort, it's not how *I* feel, all right? *This*—" Malick took hold of Jacin's hand and slammed it to the mattress. "If *this* is what you need to stay here with me, then *this* is what I want to give you. Your choice is to ask it of me. Mine is to give it. And it's not like it's some great hardship, so stop feeling like you've betrayed yourself, or... or *him*, just by needing it. All right?"

Jacin sucked in a shaky breath and cautiously opened his eyes, but he didn't meet Malick's yet. "That's all?"

"That's all."

Jacin was silent for a moment, going over what Malick had just said in his head, picking it apart so he could be sure he'd got all the nuances. He flicked his eyes up then quickly away again.

"There's... you..." No, he should be looking at Malick when he said this. He slanted his gaze upward. "That's not what you started out to say."

Malick sighed, laid his head down to Jacin's shoulder, and let go of his hand. "No. Never mind. Another time."

Sure. Fine. Jacin had no doubt "another time" would be sooner than he wanted, but "ever" would be sooner than he wanted. As long as it wasn't right now.

"You think I still let him tell me what to do, even though he's not here anymore."

"I think," Malick said slowly, muffled into Jacin's skin, "that you still... care. I think it still messes with your head. And I think you have to stop letting it. You have to stop stifling what you need because of what he might have thought of it, until you need it so bad it almost explodes out of you and takes you out in the blast. That's what I think."

Jacin frowned at the ceiling, going over that, too, wishing he had that bottle of liquor close by, because he'd stopped wanting to get away from Malick, but he'd rediscovered his desire for a soothing buzz.

He scowled. "You get what you want, so what does it matter to you?"

There was a puff of warmth across Jacin's shoulder, an ironic-sounding snort, and Malick slid a little off to the side. Jacin could breathe a bit easier than he could a moment ago, but Malick's grip was still comfortably firm enough to keep him in place.

"It matters. It *matters* here. And it's not... it's not *all* I want. Damn it, Fen, I *care*."

Jacin tried very hard to believe that last bit. To believe it wasn't all part of a trade he kept refusing to learn his part of. Sometimes he could do it. He wasn't sure now was one of those times.

The rest… it was too close to that "something" Beishin wouldn't shut up about.

Then you can know what you really are to the gods. What you are to treacherous Wolf. What you are to his own.

Fuck you, Beishin. If you see so much, why can't you see that I don't want *to know?*

Jacin should be demanding that Malick tell him everything, should be pushing and poking and prodding like Malick did, until Malick was so frustrated and disconcerted he blurted it out before he could help it like he made Jacin do.

Jacin couldn't do it. He wanted to pretend he was still flying. And Malick seemed willing to let him.

"We should clean up," he said instead, but with no real conviction.

"Mmph" was Malick's considered reply. He emphasized it by dragging the quilt from where it had slid off the side of the bed and pulling it up to cover them. "Should do a lot of things." He tightened his grip around Jacin's ribs and turned his head to plant a kiss to Jacin's throat. "Fen." He settled back in, getting comfortable while keeping Jacin right where he was, "I think—"

"Jacin."

"—maybe we should…" Malick trailed off as he registered what Jacin said. Everything about him went still. "Um. What?"

Jacin wasn't sure why he said it. Maybe he was just afraid Malick wasn't going to let the other things drop after all. Maybe he was just tired of being different versions of himself for different people, when none of them seemed to fit very well into those people's expectations. Malick didn't seem to expect him to be anything but what he was.

Maybe Jacin just wanted to give him something in return.

"Jacin." He shut his eyes, slid his fingers along the notches of Malick's backbone between his shoulder blades. "In here, it's Jacin."

⛩

Malick didn't dare even whisper it. Not yet. It was too fragile just now. Fen probably didn't even know what he'd just handed Malick, and Malick didn't want to do anything too overt and make him know. Sometimes, you just had to let Fen stay still and calm in his own self-delusion. And sometimes, you had to prod him out of it, force him to know things, see things, but not everything and not all the time. You just had to know the difference.

A bloody-mindedly determined paradox, Fen Jacin. Seeking identity by giving himself away. It would be a mighty effort for Malick not to succumb to the omnipotence Fen kept trying to hand him. Not get caught up in Fen's delusions and take up the heroic space Fen kept assuming Malick should occupy. Grudgingly assuming, which was a paradox around which Malick couldn't even begin to bend his mind.

The name was a gift, but more than that too. A sign. A real, undeniable, fuck-you-Malick-Imara-was-right-and-by-the-way-the-gods-hate-you sign.

Malick couldn't stop looking at Fen and waiting for another that would negate it.

There wasn't one.

Son of a *bitch*.

Fen was… perhaps not ready, but as close to it as he could come. Malick had no real choice anymore. He couldn't *not* see what Fen had just shown him.

Fucking Imara.

Still.

Malick had been waiting for Fen to hand him a sign, and Jacin had done it for him. Even if Malick wanted the choice, it was no longer his.

Fen needed to know. He needed to know what he was. And he needed to decide what he was going to do about it. Fen might be neck-deep in denial, but he wasn't stupid. His mind could be a brittle, unpredictable thing sometimes, but he knew something was coming, Malick could tell. How could he miss it? The Almighty Cock was going to fall off from overuse pretty soon, if Malick didn't tell Fen what Fen very obviously didn't want to know. And Malick was somewhat attached to it. He'd miss it.

Not that he was going to have much use for it for a while. Malick would be lucky if Fen didn't…

No, he wasn't going to even think that far ahead. In this one thing, Malick rather understood Fen's habit of avoiding knowledge. Because sometimes it burned and stung and stripped you raw. And Malick *knew* he wouldn't be contemplating forcing this on Fen now—tonight, even—unless he'd been forced into it himself.

He nuzzled into Fen's shoulder, careful not to wake him just yet. Soon, but not right now. Malick wanted to savor.

The trick was going to be in keeping Fen from tipping right over from sort-of-not-really-suicidal and into determined-death-wish. Because Fen wasn't quite ready, but he was as close as circumstances were going to allow, and it couldn't wait anymore.

Thing was, Fen didn't want choices. And he wasn't going to be pleased with Malick for forcing this one on him. Nor would he likely understand that it wasn't Malick doing this to him. Fen could raise his fists to the empty air and curse the gods, or he could turn his wrath on something tangible. Most likely on Malick, because he'd be handy.

Sometimes it really sucked to be a minion.

Malick stayed still, just listening to Fen… *Jacin*—a soppy little smile surprised Malick as he paused to shape the name silently on his lips—listening to Jacin dozing, his skin warm against Malick's, wire-strung nerves gone loose and pliable. Malick soaked it in, preemptively regretful, molding the shapes and sensations and textures into his consciousness, because he might not be having it for very long. Which was going to fucking *hurt*.

Loved him. Really, honestly, deep-down-heart-clenching *loved* him.

Fucking hell.

They always had their best talks after sex. When Fen was all loose and dazed and didn't remember to shut Malick out until Malick was already too deep into the "conversation" for Fen to ignore. And it had to be done. It was, after all, Malick's job.

Burrowing down tight for just another moment, Malick sucked in a long breath, firmed his grip on Fen then slowly let it loosen. He set his hand to Fen's shoulder and lightly shook.

"Jacin, wake up. We need to talk."

3

Goyo stopped in the middle of the street, head cocked, gaze distant. Entirely oblivious to the shoppers and passersby who growled at him as they jostled past him.

Something… new, but…

No, something familiar, except…

Not that, either.

Frustrated, Goyo reached, stretched his senses, dipped over toward the domain of the spirits, but only halfway. Listening. Seeking.

No stir, no sudden shift in attention, no swelling buzz in the hubbub of white noise that was the ordinary chatter of drifting souls looking for a spark of life on which to latch. Not even a tiny shock of curiosity.

He sniffed the air. Nothing. Just the smells of Mitsu—the salt breeze from the sea, the stench of guts and blood from the fishing boats in the harbor, the sweat, the hot oil from the kettles bubbling in food stalls, and here, close to the temples, the heavy perfume of incense, thick as a cloud. Nothing he hadn't smelled before. Nothing new.

"Pardon me, sir, you'll have to move."

Scowling, Goyo dragged his gaze outward, focusing on the patrolwoman who'd chided him. Though, now that he was looking, perhaps "chided" wasn't the right word. Taken an opportunity to speak with him, perhaps. There was recognition and a shy bit of admiration in her gaze. She was young—maijin newly turned, if his guess was right—and so many of the Patrol were vying for a place in the hunt right now, wanting to be one of those who brought Tambalon's *banpair* predicament under control. Goyo had never had so many trying to curry his favor before.

He adjusted his bearing to match the patrolwoman's. It wouldn't do to annoy the Patrol. Maijin though he was, he still had to work with them. And he was rather in the way, he supposed. The streets in Mitsu had never been sufficient for such a teeming mass, and those paths to the temples were always clogged. He probably could have picked a better spot for his sudden… whatever it was.

"Please do forgive me." Goyo bowed with a smile, as charming as he could make it, and moved along. He'd been heading toward Snake's temple, meaning to consult the seer-priest again, because he'd grown bored with the fruitless hunt and was hoping for new direction, however vague. He veered instead toward the Ports District. No rhyme, no reason, except whatever it was he hadn't just felt had come from that direction. Or not come from that direction. Whatever.

Perhaps he should begin visiting the inns and taverns again. There was always interesting talk, at least. Most of it rumor, true, but sometimes, if one listened properly, one could find the seed of verity inside the anecdotal entertainment. And the recent gossip had been terribly intriguing, if completely unbelievable. At least Goyo didn't believe it. He'd seen the last moments of the last Incendiary, after all. He wouldn't believe any god could be so cruel as to chance something like it again.

Too dangerous. Too much unpredictable risk in mortal form. At least, that had been the gods' excuse for eradicating the Incendiary. Goyo saw through the indefensible defense—everyone saw through it—but he accepted it, because he *knew*. Dropping an Incendiary into the world untethered was like dropping a newborn into a pool of sharks. *Temshiel* and maijin alike would sniff him out, hunt him down, and claim him for their own god, or do him in altogether to keep the others from claiming him.

Hitsuke had only survived as long as he had because—

Goyo cursed. He shouldn't have allowed his mind to wander there. A century wasn't long enough, he was continually surprised to realize every time he made the mistake of letting Hitsuke enter his thoughts. Goyo still missed him. He'd been new when he'd known Hitsuke— perhaps that was why he'd never managed to shake the gloom. Young and impressionable, and Hitsuke had certainly made an impression. And Goyo had certainly not been bored.

Maybe that was it. The not-taste on his tongue, the frisson of phantom feeling on his thumb… like when he'd wiped tears of agony from Hitsuke's cheekbone. The blood of Incendiary had a smell, a taste, but there hadn't been blood that day, only screams and tears, and Goyo had tried to wipe them away and there'd been a… tang—no, maybe more of a zest, or… something on the back of his tongue, but it had hardly even registered at the time. It hit him now with a strange vertigo of not-really-remembrance, and it made him shudder.

He hardly ever thought about that day. He made it a point not to. He hadn't remembered that not-taste until just this second.

With a shake of his head, Goyo set it aside, realized he'd wandered all the way to the piers and was staring morosely out into the gloaming over the rise and curl of the water. The breeze shifted his dark hair around his face, and he shunted out a light growl, dug around in his pocket until he found a bit of leather to tie it back. A ship's bell rang out somewhere farther down the coast, the trill of it carrying on the cool draft that flittered past Goyo's ears, tickled at his nape.

Wolf had already crested over the water, his silver face rising up as though mounting the waves themselves, only the barest red glow tingeing his flank where Raven and Dragon followed like two jealous siblings intent on missing nothing. Which was probably fairly close, Goyo thought, squinting at the horizon for a trace of jade. Owl began her secondary phase soon, riding Wolf's coattails, lending her pull to providence and purpose as the New Year approached. Goyo couldn't see the hue of harbinger in the sky yet, not with the blood of Raven and Dragon staining it.

And when had his temper swung over to maudlin?

Goyo snorted. It came out rather flat.

Bloody hell, he'd been in a good mood only a little while ago, and all it took to turn it sour was—

His head came up, eyes narrowed. There it was again. Not a scent, but a... stir. A shift. Something. Something that put Goyo in mind of the uneasy wakeful slumber of an infant child in its cradle, trying to decide if it was hungry enough to wake fully, open its mouth and bleat its discomfort; a tiny peck of a beak from the inside of a shell.

Goyo stood there for hours, meditating, reaching, stretching, but never grasping hold. Still, it was out there. He knew it. Felt it. He just couldn't touch it.

Something.

Nothing he could pin. Nothing he could identify. Something worth his attention, though. Something not boring.

Something waiting to be born.

With a narrow look up at the moons, and then a searching one at the inns and taverns that lined the piers, Goyo decided that perhaps it was time to find out if there had been any recent arrivals of interest in Mitsu.

⚏

"Incendiary." Jacin whispered it slowly, testing it out, saying it out loud to see if the shape of the word matched the dread in his chest when Malick had spoken it. It had taken him a night and a day to even attempt to try to repeat it, and now that he had...

He just didn't know. And spending nearly two days huddled in this bed and determinedly *not thinking* had given him nothing but a blank spot where some kind of erudition should be. He supposed he must have slept somewhere in there, eaten, taken care of necessities. He knew he'd smoked quite a lot, because the room reeked of it, and his lungs felt gritty. Maybe he'd been drinking too. He couldn't remember.

He remembered clinging to Malick, though. And Malick letting him. He remembered letting Malick fuck him only a little while ago. No, not letting him—begging him for it. But it hadn't made it all go away this time.

"It isn't that different, you know."

Malick's voice was quiet, almost gentle, his breath a warm spangle at the nape of Jacin's neck. It didn't lend the comfort Jacin knew Malick intended, though; in a haze of self-imposed nonexistence or not, Jacin still knew Malick had simply been biding his time, waiting for something from Jacin before he pounced. And now Jacin had given it to him. Because Malick never let up.

"Incendiary were the paradigm for the Catalysts. It was what the Ancestors intended when they made the Untouchables. Except they kinda... y'know—fucked it up a little." Malick paused, then said more softly, "Fen... this doesn't have to be as appalling as I know you're thinking it is."

Was Jacin thinking it appalling? Maybe. He couldn't tell. He still didn't seem to be thinking much of anything. There was a white roar just at the edges of his consciousness, and it was yawning wide and deep, deeper than the past two days of pretending he didn't exist had been. He wasn't sure yet if it was comforting or terrifying.

"Voices?"

Malick's grip on Jacin tightened. "*No*, Fen. Your chosen god may choose to speak through you, but it's a rare thing, or was, back when the Incendiary were... well, not such a rare thing."

Right. Back before they'd proven too dangerous for even their own gods and had been stamped out.

"But it wouldn't be like the Ancestors." Malick was keeping his tone gentle, a touch wary, and his hold on Jacin was a little too firm to be merely for Jacin's own preference of comfort. "Not dozens of voices crying insanity at you, Fen. You have to believe this. Like that day at the Girou, remember?"

Oh, yeah. Jacin remembered. A shudder rippled through him, and Malick soothed it with a firm stroke up and down Jacin's arm.

"It's dangerous." Jacin let it hang there, not bothering to tag the tone with a question, because there was no point. Malick wouldn't have been so careful about it all otherwise. Probably because he didn't know what answer Jacin was hoping for. Then again, neither did Jacin.

"It's… complicated." Malick shifted but didn't move away and didn't let go. "King-maker and god-slayer, world-changer and world-destroyer. No magic, no tricks, only the power of will. An Incendiary wants something badly enough, they find a way to make it happen. It makes you… valuable."

Valuable.

Jacin would've snorted, but all his breath seemed to be locked somewhere between his chest and his throat.

"How long have you known this?" A paper-thin whisper, not even laced with accusation, because Jacin hadn't that right. He'd been doing everything possible to make Malick keep it to himself, hadn't he?

"Since you stepped in front of my sword. Since you spoke it as you lay bleeding."

Jacin buried his face in the pillow. Right. Just one more way his own mouth had betrayed him, even if the words hadn't been his, just more insane babble forced on his mind then his tongue by the Ancestors' madness. Bloody hell, would he never get away from them?

"I couldn't tell you then. You weren't ready. But there are others who know, and I couldn't not tell you anymore."

Jacin could shut it all down now. Let the hysteria burble out his mouth in cackling laughter. Start sobbing out the hitching breaths and curses that were gathering in a hard knot in his chest.

Except he couldn't, not really. His blood still wasn't his to spill. It never would be.

"Others?"

"Like me, Fen. *Temshiel,* maijin. Word spreads quickly among my kind. No one's exactly on the hunt, because only a few know you're here, and the ones who do are scrambling for a clue from their gods for an idea on what to do about you. There hasn't been an Incendiary for over a century, and they were rare even before that. The last one—" A low-level growl was creeping into Malick's voice, a weird muffled resentment that Jacin couldn't pin. Malick cleared it away with a firm kiss to Jacin's hair and another tightening of his grip. "But rumors spread quickly, and there were others there in Ada. They heard you. And some will come looking for you."

"Why?"

"That, I imagine, will depend on who shows up. You're valuable, but some will see you as dangerous too. There's too much of an Incendiary's own will tied into their power, and their will is tied to their chosen god's. The last one thwarted Raven quite soundly and was punished horribly for it. There hasn't been one since. Not until you."

Not precisely what Jacin had meant. More like "Why *me?*"

He didn't suppose he'd've got an answer he liked anyway.

"Am I supposed care about any of it?" He set his jaw to keep his chin from wobbling. "Because I don't."

Except.

"Was… was I…?"

Tears were too close, burning behind Jacin's brow. Because the answer was imperative, *defining*, and yet he couldn't make himself ask the question.

Your sister did not have to die, Jacin-rei. That was not my doing, but yours. You have refused to be what you are…

It had stirred fury and resentment before; now the ring of it sounded too much like truth. Jacin swallowed, several times, but it wasn't helping to get breath past the chunk of old-grief-made-new lodged in his throat.

"Is this what I've always been?"

Malick stilled. Which pretty much answered the question.

"Fen, you have to listen to me, all right? You can't make this—"

"Oh, *fuck!*" Jacin curled in, dug his fingers into his scalp. The abyss opened up, vast and razor-splined, but it wasn't white and buzzing like it had been before—it was dark, blank-black, and filled with Caidi's high little voice telling him everything depended on what might rise from Fen Jacin-rei's ashes. "*Ohfuckohfuckohfuck—*"

"Fen, *no*, you have to listen to—"

"I could've saved… the *only* thing I… and *now* they tell me I could've—"

"Except you *couldn't.* That's not what this means. Even if it had been what you're thinking, it wouldn't have worked that way. You're Fate's creature, and Fate can be fucking cruel. There always has to be Balance, and the price is always bloody. *You* didn't do any of it, Fen. You were both then, Incendiary inside Untouchable, but as Untouchable you couldn't—"

"You just said *my will* is what—"

"Not *then.* Damn it, you have to *listen* to me. Caidi and too many others like her were always going to be the price of saving the Jin, the other end of the Balance that Fate demanded. You couldn't have saved her. *This* is why you have to know now. *This* is why you're dangerous. You always have to be three steps ahead of Fate to know if the price will be worth what—"

"*Worth*…?" Jacin almost gagged. "I didn't fucking *care* about the Jin. I wanted to save *her!*"

…Oh, no.

Jacin went still. "Oh… Mother. Oh, *fuck*, my—"

"*No*, that's not how it works." There was so much inside Malick's voice, too much of it Jacin didn't want to hear—sympathy, understanding Malick couldn't possibly own, tenderness and genuine compassion that made Jacin want to scream. "As Incendiary, you'll have a chance to work your will on Fate, but never forget that Fate answers in her own ways. Even the gods are tempered by what Fate allows. It's what makes you dangerous and valuable. Balance. *Always*. Even if you'd known, even had you the power then, Fate's price might *still* have been Caidi. This is why I can't let you not know anymore. I'm so fucking sorry, I'd take it from you if I could, but I can't."

It didn't stop the ache, or the sick knowledge that had birthed it—it only made everything that much more excruciating.

Jacin could almost see Caidi, sitting on the windowsill as she did almost every morning, only this time, she was shaking her head and frowning at him with a sad look of betrayal. Could almost hear Beishin, laughing at him, telling him, *You did this, little Ghost.* And Jacin couldn't argue, not even the feeble defenses he used to justify the gutless inertia that kept him from finding the will and energy to put an end to it.

"I killed her." It came out like a wounded animal's whine, and no wonder, the way it slipped out from between too-quick and too-shallow breaths. And why was Jacin just now feeling the weight and serration of the knowledge, when he'd *known* even as he'd watched her fall?

You did this, little Ghost.

"*Bullshit*," Malick snapped. "Fate—"

"That's what Asai meant. He knew, he *had* to have known, I… I didn't want it hard enough, I didn't—"

He choked it off when Malick twisted, flipped Jacin roughly onto his back, and pushed him down into the sheets. Held him still.

"See, *this* is why I kept waiting to tell you. I knew you'd—"

"How can they do it? How can they ask it? She didn't deserve it, none of them did, it isn't *fair*! They're supposed to be *better* than us—*you're* supposed to be better than us! What the fuck could they possibly need me for, and why should I even bother to pretend to give a shit what they want when 'fair' means nothing to *any* of them? They made me weak and then took my mother and my sister away because I wasn't strong enough, and now they expect me to start all over again? For them? For Fate? *Fuck* Fate, and fuck *them*."

He wouldn't. That was it. Incendiary? Fuck it. What did he care? Start again? No. He wouldn't.

Perhaps gutless inertia had been a problem up 'til now, but Jacin didn't think it would be a problem after this. Lack of knives wouldn't be as much of a hindrance as Joori probably thought it would. All Jacin had to do was wait until Malick wasn't watching.

"Bloody damn." A sharp, cynical smile curved at Malick's mouth. "I used to think it was Joori who was innocent, but you, Fen…" He shook his head, eyes hard for all his voice was still soft and laced through with gentle consolation. "How have you lived through what you've lived through and still managed to keep hold of that gullibility with both hands? You think anything's *fair*? There *is* no fair—there's *Balance*, and that's *all* there is. *Fair* is how you've ended up—" He cut himself off, clenched his teeth. "Fate's a callous bitch, and there's nothing fair about it."

"You think I don't know that?"

"Yeah, I guess you do at that. But I'm not going to let you turn this into what I already see blooming in your eyes." Malick shook his head, all at once harder, colder. "You don't want choices? You don't know what to do with them? Fair enough, then, because you haven't got any when it comes to it. Telling yourself you killed your little sister because you didn't want her to live hard enough, and all so you can add one more tick in favor of suicide, won't bloody *fix* it. You'll be gone and it'll *still* be un-fucking-fair, except it'll be even more un-fucking-fair for the brothers you leave behind."

Jacin sucked in a sharp breath through his teeth.

Malick merely tilted his head and tipped a little nod. "Yeah, love, it means exactly what you think it means. You thought I was a cold bastard before? You haven't seen what a motherfucker I can be." He leaned down, eyes sliding half-lidded, too-canny seduction, right in Jacin's face. "You kill yourself, Fen, you allow yourself to be killed, and my oath is once again my own. You understand what I'm telling you? I know you do, but just so we're very clear—as soon as the first flame touches your pyre, I will walk away from your brothers. They're nothing to me but tools to please you with, and if you're not here, I've no reason to keep them around. Wolf wants you alive, so alive you'll stay. Everything's a fucking trade, right? Here's mine—you're gone, I'm gone. Got it?"

Malick's mouth was doing that flat thing it did when he was trying too hard to be a prick, when he wanted you to think he was a stone-cold asshole who didn't care if he crushed you or killed you, but none of it was making Jacin's anger and fear any easier to suss right now. Because there was also the fact that Jacin's cock seemed to think it was all somehow incredibly sexy, twitching a little throb to make sure he got the point, and there had to be something terribly sick and wrong about that, right?

Got it? Yeah, Jacin got it. And the worst part was that he hadn't actually needed to be told, and yet here he was, naked and debauched in soiled sheets with the man who was fucking him in every sense. Worse—even with Malick's stark proclamation, Jacin had no intention of changing the current arrangement. He'd let Malick fuck him again right now, just to make it stop for a little while, and they both knew it. And they both knew Jacin would *enjoy* it.

"*Bastard.*" Jacin's teeth clenched and his jaw quivered in helpless fury. "You don't want me to blame myself for Caidi, so you'll threaten Morin and Joori?" His eyes spilled over, and he didn't bloody care. "You're s…"

You're supposed to pretend. That *was the deal. I didn't agree to* this!

"It's no threat, Fen—it's a promise." So strange, the way Malick's eyes glittered cold and his words struck sharp and precise, yet his voice was still so soft. "And make no mistake—I'll do whatever it takes to keep you here, because you're not done. Perhaps you've not pledged to Wolf, but I have, and he wants you saved, little Ghost.

"I let you die now, and we've both failed. So yeah, if I have to make it clear that you're what's keeping your brothers protected by my oath, I'll take the chance that you won't deem fucking me a more attractive alternative to listening to me anymore." Malick ran his hand, hard and rough, over Jacin's chest, up to his throat. "This may be very, *very* nice, *Jacin*, and I'd miss it terribly." His fingers settled loosely around the base of Jacin's throat, and he cut his glance upward, smirked. "But it's really not the point."

With a contradictory light stroke of callused fingertips, Malick grinned, that hard, cruel, predatory thing he trotted out when he wanted you to pay real close attention; the one that reminded Jacin that Malick could be an entirely different person between one breath and the next.

"Unless you maybe want me to blow you now to get your mind off it all for a minute. I know how you get off on shutting me up. We can pretend I won't bring it up again just long enough to bring us both off, nice and dirty. Think you can get it up again this quick?"

Jacin's teeth were clenched so tight his jaw was starting to throb. Because he'd flinched back there somewhere, a sickening lurch as his mind had tried to shy away from the razor-sharp candor of it, the precision of the verbal evisceration. And worse, his groin had tightened just a little, like some primal, ingrained response over which he had no control whatsoever.

"You're a fucking bastard."

"Yeah." Malick dropped the grin like it was a mask he could put on and take off at will. "But I'm the fucking bastard who loves you."

"*Liar.*"

"Ya think?" Malick pulled his hand away. "Believe what makes you feel better."

"I don't love you." Snarled out and venomous. Because Jacin didn't. He *wouldn't.*

"Believe what makes you feel better."

Malick rolled away and sat up, his back to Jacin as he scrubbed both hands through his hair. Jacin curled in, couldn't help but stare at the wide, vulnerable expanse of muscle beneath Malick's skin and imagine how easily a knife would slip in, right between the ribs. As if he knew, Malick peered over his shoulder at Jacin, another smirk curving his mouth, but this one was more like the ones Jacin was used to seeing on him, all smartass arrogance and knowing ease.

Infuriating.

"The gods aren't done with you, Fen. I really am sorry. If I could give you this choice, I would. You'll be what you are, or you'll fail the Cycle. I can't let that happen. For either of us."

"What the hell does that mean?"

Malick didn't answer at first, only stared at Jacin over his shoulder for several long moments then shook his head and looked away.

"I brought you here to Tambalon—Mitsu in particular—because you've a choice I can't make for you. You were born under Wolf, but you're not truly his. You're not anyone's but Fate's until you choose a god and pledge yourself. Until then, you're more or less up for grabs to all the gods, and any of their *Temshiel* or maijin who might be sent to persuade you. Unfortunately, you're also vulnerable to any of them that might decide an Incendiary is too dangerous and try to get rid of you. You're under my protection, but my magic only worked on you the once and only a little at that. I can't veil you, and I can only protect you so far."

Malick turned back again to look at Jacin, jaw set, gaze harsh.

"You see where I'm going with this?"

Jacin glared, refused to answer.

"Yeah." Malick nodded, like there'd been some kind of agreement. "You're going to have to actually try to stay alive, Jacin. Sucks to be you."

"Fuck. *You.*" Seething, *incensed* that… well, Jacin didn't really know—there were so many things to be incensed about that he couldn't pick just one. And he was sick and bloody tired of being assumed to be and accused of being suicidal when he'd already failed repeatedly to drag up the courage to prove them all right. "You don't *know* me, you don't know what I think, you have no idea what—"

"You're right." Malick turned away, rubbing at his brow. "I only know what you show me, and sometimes that's too bloody hard to read. Except sometimes you show me more than you want to, and one of the things I see is that you have no idea if you want to live or die, but you think you *should* want to die, so you'll hand over that choice to the first person who makes it for you. So until you're ready to handle that choice yourself, I'm taking it away from you. You'll live, Fen. Because *I* choose it."

There was no answer for any of that. Jacin couldn't even pretend to bluster through a bullshit response that would at least leave him a little dignity. The horrifyingly shameful truth of it all was choking him.

Malick shifted on the mattress until he was looking at Jacin straight again.

"I know that you *feel*, Fen. I know that everything hurts you more than it should, and I know this whole business is probably bloody killing you. I wish I could change it. I wish I could take it away for you. But I didn't do this to you. *None* of this was my choice. But I *have* chosen to help you. Let me."

"I don't—" The anger was still there, lumping in Jacin's chest and at the back of his throat, making it hard to form words, form the thought to make them. "I don't know what that *means*."

"I know." A long, heavy intake of breath expanded Malick's chest, momentarily broadening his shoulders until he let it flow out on a weary sigh. He slumped. "We'll deal with it when you figure it out."

Cryptic bastard. How was Jacin supposed to answer that? And why did he keep feeling like he *should* answer?

Sad, furious, confused, Jacin turned his face away. Damn it, why couldn't he make himself just get up and walk away?—from this room, from this inn, from Malick, from Morin and Joori… from everything.

"The solicitor's finally found us a house," Malick said quietly. "We move in tomorrow. He'll come for the others while you and I begin at the temples in the morning. You should decide which one you want to start with."

Jacin sat up. Temple? He had no intention of going to a temple, let alone "beginning" with one and all that implied. Fuck the gods. What had they ever done for him but torment and punish him and take away the people he loved?

"It's why you're here, Fen." Malick stretched his arm out and brushed the tangled fringe from Jacin's brow, letting his fingers linger down over the little plait that held the hair back from Jacin's left temple, until Jacin smacked his hand away. Infuriatingly, it only made Malick smile. "You start again when you make a choice. I won't make this one for you, and

I won't let anyone else, either. From this moment on, you go nowhere without me, you go nowhere unarmed. If you don't want to pick up a weapon, then you sit your ass here behind my wards like you've been doing until I personally drag you out. The holiday's over. Tomorrow we start at the temples."

"You don't *own* me."

"You're right, I don't. And I won't, even if you almost want me to. But I do actually love you, so you'd best—"

"Stop *saying* that! You don't, you *can't*, and I don't want to hear you say it anymore."

Malick's eyebrow went up, a mockery of ingenuous curiosity. "Yeah? Why can't I?"

"Because there's—" *nothing there!* Jacin choked it back. And didn't know if it was because he didn't want to say it out loud and make it true, or because he was afraid of how Malick might answer it. "It was a trade, and it's *finished*. I didn't agree to *this*, and I don't want the charade anymore. Stop *pretending*, I can't... I *won't*... This..."

He paused to suck in a breath, because air was coming a little harder than it should be doing. It didn't matter that he'd tacitly accepted the terms of this newest trade when he'd accepted Malick's kindnesses, his tenderness, his gentle words. That he'd accepted the terms before he'd even known what they were, because he couldn't make himself refuse.

He wouldn't accept *this*. He couldn't. Jacin might be slow, but he'd had no choice but to learn to recognize a setup when he saw one.

"This, all of it—all it is... it's just another opportunity... another way to... to..."

Another way to fail. And he couldn't say it. Even though it was the truest thing that was churning in his gut right now. Because he fucked up everything he touched. He even fucked up things he tried not to touch. And all this Incendiary bullshit, all the "love" distraction and probable manipulation—it only gave Jacin shiny-new ways to fall on his face and take everyone around him down with him.

As with everything, Malick refused to make facing too-obvious reality easy.

"Let me help you, Fen." So soft, so earnest. "We'll figure it out together."

Jacin only ratcheted up his glare. He'd known Malick could be cruel, but *this*...

Bloody hell, Jacin didn't need knives to bring the pain. All he needed was Malick pretending to love him.

Edging on anger now, Malick whipped out his hand, wrapped it around the back of Jacin's neck, and gave him a sharp shake. Kissed him, warm and rough.

"There is no trade anymore, you're not nothing, you didn't kill Caidi, you're going to be the most beautiful-dangerous Incendiary the gods have ever seen, and I fucking love you. Deal with it."

She waited until Wolf and Raven and Dragon all completed their descent, leaving Owl's emerald shadow lurking behind the fire-mountains, staining the sky for the brief moments before the sister suns made her a vague ghost of a sliver in day's light. But she was there—quiet, ambivalent Owl, who shrouded her enigmatic majesty from the greedy grasping of her siblings and lent subtle insight to one with the prudence to seek it. A mind open enough to hear it.

Xari opened her eyes, took her hand from the stone, and peered closely. A shift in the depths of crystal quartz, a faint swirl of possibility, but there. Less murky than it had been only last night.

She sat back, thinking. The paint of her wolf's mask was beginning to flake; it itched. She set it from her mind and concentrated instead on the blank spot in the shifting fortunes spiraling beneath her fingers.

It wasn't difficult to recognize the influence. She'd seen it before, after all. The difficulty was in following each strand and trying to suss the overall displacement of the pattern, figure out where it started and trace it to its probable end. It was wearying.

Still, it was why she was here. A penance to Wolf, though he had not asked or required it of her.

A way to… commute a debt, perhaps. She owed the boy—the Untouchable that was no more; the Incendiary even now wending through the throes of long-delayed naissance. And he was, after all, the only way Kamen would ever accept the Sorcerer's mantle.

"Come, then, all you shy little possibilities. Show me your pretty faces."

She sent another humble appeal to Owl, a wish in the form of a prayer, and set a slow, delicate swipe to the stone with the very tip of her finger. Xari watched carefully, marked the too-brief clarity from the trail of her touch, and peered through it, squinting.

She shook her head.

Unfair. The child of Wolf who was not; the Fool who would refuse his fate. And the Eremite who held the Sorcerer's mantle and still disdained to don it. He'd refused it back in Ada, and he'd *still* managed to win through, when he really shouldn't have. There would be no reasoning with him now. And Xari knew what her god wanted of her, knew what he'd wanted of her even before he'd become her god.

"You do your Fool no good, Kamen Wolf's-own." Xari's mouth set grim as she waved away the murk and waited for the smoky lacework churning beneath her fingertips to build itself into something she could see. "Hand him too much, you do, and refuse to see the heart's purpose for which he has reached for too many lives."

Exasperation kept willfully at bay—she needed a clear mind, after all—Xari sighed a breath into the stone. Whispered Kamen's name to the flux and eddy of the tendrils of haze. Combined a spell with another prayer to Owl—

Sat back with a gasp and snatched her hand away from the stone.

"Kamen, Kamen, think yourself invulnerable, do you? Foolish child, moving too quickly for—"

"You will leave it, Xari."

Xari turned, brow furrowed, and didn't try to cover her shock for Imara. Framed in the archway that led out to the gardens behind the temple, Imara stood lambent in the first tentative rays of the suns, almost radiant.

"Imara, you don't know—"

"I can guess." Calm and commanding, reminding Xari that here, in Wolf's temple, Imara was the authority, Xari a mere initiate, a priestess obscured behind Wolf's face until her induction was complete. Imara shook her head, her beautiful face pulled into what looked like true melancholy, but threaded with annoyance too. "Whatever fate it is you've seen for him, Kamen has brought it on himself. I will not be put into the position of fixing it for him. Nor will I allow him to pull you into something that would displease Wolf. He has accepted you to the Cycle, but you have not yet been initiated. I would not see you jeopardize yourself for Kamen's foolish choices."

The threat was clear. The intent behind it, however, was less so.

Xari bit her lip. "But the Incendiary. You don't know what this might do to—"

"It won't matter for much longer." Calm; implacable. "Kamen has nearly run out of time. The Incendiary will not be his concern after today." Imara lifted an eyebrow. "Perhaps you and I together can achieve what Kamen keeps refusing to hand to his god, yes? Perhaps bringing the Incendiary's oath to Wolf, as Wolf wishes, will be that final step on your path from initiate to a true maijin of Wolf."

Xari looked away. Another why, another when, any other Incendiary, and it might have been tempting.

"You treat with griefs and possibilities you cannot under—"

"Xari." Kind and gentle this time. "What happens, what will happen, it is clearly Wolf's will. It would not do for you to question your god now." The threat was wrapped in silk, but all too clear. Imara shook her head then shrugged. "Perhaps Kamen needs a lesson only Wolf can teach him."

"Wolf has marked the Incendiary's brothers. Both of them. They must be—"

"I shall see to it, Xari. I shall see to all of them."

Xari slumped back, resisting the urge to scratch at her cheek, the paint somehow heavier on her skin now, cloying. She stared at Imara, meeting the brilliance of the gold gaze squarely, meaning to argue, debate, get the woman to see sense. Instead, Xari shut her mouth, mute beneath the plain command in Imara's eyes, the reminder of who held the power here.

They had a history, Kamen and Imara. Not one on which Xari had been informed, but one that went deep, from what she'd been able to glean, which wasn't much. For *Temshiel,* they were extraordinarily closed-mouthed about whatever it was they shared between them.

Still.

This was not the end of things, merely an unhappy beginning, and Xari would keep a close watch. If the opportunity came again, Xari would not be so foolishly trusting as to allow Imara to see it. Imara had no idea what she was calling down upon one Wolf would see saved; Xari did. She'd seen what loss did to the Incendiary. And she owed the boy.

⛩

"I don't *know* what he needs, damn it, but he needs *something!*"

Joori's voice was strained, but it was more with concern than with anger, though the anger was there. Samin didn't even have to look to know the statement—plea?—had been directed at Malick.

"He's not getting any better. He's getting *worse.*"

True. Fen had seemed all right for a while there, but now...

"You're wrong." Malick sounded awfully damned sure of himself. Then again, Malick always did.

"I'm *not* wrong. Don't think for even a second that you know my brother better than I do."

No, all the gods forbid anyone should imply they might know something about Joori's brother that he didn't.

Well. Damn. Sitting them all down together for tea—"like a family again"—had seemed like such a comforting idea when Shig had put it to Samin this morning.

Samin sucked in a bracing breath before venturing through the open door and into the room Joori shared with Morin. Shig looked up from her cup with a grim smile for Samin and a shrug; Morin gave him a roll of the eyes, but Samin might have been invisible, for all Joori and Malick noticed. Samin went to the service set on the press and picked up a bowl for tea.

"Fine, then what do you suggest?" Malick asked it with an outward calm Samin was sure he didn't actually feel.

"I..." It seemed to stymie Joori for a moment. "I don't know. What about that Tatsu? The healer that—"

"Magic can't heal hurts of the heart, Joori." Malick shook his head; Samin thought the sadness was real enough. "And hurts of the mind—"

"He's not *crazy!*"

"Sure he is." Morin. Funny, how the things Morin blurted could still manage to shock Joori sometimes. You'd think he'd've learned by now. Morin noted Joori's look of stunned betrayal and merely shrugged. "He's batshit." Unabashed and getting bolder by the day. "You would be, too, if it was you. Why can't you just let him be?"

Joori was gaping. Shig exchanged a look with Malick, but neither of them seemed to have the brass to insert anything into the heavy silence that fell. Samin calmly poured himself a bowl of tea and exited, just before the dam burst.

The volume rose before he'd even crossed the threshold. His timing was getting better. Bloody hell, Joori's voice could reach decibels that would deafen the dead, and Morin couldn't help poking at hornets' nests. Samin half listened to it from the inn's hallway, out of sight of the others, because hell if he was getting dragged into that.

Annoying, perhaps, and all too frequent these days, but Samin couldn't blame any of them. He understood Joori's anxious frustration, Morin's pragmatic acceptance, Malick's stubborn optimism and Shig's uncharacteristic concern. He understood because he felt every one of them himself, depending on whether Fen's mood swings happened to be at apogee or perigee. And when you sometimes couldn't allow a man free use of even a kitchen knife for fear he'd put it through his own throat, you sort of had to acknowledge the existence of a problem. Unfortunately, you also had to admit your complete lack of knowledge about how to even try to fix it.

The tension was getting too tight around here. They needed a job or something. Samin needed a job, and hunting these elusive *banpair* might be exactly what he needed. He was actually looking forward to it. He just wished Malick would stop holing up in his room with Fen and get to it already. Samin was going to start killing pedestrians for walking funny pretty soon if he didn't get to let off some steam. There were bad people who needed dying, and here Samin was, cooling his heels.

Sighing, carefully sipping his tea as he headed down the hallway, Samin almost missed the lean figure propping up the wall, folded into the shadows between the last room on the left and the stairway. Samin paused, took a good look.

Fen was watching him from behind ragged fringe. What Samin could see of his eyes was a lot less empty than they'd been the last time Samin had worked up the nerve to have a look. At least Fen was actually dressed and groomed. Perhaps a Dark Day was taking a turn for a Good Day. Or had been.

"How long have you been there?" Samin kept it quiet enough that no one would hear if there happened to be a lull in the shouting coming from Joori's room. Not that it seemed likely. It almost reminded him of Shig and Yori's screaming matches, and he weathered the pang in his chest with bittersweet remembrance.

Fen stared at him for a moment, measuring, before he looked away with a heavy shrug.

"A little before 'batshit.'"

"Yeah, well." Samin went to take a sip of his tea to cover the fact that he had nothing of relevance to offer; he paused with the bowl halfway to his lips and offered it to Fen instead. Fen must've come down here for something, after all. And Samin didn't blame him a bit for not wanting to go into that room.

One corner of Fen's mouth turned up, sardonic, but he took the tea with a nod, said, "Thanks," and pushed away from the wall.

He was almost to the door to his room when Samin called softly after him.

"People love in their own ways, Fen. Sometimes it doesn't help, but you just have to let them do it anyway."

Fen paused with his hand on the door, then turned to look at Samin over his shoulder.

"Yeah. And yet somehow, the way I do it isn't ever good enough."

Samin had no idea how Fen meant that, and he had a dismaying certainty that it mattered. Before he even considered voicing the question he knew bloody well he wouldn't ask, about something he was pretty sure Fen hadn't meant to say, Fen had limped back into his room and shut the door. Samin stared after him for quite some time, pondering, before he braved Joori's room again for another bowl of tea.

Malick cut his glance away from Shig and out the window of her little room. Twilight was blooming, the last day of Imara's "deadline" was fading, and Malick had other things he should be doing right now besides arguing with Shig. He was just about done with interfering women.

He kept his tone calm but uncompromising. "All I need from you is for you to keep an eye on Joori and Morin while Fen and Samin and I are gone tonight. I don't want them to know Fen is coming with me." If Malick could *get* Fen to come with him. "Now, can you handle that or not?"

Shig didn't back off, not even a little. She glared, as fierce as Malick had ever seen her, almost as venomous as Fen.

"First tell me what the hell you think you're doing. Why would you even *think* this is a good idea?"

"Because I need to know if he'll fight to defend himself, and putting him in a position where he *has* to defend himself is going to be the best way to see if he will."

Shig's mouth dropped open. "Are you *insane?*"

"Well." Malick shrugged. "Guess it depends on who you ask."

"*Damn* it, Mal, I *told* you—"

"And I told *you* there are things beyond my control, things I *have* to do, whether I want to or not, so stop fucking arguing with me."

"Bloody hell." Shig shook her head, lip curled in disgust. "So full of excuses, every damned one of you. What excuse will you use when he finally kills you and then himself?"

"Fen is a grown man, a very *capable* grown man, who is—by the way, and now that you've brought it up—choking beneath all the tender care you all are forcing on him. This is Fen we're talking about, for pity's sake. Do you *really* think he couldn't have made some kind of weapon out of his henjiisticks by now, if he was as dead set on offing himself as he thinks he is?"

"Then why have you been avoiding the temples like they're contagious, when it's supposed to be the reason we're here in the first place?"

"What the fuck, Shig. Isn't it Joori's job to be Fen's keeper? Why don't you try this protective mother-hen shit with him and see how far you get before he shoves you out the nearest window."

"You know better than anyone else that he needs—"

"He *doesn't* need every bloody one of you on his back all the time, so just *back* the fuck *off.*"

"Well, *someone* needs to be there to sweep up the shattered little bits once you've broken him," Shig snarled. Snarled! *Shig!* "You wanted his submission once. You got what you wanted, and now you want to hand him life-and-death choices, when you know bloody well he doesn't know what to do with them. It's not your right to—"

"No, it isn't my right, but it's my fucking *job*—*not* yours. So how about you just shut your damned mouth for once and let me do it." Malick paused, sucked in a long, deep breath, and tried to keep himself from shaking her. "Look." Calmer; more even-toned. "He has to learn that an oath is his to give and not anyone's to take. The choices Fen has to make, he has to make for himself."

"And you keep thinking he'll just come right out and ask what those choices *are*." Shig stepped in close, and though she was at least a head and a half shorter than Malick, she still managed to look menacing. "He can't handle it, Mal. He's not made that way. If you give him the choice, he'll take self-destruction every time."

Malick didn't think he'd ever seen Shig so furious. There had to be more to her anger than the obvious, but Malick hadn't a clue what might be beneath it. Until he looked a little deeper and realized that maybe he'd been neglecting to pay enough attention to everyone else's grief and confusion while he'd been concentrating on Fen's. He'd have to fix that. Just not right this second.

"You're wrong." He said it as reasonably as he could. "I know you think you know him, but he isn't like you. His mind doesn't work the same way. He's got too much room in his head now, and he's filling it up with self-hating poison. 'Fail the Fool and fail the Cycle,' remember? This is my *job*, Shig."

"You can't save him by taking away all direction and pretending you're giving him choices! Don't you *get* that? He's too easily seduced, Mal. Look what he did for Asai. Look what he did for *you*. You can't trust him with something like this, and you can't save him by—"

"*Don't* make me punch you in the mouth. You don't know what you're talking about. There's a lot more to Fen than even you can see, things *I've* seen that you can't even—"

"He's already looking for answers to the questions *you* keep waiting for him to ask."

This? Was going nowhere. And Malick didn't have the patience for it. He growled and made to push past her.

Shig gripped his arm.

"You've got the right intentions, but you're doing it all wrong, because you think you know him better than anyone else does, except you *don't*.

If you won't give him the answers he wants, Mal, he'll look for them anywhere he thinks he might find them. And do you really want to risk him getting them from someone else?" She leaned in and up, tightening her grip on Malick's arm. "Do you really think there aren't those who are already looking for him, *Temshiel?*"

She let go of Malick with a shove, expression rife with disdain and fury.

"I *begged* you to help him. But if you're going to insist on giving him even more reasons to hate himself, then bloody well get his oath, get him Wolf's protection, *now*, before another one of you vultures gets him first."

"And hating himself is exactly the thing you can't understand." Malick was *this close* to decking her, and it was getting harder and harder for him to remember why he hadn't killed her yet. "He was already blaming himself for Caidi. Now he thinks he's been handed proof. For Caidi *and* his mother, and Yori, while he's at it.

"That's what you'll never understand, Shig, because you don't have that in you. You don't hate yourself enough that you could make yourself believe Yori was your fault. And you don't have the new burden of knowing you might be halfway right." Malick leaned in close, dropped his voice. "You *really* want to tell me it's a good idea to tell Fen he's right? You want me to tell him he wanted his vengeance so badly he accidentally sacrificed Caidi for it, when he didn't even know it was a trade to begin with? Because no matter how I say it, that's how he's going to hear it."

Shig looked away. "He's not stupid." She turned back to Malick. "If you tell him—"

"I already told him none of it was his fault, and do you know what he heard? That he could have prevented what happened. He can't hear that Fate made the decision for him. He can't hear that Caidi was the other end of the Balance that Fate demanded in exchange for the Jin. He can't hear that he couldn't have known to look for the snare in the bargain he didn't even know he was making."

Malick didn't avert his gaze or soften his voice, because Shig needed to understand this, and she wasn't listening to logic.

"Would you have traded Yori?" He blocked the punch easily, then took hold of Shig's arm and yanked her in close. He shook her clenched fist between them. "*There.*" He clapped his larger hand over her smaller one. "Now take this and put a knife in it." He jabbed a finger at her breastbone. "Take this and add in your father and the man you love telling you you're nothing your whole life, that you have nothing to give them they might want, that what you are repulses them. Add in self-hate, and getting set up for failure, and the Ancestors screaming at you for—"

"All *right*!" Shig jerked her hand away. Malick let her. "All right." Not happy, but not ready to kill him anymore, either. "You're wrong, Mal, but I can't make you see it. And I can't fight with you anymore." She shrugged wearily then shook her head. "I'll keep an eye on Joori and Morin. But if someone ends up having to explain to them why their brother put a knife through his own eye, it's not going to be me."

Malick didn't let himself flinch. If he did, this argument would never be over. And he really needed for it to be over.

"It's not going to be anyone, because it's not going to happen."

Shig was quiet for a moment, staring down at her fingers, fiddling with the fringes on the tunic that Malick was pretty sure used to be Yori's.

It seemed like it pained her to finally ask, "How is he?"

Malick huffed a sigh. People had been asking him that a lot lately. Fen hadn't emerged from their room or let anyone in but Malick since the other night. Malick had managed a little hope this afternoon when Fen actually got dressed and made vague noises about joining them for tea, but he'd never shown up. They were all starting to worry.

"He'll be all right. We'll all be all right. You have to trust me, love—I know what I'm doing, all right?" Malick gripped Shig's shoulder and gave her a gentle shake. "I wouldn't take chances. Not with this. Not with any of you."

Well...

No, all right, not even with Joori. Fen would kill him.

Shig bobbed a heavy nod. "Sure." She peered up at Malick out the corner of her eye. "Yeah, fine. Just... you have to make sure he comes back, is all." She snorted; a dry, somewhat sad thing. "And you should probably watch your own back too. It'd kinda suck if he killed you now."

And just like that, they were all right again.

Malick gave Shig a smile, and then, because he couldn't help himself and he adored her, he swooped her into a hug.

"It'll work out, I promise."

He kept the smile until he was out her door and through his own. Until he looked automatically at the bed, and found Fen still there, right where Malick had left him after allowing himself to be dragged into another bout of *fuck-me-until-I-can't-think-anymore* when he'd come back from arguing with Joori. Malick had obliged. Malick always obliged. He couldn't help himself.

It's your job, Kamen. By all means, you should do it.

Malick strangled the growl.

"H'llo, love."

He wasn't expecting an answer, and he didn't get one. Fen actually scowled at him, though, met his eyes, so Malick took it as progress.

He didn't exactly ignore Fen as he made his preparations for tonight's business; he just tried not to feel the intensity of the stare. Fen was silent still, closed off, only acknowledging Malick enough to glare at him once in a while. He hadn't come to tea or supper, but he'd apparently eaten, at least; the bowl Malick had left on the cupboard beside the bed was empty.

Malick didn't try to force conversation. That wasn't how it worked with Fen. Not if one wanted the conversation to go both ways, anyway.

Silent, Malick merely started pulling on his mail vest and digging out his leathers.

It got Fen's attention. He was clearly trying to pretend it hadn't, though. With a wary look for Malick, he limped from the sheets long enough to wash and sneer at his own reflection in the brass plate above the press for a while.

The scars seemed to fascinate him these days, like he'd never noticed them before. Malick had himself a good look, too. Heavy, silver-white bands on thigh and upper-arm, and streaks of puckered rose and almost-pearl on back and chest. The lumpy twist of muscle and missing muscle on the back of Fen's calf that left him with what was looking to be a permanent limp as legacy. The twisted divots on his forearm.

As always, Malick's gaze found and caught on the scar set just beneath Fen's breastbone. The one Malick had given him. The one Fen had given himself when he'd gotten in the way of Malick's sword. Saved Malick's soul.

Still redder and fresher than all the others. Still looking like it might open up again if given the wrong jostle. Still just as raw as Fen was.

Fen had himself a good, long look, plainly not seeing the beauty like Malick was, the tale of endurance and unwilling survival it told. Fen merely sneered again then limped away and burrowed back into bed. Clearly intent on staying there.

Malick couldn't help the frown, the ripple of disappointment that stuttered in his chest at the closed-off demeanor and the continued hush. But once he dragged his weapons out of the chest and carelessly flicked the key to the bed, he noticed something else creeping beneath the silence. He just wasn't sure what it was yet. Fen merely cut the key a glance and then pointedly pretended he hadn't.

Give him a target. That was the intention, anyway. And if Malick worked this situation just right, however tonight ended, he'd have a better measure of Fen's equilibrium than Fen did. Which wasn't exactly a new thing, but at least this time it would be useful.

"*Banpair*," Malick explained, though Fen hadn't asked, "are…" He paused. He'd almost said "vermin" but it wasn't exactly true. "They're godless maijin. Xari was… you remember Xari, right?" Malick waited for Fen to nod, as much to see if Fen would as to check to see if he actually did remember. Malick still didn't know how much of his surroundings Fen had been taking in back then, between the time Subie had eaten itself and the moment he'd more or less come back to himself in the middle of the ocean on the way to Tambalon.

Fen did nod; Malick tried not to grin smugly. If Fen was still in his *I-don't-want-to-think-about-it-and-you-can't-make-me* mindset, Malick would've gotten nothing more than a blank stare, or a *fuck-me-now* look, and he wasn't up to forcing another subject just yet. Fen could be damned immovable sometimes, and right now, he was just too… brittle.

"Xari was *banpair*. She'd lost the favor of her god when she…"

Malick covered this pause by pretending his sword belt was giving him trouble. This might get sticky. Then again, it might not. You just never knew with Fen these days. Malick cut a quick look to where Fen lay on his side on the bed, his head propped up on his hand, watching Malick with… it looked like grudging interest. Malick was pretty sure it was interest. It was grudging something, anyway.

"Xari had seen that Asai would betray Skel. She'd read it in Skel's cards. She didn't know how, and she didn't guess about the amulets. She did try to stop him, or at least she says so, but she kept the knowledge from Dragon. I can't say if Dragon would've done anything about it, but she did *not* appreciate the oversight."

Malick was eyeing Fen closely, not even trying to pretend he wasn't. Fen would know anyway. He seemed to be used to it.

Fen only watched Malick fiddle with the belt's buckle until Malick finally gave it up for too obvious and slipped it home. Malick had looped the garrote around his forearm and pulled his sleeve over it before Fen finally stopped feigning noninterest.

"So, these *banpair*—they've all done something to piss off their gods. They've been stripped of their powers. And you're meant to hunt them?" Fen paused, peering down at his fingers on the linens before lifting a hooded gaze back up to Malick. "Don't you ever get tired of doing Wolf's wet work for him?"

Words. Actual *words*. Put together into cohesive sentences. Thank all the gods. Malick was so pleased that he completely ignored the inherent insult.

"It's a purpose, Fen."

And they both knew Fen had been flailing around, waiting to figure out his own. He had one now, like it or not. All he had to do was choose what he wanted to do with it.

Easier said than done, but then that could be said for everything about Fen. He had far more needs than wants. Mostly because he didn't dare admit that he wanted at all. The man had made denial an actual art form. Drunks and poppy addicts the world over could build monuments to Fen's capacity for self-delusion.

"Anyway, they're not really stripped of their powers." Malick rooted around through the clutter on top of the press, looking for his boot knife. "They're not defenseless, so don't look at me like it's not a fair fight or something. Stripped of their god's blessing, which means they can't get power from their god. They can, however, sort of absorb it from the energies around them."

He stopped there, busying himself with his search, and waiting. It could end here, which would mean Malick had said the wrong thing somewhere back there and Fen was retreating again, or Fen would ask another question, and Malick could acknowledge another tiny step forward. With any luck, Malick would have a better idea about Fen's state of mind by the end of this… was it a conversation? Maybe not yet. Malick liked to think it might get there, though. Because this was an opportunity he couldn't let slip past, and he'd told Shig only bald truth about his intentions—putting Fen into a position where he had to fight to survive should very handily answer the question as to whether or not he *would*. And better to do it while Malick would be there, watching.

"Meaning?" Fen finally asked.

Malick very nearly didn't control the smile. "Meaning that *banpair* sort of live off the passions of others." He found the knife. With a shrug, he turned to face Fen and leaned back into the cupboard. "Mostly mortals because mortals actually *have* passion. And the strongest are the baser emotions. Anger, hatred, fear, and so on. You've got love, of course, which is also fairly strong, but it's one of those things that flares very brightly at the beginning and then settles down to a slow, steady flame. Well, if it lasts."

"And the others don't?"

Bloody damn, Fen looked so good like that, tangled in messy linens with the lamplight scudding over the angles of his face, the dark, wispy growth on chin and upper-lip accentuating the sharpness of his features. Wrinkled sheets with those pretty bare feet poking out the ends, chiseled bare chest with its intriguing map of scars, and dark silky hair slightly mussed, the perpetual raggedy fringe only obscuring the prickly gray gaze enough to make it look sexy and not contrived. And that voice. Malick would never say so, because the circumstances that had wrought it had been… well, rather terrible. But Fen's rough-raspy voice really did things for Malick. *Really* did things for him. It kind of made up for the missing braid. Which he also wouldn't say out loud.

Malick cleared his throat. "Others?"

"The other passions."

"Oh."

Right. There'd been a kind-of-conversation going on a few seconds ago. Sort of funny that Malick was the one who'd lost the thread this time.

"For the most part, no, not when you think about it. Anger, sure, when it's over something one can't necessarily fix right away." Damn. He probably shouldn't have started with that one. He decided to skip right over hatred. "Fear is the easiest, though, which is where the problem comes in. Because it's the easiest emotion to create, y'see."

Fen's eyebrows went up. "My f-father…" The hesitation was minute, but there. "My father used to tell of flesh-eating maijin. He called them *banpair.*"

Malick had heard the epithet before. He'd used it once or twice. And it always amused him.

"Not really. Metaphorically, maybe. Generally speaking, *banpair* are simply maijin who've fucked up, but not enough to be sent to the suns. They've been rejected by their god, but that doesn't preclude the possibility that another god will take them, or even that their own will take them back, if they somehow manage to impress. But they have to work at it."

He thought about using Xari as an example of how *banpair* could earn themselves a place again, but decided that would be pushing things.

"Absorbing the energies from the emotions of others isn't really forbidden, merely frowned upon. And you can't really blame someone for surviving in the only way available to them. It's harmless, really. Someone who's doing it merely to survive and maintain the strength to do the work of the gods takes only what they need, and the person they're taking from doesn't even know it. They sort of… slurp up the overflow. The problems begin when they start to… I guess the best word for it would be to 'steal' those passions. Create them so that they can be absorbed."

Actually, the *real* problem was that the rush was more addictive than poppy, or so Malick had heard.

"It's always been a danger, but the instances down the centuries have been few and isolated, because once you start crossing the line, your chances of finding a god who will take you are almost nothing."

Fen gave Malick a once-over. "You're arming yourself pretty heavily."

"Because it's not isolated this time. There are twenty-three *banpair* in the world. An even dozen of those are unaccounted for. They've somehow slipped even the sight of the gods. And no one can find the spirits of those they've killed, either. It's… worrying. And they're getting bolder and stronger."

"So you're killing them."

"Sending them to spirit. If I can find them."

Once they were sent to spirit, the gods could lay hands on them. What happened after that was not Malick's concern.

"I'm thinking it's going to be more like wandering about the seedier places and nulling out any magic I can reach, hoping I can take away whatever they're using as a veil and find them that way. Kind of a blunt, blundering approach, but no other *Temshiel* or maijin thus far has been able to find them."

Which made it somewhat satisfying that Malick would be rather pissing off the other *Temshiel* and maijin who happened to be within his range when he was looking. Having one's power suddenly cut off, regardless of what one might be up to at the time, had to be a bit annoying at the very least. Their own fault, as far as he was concerned. If they'd managed to get this under control when they'd realized it was a problem, he could have been concentrating exclusively on Fen right now.

"Seedier places." Fen's gaze wandered again to the key then darted away. "Is it… dangerous?"

Aw, baby, are you worried about me?

Malick didn't ask it. Nor did he take it lightly. Not from someone who'd had too much taken from him, and was so deathly afraid of losing what he had left. Fen spent more time talking to the dead than the living these days.

Anyway, that might've been Fen seeing an opportunity to give his choices away again. Because he might not've found the will to take a knife to himself yet, but that didn't mean he wouldn't step in front of one again, given the chance.

It was, after all, why Malick needed to get Fen to come with him tonight.

"Could be dangerous." Malick shrugged. "Not for me."

"Hmm," Fen replied then went silent.

Silent but not withdrawn, not shut down, so Malick didn't move yet. He didn't have the same need Joori or Shig had to try to pry Fen open and get him to vomit up his pain and misery so they could pick through it all, looking for… whatever. Hope, in Joori's case; Malick didn't think he wanted to know what Shig was looking for. Not that Fen would cooperate. That was what the shutting down was for. Malick had seen Fen do it in the middle of a sentence, just abruptly cut off whatever he was saying and swallow it, and then just not say anything more. Or maybe get up in the middle of a one-sided "conversation" and walk away before the other person was finished talking. Usually Joori or Shig. They took it as a further sign of Fen's fragility; Malick took it as Fen expressing his preferences.

"Samin's volunteered to come with me," Malick put in, and then he dropped it.

A sideways invitation, and Fen would take it or he wouldn't. Probably wouldn't, but Malick had to try. Fen had found balance and purpose before through justice delivered at the ends of his knives; Malick saw no reason why Fen couldn't use it as a crutch now, a way to find the focus he needed so badly until he was ready to take on the purpose Wolf had handed him.

Fen was apparently deep inside himself again—who knew if Fen was even aware that Malick was still here?—and the night was moving on. Malick needed to collect Samin and get going. With a sigh, he slipped his knife into his boot, and started for the door.

"Don't wait up."

Not that Fen would. But Malick liked to think he might at least think about it.

"Malick."

Malick turned with his hand on the door and peered at Fen over his shoulder.

Fen held the key between his fingers, watching the light shine and shift over it as he turned it. Idly, his fingertips traced the tiny braid that wove the hair back from his left temple as he stared at the key. Contemplative. Maybe even a little bit wistful.

His gaze lifted, held Malick's for a long, pregnant moment, unreadable, then abruptly dropped. He closed the key in a loose fist.

"Just you and Samin?"

It could mean anything, so Malick didn't allow it to trip up the rhythm of his heart yet.

"Yeah. Shig was never very good with weapons."

And now that her magic was gone, she seemed to have no interest in changing that. Or maybe since Yori was gone.

Fen accepted this with a distracted nod. He was silent for a while, scrutinizing his closed fist.

Malick merely waited. He could be patient, when he needed to be. When it was important.

Fen seemed lost in his Fen-thoughts for a while longer, then:

"Could you… I mean, d'you think…?" Fen gave his head a sharp jerk then set his jaw. "Does it pay?"

You really had to stop and admire the sheer depth of the self-delusion sometimes.

Malick didn't smile. He didn't sigh in relief. He didn't jump at the offer and accept it before Fen could back out. He leaned into the doorjamb and peered at Fen closely.

"It pays." He kept his tone even and direct. "You'll wear the mail. And the vambraces."

"I'm not a bloody—"

"If you're going to tell me you're not a bloody child, yeah, I'm well aware. Except for the part where you seem to 'forget' to wear things that are meant to protect you when you barrel headlong into any sort of risk."

That one rang a bit. Malick hadn't realized he'd raised his voice toward the end.

Fen looked like he was working up a retort. Malick didn't want to hear it.

"*And* you'll wear the ring."

It made Fen jerk his head back, bemused. "Why the hell would I—?"

"Because you might need the shadows if things go badly." And because Malick liked the idea of what Fen wearing it could mean if Fen were the sort to tolerate such a thing, but that wasn't the point. "You're not to die on me. I think we're clear on the consequences of that." Malick slipped the ring from his hand and held it between his fingers. "And I wouldn't take it well."

It's my job, Malick told himself. *However this turns out, this is my job as Wolf's-own.*

Just. Please, Fen. Don't hate me.

Fen merely pushed out a derisive snort, rolled his eyes, and then shot a narrow glare up at Malick. When Malick tossed the ring to him, Fen caught it.

"Give me ten minutes."

ᛏ

"Maybe I won't die on you." Jacin hunted around for his trousers then his shirt. "Maybe I'll just kill you instead."

Hated him. *Hated* him with a burning, fiery passion.

Hated himself for not really hating Malick. For grasping very little about what his life had become, but nonetheless grudgingly recognizing this one undeniable truth—no one else could give him what Malick could. And only some of what Malick gave him had to do with the physical.

Malick understood. Malick *knew*. Things about Jacin even Jacin didn't know. Things that wrung fear and cold sweats from between the cracks of dogged lethargic retreat when they needed facing, however furiously resistant to facing them Jacin might be. Malick actually sought those things. Like it pleased him to find them, no matter how ugly or humiliating. Like Jacin was *worth* knowing.

It was more than anyone else bothered to do.

So. He's finally told you what you are.

Oh, bloody *hell*.

"Shut up, Beishin."

I told you the Temshiel *were treacherous creatures. Now you know why he wants you. When will you learn to listen to your Beishin?*

"When I have one who doesn't pretend to love me while he's destroying my family."

He got a soft chuckle in response. If Jacin shut his eyes, he'd be able to see the expression that went with it, so he didn't.

Love. My boy, you are too easily tricked by its glamour. Do you really think—?

"No. I don't. So just shut up."

Touch the Untouchable. Love the unlovable. No one but I, Jacin-rei. You think he sees but he doesn't, no one does. You do not exist but in my *eyes. Only I know you. I made you, little Ghost, and only I can love what others can't even see.*

"Except you didn't. You don't. And you're *dead*."

Jaw set, Jacin snapped a throwing knife from the sheath at his wrist and whipped it in the direction of the voice. Just to see. It hit the wall beside the brass plate over the press with a *hiss* and a *twang*, hilt vibrating. Jacin stared at it, then shifted his glance to the side and stared at the hollow-eyed creature that glared back at him.

Untouchable. Unlovable.

Not Beishin's voice this time. Jacin's.

A token of his affection for you, little Ghost?

Jacin's arm was still extended from his throw. The lamps were wicked high; Malick's ring sparked in the light like a star on Jacin's finger. Jacin lowered his arm, twisting at the ring like a nervous old woman.

Or a pretty little tether to bind you with? The voice took on sibilance and an abrupt impatience that drove a shudder through Jacin while at the same time winding unease through his gut. *One such as you could do great things with such a bauble. He thinks to bind you with it, but I, little Ghost… I can free you. Your beishin can show you—*

"Shut the fuck *up!*" Growled so harshly this time it actually burned Jacin's throat.

Because if he kept listening, he'd eventually have to admit he could've been free of Malick a hundred times over already. He'd only ever had to simply walk away and keep going. Malick's magic didn't work on him; if Jacin just left and made it his business not to be found, Malick would never find him.

Not that Jacin could, even if he wanted to—there was still Joori and Morin.

More difficult to admit but even more true, there was the sick neediness in Jacin that kept him very firmly in Malick's orbit, in Malick's bed, taking the things Malick gave him that kept Jacin from skidding over whatever edge he was constantly scrambling back from. Was there even really a point in contemplating giving that up?

He wore the mail. He wore the vambraces. He wore the ring. Because it was a paying job, and Malick was the one paying, and Malick had told him to. Because Malick "wouldn't take it well," the heartless bastard, and Jacin had responsibilities. And he clearly wasn't going to walk away.

His belts and sheaths had been oiled and neatly arranged. Jacin wondered who'd done it as he unwound them and began to strap them on. All his knives were there, clean and sharp.

He hadn't been sure how he'd feel once he was armed again. He'd thought several times on the voyage here to ask for his knives back, just to see what would happen. He'd never really cared enough either way to actually pose the question. And now he knew. He didn't really feel much of anything as he buckled and strapped and tied down.

Last were the long knives Malick had given him as a "present" in his room at the Girou, back when Jacin had actually seen the abyss at his feet for the first time and taken that first willing step into it. He wrapped the snakeskin belts around his hips, tied the tethers of the sheaths snug to his thighs and pulled on his gloves. Eyes closed, he slipped his fingers around the handles of the knives, drew them, and gave them an experimental twirl.

He hadn't touched a weapon in… months now. Hadn't practiced his forms, hadn't meditated, hadn't so much as exercised his fingers to keep them limber and dexterous. The lack of calluses on palms and fingertips felt very strange.

Still, the knives spun gracefully, body-memory taking over with the familiar heft. A tiny rush of adrenaline flowed up his backbone as he reacquainted himself with the precision of the balance, the weight, the grip.

His lip quirked up. "Still… perfect."

Perfection for the imperfect. Scrabble for it 'til your fingers bleed, little Ghost. You shall never reach it. Not without your beishin.

Jacin rolled his eyes at the mocking disappointment in Asai's voice. "Yeah, I *know.*"

You can be so much more than this, if only you would believe in your beishin. How it must pain you, knowing they all look to you, and knowing you can never make the measure.

What measure? He was a minion, nothing more. Actually, he was the minion of a minion.

Worse? Better? Jacin didn't know. He didn't think he cared.

Does it hurt you, little Ghost? Almost sympathetic. *Does the disappointment in their glances cut you like the sweet-hot bite of your own blade?*

"No. Not really." Jacin resheathed the knives. "They all know I'm a fuck-up. You showed them that, Beishin. Perhaps I should thank you."

He smiled, half-expecting Caidi to appear, but she didn't. It would be difficult to fail anyone worse than Jacin had failed Caidi. All the fear and rage and just bloody *trying*—it hadn't been enough, nothing more than tragic futility. It didn't matter how Malick tried to twist the truth and soothe the agony of knowledge.

Ah, my sad little Ghost. When will you understand? I only ever tried to help you, guide you. I would guide you still, even after your betrayal. Can you say the same about your Temshiel? Can you not see all of this as the lie it truly is? Do you really believe any but I could love you?

Jacin shut his eyes, set his teeth. "Fuck you, Beishin," he whispered then yanked his hair into a tight tail at his nape and quit the room.

He wasn't surprised to find Samin standing with Malick in the hallway when he shut the door behind him. He *was* surprised by the disapproving frown on Samin's face, edged lightly with… worry?

"Fen." Samin jumped right in, like he'd been waiting to say it. "You don't have to do this. Mal and I can—"

"He knows he doesn't have to do it, Samin." Malick's tone was mild, unaffected, but Jacin was pretty sure that was anger burning behind the tawny gaze.

Jacin stared between them, eyes narrowed. All of a sudden wrong-footed. Had he annoyed Samin somehow? Jacin had to admit it wasn't out of the question—he rather thought he annoyed them all, in different ways. Then again, there was that touch of anxiety in Samin's blue eyes.

Maybe this wasn't annoyance; maybe it was the fact that it'd been months since Jacin had so much as touched anything more threatening than a comb. It had been so long since he'd shaved—because a razor was just asking for it—that the thin, wispy fuzz on chin and lip had grown into an actual bristle. Joori hated it, always offering to shave it for him— shave it *for* him, like Jacin couldn't notice the distinction—but Malick liked it and Jacin didn't much care, so he left it.

He had a limp now too. Weakness. Very obvious weakness, because he couldn't control the heaviness of it all the time, couldn't absorb or ignore or even savor the pain like he used to, and make his gait even and normal. He limped because it hurt, all the time, and the longer he walked on it, the worse it hurt and the heavier he limped.

Maybe Samin was concerned that Jacin wouldn't be able to perform, hold up his end.

"I can do the job."

Jacin could. He was sure of it.

Samin rolled his eyes. "I *know* you can do the bloody *job*."

Jacin frowned. Then what the hell?

"I'm saying you don't have to." Samin ignored the clench of Malick's jaw and angled into the middle of the hallway so he was between Malick and Jacin. "Fen." Everything about Samin was all at once weirdly gentle. "Maybe it's too soon, yeah?"

Ah. Yeah. That. It shouldn't surprise or dismay Jacin that maybe he wasn't the one Samin would choose to have at his back.

Jacin had no idea what to say, so he didn't say anything. Just held Samin's stare, until Samin's mouth pinched, and he shook his head.

"Joori won't understand." It was soft, probably as close to gentle as Samin got.

Jacin hadn't even thought about what Joori might think or understand. And he hadn't the first clue how to tell Samin that it didn't matter what Joori understood or didn't, because Joori didn't actually see Jacin, even when he tried to look. Joori understood a boy who no longer existed, who had always been going to be what Jacin was now, and Joori just couldn't understand what Jacin was now. Like the boy was real and Jacin was the ghost, instead of the other way 'round.

And wasn't that how it would always be, anyway? Jacin was born a Ghost, and he would die a Ghost—because *it isn't that different, you know*— and whether he was called Untouchable or Incendiary apparently didn't matter. It was all the same whether or not he had the braid to brand him or the Ancestors to corrode and ruin him. The deed was done; Jacin was merely trying to find a way through the rubble now.

Joori was just going to have to find his own way. Jacin had neither the wit nor the strength to find a path to wend for anyone but himself.

Selfish, yeah, but he could live with that. Failure, of course, that went without saying.

It seemed even Samin could only take weighted silence for so long.

"...Fine. Bloody-minded—"

Whatever insult he clearly intended, he swallowed it instead. A defeated slump to his shoulders, he merely backed off. But he turned a glare on Malick.

Malick lounged against the wall across from Jacin, calm and ostensibly unconcerned, but his eyes were cool and calculating as he looked between Samin and Jacin. A small smirk playing across his mouth, Malick toyed with the loop to the garrote coiled around his forearm under his sleeve, seemingly idle and patient.

So, why was Jacin so sure he could see fury smoldering behind the tolerant gaze? And why did his guts go all warm and sloppy, his groin tighten just a little, to think he could see it and Samin couldn't?

Maybe Jacin's hatred for Malick wasn't quite as fiery as it should be. Maybe Jacin cared more than he thought he did, and maybe he believed Malick cared back. That would be... dangerous, in a way that only Malick could be. The last thing Jacin needed was another risk. And after what Malick had said only... yesterday?—whatever. The blatant threats, the heartless bastard-ness.

Lust. That was all. Lust would do. Hatred and lust were not mutually exclusive. Jacin should know.

"This is on your head, Mal." Samin's voice was still quiet, but his eyes were accusing in a way Jacin didn't bother to try to understand.

"Yup." Malick's gaze flicked to Jacin, hung there for a moment, then slid back to Samin. "It's all on me."

And that...

Yeah. Good. *That*, Jacin could live with. Because he was tired of it all being on *his* head. Fucking exhausted. Let someone else make the decisions. Let someone else aim him, tell him. *You will be what the gods made you, and you will live, because I wouldn't take it well.* Fine. A mindless, heartless soldier, nothing more. Samin should understand how much of a relief it was. He'd been a doujoun back in Ada; he'd been working for Malick for years. He had to know what a comfort it was for someone else to point, and say "Kill it." Samin had let the Doujou point him, and when he'd thought to question it, he'd ended up with Malick, just like Jacin had. Jacin had let Beishin point him for nearly all his life; it was only when he'd been forced to question the direction that everything had fallen apart. Why couldn't Samin understand this?

"I can do the job." It was all Jacin could think to say, because something seemed necessary, but he didn't know what, and there was no way he could let all of what was ramming around in his head spill out. He'd learned his lesson on that.

"I *know* you can do the job, Fen." Samin huffed, resignation touched by exasperation. "I'm worried about the job doing *you*."

Jacin had no idea what that meant. He could probably figure it out, if he wanted to. It was kind of just hanging there, hovering just outside of understanding, scattered at the edges with bright, terrifying possibility, and he'd get it, if he cared to reach for it.

He didn't. He looked at Malick.

"Are we going or not?"

Malick was inspecting his fingernails now, apparently with all his concentration, but his smirk curled a little wider. His glance slid once again to Samin, shuttered, just long enough to make Samin's mouth tighten down again. Malick chuffed a little snort and shook his head. Slow and lazy, all lanky *fuck you* grace, Malick pulled out of his slouch against the wall and swept his arm down the hallway.

"After you."

He held Samin's gaze as Samin growled and stalked past him, then Malick turned his glance on Jacin. It softened, warmed. His eyes swept down to the knives sheathed low on Jacin's hips and strapped to his thighs. He smiled.

"Coming?"

Jacin hesitated then nodded at the door behind which everyone he had left was ensconced.

"Safe?"

"I've got the whole place warded. And Shig's staying. They're fine." Malick set a hand to Jacin's shoulder, gave him nudge. "C'mon, let's go."

Jacin merely checked the tethers on his sheaths again and let Malick point him.

4

"Jacin?" Morin tapped lightly on the door, not really sure he wanted an answer, but he had to try. Something had happened, something more than the usual angsty withdrawal nonsense that was the sometimes-annoying norm for Jacin these days. Something that had made Malick withdraw, too, and on those occasions when he emerged from the room—for food or more smokes for Jacin or… whatever—Malick himself had been weirdly distant. There wasn't that constant snarky laughter bubbling beneath every shift of his glance, and the smartass remarks were, if not completely absent, not half as smartassy as usual.

Morin knew there was some kind of job going on. Neither Malick nor Samin talked about it in front of them, but Morin had found that if he just sat quietly sometimes, people either forgot he was there altogether, or at least didn't seem to notice he had two working ears and a brain. And Samin couldn't whisper to save his life.

They had a job, and since Samin had more or less disappeared, and Morin and Joori weren't supposed to notice they were being babysat by Shig, Morin rather suspected they were doing that job now. Which made it a good time to try to talk to Jacin without Joori there to shut Morin up every time he opened his mouth to say something Joori didn't think he should say, or tell Jacin what he *really* meant by the monosyllabic responses that Joori didn't want to hear.

Morin tried the knob, found it locked, and so knocked again. "Jacin? Are you in there?"

Maybe he wasn't. Maybe he'd gone out on the job, too, and just chosen not to tell Morin or Joori. Morin couldn't blame him. If he were Jacin, he wouldn't want to tell Joori anything, either. Joori thought Jacin had killed all those people back in Ada because he'd had no choice. Morin thought maybe it was just that Jacin was good at it and hadn't known what else to do.

"Jacin?" Morin pressed his face right up against the door, just in case

Jacin was in there and simply chose not to answer. Jacin did that a lot. "I only wanted to tell you…" Morin paused. Because he really didn't have much to say.

He didn't know Jacin very well. He got the feeling no one knew Jacin very well, except maybe for Malick, but Morin would never dream of saying as much in front of Joori. Not only would the truth of it completely elude Joori, it would crush him too. Joori might be a sincere pain in the ass sometimes—Jacin too—but they were Morin's brothers, and he didn't have to like them to love them.

Strangely, it seemed he didn't have to know them very well to love them, either. He knew Joori a little better than he thought Joori knew himself, but Morin was only recently getting to know Jacin, and he was a far stretch from the Jacin who'd lived in their father's house in a camp in Ada all those years ago. Morin never would have thought he could love someone he didn't know, not before he'd "met" Jacin again, but he almost halfway understood now why Joori had let this whole thing make such a mess of him—almost as much of a mess as Jacin was, but that might be stretching things.

Jacin was smart, Jacin was brave, though perhaps too reckless about it. He could be wickedly funny when he actually said the things he normally just thought in his head, though Morin thought the humor was almost always accidental, and Jacin hardly ever got his own jokes, or even the fact that he'd made one. He'd smile sometimes, though, because he seemed to understand it was expected. He was terrible and beautiful with a knife in his hand, and Morin hadn't been quite sure, when he'd watched Jacin cut down guard after guard after guard, whether he wanted to run away from his brother or learn how to be just like him. Jacin was too loyal for his own good, and too focused on keeping everyone alive but himself, except when others depended on him living. And once he set himself to a purpose, he seemed to have no idea how to quit.

Morin thought that right there was a great deal of Jacin's problem—his only purpose right now was to get well, and he had no idea how to do it. Maybe Malick pulling Jacin into whatever he and Samin were up to would turn out to be the best thing, give Jacin that focus he needed. Morin was pretty sure that was how Jacin had managed not to die before, when he really should have.

He was batshit, all right, not entirely sane, but he wasn't *in*sane, either. Morin didn't know exactly what the difference was, but he knew it was there. Their mother had been crazy, but she hadn't been insane, either, though maybe she'd been getting there toward the end. Shig was *definitely* crazy, but it only made her weird and kind of wise and not boring. Morin thought the hair had very little to do with her craziness and everything to do with her weirdness, which was a distinction he was pretty sure no one saw but him. Well, Yori had probably seen it. And maybe Samin.

Maybe it was too much knowing that did it. Too much knowing tangled too deeply with too much feeling. Which made Morin kind of grateful that he was, at least according to Joori, a selfish little shit.

And that was all the thinking about it Morin wanted to do. Whether Jacin was or was not behind that door, Morin was probably better off not knowing it.

"I just wanted to say good night, Jacin," he said, and he headed back to play cards with Shig and Joori.

"You've fought maijin before. Same thing, no worries. Once I find them and take their magic away, they'll be just as vulnerable as anyone else. It's the finding them part that's going to be tricky."

So Malick had said.

Samin had known better than to count on that—a battleplan was only good until the actual battle began, and then it became less a plan and more a matter of staying alive and inflicting as much damage as possible. So he hadn't been surprised when two of the bastards had found *them*.

Thing was, he *was* surprised—and apparently, so was Malick—that it wasn't just *banpair*. There were mortals in this little pack of rabid predators, and whatever magic they were wielding was giving Samin some real worry.

"We're being watched," Malick had said, not five minutes ago, and they hadn't even been out of sight of the inn yet.

"By who?" Samin had asked.

"I don't know." Malick had looked a little scary, all narrow-eyed and distractedly attentive as he'd reached out with his magic to try to catch hold of whatever it was he felt. "It's magic, but... I can't..." He'd trailed off then, set his jaw, and reached for his sword.

It was all a blur, from then 'til now, filled with the flash of weapons in the moonlight, the shouts of their attackers, and the sounds of up-close battle. There were nine of them, armed heavily and not seeming to care in the least that they'd picked a fight with a *Temshiel* right in the middle of the Ports District and right out in the open. Samin could see the lights from the market two streets over; could hear the peal of bells on boats in their slips on the pier.

Bold bastards, and bloody strong too. It was the rare man who could challenge Samin in hand-to-hand, but it had only taken a moment for him to understand that if he didn't draw his broadsword and do some immediate damage, he wasn't going to walk away from this. And it seemed either Malick wasn't using his magic, or he was and it wasn't working.

They were masked, every one of them. Head to toe in black, hooded, and with black kerchiefs obscuring the bottom halves of their faces. Their weapons varied, but they were all armed well, with quality steel. One had a whip, until he'd flung it out to wrap around Fen's wrist; Fen had merely caught it and jerked it away. It still hung tangled around Fen's arm, but he didn't seem to be allowing it to distract or interfere. He swung it in an arc around him, drove four of them back, then let loose a little volley of throwing knives. He hit two, but neither of them dropped.

"Those three!"

Malick kicked one of them in the chest to drive her—Samin was pretty sure it was a her, from the shape—to drive her back into two more of the thugs, only to have her roll to her feet and swarm in again. Malick spared a second to point before swinging his sword in a wide arc, clipping the woman up the side as she flung herself at him, then dropping back to engage a man coming from his right flank.

"They're the ones we want." Malick swirled into nothing, reappeared a few steps away from where he'd just been and drove his sword into the gut of the one who'd been trying to blindside him. "*Get* them, will you?" He wrenched the sword up and over in a way that told Samin it would be the final maneuver for that one, at least. Empty crates splintered and garbage scattered as Malick shoved the now-corpse down the lane between a closed-up netting repair shop and a woodworker's stall.

Down to eight. No, eleven, actually, because the three Malick had pointed out were new and just standing at the edges, watching. Samin didn't see anything that marked them different from the ones doing the attacking, except they only watched while others did their fighting for them, but Malick had said so, so…

Setting his jaw, Samin tried to wade that way. He had no choice but to engage in every direction, swinging his sword a little wilder than he normally would, but they weren't giving him a lot of choice. Every time he let one of them get close enough, he took another cut or gouge to a limb, and Fen wasn't the only one throwing sharp things around. Three times, flashing little star-shaped projectiles had come whistling at Samin's head, and it had only been because he was busy defending against two or three at a time that he'd moved and they'd missed him. If this kept up, it was only going to be a matter of time.

Samin shot an assessing glance to all points, dismayed when he didn't see Malick, but he couldn't spare a second to think about it. Samin couldn't see Fen and Fen didn't make a sound when he fought, but Samin knew he was still at the center of the press of bodies; Samin made this brilliant deduction when he heard a bitten-off scream and three fingers came sailing over the melee to bounce off his chest. Good. Fen was making some progress, then. Even as Samin glanced over, one of them went down to the cobbles, and Fen spun into another, knives a whirling trail of silvery refractions in the moonlight.

Malick was suddenly at Samin's back, driving away an attacker Samin hadn't known was coming up behind him.

"Watch it, will you?" Malick was clearly winded, and *furious* about it. "I can't go and get *them*, if you're not going to watch your own back."

Samin's mouth crimped as he slammed his fist down, caught one of them on the crown of the head, satisfied when they went down, but annoyed all over again when they just rolled away and got back up. Damn it, that blow should have broken some vertebrae, at least.

"So, go and get them, then!" Samin swung his sword up and caught one in the chest. Skin and muscle, a scrape of bone, and the bugger finally went down. What the fuck *were* these people?

"I was, but I had to come back and save *your* ass." Malick flipped the garrote out in a whistling arc, and… missed. "Fucking *shit*."

Samin had to concur. Malick *never* missed.

"Fen!" Malick did a tight little spin, swiped his sword at an attacker's throat then drove in with his knife and nailed it in so hard Samin heard bone scrape. "*Fen*, damn it, the *ring*—go to shadow!"

Except Fen didn't. Samin couldn't tell if he was ignoring Malick, was too busy to spare the attention, or just hadn't heard him.

Samin parried one of the freaky bastards. Thrust at another. He was getting winded too.

"Why aren't you using your magic?"

Because as little as Samin liked the idea of just throwing magic around, they could really use an advantage here.

Malick only growled. "Just hold on for a minute, yeah? And watch this one coming up on your left." He whirled to shadow again.

Samin was too occupied with the one coming up on his left, and then the one coming up behind him, and had no opportunity to pay attention to anything else. He consoled himself by grabbing the nearest attacker by the collar and hurling him-her-it into the fountain; the impact cracked then splintered the stone figure of a raven, but that was all the satisfaction Samin got.

Somehow, he ended up back-to-back with Fen. Which was good, because Samin was getting a little tired of these people trying to distract him while one of their compatriots tried to flank him. Not so good, though, because Fen just drove and drove and drove, and Samin knew if Fen got a line to a sure kill, he'd be gone and Samin would be on his own. Probably not for long—he hadn't done so much as a push-up in months, so far as Samin knew, but Fen was still bloody *fast*—but it only took less than a second to make a difference in a situation like this one.

Damn, but they could really use Yori and her bow about now. The thought was more painful than the blade that swiped down the back of Samin's hand.

With a bit of a growl, Samin dropped back a pace when he saw-felt-sensed Fen lunge forward. Fen feinted left, and Samin mirrored the move with a cross-attack to the right. His arm was shaking when he lifted the sword above his head, his shoulder rattling an outraged twinge all down the length of it. Samin didn't have the time to pay it any mind. A black-clad figure drove in from almost dead-on, and Samin swung the sword down, timing it so the blade would hit the space where the figure would be when it descended, and hit—

Nothing.

Samin hadn't missed. The figure simply wasn't there anymore. The tip of the sword *chinged* as it glanced the cobbles, but Samin barely heard it, too preoccupied with slamming his glance to all points, looking for a trick, but there apparently wasn't one. They were all just gone, and not into shadow, because Samin would have recognized that for what it was. They'd just disappeared: there one second, gone the next.

"What the hell?" he heard Fen mutter in a tone of annoyed bewilderment.

Samin's sentiments exactly.

"C'mon, *move*." Malick stormed up to them from where the three he'd been after had been standing and watching. His gaze was flicking everywhere, narrowing at the five dead bodies on the ground, head tilted in that way that told Samin that Malick was looking with more than just his eyes. Malick took hold of Fen's arm and propelled him toward Samin. "Let's go, we need to get out of here." He looked… unnerved.

Samin had only seen Malick look that way once. He started moving, "What the fuck, Mal?"

Malick pushed at Fen until he was flanked between them. "I don't know. But I've an idea where I can find out. Back to the inn first." He paused only momentarily to snatch up Samin's arm and scrutinize where the sleeve of his coat was neatly split and dripping blood. He winced when he glanced at Samin's sword hand. "How bad?"

Adrenaline was still gushing through Samin's veins, so he likely wouldn't be able to tell for a while. But the flow didn't seem like anything to worry about now.

"Not very, I think. Stitches."

And probably not only his arm and hand, either. He was pretty sure his thigh had caught a few slices too. He scowled. Without Umeia, it would be Malick doing the sewing, and Malick kind of sucked at it. And there would be no benefit of quicker healing, either. Samin had never realized just how good he had it back at the Girou.

They both had a look at Fen, but it appeared that none of the blood splashed over Fen's face and clothes was coming from him. How had he bloody managed *that*? Even Malick had caught a blade or two, it looked like, and his lip was bleeding.

Oblivious to the scrutiny, Fen gave Malick a suspicious look.

"Where are we going?"

Malick snagged Fen's sleeve, and pushed him back between himself and Samin. With a quick, wary glance in every direction, he started walking again, dragging Fen with him.

"To The Gates of Rapture. If I'm right, the man I—"

"We're going to a whorehouse? *Now?*" Fen stopped, and even Malick's determined tugging wouldn't move him.

"*No*, it's not a bloody *whorehouse*." Malick rolled his eyes. "It's just a tavern, and if things haven't changed completely since the last time I was here, there'll be a man there who can maybe tell me how it is that *banpair* can suddenly wield old magic they shouldn't have and that I could barely touch or take away from them. Now, let's go—I don't know if they're coming back, and in case you couldn't tell, they were kicking our asses."

"They weren't following through." Frowning, Fen glanced at Samin with something like apology then back at Malick. "They never connected, not once. And they had plenty of chances. The three I killed had at least an equal chance to get me when I got them, but they didn't take it. Any of them."

"I noticed that."

Huh. Samin hadn't. Then again, he'd been a bit busy.

"Looks like they don't want you dead." Malick's voice was tight as he prodded Fen back into motion. "Or even blooded."

Samin scowled. "Well, lucky Fen, then, because they were certainly giving *me* their best shot." He kept a watch to all points as they moved, but he wasn't sure how much good it would do with people who could just pop into and out of thin air. "A snatch?"

And if so, why?

"Hell if I know." Malick did that head-tilting thing again, feeling for magic. "And I bloody *should*. They shouldn't've been able to block me like that, and I can't— Fucking *ow!*"

Samin snapped his glance over in time to see Malick slap at the back of his neck, stop dead, then yank. When he brought his hand around, it held a long, barbed shaft that made Samin's stomach drop down into his boots. He sucked in a sharp breath.

"Mal...?"

With eyes narrowed down to slits, Malick sniffed the tip of the dart, then clenched his teeth.

"Shit, shit, *shit!*" He pointed an almost panicked glance at Fen. "F-ffen." His voice had gone all at once thick, a little slurred. "Jacin. The ring. Keep it... keep it *safe*. This isn't... not your... Don't... don't..." He shook his head, sharp and quick, then turned a bleary gaze on Samin, then said, clear and harsh, "Don't let him poison himself."

And then he went down. Just dropped. Facedown on the cobbles so hard and fast Samin only stared for a few seconds before instinct took over.

"*Fen.*" Renewed adrenaline made it barbed, urgent. "Get back to the inn."

Fen didn't even seem to hear. He was staring down at Malick—or rather, Samin made himself acknowledge, Malick's corpse, because Samin had no doubt what that last look in Malick's eyes had been, nor did he doubt what was on that dart.

"Malick?" Fen crouched down, took hold of Malick's shoulder and tried to turn him over. "*Malick?*"

Samin crouched too. Not exactly a good defensive position, but at least he was a slightly smaller target. Gaze caroming everywhere at once and still seeing nothing, Samin tried again.

"*Fen*, we have to get back to the— Bloody *hell!*"

He lurched back when the first of the flames ignited, engulfing Malick's body in seconds, so hot and fast they almost singed Samin's eyebrows. He didn't have time to dwell on it; it looked like containing Fen was going to be all he could handle.

"No. *No*, you can't—" Barely audible over the crackle of flames, thin and wheezy, before Fen lurched in as though galvanized. "Malick! *Malick!*" The flames only grew as Fen beat at them, eyes wild in the flicker and flare.

Samin took hold of Fen and dragged him back, glad Fen had no knives in his hands at the moment, but not doubting for a second they were coming if Samin couldn't get him calmed down.

"It's a spell, Fen. He did it on purpose. So he couldn't be bound to the earth."

Because as satisfied as Malick had been with the fate Fen had handed Asai, he'd also been rather horrified by the prospect of experiencing it personally. He'd told Samin he'd made sure it couldn't happen, but Samin hadn't really thought about how until now.

"*No, he*—" Fen twisted in Samin's grip, still trying to throw himself at the flames. Samin wasn't so sure now if it was to put the fire out or dive into it. "He *promised*. He... he... no, not..."

With a harsh, gasping breath, Fen stilled, snapped his glance around, and slammed it into Samin's. Dark, blank nothing, just like it'd been when Caidi and Yori had died.

"To spirit, Fen." Samin tried to keep it calm and reassuring. "Not forever, he'll come back, it's just for—*hey!*" He scrabbled as Fen slithered out of his hold, but Fen could be slippery when he wanted to be, and Samin had let himself be maneuvered off his guard by that *look* in Fen's eyes. "Fen, wait!"

Fen didn't. Knives drawn and gripped in both fists, he shot to his feet and took off, his limp only noticeable because Samin knew to look for it. Too bad it wasn't going to slow him down. Samin didn't see any of the *banpair* lurking about, but as had been proven too clearly, that meant shit. Fighting them had been like fighting the air, and that dart had come out of bloody nowhere. Fen didn't seem to care. Whether he was after vengeance or suicide, Samin didn't know, but it was looking like they would be one and the same if Samin didn't do something.

Samin lurched to his feet, scanning the perimeter again, but there was only darkness and silence but for Fen's bootheels on the cobbles. Samin would never catch up. There was only one way to stop Fen.

"Malick's wards will have gone with him!" Fen kept running, so Samin notched up his shout, went for the low blow: "Your brothers, Fen! There's nothing protecting them now! You have to protect your brothers!"

It worked.

Fen stopped, just as he was reaching the end of the street and Samin would've lost him in the shadows. A tall blot of dark against dark, Fen only stood there, body rigid, knives two low glimmers at his sides.

Samin watched him, the heat of Malick's self-inflicted makeshift pyre crawling up his backbone with something that didn't feel at all like warmth.

With a hard shudder Samin could see even at a distance, Fen cocked his head up at the moons, let loose a wavering cry that sounded too close to an animal trapped in the bottom of a deep, dark well, then spun back around and headed toward the inn.

⊤

Xari jolted from her seat on the fountain's wall, snapping to her feet with a small cry that nonetheless wrenched in her chest with a sharp jag of…

It was gone. Leaving her wondering what the hell had just happened.

Pain. Grief, perhaps. Very definitely anger, but…

She couldn't tell. The feel of it was fleeting past her like a fine mist of someone else's memory. It had nearly choked her only a second ago, and now she couldn't even remember what it had been.

Nonetheless, she knew.

"Foolish, foolish, *foolish*." Xari clenched her fists, helpless. "*Warned* you, I did."

Teeth set, Xari stalked across the sward and through the garden, angling past the incense altars and up the steps to the temple. Imara met her halfway up them, on her way down in somewhat of a hurry, which didn't surprise Xari in the least. Even the worry on Imara's face couldn't stop the snarl from blooming on Xari's.

"Told you, I did! Lessons to teach, and children to chide, but Kamen will not be the one to suffer for this. Unfathomable damage you do to the Incendiary, and who will achieve Wolf's goals for him now?"

"Let me be, Xari." Imara was not quite as calm and sure of herself as she'd been the last time they'd talked. "I'm going now to—"

"Yes, go. *Go!* Try to mend that which you've just allowed to be broken. Perfect he is not, but only the Sorcerer can take Zero and make One of him, and you have just allowed the Fool's shelter to perish. *Go!* Hie you now to the Incendiary, before the break in his heart shatters his mind!"

There was no satisfaction as Xari took in Imara's stunned gaze, the anxiety on her face, nor was there any in her silence as she dissolved into shadow and was gone. Xari only stood there a moment, seething at the spot where Imara had been, fists balled tight and breath coming faster than it should be.

"Now we see." She slanted an angry glare up at Wolf. "Now we see what *your* Incendiary is made of." She shook her head, not even a little bit repentant of her blasphemy. She was Wolf's-own now and she had to obey; she didn't have to approve. She shifted her glance to Raven. "I pray he proves more than even you guessed." And then she found the hint of jade in the sky where Owl lurked. "The time approaches when all must make a stand. Pray you watch your brother's back."

Shig knew what it was. She'd been cut off from the spirits, perhaps, but she didn't suppose there could be such a thing as a complete severance, not when they'd been so deep inside her, and she in them, for so long. Like a phantom limb that could still ache.

She recognized the thick, fleeting pulse that swamped her. She only jolted a little, but otherwise stayed still, listening, reaching out and grasping for more. Blind and deaf, groping, but she caught the thin film of awareness and shut her eyes, let her cards fall to the table.

It was a shit hand, anyway.

It was late and she was tired, and didn't much feel like keeping Joori and Morin distracted so they wouldn't twig to what their brother was up to, and so she could at least try to protect them if there was trouble. Though if someone managed to get through Malick's wards and come after them, Shig had no idea what Malick expected her to do about it. Her questionable "skill" with a blade wasn't going to amount to much in the face of magic. Especially not any magic strong enough to get past Malick.

So, what now, bright little niijun?

Shig reflexively brushed at her hair, reminding herself to freshen the colors sometime soon. She kept meaning to go out and explore the city some more, and she kept not doing it.

What will you do, now that your pack's Alpha has lost his fangs?

Not a spirit-voice—her own. She knew that. Filling in the blank spaces where once she'd had to be very careful to control the flow, not allow too many in at once, pick through the comprehension that poured into her and decide which parts of it to use. Merely her own thoughts now, disguising themselves, a strange comfort-anguish, because she couldn't tell anymore how much of it came from actual *knowing*. For all she knew, she might be fooling herself just as determinedly as Fen was, because Shig had her own ghost at her edges, and talking to her dead sister didn't make Shig much saner than Fen.

"What?" Joori's tone was mildly concerned. "Something wrong?"

Oh, yeah. Something was most definitely very wrong.

Damn you, Malick. Not now!

Shig ignored Joori, let the sentient rustle ripple through her, and refused the rise of tears. Not tears of mourning—she knew better than that. More like fear. Loss of direction that had been perhaps uncertain anyway, but it had at least been something in this directionless new existence. Fen was so sure Shig had no idea what twisty things went through his head, but she'd latched on to Malick's coattails almost as desperately as Fen had, because she was just as disoriented. And now that guidance was gone, dubious and almost unwilling though it had been. Temporarily gone, sure, but gone, and anything could happen in the in-between.

Temporary? Are you sure?

Not her voice this time, not a spirit-voice, either, at least not the kind she knew. Alien. Invasive. Almost like Yori's but not quite hitting all the right nuances. Too… thick, too something. Like someone was trying to be Yori, and couldn't get it exactly right, missing inflections and tones by *that much*, and in ways only Shig would know, because no one had known Yori better than Shig.

It gave her a weird, unnerving hope. Because if she could hear this voice, regardless of its almost-malice, almost-consolation, perhaps the spirits weren't entirely lost to her, after all.

Yes, she told it, a bit of an inner snarl. *I'm sure.*

Malick would be back. Not for her, and not for Samin, but it wouldn't matter. He'd be back for Fen, and probably sooner than whoever had killed his body expected, because this was Malick, and he wasn't finished with Fen yet. Shig didn't think Malick would ever be finished with Fen.

"Shig." Joori again, and a soft rustle accompanied by a quiet ruffle of cards told Shig his abrupt anxiety had stirred Morin. "Is something wrong?"

Tell him, little niǐjun, child of light and color.

Shig almost smiled. *Niǐjun. Rainbow.* Because she'd appeared to the "eyes" of the spirits as a band of colors, given them something they saw as corporeal and longed-for when she walked with them, and they'd rewarded her with… well, pretty much everything she asked them for.

The guide-star lost tonight did not shine only for you. The Void will need all sources now, else lose the light entirely and collapse in on itself.

Now the tears almost came. *The Void.* Because they couldn't see Fen, but sometimes they could sense him, and sometimes the disjointed, tortured cries of his own spirit were louder and more incoherent than the Ancestors'. It made even the spirits reject him, in their strange, ephemeral way.

Poor Fen.

Shig opened her eyes, thought about putting on a reassuring smile, but what was the point? Joori wouldn't care that something happened to Malick—in fact, he'd probably be not-so-secretly pleased—and

Morin neither needed nor wanted that kind of fake comfort. Joori might deceive himself into living on bread and hope, just like Fen deceived himself into living for everyone but himself, but Morin wouldn't be fooled—not by himself or anyone else.

"Malick's gone to spirit." Shig waited through the confused frowns, the delayed realization, the bit of calculation in Joori's gaze and the widening of Morin's. "He went out to hunt, and he won't be coming back tonight."

They were both silent, just staring, stunned, before Morin narrowed his eyes.

"What about Jacin?"

Joori's gaze snapped over to Morin. "What about him?" He shot a panicked glare at Shig. "Jacin wouldn't have gone. He doesn't do that anymore, and he can't even… He's across the hall, sleeping." He set his jaw and stood. "*Right?*"

Shig only sighed. Sometimes, knowing what drove him wasn't enough, when it came to dealing with Joori. He was good, Shig had never doubted it. He had a good heart. He meant well. But he stumbled and flailed worse than Malick did when it came to Fen. It never mattered that Joori only ever wanted to make things better for Fen, because he always managed to somehow make it all worse.

It was the anger that got in the way of it all. The betrayal. Joori would never forgive Fen for stepping in front of Malick's sword, *making* Joori see how little Fen really thought of his own life, of his own self, making Joori see how much Fen really cared for Malick, even if Fen couldn't admit it to himself. Nor would Joori ever forgive Malick for being the one who'd been holding the sword.

And Joori would never, *ever* admit any of it. Especially not to himself.

Yori would've been so good for him. Yori would've kept him in line.

"You should probably sit back down." Shig swallowed away the lump in her throat. "It might not be safe anymore."

Joori's brow creased down, and his lips thinned. "Is he still out there? Did Malick drag him out to kill people?" He leaned in, teeth set tight. "Did he give my brother a weapon?"

Shig saw no reason to answer any of that, so she didn't. All the answers would come soon enough, and Joori could bash himself against someone else once he got them. Samin, probably, because Samin had developed a weird tendency to step between Fen and Joori when Joori pushed Fen too hard, and anyway, he was built to take it better than Shig was. Joori could whack himself against Mount Samin for years and never even make a dent.

"He's not a child, y'know." Morin's tone was neither snarky nor derisive. "You can't keep him in some kind of bubble forever." Matter-of-fact and calm, because Morin watched, Morin listened—a lot more than he talked—and Shig suspected he saw just as much as she did. Maybe more. He was male, after all—he'd understand how the testosterone-addled mind worked better than she would.

Joori rounded on Morin. "*You* want to give him a knife and see what happens?"

"For pity's sake." Morin sighed this time, then rolled his eyes. "This is Jacin we're talking about, Joori. If he truly wanted to kill himself, d'you really think he couldn't have made a weapon out of a cake of soap by now? Hung himself with a set of bedsheets?"

Shig frowned. It was so close to what Malick had snarled at her earlier.

Morin shook his head, something in his face very close to pity when he looked at Joori.

"Maybe he's not right in the head, but he's not a moron."

Joori didn't seem to have anything to say to that. Which apparently only pissed him off more. A little snarl curled at his mouth, and he jerked away from the table and started for the door.

Shig sighed, already exhausted. "I wouldn't do that, if I were you."

Joori paused at the door, as though arguing with himself. Eventually, he peered at Shig over his shoulder with a scowl.

"I'm going across the hall to check on my brother. Who is in bed, *sleeping*, and *not* out killing people." He hesitated, some of the anger draining out of his expression. "He probably won't take this well. I should be there."

"And break it to him gently?" Shig lifted her eyebrows. "You really think he'll believe you?" Joori opened his mouth, but Shig waved off whatever he was going to say. "You don't fool me, and you won't fool him. You're not sorry Malick's out of your way, if only for a little while, and I doubt you can even see all the reasons why you should be, let alone admit it. If you're a smart little rabbit, you won't let your brother see any of it."

She'd been expecting more snarls, an angry outburst. So she was a little surprised when Joori's expression turned hurt, genuinely taken aback.

"You really think I'm that cold? I don't hate Malick, I never did. But I know what we are to him, I know what Jacin is to him. And someone has to be there to put Jacin back together once Malick's through with him."

Shig thought about that very carefully, because again, it was all too close to what she'd snarled at Malick only hours ago. She tilted her head, genuinely curious.

"And what makes you so sure that someone should be you?"

Joori snorted, hollow and humorless. "You know, sometimes I really feel bad for you, because I think you miss your spirits so much you try to pretend you still have them." He shook his head. "And sometimes I think you're just a clueless bitch." He threw the door open then slammed it shut behind him.

Shig only stared after him for a few seconds, stung. That one had hurt. And she wasn't even sure which part.

"He was out with Malick." Morin's voice was low in the sudden silence. "Wasn't he?"

Shig slouched down in her chair and shut her eyes. "Yeah."

The quiet wound outward, so much they could hear Joori rapping softly on the door across the hall. Shig couldn't tell if she was relieved or not when Morin finally broached it.

"Is Jacin all right?"

"All right" was such an inclusive phrase. Shig didn't waste breath on all the ways Fen was profoundly *not* "all right."

"Even if I still had the spirits, I wouldn't be able to tell. You can't find Fen with magic. I only know about Malick because I think he found a way to tell me." Shig opened her eyes, let Morin see the apology in her gaze and shrugged. "For all I know, Fen's the one who killed him."

There was no shock at the speculation, no swift denial, like there would've been with Joori. Morin's mouth twisted, and he slumped, but that was all. He thought about it for a while, turned and looked at the door when Joori's knocking grew in both insistence and volume, then shook his head at Shig.

"No. Not unless he's lost himself completely." Morin rubbed at his eyes. "In which case, the only one who'll be coming back is Samin. Unless he got in Jacin's way."

A little shudder rippled through Shig at the truth of it. Leave it to Morin to say the things no one wanted to acknowledge but everyone needed to hear.

Just like you used to, little niijun. Have your colors dulled so much beneath the weight of your corporeal bondage?

Corporeal bondage. It sounded so... melodramatic. Didn't stop it from feeling pretty much exactly right.

Maybe that was why Joori's parting shot had stung as it had. Shig did miss the spirits, crazy bastards that they were. She missed Yori. She missed Umeia. She missed the life she'd had before she'd ever heard the name "Fen." And now she missed Malick and every bit of Fen's equilibrium he'd no doubt taken with him.

She missed being *little niĳun*.

Perhaps it was time to start figuring out who she was now. Perhaps a visit to the temple would do her some good.

Shig toyed with the ends of her hair, mouth turned down in a bit of a grimace. Perhaps it was time for some new dye.

"We should get out more." She picked at the corners of the cards on the table with her fingernail. "See the city, visit the temples." They were, after all, in the very birthplace of the gods. She'd been within walking distance of answers and direction for almost two weeks now, and hadn't been able to make herself do a damned thing about it, not even when Malick cajoled her, sweet and imposing all at once as only Malick could be. And now that Malick was… gone.

Well. She did at least need some dye.

Shig wiped at her eyes, though they weren't wet, so that was something. With a sigh, she peered up, noted Morin staring at her with a half-amused glint in his hazel eyes and a tiny curl to his lip. Shig raised her eyebrows in question.

Morin only shook his head and chuffed a tiny snort. "Sometimes you're so weird."

⛩

Damn it, he had no idea how to pick a lock. Joori pounded on Jacin's door some more, but refrained from shouting through it. It was the middle of the night, and the inn was full. He didn't need some angry foreigner shouting at him in words he couldn't understand, and he didn't need that dour innkeeper throwing them out. Though, now that Malick was apparently… not dead, but whatever it was *Temshiel* were when their mortal bodies died—now that Malick wasn't here, Joori couldn't help wondering how the hell they were going to pay for their rooms. Cold, yes, like Shig had accused, but someone had to think of these things.

He pounded again. Jacin was in there. He had to be. He just didn't want to answer, that was all. He hadn't been out with Malick, because Jacin didn't kill people just because. Only when he had no choice. He wasn't the assassin Asai had made him, he wasn't anything Asai made him, because if he kept being what Asai made him, that would mean Asai still had some kind of hold on him, and…

And Joori couldn't even stand to think it, let alone tolerate it. He might disapprove of the hold Malick had on Jacin, he might worry over it and try to weaken it a little, but it was nowhere near as destructive as the hold Asai still had. For pity's sake, Jacin still talked to the slimy bastard like Asai was standing in the room with him. At least Malick actually cared about Jacin. Even if he didn't know how to do it right. And if Malick had somehow managed to get Jacin kil—

No. He wouldn't think it. *Couldn't.* Not after everything they'd already lost. Jacin wouldn't dare risk himself like that. He *wouldn't.*

"Jacin." Joori pressed his face into the wood. "Please. Open the door. Please be in th—"

"Is everyone here all right?"

Samin's voice. Thank the gods.

Joori spun, heart hammering and breath coming in truncated little gasps. He hadn't realized how tightly he'd been wound, but when he saw Samin standing in the hallway, Jacin halfway behind him, both of them eyeing Joori a little warily, his knees almost gave. The blood registered a half a second later, and some odd little part of Joori's mind wondered if any of it was Malick's, but he wouldn't dare voice it. Nor would he dare voice the things ramming around in his head and his chest right now—the accusations, the rebuke, the *how could you?*—because Jacin had that dazed, blank-eyed look to him, and Joori needed to get rid of it, quick, before it set in and stayed. As much as Joori hated to admit it, Malick did keep Jacin in the present most of the time, chased away the "ghosts" Jacin spoke to more than he spoke to even Joori, and now that Malick was… gone, the job would fall to Joori.

"Yeah." Joori bobbled a nod. "Yeah, we're fine."

He looked both Jacin and Samin over thoroughly. Samin had clearly been wounded. A lot of the blood on him was his. Joori chose not to mention it right now. Jacin looked bloody, too, but unhurt, and cold or not, that was what mattered to Joori. He liked Samin, but Samin could and did take care of himself.

"There's, um…" Samin squinted at Joori with a strange hesitancy that didn't look right on him. "Malick—"

"We know." Joori said it mostly to spare Samin the chore. "Shig knew. She said he told her."

Samin nodded, a slump to his shoulders and a fatigue in his blue eyes that made him look older. "His wards are gone. They were *banpair*, and we think they were after—"

He broke off abruptly when Jacin jostled into his side, like he was trying to shove Samin out of the way to get by. Samin stared at him, but Jacin merely sidled between Samin and the wall and turned to stand beside Joori with his back to the door of his room. Blinked.

Samin cleared his throat again. "I don't know how safe it is here." He paused and stared at Jacin; strangely, it looked as if he was looking for guidance. When Jacin didn't say anything, Samin went on, "I want us all in the same room. Yours and Morin's is the biggest, so it should be there. I'll keep the watch."

Banpair and blood and keeping watch. *Danger!* shrieked beneath every word spoken in Samin's calm voice.

Joori didn't have a better plan, so he only nodded. "Sure, yeah, that sounds—"

"I want to be alone."

Joori didn't think he'd ever get used to Jacin's raspy voice, but even through the strain, Joori had no trouble at all hearing the inflexibility in the tone. He stared at Jacin—the hollow nothing in his eyes, the spatters of blood going to brown on his face, his hands, the knives strapped all over him like prickly armor. Joori looked back at Samin and silently shook his head.

Apparently, Samin hadn't needed the hint. He set his jaw.

"No one's alone right now, Fen, and especially not—" Samin shot a glance at Joori then back at Jacin, gaze softening, but his tone was unmoved when he went on, "They'll want to know what happened. Would you like to tell them, or shall I?"

And why was Joori detecting the tiniest hint of threat in the even question? He narrowed his eyes between them, watching the silent argument fly back and forth across the plush hallway. Something was going on, something Samin had almost said and Jacin wanted to make damned sure he didn't.

"They were after you." It came out thin, Joori's throat tight, because he knew Jacin, and knowing Jacin, it wasn't hard to figure out what he didn't want Samin to say. Joori looked at Jacin straight, but Jacin was still staring at Samin. "*Weren't* they, Jacin?"

Jacin remained silent, the gaze that had sharpened momentarily on Samin now going dull again, withdrawn. An almost a physical pulling away.

Joori had to restrain himself from laying hands on Jacin to prevent it. "Why would *banpair* be after you?"

No answer, but Joori only stood there, waiting, because Jacin could be stubborn, but so could Joori. Joori had been letting Jacin get away with not saying things lately, because he found out more when he eavesdropped on Jacin and his "ghosts" than from anything Jacin might actually tell him. But Joori wasn't letting it go this time. He knew what the stories said about *banpair,* and though he didn't think he believed in them wholly, every myth and legend he'd ever heard had started somewhere in truth. And he'd had enough experience now with *Temshiel* and maijin to know you couldn't trust magical beings for even a second, let alone the ones who were said to actually eat people.

"Jacin." Joori's teeth clenched. He couldn't help it. "I want to know what—"

It lodged in his throat when Samin all at once turned into a blur of brown and flashing blade, spinning to the side, sword raised and teeth bared. Bloody hell, he looked scary like that. Jacin, too, with his dead eyes and vicious snarl, blooded knives in his fists and body tense. They were like a pair of pissed-off jackals.

Apparently, the newcomer who'd been approaching from the stairway agreed. The woman stopped, just cresting the top step. She held out her hands, palms out, and put on a calm smile.

"Your pardon." Her voice was lilting, gold eyes placid, nearly flashing out from the toast-brown complexion of her striking face.

Temshiel. Joori knew it just by the almost unreal perfection of the features. Or maijin, maybe. Joori couldn't tell the difference between them with just a look—they all hid behind beautiful faces. Arrogant, the lot of them.

The woman dipped a low nod at Samin. "You are Kel-seyh, I should imagine." She looked between Joori and Jacin, almost bowed this time, but not quite. "Fen-seyh. Fen-seyh." She straightened. "I am Imara of Wolf. I come at Kamen's request." She gestured at the door, where Morin and Shig had slatted it open and were peeking through the narrow opening. "Might we speak?"

Morin had been out and about with Samin several times since they'd come to Tambalon. He'd seen people of different color before. Mitsu was fairly diverse, and though Morin's own olive skin was darker than most here, he'd been rather fascinated by the new knowledge that people came in more colors than what he'd seen in the Jin camp where he'd lived for all but a few months of his life. The contrast between the Jin prisoners and the Adan who guarded them was sometimes hard to see, if one only looked at physical features; sometimes you had to look at the eyes, look for the defeated notes in the gaze of a Jin to see the difference. Even in his brief experiences in Ada's city of Ikata, Morin hadn't seen so many distinctions as he had in two weeks in Mitsu. Some pale as ghosts and fair-haired, like that Tatsu, or dark as night, like Sora. Mitsu was like a big, earth-toned rainbow, every color in the limited spectrum represented.

He'd never seen anyone like this woman. Skin near sepia with an almost russet underlay that gave it a burnished depth and its own darkling glow. Her black hair was cut straight to the shoulders and slicked back so her sharp gold eyes shone out like lamps. Like a wolf's eyes, Morin couldn't help thinking.

This one probably didn't need to expend a whole lot of *Temshiel* magic to get mortals to do anything she wanted. All she had to do was point those eyes at someone and they'd fall over themselves to hand her things she didn't even need to ask for.

"…do we even know you're who you say you are?" Joori, suspicious and territorial as ever. "And if you're from Wolf, why didn't we see you when everything went to shit in Ada? Don't you people help each other?"

They'd filed in from the hall, Imara first, with Jacin and Samin keeping sharp eyes on her the whole while. Imara seemed to be trying very hard to make herself unthreatening, settling in Shig's chair, back to the door. Jacin leaned against the wall, hands blatantly curled around the hilts of the knives at his hips, though they remained sheathed. So far. Joori and Morin sat to either side of Imara, with Shig across the card-strewn table. Samin stood behind Shig, ostensibly casual, but he made sure his right hand was free and the tethers on his scabbard were loose. The fact that Imara had healed all the wounds Samin had accumulated tonight with a single touch to his shoulder didn't seem to have put Samin in a more trusting mood.

Imara's smile was soft and kind. She set a hand gently to Joori's shoulder like they were old friends.

"I was forbidden from Ada by Wolf himself. When one of our own was murdered, all of Wolf's were forbidden from Ada." She angled a look over her shoulder and peered levelly at Jacin; Jacin only stared blankly back. "The matter of the Catalyst was for Kamen, and Kamen alone. What Fen Jacin is and has always been is now a matter for Wolf."

That got a twitch out of Jacin. Imara narrowed her eyes, assessing, but when she turned back to Joori, her smile was as soft as it had been before.

"No *Temshiel* or maijin could have possibly been as valuable to Fate and to the Jin as the Paradox and the Key that was set in Kamen's hand. I don't know how the tale will be told in the annals of Jin history, but Fen Joori is a name known by all the gods and their servants."

Even if it was complete bullshit—and Morin didn't think it was, actually—it had a definite effect on Joori. He flushed, eyes glittering, and looked away.

Morin rolled his eyes. And Malick thought *he* had charisma.

The thought sobered Morin. Up until Imara had shown up, he'd been telling himself maybe Shig had been wrong. She didn't have her spirits, after all, so how could she know? Except it was too easy to believe Malick had found a way to make *sure* they knew, put them on their guard, once he knew he wouldn't be there to protect Jacin. Because Joori could say whatever he wanted, but Morin knew Jacin was everything to Malick. You didn't even have to be terribly observant to see it, and you only had to know Jacin for a little while to see it was the same for him. Except Jacin was killing himself trying to fight it.

It was a struggle Joori was only encouraging and confusing, when, really, it could've been a lot less angsty and overwrought than it was turning out to be. And all this uproar tonight was only going to make it worse. The last thing Jacin needed was *more* confusion. Malick's sudden absence, just when Jacin was starting to let himself believe a little, was only going to cast doubt where it didn't need to be.

"…brother has been through enough." Joori had apparently decided to ignore the charm and show his claws. "If I'd known Malick was planning on dragging him into this whole *banpair* thing in the first place, I would've put a stop to it."

Morin shot a look over at Jacin, just to see if that got any reaction, but it didn't. Jacin just kept staring blankly, though his hands kept flexing and fisting over the hilts of his knives, and it looked like he was trying very hard not to twitch.

Samin shifted uncomfortably. "If it hadn't been for Malick, those *banpair*—"

"If it hadn't been for Malick, they wouldn't even know Jacin existed."

"I think you're wrong there, Joori. They were waiting for us. They knew we were coming, and they waited, gave us a fight to get our measure and then struck like cowards from the shadows. I can't *wait* to see how pissed Malick is that he got it in the back and that the only blaze of glory came from his own improvised pyre." Samin shook his head at Imara. "Malick said they had magic he couldn't do much with. In my opinion, they were purposely getting Malick out of the way, trying to get at…" He trailed off and shot a tight glance at Jacin.

"So, then." Imara sighed. "They know what Fen Jacin is."

"What d'you mean, 'what he is'?" Morin couldn't help blurting. "Get Malick out of the way for what?" He looked again at Jacin, but there was still no reaction. "Jacin was Untouchable but now he's not anymore. Joori's right—if they were after Jacin, it had to be because they were after Malick." He peered around at all of them, letting his gaze rest on Samin. "Right?"

"What difference does it make?" Joori snapped. "Whatever it was,

Malick dragged Jacin into it, and Jacin has no business or reason to take it any further. If they wanted Malick, they got him. If they wanted Jacin, it was because of Malick and they can't have him." He turned to Jacin, determined. "Jacin, we're done, understand? We'll find a way to get some money, and we'll leave. There's no reason for you to get dragged into whatever Malick's business was with those… whatever they were. We'll go where they can't find you, and we'll start over. All right?"

Morin rubbed at his brow.

For pity's sake, they'd risked their souls for one another. How blind did a person have to be? Morin could understand it with Jacin—because, really, how rational could he expect Jacin to be after everything?—but there was no excuse for it from Joori. Well, there was, but not one that would help in the scheme of things.

Knowing Malick would come back wasn't going to do it for Jacin— all of this was going to hit him a hell of a lot harder than Morin thought Joori suspected, and probably sooner rather than later. If Morin knew Jacin, this threat of *banpair* coming for him for who-knew-what reason this time wasn't going to be much of a threat. In Morin's opinion, and with the state Jacin was in right now, they could set Jacin loose on the entire coven and he'd plow through every one of them, just on the tails of the anger and betrayal too obviously ramming around inside him right this minute. Joori was terrified, Morin could hear it in the stridency of his arguments, but Joori just couldn't seem to acknowledge how bloody *good* Jacin was at what he did. Or the fact that Jacin might *want* to do what was being implied. For Malick, yeah, but for himself too.

Morin couldn't tell what Imara was thinking. She didn't have that smirky *fuck you* look to her Malick always got when Joori was being a prick. Her sharp gold eyes set in her flawless face made her *other*, somehow. Less like an actual person and more like an artist's conception of what *Temshiel* should look like. Morin never really thought of Malick as *Temshiel*, because he always seemed so… normal. The only time Morin had to acknowledge what Malick really was, what he could do, was when Morin tripped over Malick's magic and didn't have much of a choice. This Imara just oozed *Temshiel*, even when she wasn't trying to.

It should have been comforting, what with Imara professing to have come to protect them in Malick's place. Instead, it made Morin vaguely uneasy.

As if she knew—and maybe she did—Imara lifted an eyebrow at Morin, tipped him a small, ironic smile, and shrugged. She turned to Joori.

"I think, Fen Joori, that perhaps there are matters of which you are unaware." She paused and turned a mild look over to Jacin, but when

Jacin didn't react—still—Imara shifted her glance to everyone else. "Fen Jacin—"

"I'm done here."

Before anyone could even blink or protest, Jacin spun, threw open the door and walked out. They were all still staring at the door when they heard the one to Jacin's room open then slam shut. The abrupt silence was so thick they heard the lock turn and catch from across the hall.

Joori jolted up, meaning to go after him, no doubt, and this time, Morin couldn't blame him. He'd just been arguing less than an hour ago that if Jacin really wanted to kill himself, he'd've found a way by now, despite any precautions. But things had changed rather drastically since then.

"Be still." Imara set a hand to Joori's wrist and stopped him. Joori's mouth pulled back in an indignant snarl, but before he could snap out a reply, Imara told him, "Be *still*, Fen Joori. I will see to it."

Shadows swirled around her, and then she was gone.

⊤

"I told you, little Ghost."

Jacin watched Asai stroll around the room, inspecting the clutter of belts and small knives Malick had dragged out before and eschewed in favor of the garrote and sword. Asai shook his head, peered into the brass plate bolted to the wall over the press, and smoothed his hair. He turned to Jacin, smiling, soft and condescending.

"This wouldn't have had to happen, if you'd listened to your beishin. When will you learn?"

Jacin had to let the gasp loose, he *had* to. He was already getting lightheaded trying to keep his breathing normal, and everything was spangling at the edges of his vision. He shut his eyes.

"You're not real. You're dead. I killed you myself."

He'd gone completely crazy, that was it. He'd started with voices, and now he'd progressed to hallucinations.

"Yes, and I must say how very disappointed I was in you." Asai *tutted*. Jacin imagined he was shaking his head in that mock-sorrowful way he had, but refused to open his eyes and look. "You fell under Kamen's spell, little Ghost, that's all. I don't suppose you can be blamed entirely. I should have taught you more about the duplicity of *Temshiel*. But he's out of the way, and we can move on to what's important to us. You still have the ring, yes?"

The touch to Jacin's cheek was cold. It startled him nearly out of his skin.

Oh, fuck. It wasn't just a voice inside his head this time—Beishin was real. He was *here*. Touching, when he'd never have touched before.

The others couldn't see him, blithely unaware while Asai whispered in Jacin's ear as they all nattered about what happened, what was going to happen, what should happen, while Jacin was busy trying not to scream every time Beishin smiled at him or spoke to him in that deep, soothing voice.

"Fen Jacin?"

Jacin jolted. That… wasn't Asai's voice.

His eyes popped open. Imara. Standing in front of him. Except… he hadn't let her in. His back was against the door. Unless she'd walked through him, she couldn't be here any more than Asai could.

Maybe she was a hallucination too. How would Jacin be able to tell?

Damn it, it wasn't fair—if he was going to be driven insane, he should at least get the mercy of oblivion to go with it. No one should have to *know* they were this crazy.

"Fen Jacin?" Imara was all sympathetic topaz eyes and soft tones. "Are you well?"

Jacin wanted to laugh. He could only shake his head and turn his glance to Asai, standing solidly right next to him, cool fingertips gliding along the jut of Jacin's cheekbone. Trying very hard not to let the crazed snigger wobble out, Jacin looked back at Imara.

"Are you real?"

Imara's eyebrow went up. "I am quite real."

Jacin supposed he'd have to take her word for it. He licked dry lips. "Do you see… anything?"

Because if even a *Temshiel* couldn't see Asai, when she used her magic to *look*, that would mean Asai wasn't real. Which would still mean Jacin was crazy, but he thought he could take that more easily than he could take Asai being alive. No one had been able to hear Asai before except Jacin, not even Malick, so if they couldn't see him, that would make some kind of fucked-up sense. But Jacin hadn't actually seen him before, either, Asai hadn't been *real*, not until Malick had—

Oh. Oh, fuck. That made awful, chilling sense.

Malick, you bastard. What am I supposed to do now?

Imara shot a look around the room. "See what?"

Jacin swallowed and clenched his teeth tight, trying to ignore Asai's too-real touch, but he was *touching*, and it was pretty hard not to notice.

"I…" Jacin choked it off—not because he didn't want to ask it, but because his throat was closing up. He couldn't breathe. "I… Asai, he… he can't… I don't *want*—"

He turned to Asai, raw desperation. "Why can't they *see* you?"

Asai merely smiled. "Because I do not wish it." He reached out again.

Jacin flinched away, nearly cringed "Don't." Thin and brittle. "Please, Beishin. *Don't.*"

"Don't what, little Ghost?"

"Don't…" Jacin's mouth flapped, air sucking frantically in, but it couldn't seem to get down to his lungs. "Don't… *be.*"

Worry etched itself over Imara's face, then annoyance when the pounding on the door at Jacin's back started. Jacin almost shrieked. He startled away from the door and stumbled sideways, but Asai was *right there*, so he pulled up short.

"Jacin?" Joori's voice. "*Jacin*, what's—?"

"He is fine, Fen Joori." Imara's tone was sharp with command, her eyes narrowed and pinned to Jacin.

Jacin could only twitch and shake and back helplessly away from Asai's advance and right into the door again.

"Ah, your beloved twin." Asai's smile was cruel now, his dark eyes hard. "Ever the watchful terrier, trying so hard to own and protect." He stopped right in front of Jacin, leaned in. "You will only get him killed too, little Ghost. And then what?"

Just like Mother and Caidi and Yori, and…

Where was Caidi? Asai's mocking had always faded to the background before when Caidi came, so where was she when Jacin really needed her? And where was Malick, because Malick made Asai go away entirely, and Jacin *really needed* Asai to go away, except, oh yeah, Malick wouldn't be coming to chase Asai away, Malick had gone up in a burst of flame, his bones probably still smoldering out on the street, and maybe Jacin would start seeing Malick's ghost, too, because why not, Jacin had been a Ghost himself all his life, so why was he—?

"Poor, poor little Ghost." Asai was close enough his breath sifted hot over Jacin's cheek.

Jacin flinched so hard he almost went over sideways against the door.

"Malick," Jacin wheezed, but it was wasted breath, because Malick wasn't here, Malick was gone, Malick was dead, and Jacin hadn't really known how much he'd depended on the safety of Malick until the safety was suddenly not there anymore. "Caidi, please."

"They can't hear you, lad. They're dead. You killed them."

"I—" Jacin wanted to say he hadn't, but he couldn't shove the words past the grating blockage in his throat. "I don't want you here," he said instead. "Go away. Go *away.*"

Imara said something then, but Jacin couldn't hear it—Asai's voice was filling up his head, making it pound.

"When has what you wanted ever meant a thing, *Ghost?*" Asai's tone had gone hard, deliberately spiteful in a way Jacin had only heard it once. "You have failed at everything you've wanted, everything you've tried. You need your beishin to tell you what you want."

The pain was so great it was like Asai had just driven a knife into Jacin's chest. Jacin's eyes popped wide as he tried to suck in air.

"Caidi?" It came out rough and shaky, more of a gasp, really, but it made Imara peer at Jacin sharply and lift an eyebrow. Jacin shook his head, trying to swallow a lumpy sob that was stuck at the bottom of his throat. "She isn't here." It seemed important somehow to make Imara understand this. "Asai comes and Caidi makes him quieter, but she's not here and he won't… he keeps… I don't want him here, I *swear* I don't want him here, but Malick's the only one who can make him go away, and Malick… he… he—"

"Fen Jacin, I don't see—"

"He's *right there!*" Jacin couldn't even lift his arm to point, because Asai was too close, and Jacin didn't want to touch him on purpose. "Can't you *see* him? Can't you… can't you make him *stop?*"

"You see Asai?" Imara's gaze had gone intense, her expression wary. "Here? Now?"

"*Yes!* I… no, it… he…"

Fuck, Jacin didn't *know.*

"*Jacin!*" came from the other side of the door, urgent, accompanied by more pounding, enough to rattle up Jacin's backbone. "Jacin, open this door or I'll get Samin to break it down!"

"Such drama." Asai huffed a *tsk* then a sigh. "Must you parade your aberrant nature so?"

"I wasn't—" Jacin cut off the protest. Because talking back had only ever encouraged Asai.

…That… that must be it. Jacin had talked back, had answered, and it made Asai more real, and if Jacin just stopped believing…

There was more noise out in the hall now, a harsh reprimand in a voice Jacin didn't recognize, then Joori snapping something back.

"There, now." Asai's mouth pinched in familiar disapproval. "You've woken the inn."

Jacin shut his eyes.

"I can't… I *can't!*" Because everything was going to sparkles and he couldn't get enough air in his lungs to shout or scream, and calling for Malick wasn't going to do any good.

"*Joori.*" Because Malick was gone, he'd left, he'd died, like they all did, and that bed only feet away—where Malick had given Jacin comfort and quiet and safety for a little while—was looking more and more like a yawning abyss through Jacin's spangling vision.

"Beishin, please." Because what else could Jacin say, what else could he do but beg the man he'd loved and killed and damned to the earth, plead with him for... fuck, Jacin didn't even *know*, just not... not *this*, whatever fresh hell this was where everyone left and those who didn't got taken away, and those who deserved their damnation came back to haunt you and drive you—

"*Fen Jacin!*" Imara shook him until he opened his eyes, gasping in sharp, shallow breaths, because his chest wouldn't expand and his throat wouldn't unclog.

Jacin flung his gaze wildly around the room, *made* himself believe it was empty but for him and this *Temshiel* who didn't belong here, in this room where Malick was supposed to—

"*Help*. He's supposed to—" Jacin's vision was tunneling. "Malick, he... Oh, *fuck*."

Not some surreal nightmare from which he couldn't wake—Malick was gone, Asai had been right there, *touching* Jacin, and now this strange *Temshiel* was looking at him like he was scary-crazy, and he couldn't deny it, because he could actually *feel* his mind teetering on some brink like it was a physical thing.

The scraping of the key in the lock right next to Jacin's hip was too loud, shattering through his head like he was standing inside a giant bell. His nerves were sentient things, juddering over his skin in wire-tight little spasms, threading out from where Imara gripped his arms and raising gooseflesh all over him.

The door shoved at Jacin from behind, Joori's voice still calling to him, but Jacin couldn't really hear it anymore, couldn't understand what he did hear, just found the sense in the word as Joori spoke his name and let Imara pull him away from the door.

Joori almost fell through it, face frantic, hair sticking to a sweaty brow, eyes both livid and frightened. A man and a woman in the uniform of Mitsu's Patrol were behind him, and Jacin had a brief moment of dismay when he realized what that likely meant, but Joori ignored them and pushed into the room. He went immediately for Jacin and pulled him away from Imara, looking Jacin over like he was afraid Imara had been trying to steal body parts. He peered closely into Jacin's eyes, narrowed his own.

"Jacin." He set his hand to Jacin's cheek, and it was so like Asai's touch that Jacin *had* to flinch back from it, he had no choice. "What the hell?"

Samin bullied his way in and demanded, "You all right, Fen?" with a suspicious cut of his glance toward Imara.

Jacin wanted to reply, wanted to say no, he wasn't all right, and it had nothing to do with Imara, but he still couldn't breathe. And even if he could, he wasn't sure what kind of gibberish might come out of his mouth if he tried to speak. He peered nervously over Samin's shoulder at the Patrol, wondering if he should just let them take him away, lock him up, take away the choices he didn't know what to do with anyway, put him someplace where he couldn't hurt anyone just by existing and where a dead man he used to love couldn't haunt him.

…Or maybe that would only trap him in some dark cell where he couldn't get away from the haunting.

Luckily, the whimper got snagged in his throat, along with all the air his lungs were trying to suck in and not quite getting.

"*This* is Fen Jacin-rei?" The patrolwoman's mouth pinched down into a skeptical frown.

Joori scowled. "It's *Jacin*. And I *told* you to wait in the hall. Or better yet, go away entirely. Can't you see we're a little busy right now?"

The woman ignored him, shot a look to the patrolman who'd come with her, and shook her head when he shrugged. She turned to Jacin.

"Fen Jacin." She looked him over with a small frown. "Goyo of Snake and counselor to the Patrol has some questions for you about the events of this evening. Please come along." She peered about, somewhat warily. "Is one of you Kel Saminil?"

Jacin only heard Joori's indignant "*What?* It's the middle of the bloody night!" from a distance. The blood pounding through Jacin's ears was much louder, the glitter and flash around the edges of his vision too distracting. Because there was Asai again, standing right behind Imara, watching Jacin, *smiling* at him.

Jacin's lips were numb. So were his fingertips. His chest had gone so tight the concept of breathing had taken on a meaning that was almost academic.

Imara's steady stare was what Jacin latched onto, because it was the only thing that was static besides Asai's mocking dark gaze. Imara looked right at Jacin, calm and unwavering, the vivid topaz of her eyes a peculiar anchor. Jacin had time to think they were the same color of the bottle Malick's uzin had come in, that night back in Ada when Jacin had tried and failed to get drunk, and instead had fallen into the morass that was Malick and the shattered remnants of his own life.

And then he had time to notice that the air had thickened and his throat had closed off completely, then, *Oh shit, I think I'm going to pass out like a hysterical little girl,* and everything just… went away.

5

*K*amen, Imara thought with a weary sigh, *when you come back, I'm going to kill you again.*

Just what exactly had Kamen been doing all this time?

Fen Joori's eyes were narrow little slits. "So, when are you going to tell me what's really going on here?" Hostile. Suspicious.

Imara couldn't really blame him.

With a stifled growl, she rechecked the wards she'd set in place last night as she'd shuffled the Patrol off with excuses and high-handed commands, and a grudging promise that she would see that the Incendiary was brought to the Statehouse tomorrow. Today. The suns were already rising.

She glanced over at the bed, and pursed her lips. "When I understand it fully myself."

She'd thought it best last night to keep watch over the Incendiary herself. The one called Kojoi Shig—the one with the mark of the spirits almost blazing out from her soul—had bullied the younger brother out the door, and Kel Saminil had kept the watch across the hall. The twin, this Fen Joori, had refused to be moved from the Incendiary's side and slumped now, trying not to let bloodshot eyes drift closed, propped against the headboard of the bed where the Incendiary lay unconscious.

Imara had been afraid for a while last night that the potion the Incendiary submissively—indeed, dazedly—allowed Kel Saminil to pour down his throat wasn't going to work, but it seemed it had finally kicked in. Perhaps she could put Goyo off a little longer; he could hardly question the Incendiary if the Incendiary was drugged unconscious, right? Imara couldn't even detect any dreams.

Then again, she supposed she wouldn't. If Kamen's magic hadn't been able to penetrate the void that was this Incendiary, Imara didn't imagine her own stood much of a chance. Though Imara had the finesse of years and knowledge, while Kamen had blunt power and the brass to use it. Not much of a match in an actual fight, but for something like this…

Perhaps.

"If you don't understand it," Fen Joori pressed, "why should we trust you to protect him?"

Imara tried not to roll her eyes. "Because at the moment, you seem to have little choice."

Fen Joori's lip curled but he went silent. Thank the gods.

Honestly, did these people think Imara had nothing better…? No, she wasn't going to let herself bow to the antagonism. She would remember that they had every right to suspicion. And she would remember that this was the earthbound who'd released the Ancestors and sent them home, and that Wolf had marked him. A Jin imprisoned all his life by the Adan, and what had *Temshiel* or maijin ever done for his people in his lifetime but use and hurt them? Well, besides Kamen, of course, but if Imara was reading Fen Joori correctly, Kamen was only a little higher in his esteem than Asai. Which, she had no doubt, pleased Kamen immensely.

A smirk threatened.

"He's had enough." Fen Joori's voice was quiet this time, fingers idly teasing at the Incendiary's hair. "You saw him. He can't take much more."

Imara eyed the Incendiary, still fully dressed and sprawled diagonally across the bed he apparently shared with Kamen, face pressed into the pillow and arm flung out as Kel Saminil had left him. He hadn't stirred, not even when Fen Joori tried to reposition him once or twice. Imara's gaze was critical, assessing, catching too frequently on the small braid that wound tangled hair back from the Incendiary's face. It made Imara shake her head, half wondering and half aghast, considering what a braid had meant to this once-Untouchable. Who would *choose* to wear such a reminder?

Pretty, in the Jin way, all high cheekbones and sharp features, echoed and yet somehow softened in his brother, even though Fen Joori's expression was locked in enmity, and the Incendiary's relaxed in sleep. Still, though, Imara could see what had caught Kamen's eye. Kamen had always been one for aesthetics. Imara didn't think that was all it was, though. Something else had snared Kamen like a man seduced to shipwreck by the call of a siren. He was such a predictably easy mark for the sort of tragedy that lived inside this Incendiary. It probably called to Kamen at least as strongly as the voice of his own god. And what Imara had seen last night did not fill her with confidence.

Kamen and his damsels. Idiot.

"Yes," Imara finally answered. She met Fen Joori's wary gaze for a moment before turning her own out the window again. "I can see that your brother is... strained." Which was putting it very, very kindly.

Bloody hell, what was Wolf *thinking*, setting Kamen to this in the first place? A pup still, really, all wagging tail and slobbering grin, until you crossed him and then the teeth came out, snapping with too little thought. Not settled enough yet, surely, to make of this once-Untouchable what Wolf obviously wanted. Kamen was only half-molded himself; how could he be expected to cast another in the shapes his god desired?—*this* other. Because this young man, lying dead-asleep and still as stone, was the embodiment of why the Incendiary had been deemed too dangerous in the first place.

This could not be the same Untouchable who'd mown through Court officials in Ada and then removed Asai's heart from his chest. This Fen Jacin could not be the soul chosen by Wolf to redefine the role of Incendiary and move the world to his whims.

Except that he was.

"So... what's your power, anyway?"

Imara turned to Fen Joori with a lift of her eyebrow.

Fen Joori shrugged and looked away. "I mean... Malick has them all. Asai—" A slight clench of teeth. "Asai was a seer, and so was that Xari. And so was Husao, now that I think about it." His mouth tightened. "All those bloody prophets, and none of them—" He shook it away. "But that Tatsu was a healer, and so was... um, Umeia." He stopped there, peering at Imara expectantly.

Imara put out a hand. "I am many things. But then, I am very old."

Fen Joori raised his eyebrows, looking her over.

Imara allowed a small smile. "Older than I look. And I have continued to learn and grow my magic for many, many lifetimes."

"So, your power is that you're... old." It was dubious and ingenuous at the same time.

Imara almost laughed. She didn't. It probably wouldn't go over very well.

"One is merely an asset to the other."

Fen Joori's only response was some weary blinking and a frown.

Imara considered for a moment. "You might understand it better as being bound to spirits, as you once had a spirit of the earth bound to your soul. Our souls belong to our gods, we can bind them to no other. Wolf took me as a healer with some small talent at interpreting the spirits and commanding fire. I have learned and grown since then. My powers are not as... dazzling as Kamen's, perhaps, but they are almost as many.

And there is something to be said for subtlety." She tried not to let that last curl wry.

It didn't seem as though Fen Joori would have noticed anyway. "Healer." He wasn't looking at Imara, instead studying his own fingers as they traced the Incendiary's braid from temple to shoulder. "Can you... d'you think you can... help?"

Imara sighed. That one hurt. Because she wanted very badly to say yes, but what she had seen so far did not bode well.

"I shall surely try." It was all she could offer.

Fen Joori merely snorted derisively then pursed his lips and shut his eyes. Imara really couldn't blame him.

She shook her head and turned to the window to watch the sister suns cresting over the distant crags of Tougei just at the bottom of the curvature of the bay, trying to push their light through the encroaching cloud cover. She shuddered. She'd lived ages, but she didn't think it would take even a few years of suffering the doom of the Jin Untouchables before madness took her. Regardless of what she'd seen last night, she had to respect this once-Untouchable-now-Incendiary for surviving it for at least a decade and with any of his mind intact at all. Imara supposed she should perhaps make an allowance or two.

Still, the sight of Kamen's ring on the Incendiary's hand appalled her. If the laws against the theft of such a thing weren't so harsh, she might consider confiscating it, just to see it out of the hands of someone so... precarious. As it was, Imara was unwilling to risk herself so. Certainly not for Kamen.

Impulsive and arrogant as you ever were, Kamen. What are we going to do with you?

What a way for Wolf's Null to emerge from his self-imposed exile. Kamen *would* make sure he did it in the most visible, dramatic way possible. Sending the Ancestors home and then claiming the first Incendiary in over a century for himself was certainly dramatic. And then he'd ruined it all by allowing himself to be ambushed in the street by *banpair*.

Imara smirked.

It flattened almost immediately.

She'd been so sure Kamen didn't know what he was doing where it concerned the Incendiary—and so far she hadn't been proven wrong. But the Incendiary was not at all what Imara had been expecting. She'd rather thought—perhaps hoped—that Kamen's nearly vicious protectiveness had been just Kamen being his arrogant self, assuming he knew more than he did and no one could do a job as well as he could. It appeared Imara had... misjudged.

There must be something to recommend the Incendiary, surely. After all, Wolf had risked the undoing of Fate itself to snatch him from Raven's hand. Kamen, of all people, had apparently completely lost his mind over his Untouchable. And the mortals all around the Incendiary too obviously both feared and loved him, though Imara hadn't yet got a complete fix on the fear. There were too many shades of it, some of it for the Incendiary and some of it of him, and all of the emotions flying around last night had been too tangled to dissect properly.

Still. The one thing Imara could see too clearly was that the Incendiary was far too unpredictable for his intended purpose. Volatile and submissive by turns, with an underpinning of violence in every move he made. And yet one hallucination of his former teacher-tormentor had undone him, reduced him to a quivering mess.

But there was the rather disturbing rub, Imara thought as she set to going over her wards yet again, searching for cracks or weak spots. Because perhaps "hallucination" was merely wishful thinking. The Incendiary had believed it so hard, he'd almost convinced Imara she'd felt something herself.

Imara pursed her lips, shook her head.

Kamen's people said that Kamen had felt something, too, just before his spirit fled, crying his message. If a Null of Wolf in his own Cycle had been so blindsided by whatever it had been, Imara didn't know what she could do about it. She'd come because the Incendiary would be Wolf's, and because she hadn't realized the warning she'd prevented Xari from offering had been such a dire one. She'd forbidden Xari because Kamen was being a prick, and because sometimes he needed a lesson. He'd been keeping something from Imara, and Imara hadn't liked it. And, she admitted, because she'd assumed Kamen had no idea what he was doing, that he was failing whatever test Wolf had set before him. She'd assumed she knew better.

Dakimo was going to flay her, and Kamen was going to do it again—much more painfully and laughing all the while, no doubt—when he got back.

Kamen had always been a smug bastard.

Imara didn't turn when the door eased open silently behind her. She merely assessed the shift in moods as Kojoi Shig crept in, stopped to peer warily at Fen Joori for a moment then, when he merely gave her a tired glare, joined Imara at the window.

Calm, this one, but she'd have to be if she'd survived the spirits with her mind intact, used them as Imara understood she'd done once. Unsettled, though. Yearning and confused, with the shadow of a fresh grief that had nothing to do with Kamen. Loyalty, but not as much as Imara had felt in Kel Saminil. Kojoi Shig had just enough calculated coldness to know where loyalty ought to end, and more than enough self-worth to end it when sense told her she should.

Perhaps in need of direction, this child of Wolf, but Imara didn't think Kojoi Shig would require much guidance in the end. Kamen had chosen well.

"All is well, Kojoi-onna?" Imara kept her voice to a low murmur. She wasn't quite ready for the Incendiary to wake yet.

Kojoi Shig snickered. "Call me Shig, yeah? I don't think I'll ever feel like an 'onna' and 'Kojoi' isn't something I feel the need to…" She trailed off and shrugged with a cynical twist of her mouth. "Just Shig."

Imara peered at her closely. Another pretty one. Blond hair set with streaks of color, a beacon to the spirits unconsciously mimicking her aura, and her sharp jade eyes belied the dulcet tones of even her reprimands. Between this Shig and the Fen brothers, Imara would have been tempted to assume Kamen recruited for beauty—which would actually be all too believable, where Kamen was concerned—but the presence of Kel Saminil rather negated that assumption.

"No formalities here." Shig's gaze was just as judicious as Imara suspected her own was, watchful with a note of wariness beneath the affability. "In fact, Samin might be moved to see how easy *Temshiel* bones break if you call him Kel-seyh one more time. He hasn't used that in years." She turned her gaze back out the window, the rose-orange rays of the rising suns catching at her hair and eyelashes, sparking gold. "Though, stick to 'Fen' with Fen Jacin. He doesn't let everyone call him by his name." A shrug that wasn't quite as careless as she was trying to make it. "I don't think he likes the… familiarity."

Ah. So, this pretty young woman would prefer to be more familiar and had been rebuffed. Interesting.

Imara turned back to the window, mild discomfort seeping in. The familiarity and invitation for reciprocation was polite. Fair. These people hadn't come to Imara, after all—she'd rather forced herself on them. It still sat odd. Perhaps not where it concerned everyone else, but giving the Incendiary a name, allowing him to become an actual person to her seemed… risky. And likely where it had all started for Kamen.

"So, what should we call you?" The lightness of Shig's tone seemed genuine this time.

Imara turned to frown at Shig. She was sure she'd introduced herself last night.

"I am Imara Wolf's-own."

"That's it?"

"What else were you expecting?"

"Overlord?" Joori's tone was a strange mix of derision and affection. "That's what Malick said when I asked him that question."

Shig snickered in agreement. "Or maybe more like Almighty Master of All Things Coitus." She shot a wry look sideways. "He has a pretty high opinion of his… skills."

Joori merely huffed something that could have been a snort or a cough.

Imara, on the other hand, had to keep herself from rolling her eyes. "I'm aware." *Everyone* was aware.

"But he's a good man, for all that." Shig rolled her eyes when Joori huffed again, but then she smirked, deliberate, and went on, "And from what I hear, his boasts are all pretty justified."

Well, they would be. That was the problem with Kamen—he was good at everything he did. He only knew what failure looked like from the outside. And he led with his heart. Always. Backed by that cocky bravado that had probably contributed at least a little to him having been blindsided by *banpair*. And if Imara wasn't much mistaken, the Incen—*Fen* had rather blindsided Kamen as well. And would continue to blindside Kamen until Kamen failed Wolf so badly that—

Imara peered, considering, over Shig's shoulder at the sleeping Fen. Was that what she'd seen last night? Was this a failure in progress?

"He was taking care of it."

Shig's teasing tones were gone, leaving only the lilting delivery common to most of those with the mark of the spirits on their souls. And the fact that her testimonial was very close to an answer to Imara's silent questions made Imara think that perhaps this perceptive child of Wolf hadn't got all her acuity from the spirits. There were some mortals who grew their own magic from the seed of the divine sorcery that made all living things, and the echoes of brilliance in the gaudy aura told Imara that Shig was likely one of them.

Perhaps Imara might acquire herself a new initiate when all this was through.

"Taking care of *us*. It's only…" Shig paused, her mouth turning down into a girlish little pout. She gestured over to the bed. "It's only that he loves him. I mean *really loves* him. And he doesn't really know how, and Fen doesn't know how to be loved, so neither one of them were doing it right, and now with Mal gone, Fen—"

"Shut the fuck up, Shig." Rough and grainy, but with force behind it nonetheless.

Imara was dismayed to see Fen sitting up slowly, bleary-eyed and already scowling, even as he rubbed at his eyes then raked a hand through his dark hair. Damn it, that potion should have kept him down for hours yet.

Fen pushed Joori's hand from his shoulder then shot Shig a blurry glare before he aimed it at Imara for a moment, more appraising. He looked back at Shig.

"We don't even know her."

Shig shrugged. "She says Mal sent her."

Like it was all the proof she needed to offer her trust, and yet Imara could tell Shig wasn't entirely convinced, either. Which was all too close, because if Kamen had known what was going to happen, Imara thought she'd be one of the last he'd call on to take his mortals in hand, let alone "his" Incendiary. And if he ever found out Imara had rather accidentally abetted his unexpected trip to spirit…

Fen stared at Shig, flat and angry. "*Mal* isn't here. And fuck if I'm going to let you pretend you know everything about me and spew it all to some *Temshiel* I don't even know." He shunted a glare between Shig and Imara. "Get out."

"Nope, sorry, can't." Shig's smile was more of a wry tilt. "Joori needs a break, because you *know* he didn't let himself sleep for even five seconds while you were out, and Samin might deck me if I left you alone without one of us to babysit you. It's what you get for being a suicidal asshole."

"I don't need a break." Joori was eyeing Fen cautiously, waiting for a reaction to see what his own should be.

Fen ignored him. "I could kill you with a fucking teabowl, Shig."

"Yeah?" Oddly, it made Shig grin. "Then maybe we'll have to take those away too."

That something so innocuous touched off such anger in Fen was alarming. His mouth curled into an actual snarl, eyes gone flat and narrow like a predator's. Before Imara had even registered that a danger existed, Fen was lurching up from the bed, throwing off Joori's attempt to restrain him like he wasn't even there. Imara didn't know if Fen's threat was even real, but there was no question he was capable of carrying it out if it was.

She put herself between Fen and Shig before she'd even really thought about what she was doing. She had to remember her magic wouldn't work against Fen. Any force Imara could use was going to have to come from her own mortal body, and though her strength was greater than that of most mortals, she wasn't armed at the moment. "Fen." Imara kept her voice calm and even. "Perhaps we can come to a compromise, yes?"

Fen didn't say anything, only glared at Shig, who was still grinning behind Imara. Well, at least Fen wasn't lunging. Progress? Perhaps Fen Jacin merely needed a firm hand.

Imara looked at Shig. "Please wake the others. You should all have time to dress and break your fast before we must leave."

And with what Imara had seen last night and was still seeing now, it wasn't going to be in answer to Goyo's high-handed summons, either. Fen was overdue for a visit to Wolf's temple, and Imara was bloody well going to make sure he made it, after all of Kamen's stalling. That was at least one part of Kamen's job she didn't mind doing herself, and none too soon, the way things were going.

She turned back to Fen. "Fen and I have matters we must discuss."

That made Fen focus the glare on Imara. "I have nothing to—"

"Can you see him right now?"

It shut Fen up.

Not Joori, though. "See who?" His expression dipped toward suspicion. "What is she talking about, Jacin?"

Fen was nearly choking on fury, but there was confusion in there too. He didn't answer. Clearly wasn't going to.

"Joori, Shig." Imara kept her gaze nailed to Fen. "I need to speak with Fen, please. Alone."

"No." Joori let go of Fen's arm and tried to step in front of him, but neither Fen nor Imara backed off to give him room. "Jacin, you've only just—"

"Get out." Fen modulated his tone for his brother, but he didn't shift his aggressive glare from Imara. "Go, Joori. Take Shig with you."

It wasn't hard to see the hurt in Joori's eyes, the sorrow and the insult. And it wasn't hard to see the determination not to care in Fen's.

Bloody hell, this family tangle could take centuries to sort and soothe.

"Fine." Joori's hollow, bloodshot eyes filled for the briefest of moments, but he kept the emotion back. "Let me know if you… right. Never mind."

With a heavy breath, he pointed a meaningful look at Shig, backed away from Fen, and walked to the door. He turned and waited for Shig. Mouth turned down, Shig followed after Joori and walked silently out of the room with one last concerned glance at Fen.

Fen waited until the door snicked shut. "Did you see him or not?"

With a tired sigh, Imara stepped slowly over to the window again, and propped her leg up on the wide sill. Fen opened his mouth like he meant to protest but then closed it again.

Imara didn't pause to analyze it, because there was already too much to analyze with this dangerously precarious Incendiary. She could pick it apart later and… do something with it. Maybe.

For now, she merely shrugged. "I did not."

It was like she'd just punched Fen in the chest. All the air went out of him. He kept the hostile expression, though Imara was sure she saw something raw and agonized in there somewhere. Perhaps she should have considered her answer more carefully.

"I don't know why I'd thought it might be over." Fen heaved something that might have been a sour laugh, but the hollowness of it turned it into something… almost eerie. Or perhaps it was the shadow of the larger implications of the comment, even if Fen didn't know what they were. "It never ends, does it." Not a question. "It will never…" He shook his head, eyes clearing, and mastered himself, control slipping around him like a visible suit of armor. "Why are you here?"

Imara blinked. "Because Kamen isn't. You and yours need protection, Fen Jacin. You can't—"

"Me and mine need nothing from you. You can go now."

A far cry from the quaver of terror that voice had husked out last night.

"Oh?" Imara's eyebrow went up. "And if Asai's spirit really is here?"

She waited, but all Fen did was narrow his eyes. Imara had half-expected the mere mention of Asai's name to trigger the frantic fear of last night, but it didn't.

So what *had*?

"You said Kamen chased him away." It was more musing aloud than statement of fact, but Imara really needed to understand this. "When Kamen went to spirit last night, his wards vanished as well. If there *is* anything here, hovering about, the only magic standing between you and it is mine. *My* wards, *my* magic." And maybe that really was it. Which would be disconcerting but also a boon, because Imara didn't think anything else would get Fen to cooperate. "Are you quite certain, Fen Jacin, that you need nothing from me? Are you quite certain that those you love need nothing from me?"

The anger and confusion emanating from Fen were almost live things. His jaw clenched, and his nostrils flared, and his eyes… bloody hell, Imara didn't even need magic to figure out what was going on in his head—it was all over his face.

So, when he finally ground out, "You're a fucking bitch," it was fairly redundant.

Imara shrugged. "Kamen has allowed the task to which Wolf set him to languish for too long. I intend to see to it now. Perhaps we might…

coexist a little better if we define and resolve to respect one another's boundaries."

"Fine. Here's my boundary: You stay out of my way, and I won't send your spirit after Ma— Kamen's."

It was small—tiny, really—but Imara saw it: a twitch, a flash of doubt and grief and fear in the truncated speaking of the name Kamen had refused to shed along with his mortal skin.

Imara almost sighed. So. That was how it was with Fen Jacin, then.

All right. Imara had seen the sort before. Bricking himself up behind rage and distrust because all the other emotions had betrayed him. Just brilliant.

At least Imara knew.

She tipped a slow nod, almost a bow but not quite. "I have no intention of getting in your way."

Not at the moment, at least. Not unless Fen didn't get himself together and pledge himself to Wolf. He'd bloody well do it if Imara had to knock him unconscious and *drag* him to the temple.

Damn Kamen to the suns and back for… for *existing*.

"We have appointments we must keep." Imara straightened, adjusting her sleeves. "You're not going to see Goyo today, Fen. We have other concerns that are much more important. Our god has… expectations, and I have no intention of disappointing him. And we all must bow to certain inevitabilities."

"I don't. I'm not going to any temple, and I won't—"

"You will do as your god commands." Imara let her eyes narrow in clear threat. "Your brothers need my protection, Fen Jacin. Do you really want to be the one responsible for taking it away?"

She'd been right—the way to Fen Jacin was through his brothers. She could see the rage all over him, but the threat reined him in; his hands had been hovering over the hilts of the knives at his belts, but they fisted instead of settling around the grips. His chin quivered, even as his eyes flared murderous fury, but all he seemed able to force out through his teeth was,

"Fuck you."

Since he merely spun and stalked out of the room and then across the hall to his brother's, Imara let that bit of disrespect slide.

᛭

"The Temple?" Morin had no doubt his eyes were sprung wide and his jaw was flapping. "You want to take *Jacin* out in public? During the day, when there are people about?"

"It cannot wait any longer." Imara seemed a bit taken aback by

Morin's admittedly indecorous reaction. "I managed to put the Patrol off for a few hours, but they will be back, and this task must be completed before your brother meets with Goyo."

"Why does he have to meet with this Goyo person at all?"

Imara looked like she smelled something foul. "Because he is counselor to the Patrol and his position must be respected."

"Yeah, well, subjecting him to Jacin isn't really going to accomplish that. He's got the social skills of a bitchy ken-ken."

And making him try to use them was sometimes actually painful. Didn't she know what a bad idea it was to allow someone of the Patrol to question Jacin at all? She was supposed to be smart—shouldn't she have figured that out just by what she'd already seen?

"After your brother has completed his task at Wolf's temple, that will hardly matter anymore."

Morin couldn't figure out if that was an answer to what he'd said or to what he hadn't said. Abruptly uncomfortable, he drew his gaze from Imara's and looked around at the others for some kind of reassurance, but there was none to be had.

Jacin was looking angry-puzzled, which was a switch from his usual angry-angry, but not much of one. Shig was trying very hard not to show any reaction at all, but Morin was getting to know her fairly well, and he was pretty sure he detected some inner giggling. Samin just looked tired, but he'd been up all night, keeping watch against whatever those things were that had somehow managed to sneak up on—

Damn it, every time the reality of it hit Morin, his stomach clenched and curled, and he wasn't even certain why. Sure, he liked Malick well enough, but Malick was *Temshiel.* He'd be back. There wasn't really any such thing as death to them; there was no sense in mourning. That wasn't what this felt like, anyway.

Maybe it was that "on our own" feeling that Morin kept shoving away, because they weren't, really. They had Shig and Samin, and while Shig could be a flighty, unreliable twat sometimes, Morin had no doubt Samin wasn't about to abandon them. And now they had this Imara watching their backs as a favor to Malick, which should have made Morin feel better, because Malick had cared enough to get Imara to do it.

Thing was, Imara wasn't Malick. Imara was here as a proxy. And probably because she had her own reasons; all her sort did. Morin didn't think her presence here was because she actually gave a shit about any of them... gave a shit about...

Yeah. That was it. Morin knew it would come to him if he thought about it, so maybe that was why he hadn't.

Malick put up with Jacin's batshit ways and near-constant grieving hostility because Malick loved him. And in his own *Temshiel* way, Malick was just as crazy as Jacin was. Malick had a vested interest in figuring out what Jacin needed and giving it to him.

Imara didn't.

"I thought it was too dangerous." Joori's disposition toward Imara was apparently just as hostile as it had ever been toward Malick. "Those *banpair* wanted to get to him badly enough to attack a *Temshiel*, and now you want to just parade him about in the middle of the day?"

"Whatever they wanted, they didn't want Fen dead." Samin was sprawled in the chair across from Morin, but his eyes were sharp on Imara. "But I can't say I disagree with Joori. They got through Mal's magic. Why not yours?"

Imara only shrugged. "I may not have Kamen's power, but I'm not helpless."

"Well, apparently, neither are *they*." Joori was leaking suspicion all over the place. "What happens if they get past you too?"

"Then we will be all the closer to knowing what they are and what they want."

See, this was why they needed Malick. He didn't have that chilly "he's just a mortal" rationality. At least not when it came to Jacin. If Malick were here, he'd be locking Jacin up in the room and hiring mercenaries to guard him.

Joori's mouth had dropped open. Morin couldn't blame him.

"Let me make sure I'm understanding you clearly." Joori was all-over budding rage. "You want to—"

"They know where he is, Fen Joori. And after last night, every *Temshiel* and maijin in the city—indeed, the world—knows where he is and what happened to Kamen. *Banpair* will not be the only ones to… seek Fen Jacin." Imara paused, peered at Jacin closely, but Jacin was busy staring off into the empty space in the corner of the room. Imara frowned then turned back to Joori. "The servants of Wolf's temple are not merely priests and priestesses but trained warriors. It is the safest place for your brother just now. Probably for you too."

"*Why?* What is Jacin to any of these people?" Joori turned a pleading look on Jacin. "Jacin? What are they talking about? I thought we were through with all of"—he waved helplessly around the room with a slight pause for emphasis on Imara—"*this.*"

Jacin was still engrossed in the shadows in the corner. Staring. Jaw clenched so tight Morin imagined he could hear teeth grinding.

Joori slapped the table. "*Jacin?*"

Jacin didn't even twitch.

"Damn it." Joori shot up from his chair and started toward Jacin. "Jacin, answer me, I want to know—"

"Stop."

It was quiet but it still halted Joori where he was like he'd walked into a wall.

Jacin didn't say anything more, merely blinked, gave his head a little shake then pushed away from the wall and walked out.

Nothing new. He did it lots of times when Joori nattered at him, and most of the time Joori chased him down. This time, Joori only looked angrily at Imara.

Imara gave Joori a level look. "It appears your brother has decided that it's time to go."

Morin wouldn't call the expression on Imara's face a smirk. But it was damned close.

⛩

He had no idea where he was going. Just *away*. Outrun Asai, maybe, outrun everyone, hide so they couldn't find him, lose himself in the streets of Mitsu where no one knew what he was, what he'd been, what *they'd* made him with their selfish "justice" and their callous indifference to those who got their bones ground up beneath the weight of their Balance.

Yes, Asai hissed, *remove the threat.* He sounded far too satisfied. *The only way to save them is to abandon them. Your mere presence is a danger, Jacin-rei.*

"I know. I *know.*"

Hadn't Asai been throwing that at him all morning? And hadn't Imara all but confirmed it? The minions of the gods were looking for him now, and if he was around people he cared about, they'd be used and threatened. It was what these people did.

I can help you. They will—

"Just shut up and leave me *alone.*"

Did Asai really think Jacin was stupid enough to just bow his head and trade one faction that wanted to use him for another? Honestly.

He knocked shoulders with someone on the stairs; Jacin jolted back but didn't stop, just regained his balance and kept going, picking up his pace so he was almost running when he hit the bottom. Malick's duster flapped around his calves, reeking of pine and sage, but the consolation Jacin couldn't admit seeking when he'd donned it didn't come.

His vision was tunneling again, graying out and narrowing, but at the end of it… *light*. A door on the other side of the inn's tearoom into which he'd just blundered, daylight slicking through its window like a beacon. Jacin aimed straight for it. There were bodies in his way, hazy enough in his periphery that he didn't bother trying to put faces to them. As long as they got out of his way, it didn't much matter.

The gods would use you still, little Ghost. Even now they send their thugs to trick you and control you.

"Get the fuck *away* from me."

Jacin wasn't sure who he was talking to. People were crowding in around him, but so was Asai, and Jacin needed all of them to just get *out* of his fucking *way*. Snarling in every direction, he rammed into some big, blocky slab of muscle and bone, staggered back a pace and adjusted his angle.

The door. He needed to get to the door.

Perfection, little Ghost. I can show you how to achieve it.

"I'm not perfect, *Beishin*." Half sneer, half shout. "I'll never *be* perfect. Isn't that what you said?"

Just another trick, another setup to failure, because that was all Beishin had ever meant for "his Ghost," and Jacin wasn't falling for it again. And now, with "Incendiary" hanging over his head, it seemed there was no limit to the catastrophic possibilities.

Another indeterminate barrier placed itself between Jacin and the door. Jacin merely lashed out with a hard fist and removed it.

"*Fen Jacin.*" It was fuzzy, muffled, and outside his head this time.

Didn't matter. There was no one who had anything to say Jacin wanted to hear, so he kept moving.

Light. Freedom. The noise of a city street to block out the whispers of Beishin in his head. And yet another obstruction in his path.

"Fen Jacin, you must—"

"Stop him, before he—"

"Step away, he belongs to Kamen."

Jacin whirled at that one, because he knew that voice, and she had no fucking right to say that, no fucking right to even *be* here, not when Malick… It wasn't *fair*, she didn't know, she didn't *see*, she didn't—

"You don't understand." He got right up in Imara's face, growled it. "You don't understand a fucking thing, you don't know anything about me, so stop—"

"You're right, I don't—"

"—pretending you give a shit, just get away from me, I don't want—"

Imara took hold of Jacin's wrists in a grip surprisingly strong, snapped his hands up between them and held them fast. Had he been going for a knife? He couldn't remember.

"What you *want*," Imara said, low and even, her gleaming eyes intense, "is about to matter very little, if you won't calm down and pretend for a moment to be reasonable." Her gaze roved over Jacin's left shoulder; he followed it, noted a big man in the surcoat of the city's Patrol, eyeing him with distrust and no small amount of anger. Imara jostled Jacin's hands until he looked back at her. "Goyo apparently sent an escort, which I've no doubt could turn very quickly to your escort to the city's dungeons." Her mouth turned down, weirdly sympathetic, for all her grip was almost cruel. She leaned in and lowered her voice. "Or to the towers of the sickhouse, Fen Jacin. Do you understand?"

Jacin clenched his teeth, peered at the man over his shoulder again, then noted the man's female companion just to the right. She was bleeding from lip and nose, one hand holding a short sword, and the other pressing a cloth to her face to blot and staunch. Jacin frowned and turned back to Imara.

"You have assaulted a guest of the inn, Kamen's solicitor, and an officer of the Patrol."

"I…" Jacin blinked. He had? He flexed his hand, still held fast in Imara's. Knuckles tight, fingers throbbing just a little. Yeah, it seemed he had. When had he done that? Shouldn't he remember something like that?

Worried now, not quite horrified but getting there, Jacin shot his glance around, noted he was quite thoroughly penned into a corner of the tearoom and nowhere near as close to the door as he wanted to be.

"This is Kamen's Untouchable?" A man of striking good looks stepped up behind Imara, black hair strung through with startling bolts of purest white, his eyes sea-blue and clear as glass. His left cheek was going red and slightly puffy, his eye watering as he regarded Jacin with a half smile that was somehow critical and forgiving at the same time.

"Don't call me—" Jacin stopped in midsnarl. Because he had no idea against which epithet he was reflexively rebelling—"Kamen's" or "Untouchable."

"I'm going to let you go." Imara's tone was incongruously gentle. "The Patrol is probably going to want to disarm you, but I'll see what I can do." She lowered her voice. "This convinces me more than ever that the safest place for you right now is Wolf's house. Give me a moment to get rid of the Patrol. Can you control yourself that long?"

Jacin shut his eyes, teeth set tight against the swell of indecipherable emotions trying to wind up his throat. He didn't want to go to this Goyo person, but he didn't want to go to any temple, either. Except he seemed to be nicely cornered. And he'd *let* it happen.

Ah, poor little Ghost. You just can't help but fail, can you? When will you—?

"Fen Jacin."

Jacin snapped his eyes back open. Hung to the gold gaze looking back at him.

"He's here with you now. Isn't he?"

Jacin tried not to flinch, but his body just wasn't doing what he wanted it to right now.

"I know you can see and hear him. I believe you."

Jacin looked away, mute.

Did she think that was what he wanted to hear? Did she think it would make it *better?*

Helpless, adrift and getting farther from shore every second, Jacin only shook his head. "It doesn't *matter.*"

Because mad or not wasn't really the point. Merely one among… hundreds.

Imara sighed. With a weary shake of her head, she relaxed her grip, tipping a small nod to the solicitor. It wasn't until he stepped in, shifting his body between Jacin and the door, that Imara let go altogether and angled away to speak quietly with the Patrol.

Jacin blinked around, noting for the first time all the eyes peering warily back at him. It appeared he'd disturbed breakfast in the tearoom. The patrons were only now beginning to resume whatever they'd been doing when the crazy Ghost invaded their quiet little lives, though they all spared chary looks before doing so. Jacin decided to pretend he didn't notice them as he let the solicitor steer him a little farther into the corner that was still too far away from the door.

"I am Naro-yi of Owl." The man dipped his head low. "I am pleased to make your acquaintance, Kamen Jacin."

The name startled Jacin, enough so he couldn't think of anything to say for a full thirty seconds. And when he finally did "That isn't my name" was all he could think of.

Naro-yi's eyebrows went up. "Ah? Well." He waved it away. "It is not meant in offense, I assure you. It is merely how our kind… differentiate." Jacin must have been blinking stupidly at him, because Naro-yi was compelled to go on, "Kamen has placed a hand of protection upon you, marked you as his, so all might know and respect his claim."

And why did that roil in Jacin's gut in a hard little ball of anger mixed with relief and gratification?

Claimed.

Touch the Untouchable.

"His claim extends, of course, to all those he has brought here to Tambalon." Naro-yi's smile was kind. "I'm told that means a great deal to you."

It had. Before. Jacin just hadn't realized how much until it was gone. "Kamen is dead."

It came out a little thin and high, laced through with anger, because damn it, Jacin had let himself depend on Malick, and Malick had let his guard down. Jacin looked away toward Imara so Naro-yi wouldn't see how speaking the words had stung.

"Is he?" Naro-yi whiffed a snort that was an inelegant contrast to the overall elegance of his manner and appearance. "So many would like to think so." His smile tilted expectantly as Imara stepped back over. "All settled, then?"

"What the hell is going on here?" Joori's voice was strained, louder than usual, and attracted all the attention that had just receded from Jacin himself. Joori didn't seem to care, stalking across the room, thunder at his brow, with Samin lumbering behind him. Joori glared at Imara, and then down at Naro-yi's hand where it was, unnoticed by Jacin until just this second, locked to Jacin's elbow. "What happened *now?*"

Jacin was sure the derisive twist to Joori's question wasn't meant for him, because it never was—always to those around him—but that didn't stop the knowledge that it was always *because* of him, and it never failed to bring the shame with it. Jacin set his teeth against it and looked away.

"Your brother is… stressed." Imara's voice was soft and sympathetic, which only made Jacin's cheeks flare up with warmth, so he shut his eyes. "The Patrol—"

They have come for the Incendiary, Jacin-rei. Hardly more than a whisper, but it nonetheless drowned out everything else, set the periphery buzzing with white again. *If you allow them to take you, you will never walk freely again.*

Jacin's head throbbed in time to his too-rapid pulse. "Shut up." Weak and watery.

They know what you are, all of them. Every Temshiel *and* maïjin *felt Kamen's spirit wrenched from the world last night when—*

"Did you do that? Was it you?"

Because that would be just like Asai. Find out what Jacin needed and then take it away, just because he could.

"Jacin?" Joori's voice. "Do what? Was it who?" Worried. And then Joori's grip landed on the arm that Naro-yi wasn't holding. "Jacin, what's wrong?"

Let me help you little Ghost.

Nowhere near an answer to Jacin's question, but it struck echoes in his head to swirl and tangle with Malick's voice, speaking those same words to him, but Malick wasn't *here*, he'd left, and Jacin was alone inside this crowd of people who stared with fear and sympathy in their eyes, even Joori.

You cannot allow them to take you. If you allow them to make the Incendiary helpless to them, you shall never see the suns again, you shall never see your brothers again. I know a safe place where none of them will find you. Come with me, little Ghost.

"I have to go."

He did. Not with Asai, but not with Imara either. Anywhere, just not *here*. He tried to wrench from the hands holding onto him, and only succeeded in shoving off Joori's. Naro-yi wasn't letting go.

"Fen." Imara's tone was too calm, too blatantly friendly, like Jacin was some rabid dog she was trying to coax out of its safe den so she could cut it down. "Perhaps we can—"

"I have to *go!*" Jacin yanked again on his arm, and again, Naro-yi merely held on.

You have to get away, Jacin-rei. They all know, they all want the power of the Incendiary for themselves. They will use your brothers against you, unless you leave them behind. For their own good, Jacin-rei. If you would protect them, you must leave them.

"And we will, Fen." Imara reached out, hand stopping to hover just over the hilt of the knife jutting from its sheath on Jacin's left thigh. "Just let us—"

"No!" Jacin backed up as far as he could, shoulder blades pressing into the wall, heart racing. Bodies were all around him, blocking off air, blocking off light, blocking off a way out.

"Jacin, please, just calm down." Joori's voice was taking on notes of entreaty and fear. "Damn it, will you just *back off* and let me talk to him?"

"Here, you've got him cornered, for the love of the gods. You think that's going to calm him down?" Samin's voice was like a firm handhold on the side of a faltering cliff. "Let Joori through."

It was like magic. One second there were blockades and obstructions pressing Jacin into the wall, and the next, it all eased back a pace. Joori stepped through the barrier, and as he shoved his way around Imara, he knocked sideways into Naro-yi.

It was enough. Naro-yi's grip slipped just a little, and Jacin shoved to the side until it fell away completely. His arm came up, forearm coming out straight to level a solid blow to… someone. He couldn't tell. Could barely see. That light from the door was like a beacon, blinding him.

Yes, Jacin-rei, get away, now, before they slap the irons on your wrists and all is lost.

Irons. Bars. Cells. All alone and unable to run from the voices.

An uppercut to someone's chin as all the hands reached for him, but Jacin was fast when he wanted to be. He spun, slammed into a solid wall of muscle and spun again.

Instinctively, his hands reached for his knives, even as he was plowing through anything that got between him and the door, hardly hearing Joori's voice back there, calling him, and Samin's voice, grinding out curses. Jacin didn't draw a weapon. He didn't dare. Just met the next obstacle with a driving run, leading with his shoulder, and rammed it with all his weight. Something broke, a shattering noise, and cool air hit his face, flooded his lungs. Shards of glass rained down on his head, sharp pain drilling into his palm. It cleared his mind enough that he realized he'd reached the door, so he wrenched it open and hurled himself through it.

He ran.

Spikes shot up the muscles of his calf, even the parts of the muscles that weren't there anymore. It hurt, but it was good, a good pain, a welcome pain. It drowned out all the other pain—the anger, the fear, the grief, the hopelessness. They'd been with him for so long, he'd been afraid of what might happen if he didn't have them anymore.

Now he knew. Jagged splines of physicality that countermanded all the emotion he didn't know how to decode. And it felt really *fucking good.*

Footsteps pounded behind him. Voices rose into shouts then several sharp whistles.

Run, little Ghost.

Jacin did. Poured on speed and slithered between passersby, shoving aside the ones he couldn't get through, lashing out at the ones that wouldn't move, until he reached the street.

"Jacin, *please!*" Joori's voice, distant, almost hysterical.

It almost slowed Jacin down, but the sound of running feet behind him was louder, so he kept going. Ran into one man then another; the second tried to grab him, so Jacin leveled him with a left hook, shaking his hand out as he regained equilibrium and took off again. More shouts rose behind him, closing in.

He ran faster.

Leapt two-wheeled carts dragged by weary-looking hackmen, their passengers gasping out in surprise as the Ghost hurdled the flimsy-framed canopies over their heads. Ducked into alleys and blew past the linens hung out on lines between buildings, the children who played Stones and Hop-through on the cobbles, then the thugs and thieves who played more dangerous games. He raced past them all, come and gone so quick he might as well have been the Ghost he'd thought he wasn't anymore but that forever snapped at his heels.

Malick's ring had jammed into his knuckle with that last punch. It was good. It reminded him he had it. Reminded him he knew how to use it, at least for this.

No, little Ghost, you mustn't—

Jacin ignored it. Not even slowing down to drag in more breath, he whispered the spell that brought the shadows and kept running.

Malick's duster fluttered out behind him, its weight on his shoulders weirdly soothing. Jacin ducked his head and sucked air, Malick's scent sliding all around him, blocking out the city smells, and he breathed it in.

So much easier this way. Shadows in the gray light of an overcast day, but all he had to do was keep to the alleys and not run into anyone, and everything else just... went away. Just the rhythm of his body as he pushed it to keep going, the soft *thud* of his boots hitting the ground— *one-two-three-four, one-two-three-four*—the raspy in-and-out of his breath, the muted jingle of a few of the throwing knives that had come loose in the sheaths strapped to his arms. The hot throb in the palm of his hand, the feel of tacky blood sticking to his fingers, and the barbs of agony traveling his leg and jolting up through his spine. Sweet and sharp, all of it, like a balm to a fevered mind.

Focus.

Control.

The shouts had gone away. The sound of pursuit had gone away. The fear and rage and betrayal that had sent him half-mad had gone away.

Asai's voice had gone away, too, and Jacin didn't want it to come back, so he ran faster. Farther and farther away, weaving through food stalls and fruit vendors, ignoring the confused shouts in his wake when a shadow cut a corner too close and clipped someone before flitting away again.

Breath pushed from his lungs, then rushed back in. Blood pumped with a furious *thud-thud-thud* in his head, whiting out everything but the next ten steps ahead of him.

No Beishin. No Imara. No Joori or Morin or Samin or Shig.

White noise. No thought at all but *Away.*

Was he flying?

Quiet, so he kept going until he couldn't go anymore. Until his lungs started to seize and his body started to shake. Until his leg finally gave out and almost dumped him facedown on the ground.

He found himself deep in the bowels of the city, in a narrow dead end between two tall brick buildings, backed by one that was sided in silver-worn, rotted wood. There was a knife in his hand, blade not quite dripping, but bloody enough. And he had no idea how it had gotten so.

Did it matter? He didn't think it did; not now, anyway. Nothing mattered but that there was no Asai whispering to him, no Imara chasing him down, no...

He listened.

Nothing alarming, no sound of pursuit, only his own gasping breaths. He wasn't taking any chances, though. Peering at the buildings, Jacin sought chinks in the brickwork, found enough suitable for handholds, and started climbing. He took off the shadows when he reached the top and collapsed on the roof. And then he passed out.

卅

"Well, what did you *think* was going to happen?"

Samin was livid as he helped Joori to his feet and made him tilt his head back to slow the flow of blood dripping from his nose. Samin spared a death glare for Imara before turning to watch the top of Fen's head disappear into the confusion and chaos of the lane that led from the piers to the street. Three of the Patrol were in heavy pursuit, but Samin knew without even having to watch that they'd never catch Fen, gimpy leg or no.

"Bloody *idiots*, every one of you." Samin made sure the murder in his tone was clear. "You corner someone, especially someone like Fen, and try to disarm him when he's surrounded by a bunch of strangers coming at him from all angles, you kinda have to expect he's not going to cooperate."

"Samin, we have to go." Joori jammed the cuff of his sleeve beneath his nose. "We have to find him, we can't just—"

"I know, Joori." Samin didn't say it merely to soothe, he said it because he agreed. Bloody *hell*, did he agree. But saying it was one thing, and actually doing it was going to be quite another.

"Where would he go?" Imara's striking face was pulled into lines of anxiety and frustration.

Good. At least Samin wasn't the only one who could see the unpleasant possibilities.

"Good bloody question. Fen doesn't know the city. Unless he comes back on his own, finding him isn't going to be easy."

If anything, it was going to make tracking him down even more dependent on random chance than it would have been in Ada. At least there, Samin had contacts and knew Fen well enough that he would've had a few places to start. Here, who the hell knew where Fen could get off to? Or—more worrying—what he could get up to.

Fen was armed, which was good, in a way—it meant he wasn't going to be vulnerable to any of the riffraff he might run into. Except it also meant it might come down to following a trail of bodies to find him. Fen hadn't exactly been in his right mind when he'd taken off, and he'd apparently sliced one patrolman pretty good while he'd been doing it. Not to mention the patrolwoman and the innocent bystander he'd decked. Plus Joori, Samin thought with a growl for Imara, and all *Temshiel* and maijin while he was at it.

"And he can't be found with magic. Right." Imara pinched at the bridge of her nose. "Perhaps the Patrol—"

"The Patrol aren't going to find a damned thing," Joori snapped, a bit muffled through his sleeve, the attempt at scathing accusation he was directing at Imara rather losing its effect through the blood and his rapidly swelling nose. "Don't you people *think*? You *saw* him last night, for pity's sake! You couldn't figure out that threatening to lock him up maybe wasn't the best way to—"

"I was not the one who—" Imara stopped abruptly, gaze gone distant, head titled to the side as though listening. She sniffed the air. With a relieved little "Ah!" she spun around, searching the crowd that still gawked toward the street or milled around aimlessly, then she turned once again toward Samin and Joori. She directed her gaze just over Joori's shoulder, then gestured to a man with white-shot dark hair and kind blue eyes. "This is Naro-yi of Owl." Imara set a hand to the man's arm as he stepped in. "Naro-yi, I must—"

"What the hell happened now?" Morin jogged out through the inn's battered door and directly over to Joori, confusion and budding anger furrowing his brow. Shig came a little more slowly behind him, taking everything in with a lift of her eyebrow but no other expression to give away what she might be thinking. Startled, Morin took in the blood all over Joori's face. "Who clocked you?"

"It was an *accident*."

Joori barked it out a little more viciously than the question had merited, but Samin understood it. He didn't believe for a second Fen knew what he was doing when he'd leveled Joori, and Joori wasn't about to let himself believe it.

Joori waved around with a sneer. "The Patrol was trying to arrest Jacin, and Jacin—"

"They were not trying to arrest him," Imara cut in, impatient.

"And what would you call it?" Samin gripped Joori's shoulder in support. "Disarming him and dragging him to 'meet' a counselor to the Patrol sounds an awful lot like 'arrest' to me. And considering that the lad grew up in a prison camp, I can't imagine why he'd think the same."

Samin usually didn't pull off sarcasm very well, but judging by the look on Imara's face, he thought maybe he'd hit it that time.

"Huh." Shig shot a dubious look at Imara. "*How* old are you again?"

Imara's pretty face tightened. She turned to Naro-yi. "He is bleeding. I can track him that way, but I have to find him before—" She cut herself off, but not soon enough.

"*What?*" Joori tried to jerk away from Samin, but Samin held him still. "What d'you mean he's bleeding? What happened?" Joori angled a desperate glance up at Samin. "What does that mean, she can track him that way? Can they *smell* it?" His eyes filled. "What the hell are these people *doing* to him?"

Samin didn't have an answer. But he was bloody well going to get one. And more than likely not from Imara. She seemed an all right sort, but she also seemed like she thought herself some sort of parent figure, set to humoring a bunch of recalcitrant children who didn't know any better. Because Samin had no doubt what Imara had been about to say: *I have to find him before anyone else can sniff him out.* Except she'd stopped herself, like she didn't want those who most needed to know to twig— like they had no right. And if all these people could find Fen by following a trail of blood like stalking hounds…

Imara looked at Joori as though she might answer, but instead turned to Naro-yi. "I have to find him before there is any more trouble."

"I should say, yes." Naro-yi seemed to find this amusing, for some reason. "Shall I contact Dakimo for you?"

Imara clenched her teeth. "I would prefer you left that to me."

"I imagine you would." Naro-yi turned. "You are Kel Saminil, I presume?" When Samin only frowned and nodded, Naro-yi sketched a shallow bow. "I am Naro-yi of Owl. I have served as Kamen's solicitor here in Mitsu for many years. As instructed only days ago, in the event of Kamen's… absence, all decisions concerning his mortal assets and responsibilities"—a slight flick of his glance to Morin, Joori and Shig— "fall to you."

…Wait, what?

Samin blinked. What the shit was this, now? How did Samin, of all people, end up "alpha" to this little pack of misfit wolves? *He* hadn't gotten a vote.

Damn you, Mal.

"Excellent." Imara clapped her hands together in front of her breastbone and bowed to Naro-yi. "It would be best to get them away. Take them to the house Kamen has purchased, and I shall find—"

"I'm not leaving." Joori pushed out his chest, teeth clenched. "What if Jacin comes back and we're not here? How's he supposed to find us?"

Naro-yi raised an eyebrow and tilted his head toward the door of the inn and the man looking it over with a thunderous scowl on his face.

"I'm not quite certain you're going to have a choice."

"He won't come back." Samin gave Joori's shoulder a squeeze when it seemed he might turn his understandable wrath on Samin. "He's smart, your brother. He'll know they'll be watching."

It sounded just as steady as Samin had meant it to—even if he had no idea whatsoever if he was even close to the truth. Who could tell with Fen, after all? He'd been obsessed with his family's safety since before Samin had known him, and losing Caidi and his mother had only sunk the obsession into something even less healthy. Fen might very well barrel right back here, not even thinking about any consequences.

Samin scowled, reluctant to say it, but—"And if they hadn't meant to arrest him before, they'll surely want to now."

They might even station one or two of the Patrol here, just in case. And by the way Imara appeared to be trying very hard not to show whatever she was thinking on her face, Samin had to assume that theory was fairly accurate.

Shig's whole body wracked in a very visible shudder. "He won't last long in a cell."

Samin had to agree. Then again, he wasn't terribly optimistic that Fen would last long outside of one, either.

Don't let him poison himself.

Literal or metaphorical, Samin had no idea, but either way, a charge from Malick to Samin, and with Malick's last mortal breath. And Samin disliked failure just as much as Fen did.

"Damn." Imara had that faraway look on her face again, and even though the way she sniffed at the air was almost delicate, it still made Samin think of a baying hound. "I've lost him." She turned to Naro-yi with a moue of frustration. "He has Kamen's ring."

She said it as though it explained everything. And maybe it did, but it didn't seem as though Imara had any intention of telling Samin why.

Except.

The nod with which Naro-yi answered seemed directed more at Samin and Joori than Imara.

Samin wasn't sure he'd picked up the meaning entirely, if there was one, but if he was going to get answers, they weren't going to come from Imara anyway, so it was worth a shot. Samin eyed Naro-yi critically before he nodded back. Because this had flown out of control far too quickly. And as far as Samin was concerned, Malick had just put him in charge. Not the calculating, manipulative sort, Samin, but he'd watched a master at it for years.

"Then *what?*" Joori turned to Samin, pleading. "What are we supposed to do?"

Samin sighed. With a long look at first Joori then Morin then Shig, he set his jaw and turned to Naro-yi.

"Take us to Kamen's house." He squeezed Joori's shoulder again and looked directly into his eyes so there was no mistaking the meaning. "I'll take care of my own."

He had no intention of leaving any of this to these immortals who seemed to care more about whatever Fen was to them than Fen himself. And he had no doubt that Fen *was* something to them—Samin was just going to have to find out what. And why renegade *banpair* and the gods' minions all seemed to want to get their hands on him.

He gave Joori a comforting pat. "We'll take care of our own, Joori." Samin just hoped he could figure out how.

6

"**R**eally? No playmates? Ever?"

Jacin shrugged, only lightly so as not to dislodge Malick's hand from where it slid up and down Jacin's arm, warm and rough. It was cold in here, cherry blossom petals too cool against his bare skin, so he pushed back on the tiny little bed until his shoulder blades nearly dug into Malick's chest. His leg bleated steady agony at him every time he moved it, so he set his focus on the dip and sway of the boat on the waves, let Malick's touch sink into his bones and soothe him. The scent of sex still hung in the air of the close little cabin, bleeding into the haze of sage and pine, and Jacin's body still tingled pleasantly, so he kept his concentration on the more agreeable aches.

"I had Joori."

The name set a light shiver of *lovepainregretshame* through him, and this he couldn't shove away. It was in his face, all the time. His failure, his complete and utter inability to give Joori what he wanted, what he needed, when Joori had spent a good deal of his life trying to give Jacin everything they both knew he couldn't have. He hadn't done right by Joori. He hadn't done right by any of them.

Maybe giving them into Malick's care had been the smartest thing. More a desperate grab from the mire of defeat than any careful decision based on the needs of those Jacin had left, but… he thought maybe he could live with that. It was better that way. He didn't dare want anything different. His wants had always betrayed him. Now he knew why.

You did this, little Ghost.

"You were very close." Malick's fingers drifted upward, skimming over Jacin's shoulder and up into his hair. "It must've hurt."

Jacin wasn't sure what Malick meant by that. Hurt to be close? Hurt because they weren't anymore? Hurt to love, to be loved, to try and just keep failing?

"You depended on each other. And then you didn't have each other anymore. It must've been very difficult."

Ah. That. Another prod, another oblique reference to Asai, even though Malick never said the name to Jacin out loud, even though he very carefully allowed Jacin to stay inside the construct of *not-talking-about-it* but for when Malick tried to talk about it without actually *talking* about it.

The boat yawed with more force, a heavy moment of vertigo, and the cherry blossom petals pelted at Jacin's skin with chill insistence. He shoved down into the hard mattress and pulled the quilt more firmly around his shoulders.

Malick was waiting for an answer. Because that was what Malick did. Jacin didn't mind it too much, not anymore. They'd be starting a new life in Tambalon. Malick was giving Morin and Joori a chance they'd never have had without him. Jacin figured giving Malick a few things in return was only fair. And since Malick always took care of Jacin's more… basic needs first, Jacin didn't mind so much. Anyway, what difference did it make? Speaking these things gave them power, yes, but they were gone and past. How much power could they have after… everything?

"I've been hurting Joori since the day we were born." It came out low and raspy, but not because Jacin was ashamed of the words or the reality he gave them in the speaking. There was no point to shame anymore, and reality would be there whether he chose to acknowledge it or not.

"No, I mean…" Malick's fingers sank firmly into Jacin's hair, tingling at his scalp. "He must've been very unhappy when As— when you were taken away."

When Asai took you. When a stranger with dark eyes and a kind smile came for you, and you took his hand with a besotted whimper and walked away, betrayed the only one who treated you like a person, and the betrayal has become such a natural thing to you now that you just can't seem to stop doing it, over and over again.

Jacin didn't answer. Because he could say things out loud to Malick that he couldn't say to anyone else, but he still couldn't say just anything. Malick wouldn't want to hear that Asai taking Jacin away had probably been the best thing for Joori back then. He wouldn't understand what Jacin meant by it, and Jacin had no hope of articulating it. He just wasn't any good at that sort of thing.

"He can be happy now. When we get to Tambalon…"

Jacin trailed off with a frown bunching between his eyebrows. Because sailing to Tambalon had never set that odd little quiver of unease to his gut before, and the icy little spikes of cherry blossom petals hitting his skin were… wrong, somehow.

"It's cold in here."

Malick dipped in to lay a kiss to the crown of Jacin's head. "That's because you won't let me help you."

"You're not—"

You're not here. You're dead.

Jacin squeezed his eyes shut tight.

You left.

He set his teeth. "You can't."

He'd spoken it softly, barely a breath, but the words themselves grew sharp edges as they left him, turned on him, dug into Jacin's chest with a brutality that made his eyes burn.

"Jacin-rei."

Warm breath wafted against his cheek in a voice familiar and deep, and with a softness that hid its razor-spined edges like the painless breach of a slick-honed blade between the ribs. And it wasn't in Jacin's head. He'd heard it. *Heard* it.

Maybe if he kept his eyes closed and pretended to be asleep, it would leave him alone. He didn't want to see, didn't want to be reminded how badly he'd failed, didn't want to have to acknowledge it every time he woke to see Caidi sitting on the windowsill of the room in the elegant inn where Malick had moved them when they'd reached Tam…

Jacin scowled and burrowed deeper into the sheets, shoving his body back into Malick to absorb some of his heat. It was fucking freezing in here. He pulled Caidi closer to his chest, chill porcelain thumping lightly into his breastbone as her doll came between them, but Jacin ignored it, tucking her curly head beneath his chin. A soft flutter of papery wings haunted his periphery, but he blocked it out, concentrating instead on the steady patter of petals that quivered over his senses, settled on his skin with a frigid pall that didn't belong, teasing at lids and lashes.

"Come, then, little Ghost, you mustn't linger."

His hands closed reflexively, fingers curling in tight, Malick's ring a comforting cold weight against his third knuckle. He pushed back into Malick harder.

"You're going to have to try to stay alive, Jacin," Malick said. "Sucks to be you."

Jacin's eyes snapped open, a snarled *fuck you* ready on his tongue, but it died aborning. The sensation of firm muscle and body heat at his back dissipated immediately, because it hadn't been there. Malick was gone, dead, poisoned, and gone up in a pillar of unbreachable flame and smoke until nothing had been left but black ash that had blown away before Jacin could even gather enough wits to—

"Jacin-rei."

Calm. Amused, perhaps.

"No." Jacin clenched his teeth to hold back whatever dark emotion was trying to knock its way through. "*No.*"

He wouldn't. Whatever game this was, he *would not* play it.

The rain was falling steadily, chilling him right through, and his leg was fucking *killing* him. And all of it scattered into a welter of fear and confusion and something else he didn't know how to suss as he lay flat on his back and shook, pinned by Asai's dark gaze. Inches above him, hovering, warm breath heating the cold rain that slithered over Jacin's skin. A shudder wracked through him, paralyzed him, as Asai pushed sopping hair out of Jacin's eyes, and tipped a smile that was both mocking and seductive.

Kissed him.

Soft and searing and somehow unholy in the mess of sensation it provoked. Deep and driving like it had been that once—just once—when Jacin had almost, *almost* had what he wanted in his hands, and Beishin had almost given it to him.

Touch the Untouchable. Love the unlovable.

Pulling away was out of the question. Shoving Asai away was… anathema. Jacin could do nothing but lie there in inch-deep water, let the rain pelt him and the cold pierce him, and accept what he'd wanted for… well, for-fucking-*ever*, and wait to wake up to yet another reality he didn't want. The one where his sister had been murdered right in front of him because he'd been too weak to stop it. The one where he'd been *this close* to peace, and been wrenched back because he hadn't suffered enough yet and living was his sacrifice. The one where Malick had promised to love him and show him how to want and *get*, and then had gone up in a self-inflicted pyre that still burned in Jacin's mind even though Malick himself was now nothing more than cold ash.

He didn't know how to feel when Asai pulled back, just a little, just enough to cease contact, and waited until Jacin opened his eyes. Jacin hadn't even realized he'd closed them.

And the game, whatever it was? Jacin had been playing it for as long he could remember, however unwitting. Had lost it probably even before that. Before he'd even been born.

Who was Jacin trying to kid?

"Come, then, little Ghost." Weirdly affectionate, for all the epithet stung like fire. "Let your beishin see to you." Long fingers stroked at Jacin's cheek, pausing to slide along the wispy fuzz that traced Jacin's jawline. "They're coming, Jacin-rei. We must away, before they find you."

They. Jacin wasn't even sure he cared who "they" might be.

He tried very hard not to shut his eyes and sigh as Asai's fingertips drifted down over his throat. "Why are you here?" Tried very hard to make his hands reach for a weapon, kill him again, and again, if he came back.

He couldn't do any of it.

"Because you need me, little Ghost. Because you need me to guide you. Because you betrayed me and doomed your sister." Asai's hand was warm against Jacin's cheek. "I can forgive you your treachery, Jacin-rei. Once. Do not disappoint me again."

A threat inside a promise. Asai had always been so good at that.

"I…" Jacin sucked in a shaky breath, tried to turn his face away, tried not to look into dark-dark eyes, but he couldn't tear his gaze away. "I don't want you here." It was weak and far too timid, all but lost inside the patter of rain.

Asai heard it anyway. He chuckled. "Little Ghost, you have no idea what you want."

With a groan, Jacin finally found some strength and shoved Asai away, jolting up on his elbows, the movement sloshing at the thin layer of water that had collected on the pocked slate of the… roof. He'd passed out on a roof. Where the hell was he?

The city bled out beneath him, hazy gray, and Jacin didn't know if it was the weather or his vision. The temples of the gods, all six of them, flared up through brakes of hackberry trees in the distance, crouching at the misty feet of the chain of fire-mountains that edged the city. Jacin didn't know if these mountains had names. He hadn't really noticed them much. He hadn't really cared.

Now he couldn't take his eyes off the temples over which they hunkered.

Do you see what you've done to me? Jacin snarled—silently, because he wouldn't give anything to Asai he didn't have to. *Are you finished yet?*

"Jacin-rei, you must listen to me." Asai's tone had gone forceful, irritated. "You cannot stay here. They're coming. I know a safe place. Let me show you."

Not here. Asai was *not here.* He was a ghost—not even a real ghost, a figment of Jacin's imagination, just like Caidi was. And even if Asai was here, he had no power over Jacin, not anymore.

Guilt. That was all Asai was now. The corporeal manifestation of Jacin's guilt, the last scraps of Jacin's heart in pseudo-physical form, a specter, someone Jacin used to love, back when he'd still thought love could save and not doom. His penance for damning another soul, for being what they'd made him, because everything was a fucking trade.

Jacin rubbed at his temples and concentrated on straightening out his leg. Bloody hell, his head hurt, almost as much as his leg, and… his palm. What the hell had he been doing? Was he drunk? No, not drunk—just insane. Jacin almost snorted, but he was afraid it wouldn't end there; he might end up in hysterical fits, and even he had more pride than that.

He blinked rain out of his eyes. "Who's coming?"

"Does it matter?"

Jacin pondered that for a moment, kneading at his calf muscle through the leather of his boot.

"Kind of."

With a growl that was strange, coming from him, Asai knelt and set warm palms to Jacin's cheeks. He waited until Jacin focused entirely on the dark gaze that was—deliberately, Jacin was sure—crowding out everything else.

"Did you learn nothing from your months with a *Temshiel* but how best to writhe beneath him?"

Heat rose to Jacin's cheeks, and he wrenched his gaze away. Asai took hold of Jacin's shaking hand and held it between them, the stone of Malick's ring dull and plain-looking in the gray of a rainy day.

"Your blood is not yours to spill. It calls to them. Every *Temshiel* and maijin who might be looking felt it as each drop teased the wind."

A shudder slithered all through Jacin. He frowned and pulled his hand away. Did he care?

"Wolf's-own all seek you for their thieving god. The rest are not far behind. They will use your brothers against you, if you try to return for them." Asai paused, dark eyes intense. "They will hold them over your head while you meekly walk into their cage, little Ghost. They will use those you love so you will allow them to use you. Or worse, lock you away and set the voices back upon you. You're weak, little Ghost—you have never had the strength to stand against such as them. Your strength was in what you offered to Kamen, on your back, but Kamen is not here, is he?"

It stung, humiliated, and froze Jacin to marrow, all at once.

Asai leaned in, face cruel, tone derisive. "Did you think the Ancestors the worst of the madness? Did you think the gods and their servants could not invent yet more spiteful methods to control one gullible Ghost?"

The nearness, the *intimacy*, rattled Jacin worse than the fact it was coming from Asai. He scrabbled back, water sloshing cold against his thighs and into his boots. He needed… space, he needed… something, he needed *not this*, and bloody hell, why couldn't Jacin every figure out what he needed when he *needed* all the bloody *time?*

Asai watched all the thrashing like it amused him, before he took a step forward, as though meaning to pursue. Except he didn't. He stopped, turned. Head cocked, his eyes went distant, narrowed at the sky—like he was listening to something that Jacin couldn't hear. Jacin couldn't help the shudder, even as Asai breathed a small sigh of… it looked like relief.

Rain pattered steadily down, runneling into Jacin's eyes and under his already soaked collar, a constant stream between his shoulder blades. He shivered as he watched Asai, wary and afraid as he hadn't been in all the times Asai had "visited" him before. Jacin was soaked through and getting soggier, and… so was Asai. Breath flowed from Asai's full mouth in thin plumes. Rain dripped in wavering rills down his face, off the tip of his nose. Heat vapor rose from his body in silvery wisps.

All of it too tangible. Breath and warmth.

It made it all shockingly real. And absolutely bloody terrifying.

With a hard set to his mouth, Asai turned back to Jacin. "You cannot stay here, Jacin-rei. They won't take long to find you."

"Who are *they?*"

"It does not matter. Or it won't. Only you matter, little Ghost. You are all I have ever needed. Let me guide you. Let me *help* you."

The words, so close to those Malick had spoken, *hurt.*

Slowly, Jacin began the process of hauling himself upright, wincing as he set his weight on his hand. Spikes shot up his arm, and then his leg as he got it beneath him, two different focal points of head-clearing pain. Jacin wobbled to his feet and settled his weight on his right leg, letting the sharp throb lance into him, riding it, until it resolved into more of an ache.

"Such a good little Ghost. See? You *can* obey your beishin when you try." Asai reached for Jacin's hand, eyes on Malick's ring. "And do you know how to use your pretty bauble, Jacin-rei?"

Jacin snatched his hand away and staggered back a pace.

He'd drawn a knife. One of the ones Malick had given him. One of the ones he'd used to crack Asai's ribcage and pull his heart out through it. When had he taken it from its sheath? He didn't remember, but there was the knife, in his hand, the blade already blooded, the tip resting right against Asai's sternum. Jacin remembered the feel of it as it had sunk through skin and bone and cartilage, remembered the thick-moist expulsion of air as he'd hit a lung, and the rip of gristle. Remembered the hot, unexpectedly firm feel of his beishin's heart in his hand.

Remembered how he'd wept and raged and *stomp-stomp-stomped* because if only Asai had given it to him willingly.

"Think very carefully, little Ghost." Asai's breath was hot against Jacin's ear, warm lips sliding down over Jacin's cheek, his jaw. "I can forgive you one betrayal. Only one."

Jacin stared down at the knife in his hand where it rested just below Asai's heart. Stared down at his fist wrapped around the hilt, white-knuckled, and wondered why his hand wasn't shaking. Stared down and wondered what the fuck he was doing, what it would matter if he did. Would Asai stop haunting him? Did Jacin really want him to? If this was all in his head, wouldn't that mean something in him *wanted* Asai here? Needed him?

And for *what?*

What would happen if Jacin just dropped to his knees and… gave up? Wept, whined, howled and begged?

What would happen if he knew what to beg *for?*

The pain in his palm was a duller twinge beneath the leg and the head and the chasm-deep ache in his chest. Jacin cast a murky glance to the wound—jagged and messy, but already clotted, and the rain had washed it mostly clean. Memories crowded. A weedy dooryard, and his brother's angry tears, and a useless little knife delivering that first spark of promise with its bite, and *How very… interesting.*

Inexplicable guilt rose, and with the guilt came thoughts of Joori, because guilt and Joori had become too intertwined in Jacin's head for it not to.

No gloves. He'd forgotten them. It was… disturbing. He'd dressed as though for battle, arming himself with nearly every weapon he owned. Mostly to piss Imara off while she waited impatiently, because she'd refused to leave him alone to dress in privacy, so he'd decided to give her as much of a show as he was capable. And yet he'd forgotten to slip the gloves over his too-tender hands where the calluses had all faded away and left the skin… his mind shied from "vulnerable" but failed to find another word he could live with.

"How are you here?" Jacin tried to push force into it, but it came out a croak. "Why are you… why can't you just…?" It was too much; there were too many pleas clogging in his throat, and he couldn't get any of them out. "Beishin… please."

"Ah, my boy. Did you think I would leave you to the whims of treacherous *Temshiel* forever? They've come for you once, Jacin-rei. Do you think they'll stop, now that they've caught your scent?"

"Come for…" Jacin's thumb slid over the stone of Malick's ring.

Malick… help.

Asai settled his hand over Jacin's torn palm with a gentleness that made Jacin quiver and made mortifying tears burn behind the bridge of his nose. That same look as in his father's dooryard all those years ago, but Jacin had thought the dark gaze kind then, full of promise.

"You don't remember any of it, do you? You don't even remember this morning."

Jacin shut his eyes.

Ghosts, too damned many of them, and Asai and no Malick to chase him away, and fuck, Asai had been right there, *mocking and leaving invisible welts on Jacin's skin beneath his scornful, demanding not-love, touching and promising, hands like chains, weighing Jacin down, choking him, and barriers between him and* away, *and deep topaz eyes that saw but didn't see at all, and—*

Guiding him. Giving him direction in his directionless existence.

Because Jacin *needed.* And Malick wasn't *here,* damn him.

"I… I want…"

"I know. I know, Jacin-rei. I've always known."

Soft fingertips swept over Jacin's temple. Jacin couldn't help the flinch.

"Love the unlovable. I can give that to you, little Ghost. You have had your *Temshiel,* but we both know what you really wanted, no? And now your *Temshiel* is gone, just like you knew he would be. Just like they'll all leave you in the end. Your kind were not meant for the love of another. Only I can give you what you need. Only I want to. You're *mine,* little Ghost. I've come back—for *you.*"

Jacin's mind was screaming, refusing, digging in its heels. His body was leaning toward Asai, and he couldn't stop it.

I am… so fucked.

There was anger in Jacin's chest, in his gut, roiling, seething, but Jacin didn't know where to point it. It muddled into itself, congealed, strung through with confusion and fear and resentment, and something that tasted like hope, bitter and biting, but he didn't know where to put that, either.

Asai had killed Caidi. Malick had left.

Jacin had allowed every moment of it.

Weak.

Failed.

Except… Asai had failed too. From the moment he'd stolen a gutless Untouchable from a prison camp, he'd stepped into Jacin's trajectory of failure.

Malick was strong. Malick didn't fail. Except Malick wasn't here, and even if he was, he wouldn't tell Jacin what to do, never, just, *I want you to live, but I'm not going to tell you how*, and *I love you, but you used to love him and I'll never let you forget it.*

"I want to forget it." A thin skirl of breath that gained absolutely no power in the speaking. "Why can't I...? I... I want..."

I don't want to love you, I don't want to have ever loved you, I hate you, I don't want you here, I want Malick, but Malick left, and all I have is you or nothing, and I can't have nothing, I can't, I've tried, but I can't stand the emptiness, and I'm afraid, and I don't know what to do.

"You don't know what you want, Jacin-rei. You need me to show you. Come with me, lad. There is nothing for you with them anymore. You're a killer, Jacin-rei, a murdering Ghost—how long, do you think, before your beloved twin stops making excuses for what you've become? How long before he sees?"

It... hurt. Which was strange, because Jacin knew Joori didn't really see him, but he hadn't necessarily thought before about what Joori *seeing* him would actually mean.

Jacin gripped the knife in his hand more firmly.

"The gods have nothing for you but more betrayal. *I* am your maker, little Ghost. By my breath do you live, by my love do you go on. You do not exist but in my eyes."

Love.

Love the unlovable.

I fucking love you. Deal with it.

A sob leaked out from Jacin's throat.

I can't. I don't know how. Damn it, how could you leave me here like this?

Asai could eat him up, swallow him, breathe him in and smother him in his own delusions. Hadn't he done it before?

The idea was... not as horrifying as it probably should have been.

You don't want choices? You don't know what to do with them?

"No." Jacin shook his head. "I really don't."

Blindly, Jacin leaned forward, eyes still shut tight. He held out the knife in an open palm. Testing, maybe, he didn't know, but waiting, wanting, mind and heart and soul all flailing and *reaching* for something— sanity, the ability to tell right from wrong, good from bad, an *answer*— while his body stood still and just... waited.

An offer—retribution. Or maybe it was a request—execution. Finally.

It would be fitting irony to have Asai dig out Jacin's heart as Jacin had dug out Asai's, and with the knife Malick had handed Jacin as a present in that room at the Girou, trying to woo him. Maybe this was Jacin's way of wooing. Knives had always been foreplay to him; no reason why they couldn't be completion too. No reason Jacin should escape the fate he'd handed Asai. Wasn't he doomed already anyway?

The scent of rain overwhelmed the cocktail of pine and sage, the smell of moist earth and ashes sitting heavy in Jacin's nostrils, tightening his chest.

Why didn't Asai smell of jasmine?

Jacin didn't know if the warm mouth that settled over his was what he'd expected. He didn't know if the firm hands that pulled him close were the ones he should be allowing the liberty—if any of this even existed outside his own head. He didn't know if the gentle kiss from the man he used to love—the man he'd killed—was right or sane or maybe even somehow erotically profane.

He knew it was warm. He knew he *felt* it, and he wasn't sure if he cared if it wasn't real.

He knew it was an answer. Even if it wasn't the right one.

"You're mine, Jacin-rei."

Breathed right into Jacin's mouth, tendriling down into his lungs, stoppering any deteriorating reason he might have had left. It pulled mind and soul loose from unsound moorings, mangled and twisted them, then crammed them back down his throat 'til he almost choked.

Jacin sucked in a shaky breath and pulled away, took his hand from Asai's and clenched his fist but not enough to break the skin that had reknit while he'd been passed out in the rain. The heat of his own blood called to him with the promise of clarity and control, but he couldn't listen. His blood wasn't his to spill.

He opened his eyes and looked at Asai. He resheathed his knife.

"Where am I supposed to go?"

Fuck, he needed a smoke.

⛩

"You… lost the Incendiary." Dakimo watched Imara's mouth pinch down, watched the anger flare in her gaze, and shook his head. "And…?"

Because by the reluctant purpose all over Imara's face, Dakimo could tell there was more.

Imara sucked in a breath. "And he was wearing Kamen's ring when he fled."

Dakimo's teabowl almost flew out of his hands. He managed to hang onto it.

"I'm sorry, what?"

"I don't think it's as bad as it sounds. He was bleeding. I smelled it.

And then it was just gone. I think he used Kamen's ring to hide." Imara held up her hand when Dakimo rubbed at his brow. "I don't think he knows all of what he could do with it. And I have to believe Kamen would not be so stupid as to give all its power over to…" She trailed off with an uncomfortable shrug.

Dakimo's heart sank. "The Incendiary is as unstable as all that?" He kept his tone mild, even though his gut had dropped all the way down to the floor. The power of the Incendiary running about loose was bad enough, but to add Kamen's powers to it, undirected… It didn't bear thinking about. And yet Dakimo had no choice.

How was he going to explain all this to Emika? To *Wolf?*

Imara paced the small receiving room before sighing and allowing herself to fall elegantly onto a plump cushion in the corner. She huffed.

"Yes. But it's more than that. He thinks he's being haunted by Asai's spirit. His sister's, as well."

Dakimo paused to take that in.

"That cannot be." He narrowed his eyes. "Can it?"

This Fen Jacin-rei was Incendiary—impossible to find through magic, and impossible for the spirits to see, let alone haunt. Even the gods couldn't always see him.

Imara looked like she wanted to cry. "I don't *know.*"

"You looked?"

"Well, of *course* I looked. I found nothing. Although… not *nothing.* Something, but…"

Dakimo set his teabowl down on the nearest table so he wouldn't end up throwing it at Imara's head.

"But *what?*"

"Nothing. I don't know." Imara ground out a sigh of annoyance. "It should not be possible to haunt Incendiary, but he was hidden inside the bondage of Untouchable for years, and that should not have been possible, either. And what were the voices of the Ancestors but haunting? For that matter, what do we know about the laws of Incendiary but that they are changeable? Isn't that the point of Incendiary in the first place?"

Dakimo nodded reluctant concession. "Answerable to none but Fate and their chosen god."

The conflict of which being the very thing that had doomed Hitsuke. This was getting out of control far too quickly.

Querulous, Dakimo waved it away. "Find Asai's spirit and you'll have your answer. At least to that." He pondered for a moment. "Set Xari to it."

"Xari should not have to undertake such a thing. I thought I would—"

"You will have other matters to attend. And perhaps look for the Incendiary's sister while you're at it."

Best to make sure.

Imara looked up, gaze narrowed. "Did you foresee what would happen to Kamen?"

"How would I have seen it?" Dakimo snapped, irritated by the sudden turn, because he hadn't seen a bloody thing, and he should have. It was his job, after all. "He was veiled down so tight I could scarcely squeeze a conversation through his shields, and he has attached himself to the Incendiary. I can barely even see the ripples of change the Incendiary initiates a moment before he initiates them." And that was with intense meditation and hours of concentration—hours Dakimo just didn't have right now.

"Xari saw it," Imara said quietly. *Too* quietly.

Dakimo rubbed at his brow. "And she told you this when?"

"It…" Imara's gaze skittered away. "Yesterday morning."

"I… see." Dakimo had to put his hands behind his back, because they'd fisted up tight and he didn't think he could uncurl them just now. "And you did nothing."

"I did nothing. And I insisted Xari do nothing." Imara lifted her chin. "I didn't know you were going to send him out after the *banpair*, and I didn't know he'd actually let them ambush him. Kamen needed a lesson. He wasn't doing his job. And he was doing the Incendiary no good; in fact, perhaps doing further damage by allowing—"

"And you thought it wise to teach Kamen this *lesson* while he had an unstable Incendiary in his care, and Tambalon was under siege by *banpair* immune to the gods?"

"I thought I could help them both by not helping Kamen. I wanted to see Kamen… chastened, perhaps, not actually sent to spirit. How could I know he'd let *banpair* fell him? How could I know how unbalanced Fen Jacin was until—?"

"Until Kamen and all his magic was already gone!" Dakimo's teeth had clenched; he forcibly relaxed his jaw. "Centuries old, and *this* is how you interpret Wolf's command?"

Imara bridled. "Wolf's command was to see that Kamen facilitated the Incendiary in his choice, Dakimo. To prevent Kamen from disobeying his own orders. That was all. Your orders were the same as mine. And they had nothing to do with trying to use the Incendiary to solve Tambalon's problems."

"Not the decisive parry I'm sure you intended. I merely hoped to take advantage of an opportunity. I did not interfere with Kamen's choices by not giving them to him, nor did I prevent another from doing so. You have erred, Wolf's-own. You have misjudged. And you have, once again, done so because of Kamen."

Imara's mouth tightened and she looked away, avoiding Dakimo's gaze as though… embarrassed, perhaps? Discomfited, at least.

Dakimo frowned. "What is it between the two of you? Why is it that Kamen can take all your years of knowledge and skill and make you seem nothing more than a mortal girl of seventeen?" He paused with a wince he couldn't help as a possibility struck him. "Tell me you're not in love with him."

"*No!*" The grimace and abrupt anger was a relief, and more of a confirmation of the denial than the actual denial. "In love with *Kamen*." Imara rolled her eyes with a scowl. "All the gods spare me from a fate such as that." She shook her head. "He is still new, and powerful. *Too* powerful. He was not ready for what was handed to him."

Dakimo's eyebrows went up. He couldn't argue with it—he rather thought the same himself—but it was very much beside the point right now.

"It is not ours to question our god. Nor to hear our god's voice and interpret it as we see fit."

Imara's mouth pressed into a tight line. "I owe him, Dakimo. I was trying to repay him."

By getting him sent to spirit and endangering the Incendiary he risked his soul to save?

Dakimo didn't say it. It would not be productive, and he wouldn't be telling Imara anything she didn't already know.

"You shall need to explain that one to me. I fail to see how allowing Kamen to be—"

"He's never failed!" Imara threw her hands out. "Never, not even in his mortal life. Skel was the closest he came, and that failure wasn't his. How can he know the danger of his power if he's never seen the consequences of it? How can he understand the risks he takes? Not just with the affairs of mortals and those he protects, but with *himself*. He risked his *soul* for the Incendiary, Dakimo, before he even knew what the Incendiary was. He'd do it again, I saw it in his eyes, and yet he won't see that the kindest thing he could've done for Fen Jacin would be to let him die when he begged for it."

Dakimo couldn't tell Imara how wrong she was. And he couldn't tell her why she was wrong. So he said nothing.

"And now," Imara went on, "Fen Jacin would spurn the gods and what Fate has made him, and Kamen would help him do it. He won't even glance at the fact that he'd fail Wolf in the doing. He risks his soul *again*, and I couldn't—"

"*Now* was not the time to make your point! Your actions have turned the Incendiary from a potential asset into a potential threat. You have set him loose in the birthplace of the servants of the gods and all the world's magic, and with Kamen's ring in his fist." Imara opened her mouth, but Dakimo cut her off. "No. The best interests of Kamen and your god notwithstanding, you have erred. You will now set yourself to fixing it.

"Where are the rest of those Kamen claimed? The brothers have been marked, as well. We cannot—"

"I *know*, Dakimo." Imara glared, but kept her tone civil. "They are protected. I left them in the care of Naro-yi."

"Naro-yi." One of Owl's. Dakimo pursed his lips. "He will do. For the moment." He hardened his gaze so there would be no misunderstandings or room for misinterpretation. "You will keep them safe. Swear them oath, don't swear them oath, I care not, but you *will* keep them safe. And you *will* find the Incendiary and do the same."

"And how do you propose I do *that*? He can't be found with magic, and I'm not—"

"I care not." Dakimo waved it off. "Set Xari to the stone, since she seems better able to discern him through Fate's mists than I. Or find the damned *banpair* and follow after them, since they apparently seek him as well, *and* managed to find him where all the gods' servants failed." The admission stung and made Dakimo's teeth clench again. "How you do it matters little, but find him you must, before someone else does. If it becomes known that he is as unstable as you say, the rest of the gods will put him down, and we will all have failed Wolf."

Dakimo paused, took the few paces over to Imara, and crouched in front of her to lay a hand to her shoulder. He softened his tone.

"You have erred, Wolf's-own. But I have every faith you will fix your mistake. You have no choice. If you would do Wolf's work, you will find and help the Incendiary." He patted Imara's cheek. "And I will do what I can to help you."

Right after he got done telling Governor Emika that they were right back where they'd started with the *banpair* problem. And that she had an unhinged Incendiary running around loose in Mitsu—an unhinged Incendiary who thought he was being haunted by the ghost of Asai, *and* had all the magic of Wolf's Null at his disposal.

Dakimo wondered if telling her the Incendiary probably didn't know how to use it would be any consolation.

He thought probably not.

Goyo wasn't necessarily surprised to run into Imara on his way into the Statehouse. He *was* surprised that she'd been paying so little attention to where she was going she nearly plowed him into a marble pillar on her way by. The pinch of the mouth didn't come until after she realized who'd just saved her from a very inelegant and public tumble down the steps.

"Goyo." Flat. With a blatantly rude grimace, she extracted her arm from his grip.

Goyo grinned as brightly as he could manage. Mostly because he knew it would annoy her.

"You're so very welcome." His bow was pure theatrical irony. "And what has you ramming through innocent pedestrians like Wolf himself has come to swallow you?"

Imara smiled in that way she had that always made Goyo wonder if she wasn't thinking about dragging him back to her web, lopping off his head, and laying her eggs down his neck. She opened her mouth like she meant to retort, then pinched it down tight again.

"You know what, Goyo? Fuck off."

Goyo stepped hastily out of her way before she could… well, he wasn't sure, but by the set of her jaw and the glitter in her eye, he thought perhaps she wouldn't be entirely opposed to an actual brawl. If the Statehouse and its perimeter hadn't been warded up so tightly, she might well have just set him on fire with her glance. Though, with the feral bit of a snarl she gave him as she stalked down the steps, Goyo rather thought biting would've been the way of it.

He smirked. He'd always figured her for a biter. Probably a screamer too.

He was still snorting quietly to himself when he stepped through into the echoing reception hall, pausing to assess the current state of affairs by gauging the urgency of the various counselors, judges, and minions who milled through on their way toward whatever business they had here today. The wards felt newish, reinforced perhaps since the last time he'd visited, which was annoying, but not surprising. Dakimo was a little too conscientious about Emika's wellbeing, in Goyo's opinion. The protection spells were almost physical, a heaviness on Goyo's chest, oppressive.

Something to do with Kamen, no doubt. The Patrol wasn't exactly buzzing about what had happened last night, but there was definite unease with the knowledge that not only had Kamen been here in Tambalon and no one seemed to have known it, but he'd been taken out by the *banpair* they'd all been ineffectively hunting for years. The disquiet was palpable, the irony decidedly unamusing. Even for Goyo, who didn't necessarily actively dislike Kamen, but had thought more than once he'd like to be there and watch as Wolf's Null was taken down a peg or two. But that it had been these *banpair* that had managed it with apparent ease…

Unsettling. Worrying.

There'd been no official identification yet, but Goyo had no doubt that the five corpses left in Kamen's wake would eventually be matched to the list of the missing. And once Goyo spoke to the Incendiary, he had no doubt more directions would open to him.

Goyo certainly wasn't the only immortal in the world who knew what a treasure-calamity Kamen had brought with him to Tambalon; it would take no time at all for the gods to direct their servants here to watch and assess. He was, however, one of the few who had a rather personal interest. And he intended to get there before the rest of them did. Now that Kamen wasn't blocking the way, there should be nothing to it.

A small contingent had been out this morning with orders from Goyo to collect the Incendiary. All he had to do now was wait until they arrived. Perhaps the unexpected summons from Dakimo would turn out to be a blessing, rather than the mild annoyance Goyo had first thought it—at least it would pass the time until the Incendiary arrived, and perhaps smooth the sharp edge of anticipation.

He was waved through three secretaries and five guards before rounding the outermost loop of the great marble building and turning down the wide hallway that led to the governor's offices. A young patrolwoman—the same maijin of Bear who'd politely shooed Goyo along the other day; he really should pay more attention to these people's names—was still greeting him and asking him his business when Dakimo appeared and bustled Goyo through and into the small, near-empty office he used as a receiving room. He practically threw Goyo down onto one of the cushions and shoved a bowl of tea into his hands.

"What have you heard?"

Goyo was too surprised to pretend that he wasn't. His eyebrows shot up.

"Only what everyone else has." He shrugged. "I doubt there's a single *Temshiel* or maijin—whether dwelling in the mortal world or the spirit plane—who didn't feel Kamen's surprise and rage as his soul fled." Goyo refrained from snorting. It wouldn't be polite.

"That's all?" Dakimo's eyes narrowed, and he leaned in, head cocked to the side. "No ripples in the spirits? No… sudden turn of attention?"

"I haven't..." Goyo tapped at his chin, eyeing Dakimo with a suspicious frown. "Why are you fishing for information, and not relaying it?"

"No new orders from Snake?"

Goyo didn't answer right away. He leaned back and took a long, slow sip of his tea. Thought about it.

Right on the heels of the chaos in Ada, Kamen had been entrusted with the first Incendiary in decades, and had promptly vanished. Again. Goyo had to assume there were immortals who'd been waiting and watching for Kamen to show up here in Mitsu eventually, but Kamen had always brazenly done what he bloody well pleased, and in his own sweet time. No one had really expected him so soon. Goyo had heard nothing more on either Kamen or the Incendiary until Kamen had been sent to spirit. And he'd been listening.

Kamen was an arrogant, self-important ass who somehow always seemed to end up diving down into a steaming pile of shit only to emerge smelling of roses. Kamen thought no one could do a job as well as he could, and the fact that he was almost always right only made him more annoying. Kamen was said to have completely lost his senses over the Untouchable-turned-Incendiary, and would know very well that every god and his or her immortals would be watching for them.

Imara had been more imperious and bitchy than usual when she'd quite literally run into Goyo. Goyo had been assuming the Incendiary would be at the inn where Kamen had been hiding, but it would be just like Kamen to leave false clues and twisty trails, and the company Goyo had sent out to retrieve the Incendiary was late. The fact that Dakimo was trying to not-so-politely interrogate Goyo like Dakimo himself wasn't supposed to have all the pertinent answers was merely one more tip-off.

"For the love of—" Goyo shut his eyes and rubbed at his brow. "You have no idea where Kamen stashed the Incendiary, have you?"

The abrupt scowl that darkened Dakimo's face rather answered the question.

"We know where he was." Dakimo seemed to twig to the inanity of it before it was completely out of his mouth. His scowl deepened. "Kamen and his bloody-minded possessiveness. And now it looks as though..." He shook his head, took a deep, long breath, and settled on the cushion opposite Goyo. "Goyo." He was clearly trying for calm. "We have need of your... discretion. And your assistance."

"Ah?" If Goyo wasn't alert two seconds ago, he certainly was now. "*We* as in Emika and Tambalon, or *we* as in Wolf's-own?"

"Both. In this, at least, it's one and the same. Perhaps more far-reaching than that, I don't know yet." Dakimo held out a hand when Goyo raised a skeptical eyebrow. "I think, Snake's-own, you will understand that this is not a matter over which to play games or employ politics. If I'm right, more is at stake here than simply which god gets the Incendiary in the end. *If* he even lives to choose."

"*Which god.*" Goyo scoffed. "Kamen is Wolf's pet. He always has been. If there is indeed to be a *choice*, Wolf's-own, we both know too well which way Kamen has been influencing 'his' Incendiary. You must think me rather dim to not see exactly why Kamen kept his presence here so bloody secret."

"Secret even from his own, Goyo. And his purpose was a secret from even the Incendiary, if Imara has assessed the situation correctly."

Goyo took another long sip from his tea, taking that in. He still wasn't sure what this was. Not entirely. Not yet. He rolled his hand.

"Go on."

Dakimo hesitated, as though trying to decide where to start. Eventually, he tipped a slow nod.

"We have reason to believe that Kamen did finally reveal the Incendiary's nature to him. Perhaps yesterday, perhaps days ago, but no more than days. The point is that shortly after the Incendiary learned what he is, *banpair* attacked and took away his protection. And shortly after Imara arrived to assume Kamen's responsibilities, the Incendiary..." Dakimo trailed off, shaking his head, the look on his face one of deep distress and... it looked like embarrassment.

It took a great effort on Goyo's part not to laugh outright. "Imara lost the Incendiary."

No wonder she'd been ready to chew nails and spit tacks. Damn, Goyo wished he'd arrived here fifteen minutes earlier. He'd have given a lot to see Imara very politely and calmly taken apart by Dakimo.

So much for Goyo's plans, such as they'd been.

"The Incendiary was... upset." Dakimo huffed a weary sigh. "From what I'm gathering, the Incendiary is always upset. Which would be beside the point, if things were not where they now stand." He gave Goyo a level look. "If Kamen's mortal companions are to be believed, the attack last night was targeted and deliberate. The *banpair* wanted Kamen out of the way. They wanted the Incendiary."

"They... Wait, what? Why?"

"Why would anyone? Why would Snake?"

Goyo hesitated, trying to decide how much to say, but Dakimo would have already guessed or seen anything Goyo knew, anyway.

"I doubt he would." Goyo opened a hand when Dakimo flashed a frown at him, because the answer was an honest one. "If I were to come across the Incendiary, I would venture that my orders would be to assess and then destroy."

He didn't know how he felt about that yet. He supposed he'd find out if and when it happened.

Dakimo rubbed at his brow. "If it were not so precarious right now, I might take that wager. But you have not been ordered so, as yet?"

Goyo hesitated, feeling for the trap. Because he hadn't been expecting one, not from Dakimo. If there was one, Goyo couldn't yet perceive it, so he merely shook his head.

"Good." Dakimo looked like it was the first good news he'd had all day. "Then we are not yet placed in opposition." He set a hand to Goyo's arm, seemingly unfazed when Goyo merely looked at it with an arched eyebrow and then back at Dakimo. "You have been leading the hunt for quite a long time." He tightened his grip on Goyo's arm when Goyo's mouth set tight. "I mean no insult. It was not a critique, merely an observation."

Goyo should hope so. It wasn't exactly easy, trying to track down beings who couldn't be found with magic, and who struck out of the blue and without pattern.

"But you have become familiar with the little predictability that exists." Dakimo lifted his eyebrows, encouraging. "You have narrowed the parameters."

"If you can call it that." Goyo shrugged, uncomfortable. "There is no particular sort—the ages all vary, the backgrounds, the color of their skin." Goyo's teeth clenched—he couldn't help it. It was bloody frustrating, and getting somewhat boring. Until a few days ago, he'd been considering leaving Tambalon and all its problems to someone else. "The only clue I've had thus far has been the disappearance of Zhiri Aika."

"Zhiri…" Dakimo's gaze went distant for a moment then cleared. "Zhiri. Yes, I remember now. She was the fifth to go missing from Hin's district. Zhiri-seyh has written twice to ask the governor for news of the hunt for his daughter. Young Zhiri Aika was no more than a girl, as I recall." He waited for Goyo to nod before he frowned. "But that was months ago."

"It was. Except then her brother disappeared."

The frown deepened as Dakimo tilted his head. "I admit it's coincidental, but I'm not seeing the clue."

"Well, I'm not so sure it is one. It's more a feeling. I didn't see it until the sister and brother. But the Zhiri boy had been making a nuisance of himself. They'd apparently been very close. He was going on about how his sister had been haunting the temples in the weeks before she disappeared. Seeking direction from the gods, it seems. And Rihansei told me that one of his monks had been counseling her as well. Seems she had traces of old magic, and could not decide between that and the call of the gods."

Goyo swirled his tea. "Do you remember the mother who'd gone missing from the sickhouse tower two years ago?"

"Yes, of course." Dakimo looked like he was waving it off as old news, but then he paused, eyebrows beetling over sharp, abruptly alert eyes. "And then her child disappeared from her bed the night after."

"Right." Goyo nodded. "And now the Zhiri children have gone missing too, one right after the other. And Zhiri-seyh swore he heard the boy talking to his sister the night before. But when Zhiri-seyh had a look, there was no one in the room with the boy. Zhiri-seyh said he was going to hire a mage for a sage cleansing, because he was afraid the daughter was dead and her body left to rot. He was afraid her spirit had been trapped and was haunting the son. The son argued against it."

"And yet you'd seen nothing when you looked for her spirit."

Again, Dakimo's statement didn't seem like a criticism, merely an observation, so Goyo didn't take offense.

He shook his head. "Nor the boy's. But here's the interesting thing—the boy's room had been cleaned, his personal possessions disposed of. As though he was… setting things in order." Goyo leaned forward, a touch of excitement curling in his gut at the interest in Dakimo's gaze. "As though he was preparing." Goyo hesitated, mostly because it sounded ridiculous to him even as he thought it, and saying it out loud… He cleared his throat. "The boy practiced the old arts. Zhiri-seyh says the boy had the seed in him too. He'd only just had his first tattoo a week before the sister disappeared."

Dakimo sat still for quite a while, thinking. "And his spirit?"

"Just as gone as the rest of them."

"And do we know how many—if any—of the other victims were the same?"

"You'll recall that the woman who disappeared from the sickhouse those years ago was rather heavily tattooed." Goyo opened a hand. "It isn't something any would volunteer—especially not to a servant of one of the Six. And we didn't know until now that it was a question we should perhaps be asking. I've already sent a few of the Patrol out to the families of previous victims to put the question to them. I don't know what I expect them to find or what I'll do with the information they gather, but it seemed prudent.

"It does seem rather odd, though, now that it's been suggested, that none of those found dead were thus adorned. All those scores of dead and not one of them of the old magic? It's too much coincidence, especially considering these *banpair* were once of the old magic themselves." Goyo took a sip of his tea. "I plan to call on Rihansei, but you know how he is. Old magic is a dying art, and he's as protective of it as—" Goyo cut himself off. He'd almost said *as protective of it as you are of the governor,* but he didn't think Dakimo was in the proper frame of mind for a good poking. "The law says he doesn't have to talk to me. I'm hoping he will."

"Old magic. Hmm." Dakimo sat back as though he'd somehow deflated. "Rihansei." He rubbed at his mouth, agitated. "*Damn* it."

"If it means anything, if old magic is a factor, I don't think it's coming from Rihansei. He would not—"

"That is not as comforting as I'm sure you mean it to be. If old magic is a factor and it's *not* coming from Rihansei..." Dakimo shook his head. "At least we know what we're dealing with in Rihansei and his monks. This..." He didn't finish, just rubbed at his forehead as though he was trying to keep his brain from bashing through it.

Goyo could only shrug. "It's another place to look. I'll go to Rihansei and ask him some more about the Zhiri children. Even if he tells me nothing, that in itself will tell me something."

"Mm." Dakimo dropped his hand, scowling. "And this Zhiri boy disappeared when?"

"Hours before Kamen was attacked."

"And I'm only hearing about it *now?*"

"You didn't exactly give me a chance." Goyo would have answered more sharply but for the weariness and sincere anxiety in Dakimo's expression. "And you seemed more interested in gossip about Kamen and his Incendiary."

"...You're right." Dakimo sighed like it was all he could do not to whack his head against the wall a few times. "My apologies, Snake's-own. I find myself lately... stretched." He tipped a small smile when Goyo waved it off, but it was strained and fell immediately, sliding into something careful and attentive. "You realize what all of this is possibly suggesting, yes?"

"That perhaps those who've disappeared haven't necessarily done so unwillingly? That perhaps circumstances are even more bizarre than we'd thought?" Goyo snorted without humor. "Of course I realize."

"And can you now take it a step further and see how, perhaps, the matter of the Incendiary and the matter of the *banpair* are not necessarily without their... commonalities?"

Goyo stared at Dakimo, utterly at a loss. He failed to see even a faint association, and that was only if he discarded reason entirely. He covered the pause and his inability to follow Dakimo's obscure logic by sipping some more of his tea.

"I suppose there's the attraction to deep emotion." Goyo shrugged, still at a loss. "One in mourning, like the Zhiri boy, would have plenty of interest to *banpair*, though if that's the case, we're more likely to find him dead eventually. Still, it's there—a faint connection, I suppose. And you said the Incendiary was always… upset?"

Though, Goyo had no idea if *banpair* could even detect Incendiary. Certainly maijin couldn't, and *banpair* were once maijin. And anyway, what would make the Incendiary's emotions so attractive to *banpair* that they'd attack a *Temshiel* to get to him?

Dakimo *hmphed*. "The Incendiary has apparently been conversing with the ghost of his sister." He hesitated, then peered at Goyo sharply. "And Asai."

Goyo didn't allow a reaction. Mostly because he didn't know what kind to have yet.

"And?"

"And." Dakimo puffed out something like an angry laugh. "And Kamen checked. Imara checked. There are no ghosts."

Ah. Goyo saw where this part was going, at least. There had been rumors, after all, and the Incendiary had once been Untouchable. Goyo's stomach didn't quite drop, but its moorings felt a little wobbly.

"So. He's mad, then."

"If not mad, then certainly… precarious." Dakimo stood abruptly and started to pace. "Bad enough, but after speaking with Kamen only days ago, I'm convinced that his dalliance with the Incendiary is more than dalliance." He stopped his pacing and turned to Goyo. "We are talking about a once-Untouchable already unbalanced, who, as Kamen put it, has lost half his family because of the events in Ada. And now he's lost Kamen. And *banpair*, who can not only slip the sight of the gods but can apparently do the same for mortals—whether by their wish or not— have sent Kamen to spirit, leaving the Incendiary unprotected."

"And now the Incendiary is missing."

"And with Kamen's—"

Dakimo cut himself off, though he was too good of a politician for Goyo to know if it was merely because he misspoke, or if there was something he didn't want Goyo to know. Likely the latter. Dakimo might be one of the more frank and trustworthy of the *Temshiel*, and his sense of honor was quite a lot more rigid than any other immortal Goyo had ever come across, but he was old and sharp. Just because he generally spoke the truth didn't mean he was always being entirely honest.

"Magic is useless." Dakimo started pacing again. "We can't find him with it, we can't read his thoughts, we can't even set the spirits on him, because they can't find him, either. And foresight—feh. Next to useless." He paused with a twist of his mouth. "Though, Xari has seen more thus far than I have." Brooding. Not quite bitter, but somewhat edged. "Perhaps I should put her to this, as well."

Another of Wolf's. And an initiate at that. Goyo had to wonder if the closing of ranks he was seeing was really there. Though, if that were the case, why was Dakimo venting to Goyo? There was no denying that Dakimo seemed sincerely distressed—not that he didn't have reason—and Goyo would wager Dakimo had not given a servant of any of the other gods as much information as he'd just given Goyo. There was more here. Goyo simply hadn't figured out what yet. And he was getting impatient waiting for Dakimo to get to it.

Goyo set his bowl on the table. "You're suggesting that the *banpair* are perhaps—?"

"I'm suggesting that they are not as immune to the pull of the Incendiary as they are to the magic of the gods. I'm suggesting that they wanted the Incendiary for something we're missing, and now they might already have him."

"All right. But so what?" Goyo shrugged when Dakimo snapped a barbed look at him. "The Incendiary has no magic. He's a Catalyst, nothing more. Perhaps the *banpair* are drawn to him—enough to seek him out and take him from Kamen—but what can they really do with him? I see no threat to any but the Incendiary himself."

Which would, perhaps, not be such a bad thing. If the *banpair* killed the Incendiary, maybe the gods would finally learn their lesson. Who knew? It might even save Goyo from having to do it himself.

"What they can do with him is a question I hope Goyo Snake's-own can answer. And perhaps keep to himself until we decide together what must be done with it." Dakimo opened a hand. "You have practically led the hunt, Goyo."

"Right into a morass of nothing but more questions."

"Really?"

The thin smile at Dakimo's mouth told Goyo the question was at least part of the snare for which he'd been waiting since Dakimo barked the first question at him.

Dakimo paced again, but more slowly this time. "Years, you have hunted these *banpair*, with no hint of even a place to start. And yet the

Incendiary is awakened to his nature for mere days, and suddenly there is a trail."

"The merest ghost of one."

Dakimo ceased his pacing. "A thin suggestion of convergence, I'll grant you, but still more than we've had since it all began. This Incendiary, without even knowing it, moved Fate to overthrow the Adan and save the Jin. He pointed the way for his brother and Kamen to set the tortured souls of the Ancestors free. Now he has been in Mitsu for perhaps a fortnight, and already the Wheels turn around the *banpair* quandary."

"Oh, please." Goyo rolled his eyes. "Even Hitsuke at his most worthy couldn't make—"

"What has Hitsuke to do with anything?"

It all but *snapped* out of Dakimo before he very visibly caught himself, like he was surprised he'd even spoken and regretted it immediately.

Goyo couldn't tell if it was a true slip, or if Dakimo had somehow wound the entire conversation to this particular raw point for his own—

...Oh.

Oh.

No, no, and *hell* no.

Dakimo knew Goyo's history with Hitsuke. Every immortal did. And it wouldn't be the first time someone had tried to use it against him. And yet Dakimo engaging in what amounted to a melodramatic stage play was as far-fetched as Dakimo saying something he hadn't foreseen and thought out very carefully first.

Still.

This had better not be what Goyo was starting suspect it was.

Dakimo was silent for a while, pensive, then a small, slow smile curved his mouth. It made Goyo narrow his eyes and pay very close attention. Diplomat with an impressive poker face or no, something had just dawned on Dakimo, and Goyo was going to have to be very careful not to let it trip him into something he didn't want to fall into.

"All right, then." Distant. Speaking to himself. Dakimo sat again on the cushion across from Goyo.

"You, better than most of those left among us, knew Hitsuke."

Goyo narrowed his eyes, chin jutting out in unconscious defiance. "I did." It probably came out more hostile than he should have allowed.

"You *saw.*" Dakimo stared, waiting for reaction; when Goyo didn't give him one, he sighed. "You suppose there is no threat to any but the Incendiary, and perhaps you're right. I hope you're right. But think back to those last days of Hitsuke. The worlds he changed for his god; the worlds he refused to change *despite* his god. Think of the worlds he *might* have changed, had he been allowed to break from Raven, as he'd intended."

"You mean when he allowed his conscience to outshout his head."

The poor, recklessly brave fool. *Conscience.* What good had one of those useless things ever done anyone?

"As you will, then." Dakimo set his hand on Goyo's arm again, as though in comfort. "He obeyed his god and took up the side of the *Temshiel* against the Jin." He paused, grip tightening and voice softening. "Until he met a young maijin, newly turned and too-brief champion to the Jin. A maijin whose ideals were as fresh as a sea breeze to such an old, jaded soul."

Goyo flinched. Not a whisper of blame had ever come to him from any direction when Hitsuke fell, except from himself, and that had never been so… tenderly put. So why was this deflected allusion tempered by gentle exoneration stinging him like fire?

"I never meant—"

"None of us ever do. Balance will be found. It is, after all, what we're for." Dakimo looked genuinely saddened. "Hitsuke found a conscience and then the strength to defy his god and follow Fate's will, as was his nature. So many of us lose our conscience when we lose our mortality."

It wasn't the first time Dakimo had expressed regret over his part in the fate of the Jin. It wasn't the first time Goyo had been privy to sideways confessions of regret from other *Temshiel*—even one of Raven's once. He'd never heard any immortal defend unequivocally the Binding War or what came of it. Defense was almost always along the lines of *I didn't like it, but I did my duty by the gods.* And Goyo certainly couldn't blame them—he would have done the same if Fate had placed him on the other side of the battle lines. Even now, with a century of distance, Goyo knew very well he wouldn't've had the brass to do as Hitsuke had done, even if Goyo's admiration for it had only grown since then.

Except Hitsuke had been punished, destroyed, for daring to change his mind, aiming his will in a direction other than that of his god's wishes, when it had only been his nature to do so. He'd been *made* for it, damn it. It wasn't fair.

"Thus far, my conscience is intact. I wish it to remain so." Dakimo sighed. "This Incendiary took up where Hitsuke left off. And suffered greatly for it. As I understand it, he suffers still. If he is mad, it is because putting right the errors of the gods has made him so." He smiled when Goyo blinked at the manifest blasphemy, and patted at Goyo's arm before pulling his hand away. "And now, consider for a moment the possibilities of a half-mad Incendiary under the influence of *banpair* who have already proven too dangerous, and the motives of whom we *still* can only guess." He hesitated, as though unsure. "Incendiary are older than the Six," he said slowly. "Incendiary walked the world when it was ancient Daichi and ruled by the One. Consider, Snake's-own, what all these faint connections might mean in *this* world, where a newly woken Incendiary walks without the protections of any of the gods."

Goyo did. And could have killed Dakimo where he sat for making him do it with the specter of Hitsuke looking over his shoulder. Which was, of course, what Dakimo had intended. Goyo had known something like it was coming.

And yet.

Was that all it took to manipulate him so absolutely? Even finally seeing the gentle trap with all its teeth, was he going to walk right into it this easily?

"You want me to take over the hunt. You want me to look for the *banpair* by looking for the Incendiary. You want *me* to find the Incendiary."

Dakimo looked away. "Of the two, only the Incendiary has been found once. And you, after all, know too well what it is you seek."

Was Goyo hearing this correctly? Was Dakimo of Wolf handing over the Incendiary—*Kamen's* charge—to one of Snake's-own?

Kamen's absence, it seemed, had shaken those of Wolf more profoundly than Goyo thought reasonable. And the loss of the Incendiary seemed catastrophic to them in a way Goyo wasn't quite grasping. Catastrophic enough for Dakimo, of all people, to stoop to invoking Hitsuke to get Goyo to help get the Incendiary back.

Goyo had to wonder why.

"And if I find him? If my god commands that I rid the world of him?"

"Then…" Dakimo paused and looked down at his hands, fisting in obvious anger, though Goyo didn't think it was for him. "If I know of it, if I see it, I will likely have no choice but to fight you for him. As will all of Wolf's-own. My god wishes the Incendiary saved."

"There is more than one way to save a soul."

Dakimo laughed this time, a harsh bark that recoiled off the walls of the small room. He looked straight at Goyo and shrugged with a bitter smile.

"We shall see."

7

Joori really wished people would stop staring at him. It was… well, it was rude. And disconcerting. And *really bloody annoying.*

Apparently, they didn't get a lot of Jin in Mitsu. There were people of every color wandering around here. He really shouldn't stand out that much. But clearly the different shape of his eyes—or whatever it was about him that was making them gape, because that Naro-yi had a bit of a Jin look to him, and even more of a tilt to his eyes—was too much for these people. Morin, with his fair hair and the gold tones to his skin, was more or less overlooked, but Joori had gotten a little tired of meeting open stares with purposefully bored looks of his own. Now he just tried not to notice. One would think the rain would've hampered the gawking.

At least it boded well for finding Jacin. He'd stand out here as much as Joori did. Probably more.

"Huh." Morin gave Joori an amused look as they followed after the others. "I don't think I've ever heard that many filthy words in one sentence without a breath between them."

He jerked his chin ahead at Samin, who was somehow managing to stalk the cobbles, loom over Naro-yi, and vent at him all at once.

If things had been a little different, Joori would have snorted. But things were rather tense, and laughing was, at the moment, something other people could do. He merely nodded, hoping it was enough acknowledgement to keep Morin from pushing, but not enough to encourage further commentary. There was too much ramming around in Joori's head right now, too many things making his chest tight and his eyes burn, and he just didn't have the concentration to keep himself in check if Morin decided there was a good poking in Joori's immediate future.

Everything was taking too damned long. It had taken forever to get things squared at the inn, and then another eternity for Naro-yi to convince the remaining Patrol that no, Fen Jacin's family did not need to be brought to the central command post—which "just happened" to be at the Statehouse—for questioning. It had been fucking *hours* since Jacin had taken off. Anything could've happened by now.

Probably why Samin was so pissed. He didn't seem to be having any luck with getting Naro-yi to either help them start looking or leave them alone so they could do it themselves.

"But I said I would be taking you to your new home," Naro-yi had insisted, "I gave my word."

Like his word was the be-all-end-all. The man was maijin—what did the "word" of any of these people mean?

"Joori." Morin's tone was even and, if Joori didn't know better, almost kind. "Stop it."

Joori snapped a look over at Morin, only just caught a snarl before it took hold, and opened his mouth—

Morin cut him off. "He's going to need you to keep it together. We can't have the both of you losing your shit, all right?"

"You're talking like you think we'll even find him."

As though they all weren't halfway dreading that maybe Jacin was already—

Joori clenched his teeth and pushed that one firmly away.

"Of course we will." Morin seemed miffed, as though he really did believe it and was offended that Joori perhaps didn't. "We've got Samin. We've got Shig. We've got this maijin person who's—"

"Yeah, and you can't find Jacin with magic." Joori nearly barked it. He was abruptly glad it was pouring and the streets were crowded, and the only reaction he got from the others was an appraising look from Samin over his shoulder. Joori lowered his voice. "Maybe..." All the gods save him, was he really going to say this? "Maybe if Malick were here..."

"Oh, *now* you're a Malick admirer?"

"*No*, I'm not an *admirer.*" Bloody hell, the very idea. "I just... I mean, if he were here, he'd be... *doing.*"

Because maybe Joori thought Malick didn't know what the hell he was about half the time, and couldn't get out of his own way the other half, that he got by on bravado and arrogance and what passed for charm. But he did seem to get what he went after a little too often. And Joori knew that if Malick were here right now, he wouldn't be calmly ambling off to a new house because some *Temshiel* they didn't know told them to and some maijin they also didn't know insisted.

Which wasn't at all fair to Samin. Samin had to have his reasons for complying—with a decided lack of good grace, but still complying. Joori just wished he knew what those reasons were, and why they called for a delay like this, when they *should* all be…

Damn it. He had no idea what they should all be doing. For all he knew, walking to Malick's new house would be just as effective as an actual all-out hunt. Because, honestly—did Joori *really* think any of them could find Jacin if Jacin didn't want to be found? And the look in Jacin's eyes just before he'd taken off had been… Well, again, Joori didn't know, but he didn't think it boded well for finding Jacin, and certainly not for finding him unharmed.

According to that Imara, he'd already been bleeding. Had put his hand right through the damned glass on the inn's door. And these people could smell it, like fucking bloodhounds, but they'd lost it, and what did that—?

"Look, Joori."

Morin took hold of Joori's arm and stopped him. Several paces ahead, Samin seemed to sense it, because he stopped, too, turned around, and calmly waited. Shig and Naro-yi were deep in conversation and only stopped because Samin took gentle hold of Shig's collar, balancing Morin's ridiculous fishbowl carefully in his big hand.

Morin waited for a clump of cloak-clad pedestrians to flow around them. "He'll be all right."

"You don't know that." Joori didn't like the way it came out hoarse and a bit whiny, but he couldn't help it.

Morin snorted. "It's Jacin, for pity's sake. He's a fucking lunatic with—"

"He's *not* a—"

"In a good way, Joori, calm the hell down, will you?" Morin shook his head, runnelets of rain flying off from the updrawn hood of his cloak. "Our brother is a well-armed lunatic. A crazy, batshit bastard who might think he wants to die but has no idea in the world how to do it. And even if he figured it out, he's so sure you and I couldn't live one second without him gutting himself to keep us alive, he'd walk back here on stumps with his own head in his hands to make sure we're all right. You're worried about *him*? I'm more worried about the people who get in his way."

Another reason to be grateful for the weather: Morin wouldn't be able to tell the rain from the sudden tears Joori couldn't hold back.

"You didn't see his eyes."

"This time?" Morin shrugged. "No, I didn't. But I saw back in Ada. I saw someone who looked exactly like my brother, but who turned into someone else entirely right in front of me. I saw him hold his own, hurt and unarmed, against a man who turned out to be a maijin. And then I saw him kill him. And then I saw him put a knife through the eye of another. And *then* I saw him mow through guards, and might-as-well-be-dead bodies, and all of this while he—"

"Yeah, all right, I get it." Joori couldn't take the subtle awe that always crept into Morin's voice and eyes when he talked about… all of that. "I know, Morin. He shouldn't *have* to… he's *not* what… I mean, I just…" He trailed off, throat aching, because it was there, somewhere, but something in him wouldn't let it come out.

He's not what Asai made him. He can't *be.*

"You just think he did all that because he had no choice."

Morin's voice was so improbably soft and even, Joori just *had* to see what was on his face. He wished he hadn't. He didn't need *sympathy* from fucking *Morin.*

"And now that he's got a choice, he should… what, Joori? Paint his face and go repent at the temples? Maybe *you've* got a guilty conscience over what you did in Ada, but that doesn't mean you should. And neither should Jacin. He's got enough guilt over Mother and Caidi—he doesn't need more for not being what you seem to need him to be. He's only being what he is."

What he is. Maybe that wouldn't be so bad, if what Jacin was hadn't been ordained and manipulated by a treacherous maijin and then perpetuated by an obsessed *Temshiel.*

Joori could feel the rage and frustration building—at Morin, at Malick, at himself, even at Jacin—instinctively throttled it down, and then realized he didn't have to anymore. There was nothing there, no frightening power inside him to keep hold of, nothing that could lash out but him. It was appallingly disappointing.

Mouth set, Morin leaned in closer. "Let me tell you something about our brother. He hasn't just gone 'round the bend—he passed the bend four psychotic episodes ago. And now he's digging grooves in the crazy-ass loops in his head, skidding along and trying to figure out how to act like a normal person so everyone will stop looking at him and waiting for him to grow some sanity. He doesn't even know what 'normal' *is* anymore. And trying to figure out how to be what other people want him to be?—*that's* what's going to push him over into truly insane." He scrubbed the rain from his face, clearly frustrated but still calm. "He's not the same Jacin you knew back in Ada, and the more you try to make him into that, the crazier—"

The swing was instinctive. So was Morin's dodge away from it. Joori didn't manage to deck him like he wanted to, but he did manage to clip him a glancing blow on the chin with an almost satisfying *crack* of knuckles. Out the corner of his eye, Joori saw Samin start back toward them then pause a few steps away, saw a few passersby jerk their glances their way and then quickly away again. That Naro-yi was staring at them, benevolent warmth radiating from him and seeping out into the rain-soaked atmosphere through his sympathetic smile. Shig looked worried.

Joori didn't care.

Neither, it seemed, did Morin. The little bastard was *laughing*.

"Yeah, I know. You think you know him so well."

"And you know *nothing* about him! You hated him, all your life—you think he didn't *know*? And then you watch him take apart a few guards, and he's suddenly your hero, you bloodthirsty, black-hearted little thug. You never even knew him. You didn't even *see* him back when it counted, because *Father* told you not to. And you bloody well did everything Father said, didn't you? Treat him like shit, treat him like nothing—for fucking *years*—and now you're going to try to make it *my* fault he believes it?

"Maybe I didn't do it right, maybe I hurt more than helped, but I only *ever* wanted to help, because that's what you do for people you love—you help them and keep loving them, even if they won't be helped and don't want to be loved. Whether I did it all right or did it all wrong, I was *there* for him, Morin—where were *you*?"

Morin was silent for several long moments, holding Joori's eye, tongue poking out every now and then to run along his bottom lip; it was going red and would probably start to swell pretty soon. And then he merely shrugged.

"Yeah, all right, you have a point." He adjusted the hood on his cloak. "Neither of us deserves what he did for us. Nobody could, not really. I think I'm not as bad off as you, though, because I know better than to try to make myself into someone who can live up to it."

Bloody hell, the soft look Morin was giving him was making Joori want to... he didn't know, but whatever it was couldn't be good.

"You've always been a good big brother, Joori, and I sucked as a little brother. Maybe I still do, I don't know. But I'm trying not to anymore, all right? And you're trying too hard to fix what won't be fixed. You can't be 'there' for him in the same way now. He's just not that Jacin anymore. He's got his own kind of 'normal' now—let him *be*."

"*I can't!*"

It came out high and wobbly, nearly hysterical. It shut Joori up, stuck in his throat. Because what the hell had he meant by that? *I can't... let him be?* Maybe. And there was something very, very wrong with the fact that the statement was true enough it had spilled out his mouth without thought, and yet he couldn't lay hands on any good reasons behind it.

Morin just looked at him with that same infuriating sympathy as before.

"Just like Father couldn't let Mother be?"

It was like a punch to the chest. It winded Joori; he could actually feel himself paling. Anger rose, hot and tight, but it was too confused to take on any form of reason. He wanted to strike back, *hurt* like he'd just been hurt, *gutted,* but he didn't know how. The snarl was building again, but it died of latent confusion when Morin reached out and patted Joori's cheek. And then the little son of a bitch *grinned.*

"He's crazy, Joori. But he's a *good* kind of crazy. He's the kind of crazy I want at my back when I walk into a room full of other crazy people. Maybe we won't find him, but he'll damn sure find us eventually." He jerked Joori in and gave him a weak, weirdly affectionate swat to the forehead. "You worry too much." He patted Joori on the shoulder this time, then just spun about and ambled back toward Samin.

Joori only blinked after him for a moment or two. Because what the fuck had just happened?

He wasn't sure he'd ever been this confused, this thoroughly jumbled. *Ever.* And considering his life up 'til now, that was saying something. He stood there, in the rain, watching Morin and Samin catch up to the others, watching them all dip their heads in a conversation Joori really didn't want to be a party to, and wondered at the white buzzing in his head.

Seriously. What the fuck had just happened? And why did Joori feel absurdly reassured?

He didn't want to feel reassured. He wanted to dismiss all the disturbing things Morin had said as the nonsense he desperately wanted it to be. But damn it, he wanted Jacin back and safe and whole and as happy as Jacin could possibly be and… that had to be more important than being right. Because Joori had never had the arrogance to think he was completely right, but he'd certainly thought he was more right than the rest of them.

Now, he wasn't so sure.

And when had Morin started making sense, anyway? Fucker.

He was growing up, clearly, Joori had known that, but he hadn't really associated "growing up" with "maturing." It was so hard sometimes to look at Morin and not see the little bastard who'd tormented Jacin just for fun because he'd learned from their father that their Untouchable brother was somehow not a real person. Had been taught that one day there would be no more Ghost haunting their run-down little house on their run-down little farm in a Jin prison camp, so why bother to get attached?

Morin had believed it. He'd loved their father, admired him, even, and why not? It wasn't as though he could have learned what a real father was supposed to be from someone else. Not until…

Joori's gaze shifted against the rain, landed on Samin.

He shook his head, still somewhat boggled, as he was every time it occurred to him, that a paid assassin was somehow a better father figure for Morin than their own father had been. Hell, bloody *Malick* was a better father figure than their father. And that was just fucking tragic.

Then again, the brother Joori loved more than life was a paid assassin—had been an *un*paid assassin—and was too bloody good at it. Had maybe even liked it in an incomprehensible, vengeful-spirit sort of way. Maybe even liked it in the same way Joori had liked it when he'd been overwhelmed by the sweet tang of blood and the sizzling-meat scent of destruction, and smiled as death came by his own hand.

And how fucking tragic was *that?*

Maybe you've got a guilty conscience…

Shit. Maybe Joori did. And maybe it wasn't about Caidi or Mother or those men he'd killed, or even for demanding more of Jacin than Jacin could give. Maybe it was for something worse than unforgivable.

Maybe it was for standing there in that overgrown dooryard and weeping like the frightened child he'd been all those years ago while he just watched Asai walk away with his brother.

Maybe it was for failing Jacin before he'd ever even really tried not to.

⁜

It took a little while for Shig to figure out what was bothering her. Not really *bothering* her, but at least giving her a feeling that she couldn't pin. Not unpleasant in itself, but unpleasant because she couldn't figure out what was not-really-bothering her. She wasn't quite sure what to make of that, so she just let it simmer at the back of her head and waited for it to make sense of itself.

The house was done in the old Jin style. Or, more precisely, in the style of the *Temshiel* who'd made the Jin, which then the Jin had adopted and the Adan had distorted, incorporating more Adan styles into it until the Jin origins were nearly phased out altogether.

Curled eaves descended from a slanted roof with a wide plateau from which three slim chimneys jutted. Shig wondered if perhaps at least half of Malick's decision to buy this particular house had solidified when he'd seen that roof. Because Malick was all about anticipating Fen, and when Fen was out of sorts, when he felt threatened, Fen went up. Height and open space. Separating himself from the world and everyone in it. Closing himself off, shutting himself down, and regrouping. Or trying to. It hardly ever worked out that way.

"Roof," Shig said quietly to Samin, then she waited out the initial look of confusion until it melted into more of an *oh, yeah, why didn't I think of that?* then gave him a smile. Samin smiled back, a little grimly, then rewarded Shig with an affectionate squeeze. He was such a sweet man, for a cold-blooded killer.

"I've arranged for minimal furnishings." Naro-yi opened the door and waved them in. "Linens, kitchenware and the like, as well—the necessities. Kamen's account, however, is at your disposal, and you may, of course, do as you like with what's here."

"Furnishings aren't exactly a priority." Joori shouldered in through the entryway and past Morin and Naro-yi to have a look.

Shig followed him in.

She wouldn't have pegged Malick for someone who appreciated such wide-open space. Whatever he'd been before Wolf turned him, he hadn't been Jin, and this deliberate-seeming embrace of the traditions and style said more about a sincere wish to please Fen than it did about Malick. Though, Shig supposed, his wish to please Fen said a lot about Malick anyway.

Kadamo mats covered the polished floor, rather than rugs or rushes. Painted rice paper screens served as partial walls, separating what must be the main living space from what Shig guessed was the dining area, with its low table and flat cushions. A small sitting room was screened off to the side of the main entrance, a low couch and table along with several wide cushions giving it a more private air of intimacy. The hallways of the second and third floors were more like galleries, open and overlooking the first floor, though Shig was pleased to see that up there, at least, it looked like all the rooms—she counted at least ten, but she couldn't see every angle from here—had actual walls and doors, instead of screens.

Most of the furnishings she could see seemed to be variations of fat, molded cushions in varying colors. Damn. She was going to miss comfy chairs and couches.

Naro-yi cleared his throat. "I can arrange some household assistance, should you wish. A boy to come and cook and do light cleaning." He handed Samin a piece of paper. "Shinji. He can begin tomorrow at breakfast, should you wish, though I imagine you'll have other more pressing matters to concern you." He paused to quirk a knowing smile at Shig, but she just wasn't in the mood to smile back. Naro-yi turned back to Samin. "He is very discreet and receptive to a steadier position, should you like to assign him more household duties, but that price"— he pointed to the paper in Samin's hand—"was negotiated for providing three meals and tea. He can start when you like."

He handed over another piece of paper. "Kamen's accounts at the moneyhouse have already been delegated to you."

Samin's eyes shot wide, and he nearly choked as he got a look at whatever was on that paper. They all knew Malick was rich, but it appeared Samin had just found out *how* rich.

"Disbursements are at your discretion, of course. Should you—"

"When will Malick be back?" Joori's tone wasn't quite snarky, but definitely impatient.

In this case, Shig couldn't blame him. These people just didn't seem to live in the same reality mortals did, where moments counted and could slip away too quickly if you didn't grab hold. She sort of understood it, but just because they had all the time in the world didn't mean every second didn't count.

Always the way of it with mortals, little niijun. Running so fast to get nowhere.

Shig rolled her eyes and waited for the not-quite-Yori in her head to fill in a wry punch line.

Except Yori didn't, because she was suddenly just *there*, right in front of Shig, staring at her with eyes just as green as her own. And no one noticed.

Shig started, squeaked, "Hey," and shot a wide-eyed glance around, caught Samin's eye, but when Samin just raised his eyebrows and didn't go white and start swearing at the sight of Yori, Shig shut her mouth and looked away. "Sorry, never mind." She waited until Samin turned back to Naro-yi then cautiously raised her eyes, stared at Yori, hard, until Yori just gave her a smile then faded away again.

Nothing at all flittered through Shig's head but a rather useless *huh*.

Maybe she really was as crazy as Fen.

"It is impossible to say." Naro-yi held up his hand when Joori opened his mouth. "But if I know Kamen, it will be much sooner than anyone expects. He has never… appreciated the complexity of the spirit world. He prefers blood and bone."

He said it like an indulgent uncle, shaking his head with a *it's Kamen, what are you going to do?* smile that Shig *almost* trusted, but only almost. This benevolent-seeming maijin might very well want nothing but to protect and please every one of them, but Umeia had taught Shig that good intentions from an immortal didn't necessarily mean the mortals around them would be walking away with smiles on their faces.

And where has your smile gone, little niijun?

Shig frowned with a shudder, that uneasy something even more uneasy now and still gnawing at her edges, an empty space waiting for her to fill it.

Yori used to be her smile. Yori used to be a lot of things. Laughter through tears, sometimes, or maybe just a bit of quiet. A lifeline of corporeal *hereness* in a sea of covetous voices.

Maybe Shig was just seeing what she wanted to see, and making a ghost of Yori for her own greedy comfort.

"That's… not very helpful." Morin took the fishbowl from Samin and set it atop the dining table. "Can't you at least give us some idea?"

Shig couldn't make herself pay attention just now, not the way she should be doing. That little niggle had grown into a full-blown itch, and it was all she could do not to start juddering and twitching, just like…

Oh. Damn.

Fen thought Shig had no idea what went on inside his head, and maybe she didn't know the extent of his particular sort of noise, but she had a pretty good idea. It was just that the noise had never reached the same level for Shig as it did for Fen, and she'd always had Yori to interpret when she had trouble getting her own thoughts through it. She kind of selfishly wished it really was Yori haunting her.

And isn't treachery a pretty thing? Handing you the shiny bauble you think you covet, instead of the brilliant gem it knows you need.

Shig nearly sighed annoyance. Because if she was going to talk to herself in spirit voices, she could at least—

Are you really talking to yourself? Yori asked, and she was there again, just for a second. *Or are you afraid that you're not?* She faded out then right back in again. *You're smarter than all of them, you always have been. Don't believe everything they tell you.* She held out a hand. *I miss you. Why don't you just come with me, love? They won't stop you. Don't you want to be together again?*

Oh. *Oh.* Well, shit.

Shig went very, very still. She shut her eyes tight then blinked them back open again, guiltily relieved when Yori was gone.

That wasn't Yori.

Her own voice, thank all the gods. And thank them all even harder, because Shig had no doubt in her mind that she could tell the difference.

Damn it. She needed to talk to Samin. She needed to talk to Samin *right now.*

"… weeks, perhaps," Naro-yi was telling the others. "No more than that, I'll wager."

Only half-listening, but Shig met the sharp glance Samin snapped at her with a grim set of her mouth and a lift of her chin. She didn't even have to look at the Fen brothers to know they were in agreement. No way were they all just going to sit here and wait for bloody *weeks*. Especially not if what had just occurred to her turned out to be anything close to provable logic and not mere hopeful conjecture. Or not so hopeful. Crap.

She *really* needed to talk to Samin.

"But I expect," Naro-yi put in before Joori had even finished his angry, "*Weeks?*" and taken a somewhat panicked step forward; Samin stopped him with a firm hand to his arm. "I expect," Naro-yi continued smoothly, "that you will not be sitting idle while you wait." He paused, making sure he had everyone's attention. His smile this time was somewhat sly. "Owl and Wolf have always enjoyed an accord. I have not been instructed to assist you. But nor have I been instructed not to."

There was a pause while everyone turned to look at Samin.

Samin only stared back for a moment before he rolled his eyes. "Right. Then we could do with—"

"I have, however, been asked to keep you all safe." Again, Naro-yi's sharp blue gaze made the rounds, peering at each one of them steadily before moving back to hold Samin's. "Perhaps you'd like to tell me how I might best do so?"

Samin's eyes narrowed, but with alertness, rather than hostility. "Perhaps you should first tell me what your definition of 'safe' is."

"Ha!" Naro-yi grinned this time, a surprisingly young-looking thing. "In this case, I should think 'alive' will do."

"Then *I* should think the best way to honor your promise would be to follow along and stay out of the way." Samin looked at Joori and Morin. "Go pick a room and stow your things. We'll be heading out shortly." He set a big hand to Shig's elbow and tugged. "C'mon, lovie. Let's see what's got you dancing about like someone put spiders in your shoes."

Despite that unsettling mental image, a weird bit of relief washed through Shig as she let Samin lead her out the back.

People didn't look at Samin and think "observant," but you only had to be around him for a little while—and be on the receiving end of it once or twice—to know he saw pretty much everything. He didn't always interpret what he saw exactly right, but he was at least within throwing distance of the mark more times than not. Shig wasn't surprised he'd twigged to her sudden almost-revelation at nearly the same time she did.

The courtyard into which they emerged spoke more to the wealth inherent to the place than the house itself did, and Shig really had to wonder who Malick was trying to impress. Fen probably wouldn't even notice the fountain—an actual working bleeding *fountain*, complete with colorful, cavorting sakou splashing about just beneath the rippling surface of the water. Or the gravel garden with its decorative-but-functional rakes. Or even the ridiculously lush and luxuriant greenery that, even for the lateness of the season and the decided chill that called to the winter not long in coming, still gave one a sense of verdant tranquility.

It hadn't stopped raining, but it had let up some, more of a chill shower now than a downpour, the scent of it mixing with the soft loam of the yard and overwhelmed by fat little pines and the last crumbling blooms of the potted sage. Which was just so fitting Shig could've pinched Malick's cheeks. Bloody hell, there was even a flat-roofed pagoda covered in kuuh vines. Shig almost chuckled as she let herself be led beneath it and out of most of the rain. She was still goggling at it all when Samin's fingers snapped in front of her nose.

"You with me, there, lovie?"

Shig blinked, met Samin's amused gaze with a somewhat scattered one of her own, and had to grin. "Sorry. I was just…" She waved her hand around then shook her head to get it where it should be. "I've been hearing Yori."

By the abrupt stillness and the slight paling of Samin's face, Shig supposed she could have perhaps come up with a better way to say that.

"No, that's not what I mean. Not in a real way."

It didn't improve Samin's expression. Damn it, Yori used to interpret this sort of thing for her. Yori would've made Samin understand.

"See, it was kind of Yori's voice, but it wasn't *really* Yori's voice. I could tell. I wasn't sure what… I mean, it's been kind of hard to figure out how I think. How *I* think, you know?"

No, it looked like Samin didn't know.

"So, I wasn't sure if it was just me missing her, or if someone was playing a trick. Except the spirits don't do things like that—they can't. Most of them forget who *they* used to be, let alone imitating someone else, and the imitation wasn't really that good. Well, I guess it kinda was, it might have fooled someone else, but it just felt really… not-Yori to me. And I'm not even supposed to hear the spirits anymore, anyway, so I couldn't tell if it was just me being… well, me."

Samin was silent for quite a while, just staring, expressionless, before he seemed to understand that Shig was waiting for a response. "Uh," was all he said.

Shig took it for encouragement. "But I think now it wasn't just me being me, and I know bloody well it was never Yori, and now it's gotten worse. She was just standing right in front of me, *this close*, and no one else could see her. Just like Fen last night."

Samin was still staring, but his eyes had narrowed. Shig didn't *think* it was in a *oh hell, not another one* way, but Samin was pretty good at keeping a person guessing about what was going on in his head when he needed to. Apparently, right now he thought he needed to.

"All right." Samin was clearly trying to keep everything calm. Including himself. "So you've been… hearing Yori talk to you, and now you've seen her. But it wasn't really Yori."

Shig grinned. She just loved it when someone *got it.*

"I'm not sure—" Samin cut off whatever he was going to say and scratched his head, the confusion obvious now. "Shig. Love. I know you miss her, but I don't think—"

"No, no." All right, so maybe he didn't quite *get it* yet. "It's not about that. I mean, I do, of course. Miss Yori, I mean. But that's not what I'm saying."

Shig paused, trying to arrange her thoughts like a normal person, but it was usually futile.

"I don't think Yori's haunting me." She said it with conviction, because it was important in several ways that Samin understood this.

Samin had loved Yori, too, and it would be awful for him to think of her being trapped in the periphery of their lives, scrabbling along with the other spirits for seeds and never being sated. Shig didn't want to see Samin's mourning for her sister reduced to pity. Plus, if he kept thinking like that, Shig would never get him to understand what she *was* actually saying.

"I think someone else is doing the haunting, and they're only pretending to be Yori."

It didn't look like that had set Samin's mind at ease.

Shig laid a hand to his arm. "Stop thinking for just a few seconds and listen. All right?" She waited until Samin nodded slowly. "It isn't Yori. She went to Wolf. She might even be on her way to being reborn already, for all I know."

She paused a moment so she could pretend that didn't make her selfishly sad. Not that Yori was perhaps right this moment safe inside some stranger's womb—some stranger who'd be a mother to her this time, who wouldn't sell her, and wouldn't hand her a sister for whom she'd have to whore herself to keep them both alive. No, this sadness came with the knowledge that, without the spirits, Shig would never know. Shig would like to know. Shig would like to see, to watch, to come across a sunny little child "by accident" one day, just to see if the smile was the same. Maybe come across that same child, years later, to see if this life had been better than the last one.

It had to be better than the last one, didn't it?

Shig blinked it away. "It isn't Yori. It *wasn't* Yori. And I was watching Fen, you know? I kept seeing him hearing, but he *couldn't* be hearing, because the spirits can't find him, they never could, only the Ancestors. It had to be inside his head, right? Just like it was all inside mine."

She shouldn't be taking such solace from Samin's nod of agreement, because Samin didn't know the same things Shig did. But she needed *someone* to tell her it was all right that she'd been just as blind as Malick had been.

"Fen had his 'ghosts' and I had mine, but I knew… I mean, I *thought* I knew where they both came from. And then I kept pushing Mal to tell Fen what he is—I mean *really pushing*—and he kept saying he couldn't tell Fen yet, Fen wasn't ready, and now I think maybe he was right, but not in the *way* he thought he was right, and now Fen's gone, and maybe his 'ghosts' weren't really ghosts, either, but how could he know that, how can he—?"

"Whoa, whoa, whoa, *wait*."

Samin's hands were a gentle, grounding weight on Shig's shoulders. It kept her from flying out in every direction, now that she knew what she meant but couldn't make it come out so he would too.

"You've been hearing someone pretending to be Yori. And now you think maybe someone was pretending to be Asai too? And Caidi, and whoever else Fen's been talking to?"

Shig could've cried, though with relief or worry, she wasn't sure.

"I thought it had to be the same for Fen. I mean, I thought he was kind of hearing… echoes, maybe, inventing ghosts where they weren't, like I was. And I *really thought* that was what I was doing, Samin, I swear. But now… well, the *banpair* had this strange magic Malick couldn't do anything with, right? And everyone keeps saying they can't find them with magic, like you can't find Fen with magic. But then Malick was gone, and all his wards and spells, and it got so much worse for Fen—really, really fast—and I thought it was just that he was… you know, being Fen about it. But maybe it *wasn't*. Maybe it was something else. Because it's starting to get worse for me, too, since Fen took off."

"I…" Poor Samin. He was trying so hard. He let go of Shig and scrubbed both hands through his hair this time. Not quite frustration; maybe more like dawning anxiety. "All right. What do you mean by 'worse'? You mean because now you're seeing her, too, instead of just hearing her?"

"Well, yeah, I guess." Shig shrugged. "But I'm wondering *why* it's suddenly gotten worse."

All right, that look on Samin's face was too easy to interpret: *Because you've suddenly lost the little sanity you had?*

Shig shook her head. "It was only the voices, Samin. Get it? When Malick was here it was only whispers and tiny little voices sometimes. Like maybe they couldn't get through his magic all the way. Or maybe when they were going after Fen, they were only nagging at me a little. And now it's worse. Like it's trying to make me think I'm crazy."

She didn't say—because why confuse the issue?—crazi*er*, she merely stood calmly and waited for a look of emerging comprehension from Samin. It didn't come. Frustrated herself now, Shig took hold of Samin's coat and gave him a tiny shake.

"Samin, I think whatever it was, it was real. I think you were right, and those *banpair* were after Fen. I think they've *been* after Fen almost since we docked. And once they got him away from us, they decided it was my turn. *That's* why it's worse. That's why I'm seeing Yori now. She said she missed me and wanted me…" She had to pause for a moment to swallow the abrupt lump in her throat. "She wanted me to come with her."

She let go of Samin and smacked herself in the head. Pretty hard too. Ow.

"I should've known." She really should've. She used to be really good at this kind of thing. "I mean, it was so quiet when we were sailing. I couldn't even remember the last time it was so quiet in my head. And it was kinda nice, but kinda not, because I do actually miss them sometimes, but…" She growled, because they were Joori's words, and they galled her just a little—not because they weren't true, but because he hadn't meant them kindly. "But it was quiet, and then we got here and it wasn't quiet anymore, and I should've seen it was the same for Fen, but it *couldn't* be the same for Fen because he can't be haunted, so I didn't think it really was. And if it *was* the same for Fen, that would mean I was going just as batshit as he was, except maybe slower, and I… well, I didn't—"

Samin shut her up by the simple but effective tactic of yanking her into his chest and squeezing her tight.

"All right." It was a soothing rumble beneath Shig's cheek where it was rather mashed into Samin's breastbone. "I think I get it. And I think you might have something."

"I think they followed Fen, Samin. I think they were trying to drive him crazy, and we were all so sure he was, and he's *always* been sure of it, and now they've—"

"I know, lovie."

"No, you *don't!*" Shig couldn't help how it came out shrill and too strident.

"All right, I don't. But I know what you're saying, and I know why it's got you in such a tizzy. So, let's calm down and decide what we need to do about it, yeah?"

Shig sniffled. When had she started crying?

TⱮT

It couldn't be this easy to sneak up on them. They were assassins, for pity's sake. And yet, there they stood, talking about things that directly involved Jacin, and quite obviously leaving Jacin's family out of it. For their own good, no doubt.

Joori kept mostly calm through almost all of it. Right up until Shig said, "I think they followed Fen, Samin." That was about when Joori started losing the thread and his mind started running around in panicked circles. Because he'd known all of this was bad—really bad—but if what he'd just heard was even close to how the situation actually stood, things had just taken a hop and a jump from "bad" and leapt headfirst right into "cataclysmic." And not without a whole lot of help from Joori.

"Fen Joori." Naro-yi set a hand to Joori's arm—whether in restraint or comfort, Joori didn't know. Neither did he care. "Perhaps—"

Joori shook him off and stalked out into the courtyard, Naro-yi and Morin both following behind. Samin knew they were coming, because his head cocked to the side and Joori could see the wide shoulders tense. Joori didn't care. Joori cared about very little right now except dragging every bit of information out of them both and then using it to find his brother.

"All right, so Jacin's not as crazy as everyone thinks."

Maybe Joori hadn't surprised Samin, but he'd certainly surprised Shig. She jolted back from Samin, wiping at her eyes.

Joori spared a moment for sympathy, but a moment was probably all they had. "Now, what are we going to do about it?"

Samin shook his head, ran a hand through his short brown hair and let it rest at the nape, like he was trying to stave off a headache. His other hand went to the hilt of the sword at his belt.

"The Gates of Rapture." He caught Naro-yi's eye and held it. "How much of Malick's money have you got on you?"

So, fine—if Jacin was delusional, he might as well just go with it. It wasn't like it was going to get any better, and fighting it had only gotten him stuck with an Asai who seemed just as solid as the rest of the world, so what was the point? Go with it. Fall and fall and fall, because there had to be a great, messy *splat* eventually. He kind of wondered why he wasn't hastening it—perfect opportunity, and all—but remembered he was gutless, and then remembered he was crazy, too, so it made indirect, ironic sense. In a demented sort of way.

He snorted.

It took a lot more time and energy to climb down than Jacin remembered it taking to climb up. Then again, he didn't really remember climbing up all that clearly, but whatever handholds he'd used had apparently since morphed into slippery, age-smoothed wood and rotting window frames. Figured.

Jacin took his time. He was tired. He was cold. The way was wet and slick, he had no gloves, and the soles of his boots were meant more for stealth than they were for this. And he certainly couldn't fly.

A small chuckle whiffled out of him this time, only halfway mirthful; the other half was a mix of disgust and anger and maybe even a little bit of hatred. He hadn't decided where that last was directed yet. There were so many directions from which to choose.

"Time is short, little Ghost. You *must* hurry."

Speaking of which.

Jacin set his jaw, took hold of the crumbling bottom corner of a storm drain bracket and set a foot more securely atop the outer sill of a third-floor window, going as quickly and quietly as he could. The rain was loud, and he hadn't yet accidentally kicked in any glass, but he could hear movement and voices inside wherever he was, and it would probably really suck if someone looked out now.

"You know," he told the side of the building, working his way past the window and down to the next, "if you insist on haunting me, you're going to have to stop calling me that." He paused to peer downward to where Asai stood in the alley, impatiently watching Jacin descend. "I don't like it. I never liked it. And I hated you a little more every time you said it. Because you knew I didn't like it."

He hadn't expected the rage to flare so abruptly or so strongly, but there it was, fizzing through his chest and threatening to fist his hands if he wasn't careful. It curled somewhat into satisfaction when Asai's mouth pinched down, but it didn't lessen it. Jacin let it sit there, right behind his breastbone. It was one thing he understood completely—so much better than kindness or apparent love—and he could certainly do with a few things he understood. The general confusion was starting to weary him. The gash on his palm was tempting, but he was already hurting and it wasn't clearing his head any. It was so much easier to give in to the madness. Because once he accepted the insanity of Asai's presence, everything else just sort of stopped mattering so much.

And really, when it came down to it, he couldn't even tell if any of this was real. For all Jacin knew, he'd imagined the whole Incendiary thing. In fact, when it came to the bizarre paths his mind sometimes took, who was to say he wasn't right now imagining that he was in Mitsu, that his brothers were safe and his sister and parents were dead, that the Jin were no longer slaves, that Malick—

He cut that one off, gripped his handholds with clawlike fingers and shut his eyes, waiting for the burning behind them to cool.

"And what shall I call you, then?"

The tone was one Jacin had never heard from Asai before and couldn't fathom now. It could've been mockery, or it could've been sincere inquiry. Jacin couldn't tell between the two, not with this Asai. It annoyed him, because the new variations could mean anything.

Had to be Jacin's imagination, all of it. He was talking to his own guilty conscience, even if he was pretty sure the guilt had never been for Asai. Or maybe Asai was an actual ghost, come back to torment the one who'd given him an entirely different sort of immortality. Maybe Asai was real—flesh, blood, and bone—and Jacin hadn't killed him at all, just imagined he had, and everything else was just...

Bloody hell, this could go on forever.

"You may call me Fen." Jacin turned his attention back to handholds and cracks and niches in which to cram the toes of his boots. Trying to do it all without reopening the cut on his palm was getting to be a real pain in the ass, but the way was already slippery enough and he didn't need blood in the mix. "Any name you have ever given me, I have since discarded."

Along with too many other things, but that was hardly the point. And he wouldn't give Asai "Jacin." Asai could've had it once and he'd disdained it. So fuck Asai. If this was all in Jacin's head, he could bloody well make a few demands, and if it wasn't... well, fuck Asai anyway.

"Jacin-rei, come down here *now.*"

Just that, a simple demand, in a voice rich with authority that made reactionary heat bloom in Jacin's gut and in his groin, no matter how tight it made his teeth clench. Everything in him leaned toward the comfort of the command, the sensual flush of acid-sweet nostalgia it stirred inside him, the bitter lust.

He was instantly enraged, and couldn't tell if it was at Asai for deliberately using that name, or at himself for letting the tone swamp through him like hot arousal.

Rage had always made him reckless. Knowing it just made it funnier. There was at least one way to test this nonreality to see just how real it was. And you know what? Fuck it all, anyway.

With a snarl, Jacin tensed screaming muscles, bunched them tight, then shoved away from the side of the building.

"*Jacin-rei, no!*"

Shouted this time, and with a swath of panic inside it Jacin never would have believed.

Airborne, for only a moment that threatened to stretch, but really only long enough for Jacin to realize that maybe this hadn't been the smartest thing he'd ever done. It was only two stories, after all. If this was real—and with his luck—the fall probably wouldn't kill him. He'd just end up making himself even more of a cripple.

Jacin clamped the free fall down tight, flipping then twisting his body in a wide arc as he plunged the last story to the ground. Vertigo took a menacing swipe at equilibrium, sending everything atilt inside his head for a few seconds, but righted itself in time for him to spring his feet forward and aim. He was surprised he remembered to spin, surprised he didn't completely blow out the joints in both his ankles, but he landed relatively smoothly, all things considered, and in time to witness with astonished eyes what seemed like genuine alarm all over Asai's face. Jacin almost didn't notice the thick spikes of agony that shot through what was left of his calf muscles, the satisfaction was that heady.

There. It was settled. No way could he have made that jump with so little leverage and with his leg screaming at him. And no way would the possibility of Jacin splattering himself—or at least doing himself some serious damage—have put that look on Asai's face.

The grin that stretched Jacin's mouth was probably not a very nice one. And it probably shouldn't be such an absurd relief to know he'd gone completely 'round the bend. And yet his chest felt instantly lighter.

"It's *Fen,*" he said, through his teeth this time, then he spun and headed to the alley's mouth.

"Jacin-rei, *stop!*"

Long-conditioned obedience almost halted Jacin, but he made himself keep walking. Limping. Fucking ow. He'd have to work on feeling no pain next. Perhaps insanity had its uses after all.

"Jacin-rei!" From behind him, and then Asai was standing right in front of him, blocking his path, dark eyes going even darker with… it looked like anger mixed with uncertainty, but that couldn't be right, because Asai was never uncertain about anything. "You will stop, Ghost, and you will—"

"And what will you do if I don't, Beishin? Kill me?" Jacin spread his arms wide. "D'you really think I care?"

"If you want your brothers to stay alive, you should." Spoken so smoothly it almost skirted right around the harsh threat.

Jacin lowered his arms slowly, hands fisting, palms itching for the grip of a knife, but what would he do with it if he drew one? He'd pulled up from inside himself whatever it was he'd needed to kill Asai once— only once, out of all the opportunities he'd had—and whatever it had been had apparently burned itself out in the doing. And anyway, it had failed, hadn't it? If it hadn't—if *he* hadn't—Asai wouldn't be standing here haunting him now, and using the one threat they both knew would work. Just like Malick. Just like Imara. Just like everyone who wanted something out of Jacin that Jacin didn't want to give. Even Samin had used it against him once.

"There is no surer way," Jacin said, softly and very clearly, "to get me to do exactly what you *don't* want me to do than to harm my brothers."

Something very strange happened inside of Jacin with the steady utterance of words he'd had no idea were so very true. A threat all their own. A weapon, perhaps, where the ones he'd been relying on for years kept steadily failing him. He peered up at Asai, met the hard gaze and acknowledged it for what he was pretty sure it was—frustration, ambition in the process of being thwarted… maybe even a little bit of fear, but that had to be wishful thinking. Except Asai couldn't see inside Jacin's head, he never could, no one could, and Asai had always been one who relied on what he could *see*.

What would happen if Jacin just… stopped showing him?

He tilted his head. Hadn't Asai told him before that the danger was from the *Temshiel?* Hadn't Asai told him before that he had to leave his brothers to keep them safe? A small frown tried to twist at Jacin's brow, but he didn't let it. Maybe Asai thought Jacin didn't remember. Or maybe the realities in Jacin's head were melting together, and he just couldn't keep them straight.

He took a step toward Asai, trying to keep the bewilderment locked down tight when Asai too obviously made an effort not to step back. Jacin couldn't understand it.

He reached out, took hold of Asai's sleeve, just to test the solidity of him. Real fabric, real flesh and bone beneath it, real rainwater squeaking between Jacin's fingers.

It was too much. He was Asai, except he couldn't be Asai, and he was real, but he wasn't, and he was not-Asai with dark-dark eyes that could swallow Jacin whole and a wicked mouth that wanted to eat Jacin's soul, gobble him with kisses he couldn't really have until he forgot he'd killed Asai, and Asai couldn't be here, except he—

"*Stop!*"

Jacin shoved back and away from Asai until he hit the building behind him and couldn't go any farther. Asai kept eyeing him warily, and Jacin had absolutely no idea what to do with that.

Fuck, he needed a smoke.

"Why are you afraid of me, Beishin?" Thin and strained, and damn it, Jacin hadn't wanted to *show* anything, but he couldn't help it. "What do you want from me so badly that you'd threaten my brothers to make sure I do it?"

And if this wasn't real, how could something so treacherous have come from inside Jacin's own head?

"The whys and wherefores are not for the little *Ghost*. You will do as your beishin tells you, Jacin-rei, or they will pay for your arrogance. You will—"

"You are nothing more than my own bad dream, Beishin. You won't—"

"Do you really want to take the chance that you're wrong, Jacin-rei?"

Jacin paused at that one, convinced he hadn't flinched, because he'd been making a conscious effort not to and he was pretty sure he would have noticed. Asai was watching him, waiting for Jacin to give in, to crumble, but it was wrong somehow, the dark gaze wasn't... confident enough, as though Asai was anxious and unsure. Asai was never unsure, not where it concerned "his Ghost," because "his Ghost" had never given him a reason to doubt. Jacin had always been obedient, had always flayed himself to please the unpleaseable, right up until he'd put a knife through his beishin's chest and dug his heart out through his ribs.

Couldn't be real. This couldn't be Asai. It was all in Jacin's own head, and if he gave in to "Beishin" now, he'd... well, he didn't know. Stay lost? Get even more lost?

Was he lost now? He couldn't tell. And wondered with a crystal-sharp moment of clarity if that would really be so bad. He was a Ghost—wasn't "lost" what he'd been meant for all along? Maybe he should just give in to that too. He'd been throwing himself at Malick for months, grasping so desperately for that illusive state of *not alone*, and it was fleeting and fickle, but he'd had it sometimes, he'd *had* it, and… well, look how that had turned out. If he'd never found it, he wouldn't be missing it so badly now, would he?

The rain had changed. Jacin thought at first it was snow, but it was cherry blossom petals, coating Jacin's skin. He hadn't even noticed until they'd dusted him in a thin layer. And none of them touched Asai.

Jacin looked for Caidi—hoped for Caidi—because she'd always come with the petals before. A thin shard of devastation spiked through him when she didn't.

"Do you think," Jacin finally answered, surprised by the hardness of his voice, the rasp of it dipping it low and perhaps a bit sinister, "that more losses could make it *worse*? Do you think that living through your betrayals once has rendered me unable to do it again?" He stepped in, right up close, and hovered his mouth just a breath away from Asai's, slanting a look at him through his lashes, because it always worked on Malick. "I'm seeing ghosts, Beishin." He slid his hand up and over Asai's chest, settled his palm over Asai's breastbone. "I'm feeling the beat of a heart that shouldn't be there. I'm…" With a slight tilt of a smile, Jacin leaned in, brushed his lips over Asai's, swiped out the tip of his tongue to catch the rain that dripped past the corner of Asai's mouth. "I'm kissing a dead man in the rain." He pulled back, let the smile bloom, let it pull up the corners of half-lidded eyes. "I really don't think you can make me *more* insane."

"Oh, little Ghost." Asai dipped in, slid his mouth along Jacin's jawbone. "I really don't think you have any idea."

"Nothing matters. Because nothing's real. Not even you, Beishin."

"No?"

With an arrogant smirk, Asai shoved Jacin up against crumbling brick, pushed in hard, a firm line of warmth that shouldn't be there from chest to thigh. The kiss was forceful and gritty, a reach for domination in the slide of lips and tongue. Asai's knee pushed between Jacin's thighs, hip grinding in with obvious purpose, and there was reaction sizzling all through Jacin, but not the sort he would've expected. Not the sort that should've been pulled from a man who was being handed what he'd craved since his beishin had strolled through the dooryard of his father's house and claimed him.

Because this wasn't real. Beishin didn't want Jacin. Beishin never had. Beishin… *wouldn't*.

Heat drove through Jacin's gut, fizzing up his spine, but it didn't blossom in his groin like it did with Malick, didn't fill his head with a cool wind that smelled of pine and sage and set him flying. There was no overwhelming scent of jasmine, and it was wrong, the absence of its heady perfume cutting through confusion, lending an odd bit of lucidity that Jacin couldn't define, but couldn't deny, either.

Jacin slanted his mouth more firmly against Asai's, strangely detached and analytical in the face of what should have been taking the last of his sense. Asai's hands pulled him in, Asai's body pressed up against him, Asai's hips pushed in and rocked with intent. And Jacin just stood there and let it happen. Shockingly unmoved.

He didn't miss the jasmine. He missed the pine-sage wind. He didn't want Asai's mouth devastating him, or Asai's body owning him. He wanted Malick's smirks, and Malick's demands—even the ones that scared the shit out of him.

He wanted to fly, and here he was, being handed what he'd wanted for so very long, even if it was all some fantasy he couldn't seem to stop imagining, and yet his feet were still nailed too firmly to the ground.

This wasn't the ethereal bliss for which he'd pined and simpered. This was base, somehow, coarse. Dirty, rough sex in an alley in the midst of a flurry of cherry blossom petals, his for the taking. And that was all.

It shouldn't matter. He'd been whoring himself to Malick since… well, since their worlds had collided. He would have willingly whored himself to Asai once, except Jacin hadn't thought of it that way back then. Giving himself. Handing Asai everything he was and begging him to accept it. And Asai hadn't. Wouldn't.

And hadn't that ultimate, undeniable realization been the one thing that had enabled Jacin to finally kill his beishin, when he'd failed so many times before? Hadn't getting it from another—from *Malick*—been what had kept Jacin haunting the world through his grief, giving in to gutless inertia, because maybe it was real, and maybe one more minute-hour-day-week would sink it home and *make* it real. And then maybe life wouldn't be so fucking terrifying.

Give me what you hide inside yourself because he told you it's not worth having.

Not a ghost-voice, but *Malick's* voice; no slant of mocking sibilance, but the credible tones of true remembrance. And a tiny whiff of pine-sage that wafted gently through Jacin's mind and bent the disorder into rational shapes.

His face was wet, but it wasn't tears, he could tell.

This wasn't what he wanted. It wasn't even close.

With a growl, Jacin shoved Asai away, panting, and wiped at his mouth with the back of his wrist.

"You know what I think, Beishin?" He dipped his head to the side and spat, then tilted another sideways smile up at Asai. He heaved away from the wall. "I think you want something from me. And I think that for the first time ever, whether you're real or in my head, you're going to have to ask me nicely."

"Jacin-rei, you will—"

The spray of blood was vivid contrast to the soft pink of the petals.

"Not nicely enough." Jacin jerked the knife to the side and down through solid muscle and thick-laid tendon, savoring the look of shock on this not-Asai's face as Jacin yanked the knife free, scraping rib on its way back out.

He watched from somewhere outside himself as Asai went down, gasping out a gurgling wheeze as he fell facedown into a puddle, guts spilling onto the cobbles. Jacin tipped his face up into the petals, closed his eyes and breathed them in until they turned to snow.

This nonreality might work out after all.

⌁

He wished he'd thought of this sooner. It was so freeing to just accept that nothing was real and nothing he did mattered.

Asai hadn't followed him from the alley. Jacin wasn't quite sure what to make of that yet. On the one hand, it was one less delusion; on the other, Jacin wasn't the optimistic sort, and he figured it was only a matter of time before something—or someone—else cropped up to push him out of the relative stasis he'd just reached. He didn't let it faze him. There was a sparkling new sense of freedom wending through him, and he wanted to keep it for a while. Maybe forever.

No one depending on him, no one telling him what he was, should be, could never be. It wouldn't be that hard to just never go back to that inn, never see his brothers again, disappear from their lives believing they would go on to live out a safe, gratifying existence without the threat of him hanging over them. They'd find vocations, marry, have families, live to be old men—much happier and more peaceful than they'd ever get with their Ghost-brother hovering at their edges. And if there came a time when they were in danger and he wasn't there to save them...?

Well. He'd never know, would he? He could go on believing they were well and happy, and he'd never have to grieve.

A young man bustled past Jacin, tipping him a nod and a friendly smile beneath the hood of his cloak. Jacin blinked after him, only realizing as the man passed and was hurrying on his way that the smile was in response to the one on Jacin's own face. He stopped on the walk, not caring that he was jostled and bumped, and touched his fingers to the unfamiliar curve of his mouth.

A high, clear laugh sounded to Jacin's left; he spun, caught a flash of gold curls moving quickly through the teeming streets. Jacin only blinked for a second then instinctively followed. He almost called out Caidi's name, but didn't get a chance. She peered back at him with a mischievous grin then ducked into the press of bodies and was gone. Cursing, Jacin tried to shove his way after her, but pulled up short when a young woman walked directly in his path and looked up at him curiously. And then Yori was standing right behind the woman.

"What the fuck" was all Jacin had time to gasp before Yori was gone again, the young woman he'd almost plowed under staring at him now, more wary than curious this time. She skirted Jacin with a nervous flick of a glance, and then a mocking chuckle was hitting him in the solar plexus. Jacin spun, saw Malick through the press of bodies between them, his wide-lanky frame leaning against the post of a shabby little stall just off the thoroughfare, a familiar smirk on his face that made Jacin's guts go all sloppy.

Jacin had already taken two lurching steps toward him when a crooked old woman, gathering a sack to her chest as she left the stall, walked right through Malick and then… he was gone. Just gone.

"Because he wasn't there." Jacin ignored the few people in his periphery who paused to stare for a quick second before hurrying on. "He wasn't real. None of it's real."

So it really shouldn't be *hurting* this much. Like a blade to the gut, and Jacin's hand moved unconsciously to the scar beneath his breastbone.

"—is the name of my trade, after all."

Jacin let his gaze drift over toward the reedy voice that somehow traveled through the damper of falling snow and the crush of pedestrians to reach him from yards away. The man was small and thin, but not with ill health; it looked like he was just built that way. He was young, perhaps Jacin's age, his clothes bright and motley, a colorful mishmash of strips of fabric sewn together into trousers and voluminous shirt that very nearly dwarfed him. Spectacles with dark-tinted lenses sat askew on the tip of his nose, giving his mien a look that was halfway jaunty and halfway enigmatic. His hair was long and satin-sleek, bound back from his angular face in a loose tail.

There were too many people crowded around and inside the tiny stall, but they all merely browsed or stood quietly, waiting patiently for the young man to get to them. The man looked up, as though Jacin had called him with his gaze, then merely smiled and tipped Jacin a wink over the rims of the spectacles and went back to speaking with the middle-aged woman with whom he appeared to be haggling.

Jacin looked again for Malick. Hope had flared so abruptly in his chest he hadn't realized what it was until it had dissolved in the acid of bitter disappointment. Now it turned to something nauseating and sour.

"I do not promise that you will walk away with what you want," the man at the stall said, "but with what you need." He waved at the placard nailed to a post holding up the roof of his little stall. *Necessities*, it read. "I assure you"—the man took the woman's hand with a reassuring smile—"you desperately need this."

Jacin couldn't see what passed from the man's hand to the woman's, but it made the woman startle back a step and gasp. Her mouth worked for a moment, then she slumped like she'd just been punched. It looked like she was trying not to sob.

"There, now," an old man put in soothingly. "Sometimes, the answer comes hard." He reached out and squeezed the woman's shoulder with a crooked hand, then went back to perusing the stall's wares.

Intrigued, Jacin took a few steps through the people weaving their way around him, and toward the stall. He couldn't hear any of their voices anymore, but the man looked up at Jacin again, just looked, that calm smile speaking a subtle welcome, even as he patted the woman and accepted payment for whatever it was he'd just given her. Sniffing, a tremulous smile slanting her mouth, the woman thanked the man, turned the smile on Jacin as he idled up to her, then went slowly on her way. Jacin watched her go.

"You look like a man lacking in several necessities." The man was still smiling, peering at Jacin with no reserve, no real caution, no discomfort. Like Jacin was a normal person. "And yet, I wager you have no real idea what you need."

Several of the stall's patrons turned to look at Jacin curiously. A girl who couldn't be fifteen yet frowned.

"I was next."

The stall's owner gave the girl a gentle smile. "Some need more than others."

The girl huffed a great put-upon sigh and slid Jacin a glare, but merely backed away and busied herself with poking about the apparent disarray, half of her grudging attention on Jacin, half of it on a small chunk of dark amber, a tiny insect trapped forever in its center. *The color of Malick's eyes*, Jacin thought with a hard pang, and wondered if he was the bug, snared inside someone who wasn't even here anymore. Then again, it would probably be more appropriate if the stone was darker—onyx, maybe—deep and fathomless, and…

Bloody hell, he really needed to get over himself and stop being such a punter.

"Now, Kyai." The young man gave the girl a chiding look as she reached out to stroke a finger over the stone's smooth arc. "You know that is not what you need."

The girl's mouth pinched down, but she said nothing, just pulled her hand away and cut Jacin a resentful scowl out the corner of her eye. She turned and made her way slowly around to the back of the stall.

The young man smiled after her for a moment then turned to Jacin. "Now, then." He rubbed thin hands together, peering at Jacin with clear appraisal. "Let me look at you so I can find what you need."

Jacin narrowed his eyes. "You can't see in me."

No one could. It was the one good thing about being him.

"I cannot." The man's smile bloomed into a friendly grin. "But I can see you."

Jacin didn't know what that meant, so he ignored it. "You're spiritbound."

It made sense, with the colors and all. He couldn't be sure, because he'd never cared enough to ask, but with Shig's hair and Xari's shawls, the apparent shared preference made sense. His mother hadn't worn bright colors, but then, his mother had lived her life trying to hide what she was.

He gave the stall's owner a curious frown. "Magic is legal here?"

"Ah, so you *are* Jin, then." The man nodded, ignoring the rest of his patrons when they all paused to shoot not-so-surreptitious glances at Jacin; Jacin found that a little harder to ignore. "I thought you had the look. Full-Blood, yes? Mitsu has not seen full-Blood Jin for ages, and now I've seen two in a week."

Jacin gave the man a suspicious scowl but stepped beneath the slanted roof and out of the steady fall of thick, wet snow despite himself. Curious, he scanned the seemingly nonsensical piles of varied goods scattered around the small space. If "goods" they could truly be called. A little mound of what looked like smoothed sea stones sat next to an oil lamp that looked like it was made of solid gold. A rusted-out length of thick chain, links corroding to russet dust, coiled around an unset beryl stone that was probably the size of Jacin's fist. Several small water-filled bowls held gossamer-finned fish the colors of bright jewels, floating in bored tedium as they stared wide-eyed at the world glass-warped beyond theirs. The entirety of the small space was a jumble of riches and just plain junk.

"Let's see what we can do with you, then." The man was squinting at Jacin, thoughtful. There were drops of water prisming the dark glass of his spectacles. "I think there are many things you need, and most of them not easily got."

He tapped at his chin, peering at Jacin intently, then turned and rummaged beneath a table draped with thick damask and heaped with books and scrolls. Jacin noticed the thick leather tie holding back the man's hair was coming loose, and reflexively tried to drag his fingers through his own. He got caught up in the tangles and gave it up.

"I wondered who might be coming for it." The man seemed to be muttering mostly to himself as he rummaged beneath the table. "Funny… another Jin rather had his eye on it; a boy with the mark of…" He trailed off and straightened, gaze sharper, more assessing than it had been. In his hands was a black-lacquered, ivory-headed walking stick. He held it out like he was offering a champion's sword. "This, I think."

Jacin shifted a reflexive look down to his leg, where his boot hid the misshapen muscle, but couldn't hide the limp. The patrons were all watching and trying to look like they weren't. Jacin didn't necessarily relish the idea of disparaging this young man's livelihood in front of what were apparently loyal customers, but magical or no, the man couldn't possibly see inside Jacin, couldn't possibly know what he needed when Jacin didn't even know himself. And the cane was just too obvious.

"Hardly magical." Still Jacin reached for the stick. His frown was unconscious but immediate; the ivory cap was carved into the shape of a wolf's head.

"I claimed no magic. Merely a necessity."

Jacin refrained from rolling his eyes. A harmless enough swindle, he supposed.

"How much?"

That seemed to give the young man pause. "I'm not quite certain." He fidgeted with the spectacles, setting them more firmly to the end of his nose. "And I don't think that's all you need."

"How would you know?" Jacin couldn't help the way it snapped out of him, edging on anger. The rest of the small gathering was completely silent, listening. Jacin didn't care. Too many people thought they knew what he thought, how he felt, what he needed, and not a single one of them did. Malick was the only one who ever came close, and even he—

Jacin cut the thought off before it could pierce him.

"That's the odd thing." The man's gaze was keen over his dark spectacles, like he was trying to remember Jacin's face, or look behind it. "I don't know. I can't see. It's like you're not even standing there, but…" He hesitated, eyes narrowing, drifting down over Jacin and pausing on—

Shit, maybe Jacin should have hidden Malick's ring or something. The man was staring at it now, head tilted to the side, then he cut his glance quickly back up to capture Jacin's. He raised his eyebrows when Jacin fisted his hand and not-so-surreptitiously slid the ring around so the stone rested in his loosely curled palm and only the band was visible.

"Hmm." The man's mouth curled, almost a satisfied smirk but not quite. "I believe I see more than perhaps I should."

"You see *nothing*."

The rage was there again, blossoming through Jacin's chest, and he didn't quite know why. Maybe it was just that it was so close all the time anymore, riding just beneath the surface, simmering away and ready to catch a boil. Or maybe it was just that he was so sick and fucking *tired* of people thinking he needed their opinions on what he bloody *was*.

A shudder rippled through him, and his glance reflexively roved over all the faces trying to look like they weren't looking back. Jacin didn't want them looking, he didn't want them *seeing*, so he shoved the stick back into the man's chest. Whether this was all one big, long delusion or not, a strange awkward shame Jacin didn't understand was writhing through him, and it pissed him off. He didn't wait for the man to take the stick back from him, just let it drop to the rush-strewn floor of the stall and turned to leave.

"Wait!" The man latched on to Jacin's sleeve, reeling back quickly when Jacin spun with a ready snarl. The man held his hands up, harmless. Slowly, he crouched down and picked up the walking stick, then tilted it at Jacin. "A gift. My wares come to me through the hands of Fate and the gods. I dispense them as those who need them come to seek them out. They pay their hearts' worth, not mine." He waggled the stick. "Perhaps it has no worth to a heart that can't find itself. But it surely has no worth to me beyond its purpose. If the one for whom it was meant turns it away, it has no purpose, and is worth nothing to me. Take it."

"I don't want it."

The young man chuckled. "That hardly ever matters." He tried to push the stick into Jacin's hands, so Jacin just fisted them. "You need it."

Jacin couldn't truthfully deny that. "How much?"

"I told you, it's a gift. Its worth is—"

"I don't *care* about 'worth' and I know you can't know anything about me or what I might *need*. I don't even care about whatever swindle you're trying to pull. Just tell me how much and I'll pay you and go."

The old man who'd soothed the weeping woman earlier shook his head and *tsked.* "No respect."

Jacin curled his lip but didn't snap back.

The stall's owner seemed genuinely nonplused. "To me, it is worthless. Fate placed it in my hands, and I now place it in yours. Its only worth is what you make of it."

He waited. Jacin merely stared at him, slit-eyed and wary, then reached out and took the walking stick. He glared down at the wolf's head then back up at the man. He wanted to smack those clever little spectacles off the man's face.

"I don't worship Wolf. I don't worship any god. In fact, I despise them all."

There were gasps and angry mutters from the stall's patrons. None from its owner. Jacin had been kind of hoping for shock and a quick retreat. He didn't get it.

The man merely smiled. "That hardly ever matters, either." He tilted his head, as though listening, and as it had with Asai on the roof, the reflection of the pose triggered an unsettling body-memory and sent a light shudder down Jacin's spine. "There is a tavern." The man's brow twisted, and his gaze went distant. "Past the fountains and several buildings down from the silk shop." He pointed. "Across from The Happy Tearoom and through the alley in the back. Rihansei is the man you need."

Jacin set his mouth tight. "Right. So I can walk right into a group of thugs waiting to mug me for what you won't ask for here in the light of day." The last time he'd walked into that trap, his whole miserable world had ended. He wasn't falling for it again. Jacin leaned in and lowered his voice. "I don't care if you're a con, I don't care if it's a trick. You don't have to prove your 'magic' in front of your followers, we both know it doesn't work, and you don't have to sic your cronies on me for making you look a fraud. I'll pay for the bloody stick, all right? Just tell me how much."

The man's eyes cleared and he frowned. "Perhaps I cannot see for you, but I can *see.*" He waved up and down Jacin's person and the sheaths strapped all over him. "No, I would not set ill will on one such as you. I think retribution, though swift and no doubt painful, would come not only from your direction, did I dare. I am Wolf's, you see. I *do* worship him, and I have no wish to anger him."

Yeah, sure. Whatever that meant. Jacin had no interest in trying to decode it. He reached into his pocket and pulled out two koins—remnants of his blood money, earned by slaughtering Blood thieves and torturing names out of a lord's vulnerable whore. More than generous, in his opinion.

The scabbed gash on Jacin's palm itched and flared as he pulled the money free. He tilted his head.

"Don't suppose you've got any gloves about, then." Something he actually *did* need. Then, a little more hopeful: "Smokes?"

When the man merely lifted his eyebrows and shook his head, Jacin rolled his eyes. Damn it, if this was Jacin's personal delusion, the answer should've been *yes*. Because he really needed a smoke. Or maybe this part was real. Maybe just the parts with Asai were the delusion. That would be a helpful indicator.

A touch more optimistic than he'd been a minute ago, Jacin handed over the koins.

The man frowned at them sitting dully in his palm. "These are Adan koins."

Oh. Jacin hadn't even thought of that. This part must be real, then. His mind might have come up with that bizarre outfit, because his mind *was* bizarre, but Jacin didn't think he had the kind of imagination that could conjure the mundane annoyance of this. Plus, everyone else in the tiny shop was openly staring now, and the discomfort felt real enough.

Jacin shrugged. "Gold is gold."

"And fate is fate, I suppose." The man sighed, but he tucked the koins down the front of the baggy shirt. "You need Rihansei. I don't know the name. I don't know where it came from or what he has for you, but the spirits say you need him. Fate is fate."

With a disbelieving scowl, Jacin turned to go, then paused. He slanted a look at the man over his shoulder. Smirking now, Jacin reached out and plucked the loose leather tie from the man's hair. There was a belated flinch back, then the man merely stared at Jacin with a questioning scrunch of his eyebrows.

Jacin used the tie to pull his own tangled hair back and secure it. "I need this," he said, flipped another koin at the young man, then he turned and left.

Though, what he *really* needed, Jacin thought as he tapped the new stick against the cobbles, was to find a vendor who sold smokes.

⚑

He found one. And just about got into a fistfight with the vendor when she tried to refuse the Adan koins, which were the only currency Jacin had. And he *really needed* a smoke. The attention the row had attracted would have made Jacin uncomfortable once; now, he didn't care.

Perhaps Asai wasn't dogging him anymore, but that didn't mean this whole thing wasn't just one long hallucination. And if he was going to live inside delusion, he was going to be smoking while he did it. And if he *wasn't* living inside delusion… well, he was going to be smoking while he did that too.

Even the threat of the Patrol wouldn't move Jacin. A hard, stony stare had finally moved the vendor. She'd taken four of Jacin's koins, more than Jacin had paid for the stick and the bit of leather, but *oh*, so worth it. He sucked the smoke greedily as he hobbled.

He'd never bought them before. He'd always nicked Shig's. Some warped sense of… he didn't know—loyalty, maybe; loyalty to Asai, because Asai wouldn't approve, and *I think that you still… care. I think it still messes with your head*, and Jacin really needed to stop letting it.

This was *his* world now, *his* insanity, and if he was to be master of nothing else, he would be master of his own fantasies, whatever form they took. If he could keep this long, drawn-out dream from tipping into nightmare, he might do all right.

8

A few new spells, Dakimo decided as he carefully dipped the brush into the henna, Emika's fine-boned hand settled trustingly in his palm. The swirls and slashes and curvettes came back to him easily, though it had been… he didn't even know how many years it had been since he'd used these wards. No need for them, really. Dakimo's magic was much stronger than anything even Rihansei could throw at him—not that Rihansei would—but there was the matter of Kamen and supposed magic he hadn't been able to thwart, and whatever nothing-that-was-obviously-something that Imara had not-felt. And Dakimo had a personal interest in keeping Emika safe.

"That tickles." Emika slanted him a speaking look as Dakimo's brush swept delicately up the network of thin bones that sloped from index finger to wrist.

Dakimo smiled and slipped a quick glance up from beneath half-drawn eyelids, met Emika's coy smile with a wistful one of his own. He didn't reply with innuendo and teasing; he merely tightened his light hold on her fingers and dipped his brush again. Pursuits of the body would wait. Concentration now.

"We are nearly done."

Emika gauged the reply correctly—she always did—and merely went back to reading whatever report or complaint or ruling she'd been studying to occupy herself while Dakimo traced over the old wards and charms on her hands and added new ones, absently whispering spells as his brush swept whorls and ancient characters on her smooth skin. There was an intimacy involved that couldn't be helped; these sessions more often than not ended with a locked door and an order left with the secretaries that the governor was not to be disturbed for an hour. Dakimo didn't think that would be happening today. Emika seemed to understand and concur equably.

Dakimo thought he might really love her.

"You met with Goyo this morning." Emika seemed to be paying more attention to whatever she was reading, and her tone was casual—pertinent small talk—but Dakimo knew her very well. She wanted to know.

"I did." Dakimo kept painting. He'd never actually used this particular ward, ancient as it was, but... it couldn't hurt.

Emika waited for a few beats, apparently finishing a paragraph, before going on, "And what news from Snake?"

Dakimo considered lying. And then he considered telling the truth. He was still caught somewhere between the two, trying to form an answer, when the noise beyond the governor's closed doors rose in pitch and volume. Dakimo stilled his brush, listening, Emika's hand still lying trustingly in his own, until the voices took on a panicked tone. And then someone screamed.

He was already rising, putting himself between the door and Emika and pulling his veil of protection tight around them both, when the door burst open.

The first thing Dakimo saw was the blood. The second thing he saw was the smile. Cold and sly beneath gray eyes set in a red-spattered face too angular and too close to perfectly shaped to be anything but Jin. Dripping knives were held in tight-clenched fists; more knives hung in belts crisscrossed over hips, with yet more tucked in sheaths strapped to thighs.

The look was feral, lethal. If the man hadn't been standing right in front of him, Dakimo would have doubted he truly existed. Trying to look at him with anything but the physical senses was like trying to catch smoke in his hands.

Dakimo's eyes narrowed down to slits. "Incendiary."

The man's smiled curled wider. "Wolf's sheep." He flipped a knife in his hand.

Jacin stopped dead when he reached the teahouse to which the strange little man had directed him. With a sharp curse through his teeth, he took a last, long drag of his smoke, then dropped it to the ground.

Couldn't be real, he decided as he ground the butt beneath his heel. Because how could that stall vendor have known? Coincidences like this just didn't happen.

Fate, the young man had said.

Maybe it was and maybe it wasn't. Maybe it was just more of Jacin blundering into an outward reality by following an inward desire. He didn't know what was real and what wasn't, so how was he supposed to know?

Like everything else, it didn't matter. Once he'd stopped fighting it, it seemed that things just started falling in to place.

Jacin stared at the sign above the door then down the alley between the two buildings that, presumably, led to another door. And didn't necessarily care what might be waiting in the stretch of darkness between him and it. Fate was fate, and he could disdain the gods, but there was no disdaining Fate. She would have him. In this case, he really didn't think he minded.

Now, this was something that Jacin would expect his warped mind to come up with.

He hadn't even known he wanted it. Hadn't even thought about the angry words Malick had spoken, like a last instruction. Hadn't even acknowledged that vengeance might be lurking inside all the spiraling emotions caroming around inside him since he'd watched Malick go down and take all of Jacin's safety with him.

Then again, what was Jacin if not a tool for vengeance?

There is no fair—there's Balance, and that's all there is.

Wasn't vengeance a balance of its own sort?

"Fate is fate."

Jacin peered once more up at the sign—The Gates of Rapture— then sucked in a bracing breath and limped down the alley, walking stick tap-tap-tapping along.

He *really* wanted this part to be real.

⚏

All right, so Malick had been telling the truth: this wasn't a whorehouse. And if it was, its atmosphere left a lot to be desired.

Jacin stepped into The Gates of Rapture with a wary eye scanning all points, taking in somewhat bemusedly the variations of the assembly.

Men and women in a wild array of apparent wealth, from moneyed to beggared, and yet all mixed together in conversation with no apparent awareness or concern about station. A young woman clad in the rich robes of the Heldes, cheekbones highlighted by the sepia strokes of elaborate tattoos; she lounged on cushions at a squat table, delicately smoking from a water pipe while speaking quietly and earnestly to an elderly man who looked like he was keeping his raggedy coat on by a few stitches and a wish. A girl who couldn't be older than Morin wagged a grubby finger at a young woman dressed in a fine satin longcoat and who appeared to be listening like her life might depend on what the girl said next. Jacin pegged the woman as *Temshiel* or maijin, because she was beautiful, without flaw, and mortals just didn't look like that.

The buzz of conversation was quiet, but more noticeable for the fact that Jacin could hear it at all. No musicians strummed or sang in a corner, no drunks bawled epithets, no doxies strolled the perimeter proffering favors.

It only took a second or two for the poppy smoke to curl into Jacin's nostrils, overlain by the yeasty smell of cheap beer and the more palpable sting of strong liquor. He wondered if everyone here was already stoned. Would that be a good thing, or a bad thing?

No one paid Jacin any mind as he wandered into the dim-lit room, just cut the occasional curious glance his way and then went back to what they'd been doing. He almost wished someone would challenge him, because there was no one tending the shabby bar, there were no maids or lads waiting tables, no clear direction for Jacin to point himself. Jacin was almost beginning to wonder if he hadn't perhaps stumbled into someone's private party when a great, whiskered man detached himself from a pile of low cushions and lumbered toward him with something a little too close to intent in his dark eyes. His hair and beard were as white as snow, both sprouting straight and lank in unkempt tufts. He was bigger than he'd looked while lounging on his cushions, a full head taller than Jacin and at least twice as wide. And nearly every bit of visible skin besides his face was covered in tattoos.

Jacin kept his hands from reaching for a weapon. He didn't want to start anything with this giant unless he absolutely had to.

"There is no magic here." The man spoke angrily, as though Jacin had offered some sort of offense.

Jacin gave him a wary stare. "All right."

"Take it off."

Jacin flexed his fingers, body tensing when he sensed another presence at his back, hovering. Yeah, well, he'd figured it was a trap of some sort.

"Take what off?"

There was the faintest of stirrings at Jacin's nape; he sidestepped quickly, only catching a minute flash of substance out the corner of his eye before it was gone and he was backing into a very wide, very solid-feeling chest. Where he *knew* no one had been a half a second ago. Bloody hell. He stilled completely when a great hand roughly gripped his shoulder from behind.

"What kind of magic have you got here, seyh? And how did you get it past the wards?"

The chatter had stopped. Every patron of the dingy little tavern who'd politely disregarded Jacin before now stared at him with varying degrees of interest.

Jacin only snapped a glare at the white-haired man in front of him. "I paid your little friend for the damned stick. If he told you otherwise—"

He already had a knife in his hand by the time the man in front of him had completed his lunge forward and snatched away the stick. Jacin let him, countering with a warning swipe of the knife that just grazed the man's beard, but the man behind him prevented Jacin from lopping a hunk of it off like he'd wanted to. Jacin stilled again, the man behind him now gripping his right shoulder and his left wrist while the man in front of him inspected the walking stick like he thought it might explode in his hands. He stroked at his beard with a narrow glare at Jacin and a curl to his lip.

All right. Jacin could still get out of this. The grip on his wrist was pretty firm, but the one on his shoulder was only just firm enough. And his right hand was still free. The man was probably used to being able to subdue anyone he wanted to with size and strength alone. Except Samin was very nearly as big as these two, and had put Jacin into this kind of hold numerous times. *And* had taught him very well how to break it. Plus, neither of these men had yet tried to disarm him. Jacin wasn't trapped quite yet.

"I can sense nothing from this." The man in front of Jacin was looking the walking stick over with a frown cut deep between his spiky white eyebrows. "Is it possible to disguise magic as nothing at all?"

Jacin muttered a curse, deeply annoyed now. This setup was much more elaborate than he'd anticipated. And just… insultingly *wasteful*. If they wanted to kick the shit out of him and teach him a "lesson" about disparaging magic in front of the little man's paying customers, why go to such absurd and convoluted lengths?

He set his teeth. "If there's magic in it, it came from *your* friend at the stall."

"Friend?"

Adrenaline was pumping. Jacin was getting impatient to get to the ass-kicking part. He could do with a target or two on which to take out some building aggressions. The man in front of him all but handed him the excuse when he reached up and took hold of Jacin's hand—the one trapped in the other man's grip—and tried to pry the knife out of it.

"There's something coming from that ring I can't—"

Jacin snapped his arm. The man behind him didn't let go, but Jacin managed a good swipe anyway. This time he took off a good three inches of length from one side of the wispy white beard.

The man let go and reeled back. The other one yanked Jacin's arm up and tried to grab the other. Jacin merely spun to face him, and when he was wrenched upward and almost off his feet, he set one boot to the man's knee and the other to a meaty thigh then launched a kick to the side of the man's head. The man let go and stumbled aside.

Jacin landed clumsily but kept his feet. He spun just in time to duck under the walking stick as it came swinging at his head, then—

"No, you can't! *Stop!*"

—everything went still as a woman stepped into the middle of the semicontained brawl.

She held one hand out in a warding gesture at Jacin's chest, the other behind her where the bearded man was hefting the stick over his shoulder for another go. Her hazel eyes narrowed with intensity over Jacin's shoulder, where he assumed the other man was likely getting ready for another attack.

"Stop. There's been a misunderstanding."

It was the voice. Jacin wasn't sure he'd have recognized her otherwise, but he knew that voice.

We were to take the earthbound and allow the Catalyst to follow.

Jacin's heart tripped up, pounding against his breastbone. Anger and loathing curled together in his gut.

One of Asai's. One of the maijin who'd tried to steal Joori so Asai's disobedient little Ghost would fall back into line and do his bidding and his killing for him. One of Wolf's who'd been more than willing to ally with Asai behind Malick's back, but had lost her nerve when faced with Malick himself.

"You know this man, Leu?"

Jacin didn't wait to hear her answer; he took advantage of the distraction and the lack of any grip on him. Teeth set tight, he flipped his knife into his palm and lunged.

The snatch and hard yank to the back of his collar didn't help. Neither did Leu's quick retreat and dive to the side. Still, Jacin managed to clip her on the arm a good one, and by the amount of blood gushing from the wound, he'd say he'd done pretty well.

Leu yelped and clutched at the gash, trying to staunch the bleeding.

Jacin merely crooked an evil little smirk as he was grabbed again from behind and placed into a hold a great deal more secure than the last one. Didn't matter. He'd got what he wanted.

"Oops. Think I got an artery."

Leu clenched her teeth. "You bloody *ass!*"

"I guess they do know each other," someone muttered. Jacin didn't bother to look around to see who it might have been, but he could feel every eye in the place on them now, where before he wasn't even sure he'd remembered anyone else was here.

"Get them out of here." The man holding Jacin dug meaty fingers into Jacin's wrist to try to make him drop the knife as he was abruptly propelled forward, but Jacin didn't let it go. His fingers were numb and would be useless in a moment, but he wasn't about to relinquish any defense he might end up needing any second now.

He didn't exactly go along as he was shoved and manhandled over toward the door, but he didn't fight as hard as he could've, either. Too many large, angry-looking men materialized out of the shadows, glaring threat, and anyway, it wasn't like Jacin was opposed to leaving. Which was good, because apparently, he was being thrown out. There were worse things.

At least it didn't seem they were going to have him arrested. He'd hate to have to kill one of the Patrol. Then he'd *really* be in trouble. Or maybe not. After all, maybe none of this was real.

"Brilliant, Fen-seyh."

Jacin cut a glance sideways to see Leu being shoved toward the door almost as roughly as he was being shoved himself.

"All the weeks Kamen spent hiding you, and *now* look. Now keep your bloody mouth *shut*."

Jacin merely snarled and let himself be shoved. He could kill her once they were outside. More room and fewer interfering thugs to hold him back.

No one came toward them, neither the patrons of the place nor the apparent…guards? Bouncers? As far as Jacin could tell, the patrons were all still sitting at their individual tables and watching the ruckus like it was a show put on for their casual entertainment.

One of the big guards waiting for them at the door reached out to inspect Leu's bleeding arm.

"You know the rules, Leu." His mouth pinched down as he peered at the wound. This one had tattoos that crawled right up his neck in the shapes of spiky flames, curling up from under his clean-shaven chin. "No magic and no fighting. This is a neutral house." He cut an irritated glance at Jacin on that last then nodded at the slash on Leu's arm. "This is mortal. Better find yourself a healer. *Out*side."

"Bloody hell." Leu rolled her eyes. "I *just* got back from spirit, damn it!"

She scowled at Jacin then shot her glance to the white-haired man, still holding onto her.

"Seb, I need Rihansei."

Seb was already bright red with anger beneath his all-over tattoos, and glaring at Jacin like he'd just taken a piss on his cat. He redirected his wrath toward Leu, opened his mouth—

"Don't argue with me and don't give me any shit." Leu leaned in close and dropped her voice. "If I go to spirit now, you'll be stuck with *this* man and every maijin and *Temshiel* who wants him. And they *all* want him. Do *you* want to be the one to tell Kamen you lost his Untouchable?"

Jacin didn't even have time to react. He was abruptly locked in a hold so strong and tight it threatened to crush his chest.

Seb went from flushed to pale by the time Leu finished speaking. "Oh, bloody *damn*." It was windless.

Leu snatched the knife from Jacin's hand. "I wouldn't spread that about, if I were you. Rihansei can only protect you so far." She looked between the gathered bouncers, mouth tight. "Bloody idiots. That's why your wards didn't catch him. They can't. And you can't see him with magic. Now get the rest of his weapons and take us downstairs before I bleed to death. I'm starting to get dizzy."

Jacin didn't know what most of that meant. He didn't much care. And he didn't have time to suss it.

A blur of movement to his right caught his eye, a flash of metal. All Jacin saw was dark eyes and dark hair, and a surge of fury moved his body before his mind could insist he'd killed the bastard twice now, and he *still* wouldn't stay dead.

With a snarl and a move that would have done Samin proud, Jacin broke the hold on him and met the charge with blades twirling.

⋈

Imara squinted up at the stately home Naro-yi had acquired for Kamen and wondered exactly who Kamen thought he was fooling. He was the bloodier end of Wolf's long arm, and Imara knew quite well that Kamen liked it that way. He wasn't some country lord, he was a killer, and as much as he was trying right now to pretend he could be something else for "his" Incendiary, Imara had no doubt Kamen was merely setting himself up for yet more risks.

Maybe he'd at least learn that lesson during his time with the spirits.

…Probably not. It was *Kamen*, after all.

She didn't have to go into the house to know it was empty. They'd been there, though, she could feel them still, could follow a faint trail of vivid color in her mind's eye that she recognized as Kojoi Shig. But the trail was *too* faint, and Imara couldn't catch a hint of any of the rest of them. Nor, strangely, could she seem to latch onto the thread that would lead her to Naro-yi.

New wards, Imara supposed, and she was glad, but annoyed too. Maijin couldn't veil. She could find Naro-yi—and, therefore, Kamen's mortals—if she took the time and effort to meditate and look, but it was irritating that Naro-yi hadn't left her some hint so she wouldn't have to.

Didn't he know she had things to do? Bad enough she'd had so little time to hand down Dakimo's orders to Xari in the first place, but it was all the worse for the rush, and Imara had been forced to leave Xari to look for her son's spirit alone. It wasn't something anyone should have to do alone, and Imara was anxious to get back and make sure her initiate didn't falter on her final steps to Wolf's path.

With a sigh that was too dramatic for its lack of an audience, Imara shut her eyes against the fat, heavy snowflakes and reached, looking for a hint of direction, latching onto the trace of Kojoi Shig's colors. Spiritbound, that one had been, but spirit-blessed she was born—a Sensitive, if Imara didn't miss her guess. The imprint was too distinct, the favor of not-quite-lost souls almost a tangible thing. Whether Shig heard the spirits or not, they still followed her, watched her, which would've been useful, had Naro-yi not obscured his path and, thus, the paths of Imara's charges.

Nothing for it, she supposed. She'd just have to follow the traces until they ran out and figure out where to go from there.

Focusing on the more vibrant threads, Imara let loose the tethers of corporeity. Slowly, carefully, she began to ease into the periphery of hazy ephemera where the spirits cried their sorrows, searching for lost reality.

Maybe she'd run into Kamen. Which would be *hilar*—

She didn't even have time to gasp.

Fen Jacin flung himself from shadow and pitched toward Imara's dissipating physicality. Wild-eyed. Teeth bared in a savage little smile. He didn't even need the long knife in his hand to announce his intentions; everything about him shrieked lethal promise.

With a quick snap and surge, Imara hurled herself into spirit, watching, appalled, as Fen Jacin's knife brutally slashed through the air where her mortal body had just stood. His arm followed the arc of the knife, hand sliding through where Imara's chest would have been, the semicontact shoving a queer tremor through a body that wasn't there anymore. Thank the gods she'd been going to spirit, rather than shadow, or the strike would have done her for certain.

Imara almost didn't hear the voices of the spirits immediately crowding in, almost didn't feel the tug and grasp of hundreds of ghost-fingers reaching for her. That she could still see Fen Jacin—when she knew very well he *couldn't* be seen from the spirit planes—shocked her. The sensation of Fen Jacin's touch shocked her more.

Dark depths and primal strength. Power she couldn't quite touch or understand, but it was there, all around her, and it tasted like damp earth and ashes. Alien and *old*.

It nearly sent her reeling from the grip she had on herself. She held on. She had no wish to stumble away from her own being and end up wandering around the spirit realm, just as lost as the rest of them. Or pulled inside whatever it was that glanced a blow to her spirit.

Because whoever this was wearing Fen Jacin's face, it most certainly was *not* Fen Jacin.

And whatever it was, it was not of the gods.

Imara stayed still, ignoring the spirits whispering their pleas, resisting and deflecting their greedy snatching, while she watched Fen Jacin's face curl into a feral snarl, watched his entire body ripple then… almost melt, before it wisped out of being like a candle snuffed.

She couldn't quite credit the relief that swamped her. But she couldn't deny it, either.

⛩

"Can't be coincidence."

Goyo muttered it to himself as he stood between Serenai and Seb outside The Gates of Rapture and listened to them snarl at each other. When they all cut their glances to the alley where Basu was emerging through the door with Ari's sheet-draped body, Serenai's fury spiked.

"This was an attack on Raven. The man was *Jin*." She spat it.

And how many Jin were in Mitsu right now, but for those Kamen had brought with him? Goyo was pretty sure the answer was very few, if any. The Jin had been an imprisoned people for over a century; it wasn't as though one often found one of their kind abroad.

Goyo didn't let his breath pull sharp or his eyes narrow. He merely listened quietly, waiting for these two to spill out in five minutes of argument what it might have taken him hours of careful questioning to get otherwise.

"I want The Gates searched and I want him found." Serenai couldn't seem to decide if she'd do better snarling it into Goyo's face or Seb's, so she divided it between them. "It was a deliberate assault."

Seb sighed, as though unfairly hard done-by. "It was a fight into which your sister stepped without cause." It was purposely calm, but Goyo could see the anger beneath it. Seb gave Goyo a hard glance. "The Patrol has no authority here. If you want to search you'll have to—"

"What he *wants* has no place here." Serenai all but stomped her foot. "It's what the law *demands*. And if this place cannot maintain its promised neutrality, then the Patrol very well ought—"

"Ari knew the rules when she walked through the door. So did you."

"And do *the rules* apply to a *Jin* attacking a servant of Raven with no consequences?"

"I think you'll find, Raven's-own, that those who saw the conflict saw Ari impose herself where no imposition was necessary and attack a man already being restrained by *my men*." Seb's eyes were bright with anger. "If you want to know the truth, Ari got what she deserved for her devious stunt. If she'd not been sent to spirit for it, I would've thrown her out. As it is, when she gets back from spirit, she's banned. Don't make me do the same to you."

"Like you threw out *Leu*?"

Goyo couldn't help the tiny jolt this time. Which was a shame, because Serenai saw it. She curled a malevolent smile at Seb and jerked her chin at Goyo.

"Tell Snake's-own how it really went, Seb. Tell the *Patrol* where you took the Jin and Wolf's maijin."

Goyo merely raised his eyebrows at Seb. He'd like to hear this. He didn't know precisely what to make of any of it yet, but he was pretty sure he knew who the Jin in question was, and he was pretty sure he knew why Leu would be involved, and he was pretty sure he knew where they'd gone. He was also pretty sure Serenai knew too. What Goyo *wasn't* sure of was why Rihansei would get involved in any of this.

"The Patrol has no authority here." Seb set his jaw. "There was a fight, it was settled, and it's over. If Raven's-own feels the need for revenge…"

He trailed off, pausing respectfully as Basu passed him on the way to deliver the mortal remains of one of Raven's-own to Raven's house for the spirit's proper release. They all waited while Basu laid Ari in the back of a cart and covered the body against the wet fall of snow. When the demure little cart was out of sight, Seb turned back to Serenai.

"If Raven's-own feels the need for revenge, we can arrange for Rihansei to meet with Raven's high priestess and discuss terms."

Serenai rounded on him. "You think I don't know what this is about? You think I don't know what that man *is*?"

"On the contrary." Seb's voice went deadly soft. "I'm quite certain you do. Which is why, I must assume, your sister went after him as she did—*in Rihansei's house!*" He paused then took several deep breaths until the choler that had risen receded to a more sedate pink. "Should

Raven's high priestess wish to have words with Rihansei, I've no doubt Rihansei will have some choice ones of his own for Raven's high priestess."

Well. Goyo had been looking for a trail. It appeared he'd found one.

Serenai cut a fiery glance at Goyo. "And will the Patrol bow to the *authority* of Rihansei, as well? Is Mitsu not a place of laws?"

Goyo found it quite funny to be chided over "laws" by one of Raven's. Serenai and Ari were probably two of the most underhanded, devious *Temshiel* he knew, but the rest of Raven's weren't really all that far behind. Nonetheless, Goyo dipped his head respectfully.

"The pillars of Mitsu stand upon the ancient foundations maintained by Rihansei and his monks. As you well know. Balance, after all, Raven's-own." He almost smirked when Serenai's mouth dropped open, but wisely kept himself in check. "It would take more than the foolishness of one *Temshiel* to shake them." He turned to Seb. "I should like to see Rihansei."

Goyo ignored the abrupt smugness in Serenai's expression as she lifted her chin at Seb. Seb didn't seem like he was capable of the same right now; his teeth tightened and his color rose again, and he turned his gaze deliberately to Goyo.

"Rihansei is engaged. Perhaps another time."

I'm sure he is, Goyo didn't say. "Surely he can find a moment. I come on an errand from Dakimo."

"*Dakimo?*" Serenai very visibly restrained herself from taking hold of Goyo. "I can understand a peddler of ancient, obsolete magic like Rihansei allying with Wolf, but *Snake?*"

Goyo kept his gaze on Seb. "I have need of Rihansei's… opinion on the matter of the *banpair*." He cut a meaningful glance at the door to the tavern. "I can wait."

Seb sighed, mouth tight, but he nodded and turned down the alley. When Serenai made to follow along with Goyo, Seb raised a hand but he didn't look back. "Not you," was all he said and kept walking.

This time, Goyo did smirk.

⛩

Damn it, Shig really wished there'd been time to visit the temples they'd passed on the way here. There was a peculiar… *pull* inside her, almost a call that, if she still had her magic, she would've plowed through danger or fire or *banpair*—or even dangerous *banpair* on fire—to heed. She paused to chuckle at that image. Anyway, she didn't have her magic anymore, so she wasn't quite sure what to make of it. And there were too many other things going on right now.

It was nearing dark when they'd finally entered The Gates of Rapture, a dingy little place that really didn't live up to its name. There'd yet to be any word from Imara, and strangely, Naro-yi seemed somewhat pleased about that.

Shig wondered if he'd been leading a solicitor's life for too long—perhaps he thought he was jaunting off on a little adventure with Kamen's pet mortals, something to spice up what appeared to be a rather sedate life for a maijin in Tambalon. Which would be fine with Shig, so long as he didn't mistake the gravity of the situation for the overwrought drama of whatever saga in which he thought he was playing a part.

She took a sip of her drink and tried to figure out how much of the conversation she'd missed while her mind had been wandering.

"… an assumption that's been rendered frequent fact over the years." Naro-yi sighed with a shake of his head. He peered at Morin's genuinely interested expression and gave him a smile. "Advocates, young Fenseyh. Not the mischief-makers some would make us. *Temshiel* are the hands of the gods, but sometimes, the gods can't see everything. Sometimes a hand can swat preemptively, and the realization of what the other hand is doing comes too late. Maijin balance out the *Temshiel.* Or, rather, I should say the *Temshiel* were made to balance out the maijin." He lifted his chin a little proudly. "We are older than the *Temshiel,* you see. And we were not always of the gods."

"And what about Asai?" Joori's tone was even, polite, but Shig could definitely sense the wariness and hostility beneath it. "Are you saying—?"

"Can we not do this now?" Samin cut in.

Joori's pause was very brief. "Sure. We can talk about all the Incendiary bullshit instead."

Shig almost snorted. Poor Samin. Shig could tell he was trying to think, and neither the conversation nor the atmosphere could really be helping.

"Not here." Naro-yi shot his glance all around the room, then looked kindly at Joori. "It is, perhaps, a subject best left for a more private setting…?"

Poor Joori too. It was kind of a lot to have dumped on him in the relatively short walk here, and he wasn't the most even-keeled person in the first place. Morin seemed to be more intrigued than upset, but he wasn't exactly happy about it, either. He exchanged a long look with Joori, both of them then peering appraisingly at Naro-yi, before they subsided with matching nods.

So cute.

Samin jerked his chin at Naro-yi. "Malick said there's a man here who could maybe help us. Can you… um." He shrugged, picked up his beer and took a healthy swallow. "Can you tell who it is?"

Shig wanted to hug him. Samin was rather out of his element here. Spying and scheming was usually Malick's job, and Samin was just too straightforward to be any good at it. And it didn't look like the crowd in this place would take terribly kindly to questions.

"Oh, goodness *no*." Naro-yi held his little cup of ginger wine like he didn't actually want to touch it, grazed its base over the warmer, then set it down delicately on the sticky table with a purse of lips. "One doesn't use magic in a place like this. I'm not sure I could if I tried. And I don't think I'd make any friends if I did." He shrugged as though trying to dislodge a heavy weight. "The wards are quite good and very strong."

"So, there's magic here besides… you people." Joori's gaze drifted as though he could see the magic if he looked. His eyes widened, then narrowed down with worry. He snapped a look at Shig. "But I thought… the Ancestors…"

Shig patted his hand. "They're gone. They can't come back. It's only that they weren't the only ones with magic."

Joori looked all but sideswiped by his obvious relief. Not that Shig could blame him. Magic hadn't ever been a cause for optimism for the Fen family.

"It's why the gods were angry." Naro-yi's voice was hushed, and he again scanned the room warily. "When the Ancestors gave their magic to the Jin, that is. It angered the gods. Mortals are not meant to be given magic—they are meant to earn it."

Joori's eyes had never lost the bit of fear; now his gaze turned distrustful. "Do I want to know how that happens?"

"No." Shig patted Joori's cheek this time to distract him, then tuned them out again. A budding crisis averted—she'd done her good deed for the day.

The grain liquor was *awful* here, she decided as took another sip and blinked against the watering of her eyes. She couldn't quite tell if it was because of the harsh fermented taste or the poppy smoke, but figured neither was going to be conducive to a clear head eventually.

She gave the motley crowd a good look while she still could.

Shig used to watch people, because if she didn't, she might get lost in the clutch and reach of the spirits and wouldn't know the difference. So, she'd paid attention to mundane things, things on which she could focus and concentrate through the haze of drugs. The way a person's jaw flexed when they tried to hold something back they *really* wanted to say. The difference in hue between a flush of embarrassment and a flush of arousal. The change in the timbre of a voice when it went from request to subtle demand.

It had been a way to hang on. A way to keep the world from flattening down to the ephemera of the spirits that constantly tugged at her. A way to keep them from dragging her to a place where physical touch couldn't be felt, where you forgot what your own voice sounded like, so you could never be entirely sure if you were the one doing the thinking. Where tactile comfort was a thing you remembered and craved, and you couldn't help tearing what was left of your mind to pieces because you couldn't have it anymore.

She'd been stoned all the time for almost five years straight when she and Yori had been yoked to the argent and his caravan. But she'd still been just lucid enough to understand how much Yori had hated letting those men touch her, yet hated even more the idea of Shig paying for it if she didn't. Shig had known for years that Yori wanted to die, that she'd hung on for Shig, and therefore made Shig hang on for Yori. And Shig had known that hating Yori a little bit for it was probably something for which she should be duly ashamed, but… she wasn't. Yori had found her own way to cope by turning it into hatred for anyone Malick told her was an enemy, and then into killing those she hated; Shig found hers by letting herself hate Yori a little bit while she loved her with everything in her.

Shig missed her spirits some, but not as much as Malick thought she did. Which was fine, because it made Malick be nice to her, even when she was a little bitchy, and it amused her to no end, so she let him keep thinking it. Malick hated dealing with the spirits, hated the greedy grasping, and hated having to harden himself so he didn't feel the sympathy and compassion that might make it possible for them to take hold. He didn't deal with them like Shig used to do—he could, but he avoided it unless he was cornered into it—so he didn't have the same remove she did, the same almost-disdain that had allowed her to half dwell with them but never let them have her.

Malick hadn't gone to spirit since Shig had known him, but she thought Naro-yi's assessment was probably too right: he wouldn't dwell there any longer than he absolutely had to.

They'd been people once. They lied, just like people did. They got angry, sometimes petulant, sometimes jealous. Some would hover and whisper and cajole, and if you took their advice, did what they said and fell flat on your face, they'd perch in your head and chuckle at you until you wanted to take a mallet to your skull. Some genuinely tried to help, but were so far gone into the inevitable insanity they had no idea their "help" was no help at all. You couldn't watch their facial expressions to try to interpret the things they said. You couldn't discern tone of voice or the reflexive tap of a foot. You had to let them touch you so you could taste it, and even then sometimes you got it wrong. Shig had let them guide her only as far as she could see for herself. Everything else, she'd backed up with real knowing.

People were so much easier. And paying attention to them was as much a survival tactic as learning how to swing a sword. In fact, for Shig it had worked even better so far.

"That man right there." Shig was careful not to actually point, because pointing in here just seemed like a bad idea.

She directed her gaze through the dim-lit tavern, over the heads of those gathered 'round tables or off in dark corners, though not doing what Shig was used to seeing people doing in dark corners. Everyone in here was talking, drinks and card games seeming more distractions than reasons to gather. The place served no food, had no musicians and no whores. It was, apparently, a place to meet in neutrality and exploit privacy. And everyone seemed to be meticulously respecting that privacy but for one man.

Burly, scruffy, and white-bearded; he seemed to be deep in conversation with another man—who Shig absently named Tall, Dark, and Gorgeous, which wasn't the point right now—but still he peered over at them unblinking from his seat in a shadowy corner not three tables away. Peered over at Joori, really, which was what made Shig stop and pay attention. Because this wasn't a look of "I want that" like she'd seen on some people looking at Joori as they'd drudged through the rain on the way here; this was a look of definite interest—just not *that* kind of interest.

Of course, the fact that most of the other patrons in here kept slipping quick looks at Joori too, and then at the man, like they were waiting for him to do something, didn't hurt Shig's conclusion that, if the man was not precisely the one they wanted, he was at least going to be a good place to start. She turned to Samin with a smile she hoped was merely pleasant, and not as smug as she thought it might be.

"He recognizes Joori. Right now, he's trying to figure out how he got a haircut and a shave so quick."

She looked around at all the bemused faces looking back at her, waited for a beat, then huffed and rolled her eyes when none of the confusion cleared.

"*Helloooo?* He doesn't *really* recognize Joori, because Joori's never been here." She grinned. "His twin has."

Goyo shifted his shoulders. It did nothing to ease the discomfort.

"Everyone seems to have new wards lately."

He took a swig from his cup. The beer here was terrible but the wine was probably the best he'd had.

"Can you blame them?" Seb shrugged. "These are uncertain times."

"Mm. Did you know that at least several of those taken by *banpair* over the past several years were of the old magic?"

Seb stilled for just a moment, but that was all. "And…?"

"And it would seem to me it should perhaps interest Rihansei."

"No more than it should interest you." Seb stared off at a spot over Goyo's shoulder. "Maijin, after all, are of the old magic."

"Maijin *were*. And those few who remained from the days when the world was Daichi are now *banpair*. Ironic, isn't it? To live so many centuries, maijin true to their gods, and then suddenly…" Goyo set his fingertips together then splayed his hand. "Poof. Gone to *banpair* then gone rogue, and no one can find them. Unless someone knows something even the gods don't."

Seb snorted. "Even you don't believe the gods to be infallible."

"No. It's why I even exist, after all." Goyo took another drink. "You do think there's a connection, or you wouldn't have said even the little you have. You're just as worried about the *banpair* as Dakimo is."

"All should be worried." Seb was still staring, but he dragged his eyes back to Goyo's for a moment, somber. "Save your questions for Rihansei. The things you want to know are not things I can tell you."

Goyo kept in a curse. "I know who he's got down at the Gate, Seb."

Seb narrowed his eyes and then pointed them once again over Goyo's shoulder. "Then you don't need my answers. And you know why I can't give them to you."

"Tell me Rihansei's not involved in this."

Seb gave Goyo a look filled with such disgust Goyo nearly regretted asking the question. Except it had to be asked.

"Rihansei is older than you are, *maijin*. If he'd wanted to challenge the Six, he could've done so long before now."

Goyo kept his expression set, though his eyebrows wanted to snap up into his hairline. "And is that what you think this is? Some sort of challenge?"

Seb sighed and set his gaze once again over Goyo's shoulder. He was silent for quite a while, just staring, brooding, then he raked his fingers through his wispy white hair.

"Even the one we do not name was nothing more than a mortal magician once. As were his children." Seb paused with a grimace, and took a long drink from his cup. "Rihansei could have surpassed the unnamed's power and ambition long ago, if he had the desire to test Fate and lay waste to the Balance." He set his glance on Goyo, frank, before pulling it away again. "One of Rihansei's greatest strengths is his lack of ambition. And his ability to learn from the mistakes of fools. Old magic is as necessary to the gods as the moons—the fulcrum between the two is the place from which Balance was born. We are the other end of the lever upon which sit the Six."

"Thank you for the completely unnecessary history lesson. But I've got too many things that are happening *now* to worry about. And one of them involves speaking to Rihansei and the man he's taken to the Gate, *and* finding out what *any* of this has to do with *banpair.*"

"Everything has to do with everything." Seb stroked at his white beard, which—now that Goyo noticed—looked like it had been caught on the wrong end of a blind gardener's pruning shears. "Balance will be found, and all Fate's creatures will play their parts. Even Goyo Snake's-own."

Goyo'd had just about enough. "Take me down to the Gate, Seb. I need to see Rihansei. I need to see the man he took there."

"You know I cannot. Once a man has approached the Gate, there is no—"

"Damn it, Seb, I'm not one of your wide-eyed students. This could very well be life or death for the—" Goyo cut himself off. He'd almost said *the Incendiary,* and though he was almost certain it would be no surprise to Seb, there was no way to be sure unless Seb said it first. "This could be life or death for the man Rihansei is hiding. Serenai won't be the only one after him, now. And not all respect Rihansei's place in the Balance. He could be in danger too. Is that a risk you're willing to take?"

"It is not my risk." Seb jerked his chin. "Nor quite yours, I'm thinking."

Goyo followed the gesture over his shoulder and turned to see a large man with a stone-cut face rising from cushions three tables away, his blue eyes very obviously on Goyo and Seb. Still, that wasn't what arrested Goyo's attention and made him stare. Nor was it the fact that Naro-yi of Owl was sitting at that same table, amiably chatting with its other occupants.

What arrested Goyo's attention was that he'd only a little while ago been telling himself that there were so few Jin in Tambalon. And there two sat at a table only paces away from him.

⁂

Jacin didn't remember passing out. In point of fact, he was pretty sure he hadn't. The thick, muzzy fog seemed more like a hangover, and the nauseating throb in his head rather lent credence to the theory. His tongue felt gritty and his throat was bone-dry, and everything else just plain *hurt*. Which just might be the result of having been out cold for who knew how long on… well, he wasn't sure. It was stone-hard and just as chilled, so he guessed it was a floor, but he didn't open his eyes yet to find out. The last time he'd woken in similar conditions, he'd had Asai hovering over him, so he took a bit more caution this time. At least it wasn't raining.

Voices muttered not too far away, but he couldn't make out what they were saying. Two of them, one of them female, which brought Leu to mind. Jacin wanted to scowl, but he didn't dare move so much as an eyelash yet. Considering what Leu had done the last time Jacin had seen her back in Ada, he wasn't expecting much better this time.

A steady *drip-drip-drip* sounded beneath the hum of voices, but it seemed distant, like it was maybe miles away and merely echoing back to him. It gave him a sense of vastness and claustrophobia, all at once. He smelled poppy smoke, a lot of it, soft and heavy in his nostrils, and a damp earth scent that brought Asai to mind, which was strange, because Asai had always smelled of jasmine. Until Jacin had killed him. Now he smelled of ash and dirt.

A deep, driving wish for the scent of pine and sage wended through Jacin, nearly choking him. He let it settle in his chest for a few moments before pushing it away.

Damn you, Malick. I need you. You promised.

Jacin took inventory. The pain in his leg was somewhat sharper than usual, but familiar and so not a concern. The pain in his palm was smaller, more of an annoying stinging itch now, so he ignored it. There were sore, overused muscles wanting attention, but nothing felt pulled or misaligned, so those he ignored as well. The only hurt he couldn't place was a small jabbing twinge at the back of his neck, just at the start of his shoulder, and since he'd seen what had taken Malick down, he thought he might now understand why he felt like he was coming down from a days-long high.

Fuckers drugged me.

It was when he tried to surreptitiously flex his fingers, get some blood flow going, in case he needed to make a quick break for it, that the scrape of metal on stone clued him in on just exactly how trapped he'd allowed himself to become. He slitted open his eyes and followed the length of the thick chains from the solid metal bands around his wrists and up to the heavy bolt that connected them to the stone wall against which he lay crumpled. A tiny, jewel-green lizard blinked lazily at him from its perch atop the metal links of the chains. Jacin squinted back and thought about how undeniably fucked he was.

He didn't even have to check to know they'd taken his knives. Even the walking stick, which he last remembered being swung like a cudgel by that Seb.

Shit.

Shit, shit, *shit*.

"… once Untouchable. No one knew. Kamen was trying to keep it that way."

That was Leu's voice, followed by a light chuckle in a lilting baritone.

"Kamen would." They sounded like they were coming closer, so Jacin shut his eyes. "There is the beauty of the Jin in him. Kamen never could resist a pretty face. Or a challenge."

"Don't underestimate the… attachment, Rihansei."

Rihansei. That was the name of the man Leu had demanded just before… whatever had happened that Jacin couldn't remember, which had apparently ended with him getting drugged and chained to a wall. It was also the name the little man at the stall had given Jacin. Just how badly had Jacin pissed him off?

He hoped he'd at least managed to take a few of them down during whatever had gone on in the small black hole in his memory. Then again, that Leu had apparently not yet bled to death, so he wasn't terribly optimistic that he'd made a decent showing.

"… if you want to stay on Kamen's good side. He won't be happy about any of this when he gets back."

Soft bootsteps sounded on stone; Jacin hadn't even realized he was lying amidst a sea of the tiny lizards until they stirred into an abrupt swarm around him and scattered, diving into hiding as Leu stepped in. From the sound of it, she stood just behind him, her boots only inches away from Jacin's curled back.

"Don't forget—Kamen risked his soul for this one. He risks it again, just by handing over his talisman."

Jacin almost frowned but controlled it. He'd known, but hadn't really thought of it in such plain terms before. Hadn't even paused to spend a bit of concern on what Malick was risking by handing that ring over to someone who… well, to someone like Jacin.

Why would Malick do that? Wasn't that how that Skel had met his end? Malick had given Jacin the ring not once but twice—and he really ought to have known better. Jacin wouldn't have trusted himself with something so… critical; what gave Malick the right? And how was Jacin supposed to keep that trust safe when Malick wasn't here to keep Jacin safe?

Damn you, Malick. What were you trying to prove? Don't you know I'm a fuckup?

Strange, how the greedy notes in Asai's voice when he'd remarked upon "the little Ghost's bauble" were only now registering in Jacin's remembrance.

"I can't imagine what he was thinking." Jacin could almost hear Leu shaking her head in dismay. "But this one wears Kamen's faith. I can't risk anyone else finding him, not with that, and not being what—" She cut herself off and went silent.

Jacin stayed limp and pliant as a hand landed on his shoulder and rolled him to his back. But when that hand settled over his, tugging at Malick's ring, he couldn't stay pliant anymore.

He snapped up and reached out at the same time, wrenching stiff limbs up into a crouch and snatching at Leu. She jolted back quickly, like she'd expected it, and the short length of the chains prevented Jacin from lunging after her.

"You see why I thought it best he be restrained." Leu's small smile was wry. "And disarmed."

Her hazel eyes had never left Jacin's; he glared back into them with every bit of anger weltering through his chest.

"It isn't what you think, Fen-seyh."

No? He hadn't been attacked, drugged and chained to a wall?

"Allow me to apologize for the… accommodations," said the soft baritone.

Jacin shifted his glance just enough to take in the man who was slowly—and perhaps somewhat painfully—lowering his bulk to crouch in front of Jacin. He was big—bigger than Samin. The hair and beard were long and straight and white, like that Seb, and there were tattoos everywhere, but the similarities ended there. This man's skin was nearly as white as his hair beneath the intricate ink, and his eyes… It was no trick of the light, Jacin decided. The irises of the man's eyes really were red.

"I am Rihansei. And this…" He gestured around them. "This is my sovereignty."

Jacin's gaze roved the small, dark space with its bare stone walls and its guttering lamps set around a small pool steaming in the center of the… room. Cave? Dungeon? It reminded him of the baths in the Girou, which made Jacin think of Malick. His eyes stung, and that just wouldn't do, not now, so he pushed it away.

More chains hung from the wall opposite, right beside a pile of bright-colored cushions set next to an ornate water pipe, which in turn sat next to what looked like a tea scuttle steaming over a small peat fire. The walking stick was propped to the damp stone wall just beside it. Dozens of the tiny lizards slouched like a spray of emeralds around the edge of the pool.

Jacin didn't know what to make of any of it.

Was he supposed to be impressed? He let his eyebrow rise and his mouth pinch down. Because he really wasn't. What he *was* was completely fucked.

You're not anyone's but Fate's until you choose a god and pledge yourself. Until then, you are more or less up for grabs to all of the gods, and any of their Temshiel *or maijin who might be sent to persuade you.*

Well, this was one form of persuasion, Jacin supposed. This Rihansei didn't look like either *Temshiel* or maijin, but Leu was. She was Wolf's, as far as Jacin knew, but she'd worked for Asai.

Unfortunately, you're also vulnerable to any of them that might decide an Incendiary is too dangerous and try to get rid of you.

Was Leu still Wolf's? Had Wolf decided the batshit Incendiary wasn't what he wanted after all? Or had Leu lost her god and gone looking for another to take her? She was maijin, so maybe she'd fucked up enough to be exiled to *banpair* and intended to snuff out the Incendiary for whichever god—or gods—wanted the abomination gone. Which might not be such a horrible thing, but there was also Joori and Morin to consider. Because if Jacin let himself die now, would Imara's promise to Malick to protect them hold? And even if it did, what would happen when Malick got back?

They're nothing to me but tools to please you with, and if you're not here, I've no reason to keep them around. Everything's a fucking trade, right? Here's mine— you're gone, I'm gone.

Jacin hadn't been sure if he'd entirely believed it when Malick had made the threat, but even so, was it a chance he had the right to take?

And anyway, what had happened to all of that freedom bullshit Jacin had talked himself into believing only… probably hours ago? Why, when actually faced with the possibility, did all of his *if I never have to know, I'll never have to care* reasoning fall apart like shattered glass? He cared a lot.

Just the thought of Joori and Morin looking at him with Caidi's dead eyes...

He should've known he'd been fooling himself. He *had* known he was fooling himself. But with Asai in his face all the time—pushing him harder than Malick had ever had the ruthlessness to do, seemingly trying very hard to deliberately shove every bit of sanity from Jacin's mind altogether—fooling himself had seemed like a better alternative. It wasn't an alternative here. If he wanted to get out of this—and he did— he'd better start paying very close attention.

"Such a busy head." Rihansei was still staring at him with those unnerving red eyes. "*Too* busy for one who so rarely hears his own voice." He stroked at the silky white of his beard. "So many lives buried inside you, although... I think not all the shrouds are of your making."

"Rihansei," Leu said, warning, "I brought him here to hide him, not so you could—"

"And once he stepped through the Gate, he ceased to be your concern." Rihansei turned a mild look over his shoulder.

Jacin snorted—he couldn't help it—and scowled between the two of them. "I hardly 'stepped through'."

"No?" Thin white eyebrows lifted. "And you remember this, do you?"

Jacin tightened his jaw. Because no, he didn't actually remember. He remembered... hands on him, and... taking a swipe at Leu, and then dark eyes coming at him, and... nothing. He slid his gaze to Leu's arm; her sleeve was cut neatly and stiff with dried blood, but the skin Jacin knew his knife had split was smooth and unmarred.

"A *Temshiel* of Raven fell to your knives before my men managed to... calm you down."

Rihansei shrugged unapologetically when Jacin's hand went to the back of his neck, the chains clinking echoes in the little dungeon. He squinted at his hands, at the smears of blood caked into the whorls of palms and fingertips.

"I killed a *Temshiel?*" Jacin peered between Leu and Rihansei, trying to fathom why they might lie about something like that, and if they weren't, why the hell couldn't he remember it? "Was I not supposed to?"

"Ha!" Rihansei slapped at his knee, amused. "In the strictest sense, I'm not quite certain."

"It's better off." Leu scowled. "Ari would've killed him. It's too obvious she knew."

"Hmm." Rihansei tilted his head. "How did you come here, little Catalyst?"

Why did people keep calling Jacin "little," anyway? He was taller than… well, he was tall. Maybe not taller than this man, but even Samin wasn't taller than this man.

"I've no idea how I came here." Jacin lifted one arm and let the chain clank loudly. "Why don't you tell me?"

"I give no answers a man can find for himself."

Leu rolled her eyes, but didn't say anything. Though she watched Rihansei warily when he lowered his hand and three of the lizards hopped up to curl around his fingers.

"Who sent you to my Gate, little vagary?"

Jacin paused, watching the tiny creatures climb over the back of the wide, bone-white hand and curl into the ink and color, almost blending right into the intricate design of the tattoo. He tried to look closer—without *looking* like he was looking—but it was almost as though the pattern shifted with the writhing of the lizards, and he couldn't tell what the tattoo was supposed to represent.

Old magic, that was what it meant to have one's body adorned with ink, at least here in Tambalon, but Jacin didn't really know more than that. He didn't even really know how he knew that much. Absorbed from Malick's random chatter, probably, hitting on one topic after another, trying to get Jacin to take an interest in something.

It made Jacin's throat close up. Because if he'd asked about the tattoos, Malick would've told him. And now Malick wasn't here, and Jacin didn't know.

"Come now, little firebrand—who sent you?"

Jacin's teeth clenched. "The name is—"

"Insignificant, as most names are. What a man *is* is hardly ever what he calls himself." Rihansei paused, thoughtful. "And, I think, your father's name is not a thing you value so much as you think you should. You spend a lot of time thinking about and being what you think you should think and be. Don't you, little vagary?" He chuckled when Jacin merely glared. "Answer the question." Stern, but the red eyes were almost twinkling, like Jacin amused him. "Who sent you to me?"

"A man at a stall." Dull and sullen, and too pissed off and thrown to care. "He tried to… He gave me your name and told me where to find you. Told me I needed you."

Rihansei's eyebrows rose. "And who told him, I wonder?"

"What difference does it make?" Jacin glared up through the hair hanging lank over his eyes. He rattled the chains again. "I'm pretty sure I didn't need *this*."

Leu sighed. "Fen-seyh, this is not what you think it is. You are not a prisoner." She reached toward the chains, but when Jacin tensed and took a swipe at her, she moved back again. She shook her head and waved at them instead. "For your protection. Until Kamen gets back."

"So, you think M— Kamen will thank you for keeping me chained up in… wherever the fuck this is until… when?"

"Kamen will probably send me to spirit again, but he'll at least do it painlessly if you're still alive when he gets back. And you'll stay here until I think I can unlock you without you killing me or bolting. The Patrol were called out, Fen-seyh. You're wanted now. You can't leave here or they'll find you and arrest you, and then we'll have no control over what happens to you." Leu cut a steady look at Rihansei. "He is Kamen's. When Kamen gets back, he'll—"

"When Kamen gets back he will, perhaps, find that what is 'his' is, in fact, Wolf's. And what is Wolf's has, in fact, never truly been."

"Don't give me your riddles!"

"*Life* is a riddle, Wolf's-own." Rihansei wiggled his fingers and lowered his hand; the lizards all trooped obediently down to the stone and scuttered off to lounge at the pool. "When Fate places a man at the Gate, it is not ours to close it in his face. He is here so that he might—"

"*We* are here because Kamen trusts you, and because you happen to have the"—Leu flipped a disdainful wave over the chains—"facilities necessary."

"Kamen trusts no one. But for, perhaps, the one who holds his heart and soul in a bloody fist." Rihansei eyed Malick's ring on Jacin's finger for a moment then turned a sly glance up at Jacin. "Why are you here, little Catalyst?"

Jacin swallowed and sent an uncomfortable glance at Leu. Whatever was going on here, she obviously didn't like it. Not that Jacin did, either, but still.

"Kamen talked about The Gates of Rapture just… just before he…" He couldn't make himself say it.

"Ah." Rihansei nodded slowly, stroking at the straight, silky length of white beard. "You're very angry with him."

"He…" Jacin looked away. "He's *Temshiel.* He should've… he was foolish to let his guard down."

And he promised.

"Kamen now and then plays the fool, but he is never foolish—not even for love. I think he sees more in you than you would like, though I doubt he knows truly what it is he sees. And you cannot bring yourself to look, though that fault, I think, lies not entirely with you." Rihansei pushed his bulk slowly upright and lumbered over to the little fire. "It is time to wake up, little firebrand." He bent over the scuttle and ladled out a bowl of… well, it looked and smelled like tea when he brought it back over and held it out to Jacin. "I haven't much in the way of hospitality. But since you are already prepared, I expect we might as well take advantage."

"*No.*"

Leu made a grab at the bowl. Rihansei easily held it out of her reach. He looked mildly amused, and mildly annoyed at the same time.

Jacin didn't know what to make of it. Leu seemed… protective.

"Give me the damned key, Rihansei." She held out her hand, demanding. "I'll take him…" Her hand closed into a fist, and she looked at Jacin, anxious. "Fen-seyh, I'm sorry. I didn't know what else to do, where else might be safe." She glared at Rihansei. "He is of the gods. You don't know what your kind of magic might do to him, and if Kamen—"

"Do not play at ignorance with me, Wolf's-own. He is not of the gods. Wolf has perhaps claimed him, but Fate made him. And now the Incendiary has found his way to the Gate. You would take away a man's choices?"

"Damn it, we've got him *chained to a wall*—you're not handing him a choice, you're giving him an ultimatum." Leu clenched her teeth and stepped between Jacin and Rihansei, threatening. "Wait until Kamen gets back, Rihansei. The servants of all the gods have respected your 'sovereignty,' but don't forget it sits in the heart of the gods' purview."

All Jacin could do was stare. And then he just continued to stare when Leu gasped as though struck and went sailing back into the stone of the wall behind her.

Rihansei merely turned back and patiently held the bowl once again in front of Jacin.

"Don't drink that." Leu tried to get up, but it seemed like she was being held down by an invisible weight. "Damn it, Rihansei, this was not what—"

And then she was just gone. Not to shadow—Jacin would have recognized that. Just there one second and—*blip*—gone the next.

Jacin continued to stare where Leu had been, no real opinion on the matter, except maybe a little shock and a great deal of confusion. What the hell was going on here? Leu had seemed like she was trying to protect Jacin—for Malick?—and yet she was apparently the one who'd brought him here and had him chained up like an animal. And intended to keep him here until Malick got back. And what was in that bloody tea that she was so adamant Jacin not drink?

And where the fuck had she gone?

Rihansei was still holding the bowl out to Jacin, unaffected. "It is not poison, little Catalyst. Merely a pathway to a long-delayed journey." He waved at the chains. "This was once a place of sacrifice. In some ways, it still is. I think this does not appall you as it would some." He paused with a smile, his red eyes sharp. "You will, however, be allowed no such... satisfaction here. Leu is perhaps misguided, but she sees clearly in this—Kamen would be displeased upon his return to find that I have allowed you to take matters into your own hands, as it were. The chains remain. I think you have labored for perfection long enough."

Jacin's eyes snapped down to slits and his hands fisted. "You can't see in me. You don't know—"

"You have no idea what I can and cannot know, little agitator. Nor can you know what I've seen until I show you. Only a fool would spurn what he most needs in his haste not to know it." Rihansei's eyes glittered like rubies in the wavering light. "Only a fool would chase the impossible, honestly hoping to catch it."

He leaned in, extending his other hand; there wasn't even time to flinch before one of the little lizards skittered from beneath Rihansei's sleeve and sailed toward Jacin. It latched onto his finger, sinking tiny stinging teeth in deep. Jacin had to shake quite harshly before the little thing let go and went flying from the end of his finger.

"What the *fuck!*" It stung. And then it *burned.* Shit, did the damned things have venom? *Poisonous* venom? Jacin hadn't even suspected they had *teeth.* "What—?"

"You are, perhaps, Fate's Fool, but a fool in truth you are not." Rihansei sat still and calm, as though nothing had even happened. "You've always known perfection is hopeless, even for gods. Was the torment of reaching for it imposed by Asai?" He paused and narrowed those freaky eyes. "Or by you?"

You are a sigh's breadth from perfection, Ghost. So little have I seen for the Untouchable, but this... I saved you for this, Jacin-rei. I made you for this. Do it now and save your family, save your people.

Not a voice in his head—a whisper in his ear. Beishin's voice with Beishin's hands reaching out for him.

Jacin was starting to feel dizzy.

You did this, little Ghost.

A strange sense of displacement settled in, foggy, as though Jacin was seeing two realities at once. The close little chamber, Rihansei's bulk settled in front of him, just out of reach, and a back alley hundreds of miles away, where Jacin's world had ended not once but twice; the bowl of whatever it was taking up far too much space in Jacin's vision, and Caidi falling silently from the sky, and the *not-sound* of her silence—

"Stop it." Jacin put his hands to his ears.

There'd been something in that lizard's bite. Had to be. Everything was turning cottony and too slow.

Not perfect, never be perfect, could've saved them and failed, walked away from the ones you had left, and what do you suppose is happening to them right now, since the little Ghost left them for—

"*STOP!*" Panting, shaking, and he couldn't stop it any more than he could stop the voices. No, not voices, only one, the only one that had mattered then, and damn it, why did it *still* matter now?

Hardly perfect, is it, Jacin-rei?

Damn it, he'd *tried*, he'd tried so *hard*, but he couldn't save… anyone.

You have not yet attained perfection, little Ghost. How it must pain you, knowing they all look to you, and knowing you can never make the measure.

"Stop. Please, just…*stop*, I can't—"

A harsh grip settled over the shackles around his wrists and wrenched his hands away from his ears.

"They will not stop, little Catalyst. They will never stop, until you silence them yourself. Even Kamen cannot take this magic away, for it is not magic at all, and nothing of the gods." The grip relaxed, and Rihansei placed the bowl in Jacin's shaking hand. "This journey can be forced." He held up a dart between his white fingers.

The small sting at the back of Jacin's neck flared, and he thought of Malick and fire that came out of nowhere and black ash on his tongue.

"But I think, perhaps, force has been too much a part of your life, no?"

Jacin glowered at the tea and tried not to actually snuffle. His head was spinning, and nausea crawled up the back of his throat. He was far too vulnerable here. He couldn't just *sit* here and accept it.

He lifted his free hand, the chain clanking heavily as he twitched and shook. "Then remove these and the question of force can be settled altogether."

"I think releasing you now would do me very little good. When your journey is complete and your head is your own, *then* we shall remove all question. I have grown too old to chase novices through their own minds, and far too old to chase *you* through the streets of Mitsu before your journey's end. The chains are as much for your protection as mine, little troublemaker."

Jacin looked down at his hand, at the rust-brown stains caking the creases. "You're afraid I'll get… violent?" That shouldn't be so funny. He shouldn't be stifling a snort. It shouldn't be so hard to *think*.

"This can be an easy thing, or it can be the end of you. Perfection is not a thing to be attained; merely an unreachable goal to guide one toward enlightenment. Not everything you did not attain was a failure, little vagary. Your Asai twisted your goals and sent you to darkness, but only because he saw the darkness gathered already within you, the echoes of too many lives to count. Such an old soul you are, and yet even I cannot breach the murk that obscures what you were." Rihansei nodded at the bowl. "It is yours to reach for the light."

Sweat was springing out all over Jacin, slick and chilled. Somewhere in the back of his head, he wanted to demand that Rihansei give him the antidote to whatever poison was in that lizard's bite, but it seemed so much less important than what Rihansei had just said.

"What do you know about Asai?"

"Questions, questions." Rihansei's smile was… kind. "And the answers are right in your hand." He leaned forward. "Would you not like to know, little Catalyst, what you were before you became what you are?"

Tears, thick and hot, burned behind the bridge of Jacin's nose. He looked away, blinked them back.

"I was Untouchable."

"But never untouched." Rihansei paused, tilted his head. "And were you nothing before that?"

Nothing, you're nothing.

Jacin kept his mouth shut and glared blearily up through his fringe.

Rihansei sighed. "You are far too resistant to those things that you need." He tapped at the bite on Jacin's finger. "You should already have your feet on the path, and yet here you sit."

"I'm… I…"

Jacin lost the thread entirely. Whatever he'd meant to say just slipped out of reach, and his tongue settled in his mouth like a dead weight. He was drifting away while sitting right where he was.

"What does Kamen see in you that touches his mortal heart so?" Rihansei stood and strode slowly around the small pool, retrieving the water pipe from beside the cushions. "What holds his Wolf's heart so enthralled that he would wrap his soul around your finger and rest a trust he would give to none other, not even his own blood, upon your choices?" He nodded to the ring on Jacin's hand as he lowered himself back down to the floor. He lit the pipe and took a long, heavy drag, blowing out a thick puff into Jacin's face. "Would you not—finally—like to believe what he tells you when you writhe together like snakes?"

Say you love me. You don't have to mean it. You can lie.

… I fucking love you. Deal with it.

Jacin flinched. He could feel his cheeks flame, and he hated it.

"Is it not your deepest, most secret wish?" Rihansei whispered on a slow, heavy curl of smoke that twisted into Jacin's nostrils and singed his eyes. "Drink the tea, little firebrand." Soft. Compelling.

More smoke wafted and settled heavily at the back of Jacin's throat. It coiled into his nose, clouding around him in heavy, sticky strands, and he breathed it in deep, even though he had a vague, slippery idea that he shouldn't. Between the bite and the smoke, his head was humming with a gluey, distracting buzz, and his limbs felt abruptly like they didn't belong to him. Red eyes flayed him through the haze, and he couldn't look away.

"What…?" Jacin's mouth didn't want to work properly, his tongue a thick lump inside of it. "What are you… doing…?"

Rihansei smiled, his red eyes burning above it, closing in, growing, swallowing Jacin up. The bowl was at Jacin's mouth, and he merely opened obediently and let the tea pour into him.

"Setting you on the path." Rihansei took the empty bowl and dipped it into the pool before setting it back in Jacin's hands. "You fight this too hard." It sounded slightly annoyed. Disappointed, maybe. "And you are far too resistant to my persuasions. Look into the bowl, little Catalyst."

So compelling. So… not seductive, but Jacin kind of wished it was. He knew what to do with seduction. And killing. He knew how to fuck and how to kill. A matched set of skills. No wonder Malick liked him. He tried to stifle the giddy laugh, but it slithered out anyway. And then it turned into a weak little sob, and *fuck*, he wanted Malick. Not that he could actually ever tell Malick that. But still. Malick would know what to do with all of… this. This was… What was this? *Where* was this? Jacin didn't want to be here.

"I want to leave."

"The bowl, little Fool. All roads begin right here."

Jacin kept losing the thread, grasping for the sense in what Rihansei was saying, but it kept flittering away. Still, a vague sense of failure filtered through, and he had no idea why he cared, but he was so bloody sick of failing, and this seemed like something easy. Just look down into a bowl. How could he fuck that up?

He blinked down into his reflection, watching him back from the murky water in the bowl. Lightheaded. Weak. Numb and weightless.

He dragged his eyes away. He didn't want to see what everyone else saw when they looked at him, because they never wanted to look, so why should he? Instead, he slid his glance sideways to where Rihansei's hand was set to Jacin's arm, the tattoos writhing all over snow-white skin now, colors shifting and shapes morphing. *Alive.* Or was it the lizards? Jacin blinked.

"Not yet." Rihansei tipped Jacin's chin up until Jacin's gaze caromed into ruby depths. "The bowl."

He had to obey. He had no choice.

Jacin skimmed his gaze once again to the bowl, just stared, wondering who that haggard-looking, blood-streaked young man was with the raggedy hair and the tiny little braid that was meant to remind him who he'd been and tell him who he was now, except he'd never quite figured out who he was, and none of it made sense anymore. His head swam in dips and blurry rises, and his reflection blinked myopically up at him, braid swinging. He only watched, detached, as the braid grew, wrapped around his neck like a noose, tightened, and even when it cut off air, he didn't reach for it.

"These are not chains." Rihansei took hold of Jacin's wrists. "Your tether. Your safety."

Rihansei withdrew his hands, and then they were… they looked like Malick's, holding on to Jacin tightly, firm body bracing against Jacin's back and shoring him up. Jacin could've wept with relief.

Except they couldn't be Malick's hands a small natter at the back of Jacin's mind insisted, but Jacin had been having a hard time deciding what was real just lately, and he *wanted* them to be Malick's hands.

"It is all right, little fool. You are safe. Pull your safety close about you and *look.*"

The hands—*Malick's* hands—tightened again and tipped the bowl closer to Jacin's face. Jacin couldn't speak, just stared down into the bowl, watching as his reflection grew larger and closer, until his nose touched the water. Thought, *drown,* just that one word, fuzzy and faraway but with a bitter tang to it, and he wondered if it was because he wanted it or feared it or was already doing it, and he had no idea which, so he just let it all go and fell into himself.

- BOOK 4 -

INCENDIARY

1

This, Samin thought with a bit of a sigh, was just not the sort of thing he was good at. He needed someone to kill. Even someone to punch would be good. This trying-to-maneuver-information-out-of-someone thing was a little too much for him. And the fact that this Goyo seemed much better at it than Samin was—and that Goyo seemed more interested in questioning Joori than he was in answering Samin—was really starting to piss Samin off.

"And you don't know where your brother would go?" Goyo's blue-green eyes were a bit too intense in his dark face.

Joori cut a quick glance at Samin, as though for guidance. When Samin merely shrugged, Joori shook his head.

"He doesn't know the city. We don't know the city. Mal... Kamen had mentioned he was planning on coming here the night... the... last night, before... um." He looked away and shrugged. "He was on his way here. We thought it was a place to start."

"Please." Goyo waved at the cushion between him and Samin. "Join us."

Joori looked again at Samin then sat slowly on the cushion, propping himself stiffly on the edge closest to Samin and staring at Goyo and Seb warily. Seb pushed a small cup toward Joori and poured something into it from the jar at his elbow that was wafting out eye-watering fumes, but that was all he seemed willing to contribute. Samin hadn't heard a word out of him since the mutual greetings and introductions.

Joori set his fingers around the cup but didn't drink. Good lad.

"So, you've seen no one who looks like me, then. Longer hair. Knives." He paused with a grimace. "Kind of a beard."

Seb snorted and shook his head, then cut a shrewd glance at Samin. Samin wasn't sure if it was meant to be revealing, but it was. Shig was right—Fen had been here.

"I only just arrived myself." Goyo took a sip of his drink, eyes on

Joori. "I work with the Patrol, you see. Seems there was an altercation. A *Temshiel* of Raven got herself skewered and sent to spirit." He smirked. "I'd like to meet the man who did it myself."

Ah. Samin was pretty sure he knew where this one was going.

"You…" Joori had gone rigid. "It couldn't… Jacin…" He trailed off and looked helplessly at Samin.

"This is *good* news, lad." Samin gave Joori a soothing pat on the back. "It sounds like your brother got into a fight and won."

Got into a fight with a *Temshiel*. And won. Samin *did not* smile proudly. He turned to Goyo.

"There's no need to try to be clever. If we knew where Fen was, we wouldn't be here looking for him." Samin took a sip from his drink, watching Goyo over the rim. "And you don't know as much as you'd like to, do you?"

Goyo didn't say anything, but his expression soured, and he shot an annoyed glance at Seb. Samin didn't know what kind of knowledge was passing between them, but he was pretty sure it was something he didn't possess himself, and they had no intention of sharing.

"So, is the Patrol looking for him?" Samin kept any accusation out of his tone, watching Goyo and Seb carefully, but neither of them gave anything away this time. "From what Naro-yi says, it sounds to me like Tambalon law stops at the door."

That made Seb chuckle!

Goyo, on the other hand, curled his lip. "Tambalon and the Gates of Rapture have a… um. Let's call it an understanding. But Raven's-own demand an accounting. And I have questions that need answering." He shrugged, annoyed. "One needs to find a man before one can put questions to him."

"Are you going to arrest Jacin if you find him?" Joori's voice was cold and sharp, but that was unambiguous fear in his eyes. "Because he won't… I mean, he can't…" He set his jaw, mouth working like he was still trying to find the words.

Samin set a firm hand on his shoulder to stop him. Whatever Joori meant to say would do nothing but give these men more information than Samin thought perhaps they should have, and take away any reason they might have to give Samin some in return.

Instead, Samin turned directly to Seb. "Was he all right?" Because there was something about Seb, something Samin recognized without really recognizing, that told him if Seb knew the answer to at least that question, he would give it.

Seb cut a sharp glance at Goyo then back to Samin. He shrugged as he turned to Joori, his big hand going to toy with the choppy ends of his wispy white beard.

"He was alive and quite… energetic when I saw him."

Samin thought Joori might break down and cry right there. He didn't. He merely let out a breath that sounded like it came up from a well of smothering anxiety, and nearly slumped over the table. With a shaky hand, Joori picked up the small cup Seb had given him and threw back whatever was in it, eyes watering and breath hitching, but Samin didn't know if it was the strength of the liquor or the emotion that did it. Maybe that was the point.

When he had caught his breath, Joori peered over his shoulder and tipped a small nod and a smile at Morin. Morin had nearly the same reaction as Joori had had, only without the liquor. Samin thought about telling Shig to get the boy some—he looked like he could use it—but Shig seemed to have wandered off. Only Naro-yi and Morin still sat at the table where Samin had left them, Naro-yi smiling placidly and chattering at Morin, apparently trying to distract him, but Morin was dividing his attention between Joori and something over in the far corner of the tavern, and didn't seem to have much of it to spare for Naro-yi.

Samin followed Morin's glance and found Shig crouched over along the far wall, smiling and with all her mercurial attention on what Samin thought at first was a spray of emeralds but turned out to be tiny green lizards. They crawled over Shig's outstretched hand, twining around her fingers as Shig chuckled lightly and spoke to them in soft words, only the tone of which Samin could make out from here.

Seb stood and abruptly clapped his hands. "Everyone out." He aimed a shrug that didn't look the slightest bit apologetic at Goyo and Samin. "I am sorry, but you'll have to take this outside."

Samin stood too. "Now, wait just a minute. I need to know—"

"Only a fraction of what you think you do." Seb clapped his hands again until all the patrons in the tavern started to slowly move, looking just as confused as Samin was. "Your friend was here and now he is not. I can't help you any further than that."

"You say that like it's any help at all!" Samin turned to Goyo, who was directing a narrow frown at Seb, looking just as unhappy about all this as Samin. "Listen, I don't want to make trouble for you, but you don't understand what—"

"Please." Joori stepped in right up close to Seb, reaching out to latch onto Seb's great, tattooed arm, but apparently not quite daring. He let his hand drop to his side. "Please, seyh. He's my *brother*."

"Yes, young seyh, I can see that. And I am sorry. But these matters are not for us. You must leave. Now."

He stepped over to Shig, who was still crouched down and playing with the lizards. She merely watched as Seb approached, blatantly not moving except to wiggle her fingers while the little creatures cavorted like puppies doing tricks in exchange for her affection.

"Little shepherds." Shig peered up at Seb with a knowing lift of her eyebrow that Samin had every intention of decoding once they were through getting kicked out. "Seen any lost souls lately?" Shig's gaze settled on Goyo. "Looking for one?"

Naro-yi pulled Morin along with him, giving Goyo a look that was canny and sharp and old and assessing as he approached, nothing like the "semisilly avuncular banker looking for adventure" he generally portrayed. Goyo didn't seem to notice; he was staring at Shig with almost the same look.

Seb took it all in and set his jaw, but when he reached down to pull Shig away, his big hands were fairly gentle. Shig didn't resist, only leaned over and let the last of the lizards hop down from her fingertip and onto the floor before it skittered away, apparently through the rough, wide-set floorboards.

"Off with you, little shepherds. You've more than one hope resting on your..." Shig peered up at Seb with a curious grin. "Do lizards have shoulders?"

"What does that mean?" Joori nearly vibrated with anxiety and confusion. "Shig? What does that mean?" He turned on Samin. "Does she know something?"

Three more tattooed men appeared to herd along the patrons who moved too slowly, and then once everyone else had been cleared out, another four came to loosely surround Samin and his little party. Not hostile, but certainly not friendly. Samin had no doubt about the message they were meant to convey. And he got it with no problem. His temper was a brittle, nasty little animal caged up somewhere behind his breastbone, and not at all happy about the confinement. He set his jaw and glared, because it was really all he could do. And because these men obviously knew something about Fen, and could look right at that desperate expression on Joori's face and deny him.

"C'mon, Joori." Samin sent glares all around, making his displeasure quite clear, impotent as it was. "We're not going to find out anything more here."

"But... Samin, they—"

"Yeah, I know. I'm sorry. But we're outnumbered, and I haven't got any magic." Samin speared another harsh look around him, letting it rest a little bit longer on Seb and then Goyo. "After you, seyh."

Goyo's eyebrow went up, but that was all. Teeth set, Samin gripped Joori's shoulder and nudged him along before all these men decided to do it a little less gently.

"We can't just *leave*." Joori was edging on panic, but his feet moved when Samin prodded him. "Samin, they *know* something. They've seen Jacin. They *have* to tell us!"

"No, they don't." Morin peered up at Seb with an unabashed curl to his lip as they neared the door. "That's the problem." He leaned in close between Joori and Samin. "Did they say anything at all?"

"That Jacin was here." Joori threw his hands up, despairing. "And he got into a fight."

Morin reached out and stopped Joori with a hand to his arm. "And?"

"And he won." Samin gave Seb another glare as they reached the door. "And now he's not here anymore."

"But that's good news." Morin grinned and patted at Joori's arm. "Didn't I say you should be worrying about the people who got in his way?"

Samin didn't say anything to the boys as he chivvied them out the door, but he did feel a little bit lighter as he did it. Because when Morin passed Goyo, Goyo smirked and winked.

⛩

Goyo had every intention of telling the Incendiary's brothers what he knew. Had every intention of setting their minds as easy as he could with what little information he had. It could do no harm, as far as he could foresee, and it might gain him some goodwill, get rid of at least a bit of the very obvious distrust for which he couldn't blame them. Not that he thought for a moment they'd run and tell him if they found the Incendiary before Goyo did—or, more likely, that the Incendiary found them—but Goyo didn't need that kind of information anymore. He knew exactly where the Incendiary was, and further knew that the Incendiary was probably safer where he was than his brothers were.

It was the blunt reality of that last thought, unfortunately, that prevented Goyo from doing his intended good deed. And it was Seb's muttered, "Watch your back," as he shut the door behind Goyo—and threw both bar and latch then tightened down the wards until Goyo almost couldn't breathe—that alerted Goyo that perhaps something more than Shig's strange little display had prompted the curt kicking out and locking up.

But it was Naro-yi's abrupt tension as he breached the barriers of Rihansei's protections at the mouth of the alley that told Goyo things were about to go very wrong.

Goyo didn't wait until everything fell apart, and he didn't need to see the trouble to know it was coming. He sent out a call for the Patrol and tried to reach beyond the wards with his magic, get a sense of what was approaching, but they were too good, too heavy, and he couldn't get past them. He was just trying to wend his way around Morin and Shig, get out of the alley so he could let his magic loose, when everything started to happen at once.

He'd never seen Naro-yi put on a warrior's face before. He'd never really even considered that Naro-yi had one. The blue-green splinter of light from the just-visible edge of Owl's moon—splattering over Naro-yi as he drew a sword and shoved Joori behind him, even before the murky ripples of not-substance warped into actual shapes—was not, Goyo decided, his imagination. Nor was Joori's sudden cry of "Jacin!" and Goyo's realization that Naro-yi was in the process of charging a young Jin man who looked remarkably like Joori, but with longer ragged hair and a face that was exactly the same except sharper, older, angrier.

Wolf's moon was fat and round, and lent silver light to the world. It glittered in the young man's eyes as he bared his teeth and charged in return. Three black-clad figures backed him up as he met Naro-yi's rush with long knives that Goyo knew couldn't have an actual sinister gleam but did anyway.

And just that quick, everything turned to madness.

Goyo drove in, past Samin, who was too busy holding Joori back to engage while shouting at Naro-yi to *wait, that's Fen, damn it, don't kill him*!

Naro-yi merely kept going, curling sputtering little balls of blue-white lightning in his hand and hurling them as he swung the sword, but neither were doing him any good. The lightning merely winked out when it reached its targets, and the attackers were too fast for Naro-yi's sword.

"That's not Fen!" Shig's voice rang clear across the cobbles, even as Joori cried, "What are you doing, that's *my brother*!"

Samin cursed somewhere behind Goyo, snapped, "Shig, hold him," then all Goyo could hear was the heavy *thud-thud-thud* of boots on the stone path as Samin barreled in.

Goyo didn't have time to look back as two of the attackers drove in. One swung a short sword with passable skill. Samin took that one. The other had a tiny bow that, Goyo learned very quickly, shot wicked little darts that zinged and hissed as they whipped past his head. Goyo all at once thought Kamen's startling fall a lot less funny.

He tried to shield with magic, tried to reach out and swat with it too, and he could feel Naro-yi doing the same. It did no good. Magic didn't work on Incendiary, Goyo knew that, so he wasn't surprised, but he *was* surprised it didn't seem to affect the other three, either.

Banpair, the ones Kamen's magic couldn't thwart, which made Goyo's gut curl, because Goyo was strong, but no one was as strong as Kamen, and if these creatures were the ones who'd taken Kamen down…

Goyo didn't have any weapons on him but the short sword of the Patrol and the small baton that had always been more decorative than useful. He drew them both now, pulling shadows in close. Those he could at least use to deflect and distract while he fought his way toward the one with the bow. Because no one needed those darts flying around in this mess too.

Two of the attackers moved in on Naro-yi with redoubled intensity. It gave the Incendiary an opening to rush through and toward his brothers. Goyo slid into substance just in front of him. He drove in close. Metal screeched on metal as Goyo's short sword met the Incendiary's long knives. Except all Goyo could really do was dodge and feint while trying not to actually kill the Incendiary.

Too bad the Incendiary had no such limitations.

"Jacin, *stop!*"

Joori broke loose from both Shig and Morin and rushed out into the middle of everything. He skirted right past Goyo, preventing him from following up an offensive swipe the way his body wanted to. He pulled the move just in time as Joori shot past and around him, avoiding at the last second the swipe of the blade that would have opened Joori's side up and spilled his insides out onto the walk. Joori didn't even seem to know how close he'd come, simply barreled in until he was between Goyo and his brother, hands up in front of him.

"Stop, Jacin, *stop!*"

Incredibly, they all did. Naro-yi's opponents disappeared right in front of him. Not to shadow or spirit—it seemed as though they winked out of existence entirely.

Samin cursed as his opponent disappeared. "Blasted little bitch can't fight fair." With a rather frightening scowl, he licked the blood from a long slash on the back of his hand, then switched his sword to the other.

"Come with me, Joori." The Incendiary held out a hand, beckoning.

Joori tried, but Samin quickly edged in behind him, knocking Naro-yi out of the way, and snagged hold of Joori's arm.

The Incendiary narrowed his eyes. "Joori, get Morin and come with me."

Morin made a halfhearted attempt to shrug Shig off.

Shig didn't let go. "That's not Fen." She gave Joori a grim look of warning. "Joori, that's not your brother."

"What d'you mean, that's not him?" Joori turned so he could glare at Shig. "Of *course* it's him, are you blind? How can you say—?"

"Because I see Yori!"

The dart came out of nowhere. Joori yipped when it lodged in his arm, but Samin snarled "Son of a *bitch*!" as Joori slapped at it, already wobbly and faltering as the creature pretending to be the Incendiary stepped in to snatch him up. Samin was already there, dropping his sword to catch Joori as he fell and putting himself between Joori and the Incendiary. Only the sweep of Naro-yi's sword kept the Incendiary's knives from removing Samin's heart through his backbone.

The *zip* of another dart sounded, and this time it was Shig who loosed a little cry. She'd stepped in front of Morin.

"Damn it, Shig, wha'd'ya do that for?" Morin swiped at the thing as Shig tried and failed to pluck it from the thick muscle of her thigh. She started to go down, too, leaving Morin to catch her.

Goyo and Naro-yi were the only two left to defend.

Naro-yi gave Goyo a speaking look. *Be ready.* He lifted his sword and jerked his chin at Samin.

"Get them back into the tavern." With a quick turn to shadow and back, Naro-yi put himself between Samin and the Incendiary.

"They're *mine*." The Incendiary whirled in, met Naro-yi's sword with both knives, locked them together, then turned a glare on Morin. "Take Joori and come with me. Don't make me have to hurt the others."

Apparently, Naro-yi had been waiting for the distraction. He swirled his sword, arc then counterarc, then leveled a solid kick to the Incendiary's midsection. It only forced them apart a pace or two, but it was enough for Naro-yi to place his sword *just so* and keep the Incendiary where he was.

The Incendiary merely lowered his knives, put his hands out to his sides.

"Morin, I won't tell—"

"You're *not* my brother." Morin had managed to drag Shig back to the alley. He glared at the Incendiary from behind the relative safety of the wards. "Who are you? Where's Jacin? Was that poison in those darts? What did you do to Joori?"

"Shut up and come here. Don't make me hurt you." The Incendiary pulled out a throwing knife and aimed it at Samin, still edging toward the alley and carrying Joori. "Don't make me hurt anyone."

"Jacin *couldn't* hurt me." Morin was all but seething. "He couldn't hurt Joori. That's always been his problem. Fucking idiot, you're supposed to get to *know* the people you're trying to impersonate."

The Incendiary pulled the knife back over his shoulder, cocked and ready, aimed at Naro-yi this time.

"Now, Morin."

"You're not Jacin, and I'm *not* coming with you."

There was a moment of stillness, breathlessness, really, as Morin and the counterfeit Incendiary stared at each other across Rihansei's wards. Goyo didn't know if the not-Incendiary reconsidered his approach because he knew Morin wouldn't be moved, or if there was simply no one left Morin cared enough about to threaten. Whatever decided him, the mask of the Incendiary fell away, replaced by almost yellow eyes over a dark kerchief that covered the lower half of this… creature's true face.

"All right, then." The voice was different, smooth where the Incendiary's—or the imitation of the Incendiary's—had been hoarse and rough. The imposter dipped a condescending nod. "Your weakling Ghost-brother could never hurt you. But you can hurt him, can't you, little Jin?"

Goyo kept quiet and so did Naro-yi, but they both saw Morin flinch.

"If you want him back, you will take your brother away from these people and come with us. We would hate to have to bear the news of your tragic death to the Ghost." The imposter paused, yellow eyes crinkling at the corners with what would likely be a chilling little smile, if it were visible beneath the kerchief. "In his state, it will be nothing at all to convince him he brought it by his own hand."

Morin nearly dropped Shig. "*Where is he?*"

A vague ripple shuddered at the edge of Goyo's peripheral vision. A presence he knew and would ordinarily not welcome made itself known to him as the ripple moved, a sinuous quiver just at the verge of magical sight. It settled on the imposter's blind side. And waited.

"They don't have him." Goyo neatly deflected the dart and the one that came after it with the flat of his sword, because he'd rather been expecting them. "I know where he is, young seyh. And whoever these… *creatures* are, they don't have him. They want you because they think you're how to get him."

"He is already ours." The imposter discarded the little throwing knife for one of the long knives as he adjusted his bearing again into one of offense. The three assailants with him popped back into sight behind him, all of them tense and in attack stance. "He just doesn't know it yet."

"What do you want from him?" Goyo asked, not really expecting an answer, mildly surprised when the imposter chuckled, something deep and bubbling that reminded Goyo somehow of black tar.

"We want our master's property returned, of course. We want what belongs to us." The imposter nodded to one of the others, said, "Get the woman too," and they all broke into a swift advance.

Imara shot from spirit with a high-pitched war cry that grated right up Goyo's spine, but he wasn't about to complain. A wall of fire sprang up between Goyo and Naro-yi and the four black-clad assailants, just as Goyo saw the first of the Patrol round the corner down by the teahouse.

When the flames finally went from a great bellow to a steady shout, Goyo ran through them.

⛩

Imara didn't emerge from the company of the spirits until she butted up against the wards surrounding the Gates of Rapture and had no choice. And when she saw what was going on, she backed away from the wards and waited. She tried to send out a shield to protect the mortals but could get nothing through, so she compromised by layering her own magic over Rihansei's incomprehensible—but all too effective—protections.

She roared as she burst from spirit, a long, ululating cry, remnant of a people to whom she once belonged, almost too long ago to remember. And when she called the fire, it came to her and splashed out at her command, feeding on itself and building a wall between the imposter and Kamen's mortals. Unfortunately, it also cut off Goyo and Naro-yi, leaving Imara momentarily alone, unarmed, and facing four creatures with power she didn't quite know what to do with, but it couldn't be helped. Seven of the Patrol were skidding into attack range, and they would simply have to do.

"Capture if you can," Imara shouted at the patrolwoman in the lead—Annaichi, a young maijin of Bear—then amended it with, "but risk nothing. Kill them all if you must."

One of the black-clad figures lunged for her, and she whipped up a wind to carry her out of range faster than what her legs could've done. Goyo shot through the flames, sword raised and glittering, and joined those of the Patrol who had already engaged.

The creatures used the shadows to parry and distract. Goyo and Annaichi fought back in kind. The effects brewed together like an especially volatile tea, creating a vortex of whirling, smoky not-substance that faded in and out as it slid and spun and gyrated amongst the spark and flash of the fire. Wavering ripples of heat slithered into the mix, making it almost impossible for Imara to follow the action, only marking hits and attacks when blades clashed and voices cried out.

Two of the Patrol had taken up positions in front of her, protective.

She growled at them. "Get in there and help as you can."

Because if these creatures wanted to come after her, mortals weren't going to stop them.

"Give me a weapon." She held out her hand to the patrolman closest to her, grimacing when he handed her only a short knife. Aggravating, but no real blame to him, Imara supposed—she wouldn't have given up a sword now, either.

Bracing, Imara waded in, sliding into and out of shadow and then into and out of spirit, depending upon which defense she needed most at the time. The shadows were faster, but her earlier encounter with the not-Incendiary told her that spirit was the safer refuge.

The mortals were taking the brunt of the fight; Imara backed them up as she could. Glimpses were all she caught of the whirling battle in which Goyo and Annaichi were engaged. Both were at least a little blooded, but the six mortals had no defense against this magic but physical skill. Imara dodged and slipped around them, heading off attacks with quick swipes of the too-small knife then darting back into shadow or spirit again for a swift retreat.

Their magic wasn't working against whatever these people were. Imara and Goyo and Annaichi nonetheless continued to fling it in a constant stream.

Imara hurled flames that merely scattered off her targets like a dash of water and dripped around them, harmless. Goyo cast small bolts of power that did nothing more than dissipate when they hit. Annaichi was new to her powers, and now she was making it too obvious, chucking it all haphazardly, not caring that it merely glanced off the creatures and bounced away. She'd already bashed in two storefronts. Chunks of street cobbles flew around in the confusing mix of shadows and physical bodies and clashing metal. Already the streets were more crater than paved stone.

One of the mortals went down with a long spike of a needle in his back, just below his shoulder blade. He fell right in front of Imara as she emerged once again from spirit. Every healing instinct she had urged her to go to him; instead she edged up as close as she dared to the flames and set her back to them. If she had to, she could dive through them and retreat behind Rihansei's wards, then figure out what to do from there if these creatures won. For now, she couldn't do much more than what she'd been doing and vow that, after this was all through, she was going to swallow any embarrassment and ask Goyo to help her find a suitable weapon to carry. She might even ask him to spar with her, brush up on too-old training she hadn't used in too long, but that might be pushing things.

It was when Naro-yi parted the flames and walked through them, a blazing ball made of what looked like a strip of his torn coat in his hand, that the tide began to turn. Naro-yi merely stood there, watching the not-quite-visible battle with sharp attention, waiting patiently with fire in his hand, and when one of the creatures solidified to engage a mortal patrolman, Naro-yi simply lobbed the flaming lump of fabric at the creature's head.

Nothing magical about it. No maijin power against which these things were immune. Physicality at its most basic and violent.

The creature's hood caught first, and then the hair beneath it. The man-shape dropped the long needles with which it had been fighting and began beating at its head. A patrolman took the opportunity to decapitate it. There was a grating curse from one of the others, and then the falling body burst into consuming flame—detached smoldering head and all. No way to identify it now, but Imara thought it rather likely that this one was on the list of the missing.

Naro-yi shook his head, mouth pursed. "The young ones always forget the old tricks." He tore off another bit of his coat.

It was unnecessary. Goyo and those of the Patrol still standing kept whirling and dodging for a moment or two, until it became apparent that they were fighting air. One by one, they stopped, but none of them relaxed their offensive stances and none of them stopped darting their gazes into nothing, squinting like it would help.

Naro-yi scowled, tossing the little ball of fabric in his hand up and down a few times, then he dropped it to the ground with a sigh. Like he was disappointed. He caught Imara's curious lift of eyebrows and merely shrugged.

"It's been a long time since one I've been told to make my enemy so clearly *was.*"

Imara had to give him that one.

She was still eyeing Naro-yi with interest when Goyo sauntered up, a little bloody, a lot sweaty, and breathing hard. He jerked his chin behind Imara.

"Could you maybe…?"

Imara blinked. "Oh. Yes. Of course."

Gathering herself, she waved the flames away. Funny, the absurd little things that could still now and then throw her.

She followed as Naro-yi and Goyo led the way back to Kamen's mortals. Imara only stopped long enough to make sure they were all still alive then turned her attention to those of the Patrol who needed healing.

The man who'd fallen nearly at her feet was already dead when Imara reached him. A woman who was very quickly bleeding out from a wound to the chest took time, concentration, and care to heal, and though she'd be fine eventually, there would be a lot of rebuilding to do; two losses for the Patrol. The others had relatively minor injuries. Imara decided they could wait for a moment and went back to Joori and Shig.

"... really matter if you're right or wrong." Annaichi's tone was rather bold for such a young maijin addressing Goyo. "Everything's going to shit and the Incendiary is standing right in the middle of it all, wherever he is and whatever his intentions might be."

"I don't understand." Morin frowned with a look of helpless distress. "Why would Jacin attack the governor?"

Imara jolted. "The governor was attacked?"

Annaichi opened her mouth to answer.

Goyo glared her into silence. He turned to Imara.

"*Dakimo* was attacked. The governor was, as always, in his proximity, and it appears she tried to... help."

"Wolf's temple too," Annaichi put in. "And Owl's."

Imara's eyes widened, and she gave a start she couldn't help.

Annaichi put out a hand. "No one was harmed." She shrugged. "But all your priests and priestesses have been looking for you."

Imara could barely process it. "And they think Fen Jacin did it?"

"They *know*." This time Annaichi ignored Goyo's glare, lifting her chin defiantly. "The man was described as Jin, dark-haired, and with gray eyes." She looked pointedly at Joori, still unconscious. "Since the Incendiary's twin has obviously not had such an opportunity, and since Dakimo's magic could not touch the assailant, nor could anyone at the temple, it had to have been the Incendiary himself."

"Or someone who looked like him." Samin looked like he was ready to bite through metal, his teeth were clenched so tight. He was fisting the bloodied strip of cloth around his hand so hard, he was wringing drops from it.

It would likely be best to distract his obviously building frustrations. Imara took up Samin's hand and began unwrapping the makeshift bandage.

Samin tugged his hand away, not terribly gently. "See to Shig and Joori first."

"Neither Shig nor Joori is bleeding. Nor have they been poisoned." Imara caught the narrowing of Samin's eyes and softened her voice into the soothing tones she'd perfected through the centuries. "Whatever was in the darts was not meant to harm, and there is none. They are merely very deeply asleep. I will get to them once I'm through with those who have more immediate need."

Mollified but still hostile, Samin let Imara take his hand back. He cut an annoyed glance at Annaichi.

"The man who attacked us was *not* Fen. I know him, I know how he fights, and that wasn't him." He hissed when Imara eased the cloth away from clotted blood and torn skin. "And I recognized one of them. I've fought her before too—the night *banpair* attacked and took Malick down. *Kamen.*" The correction came with a twist of his lip.

"Yeah." Morin stood up straighter. "And Jacin doesn't have magic. That man changed right in front of us. One second he looked like Jacin and the next he didn't. Jacin can't do that."

Annaichi lifted her eyebrows. "He has Kamen's ring, no?"

Goyo startled. "He has *what?*"

"This is not—" Imara cursed rather colorfully and snapped a glare up at Annaichi. "How did you know that?"

"Dakimo felt we should be informed."

"Nice of Dakimo to think of that *now,*" Goyo snarled.

Imara sighed. "And is that, Snake's-own, information you would have bandied about, if you—?"

"I suppose not. Not if I was the one who'd lost him in the first place."

"I didn't *lose* him, he—"

"You *lost* the Incendiary, Imara, and tonight you almost lost—"

"*Wolf's* Incendiary, Goyo. Don't pretend your interest has anything to do with concern."

"*Anyone's* Incendiary, and once *you* lost him—*wearing Kamen's ring,* for the love of all the gods—he lost Wolf's protection too. Who knows what could—?"

"He wears Kamen's ring because Kamen is an idiot. He left Wolf's protection because he doesn't know any better. The Incendiary is unstable, and ran before I could reas—"

"*The Incendiary,* has a bloody *name!*"

Samin's growling bellow shut everyone up. His normal countenance was already somewhat fearsome; his barefaced fury made it more so. Teeth set in a snarl, he jerked his hand from Imara's grip, glaring between Imara and Goyo for several long seconds, before turning the look on Annaichi for good measure.

"*Fen Jacin* did not attack us tonight. *Fen Jacin* most likely *also* did not attack your governor. *Fen Jacin* is in trouble and likely needs help very badly, and *you people* are too busy arguing over who he belongs to, instead of figuring out where he is and why *banpair* want him so badly they'd try to kidnap his brothers to get him to come to them."

He snapped a hard look at Annaichi. "Is the Patrol meant to capture and arrest him?"

Annaichi lifted an eyebrow and looked at Goyo. When Goyo nodded, she scowled, but she turned back to Samin.

"Yes. My orders from Dakimo himself were to find Goyo and have him redouble the hunt."

Samin's eyes narrowed at Goyo. "Hunt?"

"The Incend—" Goyo cut himself off and tipped a conciliatory nod. "Fen Jacin is of interest to many. It is Dakimo's theory that he is of special interest to the *banpair* that have been plaguing Mitsu. It was also his theory that if I found the Incendiary, I would find the *banpair*."

Imara rolled her eyes. "He had *you* looking for him?"

"Well, isn't that *brilliant*." Samin threw his hands up. "So now these *banpair* have the whole city scrambling, and all the gods' minions so fucking confused you can't see the absurdly simple strategy of it all when it's sitting right under your magical noses."

Morin snorted and tried to turn it into a cough. Samin dropped him a blatant wink and looked at Imara, Goyo and Annaichi, one after the other, then shook his head, expression curling into undisguised disgust.

"It's called *running to ground*. You find out where your target would hole up, and you take away his hiding places. You find out what your target cares about, and you take it hostage. You find out who trusts your target, and you corrupt that trust until everyone and his brother is ready to hand the target over to you." He looked at them all again, clearly annoyed, and then at Morin; his mien softened. "They're after him but they don't have him, lad. Your brother is still giving them a hell of a fight."

It looked like Morin was caught between puffing his chest out in pride and crying. "So they don't know where he is, either? Nobody does?"

Strangely, Samin lifted an eyebrow and peered at Goyo, expectant.

Goyo growled then shot a glare at Imara. "I can't be certain. But I nonetheless am. If I'm not very much mistaken, he entered Rihansei's Gate hours ago."

⛩

"Fen... *Jacin*. Bloody hell."

Jacin only closed his eyes, pushed his face into fine, soft sheets, and let his body mold into the mattress. Malick's breath was damp and hot against his cheek and the side of his throat, shirring down to rake shivers from nape to tailbone. Jacin shut out everything but the heat and rhythm, the sticky fusion of skin on skin, the sense of *not alone* he could only seem to catch when Malick pushed his body relentlessly into pleasure so his mind could just ride along and… *fly*.

He loved it this way. Malick preferred it face-to-face—*need to see you, so perfect*—but Jacin didn't always want Malick to see. He liked the way he could almost disappear between sheet and skin, surrounded on all sides, safe in a world made of sensation and ground-out words he could acknowledge and believe for as long as it lasted.

"Fucking love you."

Malick's voice. *Malick's* voice. Torn from shaky breaths and rasped to the cadence of long, agonizing strokes, the pleasure-pain of it too complex to narrow into word or even thought. It just *was*, and Jacin let it attach itself to the fizzy heat swarming under his skin, pooling down into a core that added to the physical weight of body but spiraled every other sense out into a soothing nowhere of mindless *now*. No intrusion of past failures, no fear of future defeats or regrets or weaknesses or losses. Only Malick's body caging Jacin inside desire and slow-rolling passion, Malick's voice and touch giving Jacin's mind a tether to grasp or ignore while he drifted on dusky wings made of cherry blossom petals.

"Tell me, Jacin." A harder shove that hitched Jacin's breath in his chest. "*Say* it."

Jacin stretched his arms out and up, taking hold of the sheets in two tight handfuls. Malick's firm touch followed, rough palms sliding over Jacin's shoulders, up his arms, callused fingers closing over his fisted hands.

"Malick." Jacin tried to push something more coherent through the mess of feeling and could only manage "here, I'm… *fuck*, here, I…" because that usually worked, even when it wasn't really true.

It seemed to be at least close to what Malick needed because he shuddered then shoved harder, picking up his rhythm.

"Yeah," Malick agreed, all thick and gaspy-sounding, ground out, "Yeah," again, and slid his arm around Jacin's torso, pulled his hips from their mindless slow humping of the mattress, and took hold of him.

Most of the time, Jacin didn't even care if he managed to chase down orgasm. It wasn't the point. Even so, Malick always took care of him. Always.

Long, firm strokes sent Jacin's body out to meet his mind in that nowhere of sensual-sensuous ephemera of untainted feeling, the rush of *now* and nothing else, hitting every sense with blinding white. He spread the wings of his mind and coasted toward climax on the push-pull of Malick's body against and within, on the shaky groans wobbling from Jacin's chest, meeting Malick's in a resonant rasp of blissed-out near harmony.

"*Fuck*, yeah." Almost a snarl into the knobs at the top of Jacin's spine. It sent more heat-shudders through him as he lingered in the in-between state of perfection of sensation just before it tipped into too much feeling. "Fucking beautiful," Malick huffed, and Jacin slid right over the edge, groaning when he felt Malick follow, wallowing in the wondrous numb ecstasy that flooded his limbs and blanked his mind.

Yeah. Jacin would agree that everything was pretty beautiful right now.

He kept hold of the feeling—greedy and shameless—as Malick tipped them to the side, somehow melding their sweaty bodies closer, even as he pulled out. Jacin refused to feel the spark of emptiness, merely tangled his limbs agreeably with Malick's as Malick gently tugged and adjusted until even Jacin couldn't tell which parts were his and which were Malick's.

Chill crept in, but Jacin didn't even consider moving to find the covers yet. He only kept sucking in breath until it came a little more steadily and easily, feeling the sluggish prickles against his skin as the sweat cooled and evaporated and stirred the fine hairs all over his body.

"Never would've pegged you for a cuddler."

Jacin could actually hear the small smile in Malick's rough voice. Not mockery, then. Merely one of those chattery little comments Malick couldn't seem to help sometimes, his version of a compliment, though Jacin couldn't figure how.

"I like it." Malick tightened his grip to strengthen his point and sighed. "And it makes sense, I guess."

Jacin frowned at that one, because it certainly didn't make sense to him, but whatever. He didn't need everything about Malick to make sense. And Malick didn't require that Jacin make sense the majority of the time, so it was only fair.

Jacin merely hummed out a low "Hmm" and kept his eyes closed.

Where are we, little Catalyst?

Out of nowhere, but right next to him too. He knew the voice but couldn't place it.

Jacin had a vague feeling it should surprise him, annoy him, maybe even frighten him. It didn't. He was getting pretty tired of the "little" thing, though, but it was far away and… trivial. He took a long breath, greedy for pine-sage-sex.

Someplace… safe.

Had he ever told Malick that? He didn't think he had, hadn't thought he should or could, but now he wished he could make Malick know it. And then he wished he could beat Malick bloody for it, because he'd given it to Jacin, made him want it, and where had that gotten either of them in the end?

That does not matter. All that matters is right now. Everything else falls away but this when and this where. You are safe here, little firebrand?

Jacin nodded, his vision going all glowy with a weird rosy patina that made everything feel warm. *I'm safe here.*

A sigh knocked loose, odd relief, when Malick's hands clamped tightly around Jacin's wrists.

Tether.

Safety.

Jacin was sitting now, with no recollection of having moved, but Malick was a firm heat against his back, so it didn't matter.

Then this shall be our touchstone. Deep breaths now.

Without thought, Jacin obeyed. He pulled in air weighted with the scent of Malick, sinking into the taste and feel of spent passion, the damp heat of the sheets and the firm muscle of Malick's chest settled against his back, the faint drips of condensation and the featherlight skittering of tiny jeweled creatures with sharp little teeth. The warmth of Malick's breath slid over Jacin's ear, down his neck, and over his shoulder.

You feel good, don't you, little Catalyst? You are at peace. You are safe and where you want to be. Every part of your body is relaxed and heavy. You are warm and safe and calm.

Yes. Tears set a light burn to Jacin's eyes, because he felt really fucking good, and he couldn't remember if he'd ever felt like this before.

You want this, don't you? And you want to obey me so that I will let you have it again.

Yes. A sob this time.

Then we are ready. Open your eyes.

Jacin was afraid at first that he wouldn't be able to, that his lids were simply too heavy, and everything would slip away from him because he'd failed this one small thing. But then he was blinking slowly, clearing blurry vision, until he focused on Rihansei, sitting in front of him in nothing more than an elaborate clout. His beard was twisted to lie over a thick shoulder, exposing a wide chest covered in ink and designs that seemed to shift and animate themselves as Jacin watched.

He licked dry lips, managed "What is that?" surprised his raspy voice had so much presence. He'd half-expected it to sound as far away as he felt.

"Only what you need it to be." Rihansei brushed a white hand across his pectoral. "This is what you have been in this incarnation."

Jacin watched, stricken and sickly fascinated as Malick's face appeared, then melted into Joori's then Caidi's then Morin's. He thought perhaps he sobbed when he saw his mother, but she told him *Don't cry, love,* so kind and soothing, so he choked it back.

Everything he'd done, everything he'd been—it spooled out before his eyes in living tattoos over snow-white skin. His father turning from him. Joori risking himself to hang on. Dani teasing him. Malick telling him things he was afraid to believe. Asai telling him things he shouldn't but did.

He wanted to look away, but he couldn't. Like living it all again, but from far away this time, so he could see everything, and how could he see all this with such clarity when his head felt like it was stuffed with sand?

"You loved him."

Not a question, but Jacin nodded and dug his fingers into Malick's arm until Malick tightened his grip.

Every lie Asai had ever told Jacin was playing out in front of him. Every manipulation Jacin had refused to see around the blinders of obsessive adolescent love now paraded before his eyes in too-stark clarity. Cherry blossom petals began to fall, and Jacin let them comfort him as he watched Asai trick him and use him and pretend Jacin mattered to him.

Rihansei held out a hand to catch a few petals. "What do they mean, little Catalyst?"

Jacin wanted to say *Death,* but Caidi's voice came to him as he sat in a carriage outside Yakuli's gates and waited for Fate to find him. "Transience."

"And where shall we go, then?"

Jacin couldn't stop watching the swirls of ink come to life, couldn't stop watching himself make mistake after mistake, couldn't stop watching himself fail as his father went into the fire and Caidi fell and Morin put their mother to rest. Couldn't even look away when he put a knife through Asai's eye then cut his throat, and took perverse comfort through Malick's touch as Jacin cracked Asai's chest and stole the heart he'd tried and failed to win.

"Away."

And all at once he was tumbling, falling, directionless and careening toward… he didn't know, but there was a sense of *Mother* as bright light flared into his eyes and new lungs filled to push out a murky little squall, but hard hands snapped a merciless wrench to his neck and cut it off. An instant of pain as he floated away, and there was a bizarre disappointment to it all, a sense of going back, moving from where he didn't want to be to a place he didn't want to go, and he knew in that moment it would never end. He'd been broken too many times, he'd been broken only a moment before, and he was going to a place where he'd be broken again, and the reprieve had been only the few seconds it had taken a midwife to pull him from the womb and turn his neck.

Falling again, not even fooling himself he was flying, trying to brace himself against… something—something he wanted but something he wouldn't take, *refused*, again and again, because *You've always known perfection is hopeless, even for gods*—and he could almost see what it was, but the petals fell thicker, blotting out everything.

"Ah!" Rihansei's white eyebrows snapped high on his forehead, nascent shock all over his face. "You were not destroyed, then. Merely hidden."

Jacin didn't have time to ask what that meant; he was already plunging into another life, another incarnation, another braid weighting his neck and chaining him to Untouchable. Life after life, slow agony after slow agony, and all of them tethered to the braid that marked him, the voices that made his ruination a thing of shame and pity. *Punishment*, and he knew when that first wave of insanity hit him—every time, every life—he *knew* it was retribution, but he didn't know from whom or for what.

He fell and fell and fell through life after life. Time after time he was born Untouchable, and time after time he went deeply and irrevocably insane. Four times he suffered the slow, excruciating pain of starvation as he raved and mumbled into the dirt from which he was too weak to raise himself. Once he somehow managed to find his way out of the camp and then wandered to the seaside, where he merely kept walking until the water closed over him. Five times he climbed and climbed and climbed, searching, seeking, not knowing for what, reaching for the heavens, and five times he threw himself down or merely fell.

And each time, the cherry blossom petals came, covered him, smothered him, and he knew they were obscuring something he needed to see, but he was just so fucking *relieved* they'd finally come that he couldn't care.

"And that, little Fool," Rihansei said gently, "is the only true failure, I think."

Jacin was weeping, slow trickles stinging his cheeks. He had no answer, so he didn't even try.

Rihansei held another bowl out to him. The tattoos on his arm were swarming and curling into shapes Jacin didn't want to see, so he shut his eyes.

"It will not be so easy as all of that." Soft with sympathy but still implacable as Rihansei put the bowl to Jacin's lips. "The veil of transience is not of your making, but it must be breached if you are to surpass it in this incarnation."

Jacin didn't care. He didn't want to know. He growled and turned his face away, but Malick held him still. Fighting was useless, but Jacin did it anyway, throwing himself against the restraint, not daring to cry out, because if he opened his mouth, Rihansei would pour that drug down his throat and then he'd have no choice.

"Malick. *Don't.* Don't let him."

Malick's hands tightened around Jacin's wrists—hard, like shackles, blood dripping down Jacin's arms—and an army of the tiny lizards stared at him from Rihansei's flanks. Jacin couldn't move. He could only flail ineffectively as Rihansei clamped a hard hand to the hinge of Jacin's jaw, poured the tea down his throat, and then closed a hand over his mouth, pinching his nose 'til Jacin had no choice but to swallow or choke. Two more little lizards had latched on during the struggle, bright little pinpoints of burning acid on Jacin's thigh and his collarbone where their teeth sank in and their venom washed through him.

"You fight too hard against the one thing that might save you." Rihansei sat back and shook his head, twisting his beard back over his shoulder again so the tattoos on his chest were unobscured. "And yet always you fight for a purpose, even if you don't know what that purpose is." He waved at the petals, still falling steadily. "This is not of your making, little lost Fool, this shroud that covers those paths your soul journeys when it is not locked into mortal flesh." He paused, leaned in, and shoved his palm in front of Jacin's nose, the fragrance of the petals cloying and thick, making Jacin's head spin, the scent of jasmine leaking in and making him want to retch. "*This* is what you fight, little Catalyst. It is both what you fear and what you crave. Only when you break through this veil will you understand those things that drive you toward despair and impossibility. Bind yourself to the safety that embraces you, hold to it, for you *will* walk this path."

Jacin heard it as if from miles away. Everything was too fuzzy, too thick. Malick's hands on him were like chains, and yet he didn't want to fight against it anymore.

Safety. Love. *Hope.* Had he ever known what hope was?

"I want to." Wobbly, and thick with tears that should be humiliating but weren't. "So badly. I want… I…"

"You have no idea what you want."

It echoed, then curled around him, suffocating.

You have no idea what you want, little Ghost. You need your beishin to show you.

I don't.

"No, you do not." Rihansei. Forceful but improbably gentle too. "When you believe that fully, perhaps then you will learn to reach for those things you both want and need. Until then, you will not be Fate's Incendiary, but merely the tool of any who offer the lies you want to hear."

"Let me go." Jacin tugged at the chains—no, at Malick's grip—but he hardly even managed a weak yank. "Please. I don't want—"

"You are a dangerous wild card. And I do not think you really want to be let go." Rihansei swept a hand over his chest, stirring ink and lines and swirls. "Hold to your safety. When you leave my Gate, you will be Fate's Incendiary, for good or ill, and you will have the resources within to keep that which you would have for yourself." He gripped Jacin's hand in a comforting hold and waved again at the thick fall of petals. "This obscures you from yourself. You will push it aside and we will look—together. No more dallying in useless lives. All the way back to the beginning now. Say yes, little Catalyst."

All the way back to the beginning.

Jacin tried to resist. Failed completely.

"Yes."

As if the answer had willed it or perhaps given permission Jacin didn't really want to give, Rihansei's tattoos swirled thicker, taking on the shapes of petals, a heavy curtain of them that grew thinner by infinitesimal degrees. And even as they revealed things that made him want to howl and shriek and weep, Jacin couldn't look away.

⛩

Where are we?

He wasn't sure. Nothing would take on shapes through the flurry of petals, and the scent of jasmine kept throwing him and making him flinch.

Who are you here, little Catalyst?

He knew this one. Almost. *Catalyst*—not what he was used to being called, but it tumbled… something. Right at the edge of everything.

Brittle. Like that last handhold astride the rim of the abyss. *Untouchable.* Past lives and loves and betrayals and griefs.

Except.

They were far away. Something he hadn't lived yet. They faded almost as soon as he allowed them to flitter over his consciousness.

Shaking, he reached out through the shroud of falling petals, and pushed it aside like a solid skein of fabric.

Tell me who you are here.

It's not that easy. There is not merely one answer.

Here, he was Incendiary. Here, he was Fate's creation, Fate's tool, his soul bound to his own will, and his will bound by Fate.

Here, he'd known Daichi, a world with no moons, only the sister suns, Tonyai and Tompai, in a sky too empty for its clots of stars.

The Bloody Fist, some call me.

You are a killer, little Catalyst?

No. Yes. Sometimes.

He'd carried a sword. No, two of them. Warrior's weapons. Weapons of honor, not those of a prowling assassin.

You are a soldier, then?

A soldier for Fate, until the One God, Mii-daichiseyh, decided all Incendiary would be more useful tools under his own rule. It was not a kind rule. The Incendiary had always been a means to Fate's whim, but now they were—

A slave. For a very long while. We all are.

Whose slave are you?

Mii-daichiseyh. He took the Incendiary from Fate's hand. And then he took the maijin. We're supposed to be advocates for mortals. All of us. But now we can't be. He won't let us.

Those mortals who would not obey him were tortured then sacrificed at his Gate, cast down into its murky depths where their mortal remains would forever imprison their spirits, a well of suffering from which Mii-daichiseyh fed and grew his power. Neither maijin nor Incendiary was immune to such fortune; many were sacrificed in Mii-daichiseyh's purge. Even his own once-faithful magicians fled from him then.

Fate did not approve. But she was a fickle thing. She saw the lot the arrogant god was making for himself, and left the wheels to turn.

She left us to him. She didn't save us.

Nor did she free the souls of the Incendiary to their own wills. Those she kept for herself, and left the Incendiary to balance her desires against the commands of the god to whom she'd abandoned them.

Mii-daichiseyh stole you, then.

Yes. Claimed us as his "children."

And set them to their labors with an iron fist, either too proud or too power-mad to understand that what he asked of the Incendiary, Fate would eventually answer in her own ways.

But you knew she had a plan, Fate.

She always does. We began to see what it might be when Mii-daichiseyh decided we weren't enough, we weren't of him, so he wanted children in truth.

He'd looked to the sister suns, and as with all things beneath Mii-daichiseyh's eye, he took of them what he wished. And as with all beings that choose to usurp Fate, Mii-daichiseyh was delivered more than he'd fancied.

Six children Mii-daichiseyh got on Tonyai and Tompai, and then six children rose up against their sire. There was war in the heavens for time unknown.

And what did the Incendiary and maijin do in the War Times?

We tended to the mortal concerns of Daichi and waited to see whom we would serve when it was all over. And we watched.

It had been Wolf who had conspired, who had led, and it had been Wolf who had called to the Incendiary and the maijin, broken them from Mii-Daichiseyh's chokehold and, for the first time ever, offered them a choice. The Incendiary had not been made to have choice; they had been made to serve Fate. They had been made to want what Fate wanted. Their wants were now their own, and then their wants were their gods', as one after the other, the Incendiary took oath.

And to whom did you swear?

I… I didn't.

One Incendiary hesitated; one Incendiary paused to consider this new choice carefully. Fate had not released the Incendiary, merely put them aside—they were still her creatures. Everything the Incendiary did, no matter how seemingly insignificant, had a price, a counteractive balance. Choice or no, blindly obeying a god could be catastrophic in too many ways.

You did not trust the gods?

Well, no, not really, but… it was more than that. I'd never had choice before; I wanted to be sure.

Wooed by gods, courted almost, though it was Wolf and Raven who stood first in this new world of choice. Bear's strict justice was an almost perfect balance to Dragon's brutal practicality; Snake's whimsical cruelty was a seamless counterpoint to Owl's indulgent compassion. But Wolf and Raven seemed to have all those things within themselves—cruel and kind, tolerant and cold-blooded, cunning and benevolent.

It had been Wolf who had gathered the maijin to the cause of the new gods, and it had been Raven who had created the first *Temshiel*—servants of the new gods to complement and balance the servants of the old.

Wolf's very nature had been… persuasive. His cool calculations, his clever strategies against his sire, his smooth promises of justice for the mortals over whom the Incendiary watched, and his sheer *power* in battle…

It appealed?

Oh, yes. It appealed very much.

And the serene, ice-blue eyes that looked upon this last undecided Incendiary with gentle lust… that appealed, as well. He'd succumbed. Once and then twice, though words of love would not fall on his ear, over his weary heart, and he had wanted it.

He said I was not his to love. Not yet. That a promise to me was a promise to Fate, and he would not offer one he might one day be compelled to break.

Wise, though perhaps somewhat cruel.

Cruelty is the way of it with gods. It hurt, perhaps, but I thought it kind at the time.

To refuse you?

To let me choose.

Because *not yet* was *not enough.* For the first time ever, he knew want. He knew need. He knew *impatience.* He was there when the first mortal feet walked Daichi, had loved them all, yet they could not love him; championing mortals did not necessarily mean pleasing *people*, and fear was not love.

It was a heady, compelling thing, to hold the eye of a god, but he'd known love only from the outside. He wanted more.

And you found it in another.

Yes, I… Yes.

Black-haired and black-eyed, fiery and strong and fierce and beautiful. The Six gods gathered in mortal forms on mortal planes to wrest Mii-daichiseyh's dominion from him, and Raven had been stunningly ferocious.

He seduced you?

He took my heart like it was a spoil of war. I offered it and he took it.

But you loved Wolf first.

Wolf was just and direct, calculatingly compassionate, but just as magnificent in his ruthlessness as his brother.

He would have me but he would not love me. He would not take from me what I wanted to give.

And Raven would?

Raven was brutal and seductively terrifying, righteous passion wrapped in darkling beauty like black ice on spring leaves.

Raven took all I handed him. I would die for him. I did die for him.

Twice, while the long, hellish war raged through the mortal world.

You returned to him when you were reborn?

Incendiary are not reborn; we simply… come back. And when I was set back on my mortal feet, I used them to run to him.

And he loved you for it?

…Maybe. My kind were not meant for the love of another. We are meant to love, not be *loved. But that could not stop me from wanting it. So I watched for it very carefully.*

Waiting. Hoping. Willing to die again and again for a mere glimpse of it in black eyes.

It was when I built the shrine to the Six that Raven looked on me for the first time with what I knew for love.

The crude little shrine had meted out the first bit of real damage to Mii-daichiseyh's spirit, the fissure that opened the way to cracks and breaks as the battles wore on.

Why a shrine?

Because mortals must believe in a god for a god to exist. Because the One feeds on the fear he cultivates, but the Six take after their mothers—they thrive on the love of their people. They need it like air. The prayers of the people are as strength for the Six. If people prayed to the Six instead of the One, they would grow and he would wither. I preached of the new gods to the mortals of Daichi, and sent the Temshiel *and maijin to do the same.*

And then stood witness as the *Temshiel* gathered great slabs of marble from Tougei to erect the first temples to stand at the edge of the city of Mitsu in Tambalon, their birthplace. No shrine stood for Mii-daichiseyh, and no temple. And as the belief and faith in Mii-daichiseyh dwindled in the mortal planes, so too did his power in the divine ones. He diminished as his children grew in strength.

The raising of the remains from the depths of the Gate was the final stroke. Each grisly corpse was removed and given the respect of a proper pyre, their souls released in what would then become the Shrine of the Dead.

And then the Six gave the One the only fate he deserved: they cast him through his own Gate and set his once-faithful to keep it. The Gatekeepers would never again speak the name of Mii-daichiseyh—they would not give him that power—but they kept the testimony of his treachery and recorded the history of the world in swirls of ink sunk into their skin.

And then you took oath?

Fate never released the Incendiary. I was still servant to her, as always I have been, and Fate must be considered when set to the tasks of the gods. My heart still could not choose between Raven and Wolf, so I asked of them the privilege of refusal if their commands left me in conflict with what I am.

Raven readily promised to have a care what he asked of his Incendiary; Wolf once more refused to offer the same. Raven gave of his god's heart; Wolf's remained his own.

No other Incendiary had done such a thing?

I'm not certain they knew they could. They were younger than I. They were not as… weary. Perhaps they trusted more than they should have. I needed the promise. I wanted the love the promise implied.

Some of the Incendiary had been destroyed. Some had destroyed themselves, committing themselves to the forever-and-ever nothing of earth instead of the fire that would only release them to renewed mortality. A string of mortal lives, one after the other after the other, was not a thing easily survived. And some had not fared well with their new choices.

He had survived. He had *thrived*. He had a reason. And even when the Six gods triumphed and climbed back to their heavens to govern from their moons, his reason remained.

Not all Incendiary could claim a god as their lover in the in-between when mortal life blurred into death and then into mortal life again. Not all Incendiary could catch the faintest whiff of jasmine and know their god was with them, watching, approving, loving. Not all Incendiary owned their god's true name, could whisper it in the depths of loneliness when mortality took on a physical weight, and expect an answer.

And what is that name?

I… I can't tell you.

Even now?

Even now.

Because it is forbidden?

Because it… hurts.

Ah. I see. Then tell me yours.

He wouldn't weep here. He wouldn't buckle. He'd made his choices.

His hands moved, feeling the grips around his wrists, tugging, just for the comfort of knowing that he was held, bound, *safe*, and couldn't tug *away*.

Hitsuke. Here, I am Hitsuke.

2

"Take them somewhere safe," Goyo told Imara, who glared back at him with a pinched mouth and a look that said *No shit*. Goyo grinned at her for no other reason than because he knew it would piss her off. He turned to Samin and made sure Naro-yi was listening too.

"They're not through. They mean to get what they want, and I doubt they'll stop 'til they do." He peered at Naro-yi. "Do you know any of the protections against old magic?" Naro-yi's eyebrow went up, but he nodded. Goyo blew out a relieved breath. "Use them."

"Why?" Samin hadn't stopped scowling, and distrust was all but shooting from his pores. "What kind of *old magic*, and what does it—?"

"If I could pause and tell you everything I know and everything I suspect, I would." It was true, but it simply wasn't possible right now. Goyo had accepted a responsibility in the Patrol, and right now, the Patrol was needed elsewhere. He laid a hand to Samin's shoulder and peered intently at Naro-yi. "Those of the Patrol who are here, I leave you as escort and guard. Where do you intend to go?"

Naro-yi exchanged a glance with Samin. "Kamen's house."

Goyo pursed his mouth unhappily, but—"I suppose it's as safe as anywhere else."

He would've preferred to send them to a temple. Any temple. But since both Wolf's and Owl's had been attacked tonight, the feelings of safety and homecoming he'd always associated with Snake's temple were somehow not quite so warm and fuzzy.

Annoyed and impatient both, Goyo shot a glance around to make sure Imara was otherwise occupied with directing two of the Patrol to carry Joori and Shig. He curled his lip before he could help it. The motivations were understandable, but Imara's easy lie still sat wrong with him. Perhaps the darts hadn't contained poison in the immediately deadly sense, but it had been poison nonetheless, and the circumstances would have been quite a lot more dire had Imara not been right there and had she not been half the healer Goyo had to admit she was.

There was no way to know, of course, what those creatures had intended for the Fen brothers and Shig, but the imposter's threats led all too easily to speculation on a few probabilities. Goyo could easily imagine Fen Jacin being presented with his poisoned brothers only to be offered the antidote with all kinds of conditions.

Damn it, Goyo really needed to know what these *banpair* wanted. Besides the Incendiary. Because the Incendiary was obviously not the end goal, but a stepping stone to it. And if the servants of all the other gods would stop to pay even a little bit of attention, they all might twig to the leverage that the *banpair* had already recognized. As it was, Goyo didn't think it was going to take long before all of Kamen's mortals ended up in more danger than even Kamen could have gotten them out of.

With a sigh and a grimace, Goyo leaned in close to Naro-yi. "You have Owl's-own to rely upon. Use them. Imara has no doubt already called in some of Wolf's." He looked again at Imara, just to make sure Naro-yi got the point, then waved to encompass all of Kamen's mortals. "These are not matters for the gods. These matters are what maijin were made for. I've a feeling I know how the next day or so will play out, and exactly who I'll be instructed to hunt down when next I see Dakimo." He paused, reluctant. "Likely by any means necessary."

"You think they're going to send you after Fen." Samin's hands clenched into very obvious fists. "You think they'll order you to—?"

"Not yet." Goyo looked away. "But… possibly soon. And just before I receive that order, I'll likely receive another to take the Incendiary's companions into protective custody." He turned back to Samin. "And I'm not certain the motives behind it will be any more honorable than those of these *banpair.*"

Samin didn't say anything this time, but his jaw clenched so hard Goyo thought he might shatter some teeth.

"The Incendiary is the business of the gods." Goyo put out a hand. "But Fen Jacin is not. And neither are his brothers."

"What exactly are you saying? I'm not good at all this manipulation shit. I need someone to speak plainly, damn it!"

"He is saying…"

Naro-yi paused to eye Goyo with a bit of a spark that yesterday Goyo would have thought amusement; after what he'd seen tonight, he thought maybe it had been cunning all along and Naro-yi was just really bloody good at playing the role he'd chosen. A small smile ticced at the corner of Naro-yi's mouth.

"He is saying the wheels of power in Mitsu will soon be turning, and not in our favor." Naro-yi pierced Goyo with a gaze so sharp Goyo would never again doubt Naro-yi knew exactly what he was doing at all times. "He is saying that while they are all busy looking for the Incendiary, perhaps it would be in our interests to look for Fen Jacin."

"And to keep your own counsel," Goyo added. "Imara is Wolf's and will do what she must in Wolf's interests, and she *will* protect you, even if it means she's sent to spirit for it. But the interests of the gods don't always—"

"Yeah, yeah." Samin waved it away, angry and impatient. "You think I hadn't got that by now?" He shook his head. "All right. I suppose I should thank you, and I do. I doubt I would've got them all out of here tonight, had it not been for..." He trailed off and his jaw tightened again. "Anyway. Thank you. And don't worry—whatever we decide to do next, we'll be sure to utterly deceive you about our intentions, and lie to you and everyone else about whatever we feel like, right to your faces."

Goyo grinned. "That's all I ask." He bowed low, then he left them all to Imara and headed for the temples.

Owl's temple was still abuzz when he got there, priests and priestesses and initiates all flapping around and eager to tell Goyo all about what had transpired. Not much, by what he could gather. Someone who looked like a young Jin man had shown up, waved some knives around, and made sure to announce that his name was Fen Jacin-rei before breaking a few things and leaving. Wolf's temple was almost the same story. Almost.

"He does not call himself so." Xari jutted her chin, still bristling from the affront of the assault. "No one has called him so since the Ancestors went home. This creature who pretends to be the Incendiary knows much, but does not know all." She tapped a fingertip to her temple. "He does not know what goes on in the Incendiary's head, only in the heads of those around him. What I saw tonight was an actor trying to play the role of another's interpretation of Fen Jacin. If we had seen the things Fen Jacin sees when he looks at himself, it would have been a much different performance."

Goyo shrugged agreement. "His brother said as much."

"Aye, his brothers would know. Even if they don't. The cards are the thing."

Gesturing for Goyo to follow after her, Xari spun on her heel, leading him into a small open-aired antechamber that let out onto the back gardens of the temple. Grim-faced, Xari waved Goyo to a seat at a small table draped with colorful scarves and centered with a fist-sized crystal quartz seeing stone, its ghost-light casting uncanny shadows that seemed to twist and move out the corner of Goyo's eye. Absently, Xari scratched at the flaking paint of her wolf's mask before taking a large deck of cards from an ancient-looking oak casket and setting them firmly between her palms. She closed her eyes, whispered things Goyo didn't hear clearly and didn't understand anyway, before she kissed the deck and laid it between them.

"I was put to seeking Asai's spirit. To ensure he was not haunting the Incendiary."

"I'd heard he—"

Xari waved it off impatiently. "A futile task. I knew before I set myself to it, but set myself to it I did, nonetheless. I must humble myself for my new god." Her mouth gave a slight twist but that was all. "I am old, Snake's-own. I knew Incendiary. And I knew the Untouchable when the Incendiary was still hidden inside him. Any ghosts that haunt such as him must come from within himself. It was never Asai." She held up her hand when Goyo opened his mouth. "I checked, because it was asked of me. I am sure. And I can't help wondering now—if an imposter could play the Incendiary, why not play Asai, as well? Why not resurrect the ghost of the beishin to confuse and distract the once-apprentice?" She paused to let Goyo take this in then shook her head. "But that is not why I have brought you here."

Goyo couldn't help his frown. "Then why?"

"Because there *is* something that dogs the Incendiary." Xari leaned over the table, the glow of the stone catching at the lines and curves of paint on her face and shifting them, sharpening them. "The art of Seeing is an old one. It is one part magic and a thousand parts learning, observing, listening, knowing. A million parts. Infinite. Even one with no magic could cast your fate for you, did they know the cards well enough and respect the intricacies of the messages they speak." She fanned out the deck facedown. "Clear your mind, Snake's-own. Sweep away the detritus and focus your thoughts on what you seek. Owl rises. It is by her grace we shall glimpse Fate's two faces."

Goyo peered at Xari curiously for a moment, then did as she instructed. He shut his eyes and tried to concentrate on nothing but what he knew of Fen Jacin. He didn't know how long he sat there in the relative dark with Xari, but when she was apparently satisfied, she tapped the back of his hand.

"Choose."

Goyo did.

Xari flipped the card over. "The Fool." She laid it faceup beside the rest of the deck with a nod, though it seemed more in rue than satisfaction. "You see? Did I not tell you?"

"Uh." Goyo couldn't come with anything to say. Because he really didn't think she had.

Xari huffed. "You cannot mistake the Fool for the simpleton most make of him. The secrets of the world rest with him, only he remembers them not and knows not how to use them." She shook her head with a pinch of her lips. "No fault to you, for I myself mistook him for the minor Fool when first I read for Kamen. I did not see the crucial Fool beneath the mask of Untouchable."

Before Goyo could ask her to clarify, Xari was poking at his hand again.

"Choose another."

Again, Goyo did, and again, Xari nodded.

"The Hawk Priest. Again." Xari's teeth set tight as she laid the card beside the Fool. "Each time, he chases the Fool, and each time, his very presence clouds his motives."

Mouth set, she laid a hand to the stone, its light seeping between her fingers before she drew them back and barely touched a swirl to its surface with the tip of a nail. Goyo could scarcely make out a smoky curl within the eerie light of the stone, but that was all. Whatever Xari saw obviously frustrated her.

"Another."

A little impatient but terribly intrigued, Goyo chose another card.

This time, Xari sighed as she laid it crosswise astride the Fool and the Hawk Priest.

"The Sorcerer. Kamen and his stubborn—" She cut herself off then *tsked* and tapped at the Hawk Priest's card. "He should not be here. He *was not* here when last I read the cards for Kamen. And now he comes between Kamen and that which Kamen wants and what he will not take."

Goyo blinked. "Am I supposed to know what any of this means?"

"He is the source of the power the Sorcerer must wield, and yet he cannot be, for the Sorcerer's power comes from the gods. Only by taking this power to his hand can the Sorcerer remove the Hawk Priest from between himself and the Fool—to *save* the Fool—but a child of the gods cannot possess power that is *not* of the gods."

Goyo stared.

Xari stared back. When it became clear Goyo wasn't following, she tapped the Hawk Priest's card again, more impatiently this time.

"*This* is who you seek. *This* is the trickster who would put down the Sorcerer before the Sorcerer has even donned his mantle. *This* is the imposter who would steal the Incendiary from Wolf's hand."

This time, Goyo frowned. Well, terrific. All he had to do was comb the streets of Mitsu until he found a man walking around with a hawk's head and wearing a priest's robes.

"This doesn't help me, Xari." Goyo said it as patiently and as kindly as he could. "Unless you can give me a name and a place to look, I can't—"

"Do you not see?" Xari's dark eyes were avid in her flaking wolf mask, her posture tense. "A ruler, or one who would be one. A father figure, or one who would pretend. One who holds power in his hands, but who has been denied such and so cannot. And yet he does." She paused, and when Goyo only kept staring, she leaned in. "You seek one who wields a power not of the gods."

This time, it clicked. "Old magic."

"Old magic." Xari sat back. "It cannot be touched with the magic of the Six. And yet." She picked up the Sorcerer's card and waved it between them.

"Kamen?" When Xari merely shrugged, Goyo's teeth set tight. "Except he's not here." Which just figured.

"No." Xari's sly smile cracked the paint along her cheeks. "Not yet."

"Do you know when?"

"No." Xari toyed with the Sorcerer's card, tapping at the Hawk Priest with it as though taunting. "But I've no doubt it will be sooner than we expect."

"*Now* is sooner than we expect, Xari." And as much as Goyo hated to admit it, *now* would be bloody helpful.

"True. And did the Incendiary have great and powerful need for his Sorcerer, I've no doubt the Sorcerer would answer the call." Xari leaned in, eyes glittering in the light from the stone. "The Sorcerer heeds always the call of the Incendiary, but it is Kamen who will take the world between his teeth for the Fool. If the Fool can admit his need and send out the call, Kamen will move the heavens to heed it."

Goyo's eyes narrowed. "What does that—?"

"Where the bloody *hell* is Imara?"

Goyo and Xari both turned startled glances to the slim figure silhouetted by the moonlight streaming down into the gardens behind them. Muddy and bedraggled, hair awry and face pulled down into a wealth of affronted hostility. Her eyes kept going from hazel to cat-slit yellow, a habit she'd never learned to control when angry. And she looked *very* angry, though Goyo supposed he was willing to give her the benefit of the doubt on this one—she looked like she'd been through a war.

"Leu," said Goyo slowly, "I was looking for you."

"Yeah?" Leu's mouth twisted into a fiery scowl. "So was I."

Goyo exchanged a look with Xari. He hoped he was getting the *She's yours, you do it* across without much trouble.

He must've been, because Xari turned an appraising gaze back on Leu. "What happened, child?"

"Rihansei." It was shoved out between Leu's teeth. "Rihansei happened. That bastard sent me all the way to bloody Haro, clear on the other side of Tambalon. You have no idea what I went through to get back here."

Considering her appearance, Goyo was almost afraid to guess. He sighed and sat back in his chair. This was going to take a while.

⛩

"Dakimo. Honestly, *please* stop fussing. I'm *fine*."

Dakimo pursed his mouth in likely pretty obvious skepticism, but said nothing. He did, however, stop "fussing," but it was… difficult. Emika had the benefit of having received excellent healing care from one of Wolf's priests last night, called from his duties at the temple, but Dakimo would have much preferred Imara. Imara, however—to Dakimo's sincere irritation—had either not received his order, or had and chosen to ignore it. The morning was a distant blur, afternoon had quickly faded into evening, and Imara had yet to show her face.

There would be words when next Dakimo saw her. Lots of them.

"You're *better*." Dakimo steered Emika away from her work and toward the cushions, pushing several together and hoping she wouldn't notice he was arranging a makeshift pallet rather than a more comfortable work area. "You're not *fine*."

Not yet. Wolf willing, she would be, but the Incendiary's knives had been long and precise.

Dakimo peered through the window at the setting suns, realized they'd missed supper, and sighed.

Last night had been… well. *Bad* sounded like such a soft word, but there wasn't a better one, at least not one Dakimo could think of in his current exhausted state. But yes—bad. The attacks had been sporadic, but shocking in their intent. Wolf's temple and Owl's had both been breached, their wards as ineffective in keeping the intruders at bay as Dakimo's had been in keeping the Incendiary from...

It *still* infuriated him. His hand clenched into a fist before he could stop it.

"You're obsessing again." Emika winced only a little as Dakimo helped her lower herself to the plump cushions. When he pulled away to gather a few more, Emika reached out with an elegant hand and set it on Dakimo's sleeve. "Stay here with me." With a soft smile, she moved her legs aside to give him room. "Please."

Dakimo sighed. "I have—"

"I know. But you've been at it all night, all day, and now it's going on all night again. Even immortals need to sleep, Dakimo. And... I miss you."

Emika transferred the hold from Dakimo's sleeve to his hand, wrapping her fingers around his and squeezing gently. The way she turned her wrist, Dakimo could hardly see the angry pink line where only last night a long slice had spilled her mortal blood all over the expensive imported carpets beneath the couches in the corner. The remaining evidence of the too-deep stab wound just below her ribs was, thankfully, covered beneath the silky formal robes of her office. If Dakimo hadn't charged precisely when the Incendiary had braced himself for a sideways slice-and-gut—

"Stay," Emika repeated, soft and fond.

He wasn't going to deny her. They both knew it.

Dakimo let himself settle beside her with a weary huff. It had been a long, difficult night and then a longer, more difficult day. And he had no illusions that any of it was over.

Where the *hell* was Imara? And Goyo, while he was at it.

"The word is it was not the Incendiary." Emika was watching Dakimo with affection as she said it, but her gaze was as sharp as it had ever been, assessing.

Dakimo frowned. "So I hear."

It didn't make anything better. And strangely, it didn't change the anger and near-hatred Dakimo felt for the Incendiary he'd never even met. Duped and used, perhaps, but it had been the Incendiary's face that had sneered as Dakimo had tried to deflect the attack with magic; it had been the Incendiary's eyes that had mocked as Emika fell.

Typical Temshiel, *letting those who love you take the blow for you. Obedient whelp of your dog-god.*

The scorn in that rusty voice resonated. The words themselves... well, they rang a little too true. Which was why they hurt.

"Dakimo."

Emika waited until Dakimo met her gaze then took his hand again. He couldn't help looking down; couldn't help staring at the dark, swirling stains of henna that had done no good.

"It was not your fault."

These words hurt too. The fact that she meant them kindly and sincerely only cut more deeply.

He'd been too slow. He'd relied too heavily on magic. The Incen—the imposter had used nothing but physical force, and still, he'd almost managed to kill Emika. Would've killed Dakimo had Emika not thought quickly and taken a ceremonial sword from the wall, thrown it to Dakimo, for which the imposter had taken his "revenge" upon Emika.

Wolf chose his own from the mortal ranks so they could deal with the world on mortal terms and never forget what it meant to be mortal, chose them to serve as the hand of their god. Because a god could never really understand mortal concerns from inside a mortal's heart.

Dakimo had forgotten. Dakimo had settled too long in the skin of *Temshiel*, and had grown arrogant in his conceit that he was better. Dakimo had watched Kamen do Wolf's work from mortal trenches— sometimes elbow-deep in the blood Wolf bid him spill—and had thought him… perhaps not entirely foolish, but… misguided. Brutal. Cocky.

With a sigh that was several parts regret and several parts resolve, Dakimo traced a spiraling pattern over the spells on the back of Emika's delicately boned hand with the tip of his finger. "I think perhaps—"

He'd been waiting rather impatiently for the stir at the edges of his wards, and yet when it finally came, rather than relieve him, it annoyed him. Their timing could have been much better.

"Imara and Goyo have arrived." Dakimo patted at Emika's hand, slipping a kiss to her silvered temple before hauling himself up from the cushions. "Please," he added with a staying gesture when Emika moved to follow, "for me."

With an indulgent smile and a roll of her eyes, Emika sat back and peered at Dakimo with an *all right, fine, you win this time* look. Dakimo smiled back and allowed a breach in the protections to let Imara and Goyo through.

Any other time, the small not-quite-wrestling-match at the door to see who got through first would have been comical. Now, it was merely another frustration. The smirk Goyo aimed at Dakimo as he pulled back abruptly and let Imara stumble through only added to the headache lying in wait at the base of Dakimo's skull.

To her credit, Imara went directly to Emika, smiling warmly and setting right to work on reinforcing and enhancing the healing Cende had dispensed last night. Dakimo held back the relieved sigh. It wasn't that Cende wasn't extraordinary at what he did—it was only that Imara was better.

Goyo made a beeline for Dakimo. "Kamen's mortals are all as safe as we could make them. After last night, we thought it best to take as many precautions as possible. We apologize for the delay." He shrugged. "Not that it will do much good, but Imara and Naro-yi have warded up Kamen's house. Naro-yi remains to guard, and I left several of the Patrol, as well. Imara called as many as Wolf's temple could spare. And there is one called Kel Saminil who seems quite inspired to keep his companions in one piece. If there is any trouble there, I imagine Samin will be the most effective and motivated in thwarting it." He looked almost fond, then he peered at Dakimo sharply. "They are understandably concerned for Fen Jacin. They wish to venture out to look for him. Annaichi of Bear suggested we take them into custody to… keep them safe." Goyo's mouth twisted in obvious disagreement, then an eyebrow went up. "I assumed you would not approve."

Dakimo pressed his lips together. "And why would I not?"

"I know the brothers have been marked, Dakimo." Goyo stared intently, as though expecting Dakimo to deny it.

Dakimo merely raised his eyebrows. "I would be surprised if you didn't. Wolf has, after all, made it obvious to any who might look. It was not something I deliberately kept from you."

"Like Kamen's ring, you mean?"

Ah. Dakimo grimaced. That bloody ring was going to be the end of him. He wished Kamen had choked on it. And not merely because it was already making things difficult and would likely make them more difficult as time went on—if there was even any time left. More because a probably insane Incendiary was walking around with the power of the strongest *Temshiel* in existence on his finger, and it seemed like only blind luck so far had prevented these *banpair* from getting what they were after.

And if that happened…

Well, Dakimo didn't know. Because he still didn't know what these bloody creatures *wanted*, damn it.

"That was… perhaps ill-advised," he admitted. "As circumstances now stand, I should have told you. As circumstances stood at the time, and with the little I foresaw, it was a necessary omission. I am sorry if you were offended."

Goyo accepted it warily. "And I am sorry if what I mean to say next offends you." He shot a look at Imara, but she was still in quiet conversation with a more relaxed-looking Emika and at least pretending not to listen. "The lines are growing clearer, and the gods are allying as expected. Snake, Dragon and Bear still wait and watch, but the attack of Raven's *Temshiel* on the Incendiary cleared all doubt as to Raven's intentions. Kamen's ring may well change all of that. I believe the only thing keeping all the gods besides yours from declaring themselves decisively against the Incendiary is the fact that he doesn't know how to use it."

"Bear would not—"

"I've no intention of debating the dubious morality of any of this with you." Goyo's gaze was not hostile, but determined. "Such matters are not for me, and I'm well rid of them. My concern is for the mortals who will pay the price when immortal battles are waged around them. And these mortals already stand to lose much more than any of us when all of this has been... settled. If the Incendiary lives through it, I will be very much surprised. I don't wish to find his kin's fingers pointed at me when the mourning begins, not when interference is so clearly unnecessary and too full of risk." He stepped in, cut a quick pointed glance to Emika, then lowered his voice to soft, compassionate tones. "'So many of us lose our conscience when we lose our mortality.'" A direct quote of Dakimo's own words only days ago. "Is your conscience still intact, Dakimo of Wolf?"

Outrage at the cheap shot of the implication swept through Dakimo first. Then guilt. And then, finally, resignation.

A moment ago, he might have ordered Kamen's mortals taken into custody for their protection. Except.

What had the best protection Dakimo had to offer done for the one mortal he would protect above all?

"The brothers are marked. They must be protected."

"They are." Goyo spread his hands as though in entreaty. "Leave the Incendiary's family alone, Dakimo."

Dakimo rubbed at his brow, the headache fully blossomed now, winding tendrils behind his eyes. His sigh was weary and resigned.

"I shall consider it. Circumstances may well force my hand to a different course, and I will promise nothing. Kamen's mortals may remain as they are, behind Imara's wards and under Naro-yi's eye. For now." Dakimo pointed a severe look at Goyo. "So long as I've your word they are protected and they will remain out of the way."

"Of what?"

"Of—" Dakimo almost answered sharply, but the question didn't seem to have been meant facetiously. "Of anything that might put them in further danger."

He supposed that was all-encompassing enough. And keeping them out of danger meant keeping them out of the way and in one place, where he could collect them quickly if he needed to. Apparently, the best way to control the Incendiary was to control his brothers; Dakimo refused to rule out any useful tool right now, no matter the aspersions on his supposed lack of morality. Wolf wanted the Incendiary saved, and a bit of ruthlessness might turn out to be necessary to do it.

He considered telling Goyo exactly who this Incendiary really was. Perhaps it would give Goyo that extra bit of incentive and drive to find Fen Jacin. Or perhaps Goyo would get it into his head that a mercy killing was in order, with or without his god's permission. Dakimo was not prepared to take that chance. Not until he was convinced the Incendiary was unsalvageable.

"If they…" Dakimo hesitated, shoulders slumping. "Just keep them out of the way. It will be all we can do to keep the citizenry safe tomorrow when the festival begins."

Both of Goyo's eyebrows went up. "I rather thought we might… downplay the festival, considering."

"*We* would."

Dakimo sent a somewhat irritated glance over at Emika, still lying obediently on her cushions and speaking softly with Imara, but he couldn't maintain the ill will for long. Death had sidled all too close last night. He shook his head and turned back to Goyo.

"The governor does not wish to allow these creatures to prevent the people from celebrating their gods. She would not see Owl slighted upon her rising. I share your concern, but I'm afraid she will not be moved. She is… devout.

"Wolf does not wish it, either, and before you ask, I have no idea why. I can only suppose that whatever is to come will happen then, and in full view of those who come to celebrate Owl's rising. The temples have all been alerted, for whatever good it will do, but the Patrol will no doubt bear the brunt of the required vigilance, and we don't need Kamen's mortals looking for trouble."

Goyo waved it away. "Fen Joori and Kojoi Shig were both still unconscious when I came to collect Imara this afternoon. Though, I suppose 'asleep' might be more like it by now. Imara says they will likely remain so for hours yet."

"So, it was not poison?"

"It was." Most of Imara's attention was on Emika, where it should be, but she'd clearly been listening. "But not meant to kill. As it was, it was hell to alter it, and even then I couldn't lift it entirely. They'll sleep through the day, at least, and probably into the morning." She peered up at Dakimo, hands still on Emika. "If it had been allowed to run its course, it likely would have simulated death, which I gather might well have been the point. The one masquerading as the Incendiary said as much. It seems his intention was to present the 'bodies' to the Incendiary and convince the Incendiary he was the one who'd killed them." She shrugged and turned back to Emika. "What purpose he had in mind for after, I can't guess."

"Those poor children." Emika's eyes were at half-mast, but still troubled. "That poor young man." Her gaze met Dakimo's. "I can't even imagine."

Neither could Dakimo. It was bad enough someone he cared for had been hurt because of him, but to be maneuvered into believing he'd done the deed himself? Unthinkable.

Silence fell for a moment as Dakimo held Emika's gaze.

Eventually, Goyo awkwardly cleared his throat. "Imara tells me Kojoi Shig is Sensitive. I saw evidence of it myself at Rihansei's. And when the imposter tried to take Fen Joori and Fen Morin last night, he also tried to take Kojoi Shig." Goyo huffed, clearly uncomfortable, before going on. "Old magic, Dakimo. We were right. Rihansei knows something, and whatever it is, it has to do with old magic. I spent rather a long time with Xari last night, and she confirms it. The *banpair* are collecting those who have old magic, and ours is simply not strong enough to thwart it."

Dakimo's glance skimmed over to where Emika was sliding off into a doze. He was guiltily glad. These matters were looking more and more like stuff of the gods, rather than the concerns of Tambalon's government.

"Xari thinks only Kamen will be able to match the power of these creatures." Goyo was seemingly unaware of the grimace the name invoked. He'd never liked Kamen much. "Something in her cards. A sorcerer and a priest and whatnot. She says the imposter plucked the guise of Asai from out of the heads of those around the Incendiary, and used it to draw the Incendiary to him. She thinks they got Kamen out of the way because they'd been unable to get through his magic to do 'a proper haunting' while he was still about." He shrugged when Dakimo cut him a sharp glance. "Her words. The point is, I believe we're in the middle of an attempted coup." He held up a hand when both Imara and Dakimo jolted. "Someone very strong with old magic. Someone who wants the Incendiary for unknown reasons, but think about it—why wouldn't a hopeful king seek a kingmaker?"

The headache was beginning to thud heavily behind Dakimo's eyes now. "And we can't fight them in kind."

"Xari says Kamen can match them."

"Which doesn't help, since Kamen's *not here!*"

"I agree that Kamen's magic kept them at bay." Imara was gently stroking Emika's brow, voice soft. "But even Kamen wasn't able to obstruct them entirely." She sighed and looked away. "I believe the 'ghosts' the Incen—that Fen Jacin was hearing were, in fact, these *banpair*, as Xari and Goyo say. Even then, they were trying to coax him away from Kamen, or perhaps merely setting the stage so he would be more agreeable to their influence once they got Kamen out of their way." Her jaw tightened. "As I said, they seemed very confident last night they would have no trouble convincing Fen Jacin he'd killed his brothers. What that would do to his mind, I don't think I want to guess."

Dakimo bowed his head, thought about it. "So, we have a band of rogue *banpair*, beings who were once maijin, made in the patterns of the old magic. And yet these *banpair* are now, it seems, seeking out those of the old magic, and turning Mitsu upside down to find the Incendiary— also a being made in the patterns of the old magic, but not of it." He narrowed his eyes and looked at first Imara then Goyo. "And you say Rihansei knows… something."

Goyo shifted uneasily. "He took the Incendiary down to his Gate."

"He *what?*" Dakimo's heart gave his breastbone a good, solid kick. "Why did you not tell me this when—?"

"And what could you have done, Dakimo?" Imara was using her healing voice, calm and soothing. Dakimo could have quite cheerfully thumped her. "You had rather your own share of excitement, no? And it isn't like we can go and get him."

She was trying to be kind. Dakimo should *not* kill her.

"I can't be certain." Goyo put out a hand. "I can only say that all my instincts tell me Rihansei knows what's really going on in Mitsu, and he now has the Incendiary. What he means to do with him besides what one normally does at the Gate…" He sighed, mouth tight. "The only thing I *am* certain of is that he has no intention of surrendering the Incendiary to the *banpair*. He's warded up so tight neither Imara nor I could even approach the doors this afternoon. If I'm reading the timing of it all correctly, Leu was there with Rihansei and the Incendiary while we were fighting *banpair* outside, but she wasn't there long enough to find out what Rihansei knows. Not that Rihansei would've told her. Oh." He put up a finger. "I forgot. Leu's back—she had quite a story to tell." The lift of his eyebrows said *later.*

Dakimo wasn't about to argue. "Do you think Rihansei can hold through an attack?"

"I think…" Goyo hesitated then, as unlikely as it was, turned to Imara.

Imara shook her head. "We have no way of gauging strength for strength. There's no way to know if Rihansei is more powerful than these *banpair*, not without testing their magic one against the other, which we obviously can't." She held out the hand that was not stroking Emika's brow. "They didn't try to breach Rihansei's protections, at least not as far as I could tell. Whether that was because they couldn't, or because they didn't know the Incendiary was there, I simply can't say. They did, however, wait until Kamen's mortals were outside to attack."

"Right."

Dakimo scrubbed at his eyes to keep himself from staring at Emika and dwelling on the guilt of not being fast enough or strong enough, along with a new culpability in giving the order he now meant to give, knowing what Emika would have to say about it were she awake. The understanding between the keepers of the Gate and Mitsu was ancient, older than Dakimo himself, and had never before been so much as questioned, let alone tested. Right now, there didn't seem to be another choice. And if the Incendiary didn't live through it…?

Well. Dakimo supposed this new development would, one way or another, tell him whether or not the Incendiary was indeed unsalvageable. With Kamen's ring on the Incendiary's finger, perhaps "unsalvageable" would be best all around.

There was, after all, as Goyo himself had pointed out only days ago, more than one way to save a soul.

"Get the Incendiary." Dakimo peered at Goyo and Imara to make sure there was no misunderstanding. "By any means necessary."

⛩

"Hullo." Morin propped his elbows on the bedside cupboard and gave the fish's jade fins a stroke. "You really are kind of boring, aren't you?"

The fish only hung in the bowl, almost exactly dead center, and stared outward, placid, its eyes empty and blank. Morin had brought it from his own room for… well, company, he supposed, though now that he actually let that thought take shape, it sounded kind of stupid.

Knowing it was absurd but doing it anyway, Morin shot yet another look at Joori, checking compulsively that he was breathing, even though Morin knew there was no danger anymore. Shig had woken up a few hours ago, after all. Still, Morin was having a hard time reconciling this peaceful-looking young man with his perpetually worried and sharp-edged brother. Which, now that he thought about it, pretty much described both of his brothers, just in different ways.

Was there such a thing as loving each other to death? Morin thought yes. Morin thought maybe he'd been watching it happen right in front of him.

He gave the fish a little poke, weirdly disappointed that it didn't go for his finger like those two at the booth had gone for each other. It merely bobbed beneath the surface and patiently righted itself when Morin stopped annoying it. He wished the man had given Samin two of them. Not that Morin would set them on each other, but he might set the bowls close once in a while to entertain himself.

Curious, he peered around the room, found nothing, although Shig's little silver case that Malick had bought her to hold her smokes—that might work. With a quick pat to Joori's knee and another reassuring look, Morin left the bedside and ventured out onto the gallery of the second floor, nodding politely to the patrolwoman who quietly paced a watch, then angling into Shig's room. She wasn't there—likely having been chivvied by Samin down to the kitchen for something to eat—but Morin didn't think she'd mind; he snatched the smoke case from the press by the door, peering at his reflection in the polished silver.

Humming quietly, Morin brought the little case back to Joori's room and flumped down on the cushions he'd dragged up to the low bed the night before. He peered at Joori a little guiltily, but Morin was bloody *bored*, and there were no books here, and staring at Joori while he was sleeping was starting to feel a little creepy and… voyeuristic. Or something.

He wasn't surprised by the thrashing and splashing when the fish spotted its mirrored twin in the reflection of the case. He continued to not be surprised as he held the case there, watching the thing bash itself into the glass, again and again. If the glass had been lined with spikes, it would have spitted itself, attacking repeatedly until it had gored itself to death. Trying to get at *itself*.

Morin's mouth turned up in a smile for a second before it slowly fell. He frowned. He'd thought this would be fun, interesting. It was turning out to be… disturbing.

And sometimes, the beauty merely hides its purpose. That's what that strange man at the booth had said.

"Sure." Morin absently wiped a drop of water from where it had splashed on the bridge of his nose. "Some purpose."

Attacking everything that looked like it. What kind of "purpose" was that? As though it hated… No, it was just a stupid fish. Fish couldn't hate. Maybe it just attacked anything it perceived as a threat. Except it hadn't attacked Morin's fingers. He wondered if it would attack a different kind of fish, or only the ones like itself. Would it go after one of those comparatively giant sakou in the fountain outside? *That* would be something to see. Morin would lay even odds on a fight like that. Sakou might be ten times the size of this little one, but—

"Stop torturing that thing."

Morin scowled. "I'm not *torturing* it." Nonetheless, he set the smoke case down flat on the cupboard and watched some more, fascinated, as the fish stopped its assault in midlunge, as soon as its "enemy" was out of sight, and went back to hanging in the bowl like a lump of docile jade. He turned to Joori. "I was only…"

He trailed off and snapped his back straight. "Hey, you're awake."

Groggy and foul-tempered, Morin could tell already, but the relief that Joori really was all right like Imara had promised was too over-whelming to let in the irritation.

Joori was still blinking myopically at the fishbowl, frowning.

Morin put on his calm face. "You're all right." He kept his voice low and smooth so as not to startle. "We're at the house Malick bought, and we're safe."

Imara had said Joori and Shig might be somewhat confused and possibly a bit frightened when they woke—and Shig had definitely been both—so Morin tried to keep everything quiet and relaxed for now. There was plenty of panic in which to indulge, and Morin had no doubt they'd get to it sooner rather than later.

"Your eyes are going to be blurry for a little bit yet," Morin said as Joori blinked some more and squinted in the too-bright early evening light streaming through the thin painted screens on the big window. Morin positioned himself so he was blocking most of it and laid a hand to Joori's knee through the quilt. "You probably have a headache too, but I've got something for that when you think you can sit up."

Joori frowned up at Morin, looking mussed and bewildered, and much younger than he was. "What…?"

"You were drugged."

Morin helped when Joori tried to sit, setting a hand between his shoulder blades until Morin was sure he wouldn't fall over. It took a moment of wobbling and grabbing hold of the bedding to try to steady himself, but Joori eventually managed to remain semi-upright, though hunched over his legs and still blinking blearily.

"Imara said it was meant to knock you out and keep you out, maybe even for days, but she did something that made it…" Morin trailed off and shrugged, because he had no real idea what Imara had done; all he'd cared about at the time was that Joori wasn't going to die, and the rest had kind of rolled over his awareness without much of it sticking. "You should be yourself again in a little while." He reached for the bowl of whatever-it-was that Imara had said to give Joori as soon as it looked like he was somewhat with it. "Here. You need to drink this."

Joori stared blank-eyed at the bowl before opening his mouth and letting Morin tip some of the… stuff in.

"Imara." It was as though Joori was trying to remember where he'd heard the name before.

Morin tipped the bowl again. Joori licked his lips and accepted another sip easily enough. He didn't seem to be wrinkling his nose at the taste or anything, so it must be all right.

Morin had given the stuff a sniff or two, but he hadn't dared try it. He had a feeling there was more in there than regular medicines and spices, and he didn't think he wanted to find out what unknown magic—meant to counteract whatever drug had been in that dart—would do to someone who hadn't been drugged.

"Imara," Joori said again, frowning down into what was left in the bowl.

Morin knew it was coming, so he set his hand on Joori's knee again and waited. It only took another few seconds before Joori's eyes widened and his whole body did a little jolty-spasmy thing, and the rest of the elixir went flying out of the bowl.

"Jacin—"

"We know where he is." Morin said it evenly. "We've been waiting for you and Shig to wake up. Samin's got a plan."

"…Plan. Good. That's—" Joori shook his head, as if to clear it, then winced and pinched at the bridge of his nose. "How long have I been out?"

Morin braced himself. "You remember going to the Gates of Rapture?" He waited for Joori to nod. "Right. Well. That was the night before last. It's now gone past suppertime."

"*Shit.*" Joori did that jolty-spasmy thing again and tried to throw the quilt aside, but he was still too disoriented to do much else.

Morin did his best to keep Joori in place. "It's going to be a little while before you can go haring off, so you might as well sit and listen for a minute, all right?"

"Where's Samin?" Joori's fear was starting to crowd out lingering confusion, and the anger was sliding in right behind it. "It's been…" He paused, thought about it. "It's been three days—almost four now, since Jacin took off. Anything could be happening. Why hasn't anyone—?"

"Just *wait* a minute, Joori. We're going to do something. Like I said, we've been waiting for you and Shig to wake up first. Samin has a plan, but there are things you don't know, and you need to know them first, yeah?"

Joori stared at Morin, hard, like he was looking for something; when it seemed like he'd found it, he slumped back—maybe defeated, maybe just exhausted, but either way, the look on his face kind of hurt Morin's heart. Trust, but not the kind to be expected between brothers—it was wary and highly conditional, and Morin had no doubt it came from a place inside Joori that saw only Morin the Miscreant when he looked at Morin like that. Joori didn't trust Morin to have Jacin's best interests at heart, and there was likely nothing Morin could ever do to convince him otherwise, so he'd best save the energy and frustration of trying.

Without another word, Morin went to the door and asked the patrolwoman standing outside it to go and get Samin. He didn't try to explain things to Joori when he sat back down again, and he didn't try to reassure him, either. He merely waited silently while Joori toyed with the empty bowl and traced the spots on the linens where he'd splashed the dregs of the elixir. He shot looks at Morin now and then, but there was no point in Morin trying to pretend he didn't know what they meant.

Joori thought Morin hadn't loved their mother, but he had. He just hadn't done it in the way Joori had done. Joori fussed and worried and made excuses and pretended everything would be all right someday, and Morin supposed that was because Joori needed to believe it would. Morin didn't see the point in that. Morin had loved their mother because, even in her madness, she'd given her children her own good heart, and had taught them, by dreamy-distracted example, that family was central, love imperative, and you simply had to accept the ones you loved the way they were; that wishing they could be something they weren't wasn't love at all. It was how Morin had managed to love their father. It was how he'd been able to draw the strength to put Jacin's knife to their mother's throat.

Joori thought Morin hated Jacin too, but he didn't. Morin wasn't quite sure he liked Jacin all that much, but it was hard to get to know and like someone who spent most of his time inside his own head. Morin didn't mind being around Jacin, though, so he supposed that was something. And he did love both of his brothers, though he didn't go about it in the flinging-oneself-into-the-breach way Joori did it. You just couldn't invest so much in Jacin. He was too precarious. Jacin was the one Morin wanted at his back, if he ever needed such a thing, but Joori was the one who you could count on in years, instead of moment by moment.

And if Morin ever found himself in a situation where he had to choose one brother over the other, save one and let one go, he'd choose Joori. It wasn't coldness or lack of love for Jacin; it was simple common sense. Practical. You saved the one who was capable of being saved. Joori would get over the loss eventually—Jacin never would. It was a halfway sick, codependent sort of love, old and deep, that went hand in hand with destruction in one form or another, and Morin prudently backed away from it. Morin loved both his brothers, but on his own terms.

He loved Joori because he was fierce and loyal and kind and he never stopped *trying*. He loved Jacin because he was strange and scary and inspiring and he needed to be loved more than anyone Morin had ever known. He loved them both because they were his brothers, all the family he had left, and Mother would've wanted him to look out for them as much as he could. And bloody hell, but they both *needed* looking after.

"Ha!" Shig sauntered into the room just ahead of Samin, Naro-yi bringing up the rear. "Don't know about you, but I think I slept enough for a year." She pointed a sly grin at Joori and shook her head. "You'd think all that beauty sleep would've done something about that scowl."

Morin nearly rolled his eyes. He liked Shig well enough, but the way she constantly poked at Joori was getting old very quickly. Sometimes she had a point, but sometimes it was just unnecessary.

"Shig, not now." Samin looked weary and ragged around the edges, but he was obviously pleased to see Joori awake and all right. "How you feeling, lad?"

"Strange." Joori narrowed his eyes at Naro-yi and outright glared at Shig before giving Samin a shrug. "Kinda fuzzy, but all right. Hungry." He paused and shot another suspicious look at Naro-yi. "Worried."

"Yeah." Samin sat on the low bed beside Joori's feet, the rope supports squeaking and groaning as he shifted his weight forward to get a good look. He leaned in, narrow-eyed and assessing, before he tipped a nod. "You'll do." He jerked his chin at Naro-yi. "C'mon, then, they'll be wanting to know why they can't listen in shortly."

Joori frowned as Naro-yi and Shig moved until they were sitting on the floor by the bed across from Morin. Morin didn't give up any of his cushions.

"Who are *they*?" Joori asked, guarded. "What's going on?"

Samin's mouth pinched. "*They* are some of the Patrol and a few maijin and *Temshiel* from the temple, left here to guard us. Naro-yi is doing whatever it is he does to block them right now so they can't hear us, but they'll wonder why eventually. Imara and that Goyo say it's for our protection, but I tried to step out to find a teashop this morning, and you'd think I was trying to break out of a prison c—" Samin cut himself off. He still got all uncomfortable and fidgety when the subjects of prisoners and camps came up. "They may well be here to protect us, but they're also here to keep us out of the way."

"Out of the way of *what?* Do they think they have more of a right to—?"

"Of course they do, Joori." Morin was just as bitter about it as Joori was, but he'd had more time to absorb it all. "Haven't you been paying attention? With a very few exceptions"—Morin shot a conciliatory look at Naro-yi—"they think we're naïve idiots who'll muck things up for them and get ourselves killed if they don't leash us up."

"I'm not quite certain that's *precisely* the thinking." Naro-yi shrugged. "But I will admit that's what it amounts to." He turned to Joori. "Your brother is safe, Joori. Kamen had meant to take him to Rihansei eventually, that much is plain now. As Samin has said before, he had apparently intended to go there the night he was… attacked. Whether Kamen's intentions were for Rihansei to do what I'm sure he's now doing, I can't be certain, but I've no doubt he would have let Rihansei make that judgment, since Rihansei is the only one who can."

Joori frowned. "And that is…?"

Morin braced himself. Because if Joori was going to lose it, it was going to happen right about—

"That I cannot tell you."

—now.

"What the *fuck* does—"

"It isn't that he won't." Shig waved her hands, as though trying to get the attention of an attacking bear. "It's that no one who hasn't followed the little shepherds has any idea where they lead."

…Yeah, all right, that probably wasn't going to help.

"Little shepherds." Joori's glare all but flayed Shig where she sat. "You said that in the tavern. What does it mean?"

Shig shrugged with a very blatant pout. "*I* didn't get to follow them, either."

Morin thought the only reason Joori didn't actually lunge at Shig was because he was still too dizzy.

"The point," Naro-yi said quickly, "is that we believe we know where your brother is, and we believe he is being protected from those who attacked us."

Joori shifted the glare to Naro-yi. "You *believe.* You don't *know.*"

"There is no way to know, young seyh. We're not dealing with the magic of the gods here. Rihansei's magic was a part of this world before the moons came. The man who pretended to be your brother was born of the same seed, though how he grew so powerful without Rihansei's knowledge I cannot guess." Naro-yi put out a hand. "Old magic, young seyh. The same cloth from which the patterns of the maijin were shaped. The same roots from which the Incendiary once sprang."

"Incendiary." Joori nearly spat it. "Is that why those people want Jacin?"

Morin couldn't help rolling his eyes. Because, *really?*

"The same magic," Naro-yi went on, dogged but kind, "that enabled the spirits to bind themselves so easily with the souls of the Jin." He reached out and tapped gently at Joori's breastbone. "You once had a spirit of the earth joined to your soul. But what seed inside you, do you think, allowed it to find you and bind itself to you so eagerly and strongly?"

Joori looked like he was going to be sick.

"Isn't it great?" Shig was all at once nearly bouncing. "Maybe I can—"

"Maybe you can do whatever it is you want to do when we have more time." Samin set a hand to Shig's knee when she frowned at him in obvious disappointment. "We have some things to do right now, lovie. And not much time to get it all straight before we do them."

He turned to Joori. "The festival starts tonight, which will make what I have in mind both easier and more difficult. Happy birthday, by the way."

Joori only rolled his eyes.

Samin grinned. "That's the spirit." He gave Joori's shoulder a pat that nearly sent him toppling, then skimmed his gaze around the room. "All right, the festival should make things easier, because the foot traffic will be breezing right by the front gates here, and once we get ourselves through them, we'll be able to blend in and move with them. Naro-yi says the interference from the crowds will make it more difficult for anyone to track us with magic. But that also means Naro-yi won't be able to track anyone else, and we're all going to be vulnerable to whatever might want to find us.

"Those *banpair* can blend in. They can look like anyone. You all saw it. And they seemed pretty determined to get hold of the three of you. I doubt they're going to pass up on the opportunity if we give it to them."

Morin caught Joori's eye. "They want to use us against him."

"Yeah, I figured that out." Nearly a growl.

"I'm only saying we can't go into this half-assed, and we stick to Samin's plan, no matter what, all right? You lose it and go haring off, you might as well just hand Jacin over to them yourself."

It was harsh, but sometimes harsh was the only way to get through to Joori. He was as disinterested in protecting himself as Jacin was, until he understood that a threat to himself was a bigger threat to Jacin.

Morin shook his head. As different as Joori and Jacin had turned out, they were twins down to the bone. In too many of the unhealthiest ways.

"I *get* it, Morin." Joori looked at Samin. "What's this plan, then?"

"Easy, really." Samin nodded at Naro-yi. "Naro-yi will be leaving shortly to go and buy us some glamour charms. He's got several people in mind who wouldn't mind getting paid to be us for a while. And I've got an ass-load of Malick's money to play with." He patted at his tunic. "Naro-yi made sure he was the one to set the wards on the perimeter, so he'll be able to muck with his own magic to get them in and us out without anyone else knowing."

Joori was giving Naro-yi a bit of a slit-eyed stare. "We seem to be trusting an awful lot of this plan to a maijin."

"A maijin who kicked the shit out of some of those *banpair*." Morin found himself bristling on Naro-yi's behalf. "To protect us, Joori."

"I know that." Joori shot a somewhat rueful glance to Naro-yi. "I do know that. I'm sorry. And... and thank you. I don't mean... it's only that—"

"The servants of the gods have not done terribly well by you and yours, young seyh." Naro-yi looked sincerely apologetic. "And magic has never been a thing for which you would ever think to be grateful, I've no doubt. And no blame to you." His hand moved, like he meant to reach out to Joori, but he didn't. "If an ulterior motive will set you better at ease, I shall give you one: Owl has ever been Wolf's staunchest ally, and Wolf has ever extended his brotherly protection to his little sister. Wolf means for the Incendiary to be saved—Owl would do anything for her brother. Something, I think, you can well understand." He smiled. "From everything I have heard, saving Fen Jacin without saving those he loves would be the very definition of futility. As Owl's servant, I must do my part where I can."

He paused, opened a hand. "If you'd like the real motive, however, I can only say that I was mortal once, and once I had a family I loved. In all my long years, I have not forgotten what it was like to lose them."

Damn it, Morin's eyes were tearing just like Joori's were. Would they *ever* reach the point where these things didn't cut them down in unsuspecting moments? Morin thought not. Hundreds of years old, and Naro-yi's grief was still plain and all too real.

Joori cleared his throat. "I'm sorry, seyh. I didn't mean to..." His mouth set tight, and he shook his head. "Either motive will do." He jerked his head up and looked at Samin. "When do we leave and where do we go first?"

Well, bloody damn. Samin was looking a little choked up himself. Morin didn't dare look at Shig, merely kept his eyes on Samin as Samin blinked several times then peered at all of them, one at a time, before leveling a steady gaze on Joori.

"Back to Rihansei's. As soon as you can stand without falling."

Hitsuke had barely an instant to bend his perception from the dregs of mortal death just a moment ago to the flight of euphoria on which he found himself soaring now.

He hadn't meant to die this time. Well, he never really *meant* to die, but this time, he'd rather been in the middle of things, and the dying had been… inconvenient. Still, not as inconvenient as it was for some. *Temshiel* and maijin, after all, were required to go through the process of restoration, meditation—sometimes even penance—before returning to the mortal plane. Hitsuke had no such strictures. Hitsuke had Raven.

"It was one of Dragon's," Hitsuke told his lord, voice a bit wobbly as he tilted his head to the side, exposing his throat for the hungry mouth that swept from jugular to jawline. "She hates me, your sister. She's accused me more than once of loyalty to Wolf, rather than y—"

"And are your loyalties mine?" Warm breath over Hitsuke's collarbone.

"*Yesss*," Hitsuke hissed, almost a whine as he pushed himself in, tilting his hips up from their soft bed of jasmine petals and against the perfect body of his lord. "Yes, yours, always yours."

"Then say my name"—a hard press of skin to skin—"and then kiss me some more."

"Daraso." Hitsuke swayed to the cadence measured by soft, panting breaths and hard, inarguable desire. "Daraso, *Dara*—"

Daraso swallowed his own name on Hitsuke's breath, pulled him into a spiral of pleasure that blanked all else, made it distant, unimportant. There was more, Hitsuke was sure of it. More repetition of the name, more words attached to it. He lost it all in the rhythm, the sensation, the want and the worship, as his god made love to him on the jasmine petals that were their bed in Raven's garden when Hitsuke lingered between life and death.

This, he'd decided a long, long time ago, *this* was worth the inevitable pain of dying. It was devotion. It was serenity. It was flying high above the world on wings made of pleasure and tenderness, then landing safe in his lord's arms.

When they were spent and sweaty, tangled limbs half atop and half covered in bruised petals, Hitsuke lay content in the arms of his lord and gave voice to his concerns:

"Your twin seeks to annoy Wolf. She is still smarting over his acceptance of the Jin and wants them gone, but Wolf's protections and the magic of the Ancestors hinder her. She cannot move until her own Cycle, and her Cycle is too long away for her liking. And she will not see that there is always a heavy price for thwarting Fate." He paused to peer up into his lord's dark-dark eyes. "She will come to you with a bargain eventually." Hesitantly, he added, "She is confident that her actions against your Incendiary will not... anger you." His mouth pinched down. "Her maijin instructed me to 'run and tattle' as he plunged the sword."

He hadn't really known what to expect, hadn't dared to hope for the reaction that his heart told him would come from a mortal lover, for his lover was not mortal, and neither was he. Still, Hitsuke had not expected Daraso to chuckle.

"My sister has always been driven by her jealousies." Daraso kissed Hitsuke's brow. "'Twas quite useful once, but now..." His eyes narrowed and he peered up through the cherry trees and into the night sky. "She was wrong. She will pay for allowing one of her own to touch you."

Hitsuke closed his eyes as Daraso's arms tightened around him. "She approves of the Binding War. She lends all her power to the Adan in hopes they will wipe the Jin from her sight altogether. I suspect she was quite gleeful when the Ancestors instructed their people to stop 'tainting' their Lines with Adan blood."

And started a war that was even now pitting *Temshiel* against maijin, threatening to leak over into the divine planes. It wasn't enough for Dragon that the mortals would kill each other and break a bond centuries in the making; she had enlisted her *Temshiel* to the cause, and had been quite certain Raven would take her side. Since it was Raven's Cycle, all *Temshiel* and maijin held their breath, waiting to see if they'd be called to a cause they perhaps did not support, but would have no choice but to defend.

"She was." Daraso sounded... amused. "It did not become her." He paused and ran his fingertips up and down Hitsuke's backbone. "Though I cannot say I entirely disagree with her desires."

Hitsuke frowned. "The Jin are more valuable to the gods than any other people. Their belief comes from knowledge, and so is unshakable.

Do you not think that was Fate's intention when she left Mii-daichiseyh to his destiny?"

"So, it was Wolf's Jin sheep who defeated a god?"

"It was Fate. The Jin were fated to lift up the Six and so put down Mii-daichiseyh. They have already converted the Adan and nearly obliterated the dying shreds of Mii-daichiseyh's last foothold. The Adan abandoned their One God *because* of the Jin. Surely they deserve some—"

"They do not even deserve what Wolf has handed them. They do not deserve to *live*, and yet live they do, with all the blessings of the magic the gods hand only to those who have earned it. The Ancestors and all their spawn should have been punished and destroyed. And because they were not, they and 'their people' worship *Wolf*, not the Six, and it will only be a matter of time before the Six becomes One again."

Hitsuke sat up, heart lumping heavily. He set his hand lightly to Daraso's mouth.

"Don't say such things, my lord. The Jin are more devoted to the Six than any other people. They perhaps offer gratitude to Wolf for protecting them, but Wolf would not—"

"No?" Daraso took Hitsuke's hand away, kissing the tips of his fingers, but his eyes had gone chilled and narrow. "My brother grows stronger with each prayer they offer him, even when he is not in his Cycle. And treachery is not a thing so alien to the Six who came from the One. Do not forget—'twas Wolf who began the rebellion against our sire."

"Because your sire was an arrogant magician before he rose into a callous god who went a little bit insane with his power as it grew. He tested Fate, thwarted her, and he paid the price. Fate always answers those who question her with the cruelty of granting their wishes. Believe me, I know."

Daraso slipped his hand to Hitsuke's cheek. "Yes. I imagine you would." He pulled Hitsuke down. Hitsuke laid his head to Daraso's breastbone, but his body remained tense, as it hadn't been before.

"Tell me, my faithful Hitsuke, Fate's Incendiary—" Daraso stopped short when Hitsuke tried to jolt up again, tender allegiance, but a firm grip kept him where he was. "To whom does such faith truly belong? *Are* you mine?" This time it was Daraso who covered Hitsuke's mouth when Hitsuke opened it to answer immediately. "I don't believe there is another soul who is more loyal to the gods, but are you *mine*? Would you do anything I ask of you?"

Hitsuke pulled Daraso's hand away. "You promised me once to take care what you ask of me. I asked for that promise because I worried I could refuse you nothing." As had been done to him before, Hitsuke kissed the tips of Daraso's fingers. "As long as you keep your promise, I will do what you ask. *My lord.*" A reminder of the delicate balance the Incendiary kept, and the promise his god had made him when he'd pledged his oath.

Daraso stared at him steadily. "And if I broke my promise, if I asked of you something Fate would not wish… Would you, Hitsuke, last of the Incendiary, Raven's-own, lover of Daraso and keeper of his heart—would you take back your oath and swear it to another?"

The thought of it would have brought Hitsuke to his knees, had he been standing. As it was, tears gathered behind his brow, burned at the corners of his eyes, but he would not let them fall, not here.

"Even gods are not invulnerable to Fate. I would not see my lord fall to her for the purpose of testing one who loves him above all." Hitsuke hesitated. "Don't ask it of me, my lord. Don't tempt me to give it to you to please you, only to see you pay for it when Fate demands her price. A worse failure to my god I cannot imagine."

One black eyebrow rose. "*Failure.*" A faint hint of a smirk twitched at Daraso's mouth, but it didn't look the least bit amused. "And yet you fail me even now, with every word of concern you speak for your god."

It *hurt.* A physical pain, right in the center of Hitsuke's chest. Hitsuke sat up slowly, pulled back.

Daraso let him go, but kept a hand to his wrist. "Do you think, perhaps, the Incendiary sees more and farther than Raven?"

"*No,* of course—"

"And yet you would refuse a request from your god—from *Daraso,* whom you love—to… what? Protect?" Daraso propped himself up on his elbows, tilted his dark head. "That smells of failure from either end. It smells of betrayal. You would betray me to save me, my Incendiary?"

Hitsuke swallowed. "Never ask of me something I cannot give you, and we shall never have to know the answer to that question."

His voice was hoarse. Horrible foreboding was leaching away all the warmth and love in which he'd basked only moments ago.

"And to whom, then, would you give your oath?" Raven asked, for it wasn't Daraso peering so intently, almost coldly, at his Incendiary. "Does Wolf still hold more of my Incendiary's heart than I would like to think?"

This was getting very, very dangerous. Exactly what had Dragon said to her twin, and how much of it had Raven believed?

"Wolf holds as much of *your* Incendiary's heart as any one of the other gods," Hitsuke said carefully. "My loyalties—my *heart*—have been all too obvious to anyone with eyes for centuries, but Fate *must* be considered. You can ask many things of me, but you cannot ask it all—I've had *your word*." He paused to set a hand to Daraso's cheek. "You would put me to the test now, my lord? Out of jealousy for a brother who wants your power and your Cycle no more than I do?"

He'd meant it as a challenge, a sharp reminder of all of the ways he'd shown his love and his loyalty, all through the centuries. He hadn't expected his god to look at him with those guarded eyes, that harsh suspicion all over his beautiful face… that jealousy and growing anger that leaked out of him to almost smother Hitsuke.

Hitsuke's heart broke—slowly and with sickening ease—as he watched his god nod his dark head, watched a cold little smile settle upon his god's red lips.

"I would." Raven jerked Hitsuke up from the bed of jasmine, Hitsuke's body already heavy, gaining substance, as Raven began the process of sending him back into the mortal realm. "I would ask *my* Incendiary to find a way to rid the world of the Jin abomination, in a way that will hint at no blame to his god. I would ask *my* Incendiary to be very careful in his choices, for his god is a jealous one, and he does not deign to *share*."

"If my lord would just listen, I'm sure he would see that…" Hitsuke was going numb everywhere, the reality of what was happening blurring over into the mortal reality into which Raven was forcing him. "Daraso, you don't understand. If I let you do this, if I *help* you do this, then I will have failed you utterly. Fate will demand a price of you, and it may be too horrible for you to pay. It is with love for his god that your Incendiary refuses. You don't walk the world, you cannot simply wipe out a people because they displease—"

"*Arrogance!* And still you think to turn me to your own heart's cause. Still you think to pretend you do this for me and not for *him*."

"My lord—" Hard hands took hold of Hitsuke, shook him.

"I can be cruel, can I not? 'Twas cruelty and resolve that brought you to me, no?" The smile turned colder. "I ask for proof, *my love*."

Angry, hurt beyond rational thought, Hitsuke tried to pull away—couldn't. "Ask for my heart in your hand, and I'll place it there myself. Ask for my soul, and I'll tear it from my body and give it with no remorse. Have I not already proved—?"

"That you are true to Fate and the gods? That you love your gentle Daraso? Indeed you have. Now you shall prove you are true to your god—to *this* god." Raven laid another kiss to Hitsuke's brow, only this one was so cold it almost burned like a brand. "Always there is Fate and your loyalties, your *choices* between us. 'Take care what you ask of me,' you tell me, and you depend upon—*play* upon my love for you to avoid those things you would not wish to do for *your lord*. Your lord's love is not without limits, and neither is your god's." He held Hitsuke away, pushing him into his mortality. "Now we shall find out where your limits lie. Raven's-own."

You are safe, little Catalyst. These things cannot hurt you now.

Then why was his chest so tight? Why did it feel like his eyes had been scoured with sand?

I want to stop now.

He didn't want to see what came next. He didn't think he could take it.

We cannot. It has already taken us days to get here. We have no more time.

Days? *Days?* It felt like moments. It felt like forever.

I don't care. I want—

Hands closed around his wrists—comfort; *Malick*—and a bright little point of pain sparked into his leg then striated out through him, made him heavy.

Stop… He licked his lips, tugging on his hands to feel the reassuring grip that wouldn't let him go. *Stop fucking* drugging *me.*

Bastard.

A chuckle, low and rolling, then: *Stop fighting me, little Catalyst. You are safe. Show me the rest.*

Like before, like always, he had no choice.

In the end, it could have been so easy. All it would have taken was a little grumbling in the tearooms, a little gossip in the shops. It would be nothing at all to put the right words in the right ears, then sit back and watch as the idea was discussed, dissected, took root. It would be nothing at all to irrevocably set the gods against the Jin and thwart Fate to please Raven. He even knew how he would do it.

It helped that the Binding War still raged. It helped that the Binding War came from unacknowledged fear in the hearts of those who had no magic toward those who had. Haves and Have-nots; it always came down to that, one way or another.

Hitsuke couldn't do it. And it wouldn't even matter, because he knew Raven would find his own way, and Hitsuke's "rebellion" would have no meaning, but for a betrayal between lovers.

He sat in an Adan tearoom with a maijin of Snake, drinking warmed wine to numb the sorrow, wondering if he really could offer oath to Wolf after everything Raven had been to him. After everything he'd thought he'd been to Raven. The thought made him want to weep.

"You're here to set the stage for annihilation." There was an odd knowing grief creeping into Goyo's gaze. "Aren't you?"

Hitsuke couldn't answer. What was he supposed to say?

He got up and left.

Goyo caught up to him only paces from the tearoom. "Incendiary. *Raven's* Incendiary." He frowned when Hitsuke couldn't help the flinch. "It's no secret what Raven would wish, Hitsuke. And it's no secret who carries out Raven's wishes for him—even better and with much more finesse than Raven's *Temshiel* and maijin. But Raven's Incendiary has always been a fair-minded man, and I can't—"

Hitsuke stopped Goyo with a wave of his hand. He couldn't stand to hear it anymore.

"It would be such a simple thing, you know." Hitsuke's voice sounded dull and dead, even to him. He wondered what Goyo was making of it, but he couldn't seem to drag his eyes from the dirt to find out. "A whisper in the ears of a few Jin, then watch them wield their magic against those who have none. They almost want to now.

"A suggestible people. Have you ever wondered why?" Hitsuke smiled, a small, weary thing. "Descendants of *Temshiel*. Every one of them. And *Temshiel* were made to obey. It's in their Blood. And thus it's in the Jin." His eyes stung. He tried again to blink it away. "That's why Wolf watches them so. It isn't love—it's wariness. How long d'you suppose their will would stand against that of Raven's Incendiary?" Hitsuke's laugh was harsh and hollow. "The gods wouldn't stand for it. Raven could call down the *Temshiel* on the Jin, and even Wolf could not save them."

Goyo was silent for quite a while as they slowly walked, his expression warping from shock to concern to confusion to horror.

"Hitsuke," he finally said, "this is not you. I know your heart, I know—"

"I have not come to Jejin to make the destruction of its people easier." Hitsuke was pleased his voice was steadier now, but still he nearly choked on what he meant to say next. "I have come to take my oath from Raven's hand."

He hadn't known he was actually going to do it until just this moment. The pain of it was like a spike to his chest.

Goyo stopped then laid a hand to Hitsuke's arm to stop him as well. Goyo's eyes were wide and shocked.

"The *hell* you say." He stared; Hitsuke kept his own gaze as steady as he could. "And would you consider Snake, then?"

Well. He wouldn't be true maijin if he hadn't tried.

"...Perhaps." It was all Hitsuke could make himself say, though he knew Snake wouldn't have him. Neither would Dragon, and Bear was too rigid to trust with his soul. Owl, perhaps, though he didn't know if she'd be willing to test her formidable brother for an Incendiary who came with conditions, who had left his god because those conditions had been renounced.

Wolf, he thought. Wolf would take him. But if Hitsuke went to Wolf now, Raven would not see that there'd been little other choice. And who knew where that sort of strife between powerful brothers could lead?

Save me, I'm really going to do this. And Daraso will never, ever forgive me.

Hitsuke didn't know if it was going to be enough that he'd never forgive Daraso, either.

Strange. He was angry, his heart was broken into a thousand pieces, and he could contemplate taking his oath from Raven with an ease he couldn't credit. But he couldn't imagine himself giving it to another. *Couldn't.*

The tears were building too quickly behind Hitsuke's eyes. Goyo had to have seen them, though he politely pretended he hadn't. Still, he took Hitsuke into an embrace that threatened to break him completely.

Goyo was newly made, as naïve as an immortal could be, full of ideals and the tenets of his god, around which he had yet to bend or manipulate his way, and too occupied with the wonders of immortality to know he would someday have to. Hitsuke liked him, maybe even loved him a little bit—loved to watch him focus on the smaller picture, *care* about the mortals over whom he had power, and leave all the bigger picture machinations to the *Temshiel.*

Maijin were almost always at their very best, what they were *meant* to be, when they were new and too young to be jaded.

Hitsuke took the embrace Goyo offered for as long as he could stand it, and then he pulled away. He placed a soft kiss to Goyo's cheek.

"I haven't the wit to choose now." Hitsuke rubbed at his aching eyes. "I haven't the wit for much of—"

"You cannot leave it. You stand before me unprotected. What if Snake wished for me to murder you where you stand?"

Hitsuke almost laughed. "Then you would probably end up with the easiest fight of your life."

Goyo didn't look amused. "And what if Raven chose—?"

"Raven's choice has already been made quite clear to me, Goyo. And mine, I should think, to him."

Or perhaps it hadn't been, not until he'd spoken the words, made them real, because even before the last syllable left his tongue, the pain hit him like a sledgehammer and took his breath. He reached out, made a frantic, instinctive grab, and found Goyo's hand locked in his.

"Hitsuke, what—?"

Hitsuke *screamed.*

He'd never felt pain like this before. He was on his knees before he was conscious of losing his footing. Goyo's hand was still gripped in his, bones shifting and scraping beneath Hitsuke's fingers, but he couldn't let go.

He screamed again.

"Hitsuke!" Goyo held on, pushing the hair from Hitsuke's face, flinching back when Hitsuke screamed yet again. "Snake!" Goyo turned his face upward. "Have mercy, take his oath while he can still—"

"*Daraso!*"

A *shriek* this time, thick and hoarse and filled with the pain that was racking Hitsuke from toe to crown. *Agony*—there was no other word for it, his soul knocked loose from mortal moorings, *pulled,* and the torture of it was like… like nothing he'd ever known. All the deaths, all the loves; none of them had even hinted at an anguish so deep and profound.

"*Daraso!*"

And he was there, in some in-between Hitsuke had never seen before, cherry blossom petals falling like a shroud, clogging Hitsuke's throat as he opened his mouth to cry his agony, and some part of his mind wondered distantly why it wasn't jasmine, but it skudded at the corners of insanity with everything else in his head. Black eyes watched him, stone-hard and cold.

"I did not think, little Hitsuke, that you would truly betray me. *You!*"

Hitsuke gasped through the pain. "My lord—"

"You do not renounce me, *my* Incendiary. You take oath to no one else. I am a jealous god—did I not tell you?"

Hitsuke could barely breathe, writhing at the feet of his god. But he forced his mouth to work, his voice to rise above a pathetic whisper.

"You cannot force me to accept betrayal and you cannot stop me from choosing another." He took a strained breath, but the pain trebled, quadrupled, and he didn't even have the wind to scream this time.

He was in Raven's arms now, looking up into black eyes that held no mercy, but a wealth of rage Hitsuke couldn't fathom.

"I can stop you from anything I like. Anything, do you understand? I am *your god* and you are nothing. This is your soul I hold in my hands, my Hitsuke. And as long as I hold it, I can do what I like with it." Raven smiled, all cruel satisfaction. "Look down."

Hitsuke had no choice. He looked down and saw his own body, twisting in the dirt outside the tearoom, Goyo bent over him, calling for

Snake to save him. Hitsuke could have told him it was useless. Snake had thought Incendiary too dangerous since his own had played with her god's laws to bring about a necessary fate. She hadn't even broken them, and still Snake had stamped her out like...

Oh.

The reality of what was really happening finally took any shred of breath Hitsuke might have had left.

Strange. Even after all the centuries he'd spent walking the world, seeing the things he'd seen, Hitsuke had still honestly thought love would save him in the end.

And the worst part? Raven was still holding him, crooning to him in the tones of a lover.

"Go on, then. Call for Wolf. Ask *him* to save you."

Hitsuke opened his mouth—not to call for Wolf, but to... he didn't know, but even now he couldn't make himself call to anyone but Daraso—but the pain hit him again, stopping everything, even thought, but consciousness would not leave him.

"You are mine, little lost soul. I will bind your spirit to mortal flesh and your heart to forgetfulness. You will be reborn under my moon again and again, and you will remember none of what you were before, but this..." Raven tapped Hitsuke's chest, ramping up the agony until Hitsuke thought perhaps he'd die from it alone. "This will remain in your heart. Always. So you too will know the pain you have caused to the one you profess to love so well." He tilted his dark head, his expression not one of pain, as he'd alleged, but more like he was... *pleased.* "A fitting sacrifice to atone for failing your god, is it not?"

"Everything—" Hitsuke choked, forcing himself to rasp it out with the very last of his breath. "*Everything*... already sacrificed... for *you.*"

"And now living is your sacrifice." Raven's smile was an icy slash. "A Jin Untouchable, I think, so none may lay hands on you but me. Let us see how the Incendiary likes being one of the people he would save. Let us see if Wolf himself will ride down from the heavens to deliver you."

He threw Hitsuke down, free fall, down and down and down, his voice echoing in the emptiness as Hitsuke plummeted.

"Beg for me, my Incendiary. Beg me prettily, and perhaps I will find mercy for the one who deceived me so cruelly."

To do so would mean he truly had failed. At everything. Including love.

Hitsuke would not. And so he fell.

3

The vendors had set up already, even this far out from where the festival would officially commence when Owl began her ascent. The scent of fried dough warmed the chill air as they strolled through the low gates of Malick's house, pausing when Naro-yi told them to until he was satisfied with the weave of his magic around the place and then around them. As though on cue, all of them at once dragged the glamour charms over their heads and dropped their false faces, then followed the jerk of Samin's chin out onto the walkway.

"Watch yourselves, all of you. Don't do anything until I tell you to, and for the love of the gods, *stick close.*"

Shig had to do a little bit of a twirl to keep from falling over as they angled around and through the crowds heading toward Mitsu's main square and the temples. She covered it with a wide, confident grin and a bow when Samin and Morin both looked at her with raised eyebrows. The floaty feeling wouldn't go away, so Shig just kind of went with it as they walked on.

Yep, still a little loopy, so she was pretty sure Joori was, too, because Joori merely cut her a guarded glance and didn't snark. She didn't say anything, though. Joori wouldn't appreciate it, and Samin might try to use it as an excuse to ditch them somewhere "safe," like he'd wanted to do before. Actually, he'd wanted to leave them all at Malick's house, but Morin had snapped arguments at him over Joori's bed while Joori was still in it and sleeping off the drugs, and Samin had eventually given in. Shig didn't know what it was about Morin that made Samin listen and acquiesce—when Shig knew Samin's main concern was keeping them all alive—but whatever it was had come in handy as she'd watched Morin argue Samin out of going back to the Gates of Rapture by himself. All right, he probably would've taken Naro-yi, but that didn't count, because Naro-yi wasn't…

Well. As Yori would've said: Naro-yi wasn't *theirs*.

Thwarting the tears that wanted to rise, Shig smiled brightly at the man who'd just nearly rammed right over her and shoved her beneath the feet of the too-close throng; the man's eyebrows went up and an answering smile bloomed as he bowed in apology and let her pass. Shig saw Samin watching it all with a smile that was both fond and tight-lipped. She made herself smirk, because that would be what Samin expected, even though her heart wasn't in it.

Damn it. Shig missed Yori right now with a bitter ache. A "job" like this one would've been like breath and blood to her. Yori's enthusiasm for Malick's various causes over the years had been the only thing that kept Shig engaged in it all. And now, without Yori, Shig was having trouble finding any meaning in tonight's business besides the burgeoning almost-possibility of touching that magic again, seeing if that kindred spark she'd thought she'd felt when the little shepherds had touched her had been real or merely wishful thinking. There was finding Fen, of course, and it *was* important and Shig *was* worried, but—like Morin—Shig had more sympathy for anyone who tried to get in Fen's way. And she was getting a little tired of *Fen this* and *Fen that* all the time.

Other people get lost too, y'know.

Shig frowned. That was a little catty. And kind of unexpected. She didn't *feel* lost. Or… well, maybe sometimes.

"The old magic is very complex," Naro-yi said softly, as if he'd been reading Shig's thoughts, which maybe he had. He'd been sort of hovering at Shig's shoulder for blocks and blocks as they'd wended through the city, dodging people who were on their way to the festival while Samin swiveled his gaze around, watching everyone's backs and broadcasting anxiety all over the place. "At least," Naro-yi went on, "it is complex where the magic of the gods is concerned." He slid his bright glance over at Shig. "You are half-Jin, no?"

When Shig nodded, Naro-yi took her hand and wrapped it around his arm. So cute and… courtly.

"Likely why the two could dwell inside you with such ease."

Shig thought about that, but… Nope, not getting it.

"The two?"

Naro-yi shrugged. "It is not a… popular topic of discussion. I suspect because there is so little of the old magic left, and those who have it keep it rather close. They prefer it that way and so do the gods. A balance is always necessary, you see. Fate requires it, and all the gods abide by Fate. But not all compromises are happy ones."

Shig wasn't watching where she was going, focused entirely on Naro-yi, so she almost forgot what she wanted to ask when he nudged her to the side so she wouldn't walk right up some woman's back. Oh, right, that was it—

"I never knew there *was* an old magic."

"Before the moons came." Naro-yi patted Shig's hand where she held lightly to his bicep. "The tribes that became the Jin were rich with it. Perhaps that is why the *Temshiel* who loved them and made the Ancestors were drawn to them. There is no way to know. There are none left among us from that time."

Because most of them were destroyed by their gods when they refused to destroy their progeny. Shig knew that old chestnut. And any immortals that had been around back then and were still walking the world were now the *banpair* that had been causing so much trouble.

"The interesting thing is the magic itself." Naro-yi gave Shig a scrutinizing look, but his smile was kind. "The old magic, you see, evolves as a seed, a part of one's own soul. The magic of the gods ripens in the Blood, a legacy of the *Temshiel,* and eats up the old magic while making itself. Like a chick inside an egg will absorb the sac before pecking its way free."

"…Uh-huh." Shig had never heard the "birth" of magic spoken of in such… respectful terms. Certainly not in Ada, and certainly not by anyone she'd ever run into.

Samin had gotten a little ahead. They were near the piers now, aiming away from where everyone else was, so the crowds had thinned, only families with small children and old people with canes straggling among them now. Samin gave Shig a look that asked if everything was all right, and Shig gave him a grin. Samin, flanked by Morin and Joori, shrugged then started walking again.

"You are half-Blood." Naro-yi tugged Shig along, increasing their pace to keep up with Samin and the boys, since they weren't being held up by oblivious pedestrians anymore. "The magic of the gods is not as strong in you as it would be in a full-Blood Jin."

"What's that got to do with this old magic, though?"

"Well." Naro-yi put out a hand. "Some believe the Ancestors gave the Jin their magic not to spite the gods, but to supplant the old magic that seeded their children, a remnant from the one god for whom the Jin had no love."

Shig really had to concentrate to follow that one. "They gave their magic to the Jin so the Jin would only have the gods' magic, and not the old?" She frowned. It sounded like Naro-yi was hinting that maybe there was a chance she could still have magic somewhere in her, but that wasn't all of it. "I don't get it."

"I'm not certain I do, either. But the Adan were of the old god, and therefore of the old magic, before the Jin converted them. And the Jin thought the dilution of their Blood through the Adan serious enough to fight a war over it." Naro-yi shook his head, pensive. "The spirits seek out those who have the seed and bind themselves to its host. New magic usurping old magic, as the Six gods once usurped the One." He sighed and peered up at the corner of the sky where the jade shadow of Owl lurked behind the fire-mountains. "I cannot help but think there's something there. I cannot help but feel we are living an echo of a past we cannot know, because none who lived it are here to warn us, but for gods who are too silent and canny to—"

He stopped dead, right in the middle of the walkway, his light, friendly hold on Shig's hand spasming then tightening down.

"Samin." Naro-yi's tone stopped Samin in his tracks, and Morin and Joori along with him. "It's begun." Naro-yi tugged at Shig's arm. Shig had time to think she'd never seen Naro-yi actually anxious before, then Naro-yi was snapping, "They've breached the Gate—*hurry*," and he yanked Shig into a run.

⛩

Samin saw the glow of the fire minutes before they barreled onto the street where the Gates of Rapture was burning.

"Well." Naro-yi bent over his knees, panting. "That's one way to get rid of the wards, I suppose."

Samin shot him a look. "You can burn wards down?"

"No. But you can burn down the structure upon which the spells are cast." Naro-yi straightened. "Rihansei is no novice. He'll have set the wards down into the bedrock, no doubt. But this…" He waved at the fire. "This is a start."

Samin spun his glance about. Seb and several of the men who'd thrown them out of the tavern the other night were trying to bully at least a dozen of the Patrol into a bucket team. And that one… shit.

"That's Imara." Samin pulled Morin and Joori back against the shattered frontispiece of a spice shop across the street. Leftover destruction from the other night. The street itself was still buckled and broken in places.

Naro-yi gave an odd little shudder, then whipped around to stare up toward the rooftops.

"There are more than just the few this time."

They all peered up. Samin had no trouble at all spotting the dozens of black-clad figures standing like sentinels atop the roof of the Gates of Rapture, and then another several dozen atop the roofs of all the surrounding buildings. They weren't attacking the Patrol. They weren't doing anything. Merely standing up there, still and somehow malevolent, like a murder of crows, watching.

Samin only had time to muse how apt that phrase might turn out to be before Joori was gripping his sleeve.

"What are we supposed to do?" Joori's eyes were wild—hope and dread and anger and fear in equal parts. He was gripping one of Malick's short swords in one hand, and one of Fen's knives in the other. "If Jacin's in there…"

He didn't have to finish. Even if these creatures couldn't get past all the protections, it wasn't going to matter. A fire to flush Fen out, and then an ambush when he broke cover. So bloody simple, Samin could've laughed.

Well, actually, no.

Naro-yi gave Samin an urgent look. "I can't veil you."

Yeah, well, Samin had kind of known that was a risk in ducking Imara.

"Fine." Samin eyed the boys. This was not going to go over well, but enough was enough, and this had turned to shit too quickly. "Things have changed. You're not going in." He held up his hand and set his face into hostile lines when both Joori and Morin glared at him accusingly and opened their mouths. "I know what I said, but it's different now. If I had my way, you wouldn't be here at all."

And how he'd let Morin argue him into this, Samin would never know, but Morin just had a way of sounding so bloody *reasonable*, and Samin hadn't been able to deny that it was Morin's right and Joori's to go after their brother. That wasn't making as much sense now as it had a few hours ago.

"There's no way in any hell you can imagine I'm gonna lead you two into a burning building that's under attack by fucking *banpair*." Samin paused for only a second, and when the boys only stared at him, a little stunned, he plowed on, "You'll stay here with Naro-yi."

Naro-yi startled. "You're still going in?"

"Well, of *course* I'm—" Samin took the unreasonable anger welling in his chest and turned it into a calm shrug. "One of our own is in there."

Naro-yi's eyebrows went up, but he merely nodded. "Shig can lead you."

That made Samin pause. It made Shig grin. Which really just figured. Without her magic, Shig wasn't much good in a fight anymore, but Naro-yi had yet to steer them wrong, and Shig seemed willing enough.

And then a knife lodged in Samin's chest.

"You must come back, little Incendiary."

He didn't think he could. The shock of pain still weltered through his body, but the shock of lost love and betrayal and anger resonated through everything he was with a brutal agony of its own.

"*Daraso!*" It burst from him in a shout, the pain through which it erupted more in his memory than in his body. "You horrible, *awful—*"

"Come now, little Incendiary, wake up, *wake up!*"

He swatted blind. "G' *off* me!"

His arm moved freely. One of them, at least.

No restraint. No *Malick*.

The shock of it stilled him until strong fingers took hold of his hand, rubbed. He blinked open eyelids that felt like they were weighted down with rocks to see Rihansei bent over him, kneading at the raw, blood-crusted skin around Jacin's wrist.

Jacin. Right. He was Jacin here. Which didn't change for a moment what he'd been when he'd been *there*. Nor that the safe grip had never been Malick at all, but shackles and fucking *chains*.

Save him, what was he supposed to do with *that?* Even now, the panic was coming at him with teeth sharper than those damned little lizards. Like he was two people at once, thinking with two minds, one bouncing right off the other, and—

No, not two. More. All of them. Everyone he'd ever been. All their memories were abruptly crushing inward, *reminding* him, making him *see*, and holy fucking shit, if he started hearing the echoes of the Ancestors, he was going to lose his shit like he'd never lost it before.

And it wouldn't stop. So much more than he'd seen in wherever he'd been. It was all spinning behind his eyes now, in his head, until he felt like it might runnel out his eyes and his ears, and it wouldn't matter that he was deaf and blind, because he'd still be able to see and hear it all.

"Are you awake now, little Incendiary?" There was a weird urgency in Rihansei's tone. "Come on, then, speak to me, you haven't much time."

The cherry blossom petals, to remind him always of what he'd lost, what he couldn't have, like a fishhook piercing his breastbone and pulling, calling to him, and something in him calling back.

No. He couldn't let it in. Except he couldn't keep it *out* it, either.

Control. Focus.

He had to get himself together. He had to get out of here. But first, he apparently had to convince Rihansei that he could unlock that other shackle.

"Incendiary." Rihansei's grip tightened. "*Are you—?*"

"*Yes*, I'm awake, quit bloody *nagging!*" It snapped out through a throat sore and dry, Jacin's voice raspier than usual. "Also, what the hell? *You're* the one who keeps drugging me."

Rihansei *tsked*, shaking his head. He reached to unlock Jacin's other wrist from the chains.

"And if you hadn't fought me so hard, we could have been done hours after we started, rather than days."

It had been Hitsuke who'd handed Raven the way to destroy the Jin, his strategy, his injudicious, weepy drivel that he'd spilled to Goyo outside that tearoom, and Raven had been listening. Hitsuke's first life as Untouchable had been one of abrupt, crushing insanity, just like all the rest.

Had Raven known the execution of Hitsuke's musings would drive the Ancestors mad, and thus the Untouchables? Had he known precisely how brutal the "punishment" would be for the one he'd promised to love?

"Days." Jacin repeated it stupidly, watching Rihansei fiddle with the key for several moments before he apparently got sick of faffing about with it and blew on the shackle. A small burst of light nearly blinded Jacin and heat flared over his skin, but the metal band around his wrist abruptly let go. "How *many* days?"

"My boy, I have lost track."

Gah. Days. No wonder Jacin felt like shit. How much of that tea had Rihansei poured down his throat while he'd been out of it? And how many of those bloodthirsty little lizards had snacked on him?

Rihansei was rubbing at Jacin's other wrist now, inspecting the damage, of which there was plenty. It looked like Jacin had fought against them quite a lot while he'd been… walking his path, Rihansei had said, but nothing about any of it felt like it belonged to him. More like echoes of someone else—too many someone elses—who shared the shape of him.

Every turn of Untouchable—he remembered them all. Remembered those he'd loved and lost, as though his love was a curse, crushing all those he dared to take into his heart. Every face, every tear, every stinging score to skin-heart-soul. Every insane Voice that had echoed through his head until he'd lost himself inside the madness, and then the petals came.

Jacin had been wrong—insanity would not be a relief. Real insanity was all too close, and it had a wide, gaping mouth with razor-sharp fangs.

He healed too fast, from hurts he probably shouldn't heal from at all, because he would live longer that way, and Raven wanted each agonizing life to stretch for as long as possible.

Liquor only temporarily numbed him, never obliterating the torment; drugs and potions only gave him a fraction of their promised reprieve. There was to be no escape from the torture of life for Raven's "duplicitous" Hitsuke.

Fuck. He couldn't reconcile it. He was Jacin, except he was Hitsuke, with all of Hitsuke's pain locked up inside him, all of Hitsuke's anger and hurt pressing at Jacin's skin, his heart, his *soul*. It was all Jacin could do to not judder apart beneath it, to hold it all in, until Rihansei finally decided Jacin's hands weren't going to fall off and got out of his way so he could make a break for it. To go where, Jacin had no idea, but he had to go, he *had* to *go*.

Pushing his way through the petals, not remembering why, not knowing what waited for him there. And each time, his god had embraced him like the lost love he wished he was. And each time, he'd wept and wept. And each time, he'd been offered a choice:

"Ask me, my Hitsuke. Tell me you were wrong, ask me to forgive you, and I will do it."

And oh, he wanted to, every time, he wanted so badly to simply fold at Raven's feet and beg. *He could do that no more than he could have willingly brought about the destruction of an entire people.*

"There is not as much time as I would wish." Rihansei's gaze was intense but full of rue. "You must go now."

Bizarre panic shot through Jacin, even as relief and the pressure to get up and flee raked him all over again. After all of… whatever all this had been, after *everything*, Rihansei was just going to set Jacin loose to… to do what?

"It is mine to show you your path and set you upon it; it is not mine to protect you from what it calls down upon you." Rihansei set a wide hand to Jacin's cheek. "Listen to me, little Incendiary. You were what you were and you are what you are. You now have the power to decide what you will be. Hand it to no one. Understand?"

Jacin didn't, not really, but he had a feeling he should, so he nodded, mute. Tears were crowding at his eyes, he couldn't help it, but letting them out now would shatter him utterly.

"You will know love, my Hitsuke." Cold and angry—hurt, maybe, though that could have been wishful thinking. "You will know love so you may know the pain of losing it." Rough hands on him, hands that had held him and brought him to bliss times uncountable, and now did nothing more than shake him harshly and bind him to one miserable mortal life after another. "Just say it, Hitsuke. Tell me you love me, tell me you were wrong, and come home to me."

Rihansei sighed and patted Jacin's cheek. "I do not think you understand, but I think you perhaps will. There is hope for you, little Incendiary. Fate never abandoned you. She merely loosened your leash. You, more than any other, know that what you ask of her, she will answer in her own ways. It is yours to divine those ways, know their price, before you ask her." His eyes narrowed down to slits, and he cocked his head to the side; a listening posture. He sighed again. "They come. And he will not be long behind. I am sorry. I thought there would be time. I did not know it was him."

That didn't exactly nip the panic, but it did give it focus.

"Who?" Jacin's whole body was strung tight and vibrating. "Time for what?"

Rihansei didn't answer; he merely hauled himself up and pulled Jacin up with him. Jacin's legs were wobbly, and everything around him immediately started doing somersaults and backflips. Fuck, weak and woozy, and from the way Rihansei was talking, trouble was coming.

"This is a neutral house, but no longer a safe place for you. Word has spread. You have to go." Rihansei lifted Jacin's hand and waved at Malick's ring. "Do you know how to use that?"

"I know how to call shadows."

"And that's all?" Rihansei's mouth pinched down. "I suppose it will have to do. You can use them if you need them to get out."

"And go *where*? I don't even know where the fuck I am."

Rihansei seemed to dither over that. After a moment he merely shook his head and began pushing Jacin off into the shadows on the other side of the chamber.

"Wolf's house." Resolute though dubious. "It is not as safe as Wolf's-own would like to think, but it is safer than here."

"But…" Jacin let himself be prodded for a few steps then dug in his heels. "I have questions. I have—"

I have dozens of crazy people in my head now instead of just me, and now you're just going to fucking leave me like this?

"Why did you do all this? What am I supposed to do now? Who am I supposed to *be*?"

Rihansei sighed, looking genuinely regretful. It didn't stop him from shoving Jacin more firmly.

"Those questions I cannot answer for you."

Jacin could have killed him. Just flung out a knife and pegged him right between his freaky red eyes.

"Then *why*—?"

Rihansei wasn't listening anymore, merely driving Jacin inexorably to wherever he was being driven. Jacin tripped over the cushions and knocked over the water pipe, almost landing with his face in the fire, which would have been just about right, he supposed. The walking stick was still propped to the side; Rihansei snatched it up and shoved it into Jacin's hands as he snagged Jacin's collar and the back of his shirt and all but threw him into the wall.

Except it wasn't a wall, Jacin realized, since he just kept falling even after he should have already rammed into it facefirst. He squelched when he hit, though, warm muck beneath his hands and knees, and he imagined all those little lizards staring at him in the dark where they could see him and he couldn't see them.

It stank. No, it *stank*.

Jacin squinted over his shoulder, gaze caroming around until it latched onto the small ovate glow from what must be Rihansei's chamber, but that seemed much too far away for the short fall Jacin had taken. It was a void of light, wherever this place was, not even a trickle of the weak glow from the chamber making it past the ragged edges.

A snarl burbled at the back of Jacin's throat. In the dark, fuck knew where, fresh from having his head split open—apparently for Rihansei's own entertainment, simply because he could—and now unarmed yet again. The stick was still in his hand, covered now with whatever goo he was kneeling in, but at least he had it. Not even any of the little knives he'd had secreted about his person were there, and he didn't even want to know if it had been Rihansei or Leu who'd got those off him.

Speaking of which—fucking Leu. Hopefully Rihansei hadn't actually killed her, because Jacin would kind of like to hunt her down and do it himself. *She* was the one who'd got him into this. Then again, she'd also been pretty adamant Rihansei not do what he'd done, and Jacin had to admit he would've much preferred she'd won that one.

It hadn't stopped rocketing around inside him— everything he'd been, every*one* he'd been, everything he'd seen, done, felt. And still, Hitsuke was who stood out; Hitsuke was where everything else came from, like a Kiwa Shuua, chasing Jacin down, rolling him under, and he had no idea if he should fight the ripping undertow or just… go with it.

He didn't have time to ponder it.

A scream came from behind him, though it didn't sound like Rihansei's voice. Still, it was bloodcurdling enough to make Jacin snap his glance toward the soft glow of the chamber's portal. Nothing happened for a moment. Another. Then.

A man's shape filled the small opening. Nothing more than a dark silhouette. And yet.

There was no way Jacin could tell who it was in the dark and from this far away. But somehow he was certain it was Beishin.

Panic took him. He froze where he was, almost thigh- and elbow-deep in slime and muck, and whispered the spell that would bring the shadows.

The figure only stood there. The hairs at Jacin's nape prickled, as though whoever it was were trying to strain sight through murk. It was probably seconds, but it felt like forever, before a great *whoosh* of flame flared from Rihansei's chamber, blinding, and when Jacin could see again, the figure was gone.

Shouts went up. A waft of smoke reached him all the way down in the muck.

Jacin decided now would probably be a good time to move his ass. And if he had any idea where he was supposed to go, maybe he would. He couldn't see a damned thing.

…Except.

"What is…?" Jacin narrowed his eyes, blinked and blinked, until the tiny glowy thing through the dark came into fuzzy focus, and resolved into… "Oh, fuck *me.*"

A faint gleam of firelight glinted off the bright green hide of one of the little lizards.

Jacin stilled. Because the little fuckers *hurt.* He could still feel the ghosts of their bites all over him.

It stared at him, which was impossible, because he hadn't said the spell to take away the shadows yet. Except, when Jacin cautiously leaned to the side and down, the little thing's faintly firelit yellow eyes followed him. And then again, when he shifted back the other way. And then it turned slowly and began to scuttle off. When Jacin only stared after it, losing its green glow to pitch darkness not four paces away, it came back, blinked at him some more, then turned around and… sauntered. There was no other word for it. It swayed its little self slowly over mud and muck, turning now and then to stare at Jacin with eyes almost as freaky as its apparent master.

Well, wherever it was going, it seemed like the smell was coming from that direction, so Jacin thought maybe he'd go the other way. Until he started to turn and the damned thing *hissed* at him. Jacin gave the thing a chary glare. Because hissing generally preceded biting. And had he mentioned that the little fuckers *hurt?* He kept still as it did its strange dance once again, walking off a waggling few paces, turning around, doing its staring-and-blinking thing, then settling in as if—

Wait.

This thing wasn't trying to get Jacin to follow it out of here, was it?

Improbable, certainly, but… impossible? They seemed to follow Rihansei's orders like little pets, so…

Another gust of flame burst from Rihansei's Gate, and more shouts filtered out to where Jacin crouched in smelly goo, staring at a fucking lizard.

"If you get me lost," he told it evenly, "I get to eat you. And any of your little friends that might show up."

The lizard merely flicked out its tongue, showing off its tiny teeth that Jacin knew from experience stung like a bitch. Almost a *Yeah, sure, we'll see who takes a bite out of whom*, and then it started to slither away again.

Wary, Jacin began to crawl after it. Because it wasn't as though he had a lot of options. And he'd certainly done crazier things in his life. Lives.

He could swear the uncanny little thing wagged its tail.

⛩

Joori's hands were covered in blood when he edged back to give Naro-yi room to have a look at Samin. It only took a moment before Naro-yi peered up, letting his gaze skip from Morin to Shig to Joori.

"I have to call for Imara."

It took a second for Joori to clear the worry for Samin and the general panic at the situation so he could interpret that expectant look in Naro-yi's eyes.

Right. If Imara knew they were here, any hope of going in after Jacin would be quashed with absolute finality.

Joori twigged at the same time Morin did.

"Joori. Someone has to do it." Morin was gripping one of Jacin's knives like he thought it should be him.

Samin's teeth had blood on them. "Someone bloody well does *not*." He was laid out on his back in the flimsy shadows against the wall of the bashed-in spice shop, blood everywhere. And *still*, he'd managed to wheeze it out like a reprimand.

The fire blazed. The *banpair* who'd been lining the tops of the buildings were now in the street, engaging the men and women of the Patrol in a battle that was looking fiercer and more chaotic by the second. They were doing their tricks with the shadows again, disappearing then reappearing, attacking from the rear every chance they got. It had been bad enough the other night, when only four of them had been up against two maijin and a *Temshiel*, but most of the people out there were mortal and heavily outnumbered. At least that Seb and his cronies seemed to be doing some damage.

There was no time for careful consideration. Samin had a knife jutting out of his chest and Naro-yi couldn't fix it. Imara could, and if they got Imara over here before someone went after Jacin, no one would be going after Jacin.

Joori looked at Shig. "Can you find Jacin?"

"I don't know." Shig tipped a jerky little nod at Naro-yi. She looked all at once terrified. "He said it, I didn't."

"The shepherds." Naro-yi set a calming hand on Shig's arm. "They know you. They'll take you."

Whatever that meant, it would have to be good enough.

Joori nodded. "Let's go." He stood.

"Hey!" Morin stood too.

Samin coughed and sent a spate of eye-poppingly filthy oaths at stubborn boys who thought they were soldiers, and everyone he knew named "Fen."

Joori ignored it all, not letting his own thoughts through, let alone anyone else's, and hauled Shig to her feet. He did a cursory check of all the weapons he'd borrowed from Jacin's and Malick's stores then started tugging Shig along the wall.

"*Hey!*" Morin lurched at Joori, managing to snag his arm and stop him. "What d'you think you're doing? You're not a warrior, Joori, all you're going to do is get yourself—"

Joori stopped him with a surprisingly—even to himself—gentle hand to Morin's shoulder. An odd calm had settled over him, a rather startling one, considering what he knew he was walking into and what he was going to have to walk through to get there. Maybe he was still high.

Thing was, Morin wasn't wrong—Joori was no warrior. And his most valuable weapon had been lifted from his soul when the Ancestors had gone home. But Jacin had become a killer for him, had made himself his own very first victim when he'd killed Jacin-rei and most of Jacin to become Fen for him. Joori owed him this much. If Joori couldn't have Jacin back, he could at least make sure Fen survived.

Anyway, Joori was firstborn; all this should've been his job from the beginning.

Joori didn't say any of that. He said, "One of our own is in there." He even managed a small smile when Morin scowled at him. "I know you probably don't believe this, but I'd do the same for you. So would Jacin. And I know you'd do it for either one of us. It's just..." Joori shrugged. "This time it's me."

And maybe it was about time.

"Take care of Samin." Joori looked away for a second then leveled a somber gaze on his little brother, who really wasn't so little anymore. "And, um... try not to die, yeah?"

Morin stared at him, firelight catching at arguments and rebuttals and denials, all glimmering in his hazel eyes. He voiced none of it, only tipped a short, sharp nod, and turned away when his chin started to quiver.

Joori turned, too, and pulled Shig along before he had time to think or Morin had time to change his mind and come up with too-convincing arguments about why Joori was a complete lunatic and about to get himself killed.

Shig took the lead almost immediately, and Joori let her. She'd been the assassin, after all. All stealth and silence, she skirted them into the edges of the shadows slanting from the storefronts along the street until they'd traveled at least two blocks, then finally crossed over, past the street where the Gates of Rapture burned and around toward the back of it. Making sure no one had followed, they started cautiously making their way back. Back toward the battle that, by the quick glimpse Joori'd had as they'd darted across the street, was looking sickeningly bloody right now. And a tavern that was going up like a spilled lamp.

"We're going to have to make it through right there." Shig pointed down the backstreet and to the right.

It was deserted back here, everyone gone to the festival, no doubt, which was... probably good. Joori didn't really know, actually. No help, but at least no black-clad figures skulked that Joori could see. Though that didn't mean anything with those creatures.

Joori turned to Shig. "And then what?"

"Well." Shig huffed with a helpless shrug. "They're little dark-dwellers." Meaning the lizards, or "shepherds," Joori supposed. "I guess that means they live... um... under."

Under.

Oh good.

"There's a drainage grate in front of that flower stand." Shig looked at Joori as though she was hoping for approval. "I figure that's gotta go under something, right?"

Joori's eyebrows went up, and his mind kind of went off on a bit of an *Ew, under what?* tangent. Still, it wasn't like he knew what he was doing. Who was he to criticize?

"Um, yeah." He gave the grate a dubious frown. "Sure."

And fuck if the little bastards weren't wriggling around in apparent lizardly welcome when Joori followed Shig over there. They even glowed in the dark. Or maybe it was more like their hides caught the light of the moons shining down through the thin stratum of cloud cover.

Weirdly, that made Joori feel a little better about it.

"You're here!" Shig's whisper was more like a high-pitched trill, obvious relief, as she knelt among them and put out her hand. Two of them hopped up and curled around her fingers. "You're going to help, right?"

Joori would swear they wagged their tails. He didn't know if shock would offend Shig, so he tried not to show it. But he was pretty damned shocked.

The grate gave easily when Joori yanked on it, like it was there for show. He found a pebble and threw it in first; he wasn't pretending to be a warrior, but breaking his legs before he'd even so much as drawn a weapon would've been pretty embarrassing. Satisfied the darkness wasn't bottomless, Joori lowered himself down until his boots touched solid rock, careful not to step on any of the lizards that spilled down after him and writhed around his feet. Joori watched them with a scowl.

"Couldn't've done that five seconds ago, *before* I climbed down in the dark, could you?"

Muttering a few soft oaths, Joori settled his footing, then reached up and helped Shig.

It wasn't anything like Joori had expected. He'd seen the grate and immediately thought *sewer*, but it was dry and solid with only a faint smell of decay. A tunnel, almost, but it didn't look like it had been carved—natural, maybe, formed by ancient lava veins from the fire-mountains that hunkered at the edge of the city. A very faint orange glow was coming from below, a distinct flicker to it, and Joori had time to hope this was an *extinct* lava vein before Shig was following the lizards and hauling Joori along behind her.

"C'mon, don't piss them off."

Yeah, Joori thought. *All right. Sure. Don't piss off the lizard-shepherd things. Fine. Because that's not crazy at all.*

Still, he let himself be tugged along. Jacin was down here somewhere, and it hadn't looked to Joori like it was going to take those *banpair* long to get to him. Naro-yi said Shig could follow the lizards to Jacin, and since Shig *was* following the lizards, Joori followed her. Because it wasn't like there was a not-as-crazy alternative.

They were going down and it was steep, so their pace was almost a trot. Joori had to snatch at Shig and then reach out for a quick hold on the rock walls a couple of times to prevent them from going too fast and losing their footing. The lizards skittered ahead of them, the soft green glow of at least one of them always in sight, and Joori found himself not caring anymore how bizarre all this was. If these things really did lead him to Jacin, he'd build them their own little shrine and leave a mound of whatever it was lizards ate on its altar every day.

…Unless it was chopped-up worms, like that fucked-up fish Morin had been keeping. Then no.

It seemed like they'd been descending for a long time when the hazy orange blush in the distance suddenly flared. Joori grabbed hold of Shig's arm, stopped her. They watched, silent, waiting, until the light flared again. Almost like a small, very quiet explosion. Joori looked at Shig; Shig blinked back. It was the only communication between them, but they apparently didn't need clarification.

They ran, heedless of the sharp slant of the gradient or the danger of tripping and careening down it headfirst.

They'd lost the lizards back there somewhere. Whether it was because Joori and Shig were moving too fast for little amphibian legs, or because guides were no longer necessary, Joori didn't know, and when they heard the scream ratchet out from the chamber at the end of the shaft, it didn't seem to matter much. A great *whoosh* of flame burst from the end of the tunnel this time, and rolled upward right toward Joori and Shig.

Joori snatched Shig by the back of her coat and flattened them both to the wall. He pressed Shig between himself and the wall, turned his head and shut his eyes, trying not to breathe, until the heat and crackle receded. Cautiously, he blinked, gave himself a quick check to make sure he hadn't caught fire, then did the same for Shig. He set a finger to his lips.

Shig nodded, wide-eyed. She was breathing just as quickly and shallowly as Joori was.

"… not your man. Another of mine, *stolen* from me."

The voice was… not unpleasant, really, but there was something deep and vaguely foul about it, though Joori couldn't have said why he thought that. Maybe because of where he was and what was going on. Which, all right, Joori didn't really know what was going on, and he couldn't stretch his neck around the bend in the tunnel far enough to see. He did it anyway, straining until he at least saw the chamber itself and the very edge of what he determined was a black-clad shoulder within it.

"They were never *yours*." This was a different voice, a lilting baritone that nevertheless dripped with scorn. "*None* of them were ever *yours*. Did you learn nothing from your long years of forced sleep?" There was a pause and then a smug chuckle. "Oh yes, I know who you are, *seyh*. I've felt your presence looming since you snatched your first lost soul. Did you not consider as much?"

"And why do you suppose I'm here?"

"I know why you're here. And I know what you've done. You will not enslave the Incendiary again."

Incendiary. Enslave. *Shit.*

Joori snapped a glance back to Shig. She shook her head at him in warning. Joori wasn't even offended. He might not be *quite* stupid enough to go bursting in there, but he couldn't deny the thought had occurred to him. Very, very slowly and as quietly as he could, Joori drew Malick's sword and Jacin's knife. With a nod this time, Shig just as quietly drew her own weapons.

"Where is he?" That first voice again, obviously angry now. "He was here. I can smell the blood."

The idea of it would never stop giving Joori the shudders. That these people could smell it when Jacin—

Oh, shit. Jacin had been here and he'd been bleeding.

"He has grown strong in this life, seyh. He has already moved worlds. I do not think he will move this one to your liking."

"He will be what *I*—"

"You made a mistake. Because you always do. You assume others share your motives and simply lack the strength to achieve them. You take and think it makes you strong."

There was a grunt then some scuffling. A small but very steady hissing noise rose.

Joori tried again to crane his neck and peer around the curve in the rock, but all he could see were small fires everywhere and the shadows they threw, and he didn't quite have the nerve to breach the chamber itself. It seemed like an unnecessary risk, at any rate; by what Joori was gleaning from this strange conversation, Jacin wasn't in there.

"You could have had what I once had, Rihansei. You could have beat me to it and had what I mean to take now."

The laugh that answered was deep and rich and long. It sounded very real and genuinely amused.

"No sane man would want what you had, seyh. No sane man, having lost it, would want it back. But then I suppose you left both 'sane' and 'man' long behind you."

Silence. Even though Joori couldn't really see anything but two vaguely man-shaped shadows casting wavering planes and angles over the stone of the chamber walls, he could swear he felt a malignant pressure building. Shig seemed to feel it too, because her small hand took hold of Joori's sleeve, and when he looked at her, her eyes were wide and scared.

"There cannot be two of us, Rihansei."

"No, I suppose there cannot. Nor can there be six, and yet there are."

"Pretenders. Usurpers."

"Children born of despoilment. What did you expect of such folly?" The voice Joori assumed belonged to the man named Rihansei rolled out in another long chuckle. "Did you really think Tonyai's and Tompai's power so weak it would not extend to their children? Their faces sear your mortal skin when you walk beneath them, don't they?" Angrier, gaining volume and depth. "And Fate dogs your every step."

"I bested her once."

"Did you?"

There was a meaty *thud* and a pained grunt, and the hissing rose in volume. A strained cry came next. This time, Joori was sure it was Rihansei's voice. He gave Shig a look he doubted she knew what to do with, because he didn't know what he was thinking, either. He turned and stretched farther, edging around the corner. He could see two men now—one with his back to Joori, wearing a dirty, bulky cloak, but otherwise unremarkable so far as build and size. Until Joori noticed that he held a much larger man up in the air, arm extended so that…

No, he wasn't holding the man. The man was simply floating in front of him. And if the bend of his large body and the set of his face were any indications, it appeared to be horribly painful.

One of the men from the tavern, or at least he had the look. White-haired and bearded and tattooed. Another lay on the far side of the chamber; Joori couldn't make out much but a lot of blood and a dead, wide-eyed stare pointing at the chamber's ceiling. Maybe the scream they'd heard earlier had come from that one. A ring of the little lizards sat remarkably still around him, like they were guarding his corpse. A sea of the tiny things writhed around on the floor, hissing angrily, leaping and crawling over each other beneath Rihansei's feet.

"Give me the Incendiary and I'll make it quick. *Tell me where you sent him!*"

This, Joori decided, had to be the man—creature—who'd been hounding Jacin. And this other man, this Rihansei, looked like he was prepared to die before handing Jacin over.

One tiny green lizard tumbled from the teeming pile and skittered across the floor in a straight line. Joori was afraid to move, afraid to attract attention, so he only watched it come until it reached the toe of his boot and scrabbled up. And then it simply had itself a seat and hissed up at him.

What the hell?

"The Incendiary is not mine to give." Rihansei's red eyes flickered over at Joori, resting for half a second before rolling back toward the man who held him up in the air as if by invisible restraints. "He seeks an end to his long existence as a pawn—*finally*. For good or ill, none but Fate will ever again hold this Incendiary. Not even his own."

It struck at Joori, like it was meant for him.

"I already hold him, fool. I own shape because *he* believes in me enough now to give it to me." The man thumped at his chest. "Blood and bone—a gift all unknowing from the Incendiary to his true master." The chuckle this time was harsh and cruel. "How horrible it must have been when you realized what path it was he walked. How bitter to know that Rihansei, *Gatekeeper*, was the one who gave me the ability to walk through *my Gate* by giving the Incendiary back to himself. He remembers me, Rihansei, he *believes*. He gives me power because *you* set him on his path. Does the irony *hurt?*"

His hand lifted, clenched into a fist, and twisted in the air between them. Rihansei reacted to it like the man had just crushed his heart. He cried out, back arching and legs spasming, then a thin stream of blood dripped from the corner of his mouth. It pattered past his feet and to the floor, the lizards diving at it and hissing angrily.

"I won't ask again." The man's fist opened then clenched tight again.

Rihansei screamed this time, but it ended in a watery chuckle. "You are a more powerful magician than I, but that is all. You cannot send me any place I am afraid to go and will not be welcomed. Can you say the same?"

"A magician uses his magic. I have watched you for a very long time now. You are nothing more than a self-righteous novice who failed to hold my Gate against me. I *am* more powerful than you. And I *will* open your mind and take what I need from it, if I must."

"Perhaps you can crash *my* Gate, deceiver-demigod, but your minions cannot. And I am not the last."

Run, Fen Joori bloomed in Joori's mind, all at once and with such force it nearly knocked him off his feet. He jerked his glance down, because as ridiculous as it was, it had the feel of Rihansei's "voice," but Joori would swear it came from that little lizard blinking up at him from the toe of his boot. *Take her and run.* Shig was already plucking at Joori's sleeve, so maybe she'd "heard" it too, but Joori couldn't make himself move.

"This does not please me." The man—*creature*—was smiling, Joori could hear it in the smug tone. "A regrettable waste of power. You would have been much more useful to me, had you listened to reason."

"*Ssst.*" Shig nudged at Joori.

Joori was too caught up in what he was seeing and hearing.

Go, Fen Joori. She would be valuable to him, if he realizes she is here, and he will know what I know all too soon.

The man's fisted hand turned and twisted again. Rihansei reared back and screamed. And then the dark mass at the man's back that Joori had thought a bulky cloak abruptly opened and spread, resolving itself into ragged, dusky wings that unfurled with a heavy *whoosh* as Rihansei writhed in midair.

Right, then. Fuck this.

With a shudder, Joori edged back around the bend of the stone, head bowed, staring at the little lizard that had come along for the ride on the toe of his boot. It hopped off and trundled into the shadows to the side, turning back to stare up and hiss.

"We have to follow it." Shig whispered it right in Joori's ear; Joori didn't know if the shudder this time was at the idea of what Shig had just said or the fact that she'd kind of said it down his collar. "The *shepherds*," Shig pressed, like it was supposed to make sense

And all right, Joori guessed he couldn't be picky since he'd followed the thing down here—if it was even the same one, because really, who could tell?—but apparently coming down here had been rather a horrible idea in the first place, and now it looked like the thing was wanting to lead them right into a stone wall.

"We *have* to." Shig half shoved, half dragged Joori toward the hissing little bit of scales and teeth and long, flickery tongue.

When the shadowed wall into which Shig was propelling him turned out to be a pitch-black passageway instead, Joori seriously contemplated squishing the glowy little lizard and running back up to the street. Instead, he sucked in a breath, reached for Shig's hand in the dark, and followed it.

╥

"You're *sure?*" Morin gave Imara a glare to make sure she knew she'd better not try to give him any happy bullshit. "He's not going to die?"

They'd dragged Samin into a closed-up teashop. The fire had been put out, but Morin didn't know how—he'd been kind of busy—but he could still hear the sounds of battle out there. From Imara's appearance and apparent distraction, he didn't think it was going well.

"He will not die." Imara was out of breath, and mussed more than Morin ever would've believed when he'd first seen her in her studied perfection. There was no telling if any of the blood all over her was hers, but Morin didn't spare any worry over it—she could bloody well heal herself *after* she'd healed Samin. "He was wise to don the mail."

Well, it would've been pretty hypocritical of him, had he not. He'd made a big to-do about searching through Jacin's things so Joori could wear Jacin's mail, and then he'd made Shig dig up an extra vest for Morin. Morin suspected it had been Yori's, but he hadn't asked.

"Your heart beats steadily already." Imara gave Samin a practiced and rather out-of-place smile, and sat back, bloody hands still set firmly to Samin's chest.

Samin peered down to have a look then gave Morin a reassuring nod. "Told you, didn't I?"

Well, sort of. He'd actually said he was *too* mean to die, and Morin hadn't argued, because it could be true sometimes, but not in general. Morin had no illusions about any of the people he loved, but there was more to all of them besides "assassin" or "brother" or even the new "Incendiary" thing. And not one of them deserved a messy death at the hands of *banpair*, regardless of what Samin might think.

Morin tried to give Samin a chuckle, but simply couldn't do it. Naro-yi was still out there, having joined the bloody, violent fight as soon as Imara had arrived—Imara had *not* been happy to see them here—and Morin couldn't believe he'd gotten attached so quickly, but he really hoped Naro-yi was as good at combat as he looked to be.

"You're veiled." Imara wiped her hands on what was left of Samin's coat, then hauled herself up, apparently finished. "I can't protect you here. I'm having a difficult time protecting anyone here." It looked like she was trying not to cry. For the first time, Imara seemed strangely... *real*. "My veil will get you out, but I'm stretched too far already. And you can't be here."

Morin gave her his best Jacin-glare. "My brothers—"

"If they are in there..." Imara sighed and waved helplessly toward the front of the shop, outside of which the sounds of battle raged. She opened her mouth as if to go on, but paused when she caught Morin's eye. Morin didn't know what Imara saw when she looked at him, but it made her shake her head and sigh again. She turned her attention to Samin. "You're not going to leave, are you?"

Samin propped himself slowly to his elbows and looked over at Morin, searching.

Morin wasn't very good at hiding things. Right now, he didn't have the wits to try anyway. Shame teased, because he was pretty sure the fact that yes, he absolutely *would* ask Samin to go back out there and try again, even after having been miraculously healed from a knife to the chest, was all over him.

Samin didn't look disappointed in Morin. Samin looked kind of... proud. He turned to Imara and shook his head.

"We can't. You've got your own and we've got ours."

Imara rubbed at her brow and nodded. Mouth set tight, she bent down to set a hand on Morin's shoulder and then Samin's, said, "Then I'm sorry," right before Morin felt a weird *push* and then a dizzy wave.

He was blinking at the fish jumping and flopping back down into the pool before he realized he and Samin were sprawled out on the green of Wolf's temple.

Imara was already gone.

⛩

Panic was a sharp-toothed bastard. All Jacin could do was try to blank his mind against it. He followed the ridiculous little lizard through the pitch of the tunnels, crawling through reeking muck, and swatting down every thought that tried to assert itself. He would not "remember" things another man had lived. He would not "recognize" people he'd never seen before and places he'd never been. He would not "relive" events that had happened to someone else.

Instead, he would focus on the darkness, the emptiness, the… worry?—that seemed too personal—the distant concern over what might have happened to Rihansei and who that might have been, standing in that firelit portal and staring through the darkness, maybe looking for—

Right. Not thinking about that, either.

One hand in front of the other, the aches all over him, inside him, the irrational, childish fear of the blank dark and the fact that he was embarrassingly relieved by the unnatural glow of that stupid little lizard. Jacin concentrated only on the physical, the vague concern over where exactly he was being led—if he was even being led at all and hadn't gone so completely insane he was imagining guide-lizards—and finding a way to get back to the inn where he'd left Morin and Joori. These were the things Jacin let himself think about as his trousers grew steadily wetter and heavier, as various parts of him complained about the abuse, as the smell grew, and as he kept crawling steadily toward… wherever he might end up.

"Wherever" turned out to be the mouth of a drainage duct that let out onto a winter-bare stretch of scrub and muddy slush along the river strand. Jacin was on his back, winded and staring up at the sky, before it registered that one moment he'd been slogging along, hand over hand, and the next his palm had settled into empty air, tipping him out of the tunnel and dumping him several feet to the ground.

Dark and cold. Getting toward midnight, perhaps, if the sets of the—

No, he wasn't going to think about the moons. He wasn't going to think about anything to do with the moons. He wasn't going to think about anything at all, just like he hadn't been thinking about anything for… who knew? As long as it had taken him to get to where he was now, anyway.

Gray, cragged peaks made silhouettes against the sky; Jacin absently took his bearings from their position, refusing to acknowledge that he hadn't known the city only days ago, and now he knew exactly where he was—beside the river that wound to the sea along the base of the fire-mountains that hunched over the temples on the outskirts of Mitsu.

Jacin stared at the curls and spires of the hulking marble structures for quite some time. Stubbornly blank. A willful void. Just a smudge of anonymous nothing lying in the mud, stinking, and refusing to remember watching the temples go up, refusing to look at the moons against which their shapes stood like sharp-edged cutouts.

It… wasn't quite working. He snapped his gaze away and looked back to the drainage tunnel from which he'd fallen.

He'd never lost sight of the little lizard. Somehow. He didn't think he'd ever been anywhere so completely void of light before. It was as if it gave off its own light. And now that it had apparently fulfilled its task, the little creature was nowhere in sight. It was bizarrely disappointing.

Jacin huffed—it wasn't like he was going to thank it, or anything—then gagged when he got a whiff of himself.

Bloody hell, he stank. There had been a point when the smell had started to really get to him, and he'd wondered if he wasn't perhaps traveling along the city's sewers, but he cut that one off before it started. Now that there was a river quite literally at his feet, he could admit to himself that yes, he'd probably just spent what felt like several hours crawling through other people's—

You know what? No.

He'd hung onto the stick. Through everything, he'd hung onto the stupid wolf's head walking stick that had started the whole bloody mess. A weapon. That was all. And the only one he had right now. The death-grip he couldn't seem to loosen was nothing to do with its ivory decorative grip. The hollow pang in his chest at the thought of hurling it into the river was nothing to do with a vivid remembrance of having—

Holy fucking shit, he'd slept with a god.

Two of them.

Had loved…

No. Just… *no.*

Hallucinations, like everything else. He didn't think he could cope if all of that had been real. Because what was he supposed to do with any of it? Except refusing to look at it was doing little good—the images-memories-useless-fucking-lives now took up space in his head where the voices of the Ancestors used to live, and he simply didn't have room for anything else. He was crazy—best leave it at that.

He hauled himself up, and took the several wobbly, squishy steps necessary to dunk himself in the river. The water was bitter-cold and salt-heavy with backwash from the bay. It froze his breath, jabbed like icy blades through his skin. But he reeked and he was sticky, and he'd apparently been out of his mind on whatever Rihansei had been giving him for days. This was the best he could do for a bath right now. And he'd endured worse.

His wrists were still bleeding. He must have really been yanking on those shackles, and for quite a long time. Anger for Rihansei sparked as he scrubbed away the worst of the caked-on blood with shaky fingertips, but there were so many other things to be angry about, and he wasn't willing to give any of them recognition. And then he remembered why bleeding was a dangerous thing in the first place, and everything else kind of paled.

If anyone found him now… Well. Frankly, they probably wouldn't get much of a fight, if they wanted him.

Still, it was probably best to keep his hands beneath the water. Water made tracking difficult for hunting dogs, right? Maybe it was the same with immortals. Unless the gods could see him. Could the gods see him?

Jacin peered at the mucky wolf's head atop the stick. That was still, *somehow*, in his hand.

"Can you see me?"

A sharp little giggle burbled at the back of his throat. He choked it back.

The panic was starting to gnaw at him. He wouldn't let it. He couldn't.

He dipped the stick, swishing the wolf's head around to clear it of sludge and other things he was going to pretend he didn't know about. Watched the ripples. Listened to the splash. Nothing else. Nothing *more*.

…It wasn't working.

The memories were just as insistent as the Ancestors had ever been, trying to wend into him, become a part of him. He couldn't let them. *Couldn't*. It had taken him this long just to be *Jacin*—whoever that was, and whatever the problems that came along with it. He was *not* going to be usurped by some quasi-immortal being who'd been stupid enough to let love—

"*Fuck!*" Jacin crouched in the freezing water, the cold seeping through to bone, his breath laden mist on the air, and clamped his hands to his head, trying to ward off the things that would not be warded off. "Malick." Weak and small. "Tell me you didn't know about this."

Because if he had…

Had he?

Malick was a manipulator who'd promised not to manipulate Jacin, but Malick "handled" Jacin all the time, even when he thought he was being perfectly straight. It was just who he was. Expecting him not to do it would be like expecting him not to breathe. He had to have known. It was probably why he'd been so bloody careful and anxious—Malick was never anxious about anything—and made his threats, because he'd fucking *known*, and he...

Damn it, Jacin couldn't even be pissed at Malick for not telling him, because he didn't want to know any of it, and Malick would have known that, too, because Malick just *knew*, even the things Jacin didn't tell him, like he could—

Shit. Had Malick known Hitsuke?

Jacin let the question blunder around inside him, refusing to look as it stumbled blind, seeking landmarks, but nothing clicked. There were no memories of a newly turned Null of Wolf inside what used to be Hitsuke. Jacin had no idea why it was such a relief, but he took it.

The shivering registered first; the bitter ache of sharp-edged cold slammed in right after it. Bloody hell, he was sitting in a fucking *river*, up to his waist, hair dripping and suspicious heat on his cheeks where apparent tears had mixed with river water. Sitting in a fucking *river*, staring at the damned wolf's head of the stick and quietly freaking out.

Was it too cold for water snakes?

After the lizards, did he care?

All he needed now was for Beishin to show up, and everything would be... well, clearly these sorts of things were normal for Jacin. And whoever he'd been.

Growling through chattering teeth, Jacin used the stick to lever to his feet, his boots heavy as he slogged his way over to the strand and threw himself down. And then remembered that he'd had smokes in his pocket.

"Bloody fucking *hell*," he muttered through his teeth as he extracted the waterlogged mess of pulp and tiny leaf bits and flung it to the ground. Damn it, he really could've used one too. Figured. He couldn't bloody win for losing.

Why didn't it just rain, while it was at it?

Still cursing, Jacin emptied the water from his boots first, debated trying to shimmy the wet leather back over his sopping stockings, and decided going barefoot might work better. He was already freezing, so fuck it.

He checked himself over again—no money, no coat, no weapons— and then he did it one more time, hoping that Leu or Rihansei had missed at least one small knife when they'd taken the rest, but no luck. Defenseless but for the stick, and he had to pause a moment to examine the implied metaphor. Because he didn't have to remember Hitsuke's experiences to know the gods were manipulative motherfuckers, and he really had to wonder now if Wolf had seen him coming and put that stick in that vendor's hands for a reason.

Some kind of message? *I am your only alternative now; you are unarmed but for me.*

Possible. Wolf had set Malick to the task of "saving" the Incendiary; there had to be a reason. And since Wolf had apparently watched what happened to Hitsuke and done *nothing*...

Had he watched? Had he known? Why did Jacin so desperately want to believe he hadn't? Jacin was *not* Hitsuke, damn it. He had no love for the gods, any of them, and certainly not for—

"Raven" escaped his mouth before he could stop it, and then, *"Daraso"* fell out right after it. Thick and choked, clotted with tears, but anger rose beneath it, *rage*, and Jacin was on his feet and stalking away from the river before he even realized he'd managed to move his frozen limbs.

He wouldn't remember, *refused* to remember, but damn it, of *course* he fucking remembered, because remembrance slid right past consciousness and into a soul he'd shared with someone who'd been so profoundly betrayed, Jacin didn't think there was a word that fit it. He'd *loved* that bastard, had put up his *soul* as collateral when that love was questioned, and had been shown in no uncertain terms exactly what value his soul—his life, his *sanity*—had to the one who was supposed to love him back. Fucking *tortured*, over and over again, sent insane by—

Had Raven been watching all those lives? Had he paused in whatever his "godly duties" were to look each time as the moment came and the Untouchable was brought to his knees beneath the Ancestors' screeching wails?

...Was he watching now?

Jacin stopped dead where he was, realizing only peripherally that he'd already passed the city's edge and was mere steps away from the rear paths that led to the temples, because all his attention was now on the sky, seeking the bloody red blot through the gap in the tops of the buildings between which he stood. He would stand beneath that fucking moon and he would look, and he would... *do* something. Scream, maybe. Rant and rave and rail, until someone called the Patrol and—

Whatever. Didn't matter. He needed to *do*—he'd figure out *do what?* when he got... wherever he was going.

He rounded the corner of the alley, paused for only a moment to get his bearings. Noise bloomed, like it had right that second sprung up out of nowhere, but Jacin suspected he'd been hearing it for a while and simply hadn't noticed. He hardly noticed now. All he could see was a tinge of red from Raven's face staining the emerald of Owl's flank through a thin stratum of encroaching clouds, so Jacin strode ahead. He was too furious to care where he was or where he was going, pushing through a clot of bodies and ignoring the indignant yips and reprimands as he knocked into one after the other.

Music skimmed from one of the wandering minstrels down the street, the melody forlorn and tenuous, as though bruised in the making. Cats screeched and yowled in battle several alleys over, the hissing wails too close to the cries of a newborn. Footsteps and then shouts and laughter all echoed from the temples. There were the calls of vendors, giggling shouts of children—it was all a hazy blur, smeared into the fury and the betrayal and the *hurt* that wouldn't stop clawing at the walls of what was left of Jacin's sanity.

He didn't have any way to stop the hurt. He'd never been good at not feeling things. But anger had always been a ready friend, an agreeable distraction and focal point. The pain was too numb beneath the cold and it wasn't helping him focus, so Jacin narrowed in on the fury, let it fill him and move him. He caught the glimmer of Raven's moon out the corner of his eye, dragged his gaze upward to give it a glare, and stalked toward the temples.

4

The scent hit him again. Goyo stopped, cocked his head.

It hit him first midbattle at the Gates of Rapture, overwhelmed him, blurring time into a vertiginous smear and sideswiping him with an odd sorrowful rage he hadn't quite known what to do with. But he'd understood this time what the scent was. What it meant. So he'd used the fury it stirred to eliminate any enemy within reach, then abandoned the battle to follow the pull toward the other side of the city.

Reaching now, seeking, he opened himself to both the spirits and every mortal around him, grasping for the thread that would lead him to the Incendiary and watching for trouble here at the festival as well. Because he had no doubt it was coming. There was a point being made by these *banpair*, and no one was quite getting it yet, but Goyo was more than certain it would be pounded home soon enough. And the creatures had already proven that the temples were just as vulnerable to them as anywhere else.

Could they discern the blood of the Incendiary too? Goyo thought probably. Too many of them had been maijin before they'd turned. For the first time, Goyo wished Fen Jacin knew how to use Kamen's ring.

He sniffed the air again. Strange; it wasn't an actual smell. More a sensation of a smell, but with a sense that was neither touch nor scent. And every *Temshiel* and maijin in the city—all of them called out on alert; all of them splitting their attention between the attack at Rihansei's and trying to prevent one at the festival—would likely sense it too.

Goyo was going to have to move fast.

He'd never understood the reasons behind the ability of the servants of the gods to perceive when the Incendiary bled. Some sort of distress signal meant to speed aid? Or a call to attack, like sharks scenting a kill from leagues away and racing in to share the feeding frenzy? Goyo didn't know, and there were none left who could tell him.

Odd, though, how when the awareness hit him, all he could see was Hitsuke, writhing in the dirt and calling his god's name.

Goyo couldn't let that interfere. There was no telling what Snake would require if Goyo got to the Incendiary first, but he wanted that option. He'd meant everything he'd said to Kamen's mortals. He wasn't even sure he cared anymore that he'd be rewarded for securing the Incendiary or killing him—whichever Snake wanted when the time came—or perhaps punished for failing. He cared that another might get that option first and… he didn't know—misuse it, maybe.

The river, he thought, tracing the feel and texture of the scent and letting his feet move without his direction. The river and the… Ah. The temples. The simplicity was almost surprising. Goyo very nearly chuckled.

He choked it back when another call hit him, urgent and far too gleeful. Not for the first time, Goyo found himself wishing the Incendiary had managed to take out Serenai too, when he'd sent Ari to spirit.

With a curse and a quick check of his weapons, Goyo picked up his pace and ran.

It was the scent of jasmine that led him. The scent of jasmine that filtered through the haze of rage covering all coherent thought. The scent of jasmine that stirred so many things inside him he couldn't possibly untangle one thing from another. So he didn't try.

Jacin merely followed the fog of perfume right over the low gate that stood before the temple, blew past too many people he didn't really see, and hurled himself up the steps and into the pillared antechamber that opened out onto the altar. Incense hung heavy, dense jasmine clouding into him like poppy smoke. Fogging. Confusing.

It was… oddly enraging.

Teeth bared, Jacin flung his anger outward like a shield, let it burn through the confusion and the memories he didn't want like a sun burning off mist. There were people in his way. Some of them tried to stop him. Jacin barreled through all of them, barely even seeing them, to hitch up—panting, shaking—in front of the altar. The altar he *remembered*. The altar where Hitsuke had once come to call upon his lover in his lonely mortality, whisper his love, and walk away with a smile and the scent of jasmine clinging to his hair.

"*Daraso!*" Jacin shoved at the little pots of ink and stacks of balsa tiles, scattering everything to the polished floor. Howls of protest rose around him, worshippers outraged by his disrespect. He spared a vicious snarl toward the blur of faces, satisfied when they backed off. The altar was too damned heavy to knock over, but Jacin tried. "*Daraso!* Face me, you son of a bitch—*Daraso!*"

"He will not answer you."

Jacin spun, stick raised instinctively. The woman who peered back at him from a few paces away neither flinched nor backed away.

Pale and beautiful, almost willowy, with dark hair and dark eyes, just like her master. Immortal. Of course. Wasn't just about everyone he ran into anymore? Jacin didn't recognize her, though, and if the lack of abrupt displacement in his head meant anything, Hitsuke hadn't known her.

Jacin assessed then dismissed her with a snarling "Fuck you" then he turned a hard glare on the few remaining worshippers until they backed farther out of the temple at the woman's discreet gesture. Jacin whirled back to the altar. "*Daraso!*"

"He knew you were coming. I have already alerted the Patrol that you are here."

Jacin spun back again, glaring.

The woman merely shrugged. "You attacked and sent to spirit one of Raven's-own. It is against the laws here."

"*Law.*" Jacin nearly spat on the floor. "As if your god gives the slightest *fuck* about any law but his own."

She laughed, a pleasing trill. "In this case, I expect it is mere convenience. Stand there and bellow all you like. The Patrol won't be long."

"So why not just kill me? I'm sure your god would—"

"If my god wanted you dead, you would have been so decades ago."

"Yeah, because it's so much more satisfying to watch me lose my mind." The mere speaking of it drove the rage up tighter, hotter, *burning* Jacin from the inside out. "Did he plan Asai too?"

Because didn't that just fit a little too serendipitously? No wonder Jacin had fallen so hard and so fast for those dark eyes; no wonder he'd just about licked Asai's boots for a scrap of approval, mercy, *love*. A sob drove up from his chest, burst out his mouth, and Jacin couldn't have held it back to save his life. He wavered, *this close* to hysteria, right in Raven's house, before his altar, like Jacin was making an offering of himself, and oh fuck, he hoped he wasn't, but he never could tell what he was doing until he was already knee-deep in doing it.

"Asai had the bad judgment to pledge to Wolf." The woman's tone seemed strangely sympathetic. "And so his actions and intentions were clouded from Raven's sight." She stepped closer and pushed still-wet hair from Jacin's eyes; Jacin couldn't find the will to flinch back. She smiled. "But even so, I think Raven would have approved. Don't you?"

Yes. Jacin did. Because it was all about revenge and punishment, wasn't it? Revenge and punishment and crushing the Jin so Wolf would weaken. What Asai had done to Jacin had certainly gone a ways toward the "revenge and punishment" part, and what he'd intended to do would have taken care of the "weaken Wolf" part. Because even had the Jin survived, it would've been as mindless servants bent to Asai's will, not Wolf's, and there was no question that Asai's loyalties had lain only with himself, not any one of the gods. Perhaps the future for which Asai had been reaching wouldn't have added to Raven's power, but it would've certainly dented Wolf's.

And none of it, *none* of it, had ever been about anything else. It was *all* about power, not love, not from any of them—not Raven, not Wolf, and certainly not Asai.

Untouchable. Unlovable. And everyone Jacin loved living under what amounted to a curse, and he was allowed to love, because *You will know love so that you may know the pain of losing it*, but he wasn't allowed to *keep* it, and son of a *bitch*, how was he supposed to… supposed to…

"I cant… I…"

I can't do this. I can't. No more. I'm tired. I'm done. Let me be done. Finish it. Whatever it is, just finish *it. Please.*

"Just… oh fuck, I…"

His teeth were chattering again, his whole body juddering, shuddering loose, and any second now, his knees were going to unlock and spill him to the floor. Falling apart, before Raven's altar, the altar before which Hitsuke had knelt and spoken to his god in intimate whispers, loving so hard he couldn't see anything else, couldn't fathom that he'd ever be betrayed, because it had never occurred to him to betray.

"I… I have to… I want…"

He wanted to die. It was too much. No one could know all this and keep going. It was amazing he hadn't simply seized up in Rihansei's chains and been done with it. But his body just kept *working*, and his feet just kept *moving*, and his heart just kept fucking *beating*, when all he wanted was for all of it to just… *stop*.

Malick!

A wail inside his head, because he just *didn't know* where to turn. His throat was spasming, cutting off air. It was quite possible he was going to retch all over Raven's altar. And wouldn't *that* just be too fitting and precious?

Malick, please, I need you. I don't know what to do. I don't know what to do with any of it. It's too much, I can't take any more, please, I don't—

Shock took him as the woman's arm curled around him, soothing.

Revulsion took its place when he couldn't make himself pull away. His nose was clogged with snot, he couldn't breathe, and tears splotched his vision, refracting smeary light, blinding him. He shook and he couldn't stop; he was shattering and it didn't even scare him anymore.

"All you have ever had to do was ask forgiveness." A whisper this time, deeper than before, so close Jacin could feel warm breath on his cheek. "Ask me, my Hitsuke. *Beg.*"

"Daraso." Thin and fractured, like a whine, and it wasn't the woman anymore who looked at Jacin steadily from black eyes. He wasn't so sure it had ever been anyone *but* Daraso, waiting for his Hitsuke in the temple the Incendiary's efforts had helped build, watching him fall apart right in front of the altar, an offering, the only kind the beaten, broken remnants of Hitsuke had left. "*Daraso*" fell from his mouth and into his god's red lips, and he couldn't have stopped it any more than he could stop the shaking.

The kiss was overwhelming, fiery and deep, and as his body molded to Daraso's, Hitsuke could feel his heart cracking apart, bit by bit, the tiny shards plummeting down into his gut and twisting. There were no cherry blossom petals now to obscure and distract, only the heavy scent of jasmine sliding down his throat, and he thought perhaps he groaned around it, but he was losing himself, he was losing everything as Daraso crushed Hitsuke to his chest and drove the kiss deeper.

Save him, it was dying and being reborn again, all at once. It was grief and sorrow, and love and hope. It was…

Memory.

Passion and wholeness turned to anger and distrust.

Faith crushed, and fidelity disdained.

Love that wasn't real, and comfort that only blinded.

Strength that turned to weakness, and promises so easily broken.

Cruelty, and betrayal, and greed, and doubt.

Fucking *outrage.*

It swamped him, choked him.

Jacin shoved back, tried to flail his way out of the relentless hold, but the arms locked around him were strong and the grip secure. Panic nipped at him yet again.

"*Jacin!*" came from behind him, the voice high and clear, and *fuck*, he'd missed her so much.

"*Caidi.*" Breathed out on a wheezy sob.

Relieved and sick all at once, Jacin tried to spin, but the arms around him wouldn't let go. He grunted, bared his teeth, then everything spun as something rammed into him from the side and he went down in a tangle of limbs and grunts.

His breath whuffed out of him, but hysteria had set him in motion and it wasn't going to let him stop until he got loose. The hold on him had broken with the fall, and he kicked and writhed and snarled as he tried to take advantage of the slack.

"*Goyo.*" A woman's voice, right next to Jacin's ear. He blinked, focused.

He wasn't tangled up with Daraso—he was tangled up with Raven's immortal, and bloody fucking hell, was *anything* about these people what it seemed? And then the name registered, *Goyo*, but Jacin didn't have time to pause and think it over, because Caidi was shrieking at him—

"Get up, Jacin, come on, get up, get up, *get up!*"

—so Jacin tried.

He wrenched away from the grasping hands. Goyo helped, however unwittingly, awkwardly grappling with the woman on the floor as Jacin slithered away from both of them.

"You *dare!*" cried the woman. "In Raven's own *house!*"

"I thought you called for the Patrol. Here I am." Goyo's grin was not a nice one. "Aw, Serenai, sorry. It's only that I thought you said you were under attack by the Incendiary. I was only trying to help." The grin abruptly dropped, and the look was fierce as Goyo held the woman down. "Funny, how Raven and his own seem to so consistently misconstrue exactly who is the injured party when it comes to Incendiary. An honest mistake, I'm sure." He shot a glance at Jacin, stopped and narrowed his eyes, mouth open like he meant to say something.

"The shadows, Jacin," Caidi whispered, frantic. "*Now!*"

And it wasn't like any of Jacin's decisions had been very good ones lately, so he did as Caidi demanded and said the spell. He was still wondering what that puzzled look on Goyo's face had been about when he backed away and out of Raven's temple.

🜨

Things were happening. Xari got the feeling they were happening very quickly, but in a place just out of her reach, and it was sending her spare. Not the uproar even now unrolling at the Gates of Rapture, though that lay over everything else like an obscuring scrim of oil atop the deceptively calm waters of a bottomless lake. A part of it, but more of a diversion; something to take the eye away from the malignant shapes of futures unfolding.

The festival carried on—outside, inside, all around—the crowds having gradually wandered from the streets and begun to queue up for a turn at their chosen gods' altars, painting their prayers and hanging their wishes for the New Year as Owl rose to flank her siblings.

Xari didn't hear the chatter, the steady *trip-trip-trap* of a thousand feet, the hawkers or the minstrels. Xari heard the thrumming nothing of dawning elucidation, that overwhelming sensation of revelation-to-come that sank through her and gripped her spirit when true Prophecy hovered at her fingertips and guided her hands.

She ignored the itch and irritation of flaking paint on cheeks and brow, paint that should've been removed and replaced hours—no, days—ago, but insight had no tolerance for comfort, nor would it wait if she didn't have her tools to hand when it chose to call. Xari patiently held her cards between her hands, head bowed over them, eyes closed, whispering orisons and spells, and waiting.

It hardly ever came like this. And when it did, it wasn't always something that could be used. The last time she'd been "blessed" with enlightenment—or rather "stolen" it from the collective ephemera of the universal divine—it had shown her Asai's betrayal, from which she'd instinctively flinched; she'd lost the singularities, the specifics, the *proof*, and so had lost her son, her god, and her place.

Xari had no intention of failing again. She knew what her new god wanted of her.

It had to be about the Incendiary. It was, after all, the nature of Incendiary to draw Fate's players, and Xari recognized the taste of the current anarchy curling at the lip of the world. An ephemeral-familiar flavor nipping at perception, a trying-to-catch-smoke sensation that hovered just outside of real knowledge and teased at instinct but never quite touched it with anything real. Faint hunches and not-quite-patterns, when it came to Incendiary—any Incendiary, really, but *this* singular Incendiary in particular. The obstructions of ancient magic that made up body and soul, and the hindrance of the Ancestors' enchantments in the gods' Blood that ran through Untouchable veins.

It was like trying to see with no eyes.

Her hand moved to the stone, and she let it. The other set the cards on the table, and she let that too. Eyes closed, all senses dwelling in that liminal transience between physical and spirit and space and not-space, Xari slipped a card from the deck and held it up. Opened her eyes.

"Kurimo." She whispered it, tracing the wheels of fire with the tip of her finger, smiling at the wild eyes of the twin horses—Force and Control—that strained at the traces.

Kurimo.

The chariot that would drive the will of her god and lay a steady hand on the reins. And the hand of Fate herself sat on his brow like a mark of protection. An invisible talisman that no servant of the gods would ignore or challenge.

The other cards almost didn't matter. The Fool and the Sorcerer, of course. The Paradox and the Templar of Swords. The Hawk Priest still chased and slavered after what was not his, and all could still fall, if he managed to catch what he sought. Xari could almost see the threads of Fate that braced the world snapping and twanging, all the carnage and misery that would follow.

With a shudder she couldn't quite help, Xari carefully collected her cards and covered her stone, rose from the table and bowed low. The time for prophecy and prediction had passed now; it was time to do.

"And we all do what we must."

Shoulders straight, she strode to her chambers to wash away the last of the dried paint of the wolf's mask from her face.

A call sizzled at her nerves, strong and insistent. Xari smiled. Dakimo had seen as well, then. She didn't answer. She didn't have the time, and anyway, Dakimo was *Temshiel* and his priorities were not Xari's. These things were what maijin were made for, and long before they bound their paths to those of the gods.

She was Wolf's maijin now, but tonight, she walked where Fate pointed. Watching in her mind's eye what possibilities sprang from the Kurimo and where they led, she rather thought Wolf approved.

┬┬

He almost fell down the marble steps. Twice.

Jacin stumbled around the worshippers who'd come to pray to their god and had ended up with a bit of a spectacle instead. The shadows were choking him, almost vibrating with a steady hum that had never been there before, so he dropped them the second he lost himself in the crush of the mob at the bottom of the steps.

"Jacin." Caidi slipped around in front of him and glowered. "Put them back on. Put them back on, take my hand, and come with me."

Jacin peered down at her dimpled little hand, stretched out for his, and... recoiled. The abrupt memory of that same hand curled loosely and lying in a pool of blood jabbed into him with too-sharp clarity.

"I'm so sorry, Caidi."

"Jacin, there isn't time."

She snatched at Jacin's hand, but he snatched it right back, because he couldn't... *couldn't.*

"I'm so sorry."

It didn't matter what platitudes Malick had tried to sell him—Jacin had killed her.

You will know love so that you may know the pain of losing it.

She'd died because of him. His father, his mother. Even Beishin.

"Jacin, *please!*"

He'd failed. In everything.

"Jacin, *now*, I mean it. Put them back on and come with me. They're looking for you. They're *all looking* for you."

Jacin didn't think he cared.

Goyo stood at the top of the temple's steps, clearly searching. Jacin only stood where he was until Goyo's glance fell on him, stayed, stared. With a helpless shrug, Jacin kept the gaze and angled slowly toward the eastern boundary that separated Raven's temple grounds from Wolf's. Goyo merely balled his hands into fists and cursed like he meant it. Several men and women in the surcoat of the Patrol hovered around him; Jacin couldn't hear from where he was, but they listened attentively while Goyo pointed and spoke and directed, and then they scattered at his apparent commands. With a vicious snarl, Goyo sailed down the steps and came after Jacin himself.

Jacin only kept shuffling away, ducking his head, moving with the throng and leaning heavily on the walking stick until he rounded the corner and headed down the alley between Raven's temple and Wolf's. He slipped the shadows back on only long enough to watch Goyo pass by, stalking toward Wolf's temple, then took them back off again.

He couldn't stand them. Almost pulsating around him, making him lightheaded and a little numb, smothering him in *pine-sage-sex*, and it made him want to just fall down and cry, because he *needed*, and he didn't know what, but Malick had always figured it out for him and given it to him, and Malick wasn't *here*.

"Damn it, Jacin, what are you *doing?*" Caidi's voice was sharp with reproach and an anger Jacin didn't think he'd ever seen on her before. And he'd *never* heard her swear. "Put them back on." She actually stomped her foot. "I mean it." She tried to grab his arm this time, but he shook her off and backed away. "Jacin—"

"I can't, Caidi."

"Can't what?" Caidi's expression slid back to concern, and she took a small step toward him. "*Jacin*. Can't do *what?*"

"You see now, little Ghost."

"No." Jacin shook his head, *refused* to look behind him. "Not you. Not *now*."

Because this voice he knew all too well. And really—*how much* was he supposed to be able to cope with at a fucking *time?*

A laugh was all he got. Close. *So* close. Hot breath fell on Jacin's ear, down his collar, and though he couldn't see Asai's face, Jacin had no trouble at all seeing the mocking smile.

"I killed you." Wheezed out through clenched teeth. "I *killed* you, I *know* I did." Twice now. "Why won't you stay *dead?*"

"Jacin…" Caidi was staring at him, eyes soft and sympathetic. "You didn't kill me."

"Because you need me, my Incendiary." Asai's arms slid around Jacin's torso, loosely pressing his arms to his sides.

Jacin didn't even bother to try to shake him loose. Asai was never going to leave him alone. None of them would *ever* leave him *alone*.

"You see how you've been betrayed. You see how the gods use and twist and lie."

"As if you don't."

Caidi frowned. "What?"

Jacin didn't answer her, every bit of concentration spent on not giving even a little when Asai tried to pull Jacin in tighter.

Jacin resisted. "As if you *didn't.*"

He tried to bring the stick up, just as full of rage for "his beishin" as he was for… just about everything right now, but Asai was *right here*, convenient, and Dar— Raven wouldn't even face *his* Incendiary.

Asai merely took hold of the stick, and stopped the truncated swing.

Jacin stilled again, gauging the hold that hadn't seemed nearly so constricting only a few seconds ago. When had Asai got so strong?

Teeth bared, Jacin grated, "Why don't you let me show you how *grateful* I am. It'll be just like old times."

"*Jacin!*" Caidi snapped. "What are you doing?"

"Ah, tempting." Asai ran his mouth along the sensitive skin beneath Jacin's ear. "But no." Asai turned them both toward the far end of the alley where two shapes were swirling into substance at the back end of it. He turned them again in the opposite direction; Jacin wasn't the least bit surprised to see two more silhouettes at the mouth of the alley, just behind Caidi.

Blocking off exits.

Jacin looked at Caidi. "Do you see them?"

Caidi frowned then peered around her. Jacin didn't need her anxious "See *what*, Jacin?" to know, because the pity in her eyes was enough of an answer. He was seeing ghosts that couldn't see each other, and it should probably be hysterically funny, but Jacin simply didn't have it in him right now. Real, not-real, punishment or callous disregard—it didn't matter anymore. None of it mattered anymore.

He jerked in Asai's grip—not hoping to get loose, really, but unwilling to just stand there. "I'm finished. I have nothing left. Whatever it is you want, whatever it is you're trying to do, it's done, and so am I. Do your worst and then… just… *leave me alone*."

"Jacin." Caidi's eyes narrowed, her tone low and wary. "Who are you talking to?"

"I think the worst has already been done." Asai sounded sad and nauseatingly compassionate. "You see now how they betrayed you, gentle Hitsuke. You have nowhere else to turn. We are the same, you and I. I've been tricked and used, as well." He hadn't let go of the walking stick. Neither had Jacin. Asai waggled it. "Wolf pulled you into his Cycle, but it wasn't to save you. It was so you could save his people, his greatest strength in the mortal world, and yet he could not be moved to save those you wanted saved. Raven punished you because you dared to be what you are, because *you weren't enough* for a god."

Except he had been. Right up until he'd made a choice.

"Every other god watched it happen, and none reached out a hand to save you." Asai tightened his grip around Jacin's ribs, so tight and constricting Jacin was getting a little lightheaded. "Do you think Wolf will accept you now? Do you think he *cares*?"

It was doing things inside Jacin, except he couldn't tell what—infuriating him one second and shattering him the next—and he couldn't seem to find a balance inside it all. Caidi was still talking at him—

"Jacin, please, there's no one here. *Please* come with me. Let me take you somewhere safe."

—still trying to tug-tug-tug him away. Except he knew where she wanted to lead him, and even if he could get loose, he simply couldn't go where she wanted him to go.

"There *is* nowhere safe," Jacin told her, because *safe* was Malick, and Malick was gone, and Asai was right—the gods hadn't protected him before, and they wouldn't protect him now.

"There is." Asai's hold loosened just enough it could've been considered a firm embrace to someone who didn't know better. The scent of jasmine was crowding in from Raven's temple, and a cocktail of pine and sage was churning with it, but the scent of damp earth and ash and darkness that weltered from Asai was what made Jacin's eyes burn. "I would have kept them all safe, Jacin-rei, if only you had listened to me."

Fuck, Jacin had heard the same accusation before, had told himself it was a lie, because Asai always lied, but now it slammed into his chest and *twisted*.

"Come with me. Bring me the bauble from your treacherous *Temshiel*. Let me show you what you and I can achieve together, and I will keep them all safe. I will keep *you* safe. Your gods would not give you the same, and your *Temshiel* could not. I *can*."

Another knife to the chest, and this one took Jacin's breath. Caidi was getting more insistent now, almost battering at him, and Jacin merely stared at the shapes creeping slowly toward them like skulking alley cats and took it. Not believing but *wanting* to.

Because he knew why now, even in the depths of madness, all those incarnations of himself had reached for the heavens just before they'd plunged to ignoble deaths. He knew now what they'd been trying to do, what they'd been reaching for.

They'd been weak. They'd believed, even in their insanity. They'd tried to fly, even as they were shown how very far they were falling.

Jacin didn't think he had that problem anymore.

"Let me love you, little Ghost. Look back onto those paths you've trod and know me. One more path for you to walk and your deceiving Daraso will never lay hands on you again. *I* will keep you safe. Let me show you what it is to be loved and honored by a *true* god."

Asai's voice was just as hypnotic as Rihansei's eyes, it always had been, and something about the comfort of giving in called to all the sick, craven places inside Jacin. The parts that were enraged at the world were shouting against it, but this thing inside him was ancient and appallingly strong.

"Why?" It slipped out of Jacin's mouth from where it had been thrashing against the backs of his teeth like the papery wings of a trapped moth. "I'm a fuckup, Beishin. What use could I possibly be?"

"Jacin…" Caidi was crying now, great fat drops down her full little cheeks. "Whatever this is, don't give up, all right? I'm going to find help. Jacin? Can you hear me?"

Jacin only half-heard it, most of it drowned out by Asai: "You were meant to stand beside a god, Incendiary. Not writhe beneath one. You, Hitsuke, are a god*maker*."

Let me show you what it is to be loved and honored by a true *god.*

Jacin… *laughed*. He hadn't been expecting it; it just surged out, loud and a little bit wild. Because really—how had he not guessed? It was so fucking predictable; so fucking *Asai*. The snorts and chuckles burbled up against the pressure of Asai's grip, then flowed out in breathless starts and stops.

"Oh." Jacin snorted. "*Oh*, that's… that's *rich*." The two prowling figures he could see were edging closer. Who knew where the other two were, but it mattered so little right now Jacin couldn't even care. He cared a lot more that one of the two he could see was smoking. And Jacin could *really use* a smoke right now. "And they're here to make sure I don't refuse?"

"My boy." Asai set a kiss to the side of Jacin's throat. "You will not refuse. You cannot. There is nowhere left for you now. You have attacked Tambalon's governor. You have killed priests and priestesses of the gods. You have terrorized the citizens of Mitsu and struck down almost a score of them. The Patrol will cut you down the second you show your face."

Jacin had to go over all that in his head a few times. He didn't remember doing most of it, but with the vague memory of Rihansei telling him he'd sent a *Temshiel* to spirit, Jacin couldn't exactly rule any of it out, either.

"It would have been better, had you seen sense, but the time for a choice has passed. And if you must be… persuaded…"

Tendons all at once stretched and burned as Asai took a fistful of Jacin's hair and jerked his head back. Jacin was abruptly staring up into the sky, a startling flash blooming dark into abrupt shocking light, nearly blinding. It took a second, but a concussive *boom* followed just as the light above exploded into a shower of colorful sparks that crackled and glittered as they fell in a brilliant, dazzling puff.

Fireworks. It was the New Year. So, that was what all those crowds were about.

Jacin couldn't help rolling his eyes. *Yeah, happy fucking birthday to me.*

…Shit. He'd missed Joori's birthday.

Another jarring *boom* thumped in Jacin's chest, stuttering against the rhythm of his heart as Asai yanked on Jacin's hair again, angling his head down this time.

"*Look.*"

Another rocket blasted in the sky. It was almost like the sound when Subie had swallowed itself; Jacin didn't think that would have occurred to him, except he was staring down onto Caidi's broken body bleeding out onto the stone of the alley. He shot his gaze around, as far as he could throw it to all sides, because Caidi had just been *right here*, and if she was still *right here*, she couldn't be *right there*.

The image changed—one moment Jacin was looking at blood in gold hair, and the next, Joori's lifeless eyes stared accusingly at him from where Caidi had just been, body twisted unnaturally and blood in a wide pool beneath him. Shadows blurred it out for a second, and then more glaring light and earsplitting explosions filled the sky as Morin took Joori's place.

"You see now, Incendiary." Low and seductive. "These are the things the gods would give you as reward for your service to them. These are the things *I* would save you from." Asai kissed Jacin's temple then slid a fingertip over Malick's ring on Jacin's finger. "I have only ever needed you, my Incendiary, and now you bring me such a lovely, lovely gift." He ran his fingertips over Jacin's cheekbone. "Your beishin will always take care of you, Jacin-rei. Have I not always said so?"

Fury was probably not the reaction Asai had been looking for, but it was what swarmed in Jacin's chest, hot enough to burn, as the images seared into his head and combusted.

"And did I not warn you, *Beishin*," Jacin said, oh so soft and deadly, "that threatening my brothers was the surest way to make sure I *don't* do what you want me to do?"

"Ah, the voice of the Bloody Fist, at last. It is still in you. You were a great warrior once, Hitsuke. And look what Raven has made of you now."

The Bloody Fist, Jacin mused. *Huh. Yeah, I was, wasn't I?*

He eyed the shapes slowly advancing, no doubt waiting for a word from Asai to close the distance. Funny how Jacin wasn't the least bit frightened. Funny how he was waiting for the signal probably as eagerly as those two were. All the aches and pains receded into unimportance.

Here, kitty-kitty.

Asai's tone dipped toward the edge of malevolence: "We are not of the gods, you and I. And the gods will not have you back. You are *my* Incendiary. You are my *Ghost*. And now that you know me, now that you *see*, you are my greatest weapon."

"Except I don't know you." Because even if this really was Asai—and Jacin was pretty sure it wasn't—it wasn't like Jacin had really known Asai, either.

"Only because you refuse to know. But that cannot last much longer. You shall see. By my breath do you live, my Incendiary, by my love do you go on. You do not exist but in my eyes. And I now exist in yours."

The smell of ash rose up as the debris from the fireworks filtered down from the sky and mixed with a new fall of snow. And none of it turned to petals.

Asai set a kiss to Jacin's hair. "You never could stand against a tender touch. It is more fatal to you than a knife to the heart. Now come with me, my Incendiary. It is time to put the Six back in their proper places."

It was… tempting, Jacin had to admit. He'd like to get his hands around Raven's neck—Wolf would do in a pinch—and he didn't think he necessarily cared if he got anything out of it but another horrible death. The satisfaction would be worth it.

Then again, he'd like to get his hands around Asai's neck too. And at least this not-Asai was within reach.

Jacin curled his hands tighter around the walking stick, narrowed his eyes at the shadowy figures stalking closer. He could see them now—black-clad from head to toe with black kerchiefs over their faces. Like the ones who'd taken Malick down and taken all of Jacin's safety and comfort with them. He wasn't even a little bit surprised. Because even if this wasn't Asai, this... *creature* still knew all Asai's tricks, knew exactly how to hurt Jacin, and was just as ruthless as Asai had ever been. More. Of *course* he'd taken Malick away, because this not-Asai wanted something, and taking away what Jacin needed was how *every fucking person* he'd ever met got Jacin to do things he didn't want to do.

Except he was the Bloody Fist. And these creatures had taken from him.

The one who'd been smoking pitched it aside, and it occurred to Jacin that he'd fucking *kill* for a smoke right now. It made him snigger. Because... well. Yeah.

Heeeeeere kitty-kitty, stupid fucking kitty.

"You never did know me as well as you thought you did." Jacin smirked, added, "And you didn't ask me nicely," and snapped his head back.

By the sharp yelp and the satisfying feel of crunching bone, Jacin guessed he'd gotten Asai square on the nose. Damn, a little higher and Jacin might've smashed bridge into brain. Too bad. Because whatever Asai was, he could apparently be hurt—his grip loosened, and Jacin jerked the stick up and back, slammed Asai in the ribs with the foot of it then spun out of his arms.

The other two were waiting for him. Make that four. Bodies closed in all around Jacin; he spun on his good leg and swung the stick in a wide arc as he went. The glint of a knife flashed in the darkness, and the slippery *ching* of metal coming loose from a scabbard rang beneath the now almost steady concussion of the fireworks, the light of them flickering sporadic brilliance down into the alley. Jacin hoped these men were having as much trouble seeing properly as he was.

"Jacin-*rei!*" Asai snarled, and then he wasn't Asai anymore.

Daraso lunged in. Jacin snapped backward, caroming into one of the others. Instinct whipped the stick back over his shoulder; Jacin felt it thunk into something solid that crunched beneath the heavy ivory of the wolf's head. He pulled it loose, swung it forward to take another one in the face.

"You failed me, Hitsuke! You are failing me now!"

Did he really think Jacin gave a shit anymore?

He lost time. Again. Everything kept going around him, and he apparently kept going with it, but it was lost in that same black hole that had swallowed his mind between the moment he'd gone after Leu in the tavern and the moment he'd woken up chained to Rihansei's Gate. Probably not a good thing, considering, but the shapes around Jacin were two less than they'd been a moment ago, so he assumed he was doing something right. The stick was broken, he was only holding half of it now, and had no idea what he'd done with the other half. He kept swinging it nonetheless, aiming for Daraso-Asai, but the remaining two kept getting in his way and he couldn't get a decent head shot. He'd got hold of a knife somehow, remembering only vaguely yanking it from out his own side, so he assumed he'd been stabbed, but the pain wasn't registering, so it didn't matter. He put the knife to better use.

Lightning flared and Subie boomed, and Wolf waged war in the heavens. Caidi was there again, shouting at him. Asai laughed at him and yanked on his braid—"You did this, little Ghost." Daraso held him then shoved him away—"*Beg* me"—as Jacin watched Caidi sail up into the sky, and then Goyo took his hand and Yori screamed and Hitsuke plummeted and Malick went down in a burst of flame.

Jacin shut his eyes, spun-slashed-bashed, and still, a gaze dark as night pierced him, shattered him, enraged him. There was no skill to what his body was doing—it was all primitive and brutal instinct. No pain, no shame, no love, no grief—no *feeling*. He was a machine. A *perfect* machine.

He didn't care if any of this was real. Some hard, nasty little thing inside him really hoped it was. Jacin let his body take over and only let his head brood over the fact that he'd fucking *kill* for a smoke. Which was still kind of hilarious.

⛩

Samin had to stop. He had to. He wasn't lying dead on the street with a knife in his chest, but he bloody well felt like it. He was weak and his head was pounding, heart hammering at it like it had decided his chest wasn't where it wanted to be anymore and had moved to settle right behind his eyes. The nausea wasn't helping, and neither was the dizziness. He held onto Morin's shoulder, and hoped Morin didn't know how much of it was for support.

Another blast went off over their heads, and more light glittered behind Samin's eyes, spangling into the thudding of his head and making it heavier.

"Samin." Morin's tone was wary. Eyes wide, he turned back and pointed to where they'd just been standing a few feet away from the fountain. "Do you see that?"

Samin squinted through another blossom of light from the sky. The marble façade of the temple was barely visible through the trees. Students of the priests—dressed in the formal white robes denoting their apprenticeship, faces painted with the mask of their god—strolled the queue, keeping an eye on both the sky and those waiting their turn at the altar.

The line for Owl's temple was the longest, in honor of her rising into her secondary cycle, the muted jade of her face just coming visible beneath Wolf's ambivalent silver gaze. Raven and Dragon glared like a set of narrowed red eyes from just below. A scrim of clouds was moving quickly to the bottom of the sky, blinding them all. Another rocket blossomed against their backdrop, making it all absurdly picturesque and a little too perfect.

None of which, Samin assumed, was what had Morin's hackles up and vibrating.

"See what?"

"I don't..." Morin took a few paces back to where he'd been pointing. "It's Caidi." He reached out to touch empty air, hand shaking and brow twisted, but a soft smile curled at his mouth, like he couldn't help it. "Samin, it's *Caidi*." His hand moved, as though he was stroking a head of gold curls Samin couldn't see.

Samin's stomach dropped. Because he really didn't need another one of them to start seeing ghosts, and especially not now that he was pretty sure he knew exactly what those "ghosts" were.

"Morin, I don't think—"

He choked it off. The look in Morin's eyes was far too close to the one Samin saw in Malick's sometimes when Malick was going all *Temshiel* on him and deciding which organ would hurt the most when extracted through the ribcage.

"Raven's temple." Morin turned back to peer down at where Caidi absolutely wasn't. "No. The alley. Are you *sure*?" He nodded then jerked his head at where the low hedge that hemmed Wolf's grounds butted up against Raven's. "She says Jacin's there and he needs help. Badly." He took a step toward Samin, waiting for the rumble of a spate of fireworks to taper off before going on, "I know what it sounds like. I know what you're thinking. But even if it's a trick, we have to check."

Samin rather doubted all three of those statements. "Morin, Caidi isn't—"

"Maybe, maybe not. But it's the first time someone I actually trust has told me a bloody thing about where my brother might be, and I'm going."

No, seyh, you are not, said a rich female voice Samin was pretty sure he knew and didn't really welcome, and especially not inside his head as it had been. By the way Morin jolted, Samin figured he must have "heard" it too.

A woman's shape melted into substance, moving toward them and backlit by the light of the rockets, gold and red and blue unfurling in the sky and lighting her features as she neared. As soon as Samin recognized the dark eyes peering back at him, the beautiful face framed by the silky dark hair, he knew things were going to go tits-up and far too quickly.

"Hey." Morin squinted, jaw tight. "I know her."

"Xari." It probably hadn't come out very courteously, but Samin couldn't be bothered with niceties right now. He felt like shit, he was miles across the city from where Joori and Shig had ventured off on some fool's idea of a rescue, Morin wouldn't bloody stop reminding him what could be happening and exactly how long it was going to take them to get back there, and he could barely stand up without his head spinning and his heart racing. The last thing Samin needed was another bloody immortal telling him where he should be and what he should be doing.

"There is no time." Xari strode purposefully up to them, looked them both over, and pinched her mouth as though disappointed at their less-than-perfectly-battle-ready state. She took hold of Morin's coat and tugged him out of Samin's grip. "Come along, then."

"*No*." Morin shook her off. "I know where Jacin is, I know—"

"Yes, as do I. As does every maijin and *Temshiel* in the city by now—the world—or at least they think they do, but this you must leave to them. The Wheels turn, but not for you. Let the Sorcerer take care of his own. Save the one you can, little brother. You always knew it would come to a choice."

Samin didn't know what to stab her for first—the fact that she was manhandling Morin like that, or the fact that she was speaking in bloody riddles like she always did. Samin had tolerated her in Ada because Malick had seemed to almost trust her and she'd done her part in taking down Yakuli. But that didn't mean he was pleased to see her now. And he really didn't need her high-handed bullshit.

Except it didn't seem like Morin thought it was bullshit, because he stopped dead, face blanching and eyes narrowing down to little slits.

"*What* choice?"

Xari looked like she was *this close* to snagging Morin by the scruff of his neck and dragging him. Instead, she took hold of Morin's sleeve, tugged.

"The one you've already made."

Morin dug in his heels. "I don't know what you're talking about." His jaw locked tight in that stubborn way all Fens seemed to share. "We have to get back to—"

"Neither brother is where you left him." To Xari's credit, it was somewhat soft and borderline sympathetic, but there was an impatience beneath it that set Samin's teeth on edge.

He stepped in and set a ruthless grip to her wrist where she held to Morin's coat.

"You don't want to be doing that. Doing things like that to one of mine won't get you anything but very, very dead." Samin didn't add *And I know how to make you stay that way*, but he didn't really think he had to.

Xari sighed and let go, both hands clenching into tight fists. She jerked her arm from Samin's grip.

Samin let her but made a point of drawing his sword. "How do you know where his brothers are?"

"And where are they?" Morin put in.

Xari looked like she wanted to punch them, but she merely rolled her eyes. Samin assumed it was at them, and he was just thinking about decking her for it, giving her a few flaws on that flawless face, but then she growled, "You track the wrong scent, Goyo," so Samin turned—

—only to watch Goyo blow past them with a snapped-out "There *is* no scent, Xari."

"Hey, wait!" Morin started after Goyo. "*Hey!*"

Surprisingly, Goyo did. Shoulders slumping with an exhausted sigh, he turned, dipped his head curtly to first Samin then Morin, then turned to Xari.

"Even when Kamen isn't here, he's still somehow at the center of calamity. The Incendiary knows one spell—*one!*—and of course it *would* be the one that makes it impossible to find him." Goyo waited until another blast of fireworks rumbled into echoes then nodded toward Wolf's temple. "He was headed this way. Surely he—"

Xari's "No, he is not" came just as quickly and urgently as Morin's "You saw Jacin?"

"Where?" Samin stepped up and shouldered Xari aside so he could level a glare at Goyo. "Is he all right?"

"I've a feeling 'all right' is a very subjective term when it comes to Fen Jacin." To Goyo's credit, he looked rather penitent the moment it came out his mouth, and he didn't even seem to need Samin's snarl and too-obvious adjustment of the grip on his sword. Goyo held up his hand. "He's alive and able to cause mayhem, if that's any consolation."

Actually, it was.

"He looks…" Goyo shook his head and glanced at Morin. "He looks like an Untouchable." He shrugged when Morin flinched. "I'm sorry. He is ragged and barefoot and using a walking stick as a weapon." His mouth pinched tight and he glared at Xari. "There was an altercation at Raven's temple, but I lost him in the crowd. I think he was heading for Wolf's house."

"But he isn't there!" Morin had to shout it to be heard over the boom of another rocket. His eyes glittered suspiciously in the flickering light from the sky. "Caidi said—"

"*Hush.*" Xari cocked her head and turned in the direction Morin had said he'd seen Caidi. She frowned. "Yes, child, we come, but all these brothers are as crucial to Wolf as the other." All of it said to empty space, but Morin was looking, too, and then peering at Xari with an anxious frown.

"You see her." Morin wheezed it, like it scared him and relieved him all at once. "You heard what she just said."

Oh, Samin really was going to kill her now.

Oblivious to Samin's growing wrath, or merely ignoring him, Xari nodded. "Wolf's magic gathers at all of his own this night. It waits only for its instrument."

Samin and Goyo both loosed simultaneous growls at whatever obscure hint they were supposed to have understood from that. They shared a rueful glance before turning back to Xari.

Xari had eyes only for Morin. She laid a hand to the top of his head, despite Morin's scowl and attempt to duck out from beneath the touch.

"Always you have followed, but Wolf has a plan for you, Fate has set her hand to your brow, and lead one day you must. Two brothers carom into peril. Two brothers pull at your heart and your conscience. And yet there is only one of you—you cannot go to them both. A choice you've always known you must make, and more than you know now hangs upon what you choose."

A shout went up from the temple. Fire flared out from one of the open-air antechambers.

They all snapped their glances over; Goyo and Samin both started instinctively toward it. Xari took hold of them both and stopped them.

Screams echoed seconds before worshippers began to stream down the steps. The fireworks continued overhead, their flash and dazzle suddenly comparatively mundane.

"Which will it be?" Xari dark eyes stayed locked to Morin's, unaffected by his obvious anger and fear. "Only one is yours to save. The other falls to the gods and Fate to shape. Tell me which you choose, and I shall tell you where to find him."

Samin could only stare, wanting with everything in him to rip Xari's head off and bash the rest of her into the ground with it for putting that look of nauseated realization on Morin's face. And the worst part was that none of this surprised Samin—the more he dealt with immortals, the more he believed Malick and Naro-yi were the exceptions. And he wasn't even really sure about Naro-yi yet. Or Malick, when it came to it.

The only things that mattered to these people were their schemes and their maneuverings, and they'd apparently trample any mortal they had to if it meant their god would look a little more favorably on them. Asai had taught him that. Husao had reinforced it. Xari had played her part in taking down Yakuli, yes, but she'd done it to save Malick so Wolf would take her into his Cycle—not because she'd given a damn what Yakuli had been up to; not because of what her son had put Fen through.

She didn't care that Morin was tearing himself in two, trying to make a choice a boy who'd already been through hell shouldn't have to make. She didn't care what he'd have to live with ever-after if the one he didn't choose didn't make it through tonight.

Samin couldn't take that look on Morin's face one more second. "Now listen, you shit-spewing little shrew." He stepped in and shoved Xari away from Morin, hard, and didn't care that he'd almost knocked her into the path of fleeing worshippers. "I've had just about enough of—"

"Joori." Morin's voice was overloud and shaky, but he lifted his chin, determined. With a quiver of the lip he didn't cover quickly enough, Morin tore his gaze away from Samin and turned it on Xari. "I choose Joori. And fuck you, by the way. Now where is he?"

⫟

His chest ached, muscles burning like fire. Every icy breath he sucked in turned to hot knives, searing his lungs. Every jolting stretch, every risky toehold sent new pain spiking through oxygen-starved tissue, jarred his bones. Sweat dampened his scalp then itched at his skin; a minor misery, almost drowned out by the near-overwhelming throb of his leg, but present enough to add its nattering nonetheless.

Jacin walled it off in a corner of his mind and kept climbing. It was ironically exhilarating. Strange, because he wasn't quite certain how he'd ended up here, scaling up the side of Raven's temple while the din of the festival rebounded beneath him.

There had been Caidi, and… he remembered fireworks, and then Subie had rumbled, which was impossible, because Subie was gone and all the way back in Ada, and they'd left Ada across the sea, except there had been Asai, too, and… *something.* Something bad. Something that—

bodies and hands coming at him from all angles. Fire in the sky and thunder in his head, and too much, everything, it was all too much

—had left Jacin with a knife wound in his side and blood all over him, but—

sharp pain in his side, and then Daraso-Asai shouting, "He mustn't bleed, damn you!" and then Jacin jerking the knife from the wound, and lunging

—it wasn't all his. Couldn't be.

The face of Wolf through a stretch of clouds limned everything silver, gave it all a monochrome cast, color-leached and stark. Raven and Dragon were twin bloody splinters, lent a ghost-green hue by the jade of Owl, just sidling into phase at the bottom of the sky. Combined, they tried for sepia, but Wolf edged them all in milky gray, overpowering them in reflected pearl as he—

blooded steel sinking into Daraso-Asai's chest, and Jacin twisted it deeper, wrenched it through bone and the heavy drag of cartilage, and then it wasn't Daraso-Asai anymore, but someone Jacin didn't know, but he thought Hitsuke had, so he made himself not know it anymore, made himself not see

—overpowered them in strength.

Jaw set, Jacin shook away the insistent haze that kept trying to muddle in and double his vision. A fall from here would just be painful and stupid. And insultingly pointless.

He lengthened his reach, set his fingers in a wide crag between blocks of marble, and hauled himself upward in an agonizing extension, then scrabbled at the next chink in the masonry. A slight miscalculation in angle necessitated a last-minute yaw then a snatch as he slid nearly an arm's length down too-smooth marble. He pitched his body back up and snagged at the carved ravens that served as molding where wall met roof. The huffed curse was completely unintentional but still satisfying as Jacin finally curled numb fingers around two of them and wrenched himself up and over. Winded, he lay sprawled on his back for a moment, staring sightless up into the sky, mind a blank white buzz, which was fine—there was nothing he wanted to know or think about just now.

The shadows were thumping into him with a heavy, vibrant throb, energy sliding into him, around him, thrumming like a heartbeat that outpulsed his own. He couldn't stand it. He took them off. Puzzled. *Angry.* They'd never done that bef—

Wait. Yes, they had. Earlier, when…

He couldn't remember. There was a peculiar sense of *Malick* when he tried, but that was all. Except. There'd been *hurt* too, with that sensation. Because of it. Not in his body, but—

"Stop." Jacin shut his eyes, willed it away. "Just… stop."

His head was already too crowded. Best he not add to it.

Dragging air, Jacin hauled himself to his feet and lurched up the gentle slope of the roof until he reached the broad plateau of its shallow peak.

The noises from the alley were a little disconcerting, but he put it all aside. It was the Patrol—he'd seen them arrive right behind Goyo—and still, Jacin couldn't shake the creeping notion that it was Asai stomping around down there, angry that "his Ghost" was disobeying him again. Which was absurd. Asai was dead.

…Except for when he wasn't. When he crouched in Jacin's head and reminded him what he really was until Caidi showed up and chased it all away. Sometimes Malick. Except there'd been the alley, and no Caidi, no Malick, and—

No, Caidi had been there. She'd been shouting at Jacin, pleading with him, begging him to…

Something.

Why couldn't he remember? Where had she gone?

"Caidi?"

Jacin waited, listening, hoping, but… she didn't come.

Just as well. He didn't want to watch her die again.

He couldn't seem to catch his breath. Sucking air, he bent at the waist and braced a hand to his thigh. The ragged clump of linen that used to be the tail of his shirt was soaking through again; he could probably wring the blood from it like a dishrag. He didn't. They could smell it, he reminded himself, which had somehow become the point, but not yet, he needed a moment. He packed the linen more securely into the wound just above his hip to at least keep it from dripping.

The new flaring spangle of pain made him hiss. Or maybe it was the abrupt revelation it brought with it—of the *life* pulsing through him, tangled like a lover with the creeping threat of death that made the bright-hot sharpness of it matter, made him *feel* it like he couldn't do at any other time. Or the nagging puzzle of why the pump of adrenaline and the near-blinding throb of agony through every inch of him seemed almost orgasmic.

He couldn't parse it. And it didn't matter anymore.

Dogged, Jacin drew himself straight, paced slowly along the roof's wide peak, and stared down over the jut of its lip. People were running and screaming. Smoke was billowing up; Jacin traced a wisp of it and noticed it had started to flurry. The clouds had hidden the moons, their faces only faint ghostly hints of color now.

How absurdly ironic.

He shut his eyes, face turned up to the sky.

Done. Just… *done.* It hurt too much, he couldn't breathe, and he was pretty sure he wasn't going to make the climb back down if he chanced it.

"Doesn't matter." Jacin shook his head, mouth quirked, eyes burning. "Not the point."

Drying blood caked his shirt to the sweat on his chest. It itched. Maddening. His skin was crawling with it, making it hard to concentrate, but if he dallied too long, Asai would sniff him out, and then… more bad things would happen. Things that kept shoving at his awareness, trying to spike through, and he couldn't understand why his mind was fighting it so desperately. He knew he'd done something terrible, something unforgivable. People had been hurt because he hadn't been fast enough this time, either. He'd tried so hard, tried to make up for it, tried to take it all back, but there'd been—

dark eyes full of lies and scorn, and they wouldn't stop looking at him, seeing him, he couldn't stop them from seeing everything, it was all over him, he stank of it, everything was leaking out of him without his permission, his own helplessness to stop it a profound

—betrayal. There'd been betrayal. He just… couldn't remember what it was. And now he didn't want to know. It wasn't the *point.* He was here for a *reason,* standing right beneath Raven's blinded eye, and trying to remember why he was doing it. Trying to remember whose blood was burning his skin. He couldn't get the reek of—

jasmine setting a stratum all over the alley, choking him, and dark eyes, mocking him—"You did this, Little Ghost"—and Beishin's blood all over him, and he couldn't get

—jasmine out of his nose, the sound of high-pitched cries out of his skull, until sage crept in, and the rest fuzzed out, except he couldn't unhear—

the sound of Caidi's screams as she fell, but that was wrong, Caidi hadn't screamed, it was supposed to be Yori, reaching, missing, falling, crying out, and

—another voice telling him *I fucking love you,* and—

magic twining with rage, weltering with the scent of burning pine from a storm made flesh that stalked the alley—"Make a fucking decision, Fen!"—and

—where the hell was Malick?

There was blood and fear, and there was supposed to be Malick to make it all go away. That was how things worked now. Promises, and confessions, and things that had made Jacin's gut clench and his heart open out at the same time—*weak vulnerable needy*—made him want to believe as he made himself *not* believe, and why wasn't Malick *here?*

Are you really surprised? Did you really expect anyone to want you? Keep you? Love you?

His own voice. No one else on whom to blame it this time. No way to hide from it. Which was better, he supposed. It made him remember what he was doing up here. It made him remember how he'd gotten here. It made him remember everything.

Daraso.

Raven.

Love.

Betrayal.

It failed to shock. It failed to confuse. It failed to do anything but strengthen resolve and wake the rage.

Right. *That* was what he was doing up here.

Jacin set his teeth and opened his eyes. He pressed the wad of shirt more firmly into the leaking wound and tried not to breathe too deeply.

"Malick."

He hadn't meant to say it. But he wasn't really surprised. No more than hopeless want made voice, really, because he could admit now he wished Malick were here. Wished he'd bothered to tell Malick how much the safety and comfort he'd offered had meant. Wished he could tell Malick it wasn't his fault Jacin hadn't believed. Because Jacin had been Hitsuke, and Hitsuke had believed and then been shown he couldn't. Just like when Beishin had taken on a role that something too deep inside Jacin had craved with a sick need he understood too late.

And this was where it had brought him. This had always been where it was going to bring him.

"Malick, I… I'm sorry. I want you. I've always wanted you. I want you here with me now, and I'm sorry."

He thought of Joori and Morin. He had to. It was too deep in him not to. But he was meant to lose the people he loved. And perhaps if things spun out like he thought they would, they'd be spared the fates of all the others Hitsuke had loved in his many horrible lives. They were not going to understand, but then again, they might never know, so maybe they'd be all right. And if they weren't…

Jacin set his teeth, straightened his shoulders.

If Joori and Morin weren't all right, if Raven still brought down on them what Raven brought down on all the others, there was nothing Jacin could do one way or the other to stop it. At least this way, he probably wouldn't be around to have to watch it.

With a last thought for Malick, Jacin took off the ring and swallowed it. It was the best he could do. There was no one he could entrust it to, and leaving it up to chance would be the worst kind of betrayal. Having that ring on his finger was like holding Malick's soul in his fist, and since Jacin thought he knew how all of this would end but couldn't *know*, he took all the precautions he could. Perhaps it would be found in the ashes of his pyre, and maybe Samin would think to look.

There were no tears as he lifted his head and found the spot where Raven glared through clouds and snow. No gasp of pain as Jacin peeled the makeshift compress from his side and curled it into a soggy clump in his fist. Blood flowed down his hip, dripped into the dust of snow beneath Jacin's numb toes, and Jacin let it, wished for a bit of a breeze to carry the scent farther and faster, but there was none. It didn't matter. They'd come eventually.

It gave him the deepest, most ironic sense of hope he thought maybe he'd ever had.

"I renounce you." Jacin's voice was raspier than it had ever been, almost soundless, but not because the words lacked the strength of resolve. "I am no longer Raven's-own."

He kept expecting a gust of wind to blow him down before he could finish, or someone to sneak up behind him and give him a sharp shove. But not even Beishin showed up to stop him.

Jacin set his jaw. "I take my oath from your hands, as I couldn't do in too many lives before."

Because the madness had prevented him from knowing he should. Because Raven didn't wish it. Because doing so would have meant failing his god and himself utterly.

Jacin snorted—it just popped out, all rough and hollow. Maybe Hitsuke couldn't take failure, but Jacin had been neck-deep in it for too long to let it stop him now.

"I loved you and I let it make me weak. I'm not weak anymore."

He held the bloody clump of linen out from his body, let it unfurl, and leaned out over the lip of the roof toward the front of the temple, so he could peer down at the chaos still swarming down the steps and toward the streets.

"They'll come. They'll come, and it will all be decided then. And there will be no petals this time to call me to your perdition.

"I'm not Raven's anymore. I'm no one's."

He didn't know what it meant. He had no idea where death would take him when there was no god to accept him, and no Fate to direct him. He thought maybe it would be a blank, empty nothing, and it terrified him, because he'd never done well alone. It wasn't enough to make him want to change his mind. He didn't think anything would be enough to make him want to change his mind. Maybe he had to be a little insane for it to make sense, but "insane" was rather the way of things once gods took notice of you.

He'd been dry-eyed only a moment ago, but he was weeping now, he could feel the tears freezing on his cheeks, but he was smiling, too, so that made it all right. He took the last half step to the very edge of the roof then raised his arms to his sides, shut his eyes. The linen flapped gently in his hand on a tiny breeze, and he let it go. He didn't open his eyes to see where it went; he kept them closed and pretended he was flying.

"It's done," he breathed, "*finally*," and for the first time in too many lives, he believed it.

He kept his eyes closed when the shouts increased in volume and urgency below. He kept his eyes closed when a small *whump* sounded and the heavy scent of smoke nearly blotted out the collective fog of jasmine and pine.

Bootsteps thudded somewhere to the side, moving quickly, running at him.

Jacin kept his eyes shut and merely waited for it. Whatever it turned out to be, it would be an end, one way or another, and more than anything, Jacin wanted an end.

The impact caught him in the side, shot the breath from him in a sharp *whoof*. His ears rang when he hit the roof on his back, cruel hands grinding into his wrists, hard muscle holding him down. Jacin didn't try to fight back, he didn't even open his eyes, and he was pretty sure he was smiling, until:

"You son of a bitch, what the *fuck* d'you think you're *doing*?"

Jacin's eyes flew open and he blinked up into a furious tawny gaze glaring down at him from a face too familiar, even twisted as it was in anger and worry and confusion, as Jacin had never seen it before. He shook his head, disbelieving, because he didn't dare, not really, but there was that odd hope again, flaring in his chest, hot and bright and hand in hand with weary desperation.

"*Malick?*"

5

They emerged into chaos. Shig only just avoided getting her nose taken off by a bloody great axe when they finally surfaced from the tunnels because Joori somehow saw it coming and tackled her to the… floor. It was a floor, smooth marble, and they were indoors, but not really. A roof, but pillars instead of walls, and the cold winter air was sharp against Shig's cheeks and heavy with the scent of pine and sage. They'd come out behind a small foyer that apparently led in from a garden—a lot like the one at Malick's house, now that she was looking—and then farther in toward the center of the structure to a… Ah. An altar.

All right, she knew where they were now, at least. Which didn't explain why it seemed like there was a war going on around them. Or maybe it did. The attackers were all black-clad and black-kerchiefed, so it wasn't all that hard to figure out.

Banpair. In Wolf's temple. Bloody *hell.*

"C'mon—*up!*"

Joori yanked Shig to her feet, keeping hold of her and shoving her to the side as one of the attackers drove in and swung a sword at them as he—she?—flew by. It missed, but it didn't really seem like their not-really-assailant cared, aiming more for the priests and priestesses in their robes and masks, and herding the bystanders who were either busy engaging or busy panicking. Flames cut off any retreat for Joori and Shig except to back from where they'd come, but Shig really didn't want to go back that way. She was pretty sure she had at least a vague idea of what was down there, and she was quite sure it knew she'd been there. Even now she could almost hear it whispering at her in not-really-Yori's voice, cajoling, coaxing, like it had done all the while she and Joori had sped through the tunnels.

"*Yah!*"

Joori swung Malick's sword at another attacker then spun under the long, curved knife that arced at his throat. He ducked low as he turned, a little clumsily, and tottered too close to the flames that were rolling across the marble floor and feeding themselves on nothing Shig could see. Seemingly on instinct, Joori's hand flailed out as he stumbled, caught hold of his opponent's clothes to keep himself on his feet; Shig had no idea if it was on purpose or not, but it was impressive nonetheless—the momentum spun the assailant down to the floor and into the flames. With another incoherent cry, Joori drove one of Fen's knives into the man's chest, rolled to his feet, and spun around to latch onto Shig.

"C'mon, *move!*"

She should be drawing a weapon or something. She'd been the assassin, after all, and Joori had been the useless baggage. She let Joori shove her and move her and push her behind him as he flung himself awkwardly into moves Shig had watched Samin teach him, ungainly but effective. Twice a black-clad figure got in their way as Joori led them along the edges of the flames that were preventing escape from the temple, and twice Joori managed to somehow—and rather inelegantly—at least do enough damage to the attackers to make them retreat, if not actually die.

And all the while, not-Yori's voice kept whispering to Shig. Not from the tunnel Shig couldn't have found again if her life depended on it—which it just might—but from beneath her, it seemed, or maybe inside her. A pull against her ribcage. Not the same as down in the tunnels—that had been... darker somehow, more smothering, engendering a feeling of dread Shig hadn't ever felt before, and somehow putting the taste of ashes on her tongue—but this was strong, too, and just as basely alluring.

C'mon, Shig, I need you. I miss you. I can give you back what you had. I can give you me. Just bring Joori to me, and we'll make Fen see.

Right. Shig was pretty sure she knew at least a little what that meant, what this was all about. And it was tempting. She didn't get it all, she wouldn't fool herself that she did, but she got enough. Because she knew what Fen was, and she'd gotten a pretty good idea what the thing that was after him was, just by what had happened down in the tunnels.

Something powerful enough to challenge gods, but not quite win. Something that needed a push to its power, and Fen could apparently give it, but Fen was Incendiary and he had to *want* it. Something that knew how to *make* Fen want it, like it had apparently made a handful of maijin and a whole lot of mortals want to throw themselves behind it and want what it told them to.

Enslave, Rihansei had said. Shig hadn't even thought of the possibility, but now that she did, she understood why the servants of all the other gods might decide Fen was better dead than alive. And if these *banpair* fed on emotion, Fen would be a banquet for them.

Speaking of which: all the fear and anger ramming around in here now probably wasn't helping the cause of the gods; it was only making these creatures stronger.

Another attacker drove in toward Shig and Joori, cutting down a priestess and a cringing man, an apparent worshipper who'd been unable to flee before all hell broke loose. The woman—yes, definitely a woman by the shape—plunged a long knife into the throat of the man then went after the priestess, who whirled out of sight in a way with which Shig was becoming very familiar just lately. It left the way clear for Joori and Shig.

Joori had managed to drag Shig along the fiery perimeter and away from the main chamber, heading toward the front of the temple where the pillars opened wider and left more room through which to try a plunge through the flames and hopefully to safety. Or, at least, Shig assumed that had been Joori's plan. Now, however, the woman placed herself between them and the ring of fire, joined almost immediately by two men. All of them heavily armed; all of them blocking even this dangerous exit; all of them staring at Joori and Shig with unmistakable intent.

And then the woman turned into Yori, like that man had done at the Gates of Rapture the other night. Green eyes twinkled at Shig with that familiar and desperately missed wry humor, pretty face turned up in a happy smile. Something in Shig knew what was happening—it had happened exactly this way the other night—but most of her wanted her sister back so badly she couldn't be bothered with reality.

"I miss you so much." Yori held out her arms, like she was waiting for a hug. "C'mon, love, you've given up enough for these people."

Shig could've cried. Because there was guilt in there, heavy and full of shame, but agreement too. She *had* given up enough for these people she hadn't even known six months ago, these Fen brothers—one who hated her, one who tolerated her, and one who probably wouldn't even be able to make himself notice if she ceased to exist altogether. Why was she bothering? Why was she risking more when she'd already lost everything?—her sister and her magic, and her home and Umeia. What else did they bloody *want* from her?

She could feel Joori's hand tighten on her arm where it had been since he'd started fighting their way across the temple, could tell his breathing had gone thin and tight. So had Shig's. Because right that second, she wanted nothing more than to pull the sword that had been sheathed at her hip through everything and plunge it into Joori's eye.

The fire went away. The temple went away. Everything but Shig and Yori went away.

She knew this feeling. She recognized it. She just couldn't make herself reject it.

"You can have me back," Yori told her. "You can have your magic back."

And wasn't that really all Shig had ever wanted? She'd never cared about Malick's causes. She'd never cared about the fighting or the killing. She'd cared that Yori had cared. Shig hadn't wanted to save the Jin or defeat evil maijin or come to Tambalon so Fen could disrupt her life even more by being something that shouldn't even exist anymore. She'd only ever wanted to live in the attic of the Girou, annoy Samin for the fun of it, watch Umeia bully gold out of silver every night, drag her feet when Malick tried to teach her sword work because it made her feel loved when he did it.

She'd only ever wanted to live a quiet, content life with her sister, watch Yori mature and change, watch her fire grow and shift and modulate into something steadier as the years passed, something deep and *important*, because Yori had that kind of potential. Maybe watch her fall in love, even, but… not with fucking *Joori*.

"Bring him," Yori whispered. "We can have it all back, love."

Shig's body had been swaying forward without her knowledge; now she took a step. Joori's hand tightened on her arm again, and this time Shig did draw her sword. She wanted this. In all her life, all of the things she'd endured and done and had done to her, this was the only thing she'd ever actually *wanted*. And she'd bloody *kill* Joori before she let him stop her.

And then, just as it had been the other night at the Gates of Rapture, Joori managed to blunder to the rescue by lurching forward and croaking, "Jacin."

Everything came back. The heat of the flames blocking their exit from the temple. The clash and screech of close hand-to-hand going on between temple officiates and *banpair* behind them. The fact that she didn't, in fact, despise Joori, nor did she want to live in some nonreality with this not-Yori giving her things that didn't really exist.

Yori wavered back into not-Yori in front of Shig's abruptly clearer eyes. The seed of pure, feral hatred that had been blossoming for Joori wilted back down into the pit of unreasoning grief where it usually lived, then withered into almost nothing.

It made Shig able to say, "That's not your brother," in a calm voice that wasn't full of hate.

Joori hadn't really been given a chance at the Gates of Rapture—he'd been brought down with a dart too quickly—so Shig didn't know what he'd do this time. She'd kind of expected grief and tears and irrational ranting. Instead, rage bloomed in Joori's eyes, so like Fen's in that moment Shig almost expected Joori to pull a couple of long knives and start twirling. Joori curled his lip, grip tightening yet again on Shig's arm, but this time, his other hand firmed on the hilt of the short sword and his whole body tensed.

"Stop. Fucking. With. *My brother.*"

With a roar, Joori lifted the sword and drew a knife, then drove into the woman like a madman. His first blow landed across the woman's ribs before she'd even lifted her own weapon in defense.

He was as vicious as Shig had ever seen Fen get, bearing down with too little finesse, but he made up for it with violent grit as he slashed and dodged and parried the more expert strikes of the woman's weapons and swung his own. There was no equality in skill, but Joori balanced it out with the sheer *want* that drove his moves, the profound *fury* that gave them strength.

Two others had been standing behind the woman. They watched for a moment then seemed to hold a mental conversation with each other before they both turned their attention on Shig. Shig's stomach dropped, and she took an involuntary step back before she made herself stop and firm her grip on her sword. Bloody hell, she really sucked at this combat thing. Maybe she could swing the sword around for a while and delay the inevitable, but it *was* inevitable. She was going to die in Wolf's temple at the hands of *banpair* pretending to be her sister, and she was probably going to get to watch Joori die first, if he didn't stop throwing himself at that woman with such fierce recklessness.

Fucking Fens.

A great bellow went up from somewhere outside, and then a tall man Shig pegged right away as *Temshiel* was barreling into the center of the temple, dual swords swinging, and followed by

"*Samin!*" Shig called, almost relieved enough to cry when she saw Morin darting through the flames after Samin and then Naro-yi appearing abruptly by Morin's side.

Morin pulled up short when he heard Shig call, eyes flying wide as he took in the two coming slowly after her and then narrowing down to slits when he shifted his gaze toward Joori. Shig had lost track for a few seconds, but when she followed Morin's glare, her heart jumped up into her throat and she screamed, "*Joori!*" just as the not-Yori's sword arced then descended, slicing through Joori's shirt and skidding off the mail underneath before it swiped back up and clipped his arm.

Blood flowed immediately, soaking Joori's shirt. He stumbled back, dropping the sword with a hissed, "Son of a *bitch!*" and clutched at the wound as the woman's sword swept up again. A second or two of forceful cursing then Joori jerked with a heavy grunt as what looked like a miniature crossbow bolt lodged between his backbone and right shoulder blade.

"Don't kill them!" not-Yori shouted.

Shig didn't think she wanted to know why. Without thinking, Shig leapt in toward Joori, who looked like he wasn't going to stay on his feet much longer. All she managed was to get an arm snagged by each of the men blocking her way. She dropped her sword, because what was the point, really?

Joori was wincing and clenching his teeth, a *lot* of blood runneling out between his fingers, dripping down his arm and puddling on the floor. The not-Yori had pulled out a small silver tube, set it to her lips, and aimed it at Joori. Shig almost thought it was a whistle for a second or two, but then she remembered those darts, and yeah, well, that figured.

Joori saw it, saw Shig seeing it, and Shig could see him understanding it too. Could see him watching Morin come and calculating odds as his glance moved between the *banpair* all around them. Teeth set, he dropped and lunged down low, rolling at the feet of the two holding onto Shig and managing to knock them all off balance. His knife jabbed up as he went, hacking at the backs of knees. There was a yelp right next to Shig's ear. The two holding onto her fell back. One of them shoved her forward. Joori made a weak grab for her, his eyes dulling by the second, but Shig knocked into him as she slid along the marble floor and he finally lost his grip on consciousness and stayed down. His hand was still clenched in Shig's sleeve, even as Shig skidded right into the snarling flames that had been keeping everyone penned in the temple like sheep at the slaughter.

It hurt. It *hurt*. Shig *screamed*. She couldn't stop. It *hurt*.

Hands were on her, pulling her back. Morin shouted, driving in with short sword swinging. Not-Yori had taken hold of Joori and was trying to go to shadow, but Morin rammed in, still shouting, and whacked his too-big sword into her neck—once, twice, three times—until her head was nearly severed as Naro-yi beat at Shig's hair and arms to put out the flames. Blood shot up from not-Yori's neck in a ruby gush, showering

Morin, but he didn't seem to notice. He yelled again, a loud, roaring, "*Yaaaaaah!*" and threw the sword at another of the *banpair* who was reaching for Joori.

The sword missed, clattering to the marble floor, but it made the *banpair* pause, and when Samin advanced—looking winded and a little green but furious, sword raised and eyes as feral as Shig had ever seen them—the *banpair* tried to back away. It slipped in blood, like a normal, clumsy mortal, and Samin got it through the eye before it hit the floor. Samin turned on the last of them, eschewed the sword in his hand, and merely reached out with the other and gripped the *banpair*'s throat—*pulled*. Shig was glad the angle was wrong and she couldn't see the bloody, twisted trachea no doubt now in Samin's hand.

As though from a distance and yet all too present, Shig noticed she was still smoking, wide patches on her face and neck and head still sizzling in excruciating agony, but she heard Morin say, "This time it was me," as he crouched down to where Joori had fallen, and then she heard Naro-yi say, "Sleep, Wolf's daughter," as he placed a hand to her cheek.

And everything just went away.

☗

Malick hated going to spirit. *Hated* it. Which was why he tried not to die when he could help it. This time had been different. This time had been... informative. He'd been Wolf's for over a century; now he knew what that meant.

He hadn't had to fight his way back this time. No deep meditations to keep himself a part of but separate from the spirits; no penitential offerings for transgressions he wasn't really sorry for. This time, he'd been shown, told, taught. And then he'd been shoved on through, breaching the barriers back to mortality with none of the usual agony and exhaustion, but a high exhilaration and a wealth of strength into which he settled as easily as his mortal skin.

Just in time, it would seem.

"Yeah, it's me, Fen." Malick put on a grin. "Who else would tackle you on a roof?"

It had the exact opposite effect Malick intended: Fen's entire body locked up with stiff-knotted tension. It threw Malick. He'd swear there'd been overwhelming relief, and maybe even some cautious hope in Fen's eyes a second ago. All Malick could see now was distrust that made his teeth clench, and fear that pricked at the soft places behind his breastbone he liked to pretend he didn't have.

"Bloody hell, Fen." He kept *fucking love you* locked behind his teeth.

Also *need you*, and *don't you dare*, and *let me help.* "You look terrible," was what he ended up saying, because the rest were all things Fen wouldn't easily hear.

And anyway, Fen really did look terrible. Bleeding and cold and damp and disheveled—Fen looked like he'd been through a war. And he'd been tottering pretty precariously on the edge of the roof.

"What are you doing up here, Fen? Were you trying to—?"

"Get off me." It was calm. Too calm, really.

So Malick didn't. "Fen." He pressed Fen down harder. "What the fuck are you doing on the roof?"

Because Malick had known, as soon as he'd realized what was in that dart and felt mortal life ebbing away all too quickly, he'd had no doubt things were going to get dicey while he was unavailable. He'd even known that Fen not being here when he got back was a possibility. He had not expected, however, that he'd actually get back just in time to watch Fen try suicide for real.

No wonder Malick had felt that fiery, all-consuming *push* to break through the barrier and pull his skin around him; no wonder he was raw all over and his nerves were so jagged he felt like every single thing in the world was trying to dig down beneath flesh and bone and rake him from the inside out. Wolf's magic, but more, too, almost a physical thing, chewing at him like insects snacking on bared nerve endings, and everything was altogether too *there*.

Strength.

Power.

And yet all it took was that look in Fen's eyes to make Malick all weak-kneed and anxious. He'd apparently arrived right at the edge of one of Fen's chasms, and it wasn't going to help that Malick could feel every immortal casting their senses toward the Incendiary, even as they all rose to the defense of a city exploding into chaos below. There wasn't going to be much time before whatever Fen had just forced came to its point.

"Get. *Off.*" It was still mostly calm, but with a little more feeling behind it this time.

Malick couldn't tell what kind yet, so again, he didn't. "Tell me what's going on. Tell me you weren't going to jump just now, Fen. *Tell me* you weren't—"

"I don't have to listen to this. You're not *here*."

"*Of course* I'm…" Some of Malick's anger and fear mutated into something softer as he peered down at the expression on Fen's face. That was despair beneath the stubborn fury. "Fen. *Jacin.* I'm here. It's me. I'm sorry I—"

"I don't hear you." Fen bucked beneath him, teeth clenched, eyes gone to storm clouds with all the same promised violence gathered behind them. "I don't *hear you*." He looked past Malick and up into the sky, blinking against the flurries feathering into his eyes. "You don't exist, *you're not real*, and I don't hear you. Get. *Off of me!*"

Malick could have held him down, if he'd tried. He'd done it often enough in more intimate circumstances, after all. And Fen clearly wasn't at his top form just now.

The panic inside the demand was what moved Malick. The almost-desolation that lurched and lumbered beneath it. The poisonous knowledge that Fen had, after all, been up here and on the edge of the roof for a reason. Something had driven Fen to this. And it wasn't what was happening in the city below.

"Fen… whatever this is, whatever's going on… let me help you." Malick kept his voice low and calm, his expression kind as he rose and dragged Fen to his feet. Fen was too wobbly, almost dazed-looking, so Malick didn't really want to let go, but it looked like Fen needed him to. With a reluctant grimace, Malick let Fen back away from him. Damn it, Fen looked like he was about to collapse, and he was bleeding. Where the hell was Samin and why hadn't he been taking care of—?

"Fucking *shit!*"

Malick hadn't been expecting the solid kick to his chest. He hadn't realized he was still so close to the edge of the roof. He watched his boots flip up over his head before he figured he'd better do something in a hurry or this was going to be the shortest trip back to mortality he'd ever taken.

With a curse, Malick called the wind, because he didn't dare call the spirits so soon after having dodged them. A great gust came as he willed it and buffered-pushed-rocked him until he was back on his feet on the roof of Raven's temple, Fen watching him with hostile, wary eyes from a semicrouch in the thin stratum of snow.

"What the *fuck*, Fen! D'you have any idea how bloody hard it was to—? Damn it *all!*"

And he was airborne again.

Well, it was his own fault for standing in the same spot twice. And at least Fen wasn't trying to pry Malick's heart out, so maybe this was more a *You bastard, how could you leave me like that?* and not a real *Die, die, die, you immortal assbag!* Then again, it looked like Fen was unarmed, so maybe Malick was being a little too optimistic.

Fuck. Fuck. And also—*fuck*.

Again, Malick caught the wind, and again, he set himself back on his feet, this time several paces away from Fen and at a side angle, so he'd have time to dodge if Fen tried another run at him. He didn't like it—it left Fen too much room to run past him and dive off the roof, if he was really that determined to do so—but Malick gave himself even odds of catching Fen if he tried it. He braced when Fen turned a glare on him of such malevolence it really should have set Malick's hair on fire, then held up his hand when it looked like Fen was tensing to pounce again.

"Just bloody *wait* a moment, will you?"

Now was *really* not the time for distraction, but there were others here now, appearing around the rim of the roof like those sentinel ravens, and Malick couldn't just ignore them. Though he did rather hope they hadn't been there a few seconds ago. *Temshiel,* maijin, every god but Dragon represented, and all of them watching to see what the Incendiary would do. Except it seemed the only thing the Incendiary was intent on doing was kicking the shit out of Malick. Which would be annoying under any circumstances, but with all these people watching, it was flat embarrassing.

"Bloody *hell.*" Malick shot Fen a scowl. "Quit with the glare before you set me on fire."

Oh, good, Malick. *Put* ideas in his head.

Fen made an abrupt forward feint that had Malick flinching back before he could help it. "Damn it, Fen, knock it off! It isn't funny!"

"Do you see me laughing?"

No, definitely no laughing here, and this wasn't Fen's twisted idea of a joke. Malick hadn't seen that look directed at him since the night he'd "met" Fen in the baths of the Girou back in Ada. Hostility. Bitterness. Wariness.

Hatred.

What the hell had been going on? Well, Malick knew what had been going on in the grander scheme—and if he hadn't, all he'd have to do was tune his senses to the chaos that was the temples below—but he couldn't follow Fen from spirit the way he could follow almost anyone else, so he didn't know what had been going on with *Fen.* And he was having a hard time guessing now—Fen's expression had shifted from hard lines of malice and was now melting into confusion.

"Are you…?" Fen cocked his head, brow twisted. "Are you… *taller?*"

…Um.

"I… no?"

Of course Malick wasn't taller. That would mean the half inch Fen had on him had bothered him, and he'd taken the time in his all-fired hurry to get back here to make that small adjustment to his height so he could be taller than Fen. Which would make Malick absurdly vain, so—

Someone snorted; Malick was pretty sure it was that Bear cub over by Xari and Leu. Right, like she'd been that gorgeous when she'd been mortal. His height was the only adjustment Malick had ever made to his appearance, thank you very much, and that after… well, he couldn't remember how many incarnations. So fuck her. He was halfway relieved to see Sora and Tatsu—Owl's and Bear's respectively—but the others not so much. Malick squinted, scowling, because that looked like… well, fuck it all. As if Goyo wasn't enough of a pain in the ass, and here Fen was, giving him all kinds of ammunition.

A small explosion whoofed from the direction of Wolf's temple.

Malick chanced a quick look over the lip of the roof and down. People were still streaming down the steps, and fire still wavered all around it.

"Shouldn't you all be down there defending your temples?"

In point of fact, Malick should probably be down there, too. This, though… He looked back at Fen. This really was more important. This was everything. And not only in the way Wolf wanted it to be.

"It seems the attack is concentrated on Wolf's house." The Bear cub wore the surcoat of the Patrol and a smirk Malick had no doubt had everything to do with the arrogance of the newly turned and nothing to do with actual talent or power. She looked rather put out when Tatsu set a quelling hand to her arm.

"You are." Fen ignored everyone else, took a step toward Malick.

Malick tensed, bracing, but it didn't look like Fen was going to try to not-really-kill-him this time.

"You… you're *taller.*" Fen sagged like all the wind had just gone out of him, and took another step. "It's really you, you self-important, sex-for-brains son of a bitch."

Malick blinked.

Right. No way was he going to try to follow the Fen-logic there. Sometimes trying to understand Fen was like trying to understand how colors worked, except while drunk and high on poppy. Nor was Malick going to huff at the insult. The several insults. Because yeah, *sex-for-brains*, like that wasn't pot and kettle, the way Fen sometimes just about *begged*… all right, no. Anyway, if being taller somehow convinced Fen that Malick was indeed Malick, well.

"Yeah." Malick kept his voice soft, because it looked like Fen was still skating the edge, and Malick didn't know where the drop-off point was. "Yeah, Fen, it's really me. Who else would—? Hey, *whoa!*"

He lurched forward with arms extended just as Fen's knee seemed to give out on him and he started to go down. Malick caught him before he fell, kept him on his feet, and this time, Fen almost melted into

Malick's chest. Fen didn't seem to have the wherewithal for an actual embrace, only wound clutching fingers into Malick's open coat and held on.

Malick glared at the immortals all around them, daring them to say something. When they didn't, Malick pulled Fen in and held him tight, noting the rigidity and the shaking, and gritted his teeth.

"You're freezing, Fen. What the hell is going on? What hap—?"

"Have you got a smoke?"

"Have I got a…?" Malick had no idea if he should laugh or not, so he choked it back. "No, sorry, I—"

"Has anyone got a smoke?" Fen lifted his head from Malick's chest long enough to have a look around at the others, but when they all sort of peered bemusedly at each other and shrugged, Fen growled and stuffed his face back into Malick's shirt. "What the fuck good are they?"

"None." Malick firmed his hold. "It's a game to them, Fen. Ignore them and let them play it among themselves."

"How about *Kill All the Assholes*? When do we get to play that game?"

Malick nearly laughed out loud. "Anytime you like. You just let me know when I get a turn."

"You have to be real. *Please*." Choked out on a raspy whisper that nonetheless broke over Malick like a heavy, pounding wave. "Be real, you have to be real, I can't… can't *take* any more."

"I am, Fen. I'm real. I'm here."

"You smell of pine and… and sage, and… you don't… you have no idea… *Malick*."

Malick thought there might be tears clogging up Fen's voice, but Fen wouldn't pull back so Malick could get a look.

"He smells of ashes. All the time, ashes. He was supposed to smell of jasmine. Maybe that's how I knew, even when I didn't know. What a stupid mistake. Keeps saying he can solve all my problems, pretending to be Beishin, except he doesn't even know enough to smell of jasmine instead of ash. And fuck it all, I need a bloody *smoke*."

Malick's brain had got caught on *Beishin*, and just sort of… hung there.

"Fen, what…?"

No, there had to be some other kind of sense in there somewhere. This wasn't about Asai, not really. Malick just wasn't following the Fen-logic the right way.

They'd all come in closer, *Temshiel* and maijin, trying to hear what Fen was muttering into Malick's chest, so Malick threw up a bit of a barrier around himself and Fen just to piss them off. There was no doubt they were waiting for an opening, watching the Incendiary not so quietly falling apart, and deciding whether to try to woo him away or kill him outright. None of them had drawn a weapon or made a move yet, and Malick thought he could at least count on Tatsu for fair warning—and Leu and Xari for backup if he needed it—so he kept his eyes and senses open and put the rest of his attention on Fen.

Fen didn't even seem to remember they weren't alone. He sniffed then shuddered, and then the floodgates opened up and *poured*.

"He has to stay dead. Please, please, *please*, he has to stay dead. I can't see him anymore, I can't *listen* anymore, he's making me… I have to… I need… I don't even *know*, damn it, *you're* supposed to figure out… I killed him, I *keep killing* him, but he won't stay fucking *dead*, and no one can see him, not even Caidi, but she was—" Fen stiffened, tried to pull away, but he was tugging toward the edge of the roof again, so Malick didn't let go. "Get off. I have to find Joori and Morin. He's going to kill them if I don't go with him, and I—"

"Go with what, now?"

Fen yanked out of Malick's grip and limped toward the edge of the roof over the alley, walking right through the barrier that was keeping the others back and then parting them before him with the sheer force of his glare. Again, Malick deftly angled between Fen and a quick plunge and took hold, because with Fen, you just never knew.

"Fen, go *where*? And who are we talking—?"

"What difference does it make? I don't want to go with him any—"

It was like every spirit of the air had gotten together and wrenched Fen sideways and down, except this was no magic of the gods that ripped him out of Malick's grasp. Malick didn't take the time to analyze it; he flung out his magic, aiming it not at Fen, but at whatever had hold of Fen and was lifting him off his feet. Malick felt it glance off of something solid-but-not, caught a momentary glimpse of yellow eyes and ragged wings, and arms locked around Fen's torso before whatever it was shook off Malick's magic and went transparent again.

"Get it!" Malick didn't wait for the others to act—he sucked every bit of magic out of them he could and hurled it again.

"What *is* it?" someone asked—Malick didn't actually care who it was, but he thought it might be Tatsu because he could feel Tatsu sending him power without Malick having to take it. Several of the others did the same, and Malick took it, massed it.

Fen's bare feet were making tracks in the thin layer of snow across the roof as he was dragged, wide eyes fastened to Malick's—confusion, panic. Malick gathered all the power out of the immortals and spirits and elementals all around him, snagged some energy from the fires snapping and crackling below, and stretched his senses until they hitched on that singular magic he'd felt stippling his nerves just before he'd gotten a dart in the back of the neck. He couldn't wield it, but he could take it away so this thing couldn't, either.

A bolt of power, everything Malick could drag through himself, and aimed right through and all around Fen this time, because it wouldn't touch Fen, but it might be enough to knock this thing off of him.

Except somehow Malick's magic *did* touch Fen, because Fen shouted like it hurt when it hit.

It lit up the rooftop, everything standing out for a split second in brilliant clarity: *Temshiel* and maijin in various states of awe and disbelief; dozens of marble ravens along the edge of the roof, sharp shadows in the snow; Fen's expression of pain mixed with a burgeoning snarl as he tried to claw his way free of the hold; the man-shape that spread its dusky wings against the sky and screeched as Malick's magic thumped into it. It jerked, lurched back, and… tripped as Goyo dove at it and struck out at its legs. Fen fell to his knees as the thing jolted and let go, wings flapping and taloned feet scraping at the roof before it disappeared again into nothing.

"Fen." Malick crouched in front of Fen and took hold of his arm. "Tell me you have the ring with you. You need to go to shadow."

The thing, whatever it was, wasn't gone. This wasn't going to be that easy. Malick could feel it like a low fizz on the bottom of his… tongue, except not—it wasn't as physical as all that, but Malick couldn't think of a better way to shape it in his head. He didn't take the time to parse it, merely let instinct move him to reach out and snag at another burgeoning swell of power that wasn't his and try to close a metaphorical fist around it. He almost recoiled at the touch, dark like a mouthful of dirt, primitive and rather crude, slick-slippery and shifting in and out of his awareness. Now that Malick knew what to look for, he could feel its contours, sense the swoop and swing in pressure as it warped and moved.

"Um." Fen sat back on his heels and looked reflexively at his hands, where a ring, Malick was only now noticing, was not. "About that."

Malick didn't even have time to decide what that meant. The swell of *Other* rose around him. He dove at Fen, just as Fen was seized again from behind, jarred right out of Malick's grip and lifted off his feet. Malick leapt after him, but all he got hold of was the ragged tail of Fen's shirt, ripping away in Malick's hand as Fen was jolted up into the air and away, disappearing altogether before he could even finish calling Malick's name.

Strange, the compulsion to fly past Kamen and make a running dive for the Incendiary, even as Xari shouted Goyo's name and the Incendiary disappeared at the very end of Kamen's outstretched hand. Goyo and Kamen both fell to the roof, Kamen rolling instantly to his feet and setting himself in an offensive half crouch, fingers hooked into claws and a ball of brilliant, pulsing power held static between his palms. He looked fierce, wrathful, the goblin-light of the physical manifestation of raw magic throbbing all around him. He spared Goyo only a wild snarl then dismissed him, turned back to where the Incendiary had been, and cocked his arm back.

Xari was there, hanging on to Kamen's arm like a little girl clinging to her father.

"*Think*, Kamen! What if it drops him?"

Kamen shoved her off so hard she paved a clear patch in the snow as she skidded across the roof. Her shoulders knocked into the queue of ravens; one thumped loose to shatter in the alley below. She didn't flinch when Kamen drew his arm back again, aiming crude force at her this time in his near-mad rage, but it seemed she didn't dare move, either.

Any of the other *Temshiel* or maijin who hadn't disappeared before took one look at Kamen and did so now. All but Tatsu, who peered around, seemed to decide that Goyo was the only one who might pay attention.

"I must consult at my temple. So must the others. But Wolf will not be alone in this. Whatever your own god demands of you, please tell Kamen as much."

And then he too was gone. Only Kamen, Goyo and Xari were left on the roof.

"You know what he is," Xari told Kamen, calm and even. "You know now what he wants. And you know now why Wolf turned you and called you to his own. Perhaps the Incendiary is yours, but you have been his since your paths collided. Wolf made you for it." She opened a hand, held it out, offering.

Kamen clenched his jaw. He never dropped the maddened glare, but the power in his hands guttered and receded back down into flesh and bone.

Xari stood slowly, wary, but she kept her gaze locked to Kamen's and lifted her chin.

"The Sorcerer's mantle sits upon your shoulders, Wolf's-own. The choice is not so hard now, is it?"

"Magic shouldn't have worked on him."

Goyo frowned when he realized he'd said it out loud, like a question, and that Xari and now Kamen were both looking at him. A bit of a frisson moved through Goyo. Xari, he was pretty sure he could handle, but he only knew Kamen enough to not like him much, and what he did know worried him. Impulsive and reckless and arrogant, and more powerful than one of his years should be. Goyo had never really understood why others feared Kamen. Strong and capable when he wanted to be, in Goyo's experience, but somewhat lazy and conceited enough to make Goyo believe all that overconfident posturing had to be covering up some kind of weakness. Goyo thought perhaps he knew better now.

Magic leaked out around Kamen like a throbbing aura, laced through with a near corporeal rage that actually *burned* at the edge of Goyo's senses. Aching to lash out. Looking for an excuse. Because all that impotent wrath had to go somewhere.

"Our magic, no." Xari kept her eyes on Kamen, still watchful and tense. "But he is not of the gods. Neither of them is. Their laws are the old laws, the magic bound to them ancient." She tilted her head. "And yet the Sorcerer's magic touched where others cannot. What more have you bound to the Incendiary besides your heart, Wolf's-own?"

"Do you know where he hides?" Kamen's voice was low as he turned to peer up at the sky, his tone too obviously under very conscious control. His empty fists clenched then unclenched, over and over again. His whole body was set in lines of overwhelming fury locked in a too-small cage, and Goyo couldn't stop feeling that steady throb of power that seemed to swell out from Kamen and swath the air. Kamen angled his gaze from the spot in the sky where the Incendiary had disappeared and turned it on Xari, coldly enraged. "Because if you're only talking to hear yourself talk," he said, flat and dangerous, "I *will* fucking hurt you."

Xari moved to back up a step until she realized she didn't have one. She shook her head.

"I do not know—"

She didn't get to finish; Kamen snarled then stalked past her, stepped off the edge of the roof and dropped down. Xari merely blinked at Goyo for a second or two then followed after, and Goyo… paused. Because the situation really seemed to call for it. This wasn't Snake's fight, whatever it turned out to be, and the crazed rage in Kamen's eyes was far too close to the glittering shards of insanity Goyo had seen when the Incendiary's wild gaze had locked with his in Raven's temple.

It was the sad resignation he'd seen after that moved him now, the exhausted grief that had struck at Goyo's heart with remembrance he had to be imagining. He'd stared down from the temple's steps as the Incendiary backed away from him and looked at Goyo with such raw sorrow that Hitsuke had risen to mind, just as he did now. The poignant resolve and the wrenching screams that were the last of Hitsuke reached out from over a century past and sent Goyo after Kamen as Kamen and Xari both parted the sea of screaming and panicking festival-goers and stalked to Wolf's house. He joined them just in time to watch Kamen split the flames then curl his arms inward; the fire leaned with Kamen's motion, followed then coiled into wisps at the tips of Kamen's fingers, as if he'd sucked the fire into himself, then he merely strode on through into the temple itself.

Goyo couldn't help the little bit of grudging awe. He'd set himself against fire made by these creatures twice now, and had only been able to call the water spirits and douse the flames that had gutted the Gates of Rapture tonight after some very concentrated effort and the expending of a lot of his power. Kamen had just done it like an afterthought.

The interior of the temple was a pit of destruction. Most of the priests and priestesses in their wolf's masks lay scattered among the ruin, dead. Trained warriors though they were, they'd been no match for *banpair* against whom their magic had little impact. A few still fought behind the *Temshiel* and maijin who'd answered the call, allowing the immortals the vanguard and backing them up when possible.

Dakimo spun and slashed in the center of too many attackers, and Imara was there, trying to serve as his rearguard, but there were too many on her too. Even as Goyo watched, a black-clad figure spun into shadow, the finest tracery of murk following after it, allowing the briefest, most minimal warning, before it rematerialized right behind—

"Naro-yi! Behind—!"

Goyo's warning turned out to be unnecessary; Naro-yi swept to the side, snatched up—bloody hell, that was—Morin and hurled him aside. With a pivot and a lunge, Naro-yi threw himself over Joori, sprawled facedown on the floor, apparently unconscious, and tried to roll them both out of the line of attack.

Too slow, Goyo thought wildly, and flung himself into spirit, leaping back through the barrier beside Naro-yi, the Incendiary's broken stick raised to deflect the axe the *banpair* wielded, and sword drawn for a counterattack.

"*Malick!*" Morin shouted, then Kamen was there, power leaping from him like invisible lightning strikes, only it wasn't the power Goyo had not-really-felt up on the roof. It wasn't a power Goyo had ever felt before, in fact—baser, more raw, something wild and saw-toothed. Goyo could almost see it leaking from the *banpair* and into Kamen like the flames had done, as though Kamen was drawing it right from their spirits and pulling it into his own.

Goyo didn't have time to analyze it—he sprang forward and swiped at the creature that had gone after Naro-yi, surprised and slightly encouraged when it hesitated long enough for him to get a good slice up its side, the tip of his sword glancing the rutted bone of ribs. He'd fought these things twice now, and he'd never before managed a decent strike, hardly even blooding them, as they disappeared in front of him and reappeared to try to flank him. This one looked like it had been trying to do exactly that, and had merely vibrated in place for too long before it realized it couldn't. Goyo probably savored the scream it loosed as his sword hit its mark more than he should have.

"Don't kill them all!" Kamen stalked among the chaos, pulling *banpair* right out of their shadows as he went, leaving them open for the swords of maijin and *Temshiel* and priest and priestess. "I want at least one of them able to talk." His gaze narrowed in at the one Goyo had just wounded, and another with a woman's shape who held a silver tube and several small darts Goyo recognized too well. She hovered uncertainly, poised to strike again at Morin, but Samin was in the way. "Those two," Kamen said, directly to Goyo. "I want them." And then he merely turned and jammed his sword into the neck of another.

"Retreat!" The woman shouted it, even as she tried one last time to snatch hold of Morin.

Morin held her off with a sword that was too big for him, and Samin was quite an obstacle, even with no magic. It looked like he was taking great pleasure in turning the tables on that one.

"Null!" The woman backed off a step. "Retreat! Null!"

Goyo hadn't thought that made any difference against their kind of magic, but whatever Kamen was doing seemed to be working. And there was no doubt these creatures knew it and feared it.

"Malick!" Samin shoved Morin at Kamen. "They're all after him and Joori. Keep him close." Bloody sword arcing, he turned quickly to jab at a black-clad figure that was trying to slide past him and out of the temple.

Goyo vaulted after it, again surprised and savagely satisfied when a mere swipe of his sword at the backs of the creature's knees brought it down to the floor with a *thud* and a cry of pain. Goyo set his boot to the creature's chest to hold it down before skimming a glance back to check on Samin.

"Told you I'd manage to get you eventually." Samin had his arm wrapped around the woman's throat, her feet off the floor, kicking ineffectually at Samin's shins as Samin tilted a nasty little smile over at Kamen. "Got 'em, Mal." He caught Goyo's eye and... winked.

Goyo only blinked back, and secured his captive.

Samin dragged the hood from the woman's face. "Let's see what you look like." Then the kerchief.

Goyo narrowed his eyes. He'd never actually met the Zhiri girl, or her brother, but he'd met both their parents twice, once after each disappearance. And this woman had the same light-brown eyes, the same bone structure to her fine features as Zhiri-onna. So many things clicked in Goyo's head he almost shook it to make sure nothing was rattling loose.

He cast his glance around to find Xari standing at the entrance to the temple, smoke wafting around her from the smaller fires still burning among the bodies and the rubble from the altar, festive banners and paper lamps nothing more than charred ash. She stood perfectly still as *banpair* scuttled around her and out of the temple, her eyes locked to Kamen, her jaw set.

Kamen was still wading through the dwindling battle, dragging Morin along as he stripped power away and struck down its wielders, trying to prevent the escape of those who'd followed the order to retreat and abandoned the fight in favor of flight. Kamen cut down at least a dozen of those, but too many streamed past, and none of the other *Temshiel* or maijin left to Wolf looked like they had it in them to pursue.

Dakimo was vibrant and thrumming with his own power as he went after the stragglers that tried to slither past him, but haggard and gray beneath it. Imara was bloodied and winded, more of a mess than Goyo had ever seen her before, and she looked at Kamen with as close to fear in her gold eyes as Goyo had ever thought to see. She looked away and dropped her weapons, hurrying to... oh no—what had happened to Shig?

"Malick!" Morin was trying to tug free from Kamen's grip, whacking at Kamen's arm and nearly writhing as he was dragged along, shoes squeaking along the bloodied marble floor with Kamen's longer strides. When that didn't gain Kamen's attention, Morin threw himself toward the floor and started kicking at Kamen's shins. "*Malick!*"

And still, Kamen dragged him along, mowing through anything that looked like an enemy as he trod through dwindling mayhem.

Leu appeared—filthy and bloody. She planted herself in front of Kamen and pulled on a glamour that was halfway between a large wolf and a bear. She kept it on only long enough to roar "*Kamen!*" then she let it drop and took a quick step back.

It was like Kamen had been slapped back into sanity. He frowned, blinked, then looked down as though he had no idea why Morin was dangling from his arm like a piece of flotsam.

"Let me go," Morin said quietly. "Joori needs me."

Kamen did, so abruptly Morin fell on his ass to the blood-streaked floor. Mute, he stared up at Kamen, wide-eyed, then crab-walked backward before lurching to his feet.

Leu stepped in again and put herself between Morin and Kamen, her expression not quite afraid but watchful, at the very least. She set a hand to Morin's shoulder and steered him toward his brother. Morin didn't take his chary gaze off Kamen until he'd reached Naro-yi then knelt to lay his hand beside the bolt jutting from Joori's back.

"Kamen." Leu's tone was careful, her whole body poised for a quick retreat. "You're frightening your mortals."

There was a smirk on Kamen's face now, something cold and nasty. He looked Leu up and down, blinked at her, slow and lazy, then shook his head and whiffed a contemptuous snort.

"Get me the girl."

※

"He wanted the Incendiary willing." The girl gasped as Kamen dipped a finger into the wound he'd made just below her ribs, crooked it. She arched against Leu's hold, juddering with pain and shock, but she still snarled as Leu kept her from writhing away. "He lost his patience. And then *you* came back."

"I don't care." Kamen's face was blank, his eyes cold and flat. "I only care where he is now." He jammed his finger deeper… *twisted*.

The girl *shrieked* this time, high-pitched and thin, as though it was ripped out of her. There were no words to it; she was clearly beyond them.

It chilled Xari. Kamen's impassive cruelty chilled her more. She couldn't tell if it had the same effect on anyone else, because she couldn't take her eyes off Kamen. She could've told him this would do no good. She didn't quite dare. Mortal this girl might be, but held in thrall to an immortal power that had managed to birth gods; torture was redundant.

It was no surprise, really, this vindictive bit of ruthless retribution. Xari knew Kamen's tactics; she knew what had brought him to Wolf's attention. She knew he wouldn't stop. And she knew what that look in young Morin's eyes meant too. She couldn't allow it to take root. Fate's hand was like a new kiss set to his brow, this young Kurimo, and it would not do for him to fear the one upon whom he might one day have to rely.

Xari turned to the maijin held fast in Goyo's grip. "Zuan." She sighed, genuinely regretful.

Zuan merely looked at her with eyes that held no reason, no recognition, even though he had been Dragon's once and Xari had known him long before Asai had even been a seed of an idea in the back of her mind. Older than she, this one, as old as time.

Xari thought she understood now why the Hawk Priest had stolen those who'd come even before he had. Maijin had been enslaved once before, after all, the seed of the old magic deep inside their souls more vulnerable than apparently even the gods had known to the leash held by the usurped who would be the usurper.

Xari wondered if Kamen had yet realized that the same seed still sat as a dormant little lure at the bottom of the Incendiary's tormented soul. And was just as defenseless.

Surely he had. It was, no doubt, why Kamen was now wrist-deep in this girl's guts, ignoring the screams and the ashen cast to the faces around him. A small bit of sacrilege in Wolf's own temple, Xari supposed, but Kamen was and had always been the bloody hand at the end of Wolf's long arm, and... well. The metaphor rather gained appalling power when made into too-vivid reality.

Xari waited until the cries tapered into whimpers.

"Kamen." She laid one hand to Zuan's arm and held the other out toward Kamen. "She can tell you nothing. Even did she want to. And you have no time to indulge your wish for blood."

"I can't smell *his* blood anymore. And he isn't using the ring, which means I can't feel him." Kamen pinned Xari with eyes that were flat as a shark's. "Have you got a better idea?"

The scent of the Incendiary's blood that had attracted all the immortals now seeking guidance in their temples had disappeared along with the Incendiary. Xari didn't know how, but there was a lot about the old magic she didn't know.

She jerked her chin at Zuan and then at Shig, still laid out on the floor and unconscious, the burns given cursory care by Imara, but not yet healed. Shig's motley hair was half-burnt and singed into kinks on one side of her head. Imara could likely save the girl's pretty face for her, but there were other matters more pressing. The Kurimo sat on the filthy floor between Shig and the Paradox, a hand on each of them, as though guarding. Xari would win no goodwill from him with what she was about to suggest.

"She maneuvers the spirits even now." Xari waved toward Shig. "Without even knowing it, she coaxes the seed of the old magic to sprout roots. They stretch and reach blind within her." She pursed her lips, but there was really no choice. She pointed at Zuan. "The Sorcerer is the channel to the power of the gods and all the spirits. It is time the mantle served the god who laid it upon your shoulders, Wolf's-own."

Morin frowned, suspicious. "What does that mean?"

It looked like he was the only one who didn't know. Everyone else merely turned their glances to Shig. Samin made to take a protective step forward, but stopped when he looked at Kamen.

Kamen hardly reacted at all, merely looked from Zuan to Shig and then down at the girl he'd been torturing. Face still blank, he nodded, pulled his hand free, ignoring or perhaps not even hearing the whining scream, and turned his gaze to Imara.

"Wake her up."

Xari could swear Imara flinched. Xari didn't blame her. Kamen had not been told that Imara had prevented Xari from warning him of nascent danger the night of the ambush, at least Xari hadn't told him, but that didn't mean Kamen didn't know. Kamen would not be distracted right now from hunting down the one who'd stolen what was his, but Xari had no doubt the business between Kamen and Imara would be dealt with in very unpleasant ways when this was all through.

It looked for a moment as if Imara's healer's instincts would cause her to balk, that she might refuse, but whatever protest she might have given died when she allowed her gaze to collide with Kamen's; it hung there for less than a second before she tore it away. Imara and Kamen both went to Shig, Kamen lowering himself to the floor and lifting Shig to lie back against his chest. He was gentler than Xari might have thought, considering the state of murderous fury he'd let grip him from the moment his Incendiary was ripped from his grasp. But his hands, covered in blood though they were, were slow, his touch considerate. He held Shig against him with contrarily protective arms then nodded at Imara.

It took only a moment. A twitch then a hiss then a long, indrawn breath let out on a thin, wheezy sob. Shig's eyes didn't fly open but squinched shut in obvious agony as nerve endings sent messages to a now-wakeful brain and informed it that the body was in a great deal of pain.

"It's all right." Kamen set a tender kiss Xari wouldn't have believed a second ago to Shig's temple. "You were burned but you're going to be all right, love. I promise. I'll let you sleep again in a moment, but I need you now. All right?"

"Mal?" Shig turned her face toward Kamen's voice. She shuddered as an obvious wave of pain moved through her.

"Yes." There was an incongruous smile in Kamen's voice, but not on his hard-set face. "It's me, love. And I need you."

"Yeah. You always have." A tiny wry smile quirked at Shig's pinched mouth. "Doesn't that just fuck with your head?"

"Well, fucking with my head is what you do best, after all."

"You're only ever sweet when want something."

"Lies." Kamen's mouth tilted, fond. "I know you're hurting, and I'm sorry."

Kamen jerked his chin at Goyo. Goyo frowned in confusion for only a moment before dragging a snarling, resisting Zuan in close.

"You cannot." Zuan fought Goyo, feral, trying to yank his hand back as Goyo forced it out toward Kamen. "You *cannot!*"

"Sucks for you, because I'm pretty sure I can." Kamen's bloody hand took up Shig's and set it to Zuan's, wrapped around both of them and held tight. "I want you to look inside, love. I want you to find out where his master hides."

"I c—"

"You can, actually. Feel that?"

"Kamen," said Dakimo slowly, "what are you doing?"

Kamen ignored him, only went on speaking in hushed tones to Shig, magic like water flowing around them and shadowed with that *Other* that Xari could halfway taste, like mud on the back of her tongue. It was as though Kamen was sucking the ambient energy out of existence itself and drawing it inward, building on it, boosting it, and turning it in his hand, making the shapes he willed with it.

It was, Xari thought uneasily, very nearly transcendent—*godlike*—and then stopped thinking about that, because they had not reached that part of Fate's plan yet.

He is Null, Xari told both Dakimo and Imara calmly. *Made to take and use the magic of others; made to bend it to his will, and heighten its power to rival the gods'.*

Had they not, after all, heard how Kamen had managed to skirt the laws back in Ada by handing this very spiritbound his magic? Did they really not understand for whom he'd done it and why?

'Twas only a lack of need and resolve that kept him from bridling all within his reach, and curling all the magic of the world in his fist. The Incendiary, as is his purpose, woke the need, and now gives Wolf's Sorcerer cause to define it. Her lip twitched—she couldn't help it. *Surely you knew the Sorcerer had other lessons to learn besides the one you sought to teach him?*

She lifted an eyebrow when Imara scowled, but Dakimo looked…
stunned. He stared as Kamen crooned and coaxed and comforted Shig
while she did as he asked her.

Slowly, Dakimo's eyes rose back to lock with Xari's.

All that power in Kamen's hand. And sealed within a drop of blood caged in the heart of a diamond…?

So then. Dakimo hadn't known. No one had. None, it would seem,
but Wolf and Xari and Kamen, and that only because Xari had told him.
How had Xari seen this—back when she'd been mere *banpair* herself;
back before she'd even been Wolf's—when even Wolf's-own too
obviously had not?

She peered thoughtfully at Kamen and wondered what Wolf *really*
had in mind for him. Because she'd thought she'd known. And now it
appeared she'd known only what Wolf and Owl had wanted her to know
and nothing more. It did not surprise her, but neither did it diminish the
abrupt unease.

Xari didn't answer Dakimo. She didn't need to. Her stomach did a
lazy little roll, as she was sure Dakimo's did, but the courses were set
and the Wheels were turning. They could only follow now where the
Sorcerer led.

"Ashes." Shig's whisper was raspy and weak. "I taste ashes."

Kamen set a gentle hand to her scorched cheek. "Sleep, Wolf's
daughter." He cut a glance up to Xari when Shig slumped against him.
"I know where he is."

⛩

Flying, he remembered flying, and he'd kept waiting to fall, but he hadn't.
He didn't think he was falling now, and he knew he wasn't flying, so he
just… drifted.

"I would have forgiven you, Hitsuke."

Daraso's hands were gentle on Jacin's face, eyes deep and dangerous
as tar pits, except Jacin kept getting flashes of cat-slit yellow, throbbing
along with the beat of his own heart, and it felt… He didn't know. Wrong.

"I would forgive you still. You are *my* Incendiary, lovely Hitsuke.
Bound to *my* will."

He arched his neck as Daraso's damp mouth stalked the thump of
blood along Jacin's jugular, but that felt wrong too—*exposed; submissive*—
so Jacin turned his head away.

"Not…" Jacin's tongue felt thick, his head light, and the thud-pulse
of yellow eyes that weren't there kept sliding through his veins, binding
him in spells he couldn't hear. *Not Hitsuke anymore*, he'd meant to say,

because he wasn't; Hitsuke's skin had been shed when Fen Jacin's eyes opened against the cherry blossom petals that had kept him blind through too many tormented lives. Or maybe he should say *Not yours*, because he was no one's—*no one's son, no one's brother, no one's father, no one's lover*—and Daraso had made him that way. "Not... not..." The smeary stutters were all that would come, and then he forgot what he was protesting, so he stopped trying.

Jasmine petals slid beneath the bare skin of his back, and it was wrong because all he smelled was ashes, and he could *see* the filthy, bloody sleeve of his shirt, so he knew he wasn't naked. Still, the feel of Daraso's skin slicking against him sent a hot thrill through him, spangling out and covering his mind in blank-white heat as Daraso entered him. His back arched, his hips rocked, and a low moan shuddered loose from down deep in his chest, and still, it wasn't right somehow.

...Where the hell is Malick?

The name rolled around in Jacin's head, slowly gaining substance—presence. Because Malick had been there, only a little while ago—*I'm real, Fen, I'm here*—Jacin *knew* there'd been Malick, he could still feel the touch on his skin, and the touch that was Daraso couldn't rub it out of his awareness.

"Can't..." Thick and slurred and ten different kinds of disoriented. "Can't do this, I can't—"

"You will do as your beishin tells you," Asai said against Jacin's throat, driving into him with a gentle, relentless force that strung out every sensation Jacin had into never-ending loops, curling back into themselves.

Smoke rings. Circles. Perfect circles.

Something echoed, but the want and the craving and the *finally* drove it all sideways as Asai rocked Jacin's body and soothed the eternal craving of unanswered desire.

Say you love me, just say it.

He'd always known it would be like this, all dreamy and quietly passionate, then faster to blank out awareness. All those years of wanting, and if only Asai had given it to him...

It made Jacin frown, but then Asai's teeth sank lightly into the lobe of Jacin's ear, and all the vague thoughts trying to take shape scattered into—

Petals.

Ashes.

The stink of them, the taste of them on the back of his tongue. And the thick, metal scent of blood.

The eyes went to yellow again, a wild pulsation battering at Jacin's mind like the frantic beat of a moth's wings—*thwip-thwip-thwip*—and a desperate ache for Malick bloomed in his gut.

Help.

He'd been there, Malick had *been there*, damn it, he'd come back, but now—

"You fight me." Daraso dragged Jacin up from a hard stone floor that wasn't a bed of jasmine petals; curled his fists into Jacin's filthy shirt that wasn't bare skin heated by breath and caress. Yellow eyes that weren't black or even deep-dark brown narrowed into him, skewered him and set his head spinning, and a voice that was Daraso and Asai and Father but none of them told him, "Fen Jacin-rei taught you how to fight, my little Hitsuke. Fen Jacin-rei brought you to me. But now it is time for Fen Jacin-rei to be gone."

Jacin nearly snorted, because it was kind of funny, considering, but the choked-off laugh turned into a gasp then a truncated shout as Jacin was lifted off his feet and slammed into… shelves. A wall of shelves.

Ornate urns made of clay rocked and fell and shattered as Jacin flew into them then slithered to the floor, stunned. Billows of thick, greasy ash fanned up around him and slid into his nose, down his throat. He coughed when he realized what they were, what it meant—the dead, all over him—and tried to lever himself up and away, but those same hands lifted him and threw him again. More urns shattered and more ash covered him, making his skin crawl, strangling him.

There were others here. Lots of others. They stared down at him, fierce-eyed and avid, watching Jacin getting thrown across the dim-lit chamber by someone who could reach right down into the core of him, show him what he wanted and why he should never have wanted it at all. Watching him writhe to a touch that wasn't there, return kisses he couldn't have, twist and thrash beneath the ghosts of lovers and not-lovers that mocked him and crooned to him in their simulacrum voices that went right to the soft underbelly of his soul and *wrenched*. Watching Jacin's mind opened up and ripped apart in the Shrine of the Dead, where everything tasted like ashes and nothing else was real.

"You know who I am." This voice wasn't any of the other glamours this creature had been wearing for him, but Jacin knew it, something way down deep inside him turning toward it before he could help it. "Say my name, little Hitsuke."

He tried to drag himself up off the cold stone of the floor, but it was as though he was broken into a million pieces—*hahaha, broken, no shit*—and nothing would move right.

Mii-daichiseyh curled in Jacin's throat, like a compulsion, but even if he'd wanted to voice it, he was suffocating, couldn't even get enough air for a decent breath, let alone speech. The other voices did it for him—"Mii-daichiseyh"—like a prayer or a chant, and a ripple went through all of the hostile-eyed sentinels watching Jacin trying to find his mind as it was steadily thieved away from him.

Again, he was picked up, and again he was pinned with his back grinding into the shelves behind him, the dead in little jars clinking protest. He stared into yellow eyes that glowed and pulsed and slithered into him through his own eyes and wriggle-twist-slunk down into his mind.

"You know who I am," Mii-daichiseyh said again, and for the first time in centuries, Jacin could see his face, could see the beauty of the intricate tattoos that covered his skin, the swirls of colored ink that writhed and coiled into shapes Jacin's mind couldn't quite grasp. "And you know what I can do. Don't you, little Incendiary?" He leaned in, close enough for a kiss.

Bile rose to the back of Jacin's throat.

"We can do this the hard way, Hitsuke. And oh, indeed you merit the hard way, yes? After what you did to your god?"

Which one? Jacin thought, but the grip tightened and Jacin was pushed harder into the shelves, bones in his back creaking and shifting.

"I think I shall have you begin with the Adan. The last of my devoted mortals brought back to the faith by the Jin Untouchable who was once the Incendiary who stole it away. Won't that be nicely circular and poetic? Perhaps I shall have you build me a temple, yes? Perhaps I shall have you walk the world until your feet bleed; build a temple to Mii-daichiseyh in every land until your whore's-body is of no use to anyone, not even you; preach of the One God until your throat cracks and your tongue splinters in your head.

"Do you think, my Hitsuke, it would cool the rage that has been burning in my heart since I was cast down by those *you* helped lift up? Do you think any of them will save you now?"

It was so strange, Jacin thought with some part of his mind that insisted upon staying present and paying attention. His hands were free, and yet he couldn't move them, couldn't move anything, could only hang there and let himself dangle like a broken doll. Slit-yellow eyes were almost physically burning him, flaying and searing something inside him that scorched like acid, and yet he couldn't look away, couldn't scream. His body wouldn't listen to him. His mind was nearly nodding its empty head in agreement with all of the vitriol this would-be god was spewing all over him.

Jacin tried to parse to the accusations… couldn't. Remembrance was there but not, all of it at a strange remove, as though he'd been there and watching, but not like it had actually happened to him. The memories were real, he knew it had all really occurred, he recognized people he'd never met before. But up until now, he'd been weirdly detached from most of it.

This, he remembered. This feeling, this helplessness, this watching as a spectator as someone else made his choices for him, someone else gave his body commands, and his mind only sat in his head, numbed and useless, along for the ride while his body did what someone else told it to.

He'd betrayed and fought and killed to save his mother from this. Was there anyone who could save him? Was there anyone who *would?*

Malick… please, I need you.

Magic wasn't supposed to work on him. He was Untouchable, a void for it. Except he'd been Incendiary first, made of the same stuff Mii-daichiseyh was made of, and the slavery to which Fate had abandoned the Incendiary had been all too real. Mii-daichiseyh had caged Hitsuke with magic once before; Jacin hadn't recognized the bars and locks until they'd already snapped shut around him.

Help, someone, I need…

He'd never been able to complete that desperate cry-thought-wish, because he'd never really known what he needed. He knew now. He needed Malick.

No. He needed the stone-cold bastard that lurked behind Malick's eyes.

He needed Kamen.

And Kamen wasn't *here*.

"I would have forgiven you, Hitsuke." A whisper, soft and sonorous. "I would have had you willing. The power of your will is so much more effective when it's turned to something you truly want. But even after I *showed* you what the gods have done to you, still you remain theirs."

There was no such thing as resistance. No such thing as rebuttal. Jacin wanted to say, *No, not theirs, I hate them,* because it was mostly true, but he hated Mii-daichiseyh more. Mii-daichiseyh had shown him what slavery meant, had shown him inevitability, had taught him to resign himself to the yoke he'd worn for one god then traded for the bondage of another, oppression disguised as love, until he'd finally broken beneath it and stood on the roof of Raven's temple to cast it off. Mii-daichiseyh had shown him gods could not be trusted—they wouldn't protect him, they wouldn't protect those he loved.

Jacin thought he'd give anything right now to have the ignorance of belief back again.

"But you are not truly theirs, are you, Incendiary? You are, and always have been, mine."

"Yes," Jacin wheezed, because Mii-daichiseyh willed it, yellow eyes boring into Jacin's soul and slaughtering all choice, tattoos lacing into spells on Mii-daichiseyh's brow, burning into Jacin's mind, bending it.

"You are mine now, Hitsuke." Harsh. *Mocking.* "Mine, as you've been since the birth of your One God. Aren't you?"

"Yes." Tears slid out the corners of his eyes, *Malick!* purling at the back of his tongue and clogging there hard enough to choke him. "Yours."

Someone… help.

"*Yesssss.*" Mii-daichiseyh pulled Jacin away from the wall and the urns filled with the dead, and hugged him close. "And do you know what you will do first, my Incendiary?"

Jacin knew. Hitsuke knew. Every incarnation of every insane Untouchable that lived inside him knew.

"I…" Jacin gritted his teeth, shoved it out. "I swallowed it." One thin hope. One betrayal he couldn't be forced to make. "It's gone."

"Is it, then?" Mii-daichiseyh's smile was chillingly satisfied as he set a hand to Jacin's torso, just below his breastbone. "Mm, yes, I can feel it pulse within you." He pressed harder, thin tendrils like tiny little strings of lightning threading into Jacin's gut, piercing him. "I told you it would be useful to me, did I not? Perhaps I cannot wield the power of Wolf's-own, but my Incendiary can, no?"

Pain had been Jacin's ally for years; he'd inflicted it himself with precision, knowing the depth and length and location that would bring the clarity when he needed it. He hadn't remembered what *real* pain was until just this second. The tendrils turned to thickset cords and then to great swathes that cut right through him and would have sent him to his knees had Mii-daichiseyh allowed it. He didn't. Jacin could only hang there, held in Mii-daichiseyh's grip, strangling on agony he didn't have permission to voice, until Mii-daichiseyh chuckled like Jacin was a pet that had performed a favorite trick. And then Mii-daichiseyh simply let go.

He held out a hand. "You may scream."

Jacin fell to his knees and screamed.

6

"**T**his part is mine," said Kamen.

The scent of the Incendiary's blood filled the wide space like a grisly perfume, the simpler scent of ash and mortal blood cloying beneath it. Dakimo thought at least part of the wild glint in Kamen's eyes was visceral reaction to it. He was sure the sudden rigidity that rippled through the others was.

Seb and the other monks who'd arrived fresh from the battle at the Gates of Rapture merely accepted Kamen's assertion with serene nods. Oddly, none of those *Temshiel* and maijin who'd followed were yet balking at Kamen's bit of assumed authority. Dakimo would like to think they'd all come to help and not merely watch to see what happened so they could decide how best to take advantage. But since Dakimo wasn't even sure what he himself intended to do, he had to assume at least those from gods other than Owl and Wolf were here to vie for the outcome most advantageous to their own gods. And he had no doubt Serenai had very specific orders from Raven.

"There are others back there." The glimmer of Kamen's eyes seemed to shift toward malevolence in the low gutter of the scattered lamps. "In fact…" He paused, head cocked. "They seem to be heading this way. You just keep them off me."

"Kamen." Dakimo set a hand to Kamen's arm, preventing him from going after the Incendiary like Dakimo could tell he was desperate to. An ephemeral tingle of strange magic was rippling over Dakimo's senses, and shadows were oozing from the entrance to the Hall of Relics. "Charging in blind is not a strategy. We must—"

"I have a perfectly good strategy—I'm going to kill anything that moves. How about you do the same? Or"—Kamen waved toward the others—"you can just stay out of my way while you form a committee and discuss it."

Dakimo set his teeth, and took quick stock.

Leu and Xari were here; combined with Kamen and Dakimo, there should be enough power between them to take on anything. Naro-yi had not come for Owl, though Sora had, and there was no question that Owl stood with Wolf. None had come to represent Dragon, though that was no surprise; Dragon rarely took a stand until an outcome was assured. Tatsu and Annaichi were here for Bear, and Goyo for Snake, and though Dakimo couldn't say circumstances wouldn't change, right now they were allies. The only one here who clearly wasn't was Serenai, Raven's-own, though she nonetheless seemed to be readying to deal with the emerging shadows just as everyone else was.

It might be enough. Still, Dakimo didn't let go of Kamen just yet. He held on tighter.

"There is more to this than rescuing a lover. If this is Mii-daichiseyh risen, as you say, he has already enslaved the Incendiary once. With your ring—"

"You have your priorities." Kamen gave Dakimo a violent shove to shake him off. "And I have mine."

Dakimo hadn't even recovered his balance before Kamen burst into abrupt, deadly movement. Blank-faced, almost casual, he advanced on the shadows that had sprung up like a picket. He parted them, ripping them away and exposing the creeping *banpair* before they could assemble for a proper ambush. The insouciance was galling even to Dakimo as Kamen dropped three surging opponents on his way through them, quicksilver sword strikes—one, two, three—an economy of effort as though he didn't even have to *try*, then spun to shadow and winked out before Dakimo could reach for him again.

Dakimo wouldn't have, at any rate. If there had been any question before that Kamen's concerns were not the same as Wolf's-own, Kamen's own words had just neatly answered it.

It was... regrettable. There were only so many deviations from the chosen path Dakimo could allow when it came to the Incendiary. An Incendiary apparently now held captive by one who'd already once held him in thralled bondage. And now the Incendiary held Wolf's power bound to a token handed to him by a foolish, impulsive, too-powerful *Temshiel*. Love, infatuation, obsession—whatever it was Kamen felt for this Incendiary, Dakimo's responsibilities were all too clear here.

Just where do your loyalties lie in this, Wolf's-own? Kamen had asked Dakimo only days ago. Dakimo had answered truthfully—in this, as in all things, his loyalties lay with Wolf.

Dakimo watched the minions of gods and a would-be god engage in violent battle, and gripped the little crossbow he'd liberated from a dead body in Wolf's temple. He didn't think about what he was doing; he thought of Emika's eyes as she'd watched the specter of Fen Jacin charge toward her, and still she'd advanced, rather than retreated. Kamen probably thought Dakimo had no idea what was in his heart for Fate's Incendiary. Kamen would be wrong.

Rueful but resolved, Dakimo followed Kamen.

Something was off.

Malick paused when he reached the Hall of Relics and found Fen standing beside the man who would call himself a god, tattoos flaring and whirling around yellow eyes, his hand set proprietarily to Fen's shoulder. And Fen was just letting him.

The scent of blood was everywhere, and not only Fen's. It had sunk into the very stone, merged with ash so thoroughly there was no separating one from the other. Malick figured he knew now where the *banpair* had taken their victims to torture them and slurp up their pain and terror.

A steady tug was rippling at Malick's magic, centered *in* Fen, like a tether from him to Malick. Not pulling at Malick, really, but undeniably there, and with a foreign flavor to it that sat beside Malick's magic like a malevolent twin.

Mii-daichiseyh smiled, condescending, but he didn't otherwise react to Malick's presence. He merely gave a minute flick of his fingers, and a second later, an alarmingly dazed-looking Fen took a stumbling step forward. His breath was coming shallow and raspy, and sweat was sticking his raggedy dark hair to cheeks and brow. His eyes were glazed, unseeing as they stared through Malick, and he was covered in ash, bloodied and bruised and just plain beaten. His mouth moved, though no sound emerged, but Malick didn't think it had anything to do with arrogance when he recognized the shape of his own name on Fen's lips, over and over again.

"What…?" Fury swept Malick, but he didn't let it distract him from pulling splotches of energy into his balled fists, flexing them so power spat and hissed at the ends of his fingers. "What is this? What did you do?"

"I forgave him."

Malick didn't really understand what that was supposed to mean, but he now knew everything Wolf knew about Mii-daichiseyh and the role Hitsuke had played in bringing him down. And whatever was wrong with Fen right now didn't look anything like forgiveness.

"*Forgave* him." Eyes on Mii-daichiseyh, Malick reached his senses out to Fen, probing at that odd magic that shouldn't be there, and was unpleasantly surprised when his own power answered. A shifting aura that was his and yet not his, a shadow looming over it with a too-familiar taste. Malick's magic, matched and rivaled by Mii-daichiseyh's, and yet when Malick gave it a tweak to test it, try to direct it, Fen gasped and juddered in place.

"It was probably wise of you to keep the important spells from him." Mii-daichiseyh peered at Malick smugly with those freakish eyes that kept glinting in the lamplight like a feral cat's. "I had a slight difficulty in determining that he simply doesn't know them. The process was"— he reached out and pushed Fen's hair back from his brow—"rather painful for him, I'm afraid."

That smile. Malick strained to keep himself in check until he knew exactly what was going on. *When I pull your guts from out your lying mouth, it'll be for smiling like that while you talk about hurting him. While you touch him.*

"I imagine his second task will have to be finding someone who can give him the spells so he may use the magic now locked inside him. After he's completed his first, of course." Mii-daichiseyh tilted his head, eyeing Malick with a raised eyebrow. "Although, perhaps the first and the second might be one and the same."

So. Malick was pretty sure he got it now. Mii-daichiseyh couldn't wield the magic of the gods any more than Malick could wield that of Mii-daichiseyh. But Fen—with the soul of an Incendiary and the gods'- Blood that ran through Jin veins—could wield both. And there Fen stood with an invisible leash around his neck, its tether set in Mii-daichiseyh's hand.

"The..." Dakimo emerged from shadow at Malick's side. "The *magic.*"

And now Malick had to hold himself back from going after Dakimo too. Because Dakimo—Wolf's voice here in Tambalon, as he reminded Malick a little too often—had known all about Hitsuke even before Malick had. And he'd never said a bloody *word.*

"It comes from inside him." Dakimo turned a worried, suspicious look up at Malick. "How is this possible?"

It wasn't, not really. Except that Malick's ring seemed to be *inside* Fen, had somehow enabled Mii-daichiseyh to bind the two magicks together, and they now sat inside Fen like parasites, curling around each other and becoming something new, something other, something that could be taken up by a powerful hand and turned against... well, anything. The old magic and the magic of the gods would both be susceptible to it, and if directed by the will of an Incendiary, an Incendiary bound not to the will of Fate, but to a fallen god who'd already enslaved him once...

Dakimo was looking at Fen like he was staring out over the end of the world, and Mii-daichiseyh's smile was just too telling.

"I only wanted him to bring it with him when he finally came to me, you see. When he remembered me and believed in me hard enough to give me shape; when I could lay physical hands on him and *take*. I hadn't thought of all the… possibilities."

He'd been nothing but a spirit before, pretending to be Fen's ghosts, sending his glamoured minions disguised as Asai after him, until Rihansei walked Fen through his past and showed him Hitsuke. And once Fen—the Incendiary—remembered and believed, it gave Mii-daichiseyh power to *be* again. Malick wondered if Fen's twisty mind was responsible for those ragged wings Mii-daichiseyh had sported before, and thought with bitter irony that he probably was. Without even realizing it, Fen had forced Mii-daichiseyh's spirit into the physical manifestation of Fen's own demons.

Mii-daichiseyh shrugged. "The fool swallowed it. To protect his *Temshiel* lover. What else could I do?"

It should have hit Malick like a punch to the gut. It should have paralyzed him with fear for his own soul.

It enraged him. It *out*raged him. It tapped at a pit of cruelty and violence he rarely let loose, because when he did, it was hard not to let it take him utterly. He'd terrified Morin in the temple. He'd deliberately caused Shig pain. And that wasn't even as bad as Malick knew he could get.

There was no one to terrify here. And pain…?

Well.

"Incendiary." Mii-daichiseyh's tone was bored but his smile was small and cruel. "Bleed."

As though abruptly jerked by strings, Fen spasmed violently, then coughed up a jet of blood.

Malick merely stood there and made himself look. A show of power, a *You see how completely under my control he is*. And bleeding on command was certainly convincing.

Dakimo tensed beside Malick, that funny little crossbow in one hand and his sword in the other.

Smiling, all eyes for Malick, Mii-daichiseyh pulled Fen to him. Fen's eyes were still dull and clouded, not really seeing anything, but the tremor that went through him told Malick that Fen knew on some level what was happening. And was as repulsed by it as Malick was.

"He will serve well in his new life." Mii-daichiseyh cocked his head to the side, the tattoos shifting and whirling, almost hypnotic in combination with the pulse and shiver of those freakish eyes. "I wonder if he will serve Mii-daichiseyh as well as he served Raven. As well as he served Wolf's *Temshiel.*"

The possessive way Mii-daichiseyh tightened his grip, the suggestive way his hand caressed Fen's arm…

All right, *now* Malick was pissed.

Fen's mouth was moving, Malick's name tripping silently from bloody lips. Until Fen stopped. Gasped. Shaped another.

Kamen.

Plea, demand, permission—there was no way to tell, so it couldn't be allowed to matter. Malick receded and Kamen rose to the fore.

He let a bellow flow from the pit of his chest as he surged forward. His sword was blocked and countered a little too easily, so Malick had to settle for ramming into Mii-daichiseyh and shoving Fen away at the same time, snagging hold of his own magic and coiling it around that stratum of *Other* that swarmed around and inside Fen. He heard Fen scream, acknowledged it, but it was distant, unimportant. Malick rolled his body aside, dodging Mii-daichiseyh's physical strike and sailing headlong into the magical one, wrestling a handhold in the dual magic for which Mii-daichiseyh was grappling.

Mii-daichiseyh's hold was too strong, the belief of the Incendiary too entrenched. Malick didn't have enough magic. And pulling it from every other immortal and spirit around him wasn't going to do it.

The Sorcerer's mantle—Xari's voice, in his head, and he didn't know if it was really her, or simply a memory of too many times when it had been. But that same flinch rocked through him as it had done every time the choice was put to him, that same shying away from *too much* and *too big*, and everything that would come along with it if he took it.

He watched Mii-daichiseyh command Fen to get up. Watched Fen obey. Watched Fen's whole body ripple through a spasm of pain as Mii-daichiseyh's magic curled around Malick's, tightened. Watched Fen open his mouth on a silent scream then move it again to shape a word, only this time, it wasn't a name:

Help.

Malick called out to his god, *reached.*

It hit him immediately, swamped him. Everything lit up behind his eyes, clarified and lush with brilliance. His skin tingled and his whole body vibrated with the energies of every immortal, every mortal, every creature that crept and every spirit that hovered at the edges of it all. Malick sucked it all into himself and reached again.

Everything that came to his hand he took. And just as he curled it into himself, it scudded back through him and drove at Fen.

Link. Tether. *Noose.*

Malick almost lost his grip, almost let it all slip away in his surprise. He held on, let it wash through him then direct itself at the small drop of blood, that little piece of Malick himself that bided now inside Fen. Power exploded through them both, and though it didn't hurt Malick, it was too obviously excruciating for Fen. Malick could almost see it all behind his mind's eye: a column of force that blasted down from Wolf himself, skidded through Malick, and plowed into Fen.

Fen shrieked this time, a wild, agonized cry that bounded against the chamber's stone walls. Malick ignored it. Because he hadn't expected *this*, but oh, he understood too well now what was happening. And he hated Wolf for it, but still he kept his grip, still he let it happen.

He was deliberately a second too slow when Mii-daichiseyh hurled a bolt of raw energy at him then came at him with what looked like one of Fen's own knives. Malick let Mii-daichiseyh's magic hit him full force, tried not to yelp at the breath-stealing impact, then sucked it in, held it, built on it. It winded him, and this time he really was too slow when the knife came at him; he dodged just in time to avoid a slash across his face, countered with an arcing sweep of his sword, only pulling it when Fen was suddenly in front of him and Mii-daichiseyh retreated.

"Incendiary!" Mii-daichiseyh's smile bloomed with malice as Malick snarled and Fen groaned in pain at the sound of the command. "The *Temshiel* must die. Your beishin wishes it."

"Dakimo," Malick said, calm and even, "hold him."

Just in time, too, because Fen's whole body juddered then wrenched, as though fighting against invisible wires, then he moved to lurch in. Dakimo already had a grip on him and he strengthened it now, but Malick knew Fen, knew what he could do, and Malick didn't think the hold was going to last long. He hoped he wouldn't need it to.

Teeth set, Malick reached again, this time toward Fen, latching onto the pulse that thumped steadily from inside him. Fen was fighting it, fighting Malick as Malick took hold, fighting both of the magicks coalescing into something completely new, but Fen kept trying to push it all away and shut it down. And he probably didn't even know he was doing it.

Malick couldn't allow it. Whatever this turned out to be, it was making itself a part of Fen; Malick wasn't going to be able to do a damned thing with all that power if Fen didn't choose it, and right now, Fen's choices didn't belong to him. Malick closed a mental fist around it all and *squeezed.*

He couldn't help the wince when Fen loosed a breathless shout and clutched at his chest, wrenched away from Dakimo's grip and went down, but Malick didn't have time for much else. With a silent curse for all gods and a desperate hope that he knew what he was doing, Malick poured all the magic he'd been sucking up since all this started, wrapped his own around it, and set it to devouring the other.

The screams and howls were enough to crack his chest and spill out his heart, but it was Malick who owned a heart, and Kamen couldn't be bothered with one.

Mii-daichiseyh *laughed.* "Your own gods thwarted you centuries ago. You cannot touch an Untouchable, *Temshiel.* You cannot touch an Incendiary. The magic of the Six cannot best the magic of the One."

Maybe not. But it could latch on like a leech and eat it up.

Malick didn't let anything show on his face. He merely set his jaw when Mii-daichiseyh said, "He is made from Daichi, your Incendiary. And so he belongs to *me.*"

Mii-daichiseyh spun in with Fen's knife. Every bit of Malick's power was directed at and bound up in what was happening inside Fen. He didn't have the magic available to feint and retreat like he should have done; he took a slice to his neck that was a little deeper than it could have been, but not enough for a dangerous bleed-out, so he disregarded it. Another swipe went for decapitation, and Malick ducked just in time, the tip of the knife sinking deep enough to scrape the bone of his skull across his forehead. With the exception of the fact that now he had blood running into his eyes, Malick ignored that too.

But when Mii-daichiseyh called, "Incendiary! Engage!" and he threw the knife at Fen, Malick couldn't ignore it. Because Fen's hand came up, deep-set reflex, caught the knife and spun it until the hilt lay in his hand in his preferred reverse grip. He swiped it at Dakimo behind him, a cut deep enough to make Dakimo let go, and shook him off. Fen's gaze was clear now, that dazed-glazed look gone, completely aware.

Telling—*I have no choice.*

Asking—*Help.*

The knife twirled. Fen's body tensed into a too-familiar offensive stance. Pain crouched beneath everything about him as his body was forced into motion around whatever agony was wracking through it— agony Malick knew he was causing by keeping a stubborn grip on magic that shouldn't be there.

Dakimo was readying for a tackle from behind, but Malick called him off.

"Don't. It won't help."

Mii-daichiseyh wasn't even bothering with a defensive stance. He merely stepped back with a sweep of his arm.

He's all yours.

Malick let his lip curl up, but that was all. He kept a hold on the magic that tethered him to Fen, and steadily but far too slowly drew away at the other while he set himself to not letting Fen kill him.

The first strike was predictable, a driving rush. Malick easily dodged it then feinted. Fen staggered past him, pulling up *this close* to Mii-daichiseyh. Malick could see Fen's whole body leaning, *trying*, but when Fen lifted the knife again, he spun it in his hand and came at Malick. Because Mii-daichiseyh wanted it, and the Incendiary had no choice now but to want what Mii-daichiseyh wanted.

Again, Malick dodged, and again, Fen went past him, but this time, Fen flipped the knife into his near hand and swiped a vicious undercut toward the back of Malick's leg. Malick only barely managed to fling himself forward and spin before Fen was coming at him again, rolling down low then springing up in a flying leap. There was nothing for Malick to do but duck out of the way, which left nothing between Fen and a careening collision with the wall. Shelves cracked and split, and jars shattered, dust and ash puffing up in heavy clouds and coating everything, including Fen.

"His mind, such as it is, is his own, trapped in a body that moves to my will." Mii-daichiseyh chuckled. "Perhaps, my Incendiary, I have not forgiven you after all." He growled. "*Kill him!*"

It was almost like watching an invisible hand pick Fen up, the way his bones moved oddly, the clear attempt at resistance that jerked his limbs at anomalous angles, shifting his center of balance from practical elegance to ungainly stumbling. Still, he lurched roughly to his feet, swayed there for a moment, then firmed his grip on the knife.

Malick couldn't wait anymore—if he let it go on, one of them would end up dead, and Malick knew without a doubt he'd never be able to bring himself to kill Fen. Which left only the alternative. He could stand it if Fen killed him, but Fen wouldn't be able to take it. Even if Fen had no idea how he felt about Malick, Malick did. And Fen had lost too much already. Anyway, if Malick was gone, who would help Fen? It wasn't like they'd done a bang-up job when Malick had gone to spirit for a few days.

Before Fen took a step toward him, Malick reached for the magicks, and *yanked.*

Fen's eyes went wide and his mouth dropped open in too-obvious agony. But his body, exhausted and hurt and not in his control, kept coming.

Malick let him, waited for the attack. When it came, Malick feinted then swept in, sacrificing a vicious slice to his forearm that almost cut through to bone as he lashed out with a bolt of the magic. It was powerful and precise; Malick had been sucking it steadily from what Mii-daichiseyh had left pooling in Fen, meshing with Malick's own, and now he aimed it for a pinpoint strike at Fen's arm.

Breathed, "Holy hell," when it worked and the knife flew out of Fen's hand, because it *worked*, and Malick hadn't really let himself expect it to. He didn't have time to boggle—Fen had some deadly reflexes—simply took advantage, got hold of Fen and didn't let go.

"Dakimo!" Malick jerked his chin at Mii-daichiseyh. "Get him."

He had no illusions that Dakimo could do much more than distract, but hopefully that was all Malick would need. He secured his hold on Fen and dragged him in, his back to Malick's front, wrapped him in tight and set his hand to Fen's torso—right over the scar from Malick's own sword. With a snarling curse for Wolf, Malick pushed everything he'd been storing inside himself into that bit of his blood that bided now in Fen's body.

Fen didn't scream this time, which was worse, really, because Malick had no doubt what this was doing to Fen. It must be like being ripped in two from the inside. Pain with each twist of magic in Malick's hand; pain with each surge and flux as Mii-daichiseyh grappled for it.

Malick couldn't heed it; Kamen needed more.

Channel to the power of the gods and all the spirits.

Xari had said that. More than once. A halfway-bitter rebuke, pushing Malick to reap what Skel had allowed to go fallow in his hand. Malick had never wanted it, never needed it. Because there'd be no going back from it, once the channel was opened and all that power was his. Asai's mistakes would be so easy to make.

Except Wolf had said *fail the Fool and fail the Cycle.* And more than anything, Malick didn't want to fail Fen.

There was only one way to win here. And if Fen survived it, he'd probably never forgive Malick. Yet, considering all the "rebellion" in which Malick had indulged over the years, he'd never once truly disobeyed his god.

Malick ripped power from all around him, every mote of it within his reach, regardless of from which god it came. Refusals and attempted rebuffs were minor annoyances; Malick blew right through them without even a snag and sucked the power in.

The world—the universe, infinity—lit up inside him in bright-beautiful constellations. He let it surge through bone and blood and skin and sinew, let it welter up and through, brightening consciousness like a never-ending surge of lightning, jagging over him, through him, sliding the strength of gods into his soul and setting it like a gem in his palm. For a moment, Malick *was* a god—immortal in a way he hadn't fathomed in his already long life; invulnerable and invincible—and the power was overwhelming and exquisitely, terribly seductive.

He didn't let it take hold. He couldn't let it show him what he could have, what he could be. He took all the coiling magic, obedient now to *his* will, and shoved it into Fen.

Fen didn't flinch or moan or hunch in or weep. He merely seized up and vibrated as Malick held on, as Fen's body fought him, still trying to obey Mii-daichiseyh's last command. Malick dipped down, whispered, "Sorry, I'm sorry, I love you," into Fen's ear then curled a mental fist over every bit of magic inside Fen and *heaved.*

Mii-daichiseyh shouted, "*No, you cannot!*" and Fen finally screamed and bucked in Malick's arms. Malick whispered to him again, "So sorry, I'm sorry, Fen," and looked up to see Dakimo with the crossbow raised and aimed directly at Fen's chest, just as Malick felt Mii-daichiseyh's grip on the combined magic slip and Malick took solid hold of it.

"Dakimo," said Malick, low and measured. "What are you doing?"

Dakimo shook his head with a remorseful cast to his gaze. "What you cannot." He loosed the bolt from the crossbow.

Malick didn't even have time to dodge.

⛩

The stick was still tacky with *banpair* blood. Goyo didn't know what had compelled him to take it from the alley and arm himself with it like a club. He'd only had his Patrol-issued sword and baton when this never-ending day had begun; still, he'd seen enough dead bodies armed with weapons that hadn't helped them, and he'd had plenty of opportunities to arm himself better.

He'd taken the broken stick with its bloody wolf's head.

The hoarse scream that echoed from the pits of the Shrine of the Dead didn't answer his vague question, but it made it not matter anymore. Once again, the present rebounded against the past. Goyo didn't question his own instinct—Goyo wasn't questioning a lot of things he should probably be questioning right now—he merely suspended thought and followed the echoes, abandoning the fight going on around him in the Shrine of the Dead and diminishing into shadow, tracking the screams.

Again, the past hit him with sharp resonance as he slid back into substance in the Hall of Relics and saw the Incendiary writhing in Kamen's grip. Screaming. A throbbing pulse of magic drenched the air, nearly choking. And somehow coming from the Incendiary.

The ghost of Hitsuke rose, overlapped, jerking when the Incendiary jerked, arching when the Incendiary arched. The yard of an unremarkable tearoom overlapped the reality of stone walls and broken shelves. Instead of torches, it was sunlight that glinted in Goyo's eyes as he stood stunned witness to a god renounced; rather than stale air and the taste of ash, it was a warm breeze that carried the screams of a soul wrenched from its body and damned.

There was no Kamen, holding the Incendiary up and asking "What are you doing?" There was no voice answering "What you cannot," barely acknowledged.

There was only Goyo, lurching in toward Hitsuke as he sent a prayer to—

The sharp, thudding pain in Goyo's ribs was a bit of a surprise. The fact that it had come from a weapon brandished by Dakimo was a bigger one. By the time Goyo looked down and saw the short bolt protruding from just beneath his ribcage, the surprise was giving way to belated fear and serious pain. Instead of further muddling past-present, it clarified; Goyo's eyes were clear and his mind at least tracking the present as he watched the thing that had to be Mii-daichiseyh fly across the wide chamber and hurl itself at Dakimo, a cry of "He is *mine!*" like grating metal.

Goyo didn't see much of the fight. He was down on his knees, his hand curved lightly, protectively, around the bolt in his side, before the vertigo registered. He watched Dakimo hold his own for several sweeping drives, and then he watched Mii-daichiseyh's knife sink into Dakimo's chest then slash at Dakimo's throat. Dakimo went down with his stare locked to Kamen's.

See, thought Goyo, *this is why Kamen is the assassin and Dakimo the diplomat.*

Lucidity had apparently been temporary. Goyo was all at once feeling uncomfortably woozy.

The Incendiary was still screaming, raspy and thick, trying to wrench from Kamen's grip, body arched and head thrown back.

"Sorry," Kamen kept repeating, "I'm sorry, I know, I love you," like he was the one making the Incendiary scream like that.

…Was he?

It seemed incongruous to what Goyo had heard about Kamen and "his" Incendiary, and what Goyo knew about Kamen in general, his possessiveness, his viciousness where it concerned keeping hold of what he'd deemed "his." Then again, deciphering Kamen wasn't exactly a productive or favorite pastime.

Muzzy, pain spiking, Goyo reached out to Hitsuke—no, not Hitsuke, Fen Jacin, but *Incendiary*, and it all kept blurring together—reached out, meaning to do better this time, still no idea how, but so few things mattered when mortal death stalked too close. The broken stick was still in his hand and weighting down his arm, so he dropped it, the wolf's head grinning up at him with a narrowed, blank-white stare. A long knife lay beside it; Goyo had a vague notion he should pick it up, maybe do something with the sword in his hand, too, while he was at it, but it seemed so far away, and the pain was *right here*.

Mii-daichiseyh spat on Dakimo's corpse then turned eyes on Kamen that were flashing yellow and made Goyo think "angry maijin" like he did every time Leu slipped and let her eyes go all catlike. With a snarl and another, "He is *mine*!" Mii-daichiseyh threw his arms up, demanded, "*Kill him*!" and ash flew up on dozens of little whirlwinds, grit peppering into Goyo's eyes and making them tear. Though, he supposed, that could be the pain. Where was Imara when you needed a pissy, overbearing healer, anyway?

Jars flew and shattered and more ash rose, swirled. Pieces of broken shelves turned to projectiles and caromed with the tumult. Kamen threw up a shield that thankfully encompassed Goyo where he knelt bleeding on the floor, probably dying, watching Hitsuke die all over again, except it wasn't Hitsuke, it was Fen Jacin, but Goyo couldn't stop seeing them both, smeared and twinned.

Wind howled in the chamber, meeting and matching the pained howls of the Incendiary. Fire erupted to join the reeling ash and shards, spinning around the room and flaring at Kamen's shield.

Goyo dazedly curled his lip. He'd known Kamen's power was the only one that might have a chance of standing against what Mii-daichiseyh wielded, and it was certainly coming in handy now, but still. There would be no living with Kamen after this.

"Incendiary!" Mii-daichiseyh snarled. "To me!"

The Incendiary's body jolted then arched when Kamen said, quite calmly, "No, Jacin. I've got it now. You don't have to."

A pathetic-sounding whimper knocked loose from the Incendiary, and he gasped. "Maaa-*huhn*-alick… *ah*! Help, I—"

"Control, Fen." Kamen's voice was soft but still audible above the wind and the shouts. "You can feel what I'm doing, I know you can. You can help me, or we can both stand here and wait for him to get it back, because I can't hold onto it forever. *Focus*."

The Incendiary's body went rigid as he sucked in a long, ragged breath, teeth gritted, eyes squeezed shut. He set a clawed hand over

Kamen's, resting just beneath the Incendiary's breastbone. Gasping. Shuddering.

"Out. Get it *out*."

"It's too late. A channel. And now you're part of it." Kamen tightened his hold. "I can't do anything with it if you're fighting me—it's all on you. Want it. Use it. *Take it!*"

Goyo vaguely knew what it meant. Xari had been warning cryptically of it since all this began. And Goyo had seen Kamen hand his magic to one of his mortals and command her to use it, just as he'd done when he'd tricked a victory out of what should have been a soul-forfeiting loss in Ada. And if the Incendiary could break his spirit loose from Mii-daichiseyh's hold and *want*...

Apparently, the Incendiary could, because everything that was flying around in the wide chamber abruptly collapsed down into itself and coalesced into a great, burning glob that wheeled up to the high ceiling then down at Mii-daichiseyh. Mii-daichiseyh tried to deflect it, Goyo could see his hand rising against it reflexively and his mouth moving in spells Goyo couldn't hear, but it only dissipated a little before it hit him square-on and engulfed him.

Kamen jolted. "Shit, no, wait, not fire." Cursing, he reached out a hand then curled it into a fist.

Mii-daichiseyh shrieked, an animal's cry, and the flames coiled down into a spiral around him, slithering along the floor at his feet. Smoke whorled up from his charred body, tattooed skin sloughing off in flash-burn patches. He smiled around it.

"Incendiary." All coy and seductive. "*Break.*"

The Incendiary gasped; so did Goyo when he heard the very distinctive sound of a bone snapping, and the Incendiary's right arm took on a warped, misaligned shape in Kamen's grasp.

Kamen roared, audible rage, and the flames around Mii-daichiseyh flared up again. Mii-daichiseyh reached for them, fingertips twitching and making them jump, then snarled when Kamen's hand came up, too, and did the same. Kamen's arm rose and his hand cupped, fingers splayed, the fire mimicking the shape and making a wavering cage around Mii-daichiseyh.

"*Focus*, Fen." A grating command through Kamen's teeth, obvious effort as he fought to maintain control of the power. "You've been using pain for it all your bloody life. How badly do you want him dead?"

The Incendiary was sweating, shaking, still in obvious agony, but he shoved out of Kamen's grip and wobbled a few steps before he fell to his knees. It didn't stop him—he crawled on his good arm toward Goyo.

Hair in his eyes, sweat dripping, a small runnel of blood spilling out from between curled lips. With a filthy, trembling hand, the Incendiary groped for the fallen knife, came back with the broken stick.

Face pulled up in a grimace of rage and pain, the Incendiary set his teeth, snarled one word—

"*DIE!*"

—then cocked back his arm and flung the stick.

End over end; the weighted ivory wolf's head gave its trajectory impressive force as it flipped top over jagged tip. Everything blurred for Goyo, and then Mii-daichiseyh bellowed, and it all flared up and swirled.

Goyo wasn't sure if he collapsed first or the Incendiary did, but they both ended up facedown on the ash-covered floor, staring at each other from what was really a few inches away, but seemed much farther. The fury-filled screech coming from Mii-daichiseyh was abruptly cut off, and Kamen panted, "Bloody hell, Fen, you did… *shit!*" but didn't come to him. Goyo vaguely noted Kamen's bootsteps were moving toward Mii-daichiseyh, and then he stopped caring.

He didn't register much of it, didn't register the hurried footsteps from outside the chamber, or the abrupt swirl of voices all around them. He stared into the Incendiary's eyes, not really looking for or expecting the realization dawning slowly but inexorably, but it came nonetheless.

It was the eyes. Not their color or their shape or the way they were set in a face far too striking to be mortal, despite the current wretched state in general. It was what was behind them. It was how they looked back.

Goyo hitched in a breath, wheezed, "Oh," then let his eyes slip shut.

ᛝ

"Kill them all. There's no other way."

"Most of them are mortals. They don't even know—"

"They know about *him*, they believe in him, they give him power. Send them all to the gods and let *them* sort it."

A slight shiver cambered through Jacin at the ruthlessness in Malick's voice. Not a bad shiver. There was probably something very wrong with that, but everything was very far away right now, so Jacin didn't spend time on trying to figure it out. He didn't try to figure anything out, and feeling anything but thudding pain and creeping terror seemed quite beyond him. He lay where he'd fallen and tried to keep very still through the knot-screw-coil in his guts.

"Out." The ash stirred over the stone floor with his breath, but the word made no sound, no other impact on the world than a few disturbed motes of grime. "I want it *out.*"

A little glint of emerald skittered into his hazy field of vision, bulbous eyes and long, flickering tongue. It stared at him, unblinking, weirdly… stern or some other hard-set look Jacin couldn't quite decipher. It turned in a circle, pausing for a moment to peer at Goyo, then it merely wandered on, leaving Jacin to his misery, tiny little footprints and a swishing track from its tail in the layer of ash. It made Jacin sad and he didn't know why, some strange sense of loss moving right through him, like light through clear glass.

He should be used to this. The hurt and desolation, the bloated sense of nonreality in the aftermath of not dying. The confusion that whelped tiny baying beasts—fear; panic—then warped them into a leviathan of shock that rammed through the centuries and ambushed him, turned it all into something surreal and far away. Turned *him* into… not him.

Not me. He isn't me. I'm not him. I'm—

It echoed and turned on itself, swallowing its own tail.

—nothing, you're nothing.

Smoke rings. Perfect circles.

He wormed the arm he could still move beneath him, clutched at the spot beneath his ribcage from which the stutter and churn whip-cracked over… everything. The vertigo was almost routine. Jacin stared blankly at the tracks the lizard had left behind until they blurred out of focus and thought… nothing. Memories and the emotions that went with them were haunting the jagged edges of Hitsuke that splintered over Jacin's perception, wispy gray moth's wings with razor splines—*thwip-thwip-th-wip*—but if they were slicing him up in there, he couldn't tell the difference.

His knife was lying there, only inches away, a lackluster gleam beneath a muting coat of ash. His, he was sure of it. One of the ones Malick had given him back in Ada. Jacin had last seen it… when? In that tavern, before Rihansei. How had it…?

Didn't matter. He didn't care.

He slid his hand through ash and dust and wound his fingers around the knife. Comforting. He'd used this on Asai. Had sunk it right through bone and gristle, and taken what wasn't his, what hadn't been given. His fingertip slid along the cool ironwood grip. A present. From Malick. *I'm trying to woo you here, and you're not making it easy.* Jacin had killed his beishin with it, and then he'd damned him with it. Malick had cut the hated braid from Jacin with it. And in the confusion of loss that had followed, Jacin had let it be taken from him, locked up and away, because he'd been afraid of everything it represented. Every loss. Every failure. Every potential loss and every latent failure. He'd taken it back only to have it taken it away again. Now it was here, stained with Malick's blood.

Circular. Somehow. No way to suss it; Jacin didn't have the capacity.

Maybe he could take the knife, turn it, slide it in and dig out this…
whatever it was, and maybe he *should*, or… or shouldn't, or…

Out. Get it out, *I can't… can't…* be *this.*

He pulled the knife to him and curled it close. And breathed a little
bit easier. Yeah. Comforting.

"No, I need Seb." Malick's voice, edged sharp and tilted dangerous. "We
can't let him go to spirit. I almost fucked it all completely with the fire."

It threaded its way into Jacin's head, stumbled around for a while.
He almost frowned, but it seemed like too much effort, and he supposed
whatever Malick was talking about made sense to someone. Nothing
ever made sense to Jacin, and it never mattered, because the world just
kept going and going and going, and dragging him along behind it.

"You cannot keep me bound forever." The depth and familiar timbre
made Jacin shudder, even through the liquid, gurgling tilt of it. "I hold
his leash, *Temshiel*, I always have. And he *believes*."

A shriek sounded every atom of ashy air in the hollow cavern, vibrating,
clay jars clacking and jittering on their shelves, like the dead themselves
were protesting. Jacin cast a blurry glance across the chamber, saw Malick
hunched over Mii-daichiseyh's writhing body, the broken walking stick
in Malick's hands, piercing Mii-daichiseyh's chest, the wolf's head coated
in blood but still leering and grinning, its eyes no longer blank but washed
in red. The scream cut off abruptly to a silence that was almost charged,
like the prickly scent of ozone before a summer storm.

Malick's angry mutter came from all the way across the chamber, but
Jacin heard it clearly:

"'S what you get for fucking with mine."

Jacin let his eyes drift back to the broken jars and the ashes of the
dead all over the floor.

Mine.

He shaped it on his lips, but it didn't go any farther—no sound, no
resonance, no warmth in a body chilled through to bone, lying
facedown and broken on the floor of a tomb.

Mine.

And the thing was, Malick meant it, Jacin knew he did. *I love you*, over
and over again, mixed in and fuzzed with *I'm sorry*, and Jacin believed all
that too. *Mine*, and even after everything—Hitsuke and Raven and Asai
and Untouchable, and every single corner and cranny of everything in
between—it still filled up empty places inside Jacin he knew were
dangerous, *knew* it, but it didn't matter in the face of that one word.

Except.

Leash.

It sort of did. Matter. Or it should. It was only that… it didn't seem to matter *enough.*

You are mine, little lost soul.

My Ghost, my gentle mercenary.

And yet, that single word in Malick's voice—*mine*—rang loudest, rumbled deepest.

Everything went blurry. Jacin's eyes stung. He couldn't think of any reason to keep them open, so he didn't.

The knots in his gut looped and cramped, twisted, and even the whimper that skirled out over the layer of ash was soundless. He tried to will himself to vomit—*out, get it out*—but couldn't make himself move. Tried to sink inside the pain—*Focus, Fen*—but it was too scattered.

His arm was broken, no question there, he'd felt the sick screw and snap. There was something very wrong going on inside him, writhing, squeezing his guts like a closing fist then fizzing out all through him. And he couldn't fight any of it. The pain was not giving him clarity—it was only making everything worse. Blood coated his mouth in copper, and ash gave it all a sludgy-thick feel, nostrils filled with burnt-black phantoms, and throat clogged with soulless not-breath.

A light patter fell over Jacin's cheek, his eyelid, the side of his nose. The stench of ash covered everything, overwhelming the cloying scent of the petals beneath it, but Jacin knew the petals were there. Waiting. Beckoning.

"Caidi." A plea carried on a windless whisper, barely a breath, weak and noiseless, but he had to try. Caidi sometimes came with the petals, and Malick was all the way over there, *not here.* And Jacin *needed.*

"Have you wandered, lost and lonely, long enough, my Hitsuke?"

That voice. *That* voice. The black eyes that went with it were boring in through skin, Jacin could feel them, but he wouldn't open his own. *Couldn't.*

Gentle hands settled over him, turned him, lifted him, and Jacin just… let them. Maybe moaned a little as he was handled like a doll, but didn't even try to resist. He let it all happen. Propped up in a tender embrace, knife clenched tight to his chest, bones in his useless arm grinding together, making nausea rise and light explode behind his eyes. The torsion in his gut wound tighter, turned to a nest of writhing snakes in his belly, saw-toothed and venomous, and why did the picture that went along with that seem too utterly fitting?

"All you have ever had to do was ask for my forgiveness. Even now I would give it to you."

Fingertips brushed tangled hair from off Jacin's brow; soft lips followed.

Voices carried on behind him, Malick's and others Jacin didn't recognize, and Goyo still lay beside him, unconscious or maybe dead. None of it mattered. None of it was as real as the hands on him, the voice, what it was saying, and what it all meant.

"Ask me, Hitsuke."

But I'm not him, not anymore.

Jacin shook his head, unable to voice it, unable to pull away.

And he wasn't wrong. He didn't deserve what you did to him.

Maybe Hitsuke had defied his god, but he'd had the *right* to it, he'd made sure of that, the first real choice he'd ever made, the first and only promise he'd ever asked for. That rebellion had sprung like a poisoned byproduct of a love contaminated with possession and jealousy didn't make it any less Hitsuke's right. He'd sought to protect that right—to protect Daraso from Fate's vengeance, for fuck's sake; he'd done what he'd done mostly *for* that love, contaminated or no—and all he'd gotten for it was the wrath of Raven.

Just like Jacin had sought to protect his family, and all he'd gotten for it was death and loss and betrayal.

Hitsuke had loved and he'd lost. Spectacularly. But he hadn't been wrong. He hadn't *failed.*

If anything, Raven—no, *Daraso*—had failed Hitsuke.

Jacin opened his eyes, glared into the deep-dark of Daraso's, ignored the petals fluttering down between them, and set his jaw. It took a huge amount of effort to pull away and sit on his own without wobbling, but he did it. Daraso kept a grip on Jacin's arm, but at least it was the one that wasn't broken.

"I don't love you anymore."

It didn't quite resonate, but it wasn't soundless. The roiling in Jacin's gut didn't calm, the agony of his arm didn't recede, all the other pains that littered his awareness didn't fade. Nothing changed. No cleansing breath, no lift of invisible weights from his chest. And still, it felt good to watch Daraso's mouth set thin, his black eyes narrow.

"I don't love you." It scraped Jacin's raw throat. "I don't love Asai. I'm not Hitsuke, I'm not perfect, and I'm no one's. Now get your fucking hands *off* me."

Demand, plea, deep-down bloody *yearning.* It didn't matter. He didn't want this. Couldn't stand it. Couldn't stand hands on him, couldn't stand to be touched, not by anyone, and Jacin didn't think he could fight his way out of a toddler's hold at the moment, but *fuck*, could someone *just once* do what he asked just because he asked it?

Daraso didn't—of course. He strengthened his grip instead.

"Your twin is still mine, Fen Jacin-rei. The last born under my moon." Daraso's hand swept gently over Jacin's cheekbone, settled there, warm and firm. "It doesn't have to be like this between us. It never did. I have loved you always, Hitsuke. I never stopped. Even now, when you still think to betray me with your Wolf's *Temshiel*-sheep, I would give you a gift for which you never would have thought to ask." The tender touch at Jacin's cheek turned to a harsher grip at his nape when he tried to pull away. "How much would you give to forget, Hitsuke? What oath would you give to a god who took away all the pain of remembrance?"

Everything in Jacin went very, very still.

Forget.

Hitsuke—gone. All his memories, all his pain, all the Untouchables he'd been, including Fen Jacin-rei. All of it gone, wiped away, and all the hurt with it. He could start again. For real, this time. A clean mind, uncluttered, free of everything that made him a lure for manipulative gods and everything that made him "batshit" and a danger to everyone he loved. Free of…

The clamor and hum in his head abruptly shaped itself into a hot rush of blood in his ears, ribboned out and unspooled all through his chest.

Another promise, spoken in another where, another when, and to someone else entirely, but it had the same ominous ring beneath the soothing purr. Because wasn't this "gift" the same curse Raven had hurled at Hitsuke as Hitsuke had fallen from Raven's "grace"?

You will be reborn under my moon again and again, and you will remember none of what you were before, but this… this will remain in your heart. Always.

Free. Sure. Free of everything that had taught him why no god could be trusted.

And the worst part? Jacin had come *this close* to falling for it. No wonder he was constantly getting fucked over, up, down and sideways— he couldn't seem to stop bending over and bloody *asking* for it.

Jacin ignored the burn behind his eyes, ignored the flare and churn in his gut where something was wrong and going more wrong, ignored the touch that could still make him shudder with want if he forgot for a second why he couldn't let it. His teeth set tight, and he jerked away—

—only to watch from a new, abrupt surreal bubble as Daraso's eyes widened and his body stiffened, and the bright thin shine of a sword's blade erupted from his chest. His grip tightened painfully on Jacin's arm and nape, and his back arched. And then he wasn't Daraso anymore, but the *Temshiel* who'd pretended to be her master in Raven's temple.

"Nice try, Raven's-own." Malick twisted the blade.

A thin wheeze slid from her chest and a rivulet of blood spilled from the corner of her mouth. Her dark eyes dulled as she slumped forward, black hair fanning over Jacin's arm where her head dipped down.

Malick pulled his sword from out of her back, kicked her to lay crumpled on her side in front of Jacin. Malick's tawny eyes glared at her body and his jaw clenched. His gaze shot up, pinned Jacin, almost cold.

"I'm sorry, were you not done with your negotiations?"

Jacin only stared. The petals were gone. Had they been there at all? Had anything been… had he actually heard… was any of this…?

"Did… did you see him?" Thin and wheezy, but Jacin forced it out from a chest gone far too tight. He couldn't tell what was real anymore. And he had to know.

"I saw *her*"—Malick pointed his dripping sword-tip down at the woman's body—"all glamoured up and trying to get her claws in you. And you sitting there and *letting* her."

That… Did that answer the question?

Jacin shook his head. "But did you see *him*?" His breath was coming too hard. "How much did you know? Did you know about Da—" Fuck, he couldn't make himself say the name. "How much did you know about Hitsu—?"

"That isn't something we can discuss here." Malick's glance shot around, warning, before narrowing back on Jacin, borderline hostile. "What did she promise you, Fen? And why the fuck were you listening?"

"It wasn't… because the… he… I didn't…" The knots and tangles in Jacin's stomach arced up into his chest and cut off air. He wasn't sure he minded all that much. Because the alternative would be explaining to Malick that Jacin had been sitting here listening to his once-lover pretending he still loved him, and some gaping pit of need inside Jacin had really wanted to believe it.

"Fen?" Almost glaring. Waiting for an answer.

Typical—Jacin didn't have one.

What was he supposed to say? That it didn't affect him? That it had been tempting until he'd figured out it was the same fucking thing he'd been living over and over in a slightly less horrifying package? That he hadn't even the slightest clue what the *fuck* he was supposed to be or say or do, and if Malick didn't get that by now, *he* was the one who was batshit? That he *hurt*, and something was wrong, everything was wrong, and someone needed to either help him or put him out of his misery because he couldn't think but he could *feel*, and he couldn't take another second, not one.

Tatsu came up behind Malick, looked between them, then merely shook his head and knelt down beside Goyo.

Jacin couldn't pull his eyes from Malick's. He couldn't do anything at all except open his mouth and then close it, eyes still burning, nose and mouth and throat still coated in ash, and everything—inside and out—throbbing with a resonant hum that *wrenched* and twisted and threaded pain so tightly through him he thought he'd never get loose.

"Malick." Thin and hoarse, hardly anything to it at all. Jacin's right arm was a throbbing agony, but whatever was going on inside him blotted it out. His hand went to his torso, fingers still wrapped around the knife, and he laid it over the scar from Malick's sword. Jacin imagined he could feel calluses on his fingertips through the thin weave of his filthy shirt, and he didn't, he couldn't, but it made his chest unlock a little nonetheless. "I… I need…"

As usual, he had no idea what he needed, but Malick seemed to think he did. He knelt down in front of Jacin, and gave him a smile—a small, warm thing that took the chill from his eyes and made the burn behind Jacin's flare and smear his vision.

"It's all right, love." Malick set his hand over Jacin's, wrapped around the knife, the heat of the touch bleeding right through and calming the heave and pitch of whatever was wrong inside him. "Let me help you."

A harsh breath burst out of Jacin's chest, a sob he couldn't help that *ached* as it broke loose.

Sure. *Help.* If only there really was such a thing.

⛩

"Kamen." Tatsu's hands were busy on Goyo but his gaze was nailed to Malick. "You are no healer. You can't—"

"No one touches him but me." Deliberately vicious. Malick narrowed his eyes to flinty little slits. "You saw what she was trying to do. Are you going to tell me you're not the least bit tempted?"

"Tempted to do what, exactly?"

"To—" Malick locked it behind clenched teeth.

Tempted to kill him where he sits. Tempted to try to get him for yourself and your god. Tempted to try to pry out what's right this moment turning him into something shiny-new and even more dangerous as we sit here and argue over it.

Because maybe Tatsu was an ally, sometimes almost a friend. But this thing inside Fen now changed everything, and no one could be trusted. Apparently, not even Wolf's-own. At least when it came to

Dakimo. Who was very lucky Mii-daichiseyh had got him, and as quickly as he did, because if it had been left to Malick…

It took all Malick had to relax his clenched fists and soften his gaze when he turned it on Fen. Carefully, he gathered a gentle tendril of power, slid it at Fen, and gently prodded. Testing.

"G-*ah*!" Immediately, Fen flinched away with a heavy gasp and an accusing glare at Malick. As though he could tell what had just happened and who'd done it. "*Out*, I… you have to get it…"

Malick backed off right away, pulling a knee up and setting an elbow to it, contemplative.

"You're fighting it, Fen. That's why it hurts."

Which was true, but likely worthless. It wasn't as though Fen would stop fighting because Malick said so. And neither of them had a say in any of it. This wasn't going to stop until it was through making itself into whatever it meant to be.

It was different again. It was different every time Malick reached for it. Growing. Changing. Mutating into something that was ancient and new all at once, his and not his. He could still take hold of it if he wanted to. His own magic had settled around Mii-daichiseyh's like a constricting cocoon, gnawing at it steadily. And whatever it was becoming had somehow intertwined with Fen himself, latched on to his being like a parasite clamped adamantly to his ribcage, wrapping around blood and bone and clinging tight.

Trying to use it right now was out of the question; if even touching it was causing Fen that kind of agony, using it might actually kill him. At least if Malick were the one doing it. And yet, with the right spells at his disposal, it was entirely too possible Fen could…

A small, cold pit Malick had been insistently ignoring opened up in his gut. An obscure fear while it had been happening. A *what if?* A formless, wary *I don't want to be right about this.* Now it looked like the nebulous possibility was too fast becoming hard reality.

That was *his* magic inside of Fen, *his* talisman made from *his* blood. And he was responsible for how it was used. The misuse of it would mean Malick's soul. And there it was, sitting inside someone who kept casting about, looking for someone to tell him who to be.

"Kamen." Tatsu was using his calm healing tone. "His arm, at least, needs setting. He needs—"

"I know what he needs. Keep your damned hands—"

"I have yet to put my *damned hands* near him, but I won't simply sit here and watch him suffer."

Tatsu's mouth was set tight as he pulled the bolt from Goyo's side and laid a hand to the wound. Goyo groaned and stirred, breathed something that sounded like a blurred string of curses, and blinked open hazed eyes. They caught Fen's immediately, held.

Fen only shook his head, a wordless, helpless nonanswer to the knowing spark in Goyo's gaze. And then he looked away.

"He didn't make a new one." Goyo pulled in a wheezing breath. "He went and brought the last one back." His somewhat bleary gaze sought Malick's, accusing. "You would *dare*."

Shit. How the hell…? No, it didn't matter.

Malick set his teeth, fully prepared to undo any healing Tatsu had managed if Goyo didn't shut up. Because the Hitsuke thing belonged to Fen, not all of these people, and it wasn't up to Goyo to throw that information around.

"Not here, Goyo." Malick dipped his voice as low and threatening as he was able. "Not now. And *I* dared fuck-all, so don't start with me."

Goyo's eyes narrowed, but when he peered over at Fen again, his gaze softened. He didn't look at Malick, only turned to Tatsu and set a shaky hand atop the leaking wound in his side.

"You going to fix this or not?"

Thankfully, Tatsu didn't seem to know exactly what was going on. Though he clearly knew something was.

"Another moment." He wasn't looking at Goyo. Eyes narrowed, Tatsu snapped a hand out, and before Malick could react or protest, sent a bolt of healing power to tingle at Malick's skin. Malick could have refused it, but it was there and halfway necessary, so he let it knit his wounds back together and ignored the smug hostility in Tatsu's expression. "And yet you would deny as much to the one you profess—"

"Shut the fuck up, Tatsu. You don't know even half of what you think you know."

Tatsu opened his mouth, hesitated, then sent a kinder glance to Fen. "I can help you. It is not Kamen's choice, but yours. If you would—"

"The *hell* it isn't my choice." Malick set a hand to Fen's shoulder, proprietary, and Tatsu could say what he liked about it, but too fucking bad. "He was Untouchable, Tatsu—you can't heal him without my help, and I'm not letting anyone's magic anywhere near him. Dakimo tried to *kill* him, for fuck's sake." He waved in the general direction of Fen's torso. "That's *my ring* sitting in there."

Tatsu paused, obviously surprised, but only for a moment. "So get it out."

Malick could have choked him. "You think if it was that easy I wouldn't've already? It's too dangerous."

"Dangerous or no, it's clearly causing him a great deal of pain." Tatsu's tone was softer; Malick almost believed the sympathy this time. "I don't know what any of this means, Kamen. But I can see you think you do." Tatsu nodded over at Fen. "None of which, I think, matters much to him just now. Fen Jacin." He waited until Fen lifted a muzzy gaze from Goyo to Tatsu. "Kamen is right—I can do nothing for you without his help. Perhaps he will give it if you ask it for yourself."

Oh, cheap fucking shot. Malick's jaw set rigid, and he only just kept his grip on Fen from tightening hard enough to inflict pain. With all his quickly unraveling control, Malick turned to Fen and dipped in so he could drop his voice.

"I know I'm being a bastard. I know you're hurting, and I know you don't believe me, but it's fucking killing me." He had to stop for a second so he could clear the pathetic quaver out of his voice, because everything he was saying was bald truth, and yet he was still going to do this. "You can't let anyone in. Not even for this. Do you understand?"

Fen only stared at him, not really blankly, but not entirely with it, either. "It hurts. It's… doing something in there. I want it *out.*"

"I know. And I can't. If you can just make yourself stop fighting it…"

Fen chuffed out something thick and watery, already hazy eyes going too distant, retreating.

Malick slid his hand up to Fen's nape, gripped firmly but gently, and rubbed at his brow, trying to will away the burning behind it.

"You swallowed it, Fen. To protect me. I don't have the words to tell you what that does to me, and I don't really know what happened that made you do it, but it's done and there's no going back. It can't be fixed, it can only be endured until it's finished. And I can't let any of these people get their hooks in you, because… because."

Malick couldn't say it, not out loud, not here. None of these people knew exactly what had happened yet, but they knew enough. And when the whole of it dawned on them, it wasn't going to be pretty.

"Fen." Again, Malick had to pause and swallow to make his voice work right. "My magic—it's in you. Understand?" Malick could see that Fen kind of did, and that it didn't make him feel any better, but Malick really didn't think Fen understood all of it yet, or he wouldn't be sitting here waiting for Malick to make sense. He'd be taking that knife still curled in his fist and digging Malick's heart out with it, and then maybe his own. "If I let anyone touch you with magic, I'll be handing them mine." He set a hand over Fen's fist bunched around the knife and resting just beneath his breastbone. "That's *my soul* sitting just beneath your heart."

Right alongside whatever was still busy evolving inside Fen himself. And if these people knew, if they got their hooks in there…

Fen didn't say anything for a while, only stared at Malick—hurt and betrayed—then he looked down, fingers tightening on the grip of the long knife.

"I don't want this. I don't *want this*."

The grip tightened; Malick strengthened his hold on Fen's hand, an instinctive preemptive move, because he'd seen that look in Fen's eyes before, right before Malick had collected all of Fen's weapons and locked them in his small armory trunk. Bloody hell, were they really all the way back to this? Had they never really left it behind? Unwilling, Malick remembered the look of blessed anticipation on Fen's face, that terrible-beautiful state of grace in extremis, as he'd stood on the roof of Raven's temple.

"You should let me. Goyo should've…" Fen jerked his hand, but stopped when Malick wouldn't let go. "There's nothing… it's not… not worth it. You know?"

Unfortunately, Malick did. And he really didn't think Fen had a clue. *Fail the Fool and fail the Cycle.*

This was what Wolf had made Malick for, Xari had said. And whether he liked it or not, Malick was Fen's, but Kamen was Wolf's.

"I'm sorry." Malick could only shake his head and gently take the knife from Fen's hand. "I can't."

Not yet. Not until Malick knew that Fen understood what he was really asking for.

Tatsu was shoving out curses under his breath. Goyo said something about arrogant thugs and the gods who made them their "pets." None of it mattered. None of it *could* matter. Not to Malick.

"I'm sorry." Malick laid a wobbly kiss to Fen's slack mouth. "I'm *sorry*, Fen, I didn't…" *Didn't mean it, didn't know it was even possible.* "Please." Too shaky, breathed over Fen's still lips, across his dirty, blood- and tear-streaked cheekbone. "Please, Fen, I'm sorry, I'd fix it if I could, I'm—"

"Is he dead?" Fen waited until Malick pulled back. His face was blank, his tone harsh. "Mii daichiseyh. Is he *dead?*"

"No, he can't… I mean, killing him would only make it worse. It would free his spirit. And then he could come back." Malick let his thumb run up and down the tendons of Fen's nape, soothing, and jerked his chin over his shoulder. "Rihansei's monks will take him. He's the same as them, which makes him their problem now."

"Will they kill him?"

"Yes. For good this time."

"How can you be sure?"

"Because I intend to be there and watch."

Fen's dull gaze roved to where Seb and the rest of the monks were whispering binding spells over the mortal form in which Fen had, all unknowing, trapped the insane, grasping spirit that was Mii-daichiseyh. Slowly, his eyes drifted back down to where Malick held the knife in a loose grip between them.

"I want my brothers."

"All right." Slow and careful. "If you think you can walk, we'll go find them."

Fen nodded. "My arm is broken. And I think… I think I remember… I was stabbed… somewhere." He pulled back, but he didn't shake Malick off, didn't growl or snarl or snap. "Can I at least get some drugs without risking your soul? My arm fucking hurts."

Malick only nodded, took his coat off, and set it around Fen's shoulders before turning to Tatsu.

"I'll get him to a sickhouse."

The *Are you fucking happy now?* was implicit.

7

"It won't come near me."

Shig dragged burning eyes up to squint at Imara where she sat beside Shig on the thin pallet on the floor.

The sickhouse was chaos, a little bit frightening. Casualties from the attacks on the temples littered the floor, a sea of injured every direction Shig looked, so she didn't look. Healers and helpers and priests and priestesses all fluttered among the hurt and dying, but it seemed more just kept coming. The lamps were too bright, the noise was too loud, and the blood was too red.

Samin sat on Shig's other side, between her pallet and the one where Joori lay, apparently sleeping peacefully. Both of them, actually. Samin's head was titled back against the wall and his eyes were closed. Morin sat on the other side of Joori, gaze darting everywhere, still watchful and wary, and his hand was set protectively to Joori's arm. None of them stirred or looked over when Imara spoke.

Imara nodded down at the little lizard that kept curling around Shig's index finger, pausing only long enough for Shig to rub her thumb over its smooth little head now and then before resuming its odd circuit.

"I tried to shoo it away, but it hissed at me and hid somewhere in your clothes until I moved away." Imara's mouth quirked, wry. "I assumed you'd prefer I didn't go searching about." She set a hand to Shig's knee. "You won't scar. You may have a bit of pain for a day or two, but I'm sure you'll agree it's nothing like it was." She smiled when Shig nodded, but it turned to a sympathetic grimace when she touched Shig's hair. "Nothing I can do about this, I'm afraid, but… it'll grow back."

Shig touched at the stiff, kinky wisps that were all that was left of her hair on the left side of her head. She breathed in deep and tried to sigh away the residual pain and frustrated anger, but most of it clung. Because it wasn't going to get better. It was going to get worse.

Someone shrieked down at the end of the wide room, several

calming voices rising to shush and soothe. The woman lying on the pallet behind Imara stirred and clutched at her chest, but only groaned a bit and went silent again.

Shig shut her eyes. She just wanted to go home. Except "home" was the house Malick had bought, and she'd spent all of a couple hours in it—awake, at any rate—and it really *wasn't* home yet. Nowhere was. And the presence of Samin and Morin and Joori wasn't soothing her like she thought it should.

She didn't know if she could do this anymore. She didn't know if she had it in her. And somehow, the absence of Yori made the prospect of endurance rather… depressing, maybe. Yori was the one who'd been driven; Yori was the one who'd given what they did purpose. She would've reveled in what had gone on tonight. Even back when Shig had been able to look into the hearts and minds of those they hunted, *know* their souls were too dark and hateful to be allowed to continue with whatever evils they wrought, still, Yori's conviction, Yori's *faith*, were what had made everything their little Wolf pack did seem right and good to Shig.

Shig's faith had been nothing more than a parasite of Yori's, and so had died with her. Their pack had been splintered, and all of them—with the possible exception of Samin—were merely hanging onto the fragments out of loyalty, habit, and a lack of alternative. They didn't even sit down to eat together anymore.

"How's Joori?" Shig kept her eyes closed, her apparent new pet finally settling into the crook between her thumb and forefinger for a nap. She stroked gently at its tail with her thumb.

"He only sleeps now." Imara's cool fingers swept along Shig's brow, a brush of healing relief skirling beneath them. "He'll wake shortly." Imara paused with a soft sigh. "Kamen has brought the Incendiary here for healing." She held up her hand when Shig's eyes flew open. "A broken arm is apparently the worst of it. He was stabbed, but not badly. Some sutures, that's all. Battered, perhaps, but." Imara shrugged. "I have not yet alerted Kamen that you are here, though he probably knows. I thought perhaps you and I should talk." She met Shig's gaze, thoughtful, then peered over her shoulder.

One of the men from the Gates of Rapture stood near the door where healers and nurses flitted in and out of the ward. His posture was one of watchfulness, perhaps benevolent watchfulness, but Shig couldn't really tell. Silent and still, he stared at Shig and Imara, but with an expression of unending patience and perhaps even… kindness. Maybe. A priestess of Wolf stood beside him, the same look on her face beneath the painted mask that somehow didn't out-vivid the tattoos on the man's skin, even though it was more elaborate and obvious.

"You have choices, Kojoi Shig." Shig looked back at Imara, frowning. "You have more to offer than you know. More than Kamen would like." Imara shook her head when Shig's eyes narrowed. "Only because I've no doubt he prefers 'his own' to remain so. He would give you the choices he is able, I'm sure, but not all of them are in his reach. In truth…" Imara paused, looked over her shoulder again, and sighed before she turned back to Shig. "In truth, I myself might have kept this choice from you, kept you for Wolf before you even knew you had one, but…"

Shig waited, but when Imara didn't finish, she prompted, "But?"

"But." Imara smiled and peered at Shig through her lashes. "I meant to teach Kamen a lesson, and I instead learned it for myself. The designs of the gods are not ours to understand. Not even those of us they have made weavers of their threads. It's why so many of us have hardened our hearts." Her mouth pinched. "Kamen has never been so fortunate. His heart belongs to the one he must break to save, but never doubt he will spend his last breath in the saving."

"I don't."

Morin was still merely sitting there next to Joori, oblivious. Samin looked like he was sleeping, which Shig could almost understand, because Samin hadn't been entirely right since he'd taken that knife in his chest, and he was probably still healing. Still, Shig had never known Samin to so much as shut his eyes when he was in protective mode. Shig wondered if Imara had woven some kind of spell over them, because Morin wasn't even listening, and Morin listened to everything, whether he was supposed to or not.

"I just…" Frowning, Shig gave the sleeping lizard a gentle stroke. "Mal doesn't… he can't understand, he can't *know* what it's like to—"

"I know. But you can't save your own heart and faith through the saving of another." Imara's voice was still low and soothing, but her gaze, when Shig finally met it again, was stern and unbending. "Twin souls you may share with your Fen Jacin, even more so than the one with whom he shared the womb. But your soul is as different from the Incendiary's as his is from his twin of the flesh. Your way can't be his way."

"And is his way Kamen's?" Shig shot a glance at Morin then at Samin again, but it was as though Shig and Imara were invisible, conversing in voices outside of mortal hearing.

Imara smiled kindly. "The point, Kojoi Shig, is that he must find his own way."

"And what if he can't?" Everything in Shig was somehow abruptly frantic for an answer, and she had no idea why. "Malick keeps expecting him to know how to decide for himself what's good for him, except he *can't*, he doesn't know how." She waved at the hurt and injured all around them. "Look what happened tonight because of him, and Malick won't *listen*, he won't—"

"An admirable maijin you would make, Shig, but a terrible immortal. Perhaps even more tragic than Kamen." Imara leaned in and pierced Shig with a stern look. "Since Wolf peeled away the glamour of Untouchable and revealed the Incendiary for what he is, Kamen has labored to hand him choice. Should he have done less?" She tilted her head, her gaze shrewd. "Should he do less for you?"

Shig's heart lost a beat. Her breath stopped. Was that what it came down to? Had she been aiming for it all along and just hadn't known it? It made her feel empty and filled at the same time, joyous and grieved, and she still had yet to articulate it inside her own head.

She was still sitting there, staring at Imara, when Imara finally sat back and waved a hand, as though bringing the world back into focus for them both. The busy background noises of the sickhouse came back to Shig, and Samin started from his "sleep" with a snort and a guilty look to all sides.

"Kamen is on his way," Imara said with a nod, and the last of the strangeness shattered completely with her matter-of-fact tone. She got up, made her way around the foot of Shig's pallet, and then crouched down beside Joori's. Morin watched her warily, but he shifted aside, grudging, to let Imara set a touch to Joori's brow.

Joori stirred.

"Joori?" Morin seemed somewhat cautious, but obviously relieved when Joori's eyes flickered open and he turned a fuzzy gaze up at Morin.

Imara looked only at Shig. "It's only that Kamen doesn't know he holds this choice. Not that he wouldn't give it if you asked it of him." She smiled and patted at Shig's knee then turned another significant look on the monk and the priestess across the room. "I hope you choose Wolf, but…" She trailed off, shrugged, then merely stood and walked away.

Shig stared after her, gaze drifting toward the two who were apparently waiting across the room. For her. Or something. The little lizard stirred, its tail tightening a touch around her finger. It roused a flutter in her belly, something loosening abruptly, and she couldn't decide if the feeling it engendered was some kind of vague elation or sick vertigo.

She didn't get a chance to suss it; a flurry of urgent voices erupted at the entrance of the ward, a man screaming, "No! Kula! *Kula!*" Several of the healers and nurses were gathered 'round him, trying to pull him away from his apparently dead daughter, holding her small corpse to his chest, his face buried in her wavy gold hair. One of the healers laid hands on him, and he fought, hysterical and enraged, lashing out and crying his grief as they tried to drag his child away from him. He called on the gods as they surrounded him, entreating them to save his Kula, but whatever healing the father had sought at the sickhouse had apparently failed.

"Get the restraints!" one of the healers called, and several of those gathered around the man split off to do as instructed—

—revealing Malick right behind them, Fen at his side, rigid and staring, filthy and hollow-eyed, with his arm in a sling. Fen stared at the scuffle going on in front of him, too clearly affected, watching with something like empty shock as the child was pried away from her father and the father was pinned then bound with straps of padded leather one of the nurses brought, screaming grief and protest and pleas to the gods all the while.

"Get him to the tower," someone said.

As if she'd called it, Fen's gaze crept up, met Shig's. No recognition, no understanding of the reality around him. Shig had to wonder what Fen was seeing in that little body topped with long, gold waves, what he was hearing in the grief hurling from the man's chest and rebounding against the walls.

Shig would probably never know, because Fen merely shuddered so hard Shig could see it from across the room, then turned abruptly and limped away.

⛩

Morin shot up from his seat when he saw Malick pelting after… that was Jacin. Only distractedly did Morin lean down and help Joori up when Joori latched onto Morin's trouser leg and wouldn't let go. Samin helped, hauling Joori up and hurrying them along as the three of them shot off after Jacin and Malick. Morin had the presence of mind to look back at Shig.

She only tipped him a small smile with a "Bye, love" and waved him off.

They wended through the maze of bodies sprawled on their pallets on the floor, and emerged from the sickhouse into the light-falling snow only a few dozen paces behind Jacin and Malick. Jacin had apparently slowed the flight with a limp that was more pronounced than Morin had ever seen it.

"Hey!" Joori shook Morin off and quickened his pace. He didn't fall over or pass out, so Morin merely followed, with Samin bringing up the rear. "Jacin, wait!"

Jacin didn't, but Malick did, halting them both as Joori shoved through the thin stream of wounded still trickling in and out of the sickhouse and across the street, back toward the square and the temples. Malick was dipped down, speaking calmly into Jacin's ear, but Morin didn't think Jacin was hearing whatever it was. He wouldn't look at either Morin or Joori as they approached, merely angled behind Malick and stared at the ground. Something in Morin made him halt several steps away from them, and something else made him reach out and halt Joori too.

Joori stopped, but he craned his neck and narrowed his eyes at the way Malick tipped his left shoulder forward so Jacin, under Malick's arm now, wasn't clearly visible. The relief on Joori's face at seeing Jacin was plain.

"Jacin, thank the gods! Are you all right? What hap—?"

"Not now." Malick stepped back, an odd awkward shuffle, as Jacin tried to pull away; his bare feet only slipped in the snow. Malick tightened his grip. "Where's Naro-yi? Get him to take you home, all right? We'll be along shortly."

Morin was still processing his own relief when Joori's "Oh, *no!*" set the grateful sigh in Morin's chest into a wheezy gasp on its way out. Because Malick had been forced to shift so Jacin didn't dislodge him, the duster set loose around Jacin's shoulders flapping open with the quick stumble, and Morin got his first look at Jacin at the same time Joori did.

"*Shit.*" Morin watched Malick half-prop a very bloody, very bruised and broken Jacin in a firm grip. "Did he break his arm? And where the hell are his boots?"

Samin was behind Morin, cursing quietly, but he had the presence of mind to wave down Naro-yi and Xari when he saw them approaching from the direction of Wolf's ruined temple.

Naro-yi, quickly assessing, turned to Xari. "I'll see to Shig, shall I?" He didn't wait for anyone to answer or acknowledge, just kept moving, while Xari pursed her mouth and gave Malick a glare as she stopped in front of him.

Whatever passed between them made Malick scowl, but he nodded. "Fine, then." He turned to Samin. "Take them home. I'll—"

"No fucking way." Joori's growl was low and through his teeth. With a glare for Malick, he moved in and set an arm around Jacin's torso, adding to Malick's support. "It'll be all right, Jacin."

Jacin only bowed his head and shook.

Samin stepped up to Malick. "He's right." He tipped a nod at Joori. "You can't keep taking him away from them, Mal. They almost died for him tonight."

Jacin flinched, hard, then tried to pull away from both Malick and Joori, but neither would give up their hold. It was eerie, the way Jacin did it all without a sound, without a word or snarl. And then he just gave up, went still, and sagged in both their grips, retreating without moving a muscle.

Xari pursed her lips, as though disappointed. "Come, then." She didn't wait for agreement, merely turned and headed for the temple.

Malick's sigh sounded almost close enough to a growl, but he didn't say anything, just followed after Xari and scowled something at Samin that very clearly said *We'll deal with this later, and I doubt you'll like it.* Samin only glared back, set his great hand to Morin's shoulder, and prodded him along.

Joori was remarkably calm, speaking steadily and softly to Jacin as they followed Xari up the scorched and littered steps of the temple and then over the still blood- and detritus-covered marble floor. All the bodies, thankfully, had been taken away, but the stench of blood and ash still covered the place like a smothering shroud. Morin couldn't stop looking at the too-wide blood stain on the back of Joori's shirt, the ragged hole in the middle of it that revealed the dull shine of breached mail, and then casting his gaze around, trying to find the exact pool of blood on the floor that was his brother's.

"I shall call for a cart to take you all home," Xari said as she led them back through a wide hallway that opened out onto what looked like a series of private chambers. One or two white-robed initiates paused along the way to stop and stare, but Xari and Malick both ignored them, so Morin did too. "I believe your Shig won't be joining you, but Naro-yi will see to it that—"

"What d'you mean she won't be joining us?" Malick's tone was blunt with threat. "The healers at the sickhouse said—"

"She is well and gaining strength." Snappish. Not at all what Morin would expect from someone trying to reassure. "She has new choices set before her, Wolf's-own."

Morin had no idea what that meant, but Malick seemed to. He glared but said nothing as Xari waved them through a door and into the small kitchen of a private apartment.

"There is water prepared for tea. No one will disturb you here. I'll see to the cart."

As soon as she was gone, Joori asked "How bad?" as he angled toward the cushions set in what looked like a small lounge beyond the kitchen then seemed to think better of it; he pointed them all toward a straight-backed chair by the stove instead. "What the hell hap—?"

"I'm fine, Joori." Jacin sounded like he was speaking from the bottom of some deep dark pit, all hollow and... small. "It's not that bad. It's only—"

"Not that *bad*?" Joori's face was turned away, but Morin knew what it looked like just by the tone of his voice—aghast, worried, angry, scared. "Your arm is clearly broken, and you're covered in blood, Jacin. How could it *not* be 'that bad'?"

"Most of the blood's not his, at least." Malick dragged the chair away from the wall with his foot and stooped to set Jacin in it.

Joori held onto Jacin until he was safely seated then snapped his back straight and set a glare on Malick. "Then whose is it?"

"*Banpair.* Whose d'you think?"

Morin rolled his eyes. Predictable, the both of them. Joori overreacted, and Malick just kept poking him until he went over the edge entirely. And *then* acted all shocked and annoyed that Joori had gone over the edge. Sometimes, it was fun to watch, and other times, it was just tiresome.

Joori's jaw set tight, his eyes flared, but, amazingly, he didn't snap to Malick's bait. He set his gaze instead on Jacin, voice softening.

"Where are you hurt? *Besides* the arm."

Jacin's good arm had gone around his middle, so it was fairly obvious. And yet, as though he really thought he could lie his way out of it, he shook his head at Joori.

"It's nothing, only a little—"

"They were *banpair.* You really expect me to believe they stood there and let you kill them and didn't get you at all?"

Morin almost winced at the spark of... something—shame? panic?— that flashed over Jacin's face. And while Morin could feel kind of bad for Jacin, he couldn't fault Joori, not for his anger or his worry, not this time. Morin was feeling different strains of both himself, and the weird new anxiety in Malick's eyes as he kept failing to stop whatever this was from spiraling out of control wasn't helping.

With a sigh, Samin knelt without comment by Jacin's chair, trying to pry Jacin's arm away and get a look under the bloody shirt.

"You..." Jacin's chin quivered, and he pulled his gaze from Joori's like it burned him. "I don't... can't remember." He sucked in a long breath, shaky and thin. "I can't... I'm sorry."

"You're... *sorry*. You don't *remember*?" For once in... Morin didn't know how long, maybe ever, Joori didn't seem entirely sensitive to Jacin's angst. Seemed, in fact, as though it was only fueling his own. "Right. *I* see. Almost a fucking *week* you've been gone, and now you show up, broken and bleeding, and you don't bloody *remember*." He pointed at Morin. "We were almost *killed* tonight, Jacin. No, wait, not just tonight—we've been running around the city, looking for you, dodging *banpair* and maijin and *Temshiel*, all the while wondering if you were already dead and burned up or buried somewhere and we'd never know, and you don't bloody *remember*! I was *shot*, Jacin, a bolt to the back— wanna see it? Shig was set on fucking fire. Samin got a knife in the chest. And you don't bloody *remember*!"

Jacin looked like he was going to be sick.

"Joori, that's enough." Malick's tone was warning. "He didn't do anything wrong. Would you *rather* he'd shown up dead?"

Morin actually flinched. Not only because it was so bald with what could have happened, but because he knew exactly what Joori's reaction would be.

"Don't," Joori said, slowly and through his teeth, "*ever* say something like that me again."

"Then think before you open your bloody mouth!" Malick set a hand on Jacin's shoulder. "You don't even know what's going on, and you have no idea what the things you say sound like to—"

"Oh, *fuck* you, Malick." Joori's glare was just as deadly as Jacin's had ever been. "Don't try to twist what I'm saying, don't try to pretend you've some kind of right to defend my own brother to me when I wasn't accusing *him* in the first place."

"Oh?" Malick's eyebrow went up. "Care to tell me who you *are* accusing?"

Morin kept expecting Jacin to say something, but he kept not doing it. He only sat there with those dead eyes, staring blankly at the pile of tea-makings someone had left on the bench by the stove.

Joori didn't seem to notice. "*You*," he snarled at Malick. "*You're* why—"

"*I'm* why you're still breathing. Although every time you pull something like this, I get closer and closer to—"

"If it wasn't for *you*, none of this would've happened in the first place! If it wasn't for you—"

"*Joori!*" Samin big hands rose, outstretched, like he meant to stop Joori's words before they could emerge.

Joori hesitated. Because it was Samin and you just had to. They hardly ever saw Samin the way those who died at his hands must, but when it flashed through his usual even-keeled disposition, a person just had to stop and pay attention.

"It's been a long, difficult night." Samin stood. "We don't need to make—"

"*Don't* tell me what I need." Joori flung his arm out, pointed at Jacin. "Don't tell me what *he* needs." That one was directed at Malick, and so was the murder in Joori's flat glare. "I've been listening to you people for fucking *months*, and I've got nothing to show for it but death and more death, and a brother who talks to ghosts and kills people and then can't remember it, but he apparently makes a good enough fuck-toy for a *Temshiel*, so that's supposed to make it all right."

Oh, shit.

"...Joori."

Morin's voice came out too hoarse, too quiet, but he couldn't unknot his throat enough to do better. And even though he knew too well what Malick was, what Samin was, what they could do, that they'd both been killers since well before Morin had even been born, still, Morin's eyes were nailed to Jacin, who'd gone stiff and blank. Somehow, that tension and the emptiness inside it were more terrifying than any threat Malick and Samin could muster between them.

Malick's laugh was almost wondering. "You spiteful little *shit*." He took a step toward Joori, checked himself, and blatantly ignored Samin tensing up.

Morin might not know these people as well as he liked to think he did, but he had no doubt Samin was positioning himself to protect Joori, if necessary. After watching Malick tonight in the temple, Morin couldn't make himself believe it might not be necessary.

And Jacin was merely *sitting* there, taut and vibrating, like he was made of wire, but with those blank eyes that made Morin absurdly uneasy. It was worse than that night Shig had pushed Jacin over the edge; at least then, Morin had been able to see Jacin in there somewhere. This was like that night at Yakuli's, when Jacin had taught Morin, all flat and empty-eyed, how to kill those who were as soulless as Jacin looked now.

"There's a word for what you've just called your brother." Malick's voice was deadly soft. "The brother you claim to love more than life." He leaned in, only a little, only enough to make Samin brace even more and Joori rear back despite the fury burning in his eyes. "Why don't you grow some balls and say it out loud, so he knows without a doubt what you really think?"

"That isn't what I meant and you know it. Jacin, listen to me." From enraged to anxious pleading with the turn of his head. Joori knelt in front of Jacin's chair and took up his good hand, either not noticing or not caring that it was caked with dried blood and clotted filth. "It's not getting better. These people aren't helping you. This isn't who you are. My brother is *not* the assassin Asai made him. You can't—"

Jacin shot to his feet as though he was spring-loaded, tried to back away from Joori, but only managed to knock the chair over behind him. Joori followed him up and kept tight hold of Jacin's hand, despite Jacin very obviously trying to wrench it free. Samin was still tensed and ready to step in, but he didn't seem to know if he should. Neither did Morin. Malick—obviously furious, obviously wary—simply watched and took a step back.

"You can't keep walking away from me," Joori said frantically. "You can't keep pretending you're what Asai made you. You're *better* than that, better than—"

"*You*," Jacin nearly spat, "don't know a fucking thing about me."

And then, to Morin's profound shock and sick horror, Jacin broke his hand free of Joori's grip and shoved him back so hard he stumbled into the bench several paces behind him. Jacin didn't stop there; he advanced on Joori, almost stalking him like cowering prey. Morin had time to take in Joori's wide eyes, Jacin's chipped-ice stare, and wonder if this was what all those men Jacin had killed for their mother had seen as they'd sucked in their dying breaths.

"Don't I?" Joori was either foolishly brave or foolishly certain. "You think you're nothing. You think it should've been you. You think—"

Teeth bared, Jacin took hold of Joori's shirt and shoved him harder into the bench.

Joori only paused long enough to snatch in a shaky breath. "You think you're everything Asai told you you are, nothing more than—"

Jacin *snarled*, pulled Joori in then slammed him back again.

Like those fish, Morin's mind babbled, all throttled panic and too-knowing dread. *Like those fucking fish.* Except he couldn't tell if Jacin was going after another fish in the water, or his own reflection warped back at him through Joori's desperate words. Jacin's mind was so alien, there was no real telling how it worked.

It had to stop before it got out of control entirely, and no one else seemed to have any intention of doing it. Boldly, Morin stepped in and laid a hand to Jacin's arm.

He never saw it coming.

Jacin spun so fast Morin was on the floor with a throbbing jaw and Joori was hurled across the room against the other wall before Morin even registered the fact that Jacin had hit him. He could only stare, stunned, as Jacin went after Joori again, this time pinning him up against the wall with his splinted arm across Joori's throat.

It finally spurred Samin and Malick to intervene. They each took a side, hands on Jacin's shoulders, speaking commands to back off, sternly but with even tones.

Jacin didn't. He growled, low in his throat, like a wild animal, and shoved up hard with his arm under Joori's chin.

Joori went completely still in Jacin's hold, staring at Jacin with such grief and betrayal it hurt Morin's heart to look at it.

"Jacin." Joori's voice was wobbly and thick with tears. "Please. I want my brother back."

It seemed like it knocked the wind out of Jacin. His stony stare shifted all at once into sick realization. Everything about him shattered inward, his posture sliding into defeat and the tension runneling out of him without any actual movement. Slowly, he relaxed his grip on Joori's shirt and took his arm away from Joori's throat. He held up his blood-caked hand as he let Samin and Malick pull him back, eyes locked to Joori's, misery and apology in everything about him now, where before there'd been blank, empty nothing.

"You don't know me." Jacin turned his hand, shaking badly now, so there was no missing the blood-rust stains caked into the cracks and whorls of fingertips and palm before he curled it into a fist. "Do you see? Do you *see*?" He shook his head, stumbling against Samin's chest as Samin and Malick continued to inch him backward. "He's not here. He's *gone*. There's nothing *left*!" He wrenched out of both Malick's and Samin's holds with a snarled "Get the fuck *off of me*!" and staggered back.

Wary, tracking everyone in the room, Jacin shunted a glance down at himself—the bloody shirt, the bloody hands, the splint—then narrowed his eyes as he scanned over Samin first then Morin and Joori, and then, finally, Malick.

"Fen?" Malick's tone was strangely mild and calm.

It didn't seem to matter. Jacin flinched like he'd been struck then spun around and caromed out of the kitchen.

"Samin." Malick turned a level gaze on Joori. "Take them home." He waited for Joori to argue, and when he didn't, Malick left the kitchen of the borrowed rooms, calm and unhurried.

The pretense lasted until he shut the door behind him, then he took off after Fen. Relief swamped him when he reached the ruined temple floor and caught the flap of his own duster, still around Fen's shoulders, as Fen hobbled too quickly out of the temple and down the marble steps, skidding on the cover of snow.

He hadn't gotten far. Mostly because he didn't seem to have much in the way of equilibrium, angling over to the gate along the boundary between Wolf's temple and Raven's so he could use the building and fence to stay upright and moving. He'd reached the alley when his vague glance careened over his shoulder and he spotted Malick.

Fen's jaw tightened in some half-assed show of determination, and he straightened, shoved away from the wall, and redoubled his efforts at staying vertical. It was like following a drunk.

Malick held onto his temper, though it was difficult. There was only so much drama a man could take in one night, after all. And by rights, Fen should be laid out and unconscious right now, not trying to stagger off to... wherever the fuck he thought he was going.

"Where are you going, Fen?"

"Boots" was all Fen said.

Malick didn't try to make sense of it. And at least it was better than a lot of answers Fen could have given him.

"Fen." Malick kept it even and nonthreatening. "Fen, come with me and let me take you home, all right? You're not well and you should—"

A hoarse bray of laughter knocked loose from Fen's chest, skittering up Malick's backbone with its too-obvious inclination toward blatant hysteria. Fen didn't answer, though, only kept stumbling along, sliding on the snow now and then, reaching for handholds when he could, and somehow staying on his feet. He allowed Malick to catch a pace beside him, though otherwise ignored entirely the fact he wasn't alone, only carried on with a conversation he'd apparently been having with himself before Malick showed up and disrupted it.

"I should've let them. Caidi... if you hadn't warned me, I could've just..."

It went on, weird babble that went from sense to nonsense and back again in raspy, truncated circles. Except it wasn't nonsense—Malick *knew* what Fen was talking about, what he was lamenting.

They'd gone perhaps two dozen steps before the rage and delayed panic started to overtake Malick. He made himself eat it for as long as he could, until it started to eat him, then he set his teeth tight, snarled, "Fuck it," and heaved Fen against the marble wall of Wolf's temple. Before he even realized what he was doing, Malick was shoving up against Fen and his hand was around Fen's throat.

"Do you see now what you're doing to yourself?"

Fail the Fool and fail the Cycle. Malick was failing now, and he couldn't have that.

Fen looked dazed, like he wasn't sure exactly where he was or who was in front of him. He didn't fight back, didn't struggle against Malick's hand on his throat, didn't do anything but go limp against the marble and stare at Malick with wide, bewildered eyes. Snowflakes caught in his thick, dark lashes; for whatever reason, it ramped up Malick's fury, and he tightened his grip, shoved harder.

"Do you remember *any*thing, or are you *trying* to forget it?"

It wasn't an idle question, though Malick had no real hope of getting an answer. And he really wanted one. Because he had to wonder if Fen didn't remember because he hadn't been Fen at the time; he had to wonder if Fen didn't remember because the remnants of Hitsuke had risen when Fen had needed the Bloody Fist. He had to wonder if it had been happening all along.

Malick couldn't be altogether perturbed by that idea. He rather thought he understood the trinity that was Fen and Jacin and Jacin-rei a lot better now. And he rather thought he knew where they all came from.

"This isn't the end of the world, Fen. It isn't just about what the gods want, and it isn't just about you. There are people who *give* a fuck, damn it. You scared the shit out of your brother, y'know. I can't say I'm too broken up about Joori, but Morin didn't—"

"Joori." A low whine leaked from Fen's throat, Malick could feel it against his palm. Fen shut his eyes, face twisting in pain and unwilling remembrance. "My fau—"

Malick shook him so he wouldn't have to hear it.

"What happened while I was gone, Fen? Why were you listening to Raven's bitch, and what were you doing on the roof of his temple? What happened in this alley? Were you trying to get yourself killed?"

Because maybe Malick knew the answer, but Fen didn't. And he needed to know. Otherwise, he'd keep trying until he got what he thought he wanted before he realized he didn't actually want it. And then it would be too late.

"Beishin." Fen snorted—*snorted*—with a ghost of a smile, all faraway and dreamy. "Except he wasn't. He was… They said I'd taste sweet, and then Beishin said it was my fault, because Caidi couldn't get help, so she died again, but—"

Malick slammed him into the wall harder, just to make him *shut up*, which was really fucking ironic, because this was *Fen*.

"Beishin *wasn't there*, Fen. It was a trick, a glamour, and you fell for it because you can't make yourself believe anything but what he told you. Asai is dead and he's *not coming back*. He can't—*you* made sure of it. You *beat* him, he's done, they all are. How long are you going to let your own mind haunt you? Why won't you just let me help you?"

It sounded so desperate, not at all like Malick. He didn't think he'd ever felt the sort of reactionary fear that swamped him now, when he could see all too clearly how it all might have gone, what could have happened, what *had* happened in the kitchen only a little while ago, and his hold on Fen tightened reflexively in its wake.

Fen was having a hard time breathing through the grip on his throat, and still, that weird little smile flickered at his mouth, and his eyes were too remote, *this close* to not there at all. He laughed this time, something grating and breathless, the cords of his throat bobbing against Malick's palm.

"You want to help me?" Fen looked right into Malick's eyes, the far-flung gaze narrowing down, teetering between devastated and just plain blank. His hand moved to that same spot beneath his breastbone he'd been worrying since he'd taken down Mii-daichiseyh before it skittered toward Malick, landing on the hilt of the knife Malick had taken away from Fen and shoved in his own belt. "Then *help me*."

Plea or mockery? Malick couldn't tell. The eyes were almost begging but that not-smile was *this close* to scornful.

Malick's jaw clenched tight, delayed fear and the resulting rage crowding out everything but Fen's eyes and whatever they were trying to tell him that Fen simply couldn't. He leaned in, pressed his brow to Fen's, hand clamped so tight around Fen's throat he was cutting off air. Fen's pulse battered at his fingertips, and somehow, it only made everything spike in Malick's gut with bright-sharp desperation.

"D'you want to die that badly, Fen?" Fen's eyes widened, just enough to let Malick know he was registering the present, was seeing him. "Is this what you *really* want? Is *this* the help you want from me?" He dropped his voice to a seductive murmur. "Think about it, love, because I'll give it to you. You don't have to go looking for it somewhere else."

He loosened his grip, just for a second, just enough to let Fen pull in a reflexive gasp, then clamped it back down again. Fen's good hand had come up and settled on Malick's wrist, but he wasn't trying to break the hold. Reaction, but only barely. Not enough.

"Quick and painless." Malick reached up with his free hand and pushed Fen's tangled hair out of his eyes, tender and warm, in direct opposition to the unrelenting hold on Fen's throat. "A clean snap, what do you say? One nod of your head, and it's all done."

Fen's face was going red, so Malick let him have another breath before he cut it off again. Gray eyes were glittering, aware, *understanding* what was being offered.

And it *was* an offer—Malick meant it. Because no one was going to stop a determined Fen, and if he really couldn't let go of what he thought he wanted, Malick would rather see it end here for him. Simple and over quickly, and not some messy, painful end at the hands of someone who wouldn't have any clue what sort of blighted gift they were handing him.

Malick snaked his hand down, slid it to Fen's groin… smirked when he found exactly what he'd expected.

"Look at you. Wobbling on the razor-edge bridging life and death and you're half-hard." Fen's eyes slid shut, so Malick rammed him into the wall again until they snapped back open. Malick shoved in good and tight. "Are you hard for me, or for my hand around your throat?"

He loosened his grip for another quick, rough breath, then tightened it back down again. Tender, in deliberate contrast, he ghosted his mouth across a bruise darkening Fen's cheek.

"Did you think no one else in the world feels the rush so intensely when life and death curl around each other like grasping lovers? Did you think I couldn't understand, that I didn't *know*, couldn't *see*? You may be damned stingy with words, love, but your eyes are never silent."

Fen's fingers tightened around Malick's wrist, dug in, and his throat worked convulsively beneath Malick's hand, trying to suck in a breath that Malick wouldn't allow. Not yet.

"Whatever would Beishin think, little Ghost?"

The pressure on Malick's wrist increased. And still, that was all.

"Tell me what you want, Jacin. Does it end here? You wanted so much more from Asai. Is this all you really want from me? Of all the things I can give you, is *this* what you'll choose?"

A shove this time. A small one. Reflex of the body, perhaps, and it wasn't good enough. A fight, a conscious decision—anything; Fen needed to give it more than Malick needed to get it.

Malick let Fen have another breath, ragged and painful-sounding, then secured his grip again.

"I can give you what you want, or I can tighten my hand and give you what you *think* you want." Malick laid a soft kiss to Fen's temple. "But I won't watch you flirt with suicide because you think it'll make everything better. You've already seen how much worse it can get."

Teeth clenched tight, Malick pressed in hard, pinned Fen's entire body to the marble, squeezed his throat until Fen's eyes widened and his face took on a faint blueish tinge. Malick bared his teeth, set his gaze hard and cold.

"All you know is what you've had, what you haven't been allowed to have, what you want and what no one will give you. You think you know how it all goes, but you don't know me, love, you won't let yourself, and I can guaran-fucking-tee you—you've never seen anything like me before. So, here it is, then, it's all on you this time." He gripped, shook. "Make a fucking decision, Fen."

And then he watched, wary, as Fen did. Malick could actually see it happen, could count the rabbiting beats of Fen's heart through the pulse beneath his fingertips, could *feel* it move from Fen's skin to his as Fen's body fought for air, and his mind fought itself. No baring of the throat this time, no wordless submission—Fen's gaze sharpened, narrowed, and his lip curled back from his teeth.

Malick didn't register movement besides a quicksilver blur before his hold was abruptly broken and Fen's knee was planted solidly to Malick's gut. Malick didn't even have time to suck a breath before a kick followed, like a fucking *anvil* to the chest, shoving Malick back until he stumbled across the alley and fetched up against Raven's temple opposite. Fen didn't stop there—eyes blazing, he stalked after Malick then slammed his jaw with a roundhouse that knocked Malick down flat.

Fen collapsed, then, down to his knees in the snow covering the stone of the alley, coughing and sucking in air, splinted arm across his middle, holding himself up on his good hand as he tried not to retch.

Malick gave his head a small shake to clear it, rotated his jaw to make sure it still worked, then crawled across to Fen. He should be wary of touching, but he couldn't make his hands not reach. There was a jolt as Malick laid his palm between Fen's shoulder blades, but Fen didn't actually scrabble away, so Malick left it there. He waited until the heaving and coughing calmed to gasping then pulled Fen up and dragged him in.

Fen fought him a little, but not much. Malick merely wrapped his arms around Fen's ribs—careful of the splint—and pulled him in close, huddled with him there, on their knees in an alley in the middle of the night, and told himself his eyes were only stinging because Fen had a punch that could fell a giant.

"I've fought wars," Malick breathed into Fen's hair, almost unwilling. "I've lost people I loved. I've betrayed and been betrayed. You—*you*—are the only one who can undo me."

"*Bastard*," Fen managed to wheeze, but he'd stopped resisting Malick's hold, had in fact sort of crumpled into it and let his head fall to Malick's shoulder. His puffing breaths were warm on Malick's throat, and Malick could feel Fen's heart thumping through his own breast-bone. "Fucking *bastard*."

"Yeah. But I'm the fucking bastard who loves you."

"You don't. I should never… I shouldn't've made you… made you *say*—"

"You'd like to think that's all it is, wouldn't you?" Malick dared a kiss to the crown of Fen's head. "Because then you wouldn't have to feel so ashamed for wanting it, and so horribly sad because no one's ever meant it before and you can't make yourself believe it."

It took a long time for Fen to answer, and when he did, it was in hesitant stutters. "I… don't know what… I… I… but…"

He trailed off, stopped trying to force out the peculiar truncated confessions, quivering as though in pain, like every nonsensical word was an admission that cut him to bone. Malick supposed it was, in a way, and he really wished he had the key to decoding it.

"Can you only crave love from the ones who won't love you, Fen? Are they the only ones safe enough for you?" A hint of mockery, just enough to draw reaction.

"Fuck you."

Malick smiled. "I shouldn't let you go, you know. With what's in you now, I should kill you outright, or keep you chained to me, use you every chance I get." He shook his head and closed his eyes. "I'm not going to, and I don't care what it means for my soul. I want you with me, Fen, but not like that. Your choice now. Ask me to let you go and I will. Everything is always your choice. Just… I don't want you to ask me to."

"I don't—" Fen paused, like he was choking. "I don't want to die." Strengthless, like it sucked everything out of him to admit it.

Another twisty shift in Fen-logic, and Malick couldn't quite follow the thread, but it had been the point ten minutes ago. Even with everything else that happened tonight, it had been what had pissed Malick off enough that he'd offered the threat. So he merely shrugged.

"Yeah, I know. Kinda the point."

"*Fuck. You.*" A little more volume behind it, but Fen still didn't pull away.

"It's not something you're meant to be ashamed of, love."

A strangled little sob spiraled from Fen's throat, and he went abruptly limp in Malick's arms.

"I didn't ask for this. I don't want to be… *this*, whatever I am. It wasn't supposed to *be* like this!"

Malick sighed. "You're right. It wasn't. Would you like to know what it was supposed to be like?" His hands came up, cradled Fen's face and lifted it until Fen looked him in the eye. "They were all supposed to die that night. The lot of them, slaughtered in their beds, their spirits bound to the earth, your mother and brother caught soulless in Yakuli's strings. I've seen their stories written in Fate's hand.

"You were supposed to be Mii-daichiseyh's weapon, his *slave*, his gateway back to power. *You* changed it. *You* did."

He leaned in and laid a careful kiss to Fen's mouth, soft and chaste.

"Incendiary, Fen. That's the answer you're looking for. That's the purpose you think you don't have. A wild card for Fate, and a foil for all the gods. A *true* Catalyst. You don't even know what you've already done to change the world. And it doesn't have to be like anyone else thinks it is, because you have the power now to change everything." Malick tapped gently at Fen's breastbone then traced a fingertip down the mussed, matted braid at Fen's temple. "Stop fighting it so hard and it will stop hurting."

Tears melted the snowflakes on Fen's cheeks, glistening tracks down to his jawline. "I don't even know what that *means!*"

"I know." Malick swept his thumbs through the tears. "Let me show you. Let me help you."

Fen reached up, locking his hand to Malick's wrist like he was afraid if he let go he might fall or slip away.

"I'm so fucked up, I don't even know what… Caidi said… and Asai, but I don't… I mean, Hitsuke, he kept… there's no flying, it's all falling, it's all *falling*, all the fucking *time*, and I can't tell what…" Breathless, Fen squinted up at the sky through the snow still falling lightly, then back at Malick. "Maybe they're petals—I don't *know*—and maybe that was Goyo, but maybe it wasn't, except Asai's gone, I kept killing him and he kept not being dead, and now he's *gone*, so maybe… *maybe*… except maybe it *isn't*. I can't tell what's in my own head, I can't tell what's—"

Malick strengthened his grip, though he kept it gentle, only enough pressure to head off the panic boiling beneath the babble.

"Yeah, you're fucked up, baby. 'S part of what I love about you." A silky murmur against Fen's mouth. "Can you say that about anyone else in the entire world?"

Malick drew back, just far enough he could look Fen in the eye.

"Everyone's going to want a piece of you now, Fen. Good intentions or bad, they're all going to want something. You want something for yourself? I'm handing it to you. Take it."

Fen's hand tightened on Malick's wrist. His face twisted, hope and despair all at once.

"You'll leave. You'll get tired of me."

Except Malick heard *You'll betray me*. Because that was what people did, as far as Fen knew.

"You'll get tired of dealing with… with *this*, and you'll leave. You'll get me to love you back, and then you'll stop."

Malick sat back, peered at Fen very closely. He could make promises. He was almost sure it was what Fen wanted to hear. And Malick could give them, take advantage, hand Fen what he wanted so he would take the first step onto the path Wolf had set for him. Malick was good at it. A master manipulator. And he always got the job done. Fen could have power over Malick, with what was still making itself into something big and kind of scary inside him, and Malick should really be fucking terrified for his soul here.

Except, see, the *really* scary thing? Malick had power over Fen now, too. That omnipotence Fen kept wanting to hand him. Malick had it now in an entirely different way. And he could use it. He really could. He was pretty sure Fen wanted him to, begging him with eyes that said everything Fen wouldn't or couldn't. And when someone looked at you like that—*Tell me what to do, tell me who to be*—how could anyone not get a little weak-kneed high with the temptation?

And that—*that* was fucking terrifying.

Funny, though. It didn't really change anything. Not for Malick.

"Wolves mate for life, Fen. Kinda shocking, even for me, because I actually mean that. Go figure. But I can't guarantee how long that will be. For either of us. I can only guarantee that right now, right this minute, I can't imagine a time when I won't want to plummet into your eyes and stand at the center of you. I can't imagine a day when I'll reach the end of you." This was it, this was everything, all cards on the table, so Malick let the rest come: "I can't help it, Fen—Jacin—I love you. I want you. And I want you here, with me. Whatever you choose to be, I want to be there and watch you make yourself into it."

"I'm not… *He's* not—" Throat working, teeth clenched tight, Fen took hold of Malick's coat, shook him. "You think there's some great mystery here for you to figure out. You think there's more, something that'll make it all worth it for you, and I just haven't shown it to you yet. There isn't. I'm not him anymore. Hitsuke is dead. This is all there is."

Malick couldn't help it—he laughed. "Fucking hell, Fen, is this what's been…?" He dragged Fen in again, locked him in his arms, and held on tight. "This right here—this'll last me for lifetimes. It's worth it *now*." He squeezed harder. "I won't let you fall, Jacin. You fly all you want, I won't let you fall."

"I don't… I don't have anything to give *back*."

Bloody hell. Would they never get out of that particular trap?

"No more trades." Just the truth, genuine and naked. "Something for you, just you. Something you *want*. Just… bloody *ask me*, Fen."

"I… I want, I… *need*…" Fen's mouth moved, but the words just… stopped. As though he couldn't shape them properly, or maybe he just didn't know how to finish.

Silence, only Fen's harsh breathing against Malick's chest, the quiver of overused muscles vibrating through them both, then, small and shaky and so very quiet:

"…*Help*."

╥

They sat there for what seemed like a long time, until the snow fell thicker and coated them both. It was, in reality, only several quiet moments, made longer by the uncomfortable tingling in Malick's legs and the steadily thumping throb of his jaw.

Cautious, Malick set his hand gently to Fen's torso. A tiny, gentle prod, a call to his own magic then a reticent answer, but it didn't feel all spiky and thrashing like it had before.

"Still hurts?"

It was silent for so long Malick wondered if perhaps Fen had passed out. But he stirred eventually with a small, throttled groan, movements stiff and careful as he pulled back. He took a long breath, like he was bracing himself, but he didn't answer Malick's question.

"They're safe?"

More Fen-logic, but this jump wasn't so hard to interpret. In some things, Fen was still entirely predictable.

"They're safe." Malick waited some more. It would come. Perhaps not right this minute, but it would come. Fen was ready for it now.

"All right, then." Slurred and sloppy. "Tell me what your greedy god wants from me to keep them that way." Before Malick could reply, Fen's hand came up and gripped his arm. "No, wait, not here." He sagged like dead weight into Malick's chest. "All the shitty things always happen in alleys."

And then he did pass out.

8

Imara couldn't remember if she'd ever been this exhausted. It was well into morning now, and she wanted this business done.

The charred mortal remains of Mii-daichiseyh lay beside the little pool, just across from Rihansei's body, lying in respectful state on the other side of his beloved Gate and dressed in an elaborate formal clout. Imara had known his long life had called for a wealth of ink, but she'd never actually seen any of the tattoos besides those that the occasional errant sleeve would uncover. Every inch of his large body but for his face was thus adorned, the colors and outlines starker over his death-pale skin than she'd expected, and stagnant now, their constant shift and reshaping gone as still as his heart.

His "shepherds" climbed him sedately, a constant, solemn parade of swarming green that seemed absurdly respectful but still gave Imara a heavy twinge of unease. She turned away.

It didn't seem right that Mii-daichiseyh was here. It didn't seem right that his body lay so close to Rihansei's. Imara didn't say anything. Seb and the rest of the monks knew what they were doing. They had their own customs and traditions that had nothing to do with the gods or their servants. Imara was here by their sufferance so she kept her mouth shut. They hardly ever let anyone down here, and certainly not *Temshiel* or maijin. None except for Kamen, she thought with a twist to her lip, and she peered across the cavern to where Kamen pretended he wasn't being disrespectful by arguing quietly with Goyo and Tatsu.

The argument seemed to center on a walking stick that Goyo kept twirling until Kamen finally snatched it out of his hand. Goyo let him, looking smug. Kamen looked like he wanted to hit Goyo with the thing, but he managed to restrain himself. For a change.

A chuckle ratcheted up Imara's throat, and she throttled it back. She had no doubt what the argument was really about. Goyo wouldn't bloody shut up about it. She rather thought Kamen had just acquired a very opinionated, very vocal conscience in the form of Snake's maijin, and it was more than Imara was worth to step into the middle of it. It was probably a good thing that Kamen couldn't kill Goyo. Or the other way around, come to think of it. Goyo looked very angry. He should perhaps watch it, or he might find himself called by Wolf, and wouldn't *that* be a fun decision to watch him make. Imara refused to let that thread fray out into an actual skein of tangled thoughts. Kamen would see to any difficulties that might threaten the Incendiary, no doubt.

Imara caught the thought and scowled at herself.

She would never understand it. She didn't think anyone would. Kamen broke all the rules, skirted the laws, and still Wolf handed him everything he needed to keep doing it, still Kamen won everything he set his hand to winning. It defied logic. He was a child. A reprobate. An arrogant thug. And yet he'd managed to snag more power to himself than any immortal but for the gods themselves, and what had he done with it? Fed it into the Incendiary and bound the Incendiary to Wolf in a way that had been incomprehensible to any other until it was done. If the Incendiary loved Kamen—and he did; Imara had no trouble seeing that, even if the Incendiary didn't—he would not thwart Wolf's laws and risk Kamen's soul. And if Kamen loved the Incendiary—Imara only rolled her eyes—he would not use the magic against the Incendiary's will, for the magicks working in anything but complete concert would cause the Incendiary pain so great as to rend his soul. At least that was how Goyo had understood it and explained it to Imara.

Perfect Balance.

Imara shook her head, marveling. How did Kamen *do* it, damn it?

"I don't think he plans to send you to spirit."

"No? Well." Imara gave Shig a small grimace, and shifted her shoulders. "It wouldn't be the first time."

In fact, the rest might do her some good. Kamen could make the killing part hurt like none other, but Imara had withstood much in all her lives. She'd stopped caring how this one might end.

"Naw." Shig jerked her chin at where Emika clutched at the arm of one of the monks and stared around the chamber in stately mourning. "He said something before about someone having to take Darama's place with the governor."

"Dakimo," Imara corrected absently.

No telling yet how right Shig—or Kamen, it seemed—was about the speculation. Emika had been marked by Wolf since the last time Imara had seen her, and Imara thought perhaps there were other plans for Emika than a mere governorship. If Dakimo had anything to say about it, at any rate. Considering where Dakimo was now, Imara thought he probably did.

With a sigh, Imara looked down at the small company of lizards that hovered around Shig's feet like her own little corporeal aura, then peered closely at Shig. The blonde hair was cropped short all over now, the burnt kinks trimmed away, along with the last of the bright colors that had streaked her head in a motley halo. Imara reached out to run an assessing touch to Shig's cheek then her brow and temple, satisfied when her touch revealed nothing but newly knitted skin, the hum beneath it calm with no sharp jags of pain, only a residual tenderness that would fade shortly.

"It is well?"

Shig grinned. "It's amazing. A little tight still, maybe, but it doesn't hurt." She ran a hand over her shorn hair, somewhat rueful. "Wish you could've done something about this, though."

"You're gorgeous as always." Kamen sauntered up, twirling the walking stick he'd snatched from Goyo. His tawny eyes caught Imara's a little coldly, but the smile he pointed at Shig was warm and real. With a familiarity that made Imara feel somewhat intrusive, Kamen set an arm around Shig's shoulders and gave her a little squeeze when she sank into it and leaned into his side. "Just watch, it'll be all the fashion by next week." He grinned and tweaked Shig's nose, then gave Imara a brief nod.

Imara merely blinked. She hadn't really expected Kamen to break her neck right here, in front of all these people and at what amounted to a funeral, but she hadn't expected anything resembling civility from him, either.

"Where'd you get that?" Shig poked a finger out to trace a pointed ear of the ivory wolf's head atop the stick.

Kamen's jaw set tight. "A 'gift' for Fen. Goyo had the cap set on a new stick. Said I should be glad he didn't switch it to a snake."

"Shouldn't he be giving it to Fen himself?"

"No." If Kamen hadn't been keeping his voice down, it would have been a bark.

"But wouldn't it—?"

"I said *no*. Drop it, Shig."

"Hmm." Shig peered up at Kamen, all innocence. "Should you be worried?"

"*Worried.*" Kamen scoffed. "About what, exactly?"

Shig was grinning now, like she knew something Kamen didn't want her to know. She seemed to think it rather hilarious.

"About... well, anything."

Kamen hesitated for only a second before he smirked. "Am I ever?"

Shig rolled her eyes.

Imara resisted the temptation. She knew what that stick had been used for, and she knew Goyo had to be up to something, and she knew Kamen probably *should* be worried. She also knew Kamen wasn't. And she really didn't want to know even that much.

"What are they going to do, Mal?"

Shig's mercurial attention had apparently been snared by the monks detaching from whatever they'd been doing and converging together into a tight knot off to the side. Their lips moved, though no words emerged, at least none Imara could hear, yet still, it seemed the air thickened and grew heavier, hushing whatever chatter that lingered into silence.

"Rihansei wished for his spirit to remain within the Gate," Kamen whispered. "Most of the Gatekeepers do, from what I'm told, though I've never known another. Rihansei has been here since long before I came along."

"I knew the one before him," Imara put in, just as softly. "Tanamon." She gave Shig a small smile. "Knew of him, at least. I understand he did the same, except his mortal death was more… seemly." She shrugged. "He simply decided he was tired and entered the Gate."

"Mm." Kamen ran a gentle hand up and down Shig's arm. "Mii-daichiseyh will be…" He paused, mouth pursed.

Imara leaned in, attentive. She had no idea what to expect out of this, and it mattered. Rihansei's monks had apparently kept Mii-daichiseyh's mortal body alive with his spirit trapped inside it, and Imara was at a loss as to how it could be destroyed completely without his spirit being sent to the suns, which the magic of the gods couldn't do.

The toe of Kamen's boot nudged at one of the lizards lounging at Shig's feet. "Your little shepherds will take care of Mii-daichiseyh." He smirked when the lizard hissed at him.

Shig stared down at it for a moment, frowning, until the meaning of what Kamen had just said seemed to dawn on her. She wrinkled her nose.

"Ew."

Imara agreed. And she'd actually *solicited* Seb to let her be present when the deed was done?

"He was sent through the Gate once before, and he managed to break free." Kamen was still squinting down at the lizard. "His strength doesn't come from prayers as the gods' does; it comes from those who believe in him. Fen believes in him. We can't take the chance."

He shot a narrow glance at Imara, clearly daring her to suggest handing the Incendiary the same fate Kamen had handed to Mii-daichiseyh's hapless followers last night.

Imara had no such intentions. She had no doubt who'd win a challenge with Kamen, and she simply didn't have the strength.

She did, however, wonder if it had yet occurred to Kamen that perhaps he'd come out of all of this with his soul intact, and with his already gigantic ego justified, because his Incendiary had believed he would. She decided to keep that one to herself, but couldn't help the tiny smirk that threatened at the corners of her mouth.

They were silent for a moment, gazes roving from Rihansei's body to Mii-daichiseyh's, and then to the monks who struck up a quiet chant as they… did whatever it was they were doing. Calling their magic together or something, Imara thought, because the army of lizards that still clambered lovingly over Rihansei's body now began to dismount and assemble on the other side of the pool, even the ones that had been lingering by Shig. All but one; it climbed up onto the toe of Shig's shoe and curled its tail around its body, apparently content.

Kamen leaned down so he could whisper to Shig. "Have you decided yet?"

Imara carefully kept still, pretending not to listen. If Kamen caught her at it, he'd make sure she didn't hear the rest. And she desperately wanted to hear the rest.

Shig sighed and rested her head on Kamen's shoulder. "I'm told I don't have to yet. I'm told I've a place here or in the temples, whichever I choose. It's been suggested I go to Tougei for a while to meditate before I make a decision."

Imara had suggested that. She could hardly credit it. She should have been urging Shig to come to the temple, where Imara could lend subtle influence and direct her and all her latent talent toward Wolf. Instead, Imara had taken great pains to inform Shig of all the options open to her, with only a caveat at the end to describe Imara's own wish to have her as an initiate.

Maybe Imara was getting soft. Maybe Kamen with his squishy mortal heart was a bad influence.

Kamen was silent for a while, gaze trained on the slow-moving swarm of lizards. "So, you're not coming home, then."

Imara was sure the tone was disappointed. And hurt, maybe.

"It's not my home, Mal. It hasn't been since Yori died. Y'know?"

"No, I don't. Shig, you—"

"You're a really good man." Shig smiled, all sincerity as she peered up at Kamen. "And you try really hard to give all your people exactly what they need and want, even when you're pretending you don't know or care what they need or want. But see, the problem with that is sometimes you take choices away when you think you're handing them over. You keep wanting to save everyone, even the ones you have no business saving." She shot a quick rueful glance at Imara then back again to Kamen. "Sorry, Mal, but probably the best thing you did for Fen since you met him was die on him for a little while. He'd never get over all this if you'd been there to save him from it. And he *will* get over it. But he needs to save himself and in his own way—alone."

Perhaps Imara had a little more pull with Shig than she'd thought. It gave her hope.

Kamen's jaw set tight. "That's probably the shittiest thing you've ever said to me, Shig. And you've said some shitty things to me over the years."

"And that's part of your problem—the important parts of what I said weren't about *you* at all. And none of it means he doesn't need you." Shig paused and drew in a long, slow breath. "He's broken, Mal." Her voice was kind but implacable, though she still leaned into Kamen's side, almost snuggling, clinging. "Luckily, that's part of what you love about him."

Kamen opened his mouth; Shig set gentle fingers over it, silenced him.

"You wanted to know if he'd fight for himself. Now you know. And so does he. But the broken parts will always be broken. And so you'll never get tired of him, because you'll never be able to really save him." She tipped up to kiss Kamen's cheek. "It's a *good* thing, Mal. For both of you. In a weird 'unhealthy addiction' sort of way, but still. Neither of you will ever be good for anyone but each other anyway."

"Bloody hell, Shig, are *trying* to be—?"

"He's always going to *need* you, Mal. Even when he pretends he doesn't. And you're always going to need him, because he keeps you trying." Shig watched Kamen until his glare softened, his mouth closed, and he looked away. Her smile was soft, a bit sad, when she looked back down and shrugged. "I'm not broken. And it's time."

Imara only stared. She had mixed feelings about… well. All of it. It seemed a kind way to say *you two deserve each other, and no one else would have you anyway*, which would've been bloody *hilarious*, had it not been for the "broken" thing that sounded like…

Right. No. That's how she'd gotten herself in trouble last time, and she still wasn't sure Kamen wasn't going to make her pay for it.

Apparently, Wolf wanted Kamen to be the one beside the Incendiary. According to Xari, Kamen had been turned over a century ago expressly *for* the Incendiary. Imara apparently had no say in any of it.

She didn't think she wanted one anymore. She was fast coming to agree with Shig that Kamen and the Incendiary deserved each other. And the gods help the world and all its inhabitants.

"We'll miss you," Kamen whispered as the monks' chants rose in volume. The air grew more weighted, and the throng of lizards began a weirdly decorous march toward the body of Mii-daichiseyh. "Samin won't understand, y'know. And Morin will—"

"For pity's sake, Mal, I'm not *dying*." Shig elbowed Kamen in the ribs. "In fact, I've no doubt I'll live longer, once I'm *not* around you and Fen anymore. Now shut up, I want to watch this."

Imara held back the snort and followed Shig's gaze over to where the lizards scrambled up and over Mii-daichiseyh like an emerald cloud and began to nip and tear at charred flesh. With a grimace, Imara looked away, gaze accidentally catching on Kamen's, so she was looking right at him when his smartass smirk bloomed.

Imara scowled and rolled her eyes.

"Mal?" Shig drew back with a slight frown.

Kamen gave Shig a quick peck on the nose then pulled her back in. "Yeah, love?"

"Are you taller?"

☖

Joori woke to… nothing, really. Blankness. Numbness. Perhaps he was in shock. Perhaps he'd felt everything there was to feel and now there was nothing left.

There was bright sunshine slanting in through the sitting room's windows, burning red through his eyelids, but the warmth of it escaped him. He didn't bother to open his eyes. What was the point? Maybe he could simply lie here all day and pretend he was invisible. Or better— nonexistent. One day of wallowing and avoidance before he had to open his stinging eyes and face… everything. Then again, perhaps the sitting room wasn't the best place to expect solitude.

He'd slept heavily, when he hadn't thought he'd sleep at all. He hadn't meant to, in truth. He'd just sort of collapsed on the couch when he'd heard Malick finally dragging Jacin back home, and instead of charging out to confront them, Joori had… cowered. Afraid to face his brother, hiding, really, and… that was all he remembered. He didn't remember hearing Malick taking Jacin upstairs, though Joori supposed he must've done.

Maybe Joori had closed his eyes in relief and then simply hadn't opened them again. He didn't think he'd even stirred. His muscles felt sore and blood-heavy from lack of movement. Imara said his back was going to feel bruised for days, and bloody hell, did it ever. And he was still exhausted. Wrung out. Incredibly fucking sad and scared and sorry, and the well of his emotional endurance was bone-dry.

Beaten. Not in the physical sense, of course, but that had been a real possibility for a few terrifying minutes. He'd been shot, had almost died, according to Morin, and still, Joori's most vivid memory of last night was Jacin. He could still feel the shape and pressure of that splint against his windpipe, could still see the feral rage, and yes, that had been murder in his brother's eyes. Eclipsed almost immediately by realization and desolation, but it had been there. Joori hadn't really needed anyone to tell him Jacin was never coming back, not after that; one look into Jacin's eyes last night, and Joori couldn't pretend anymore.

It wasn't going to go away. It wasn't going to get better. Joori wasn't going to wear this new Jacin down until his brother emerged from the ashes. This Jacin was practically made of endurance. Joori apparently wasn't. He'd lost. Badly.

He'd thought it would be better. Nothing left to fight, right? They'd won. Except Jacin wasn't done. Jacin would never be done. What Jacin was now was so far beyond Joori there was nothing left for Joori to do but… let go.

Jacin was Fen now. And Fen was Incendiary. More godly machinations and directives, against which Joori couldn't fool himself into believing he had any kind of influence at all. Jacin was what he was, and the Jacin that Joori knew just didn't seem to fit in with the Jacin that was now. And certainly, what Joori was didn't seem to be doing Jacin any good.

So, now what? Besides mourning. Again. Joori didn't know if he had the energy for it. He'd been mourning for as long as he could remember.

He could leave. He had legal papers, and it didn't seem like being Jin was a problem here. The shape of his eyes and the set of his cheekbones were fairly distinctive, compared to the people here, but he'd seen several in the crowd last night who, if they weren't entirely Jin, at least had a good deal of Jin in them. And none of them had that weary, resigned-hunted look in their eyes that Joori had seen for so long he hadn't realized what it was until he didn't see it anymore.

He could be Jin here. He wouldn't be arrested and thrown into a camp. He wouldn't be stolen in the middle of the night for magic he no longer had and didn't miss in the least. He wouldn't be sneered at or glared at or watched or hunted. He could give up, give in, and stop being… *this*.

Because *this* was grinding Joori down into something he didn't even recognize anymore. And it was killing Jacin.

Tears rose, hot and sticky.

He wouldn't fool himself that he would've been able to bring Jacin home last night. Malick had gone after Jacin and Joori had merely stood there and watched, because there'd been no doubt that if had been Joori doing the pursuing, Jacin would've run farther and faster, gimpy leg or no.

Morin had said Joori was going to have to let go, and Joori no longer saw any alternative. He wasn't helping Jacin, he was hurting him. And Joori still wasn't sure if he was grateful or insanely fucking envious that Malick seemed able to do what Joori couldn't. Perhaps it really would be best for Joori to just… remove himself. He couldn't help being who he was any more than Jacin apparently could, and who Joori was only seemed to be making things worse. After last night, only a heartless bastard could look away from the cold facts; Joori was perhaps many things, but heartless had never been one of them, more was the pity.

Malick wouldn't hold Joori here. He'd probably pack Joori's few belongings for him and help him out the door. And Joori could no longer pretend his brothers needed him. Morin still mystified him sometimes, but Morin had very clearly been able to take care of himself for a long time. He didn't need anything from Joori. He seemed to get on with Jacin better than Joori did these days. And Jacin… well. Could there have been more damning or conclusive evidence than last night that Joori was not the one to save the brother who'd saved him?

His hand curled into a fist, fingertips settling over the scar on his palm, and his eyes burned hotter. His chest knotted. A small, strangled sob leaked from his throat, and he clamped his teeth against it.

"I figured you were awake."

Morin's voice was soft, and though it startled Joori, he didn't flinch or gasp. Everything was too heavy for that.

"Go away, Morin." It was too quiet, raspy, like Jacin's voice, which only made Joori's eyes feel like they might as well be spouting flames. He squeezed them tight and didn't even care that they leaked tears out the corners when he did it.

"Can't," Morin said. "Samin said to come get you up. We've got company."

That got Joori's eyes open. Morin looked tired, but not terribly concerned, so it didn't seem like the "company" was bad news.

"Who?" Joori dragged his sleeve over his face as he sat up, then scrubbed at his eyes, as though to expel sleep. He figured Morin knew better, but still.

Morin shrugged. "Malick said Tatsu, and somebody else, some Anna-something-or-other. They followed him back from someplace this morning, and bloody hell, was he *pissed*. He wouldn't let them past his wards for a while, but I guess they wouldn't stop messing with the spells, and now he says it'd be less annoying to just let them in. He didn't look happy, but Samin doesn't seem worried. Only alert. Naro-yi looked kind of amused, so I figure it must be all right."

"Malick's up? Where'd he go?"

"Dunno." Morin didn't look terribly interested, either.

"What time is it?"

"It's just gone lunch." Morin waited for Joori to stand, then handed him a bowl of tea. "And no, Jacin's not up yet." It was matter-of-fact, no snark or sneers. "But Malick says he's all right, and don't be surprised if he sleeps through the day."

Joori only nodded, and took a sip of the tea. "You, um…" He waved the bowl toward Morin's face. "You probably shouldn't tell Jacin how you got that."

"This?" Morin smirked, and rubbed delicately at the swollen bruise on his jaw. "I figured I'd find a way to blame it on you. I haven't decided yet if I want to make you look clumsy or bitchy, so I'm undecided between an accidental elbow and an unreasonable hissy."

Joori was surprised to find a small smile ticcing at the corner of his mouth. "I guess either would do just as well." Though the latter would probably be more believable. The smile sort of shriveled.

"You know." Morin turned slowly and started for the gap in the screens that separated the sitting room from the rest of the house. "If Jacin hadn't pulled it like he did, I'd've been lucky to get away with a broken jaw." He shot a glance back over his shoulder. An eyebrow went up. "He probably could've killed me. You know—if he hadn't pulled it."

He wouldn't have hurt you. He couldn't.

Morin wasn't saying it, but he was *saying* it.

"…Yeah." Joori huffed a derisive snort. "Sure."

Morin turned back to fix Joori with a steady look. He still had that smartassy tilt to his demeanor, but his eyes were somber.

"You're a good brother, Joori. You and Jacin… you're a lot more alike than you think you are."

Joori had no idea how to take that. This was Morin, after all—it could be insult or compliment, or both at once.

"I mean, you both kind of…" Morin waved his hand around. "You go at things with everything in you. There's no give. You either win everything or you fail completely. Or you think so, anyway."

Right. Insult, then.

Something must've changed on Joori's face, because Morin held up both hands, palms out.

"I only mean that there's such a thing as fighting for what you can win. We lost… well, a lot." Morin paused, swallowed. "But we walked away with a lot, too, and… well, I need you too, Joori."

Joori jerked his glance up, surprised to see Morin actually flushing. He held Joori's gaze for only a second before he turned his own to the floor and shrugged uncomfortably. Strange. Very un-Morin-like. Then again… maybe Joori simply hadn't been paying all that much attention lately.

"I, um." Joori cleared his throat.

He never got to answer. The front door opened, and Malick's voice came rolling through the entire house:

"…consented to anything yet, so douse the fire in your knickers before I stomp it out myself."

He sounded *pissed*.

Morin and Joori both poked their heads around the screen to see Malick, thunder at his brow, shooing… ah, that was definitely Tatsu—that profile and wavy bright hair were very distinctive. He preceded Malick with a serene smile on his face, caught Joori's eye, and dropped a wink that almost made Joori smile too.

Joori couldn't say there'd been much opportunity to get to know Tatsu before they'd left Ada, but what Joori had seen and gotten to know, he'd liked. And Tatsu had healed Jacin, so what more did Joori need? After last night, Joori would've been willing to throw rose petals at Tatsu's feet if he could do something for Jacin this time, too.

"And I'll tell you something else." Malick was waving a walking stick around like he wished it was a sword. "I *don't* appreciate this 'summons' business. It was bad enough coming from Dakimo the last time, but this is beyond the pale. She may be *the* governor, but she's not *my* governor."

"That may be so," said a cool, feminine voice behind him, "but she is the governor of Tambalon, where you have chosen to bring your charges. She is, therefore, *their* governor."

The gravity of what the voice was actually saying was just sinking in when Joori got his first glimpse of the woman from whom it came. The little start at recognizing the surcoat of the Patrol was almost incidental. He'd never seen anyone so… startlingly striking and altogether bloody *gorgeous*.

Her skin was like burnt henna, flawless but for the darker hints of an ornate tattoo on the entire left side of her face that almost-but-not-quite blended into the color of her skin. Her hair was stake-straight and short, just brushing below the high collar of her surcoat, a faint blue cast to silky ebony. And her *mouth*.

Joori's mind went to places it really shouldn't, his gaze locked tight to lips wine-dark and plump. Until the woman's glance landed on him, and then his mind went completely blank.

"Oh," he vaguely heard Morin mutter, "it's *her*."

It sounded somewhat acidic. Joori couldn't make himself care.

He'd thought Yori's eyes had been the greenest he'd ever seen. He'd grudgingly admitted that Shig's eyes were the same jade as Yori's, but something about Yori had made the color of Shig's eyes incidental. This woman's eyes were more of a minty green, but even so, it seemed they were the definition of the color itself. Bright and watchful, sly and intelligent—catlike in the overall effect.

Had to be maijin or *Temshiel*. No mortal looked like *that*.

Tatsu smirked as he sauntered past, reached out and gently set a finger to Joori's chin, presumably to close his hanging jaw. Joori beat him to it, but not before Tatsu snorted.

"Ah, so this is the twin, then."

Joori had been so busy with highly inappropriate mental pictures that he hadn't realized the woman had stopped right in front of him. Joori only tilted his head like a curious pup. Which wasn't terribly far off the mark. His libido was all ready and willing to sit up and do tricks.

"And what is your name, then, young seyh?"

"You don't need to know anything about him." Malick's tone was downright malignant as he angled in front of Joori.

"I really don't mind," Joori heard himself murmur as he watched Malick compel the woman past the sitting room and toward the kitchen. Joori stared after them for quite a long time before he turned to Morin. He blinked.

Morin blinked back, then raised his eyebrows with a twitch of a grin. "From what I saw, she's kind of a bitch, but… you look like maybe you want more tea."

Maybe Joori should go check on Jacin, see if he was awake. Maybe he should…

Joori peered down into the bowl Morin had handed him only a few moments ago, and from which he'd only actually taken a sip or two. Still steaming, even. He gulped the tea in one swallow, and didn't even care that it nearly seared his throat.

"*Oh*, yeah."

"Hey," Morin whispered as he and Joori followed the others toward the kitchen. "Does Malick look taller to you?"

Jacin was still trying to process the fact that the strange, roiling pain in his gut was gone when he woke, so it took a while for him to realize his mind was relatively silent. No Asai, no not-Asai, no ghosts, no scent of cherry blossoms. Caidi hadn't appeared to chide him since… damn it, he almost remembered the alley, but every time he reached for it, it wheeled farther from his grasp. Along with most of last night in general. He remembered killing Asai again, and then he remembered that Asai had turned into someone else entirely before he'd hit the ground, but Jacin didn't really remember much after that. And what he did remember was all smeared together into a kind of screaming blur that spun away and dissipated every time he tried to pin it down.

Probably just as well. This new thing was more than enough to keep his attention.

Malick had helped him bathe last night. Again. Had washed his hair for him. Again. Had even woven the little braid at his temple for him. Had spoken softly to him through it all, kept him *here*, and Jacin hadn't really minded. He kept thinking he should be embarrassed when Malick did things like that for him, but… somehow, Malick simply being Malick wouldn't allow "should" to become "did."

He didn't think he'd meant to cling to Malick like he'd apparently done But he'd woken to Malick trying to very delicately extricate himself from Jacin's hold without waking him, while Jacin only kept winding around him like a starfish. He'd pretended he was still asleep, let Malick break the hold, and rolled over to bury his face in the pillows. Now, he lay on his back, staring at the unfamiliar ceiling, absently acknowledging the thump of pain in his arm and wishing for a smoke.

"Incendiary." He said it out loud, as loud as his raspy voice would go, and it didn't echo back into him with the acute bite of fear he'd sort of expected.

You're not the last, Malick had told him when Jacin had said it last night. *You're not the last of anything. You're the first. This is not something you have to be, but something you have to make. You're shiny-new and completely your own, Fen. You can't fail, because no one knows what to expect to begin with. I know you don't believe that yet, so I'll just keep having to show you.*

A purpose. A choice. A direction. Terrifying, yes, but a relief too.

He could actually think again. And his thoughts were strangely calm.

No voices? Ever?

Jacin could remember the stilling of his breath when he'd asked that one, plastered to Malick's ribs with his good arm, the splint between them and far too annoying for the distance it forced.

No voices, love. No voices. Never again.

Jacin had clung. *Really* clung. Malick had let him, and said all the things lovers were supposed to say, had called Jacin beautiful. Jacin had chosen to believe it.

Funny, that Malick offering to kill him was what had finally sunk it home for Jacin. Probably more typical than funny, now that he thought about it. There was still the batshit thing, after all, but Jacin had seen too much of himself in that poor man who'd been dragged to the tower from the sickhouse last night, and... he hadn't liked what he'd seen. It had been rather terrifying, really. Humiliating, to think that was what Morin and Joori had been seeing every time they looked at him. Who could love that?

Malick kept telling Jacin that he could. Jacin could admit now that he'd been wanting to believe it since the first time he'd coerced Malick into saying it. Still, Jacin hadn't *really* believed until Malick's hand was wrapped around his throat and the offer was all too clear in tawny eyes. Because it *was* an offer. And how could Jacin not love the man who would give him that, if he really wanted it?

He'd wanted sex when Malick had finally brought him to bed, that last solid connection, but he hadn't been able to gather the strength. Anyway, the arm probably would've gotten in the way.

Jacin rolled carefully to his side, mindful of the splint, and slid a pillow over his head against the bright sunlight streaming across the bed. His arm hurt, his head hurt, his whole body hurt, he was still tired and a little bit nauseous, and he just generally felt like shit. His mouth tasted like he'd been licking dirty socks. But the other pain was gone, so he let himself believe the rest would eventually recede, as well.

He'd stopped fighting it. Somewhere in all the blur that was last night, Jacin had stopped denying what was going on inside him, and the pain had simply gone away, like Malick had told him it would. Strange that Jacin couldn't pinpoint exactly when that had happened. It had been all-consuming for what seemed like forever and then it wasn't anymore. It seemed like something he should remember, but he couldn't. He decided to stop trying.

The bed was soft, the sheets smooth against his skin, and the quilts warm. He dozed, not thinking about much, really, and with no dreams to trouble him. He bided in a cocoon of relative safety, comfortable but for the rampant zings of pain in his bones and joints and muscles every time he moved. As he'd done several times in his sleepy little stupor, he let his fingers creep up to the bruises on his throat. Pressed.

Real. A lot of last night was still a hazy murk, but that part Jacin remembered. There was not-Asai in an alley before that, and it still hovered in the fog, indistinct and unreal, but that other alley… It had really happened. The bruises proved it. The soreness of Jacin's throat when he swallowed proved it. *Real.* Malick had shoved Jacin's face into the reality, and Jacin had looked for the petals, but couldn't find them. That illusion had been taken from him. There would be no warrior's death with the false promise of the reward of rest, only to have it snatched away by a god who twisted love into betrayal and betrayal into love.

There would instead be what Jacin chose. What *Jacin* chose. And he chose *this*. This feeling, this calm, this… contentment.

Somehow last night—dangling over the chasm between life and death, love and hate, rage and hope, confession and deception—a strange peace had descended, settled over his spirit like a warm, heavy shroud. Acceptance, but probably not the sort Malick had been aiming for.

Daraso had perhaps loved Hitsuke, but in a selfish way that made it impossible for Hitsuke to be what he was. Beishin hadn't loved Jacin at all, had not-loved him in such a way it made the Hitsuke left inside him strive to be what Beishin wanted him to be, just so he could pretend the love was real. Jacin wasn't perfect and never would be. He'd let Caidi die, he'd let Yori die, and he'd been too late to save his mother and father.

If Jacin was going to choose to accept the reality of Malick, he was going to have to accept it all. Including his own failures. And that Malick knew every one of them. Some of them intimately. Malick knew exactly what Jacin was and wanted him anyway.

Can you say that about anyone else in the entire world?

No. He really couldn't.

…you've never seen anything like me before.

And, well. That was true.

Daraso had betrayed Hitsuke. Asai had risked Jacin and everything Jacin loved. Daraso had put Hitsuke through torture that sickened even immortals. Asai had taken everything from Jacin, then pretended Jacin could have it back, if only he'd be what Asai wanted.

Hitsuke had been good enough for a god until that god had tried to take his choices from him. Had tried to make his choices *for* him. Asai had never even allowed for the possibility of choice.

Malick didn't want to make Jacin's choices for him. Malick said he wanted Jacin any way he could have him, had already given Jacin everything he was still capable of having, and all Jacin had to do was exist. *Choose.*

I won't let you fall, Jacin. You fly all you want, I won't let you fall.

Jacin had been falling for such a very long time. He wanted to fly. He'd always wanted to fly.

"Incendiary," Jacin said again, a tiny, serene smile tugging at the corner of his mouth. "No one's but Fate's." Even the gods answered to her. She'd loosened his leash, Rihansei had said. Jacin felt pretty free right now, so he supposed he believed it. And he didn't think she'd done the same for the gods. The smile pulled just a tiny bit wider. "I'm not nothing. I'm…" He paused, just to make sure the lack of knots in his chest was real, then he sucked in a long, deep breath. "I'm Incendiary."

It didn't resonate. But it didn't hurt.

"So, he's told you everything, then."

Jacin wasn't surprised to hear Caidi's voice, even though he was *sure* he'd watched her die again last night. He lifted the pillow to see her sitting cross-legged beside him on the bed, her Caidi-grin bright and warm. He let the pillow fall back over his eyes then shut them.

"He told me."

The sunlight was falling almost fully over the length of the bed now, warming through the quilts and sheets and setting into muscle and bone. Maybe he'd sleep a bit more.

"You seem strangely all right with it."

"The way Malick tells it, it's really the same as being what I was, except no voices."

"And the rest?"

"It's stopped hurting. Malick said it would when I stopped fighting it. And it's…" Jacin paused, thought about it. "It's not quite as horrifying as it probably should be. I don't know how to use it, and Malick can't, not unless I want him to, or unless he's willing to kill me to do it. He's not."

"Well, yes, but… I was sort of talking about Hitsuke."

"You thought I'd be surprised all of my past lives have been lived in madness and misery?"

"I suppose I thought it would… upset you."

Jacin pulled the pillow off his head and stuffed it under his chin. He squinted up at Caidi, pensive.

"It does, a little bit. Or did, maybe. But not in the way it probably would've done a few weeks ago."

Maybe Jacin was getting… "better" didn't seem like the right word. He frowned.

It's not getting better. These people aren't helping you.

Joori's voice, but Jacin couldn't remember when Joori had said it, or… anything else about it. Except for the fear in Joori's eyes. Or maybe they'd been Jacin's own, reflected back at him, distorted with a strange curvature of some inner mirror that showed him the true nature of his warped soul.

He shook his head. Because he didn't think it really mattered. He didn't think it ever had.

"I don't think—" He cut it off, thought more carefully about what he wanted to say. "I don't think I care much that I was Hitsuke once. Or even hundreds of times. I'm not entirely certain why I'm supposed to. He defied his god for the love of him and was betrayed and punished for it. The story isn't exactly unfamiliar."

"'Punished' isn't quite the word I'd use. Raven knew what Hitsuke would choose, or he should have—it was the only way an Incendiary *could* choose. Raven just didn't like it that Hitsuke would dare heed any but him, even Fate. If you ask me, Hitsuke was set up. Raven got the pleasure of retribution, a demonstration of his power, and no one else could have 'his' Hitsuke." Caidi's lip curled. "I wonder if Raven thought one day he'd bring you back, make you forgive him, and use you some more."

Jacin snorted. He had to. It was just so… circular. Fucking smoke rings.

"The madness of the Untouchables must have seemed like poetry to Raven." Caidi grimaced. "All those lives."

She sounded so genuinely sad. So genuinely incensed.

Jacin watched her steadily. "And no one knew he was being reborn again and again." He tilted his head. "Why d'you suppose maijin and *Temshiel* didn't notice?"

"No one was looking for him. They thought Raven had destroyed him."

"Surely the gods knew."

"I should think."

"He could've changed gods."

"Not if he didn't know what he was. And by the time he would've been able to understand, or perhaps even speculate about the possibility, the madness of the Ancestors would've taken him."

Almost exactly the words Malick had used when Jacin had asked that same question last night.

"And the gods did nothing."

"I suppose they could've called upon *Temshiel* or maijin to put Hitsuke out of his misery each time, but only Raven's could follow that command, and Raven would've seen to it they didn't. Which is why I imagine Wolf waited to pull you away from Raven at the end of the Cycle. Not much Raven could do about it then."

Jacin regarded Caidi calmly as he watched her hazel eyes flare outrage, watched her pretty face set a bit hard.

"Did you know him?"

"Hitsuke?" Caidi shook her head, bright curls flopping around her shoulders. "I never met—" She stopped, mouth hanging open, eyes wide.

The only thing shocking about it was how bloody *easy* it had been, how very clearly he could see it once he stopped letting his own wants and regrets get in the way.

Jacin kept his voice completely even, his mien blank.

"So, then," he said quietly. "Who are you, really?"

☖

"I'm supposed to do *what?*" Morin turned his gaping stare from Malick to Joori then back again. "You're crazy."

"Probably." Malick shrugged. "But there it is."

Morin had been almost all right a few minutes ago. It had been fun to watch Joori leering over Annaichi. His tongue had almost been hanging out. And Morin hadn't minded looking all that much himself, even though he remembered her a little too well from that night at the Gates of Rapture. Morin had decided to put it out of his mind in favor of ogling with his brother.

Anyway, he'd been in a pretty good mood, all things considered. Naro-yi had offered to cook something, and Morin had been next to blissful to learn that Naro-yi couldn't only cook, but *cook*. Blissful because he couldn't remember the last time he'd eaten, so Joori and Morin had rather made fools of themselves over the sweet potato hearts, braised with cinnamon and butter then spattered delicately with caramelized sugar. Which was fine, because they'd already made fools of themselves over Annaichi, so expectations were suitably low.

That had all crashed to a halt rather quickly, as soon as the word *Incendiary* had come out of Malick's mouth. And then *Kurimo*.

Samin's silence was thunderous as he stood behind Malick's chair. He looked like he'd happily kill every immortal in the kitchen, Malick included.

Morin wasn't sure yet if he agreed. He looked away from all of the eyes on him and turned his glance again to the walking stick Malick had propped against the low table. Funny. Morin could swear it was exactly like the one that strange little man at the stall had chided him for touching.

"So, this… boy." Annaichi was eyeing Morin in a way that probably should have been insulting, but Morin couldn't get past the shock enough to care. "He's meant to lead the Jin in reclaiming their lands and their sovereignty, and the Incendiary is meant to help him do it." One perfect eyebrow went up when Malick nodded.

"And Jacin agreed to this?" Joori asked calmly. Surprisingly calmly, actually. It was Joori, after all.

"He hasn't agreed to anything yet." Malick peered at Joori steadily, not unkindly. "There is nothing for him to agree *to*. He is what he is. You know what a Catalyst is—an Incendiary is the mold from which they were made. God-maker and god-slayer, world-changer and world-destroyer. No magic, no tricks, only the power of their own will. They want something badly enough, they find a way to make it happen. And if Fen doesn't want Morin to be the liberator of the Jin…" He shrugged and left the rest hanging.

"It is why Incendiary are both so very valuable and deadly dangerous." Tatsu leaned against the bench by the stove. "It is also why they are changeable, and rarely serve one god for all their lives."

"*Short* lives, I'll wager," Samin grumbled.

"If their will clashes with that of their god, if the command of their god is forsaken, the punishment can be… cruel. But they are free to choose their god at will, and hold oath only until they choose another."

"But Fen is different." Malick's gaze was bright, not nearly as somber as everyone else's. "Something new and not of the gods. Except he could wield their magic—my magic—if he wanted to. He can be anything he wants, *do* anything he wants. He's Incendiary, yes, but I think Fate's made sure *this* Incendiary can't be punished like…" He shot a quick glance at Tatsu, but merely let whatever he'd been about to say lie. He looked awfully satisfied, though, where Tatsu looked uneasy.

"So, you said…" Joori stared at his hands, clearly unhappy, but relatively composed. "Were the Untouchables modeled wholly on the Incendiary? I mean…" He peered up at Morin first, eyes sharp, and then at Malick. "Jacin is Wolf's. Can no one but Wolf's touch him?"

Ah. Morin wouldn't have thought of that.

"He was born under Wolf," Malick said, cautious, "but he hasn't yet taken oath to him. He has *my* protection."

"And that means what? Is he safe or not?"

"He is not." Annaichi leaned in, green eyes hard but not mocking. "He is what you might call open game. Kamen has done well to keep him hidden as he's done, but now that the word is out, the servants of the gods will be most eager to seek him out."

"There will be those," Naro-yi added, "who will try to seduce him to their own god. There are those who have allied with Wolf and will assist as Kamen wills it. While I am here at Kamen's request, Annaichi and Tatsu are both here at Bear's command."

"And if I'm hearing what you're *not* saying"—Samin flashed a glare at Malick—"there will be those who seek to put him down altogether."

"Yeah, but." Morin peered around, unable to gauge all the expressions on the faces looking back. "All he has to do is swear oath to Wolf." He turned his glance to Malick. "Right?"

He almost wished he hadn't asked. Malick didn't look at all reassuring. In fact, he looked a bit cagey.

"There's more to this than Incendiary. There's Fen. There's Jacin. There's choice."

Annaichi rolled her eyes and sighed at the ceiling. Tatsu was carefully neutral.

Malick leaned into the table and split his gaze between Morin and Joori. "He has never in his life—in any of his lives—been permitted to be what he is. He won't be pushed into an oath." He shot a glare at Annaichi. "I won't *allow* him to be pushed into an oath." He turned back to Joori and Morin. "There is a soul at stake here. You know what he did for me. I owe him at least this."

"And if he chooses Raven?" Annaichi asked, ostensibly mild but her brilliant eyes had gone narrow and a little bit chilly.

Malick's mouth tightened. "Then I will deliver him to Raven's temple and wish him—"

"You will *not*!" Annaichi pounded a fist to the table. "Not with your power locked inside him like a smoldering coal. He could raze the world, and Raven would merely have to point him. I would see him dead first. I'd do it myself. You *will not*—"

She yipped as she went flying right off her cushion and into the wall. She hung there, like she'd been nailed in place, green eyes wide and a little bit frightened, but furious too.

"Don't test me, maijin." Malick's voice was deadly soft, pulses of power radiating from him and brushing at Morin's skin 'til Morin thought his hair was standing on end. "I'm giving you a warning as a courtesy to Tatsu and your god. You won't get another."

No one else had moved, stunned where they sat or stood, staring.

Everyone but Tatsu and Naro-yi looked on the edge of frightened, even Samin. Tatsu and Naro-yi just shared an oddly amused look. Whatever unspoken contest they were having, Tatsu apparently lost; he took a step forward and laid a hand to Malick's shoulder.

Morin was pretty impressed. He certainly wouldn't have gotten any closer to Malick right now. In fact, he'd been thinking about edging away, but he didn't think he could get himself to move.

"She is young, Kamen," Tatsu said. "Newly turned. As I recall, your ideals were a bit… enthusiastic once too."

Malick's lip twitched, but that was all, until he flicked his fingers and Annaichi slid down the wall. Samin reflexively helped her up, but by the look on his face, he wasn't happy with his own reflexes. He let go of her as soon as she was on her feet. Annaichi didn't even try to hide the flinch when Malick swept a hand toward her.

"If she's here on Bear's orders, why does she think she gets an opinion? Why does she think she has a *right* to—?"

"I have every right." Annaichi was admirably cool and collected, for all that she'd been stuck to the wall a moment ago. "Every servant of the gods has a right. Goyo recognized the soul that bides in your Incendiary, I saw it. Goyo is Snake's, and if Snake decides to ally with any of the gods, it will be Raven. If the Incendiary—"

"He's got a *name*, you insolent little—"

"*Children.*" Tatsu waited for a beat to be sure he had the attention of both Malick and Annaichi. "We are wasting time." He looked at Annaichi. "You are young. There is much you don't know. And it was not Bear's order to inform the governor of Kamen's doings, or those of his… of young Fen-seyh." He held up his hand when Annaichi opened her mouth as if to protest. "The damage is done, and you will be held accountable by Bear herself, should an accounting be desired. I have already washed my hands of it. Heed Kamen's warning, and perhaps I will not be compelled to repeat it."

Morin would swear Annaichi's tattoos were standing out more plainly as she dropped her gaze. He almost could've felt sorry for her, if she hadn't just reminded him so starkly of that Husao, more worried about how Jacin may or may not benefit her god, and disregarding entirely the fact he was a thinking, feeling person.

Tatsu turned to Malick. "If it is choice you would give Fen-seyh, then perhaps we would do better to discuss these matters in his presence."

"You think I haven't?"

"I think you have a unique way of making a person believe they are flying, while they are in truth plummeting to their doom."

Strangely, Malick twitched at that. Tatsu saw it, too, Morin could tell by the way he paused and tilted his head, waiting, but Malick gave nothing more away.

Finally, Tatsu shrugged. "We won't be the only servants of the gods who come to make their case to Fen Jacin. I thought you would appreciate a more private setting than Bear's temple."

Malick sucked in a breath, like he was trying to suck in control, when he very clearly wanted to punch something. Something made him jolt as though he'd been poked, but he only scowled and shifted his shoulders.

"Goyo's outside, scratching at my wards." The grimace was all too telling. He picked up the walking stick and turned it in his hands until he was frowning into blank ivory eyes. He shook his head then looked over at Samin. "I'm letting him through, but keep him down here. And keep our guests happy for a bit, yeah? I'll go see if Fen's up yet."

There was no panic when Fen wasn't where Malick had left him. There was *almost* panic, and a few unkind—though admittedly somewhat provocative—thoughts about leashes, but then Malick noted that the quilt was missing from the bed too, and he had an idea what that might indicate. It was, after all, part of the reason he'd chosen this house.

He tossed the stick onto the bed with a tight set to his jaw and left the room. *A gift for the Incendiary*, Goyo had told Malick smugly. And then had the gall to ask when would be a good time to call. He apparently hadn't accepted "never" as an answer. Malick hadn't really thought he would. Malick had no doubt Goyo was going to make his life hell for some time.

He found Fen on the roof, sitting wrapped up in the quilt against the cold and staring out over the part of the city that could be seen through the trees. Smoking.

Fen didn't turn when Malick trod up behind him, nor did he look when Malick brushed the light coating of snow away and sat down next to him. He only flicked his smoke away over the roof's edge and leaned into Malick, almost burrowed into him, and allowed a small sigh that sounded like pleasure flutter out when Malick's arm automatically rose and wrapped around him.

"He's dead?" Fen asked in his rust-rough voice that never failed to chase a bolt of heat up Malick's backbone.

Malick nodded. "He's dead."

"You're taller."

Ah. It was going to be one of *those* conversations. Malick tried to relax into it, because the randomness could be kind of weirdly charming, or it could be kind of headache-inducing if he tried too hard to follow the Fen-logic.

"I'm taller."

What was the point in denying it? It was vain and it was absurd, but so was Malick.

Fen snorted. "You're such a freak." He adjusted his splinted arm until it rested at a more comfortable angle against Malick's hipbone. "'S kinda… cute."

Cute.

Malick raised his eyebrows but didn't comment. He didn't want to say anything that might make Fen move.

Funny, though, that Fen of all people had turned out to be one of the most tactile people Malick had ever come across. It made sense, in an awful, sad sort of way—Fen had spent this life being rejected, so many more as an Untouchable still craving touch, so it wasn't really surprising he'd take it when it was safe to do so. Malick tried not to make too much of the fact that Fen apparently felt safe accepting it from him.

The notion that Malick's eyes were suddenly hot and blurry was, of course, absurd. He was merely adjusting to the cold, that was all.

"You never had any intention of leaving my brothers to themselves if I died." The pause was very brief, but Fen added a "Did you?" to make it clear he wanted an answer.

No point in sidestepping; the tacked-on question made it pretty obvious that Fen already knew.

So Malick simply said, "No," and left it there.

"How much do you know about Hitsuke?"

Malick must be getting used to the randomness, because he just opened his mouth to answer without pausing to consider the most advantageous one.

"I know he… um… that is, I know *you*—"

"He," Fen cut in, but it wasn't harsh, and he didn't stiffen up and pull away. "I'm not him."

Firm and just bordering on aggressive. It unknotted something in Malick's chest, but he didn't really know what. He decided not to care.

"All right." Malick set a kiss to the crown of Fen's head and watched the snow melt from the boughs of the trees by the gate. "I know he was used by Mii-daichiseyh and then by Raven. I know he was set to the task of stamping out the Jin for Raven, and when he refused, Raven punished him. I, um…" He set his jaw. "I'd rather not have to recite what that punishment was."

"No. You don't have to."

Fen grew quiet for a moment, leaning in more heavily and tucking his head beneath Malick's chin. Burrowing. *Nuzzling.*

Bloody hell, it was freezing up here, and Malick really thought he might be melting. What the hell?

"And that's all?"

Malick frowned. "Isn't that enough?" He peered down at Fen. "Is there more I should know?"

Fen seemed to think about that for a while. Eventually, he looked up at Malick, gray eyes clear, expression thoughtful.

"No."

He tipped his chin, gave Malick a brief, soft kiss before tucking back up and digging in closer. He shivered.

"Are you—?" Malick had to clear his throat. "Are you cold?"

"Not especially. Arm still hurts."

"What about… um." Damn it, Malick was really having trouble finishing sentences.

Fen sighed. "It doesn't hurt anymore. I don't…"

Malick half-expected him to say he'd made up his mind, made the choice Malick had shoved in his face last night, and he didn't want any part of Malick or the magic that had somehow latched onto him and made itself a part of him. Not quite resigned to it, but still, Malick found himself bracing for it, preemptively hardening his expression and trying to harden his heart.

"I don't know what all of this is supposed to mean," was what Fen ended up saying. "I don't know what's expected of me. I know I'm supposed to go to all the temples. I know I'm supposed to listen to the high priests and priestesses of each one make their case. At least those that don't actually want to kill me. And I know I'm supposed to choose a god." He shook his head. "I'm not quite clear on why."

"For protection. To keep those who do want to kill you from doing it. For… direction, I guess."

Fen pulled back to look at Malick. "Isn't that what you said you wanted to do for me?"

He wasn't being a smartass—the question was sincere. And Malick really had to think about this one before he answered.

"Well… yeah."

"Would you still do it, even if I chose a god besides Wolf?"

Strangely, this one Malick didn't have to think about at all. "Yeah. Yeah, I would."

"And would you be punished?"

It made Malick pause, but only for a moment, because he hadn't forgotten any of the directives he'd been given lately, and *Fail the Fool and fail the Cycle* still rang the loudest.

"No. And I don't care." Malick leaned in to drop a kiss to Fen's mouth. "I really don't think you get this—I *love* you. You're beautiful, you're perfect, and I want you with me. I'll take you any way I can get you. And I don't care if I end up godless."

Fen stared up at him for a very long time this time before his eyebrows drew together, like he was confused. "You really do mean that, don't you?"

"Well, of course I mean it!" Malick pressed his hand more firmly beneath Fen's ribcage. "Do you *get* what this means, Fen? No, I didn't see it coming, and I didn't want it to happen to you, but it has, and I really should just kill you and avoid the risk, but I can't, I won't, and I won't let anyone else do it, either. And I don't even really trust you not to do something stupid with it, but I'm willing to take that risk, because I can't imagine not having you here.

"Ever heard that love makes a person's brain go wobbly? I've become a bloody, blazing *moron* for you, Fen. I'd let you top me if you wanted. I hardly ever do that. I've fucking *swallowed* for you. What else can I do?"

The stare this time was bemused, still calm and almost… serene. It made Malick wonder if someone had given Fen an extremely potent draft Malick didn't know about.

"But *would* you end up godless? Would you be… punished? If I didn't choose Wolf, would Wolf take it out on you?"

Malick sighed. Well, this wasn't going like he'd hoped.

He cast his glance back out over the trees. "Probably not." He thought about it, shook his head. "No. I wouldn't be punished. I think… if Wolf saw this coming, I think he… allowed for it. Or something."

… you know now why Wolf turned you and called you to his own. Perhaps the Incendiary is yours, but you have been his since your paths collided. Wolf made you for it.

Xari's words had been, for once, clear and lacking her usual riddles. Malick shook them off anyway. Maybe Wolf had turned him for this and maybe he hadn't—Malick didn't care. He tightened his mouth and sighed, great billows of frosted steam wafting from his nostrils like dragon's breath.

"There aren't any like me, either, y'know. There's a reason for that.

Too much power, it… goes to one's head. I think… I think it's what killed Skel, in the end." It felt strangely like a confession, though Malick was almost sure that wasn't how he meant it. "Watching other immortals for a while, I think it made me wary of all I could have, all Wolf was handing me, all of what Xari wouldn't stop nagging me to reach for. And I got along without it, for over a century, and I still managed to get the job done. Until last night." It was probably cowardly to avoid meeting Fen's eyes, but Malick was doing it anyway. "Even when I realized what was happening… I *had* to take it. I *had* to… do what I did with it. I couldn't lose you like that, not to him, not to whatever your life would've been if he'd won. I *couldn't*. I'm sor—"

"No, don't." Fen was still watching him, but Malick couldn't make himself look back. "You already said that. Lots of times. And I do… understand. Why you did it. And I think I'm grateful."

Malick jerked his gaze back to Fen. And saw nothing there but truth. "Yeah?"

Fen looked a little surprised himself. "I think so, yeah." He broke the gaze to butt at Malick's chin until Malick lifted it so Fen could fold in again. "I don't want to die, you know." So matter-of-fact; so blunt. "I'm pretty sure I didn't before, I only wanted… I wanted to stop feeling like… like I should've. I wanted to stop hurting. I wanted to stop hurting other people because *I* couldn't stop hurting." He shrugged. "I've been reminded just lately what real pain is like. And I think I'm afraid to die now. I don't know what would happen."

Malick frowned. "You'd go to your chosen god, of course. It'd probably—"

"I'm not choosing a god."

"—work the same… Um. What?"

"I'm not choosing a god." Fen's hand had been holding the quilt closed in a knot in front of his chest; now, it crept beneath and settled atop Malick's, wedged beneath the splint and resting warm against Fen's breastbone. "I think maybe Wolf meant to help me—help Hitsuke, I guess—but I also think maybe he didn't, that he just knew I'd come in useful and so decided to wait and use me. And you.

"Balance, you know. It's so bloody important to them. Everything's a fucking trade." He huffed, derisive. "Umeia said you and I would balance each other out. See? Trade. Balance. They're bloody mad for it. And now Wolf's knotted me up in a neat little bow. Whether I choose him or not, I won't go against him if it risks you. He gets what he wants either way. Which means I don't think Wolf did a damned thing for me, or Hitsuke, and I don't trust any of them. So they can all just fuck off."

He sighed then shrugged. "Kind of sucks, though, not knowing what'll happen when I die. I don't know if I'll be reborn, like the Untouchables, or if I'll just come back, like Hitsuke. Or if I'll just… stop altogether. Cease to be. Or… well, there are worse things." A small shudder rolled up his back and out through his shoulders.

Malick was just kind of staring stupidly at the top of Fen's head, bobbling small nods in places, because it all made too much sense. It was, in fact, very close to what he'd started to say only a moment ago. Except for the not-choosing-a-god thing, which almost made him groan out loud, until he realized—it was a choice. A real choice. And Fen had made it. Last night, Malick had actually had to throttle him to make him choose between life and death, and now Fen was deciding something like *this*? It seemed like—

Wait.

Malick's eyes narrowed. "Did you just say *Umeia* said?"

"Oh yeah." Fen patted at Malick's hand beneath the quilt. "Umeia's back. She's been pretending to be Caidi, trying to help. I guess she did. I don't think it was her in Ada, though. Should've asked her, I guess, but… I want to think it was Caidi." He paused, thoughtful. "I should probably be glad it wasn't really Caidi, what with the… well, you know, but… in a way, it's almost like losing her again."

Maybe Malick should be offering some sort of comfort for that last bit, but he was still just sort of staring at Fen's head with his mouth hanging open.

"How the hell…? Wait, today? Just now?" When Fen nodded against his chest, Malick winced. "Fen, that's impossible. I've got the whole place warded up. She couldn't have—"

"Yeah, she said to tell you that you used the same spells you used to use to protect the Girou. She apparently didn't have a problem, since you taught them to her. And I'm to call you a dumbass. I said you'd probably give me plenty of reason eventually to come up with that one myself. I mean, for pity's sake, you're *taller*."

Malick should probably stop staring at Fen's head. Anytime now.

Umeia. Back. Malick had no idea how to feel about that.

"Anyway." Fen pulled his legs around so they were draped across Malick's. "She said I wouldn't have trusted her, so she came as Caidi. Which is likely true, but still. And she said it would probably take you forever to break the news about Morin to me, so now that I knew who she was, she figured she'd do it.

"But I don't want to talk about that right now. Except to tell you that she said she'll be sticking to spirit for a while and avoiding you. That you can find her when you want to, if you ever forgive her. I keep going back and forth on whether I think you should or you shouldn't, but it's not really up to me, I guess."

Malick didn't know where to start, but his mouth did—"I would've told you! I told Morin already, even Joori knows, so you *know* you'd've heard about it soon enough. I was going to come up and talk to you, if you looked like you were ready to hear it, but Tatsu is here with his Bear cub, and then Goyo showed up, and I had to—"

"Something you should know." Harsh. Forbidding. "I'll *never* look like I'm ready to hear something like that. I'll never *be* ready to hear something like that. But if you try to keep anything like it from me again, I'll cut your fucking heart out. Understand?"

Despite the frisson that never failed to move up Malick's backbone at the thought, he couldn't help the grin. All right, see, *this* was the Fen he knew and sometimes feared.

Malick gave Fen a little jostle. "And if you ever joke about that again, I'll have to kill you."

Fen nodded peaceably. "Wasn't really joking, but fair enough."

There was probably something very wrong with the fact that an exchange of death threats made Malick all warm and fuzzy, but there it was. Still, the thing with Umeia was interfering with the pleasant buzz he was beginning to feel, so he cleared his throat.

"I'm sorry."

"Why?" Fen shifted, but he didn't pull away. "What'd you do now?"

"I meant for… for not believing you. When you said you'd been talking to Caidi. When you said… well, you never actually admitted to Asai, but I knew it had to be him, and all the time—"

"I wouldn't have believed me, either." Fen's tone was abruptly weary. "I'm batshit, I know that." He must've felt Malick twitch, because he went on, "No, I am. I get that. You're a little bit crazy too, so I expect it works well enough." He shrugged. "This is how I am, you know? It won't be changing, I don't think, and I can't really pretend. I tried. It only made things worse. So I'll keep being like this, and you'll be like that, and we'll see how long before we kill each other. I don't think that's so terribly different from most people."

Malick let all the other row-inducing things in that pass him right by in favor of the one that needed immediate attention. There would be other times for all the other… stuff. And with what had happened with Joori last night, it seemed like it should have priority.

Ah, Joori—couldn't live with him, couldn't chop him up for stew.

"I'm not the one you need to convince, I don't think," Malick said. Then braced himself.

But Fen failed to explode into a brother-defending dervish of death. He only sighed.

"I think that's the most terrifying thing about all this… love. Stuff. Whatever. That you can hurt someone so badly just by being what you are."

Maybe it was simply because the subject was right at the top of his mind, but Malick couldn't help but think of Umeia. And then he thought of Shig and Yori, and his throat went tight.

"It's not you doing the hurting. And he *does* love you, Fen. It's… he's…" Malick paused. Because it was important he get this right. "You're more alike than you think you are, the two of you. Which is strange, because I've never once had the urge to fuck Joori into next week, and all I have to do is look at you and I want you. But the sameness—it's there.

"You're both so bloody protective it's amazing you haven't eaten each other up. It's only… you've always had much bigger things to fight, and I really don't think you know how to *stop* fighting, but he watches you turn that on yourself and it kills him, and he doesn't know how to fight that so he fights you. Or me, if I'm handy." Malick's eyebrows went up. He gave himself a mental pat on the back. That was kind of profound. "He loves you, Fen, which is the only thing that's kept me from arranging an accident for him. He just—"

"Not funny."

It was rather mild, just bordering on actual threat, so Malick ignored it.

Anyway, it was too funny.

"He just has to figure out how to do it properly," Malick went on. "Sometimes he gets it right, and I can see him knowing it when he gets it wrong, so… there's hope. Just let him keep trying, if you can stand it."

Bloody damn, had he just defended Joori? What the hell? All the warm fuzzies must be going to his brain and melting it to slush.

"He's still Raven's," Fen said. "I want that fixed. Now. Today."

"He isn't, Fen. He's Wolf's now. One doesn't necessarily have to go to a temple and renounce to defect from a god."

Joori had been marked by Wolf as clearly as Morin had been. Malick just didn't know why yet, so there was no point in getting Fen all knotted up by telling him everything right now.

"But I think it's going to be interesting to watch what happens with Raven now. The word will spread about Hitsuke. Goyo knows, and he's really bloody pissed off about it. It's only a matter of time before it's not-so-common knowledge, but even whispers do damage. Some of Raven's maijin and *Temshiel* will defect, I've no doubt, and the mortals will follow. His power will shrink, mark that. He wanted to be more powerful than Wolf, and it's miscarried quite stunningly. Only what he deserves."

It came out kind of vicious. Maybe Malick could tell himself—and Fen—he wouldn't care if he ended up godless, but he couldn't really deny he was Wolf's, blood and bone. He could make the choice if he had to, and he knew if it was put to him right now, he'd choose Fen. He just really hoped he'd never have to.

"Hmm," Fen hummed, skeptical, then he went silent again. It lasted for quite a while this time before the Fen-logic made another sharp turn:

"I don't think I can take Goyo today. I don't think I can take anyone today, but especially not Goyo."

Malick's eyebrows rose. Because all that talk about love and such, and it was too obvious that Goyo had known Hitsuke, and now Fen was bringing Goyo up, and—

"Mind if I ask why?"

Fen hesitated then shook his head. "I don't have an answer for you right now. And certainly not one you'll like. Another time, only… not now. All right?"

No, it certainly was *not*.

"Yeah, all right."

Malick clamped his teeth together, annoyed with himself. Bloody hell, that had the definite ring of *Goyo and Hitsuke used to fuck like minks in heat, and I don't think you'll react very well to hearing that, so I don't want to tell you*, and here Malick was, nodding agreement like a simpering sop and hugging Fen closer.

Malick really would do anything for him. Fucking *anything*. Fen would be the death of him, one way or another, he just knew it.

Ah, but what a way to go.

"I want a smoke." Fen slurred it into Malick's chest. "But I don't want to move. And my arm hurts."

It was the admission—and the fact that it was the second time it had been voiced—that made it dawn on Malick, but he really should've twigged when he realized he was having a real conversation. With *Fen*. And Malick hadn't even had to fuck him stupid first. Which was what made Malick understand that he wasn't really having a conversation with Fen; this was Jacin.

"You should probably still be in bed." Malick rubbed up and down between Fen's shoulder blades through the quilt. "It's cold up here, and I know you haven't eaten yet."

Fen snorted. "I can't remember the last time I did eat, actually. But I really don't want to move yet. All right?"

Malick didn't really want to move yet, either, so he merely rested his chin atop Fen's head. His ass was cold and the suns were peeking through the clouds, blinding him with reflected light on the snow, his back was starting to stiffen up, hunched over Fen as he was, and his legs were losing feeling. And still, the gods and their minions all combined couldn't have pried him away.

They were quiet for a long time, just sitting there huddled together, Malick squinting against the suns and watching snow melt, and Fen half dozing against him. Malick was absently trying to see if he could spot the temples from here when Fen finally stirred.

"He'll need to be trained."

Morin, of course. Malick was getting very used to the randomness of Fen-logic.

"Obviously."

Knowing Samin, he'd already started.

Fen was quiet for another few moments before he mused, "We'll have to go back to Ada eventually."

"Yeah. Will you be all right with that?"

"Does it matter?"

"It does. You have to want it, Fen. That's the point."

"What if I don't know what I want yet?"

"Then we wait until you do."

"I don't…" Fen shifted, pulling the quilt up to his chin. "I don't want Joori…" He paused again with a tired sigh, then slumped against Malick.

When Fen didn't go on, Malick ventured, "Naro-yi can find out what he's good at. Get him a trade. He can… he can maybe even apprentice with Naro-yi or something. Take care of my money. That way he'd always know what we were doing. And he could stay here, out of danger. Take care of the house and such."

"I… Maybe. He won't like it."

"He might, actually."

And if anyone could figure out how a person could be the most useful, it would be Naro-yi. Joori could be talked into liking just about anything if he could be useful to his brother while doing it.

"It'll work out," Malick said. "Shig will be staying here, one way or another. She can keep him in line." Malick still hadn't reconciled himself to that new circumstance, so his brow furrowed and a bit of a lump rose in his throat. He cleared it. "So there's that. And besides, we've years yet before we have to worry about sailing back to Ada for adventure and political coups."

"I think the worst part about it all," Fen said slowly, "is that it makes such horrible sense. Morin is practical and ruthless, but he has our mother's heart in there somewhere. He could make a great general. I just... I just wish—"

"I know." Malick dipped in to drop another kiss to Fen's hair. "We'll figure it out, Fen. We'll make it work. You and me, yeah? We'll be amazing."

"You and me." Fen said the words slowly, softly, like he was tasting them, trying them out. He nodded then pulled himself in so close he was almost sitting in Malick's lap. "I'll want to think it all through very carefully. You're good at all the manipulating and game-playing, so you should be able to spot the traps. Lay it all out and find the catch, see what the price might be this time and know the sum of the trade, before we do a damned thing. We'll give the gods their fucking Balance, but *we* decide how and what we'll pay in return. Yeah?"

And that right there was why Malick thought it was Fen sitting here with all that magic inside him, and all that control locked down around it. Because no one embodied control and focus like Fen, and no one Malick had ever come across could direct what was to come with an eye toward the least damage done to all sides. Focus and precision, that was Fen, and Fate had made him, but too many lives had tempered him into the meticulous tool of the gods he was now, whether he chose one or not.

I'm tired of shit happening to *me*, Fen had said once. It appeared that sentiment had finally taken hold. And Malick didn't think any of the gods—including Wolf—had a single bloody clue what to expect from this new Incendiary with a mind and will of his own and the determination, *finally*, to use them. There had, after all, never really been such a thing—it was up to Fen now to redefine Incendiary, and himself while he was at it, and Malick couldn't wait to watch him do it.

It didn't matter what Shig had said. There was nothing truly broken about Fen. Cracked a little, maybe, definitely bruised and somewhat frayed. But this was not broken.

Malick sighed. Because they'd touched on what had gone on and what it meant, but they hadn't really done much more than that. And it was pretty fucking important. There was something new and very powerful hunkering inside Fen, and Malick thought Fen was probably too right—Wolf had known, and it had happened for a reason. Maybe that reason was to put Morin in a position to lead the Jin out of the desperation generations of slavery had left behind, but they were talking about gods and their whims here, so maybe it wasn't.

Either way, word would eventually spread. The servants of the other gods were not going to stop coming for Fen. And without taking oath, all Fen had between him and them was Malick. Malick thought anyone—gods included—who found themselves on the wrong side of Fen might be in for a hell of a shock, but still.

"Fen, we really should talk about—"

"Malick?" Quiet and almost tentative, but it stopped Malick quite effectively.

Malick felt the need to set another kiss in Fen's hair, so his "Yeah?" was a little muffled.

"This is how I am. This is all there is. I can tell you I love you, but I don't know what that's worth when I'm not really sure if I know how to do it right. I know it was… very difficult when you were, um… gone. I know I needed you, and I wanted you with me. But…" Fen pushed Malick's hand more firmly into his breastbone. "I won't risk what's in me. If that means anything. You said you think I'm protective. I'll protect this. Even from you, if you ever make me. It's… I'd rather it wasn't there at all, but it is, and I'll keep it safe. I think that's… I think it's how I love." Fen lifted his head and peered at Malick steadily. "Yeah?"

Malick kind of wished Fen wasn't looking at him, because he knew his eyes were getting damp, and it was fucking embarrassing. He swallowed, managed to croak, "Yeah, Fen, that's… yeah," before his throat closed up altogether.

Fen leaned up and set a light, soft kiss to Malick's mouth. "I like it better when you call me Jacin." And then he just tucked back in against Malick's chest and went quiet.

Malick thought he might choke to death before all the soppy emotion in his chest settled down again to let him get a decent breath.

But oh yeah. What a way to go.

CAROLE CUMMINGS

lives with her husband and family in Pennsylvania, USA, where she spends her time trying to find time to write. Recipient of various amateur and professional writing awards, several of her short stories have been translated into Spanish, German, Chinese and Polish.

Author of the *Aisling* and *Wolf's-own* series, Carole is currently in the process of developing several other works, including more short stories than anyone will ever want to read, and novels that turn into series when she's not looking. Carole is an avid reader of just about anything that's written well and has good characters. She is a lifelong writer of the 'movies' that run constantly in her head. Surprisingly, she does manage sleep in there somewhere, and though she is rumored to live on coffee and Pixy Stix™, no one has as yet suggested she might be more comfortable in a padded room.

...Well. Not to her face.

www.carolecummings.com